## PRAISE FOR RODRIGO FRESÁN

"Rodrigo Fresán is the new star of Latin American literature. . . . There is darkness in him, but it harbors light within it because his prose—aimed at bygone readers—is brilliant."
—Enrique Vila-Matas

"I've read few novels this exciting in recent years. *Mantra* is the novel I've laughed with the most, the one that has seemed the most virtuosic and at the same time the most disruptive."
—Roberto Bolaño

"A kaleidoscopic, open-hearted, shamelessly polymathic storyteller, the kind who brings a blast of oxygen into the room."
—Jonathan Lethem

"Rodrigo Fresán is a marvelous writer, a direct descendent of Adolfo Bioy Casares and Jorge Luis Borges, but with his own voice and of his own time, with a fertile imagination, daring and gifted with a vision as entertaining as it is profound."
—John Banville

"With pop culture cornered by the forces of screen culture, says Fresán (knowing the risk to his profile of 'pop writer,' even coming out himself to discuss it), there's nothing left but to be classic. That's the only way to keep on writing."
—Alan Pauls

TRANSLATED FROM THE SPANISH
BY WILL VANDERHYDEN

# THE DREAMED PART

## RODRIGO FRESÁN

OPEN LETTER
LITERARY TRANSLATIONS FROM THE UNIVERSITY OF ROCHESTER

Library of Congress Cataloging-in-Publication Data: Available.
ISBN-13: 978-1-948830-05-8 | ISBN-10: 1-948830-05-1

*This project is supported in part by an award from
the National Endowment for the Arts*

Printed on acid-free paper in the United States of America.

Text set in Caslon, a family of serif typefaces based on the designs
of William Caslon (1692–1766).

*Cover Design by N. J. Furl*

Open Letter is the University of Rochester's nonprofit, literary translation press:
Dewey Hall 1-219, Box 278968, Rochester, NY 14627

www.openletterbooks.org

*For Ana and Daniel:*
*dreams made reality,*
*reality made dreams*

# THE DREAMED PART

What are dreams?
—Vladimir Nabokov
*Ada, or Ardor*


The depths of many marvelous moments seen all at once.
—Kurt Vonnegut
*Slaughterhouse-Five*


Each man is given, in dreams, a little personal eternity which allows him to see the recent past and the near future. All of this the dreamer sees in a single glance, in the same way that God, from His vast eternity, sees the whole cosmic process.
—Jorge Luis Borges
"Nightmares"


It's only in dreams that things are inevitable; in the waking world there is nothing that cannot be avoided . . . Let us say, the present is where we live, while the past is where we dream.
—John Banville
*The Blue Guitar* and *Time Pieces*


And somebody spoke and I went into a dream.
—John Lennon & Paul McCartney
"A Day in the Life"


And suddenly it all went black. And that time was gone forever.
—Denis Johnson
*Train Dreams*


Listen, I tell you a mystery: We will not all sleep, but we will all be changed—in a flash, in the twinkling of an eye.
—The Bible
*Corinthians 15:51-52*


As night unites the viewer and the view.
—Vladimir Nabokov
*Pale Fire*

I

# THAT NIGHT
## (FOOTNOTES FOR AN ENCYCLOPEDIA OF SLEEPWALKERS)

*All* that we see or seem is but a dream within a dream.
—EDGAR ALLAN POE
"A Dream Within a Dream"

I have dreams of a density I would like to bring to fiction.
—JOHN CHEEVER
*Journals*

A dream, all a dream, that ends in nothing, and leaves the sleeper
where he lay down, but I wish you to know that you inspired it.
—CHARLES DICKENS
*A Tale of Two Cities*

I think we dream so we don't have to be apart for so long. If we're
in each other's dreams, we can be together all the time.
—A. A. MILNE
*Winnie-the-Pooh*

All men dream, but not equally.
—T. E. LAWRENCE
*Seven Pillars of Wisdom: A Triumph*

Dreams are toys.
—WILLIAM SHAKESPEARE
*The Winter's Tale*

The dream is, here, the body of the text.

There it is.

The body: in repose and asleep, yet always alert.

The text—in the most suspended of animations—opening its eyes when the book opens, every time it is read, as if upon entering that place a light turns on so the light can shine out. In *shhh*ilence. Without a sound beyond an onomatopoetic and contagious opened-mouth *yawn*, and, every so often, stretching its arms out wide, until its bones creak.

And that's all there is to say about the outside as this procession is headed inward, line by line, lining up into a litany.

That's why, always, after centuries of reading aloud, we learned it was better to read soundlessly: lips moving just enough to let air escape between teeth, and little more. With that combination of devotion and fear that overcomes you, in the dark, watching a luminous and illuminating loved-one sleep. And, just then, acknowledging and being fully aware, inside a darkness all our own, that the person we love will never be entirely open, known, legible, and comprehensible to us.

When someone is sleeping, that person is a mystery and yet, at the same time, as they *really* are. Lacking the sophisticated and artificial poses of waking life, when all of us are so awake to how we're being perceived.

Asleep, on the other hand, limited possibilities: face down or face up or on one side or sprawled out or contracted in fetal position, like when you floated in the shell of your mother, fantasizing, like Hamlet, about being "king of infinite space," where there's no room for bad dreams. Easy to perceive, and yet, in its deceptive simplicity, a body that, like the numbered verses of a poem, we could recite from memory, yes; but, again, without ever fully understanding it. Like what happens in and with many poems.

And possible meanings and interpretations are but footnotes. Notes in smaller font—the secret and definitive clauses. Under or at the foot of the bed. Feet reaching out and seeking the heat and company of other feet. Or, at least, of that hot water bottle resembling an organic prosthesis of a mollusk-like consistency, there, in the lower reaches of the bed, under a blanket of aquamarine blue. Feet moving to the somnambulant rhythm of a song sung in its sleep, rocking back and forth. One of those cradle lullabies that, when they grow up, awaken transformed into bedtime songs and, in the end, stop dreaming of little angels, dreaming instead of their increasingly certain non-existence, and waiting to perform and dream the funeral march. They dream of the bluesy beat being played beside that supine body, just there, in the bed of a coffin, resting, supposedly, in peace.

And—*aaaaah ah-ah-AH ah-ah-AH AH-aaaaaah aaaaah aaaaah aaaah ah-ah-AH aaaaaaah*—somebody spoke and I went into a dream, singing, one night in the life, "A Day in the Life," in the language of dreams which is the language of all time, all times, at the same time. The free words, the present; the ones between quotation marks, the past; the ones between parentheses, the future.

But all of them being told right now.

"Tell a dream and lose a reader," someone told us.

Who said that and who sang that thing about going into a dream?

What did they do? Did they have some personal problem with the act of dreaming, some nightmare trauma, some unfulfilled longing?

What authority could somebody possibly have to chisel such an irrefutable maxim or to sing that symphonic and floating sigh?

What does it matter?

Because, oh, he's now—again, as is already custom—prepared to lose multiple, many, maybe all his readers.

He's going to tell them a dream.

Luckily, he's not a writer.

Or better: he's no longer a writer; which is more or less the same thing. He's an *exwriter*.

To be an exwriter isn't only to no longer be a writer, it is, in a way, to never have been one: when a writer stops writing, unlike any other profession where what's done remains, the condition and race and species and not-necessarily-super power are lost. The books remain, the work, yes. But in the past, and ever further from life itself, and as if they were no longer yours. Because if that mysterious mechanism that turns on *during* (in the most private and ineffable moment of the profession, in the act of writing itself) isn't cyclically rereleased, everything written in the past begins to reject its author. To cross over to the other side of the street when they see their writer coming, rambling to himself and wandering in spaced-out esses when he should be doing hallucinogenic zees. Not acknowledging him the way kids don't acknowledge their awkward parents who show up at their parties to drink and dance and shout. Going off alone and on their own and not returning his greeting or helping him up when he stumbles and trips and falls. Something that happens more and more: exwriters—like the elderly; and he's an exwriter *and* someone who he feels so old—stumble and trip and fall at the slightest obstacle or over the same stone. Few things are more fragile than someone who has been left without words and whose infrequent handwriting, always, seems to spring forth from the private earthquake of that atrophied claw, once a flexible hand of movements both harmonious and forceful, like a conductor.

Not anymore.

Now, the emperor's thumb forever pointing down, making it impossible to even sustain the weight of a pen and its ink.

For a while now—a long while; because his old age has turned out to be far longer than his childhood and youth and middle age put together—all his events precipitate. And he with them; almost letting himself fall, free but a prisoner of the gravity of the moment. With the almost-secret hope and fantasy of, maybe, never having to get up again and the comfort of resigning himself to staying down, wounded.

But no such luck (good or bad) and something forces him to find a wall to lean on (though he doesn't seek any type of special assistance) like he once leaned on a blank page or screen.

And there he goes, "Once more unto the breach, dear friends, once more" and "Lasciate ogni speranza voi ch'entrate": the same quotes as always, functioning in the way of ארבדכ ארבא (the abracadabra that means "I create like the word") or اﻓﺘﺢ اي ﺳﻤﺴﻢ (that thing you say to open the door to the cave housing stolen treasures or the body to be resurrected in whose name so many will steal).

So there he stays, noteworthy for nobody, but standing all the same and with all these notes at his feet.

Footnotes that scrambled up from the bottom of the page, like in a Wonderland dream, and were integrated into the main text, indistinguishable but never refusing to be turned into his other voice. An accelerated and particular and messianic voice, when he imagined combining the end of his world with the end of everyone's world, typed in the belly of an apocalyptic Swiss particle accelerator. A voice that speaks in the clacking but incessant clickety-clack of an American Typewriter, in a landscape, ever more uniform and obedient and digital and without fingerprints and always bowing down in prayer to Sans-Serif. Skipping entire paragraphs when the descent, from the top to the bottom of the page, zigzagging left to right, grows more difficult. A font that at one time so many people found so hard to read (and that they complained about so much, though they never complained about spending their lives reading tiny text on tiny screens), that fluid font he always liked so much to write in, first on acoustic and later electric typewriters.*

---

* A footnote like this, right here right now, but not for long. A footnote that will be the only one so far down the page. And that is already preparing to leap—hooks and ropes and sails like sheets and asterisks like the emblem on the banner—and shout "All aboard!" A footnote that steps on the laces of its own sentences and trips and seems about to fall but keeps its balance and is followed, enthusiastically and obediently, by all the titles and names of its companions, stowaways, vagabonds, meddlers, misfits, wanderers. Encyclopedic and general and telegraphic and enumerative notes mingling with the personal and nontransferable winks and all of that. And he remembers that, when he was young, there was that book called *The Book of Lists* (in the library of the house of his summertime, end-of-the-world grandparents, edited, along with his children, by best-selling author Irving Wallace), which was nothing but absurd lists ("The Five Most Famous Prophetic Dreams" or "The Five Most Celebrated Insomniacs") and whose principal charm was that you could pick and choose one or two here and there. Open the volume to any page and close it again convinced you'd learned a little bit of nothing (don't forget that, around that time, there were also enumerative lists of sex positions and rankings of lovers and of different sizes to widen and moisten the eyes of that boy he once was and will forever be), like a primitive version with the traction of ink of floating around the Internet. A false and self-assured feeling of victory and accomplishment with minimal effort. Now, so long after, footnotes that are, actually, notes fallen to their knees, beaten, accumulations of data and lists of possible "things" to write that, if he goes on *like this*, his fire dwindling, will never be written. Notes about something you forget as soon as you remember it or as soon as

Footnotes growing like plants that wrap around and ensnare him. Footnotes you can do several things to: kick them, pick them up, leave them lying out in the rain so they're swept away by the water as it drains or so—accumulating remains—they germinate and turn into footnotes that ascend into the heights.

Foot-tapping footnotes that lose more readers than telling dreams. And that make you lose more listeners—like reading with the ears—than speeches. And that here are part of the problem, of what went wrong when a reasonable and maximal utilization of the time of men was sought. Even of the time that passed while they were dreaming.

And, yes, what it ended up producing was something monstrous.

Nothing too very scientific, but even still, now, a direct consequence of the experimentation.

Of experiments gone awry.

Dreams that—scholars of the matter insist in interviews and documentaries, with faces like those of lying children—are nothing more than electrochemical reactions. Small gusts of energy leaping from cell to cell. Imprecise stimuli nobody really totally believes in. Nobody really knows where dreams come from, and where they're going, and what they're for. You could say—with equal certainty—that dreams are, actually, the thoughts of guardian angels. And nobody could dispute it; because if dreams exist, why can't angels who dream them also exist. Series of dreams like accelerated particles where nothing comes up to the top, but even still, falling from on high like hard and heavy rain; and he folds his umbrella to let himself be drenched, not thinking of anything specific or making use of any intricate scheme or looking for an exit in any direction. Dreams where—in the moment of dreaming them, as if he were writing them down as someone else dictated—you don't make any great connection, or think all this would pass inspection or the cards you're holding (dreams like Tarot cards or one of the

---

you remember what you're going to forget. Terminally ill notes of one who no longer counts or has anything to recount. Neither counting nor sheep, neither rabbit holes nor looking glasses to pass through, in the insomniac and dark night of the soul. In bed like a ship adrift and with no stars in the sky (concentrate specifically on that one, on the second star to the right) by which to regain direction and sanity and destiny. Broadcasting *Last Footnotes of the World*; and more sordid details coming up.

other many and enthusiastic and optimistic methods people buy into when it comes to interpreting something) will be any good for you, unless they come from another world.

Dreams like irrefutable evidence that you have a nocturnal life, that at night and in the night and through the night and with the night you're more alive and awake and alert than ever.

Enough of this.

Better to stop here, before everyone falls asleep.

That's where we're headed.

Come in and dream.


When he longer had anything to sell, he sold what one should never sell: dreams.

His dreams.

He didn't like the idea of doing it, of course.

Nothing was more disturbing to him than selling with eyes open something made with eyes closed. Something only you see and whose description or recreation will always be partial, imperfect, nontransferable. The memory of a memory of a memory. The most faithful portrait of the wind, when you know what gives stature and profile and shape to the wind are nothing more and nothing less than the things the wind sweeps along. All the things the wind suspends in the air, as if they were letters to be arranged, scattering them across the solid ground and ready and set and aim and fire at some obscure moving target. All of that, there, blowing in a wind that doesn't sound like wind but like wind sounds in the movies. Or, closer, dreams like a movie that ("I saw it, but I don't remember which one it is!" we exclaim) we only catch a few minutes of, drifting in the ether of a midnight TV channel, back in days when it was impossible to instantly know what was being broadcast, because you didn't have the remotest control over all of that, over pausing or rewinding or fast-forwarding what was happening on not-flat-but-cubic screens. Or, finally, dreams like a song we catch already underway, on the radio, and whose performer and name we don't know; just that chorus that's been stuck in our ears and is fading away to then hammock all day, until all we've got left are stray verses and notes. And more details about dreams and movies and songs coming up, if and when, by then, he hasn't forgotten all of this, all of that, and all of that other one too.

But yes: nothing is more unsettling than selling—to part with something invisible, yet so intimate and personal and private and unique—dreams. Something with neither body nor weight. Though nothing is as solid as something that appears to be nowhere but is actually in all places. Here and there and everywhere: like what was said about some old gods nobody believes in anymore because it was definitively proven they do not believe in us; they no longer believed in the people they had first dreamed to make a reality later. Yes, the gods departed of their own volition or never existed. And nobody took seriously anymore that ploy whereby man first created the gods in order to, maybe, later, be able to create a story where the gods create mankind. After the curtain of faith and of myths dropped—when nobody any longer dreamed that sacred dream of which nothing remained—all that was left were dreams.

Our divine and ferocious dreams.

And later not even that.

And so the few dreams that were still alive, "awake," became very valuable and people paid a great deal of money for them.

And more details about all the foregoing forthcoming.

And—again with the recurrence of dreams, with that persistent insistence that also belongs to memory, just not asleep but in a trance—nothing is more disturbing than selling something you know to be yours and only yours and not resembling that of anyone else. * ("Of all memory only the illustrious gift / of recalling dreams is worth anything," Antonio Machado.)

Dreams—like the pupils of our eyes and the fingerprints of our fingers and the lobes of our ears—are unique and nontransferable.

Dreams are the DNA spirals of the mind.

And even those dreams that are dreamed en masse, dreams everyone dreams * (those sticky and somewhat banal and automatically-humma-ble oneiric greatest hits in which you find yourself naked in public, falling from the sky, swept away by a giant wave, chased through the darkness, weeping for the death of a loved one, suddenly rich and famous or making love to *that* person or being raped by *that other* per-son, and worst of all: back in high school, taking an exam you didn't study for), are never identical, not even close, to those of other dreamers. * ("We live as we dream: alone," wrote Joseph Conrad; which could also be read as "We dream as we live: alone.") Nobody falls the same, nobody is the same when they're naked, every person is so *personal* in the moment of the agonized cry or the orgasmic moan and, of course, no two waves are the same, and the answers to *that* exam are never repeated . . .

But he had nothing else left, he had nothing left.

He'd already sold everything sellable: his car (that he never learned to drive, and that was the legacy of a suicidal and insomniac friend, who went out driving it at night, imagining he ran himself over and didn't stop to help himself); his books and his collection of films and LPs * (that were many and many and many; and that were so valued and loved and necessary; and for which he was given just a handful of wrinkled bills, because nobody read or watched or listened anymore); his house * (that, already empty of writing and music and scenes, was just an empty, impersonal space, which he let go of like someone taking off their clothes, all alone, almost without realizing they were taking off their clothes, because it'd been so long since anyone had seen them naked). There, almost a bubble, transparent and fragile, in whose center floated a firm mattress, and a less and less cool refrigerator, and a desk * (that reminded him more and more of one of those empty parking lots beside a shopping mall where all the stores are vacant and horrible teenagers meet up to do nothing, to not look each other in the eye but only at their screens), and a chair, tired of holding him, where he only sat down now to *not* write.

Then, when there was nothing left for him outside, he began to sell himself: his blood * (which proved to be light and of the most banal and innutritious type, even for the thirstiest vampires) and his semen * (which turned out to be weak and impotent and made up of spermatozoids of the kind that don't feel the least hurry to arrive to an ovum and fertilize it, because they don't want to be babies in the first place and much less parents later).

And so, again, his dreams.

His sleeping dreams, sleeping yet more awake than the dreams of most everyone else.

Dreams that, yes, were coveted specimens of a race on the brink of extinction.

Dreams that were worth a great deal and that he surrendered, one by one, like someone removing secret parts of a model to be assembled or important pieces of a puzzle to be completed elsewhere, far away from the dreamer and in the vicinity of those who could no longer dream.

And, of course, money, yes.

A great deal of money in exchange for his dreams.

But, also, the answer to the question of his growing need to let her go, to forget her, to never dream of Ella ever again.

So here he goes, here he is, here he comes.

Recounting all of this in the same voice with which others count sheep.

A voice-over about to turn off.

A countdown voice.

A voice as if he were, at the same time, under the influence of a hypnotic pill and, also, the sedative diction of a hypnotist who counts down from 10 to 0.

A voice speaking strangely; with a strange cadence.

An inverted voice, unpronounceable and yet comprehensible.

A ventriloquist voice busting out of the belly of his mind and sounding like that voice made of random words that come together automatically and that, at one time, informed you of the exact time on a telephone as heavy and as dark as those nights when you couldn't sleep.

A voice that sounds first recorded, then listened to in rewind, then with repeating and recording the rewound part, then playing it back and listening to it straight through, sitting in a red room where a dwarf dances. Yes, *that* dwarf.

A voice that's like the flipside of a language and not the language it speaks, as if it were the shadow of the voice and not the voice itself speaking.

A voice running in reverse, yet moving forward, never looking back at everything it leaves behind.

A voice climbing the hill that leads to the Onirium to sell its dreams, another dream.

Or—to be more precise—to sell the only dream it has left.

The most coveted and desired dream of all.

And the dream most cherished by him.

A last dream, yes; but a recurring dream.

And also—and this is what has made it such a rare and valuable specimen for those in charge of the Onirium—a dream that came true.

His dream of you.

Your dream of his.

He ascends to the Onirium with an elastic and floating step, the way you move in a dream. Like at the beginning of that old and nineteenth-century and gothic and lonely novel. A singular novel. That's how he likes to imagine himself: moor and fog and him like that man to whom a good story will be told so, in turn, he can tell how it was told to him. As if he were Mr. Lockwood heading up the path that leads to a house known as Wuthering Heights, and arriving there, and being poorly received by its occupants. And lying down in a small bed with names carved in the wood. And falling asleep and dreaming a dream within a dream in which not a tree branch but an arm reaches through a windowpane and a hand with cold fingers grabs you and beseeches you and broken glass and blood on the sheets and a voice telling you it has been lost for a long time and asking you to let it in * (and, oh, he cuts himself off, he can't, he shouldn't speak of that book. He's not allowed to. It's a book that already has a mistress).

And, as if in a dream, everything changes direction, though he keeps climbing, up the path. Again: as if in a dream. A dream in which, above and beyond any drifting of those who tend to drift in dreams, it's unclear what's up or what's down or what's in front or what's behind * (though what's behind—as postulated by the insomniac harlequin-mentalist Vadim Vadimovich and as already explained to him in the Onirium—doesn't exist in dreams: in dreams there's neither past nor memory nor previous stops; in dreams you cannot walk backward like a perfectly broken toy); but a dream in which he's always certain he's moving toward Ella.

Her name, of course, isn't Ella (she tells him her name in his dream, but he doesn't manage to hear it, to hear her), but it's what he's decided to call her: a bit impersonal (especially in Spanish, as Ella, in addition to being a name, is the feminine pronoun meaning she/her), but at the same time, a personal and appropriate way to understand her. Ella is a way to identify her without forcing her to be someone she's not or to send her down a path not hers, Ella's, and from which there's no escape in any sense.

Ella is not, but somehow resembles, someone who left. And now she returns the way those who have left return: in dreams, in dreams that are the Great Beyond reaching out to us here, when we sleep and dream of people who have departed returning as ghosts, seeping and slipping in through cracks and holes, like smoke and rain.

And now, a slight detour, he remembers how yesterday he listened to that song about dreams, about other dreams.

He doesn't mean that one named "In Dreams," sung in an operatic voice and with deadpan and sinister face, by a man with dark sunglasses who looks like a wax sculpture of himself and whose name he doesn't remember. * (His name is Roy Orbison; and, great Roy Orbison anecdote: Bono dreams and composes in his dreams a song titled "She's a Mystery to Me" and he wakes up convinced it's a song that already exists by Roy Orbison; he sings it to his U2 bandmates, who listen to it and diagnose: "Orbison"; but they look for it and can't find it anywhere; and that same night, after the band's show, someone knocks at their dressing room door. It's Roy Orbison, who smiles at Bono and says: "I think you have a song for me, don't you?") And he always thought there are few things more unsettling than seeing someone sing, hiding their eyes and saying things like "It's too bad that all these things can only happen in my dreams / Only in dreams, in beautiful dreams."

And he's not talking about that other song either. That white-piano ode, barely hiding the solipsism and the do-nothing-so-that-everything-disappears: the comforting idea of utopia concealing entropy's ultimate desire, for everything to come crashing down and disappear. The one with that bit about "You may say I'm a dreamer / But I'm not the only one." And, now that he thinks of it, isn't it a little odd, like something out of a dream, that the piano isn't a string instrument? And, yes, he's not that surprised the man who wrote that song * (the one who also wrote "I'm Only Sleeping" and "I'm So Tired" and "Good Night") and who sang it with the voice of someone just waking up or just falling asleep and the cadence of a hypnotic hymn—suggesting to listeners they imagine various impossibilities—has, unexpectedly, ended up with his body shot full of lead. Because, yes, it's not advisable to suggest certain things, to open certain doors, to dream certain dreams. Inviting people to imagine absolute nothingness as the perfect form of harmony is tantamount to saying there is *also* too much of you; you are too much; there's nothing for you to do there; it's better to fade into the fog of dreams. To kill the messenger and there's no dreamer more perfect or definitive than a dead person. * (Now one of his best bad jokes, told to him by his Uncle Hey Walrus, the last time they saw each other: "I do remember perfectly where I was and what I was doing on the night they assassinated John Lennon, signed: Mark David Chapman"; and he laughs alone in the dark of the night, and how strange your own laugh sounds when you hear it on your own; thinking there is nothing more dangerous than saying "I have a dream," in front of multitudes; because dreams are not possessed, they don't belong to the one who dreams them. And if you describe them as your own in public, dreams end up biting the hand and cutting off the head of the one who dreams them.) And it doesn't surprise him that "Imagine" was, someone told him once, the favorite song of his mother, may she rest in peace, may she dream in peace.

But no, it's not "In Dreams" or "Imagine."

No: the song he's referring to, the one he's listening to now, is another song. Not the old man with the dark glasses * (Roy Orbison) and not the young man with the grandma glasses * (John Lennon). And he still hasn't figured out whose it is or who sings it. And there's nothing funnier to him than saying here he doesn't remember the title or performer * (it is, he's sure of it, one of the songs by his favorite songwriter, whom he went to see live so many times and with whom he crossed paths, unplugged, in hotels here and there, and the last time on . . . on . . . on that night when he planned to destroy himself and the whole world with him, in Switzerland, pressing buttons and pulling levers in that collider of hadrons and accelerator of particles, and was all that real or was it a dream he dreamed once and will never dream again?) and convincing himself he cannot pin it down, in the name of making it all work better as what gets told with eyes half closed.

Then he decides—because it suits this story—he can't remember particular features of that song, but he can remember the moment he heard it for the first time.

And it's just that there are songs that—when you hear them for the first time—function in the way of photography: they trap an instant forever and reveal it and fix it with the liquids of epiphany, so that, every time you hear that song, you can return to that definitive moment. Again and again. Everyone has their own: *that* song that functions like the key to the lock of the door of their lives * (not the eye of the keyhole but the ear of the keyhole where you rest your own ear when the eye sees nothing there) and to which they return again and again. Listening to it is more than remembering. Hearing it again is like accessing the possibility of suspending the undeniable and tyrannical laws of time: what was running before, suddenly, slows down and stops and . . . Listening to *that* song is, he understands all of a sudden, like a waking dream.

Here it comes again.

He hears it now coming uphill as he ascends to the Onirium. Jumping from the window of some burning building, playing again randomly on some eleventh-hour radio, tuning it in in the middle of the song, when the songwriter's name has already been announced * (and, ah, in this sleepless and dreamless world there's an overabundance of midnight DJs: a profession now as prestigious as that of a lawyer or doctor or soldier or priest). A song that is, at first, a series of possible dreams, a list * (and he loves making lists because lists end up making you and explaining who you are and what you're like) of waking things corrected with the help of horizontal bodies and closed eyes. Nothing too spectacular, not anything specific, nothing too very scientific.

There, in the song, again, a list of frayed events and disjointed objects. As if the song were more the dream of an object than of a person. No direction or any great connection, cards, numbers burning, folded umbrellas * (opening it up for conspiratorial and nightmarish interpretation of giving the signal to a sniper assassin or, waking explanation, reminding a president about to be killed of the past disgraces of his father / see-research JFK / The Umbrella Man / idea for a story or story for another one of those ideas that he'll never tell?), to completely stop and, at last, running and climbing and witnessing a crime impossible to solve yet so easy to see. An exhibitionist crime. A crime that feels no guilt at all for being a crime. And that crime has always taken place in the past: in that place where we're all guilty and for which we always invent excuses, alibis, an I-wasn't-there or an I-was-sleeping-and-dreaming at the exact time when all that went down.

Let's see.

Let's listen.

When he was born * (when he was born one of the many times he could've been born, the time he chooses for tonight like others choose the clothes they'll put on the next morning), his mother was dreaming. And his first cry didn't wake her * (it's always been said, since the very beginning, it was all quite clear: you arrive to the world, you wake up to life after a nine-month dream, crying and not laughing; there must be some reason). Her own cries of pain didn't wake her either, because his mother, fast asleep, didn't make a single sound during the birth. So, in a way, he is more the child of her dreams than her child. He never knew her, but, in a way, he knew her better than anybody; because there's nothing more intimate and personal than dreams. And she and he dreamed the same dream day and night for nine months. There were no borders for his mother's dreams. Nothing interrupted them. They were, yes, perfect dreams; because they had nothing of that uncomfortable, immodest, embarrassing moment of being recognized and acknowledged as dreams, as *just a dream*, when you wake up and, the first thing you think, like, the most automatic of reflexes, that whole: "Oh, it was a dream."

* (But he's not being clear, not explaining himself well. He begs your pardon, but the imprecision is inevitable: because he's talking about his sleeping dreams with the liquid grammar and gaseous logic of waking dreams, of the dreams of someone not yet asleep. Let's see, he's going to give it a go. And it won't be easy: it's clear his mother and father aren't the ones who appear here wearing their faces. But that's what's good about his mother and father, their definitive gesture with respect to him, his inheritance: that they disappeared so

long ago and so spectacularly gave him—they gave it to him, so he'd give it back—the chance to alter and transform them the way people change in dreams, given that dreams are an accumulation of ways of being awake distorted by the fact of being asleep. For example: his true but oh so difficult to believe parents: terrorist parents for many but terrified ones for him, addicts of being *en vogue* and shaking from the withdrawals brought on by being *passé*, of passing out of fashion, of no longer being there. But now they're coming back, now they're coming back again, rewritten by him with a finger in the air of the dark night, as if he were conducting a brief nocturnal score to be executed by two soloists already executed so long ago.)

His mother * (this variation of his mother that he now composes and that performs here and that, yes, it's true, also has something of his sister's story) wanted a child but not a husband. So, in the tumult of one of those sleepless parties, her fertile ova dancing their dance in her belly, his mother approached—after a months-long investigation—someone who seemed to her the most genetically perfect specimen: a classmate who didn't want a child but wanted his mother. If only for one night. All good then. Quick accord. No promises made. In and out and good luck and *adiós*.

And so it was.

His mother emerged hot and burning from the fire of that party, all her normal systems functioning to perfection while inside her body lights were turning on that'd never been turned on and buttons were being pushed and needles were jumping that'd been patiently waiting for that moment. Her biological clock struck the exact and precise hour and there he was, there inside, the future suddenly turned present. A dream made reality.

His mother, of course, knew right away, right after; with the sorceress' certainty only newly-minted mothers possess. His mother left that party smiling and, blind with joy, crossed the street and didn't see the car coming at top speed * (driven by an insomniac man, a man who only stops to fill up with gas and then returns to the highway and there he stays, at top speed, counting those brief dashes and dots Morse-code style down the center of the asphalt, certain he's reading faster and faster and unable to stop the best novel-in-code ever written, and so anxious to find out what'll happen in the next chapter after having run over a woman in the last one) that ran her over and didn't even stop to see what'd happened.

His mother never woke up.

The doctors diagnosed brain death, deep coma, one-way trip with no return ticket. At first, the doctors didn't detect his presence, didn't see him. The doctors were concerned with other things; and the concern gave way to resignation when it was decided the best thing, the most merciful thing, the most humane thing, was to pull the plug. And that's what they did. But his mother—to the joy of his grandparents, who'd never been fully onboard with shutting down and burying the thing they loved most—kept on living and breathing and dreaming. Thus, his mother attained certain fame. The troubling fame of miracles. Magazines and TV channels devoted entire pages and long minutes to her, giving her a name as obvious as it was appropriate: "Sleeping Beauty." Because his mother was, indeed, very beautiful. And very beautiful women are even more beautiful when shrouded in dreams. * (And his mother was even closer to the original version of Sleeping Beauty, in which the prostrate young woman is impregnated in her dream by the prince, more shady than charming, and gives birth, nine months later, without ever opening her eyes.) And the dreams that shrouded his mother were perfect, invulnerable, nothing could wake them up. Dreams without any meaning. Abstract and brilliant shapes multiplying themselves in abyssal mirrors, as if trapped inside the circle of a kaleidoscope aimed in vain and out of pure vanity at the stars.

When, after a couple months, it emerged that his mother was pregnant, the power of her miracle doubled and the weeks were counted down to the big event. The TV news devoted a special segment to his mother (and to him), every day, after the weather report, a contest was organized to come up with a name for him, and pretty soon his first ultrasounds were broadcast live and direct.

There he was, dreaming inside his dreaming mother. Sharing her dreams, feeding off them, dreams that weren't like the dreams of people who dream only a few hours of the day with the rapid movement of their eyes under the soft and nearly translucent sheets of their lids.

No: his mother's dreams stared, and they were staring at him.

And all around and outside her, multitudes assembled to pray. * (They prayed not in the name of the resurrected though as-if-half-asleep Lazarus of Bethany—whose figure was complicated and volatile, because it competed with that of the Messiah and for that reason the wise men decided to assassinate him a few days after his return, and dismember his body and spread it across the world—but in the name of the lesser-known Daughter of Jairus, whom Jesus awakens from a deep sleep with an Aramaic and commanding "Talitha Koum," meaning "Little girl, I say to you, get up.")

Miracle.

He was born in the middle of a winter night.

Lightning and thunder.

Dogs barking and cats meowing and one of the nurses starting to speak in tongues and astrological conjunctions. Many wonders. All the typical clichés of the atypical.

His mother gave birth to him and then sank forever into the darkness, perhaps, though he couldn't understand it at the time, saying goodbye in her dreams with an "I'll only be gone for a while," with that oh so studied style of those who leave and never come back, and—as that *other* song explains—that's why God made the movies.

His grandmother—who'd always studied the world of dreams with the devotion with which others study the twists and turns of telenovelas or the ups and downs of their finances—told him that his mother opened her eyes when she died, that she died with her eyes open, that she woke up to die, but before she did, she saw him. And she smiled one last and perfect smile; because his mother knew that not only had her dream become reality but that, in addition, now, reality was part of her dream.


He writes all of this—not his book of dreams but his series of dreams, numbered and addending and always following a †—in one of his biji notebooks. * (The biji—筆記—is a genre of classic Chinese literature that appeared for the first time during the Wei and Jin dynasties, and reached peak maturity during the Tang and Song dynasties. "Biji" can be translated, roughly yet more or less faithfully, as "notebook." The different items in a biji can be numbered, but, also, can be read without following any order, making your own way, starting at any point and jumping back and forth or up and down or side to side. Beginning at the end and ending at the beginning. And a biji can contain curious anecdotes, nearly blind quotations, random musings, philosophical speculations, private theories regarding private matters, criticism of other works, and anything its owner and author deems appropriate. Example:

† Always put in a book—though not always on the first page—the completely unnecessary and simultaneously indispensable inscription: "Any similarities to reality in what is described or in descriptions of an individual or in individual descriptions in this book are purely coincidental.")

He writes that and can't help but feel moved by all those oneiric obsessives who sleep with notebook and pen beside the bed. And who (because the recommended average of eight hours already passed, because somebody turned on a light, because they were stabbed by the stinger of a nightmare and the flash of their own scream woke them) write it all down as soon as they wake up, frantic. Scribbling a murky chronicle of what happened to them but never took place on the other side; feeling how, as the seconds pass, the light material of their dreams dissolves and all that's left is the somnambulant and imprecise memory and confused reading of what they dreamed. Night after night until—like he read in a book, in the first book of a last youth—they reach the climax of a dream in which they appear reading a notebook containing their own dreams. Those dreams that surround this brief life and that, for many, are an important though not entirely visible part of it. The dream like the tip of the theoretical iceberg. That which some will recite imperfectly, like a poorly learned lesson, to a psychoanalyst who will apply general notions and statistics to something unique and irrepeatable. While the patient, there, on the divan, sleeping awake and needing so badly to believe in the trance of absolute truth or of that which, the patient supposes, should be absolutely true. Something like that.

And he's said it before, thought it before * (those dreamed repetitions, those refrains so characteristic of dreams), but now he writes it down:

Dreams are the fingerprints of the brain.

Dreams are the pupil of the unconscious.

Dreams are the lobe of the ear of DNA.

Someone said it before, someone talking in their sleep: no two dreams are the same. And so—though classic motifs repeat on more than on occasion, again, greatest hits like falling from the sky, walking naked through the street, teeth falling out in public—there are, in the event that dreams might have some meaning, no two dreams that end up making the same meaning of the same thing. Just like—depending on the reader—no two David Copperfields or Martin Edens or Dick Divers or Hugh Persons are the same.

He finds it hard to believe.

He finds it hard to believe anyone believes in that.

He finds it even harder to believe anyone could end up believing it's possible to make some kind of believable message about why you should believe in all that; but it's also true that people believe in the whole no two people in the universe have the same fingerprints or the same eye pattern and color or the same earlobe shape, without wondering how such a certainty was arrived at, how it was proven. Or does anyone really have the power to crosscheck the fingerprints and pupils and ears of everyone who lived or lives or will live?

Dreams, on the other hand, *never* resemble each other and are hard pressed to repeat. So-called recurrent dreams * (he'll get back to those later on) are nothing but the increasingly diffuse echo of the first and original aria of a dream we refuse to let go of or (his case) the stage with fixed scenography for performances with no fixed lines.

Dreams, for the majority of people, are nothing but the tatters of a fallen flag, flapping in the wind just before being lowered and—among all the theories impossible to elevate to theorems and, as such, inapplicable to his situation—is left with that which postulates hypotheses regarding how these loose threads of conversations and landscapes and moments are nothing more than the way the brain self-regulates, eliminating all that which serves nothing, which upsets, which takes up too much space, which sullies. Extra pieces of the puzzle of puzzled brains, white noise or that ghost sound that—if you listened carefully—you could hear, between one song and the next, in the deepest grooves of those old LPs. Others, on the other hand, are inclined to think dreams are life itself: that in dreams fantasies are realized, that you are there and you live and you think the way nobody dares to think and to be here.

His dreams, on the other hand, are something else.

His dreams are different dreams.

His dreams are laser and digitalized.

His dreams have the precision of something unforgettable. They aren't dreams like everyone else has. They aren't mute and wavering sequences that can make enormous plot leaps, moving from a house to an airplane, from a mattress to a gallows, from a relative to a monster, always in black and white * (and to be honest he never really understood how anyone could ever specify something like "Dreams are in black and white").

Could it be that once movies started getting made in color, black and white was relegated to the realm of dreams and memories?

Are memories in black and white?

Remember: in films someone dreams and the red is black and the yellow is white. He doesn't know, it doesn't seem like the most solid of claims.

In any case, his dreams are in color and in CinemaScope.

And their plotlines are linear and clear.

Nothing of passing through Z after leaving A and before arriving to B.

His life is—as, if you think about it a little, everyone's life is—much more digressive than any of his dreams. And so, arriving to this point and before moving on—continuing the waking dream—he should insert a small clarification.

In color or in black and white.

Either way.

And here it is: the woman of his dreams is not his mother; even though once, long ago, for nine months, they dreamed exactly the same dream, and her dreams were his and his dreams were hers.

The woman of his dreams is Ella.

And every time Ella appears in his dreams (in his sleeping dreams, he means) he wakes up, he manages to wake up, forces himself to wake up. It's been a long and arduous training, like that of an Olympic athlete or, better, an oneiric athlete. Waking up—every time Ella appears—is to reach the goal interrupting the race, thinking that thing about "I'll never know you, but I'm going to love you all the same," something like that. The guarantee that what's interrupted turns into a constant (*to be continued . . .*) that guarantees he'll dream again of Ella and wake up when he sees her and . . .

And so Ella signifies his sleeping dreams are drawing to an end so his waking dreams can begin.


And he's going to say it now and quickly and without overthinking to avoid having time or space to regret it.

He has the power to make his dreams not come true.

He'll get back to all this later on.


And something else that always intrigued him: that whole thing where people count sheep or lambs to fall sleep. Why count? And why lambs or sheep. It's obvious there's a relationship between sleep and counting: the countdown of hypnotists sinking their volunteers into the most docile of somnolence. Not a comma but an ellipsis where the will is suspended and surrenders to the dictums of the magician: "Now you're a sheep, one of those sheep someone counts so they can fall asleep." And off that poor guy goes * (like Uncle Hey Walrus, more details coming up). Hopping across the stage while in the audience everyone laughs and some wonder, for a few seconds, whether they've been hypnotized for years or minutes, in a trance they understand as their lives. Whether their entire lives, poor dreamers, are but the hypnotic command of the illusionist. An illusionist who at any moment will snap his fingers and humankind will discover that, in reality, they were nothing but an ancient and dreamed fiction.

He, to get to sleep, counts and recounts dreams.

"Tell a dream, lose a reader," warned * (how could he forget it'd been he who'd said it? symptoms of a lack of nocturnal life? liquefaction of memory due to a lack of dreams?) the writer Henry James.

He hopes it isn't true and this dictum isn't operating in these pages.

Because he has several dreams to tell.

He can't not do it.

Dreams within dreams, as well.

Chinese boxes in the hands of Russian dolls facing the abyss.

Dreams are an inextricable part of his waking life and—at the indivisible nucleus of them all—of the life of the woman of his dreams.

Of Ella's life.

Yesterday he saw her again.

Ella works in a bookstore (there's no profession he finds more attractive in a woman) and *in addition* she's the most beautiful woman in the world. He doesn't know if she thinks the same thing concerning his beauty, as he learned in *another* song, which would require an understanding of what he is. No mean feat. And he's not entirely sure she intuits that. But it seems she suspects *something*. What he's sure of is Ella is sure she's not really interested in the fact that he thinks she's the most beautiful woman in the world. There are beautiful women—like Ella—who figure out how to put their beauty in the eyes of their beholders. They know, they intuit, that an awareness of their own beauty would be too great a burden to bear and so—rationally and intuitively—they decide it would be best for everyone else to bear it, that weight. Maybe that's why Ella has that tattoo on her forehead, right where her third eye should open. But no. Ella's tattoo looks like something designed to shut that supposed third eye and to enhance the power of her other two eyes. Something that might be a cross or a sword and that looks like this † and that, he thinks, Ella had tattooed on her to distract a little from her beauty, for all those who stare at her and can't stop staring at her eyes. That † like a lightning rod and a shield and a mirror that deflects adoring and uncomfortable looks. That † like an evasive maneuver that, at least for a few seconds, makes you wonder what it might mean instead of wondering where a woman like that has come from.

Yes: there are women enslaved to their beauty and there are women who, with their beauty, enslave everyone else.

And Ella doesn't want to be either.

And there are days when, for this slave, Ella's beauty becomes indomitable and dominant and, looking at her, he wants to fall to his knees, to sleep, and to dream that he wakes up and she is still there.

Now it's one of those first afternoons of autumn when it seems the whole world is a half-finished drama or a comedy, and everything has the look and feel of an intermission between one act and the next. And when, as the actors return to their places, it will become apparent—with little surprise—that it's a different show now, that what's happening now has nothing of the look and sound of everything that came before.

In the first moments of bygone autumns, people dreamed more because their dreams were changing wardrobe. And, in the mornings, when the sun no longer rises so early and so quickly, when everyone emerges onto the streets bleary and fresh out of bed, he can still see the remnants of dreams wrapped around their necks like scarves, covering their mouths, refusing to release their possessed masters.

The beginning of autumn is his favorite time of year and, also, the season when he feels best in bookstores, the perfect climate for spending hours standing around, there, inside.

He enters the bookstore.

One of those bookstores that used to be just a bookstore but recently has been mutating and, like the mythic creatures from ancient bestiaries, combining the features of multiple species * (if there's something more interesting than a lion it's a lion with wings and the face of a woman and questions in its mouth and delusions of divine grandeur) and this one is a bookstore-café-record store.

He pretends to look for something: *Todavía Estamos Aquí*, the latest album from Los Dinosaurious Inextinguibles, for example. Or some edition of *The Glass Key* by Dashiell Hammett, so he can read again its soothing ending—after all that betrayal and death and revelation—where a girl recounts a dream. One of the endings and one of the dreams he likes best in the history of literature, in a detective novel that, along with Raymond Chandler's *The Long Goodbye*, can be read like a daydreamed variation of *The Great Gatsby*, that almost-detective novel and . . . Oh, the things he thinks about in bookstores in general and that one in particular to keep from thinking about Ella.

The bookstore belongs to a man named Homero.

No, he's not blind and, yes, he is Ella's father.

And one night, to his immense displeasure, he dreamed Homero was his own lost father, who had once driven a car blindfolded, and he woke up with a smile of relief: no, Ella was not his sister.

He opens and closes books. He reads random words that, always, refer to the same thing: "Writing is nothing more than a guided dream," "Dreams are the genus; nightmares the species," "Dreams are an aesthetic work, perhaps the earliest aesthetic expression," "We have these two ideas: the belief that dreams are part of waking, and the other, the splendid one, the belief of the poets: that all waking is a dream," "If we think of the dream as a work of fiction—I think it is—it may be that we continue to spin tales when we wake and later when we recount them," "We don't know exactly what happens in dreams" * (Jorge Luis Borges; he still remembers that name, luckily; who knows how much longer he will, how many nights he has left before that prison he writes in fills up with sand that, grain by grain, covers and chokes and buries and erases him).

Annoyed, he closes the book that—as everyone knows happens in dreams, this is one of the quickest and most efficient ways to know you are dreaming—changes title and subject and genre because dreams are not attentive readers and their capacity for concentration is minimal. The speed of dreams is greater than the speed of sight. And so, putting the book down to one side, he nullifies his desire to have it in his dreams, and slips—without losing sight of Ella, behind the counter—into territories he feels are safer. He takes the long way around to avoid getting anywhere near the esotericism section * (where there abound those absurd dictionaries of oneiric interpretation and all of that) and shudders a little as he passes the self-help section (and wonders the same thing as always: how are there people desperate and deluded enough to believe in the efficacy of those manuals; how can those people who can't help anyone think they can help themselves by following the instructions of something written by people they don't know, whom they know little or nothing about, and who don't know them and who are, inevitably, as in-need of help as they are, and who can't help themselves except by writing these books). So he stops in the comics section. * (Do those DC-variety comics still exist that, when he was a kid, produced in him a combination of fascination and disdain? The ones that announced themselves as belonging to those "imaginary adventures" that toyed with impossibilities like Superman dying or Batman retiring—with things that ended up really happening so many years later—that at the time could only be understood as waking dreams?). He'll be safe there and, also, have a good view of her.

It's a good position from which to watch Ella.

A boy with robot airs studies him around the borders of a manga magazine. A kid with zits and tattoos * (or maybe it's the quantity of zits that makes him think of one of those surfing, whaling Maori warriors) gives him the defiant face of the modern and psychotic Batman, and he has no doubt he's there to get a better view of Ella too.

He pretends they don't exist (his grandfather always warned him that there are certain rare animals you should never stare at because it's like an invitation to fight or for them to sink their teeth into you) and * (again, please, none of those compilations of "imaginary" and dreamed "adventures" of Superman where he marries Lois Lane or dies or goes out into the street without his Superman suit or falls from the sky having lost the ability to fly) picks up an album dedicated to one of the specimens of the genre: outlines of childish animated drawings devoted to performing brutal actions where everything has the rhythm of onomatopoetic nightmares. He opens it and there's that little monster barely captured in the panels: sleeping with an open mouth that lets out a *zzzzzzzzz* and, above his head, inside a bubble, a saw sawing a tree trunk and . . . he closes it. The little monster from the comic could be a more or less close relative of Manga Boy or Freak Batman, he thinks.

And, suddenly, over the bookstore sound system, a song comes on, *that* song that's a series of dreams. And maybe that was a good way to make contact, he thinks. To approach Ella. To ask her if she knows the name of that song he can't remember and maybe then, at the end, in a brand new and freshly added verse, the song will sing about a bookstore and a beautiful woman and . . .

. . . then something happens. Something happens so it won't happen again. Something happens so it won't have the obligation or the right to happen.

He walks toward Ella and his steps are interrupted * (he doesn't like how that phrase sounds, it sounds like a poorly-aged translation, but, he understands, there's nothing he can do about it: after all, dreams are the translation of a translation; and his is a cursory translation, rushed out of fear they'll start to disappear, that his dreams will start dreaming and will be forgotten by the one who dreams them thereby provoking their oblivion) because, now, she's coming toward him. Walking, but in that way some women have that's like running in slow motion. And Ella smiles at him; but there's something terrible in that smile: it's one of those forced smiles, like a happy death's head. One of those open-mouthed and air-sucking smiles with which synchronized swimmers come up before diving back down to smile underwater, a hermetic smile where their clenched teeth keep them from filling up with water and drowning.

And Ella opens her arms and her lips and it's as if he could see, there, inside her throat, how those words he wanted so badly to hear but she shouldn't say, here and now, were taking shape; because saying them, giving them sound and releasing them into the air, would mean bringing about the end of everything.

So he shuts his eyes to keep from seeing them and opens his eyes here, far away, where he can no longer hear them.

He walks toward Ella and his steps are interrupted (again, the same phrase: the horror that writers, in addition to having recurrent dreams, have dreams with recurrent phrases and dislike how they're written and dreamed) because he feels a terrible pain first in his left arm and then in his chest; but it doesn't matter because it's a pain that'll make him collapse right there in front of Ella. He regains consciousness inside the ambulance and is so happy to discover that Ella is not traveling beside him, not holding his hand throughout the ambulance ride. And there's something beautiful in the way cars and buses and even empty ambulances move aside to make way for the high-speed and wailing red light of his love for Ella, who, luckily, isn't there. So, quite content, he keeps on dying, feeling more alive than ever.

He walks toward Ella and his steps are interrupted (ugh, he's not going to mention this again) and now Manga Boy and Freak Batman have that final look—like an inverse sketch, the sketch you only arrive to after the finished work, the signed portrait—that distinguishes the terminally ill. Eyes tired with the awareness of everything they won't ever see, youthful wrinkles that only appear on the faces of those who won't have a chance to grow old, their hairless heads showing skin reddened more by the moon than the sun.

He pauses in the used books section and opens an old compendium of advice for home gardeners and, from out of its pages falls what appears to be an ancient manuscript inked with numbers and cabalistic symbols. And somehow he understands it's a formula capable of curing all the ills of this world. And Ella understands this too; because she comes running toward him, tears streaming down her face, overcome with the transcendence of his discovery, her eyes open so wide he can't help opening his until he hears them groan from the effort. His eyes wide open like two mouths opening in a kiss.

He walks toward Ella and his steps are interrupted because Ella comes toward him and slaps him. And it's the best slap of his life. * (A close-up and Golden-Age-of-Hollywood slap.) Ella is a mark tattooed on his cheek. And Ella is so strong his head jerks in a bad way and from then on he'll, happily, spend the rest of his life with a terrible pain in the neck. And yet, he understands, there is a kind of passion in that slap. There are motives behind that slap that are not for him to know, so he leaves that place to enter in another. Into a bookstore where Ella works, for example.

He walks toward Ella and his steps are interrupted because Homero comes toward him from the bestseller section and accuses him of stealing books. He runs toward the door, leaving behind, falling from the secret pockets of his book-stealing jacket, multiple tomes of the complete works of an author he idolizes but whose books are unavailable, because they were never written. Because that author doesn't exist on the side of life that's not a dream.


He walks toward Ella and his steps are interrupted because they hear shouts and songs and, outside, everyone is kissing and hugging and, yes, at last, that dictatorial and dynastic government has fallen. The end of years and years under the banner and boots of a single surname. And he and Ella know the thing to do is hug and kiss the person closest to you, and neither he nor she is about to throw themselves into the arms of Manga Boy or Freak Batman, so he decides to run away, to get out of there as quickly as possible, making his way through the people who are kissing and hugging and toppling bronze statues in plazas and parks. They bring them down so that, in their place, nothing is perfect, new bronze statues inevitably grow with arms raised, all of them pointing nowhere, but so certain nowhere is in that precise direction.
There.


He walks toward Ella and his steps are interrupted by a great noise coming from the street. The murmur of a cataclysm descending from the heights. He and Ella go out into the street bound together by fear and curiosity * (curiosity and fear are powerful accelerants of human relationships and, suddenly, she and he are strangers who know each other perfectly) and they see people running and cars crashing and, in the sky, what at first looks like a metal cloud and subsequently turns out to be a spaceship of interplanetary fabrication. The grace of its curves, the elegance of its lights, cannot be things of this world, he thinks. Human beings are not yet ready to imagine or create such things.

The spaceship delicately alights—like an insect on a flower—and from inside it emerge two transparent creatures. They approach him and Ella with wise smiles and, with the silent and telepathic flow of their thoughts, explain to them they've come to save humanity, to do away with all the evil and evil people on this planet. And the only thing they ask in return—after having studied earthlings for years—is that he and Ella go with them, that they climb aboard the spaceship and accompany them back to their world. They say the two of them are the most perfect humans they've ever seen; he and Ella were made to be together and take the best of their species to the farthest reaches of the universe. "You're the new founders of a new history," they say. "You're the first two names in the first chapter and it'll be your children who will follow the example of our love on a new Earth where there will be no war and no sickness. That's the price you'll have to pay for us to prevent the millions of inhabitants of this damned old Earth from continuing down the path toward self-destruction."

He and Ella look at each other and smile and then, before it's too late * (saying to himself that aspects of the plot of one of his favorite novels whose title he doesn't remember have been combined with one of his favorite songs whose title he doesn't remember) he forces himself, once more, to open his eyes, to remember.


He walks toward Ella and his steps are interrupted because Ella is walking toward him and they stop in front of each other, without a word, looking at each other in a strange silence like fire that freezes or snow that burns. And here the question is and will forever be which of them will dare to break that strange silence—that ever so eloquent silence—to say the thing that can only be said once. Those slumbering words that, once awakened, will never be able to close their eyes again. Those invisible words in a silence that—unlike what's falsely claimed concerning the visibility of the Great Wall of China from space—*can* be seen from the moon. Because that silence is the greatest structure ever constructed by man and woman, by a man and a woman.

See it.

Open your eyes.

There it is.


It's not easy to open his eyes, to interrupt the trajectory of his dreams in that exact moment, just when he and Ella are about to be bound together forever.

It has required a difficult training, an arduous programming.

It hasn't been easy, but it had to happen.

The possibility that Ella might someday come to love him in waking life depends on him waking up just before Ella begins to love him in his dreams, he tells himself.

He said it before, but maybe he wasn't entirely clear.

Or maybe it was so clear it wasn't understood.

This tends to happen with simple pronouncements and complex dreams: people distrust their simplicity and discard them without taking into account that they're complex entities, and that's when all the trouble begins.

So, better, just in case, it bears repeating:

He has the power to make his dreams not come true.

And, of course, this is the part and the moment when, he thinks, many will smile with that pity, born more of scorn than commiseration, and will say: "What's so special about that? I have the power to make my dreams not come true too."

To which he will insist:

He has the power to make his dreams not come true.

And he'll add the following, something difficult to say and put in writing; because certain things are not easy to confess:

When he says he has the power to make his dreams not come true, he means nothing he dreams will ever take place. His dreams are always too fast asleep to wake up and come true. Everything he dreams is automatically eliminated from the plot of his story and the waking story of humanity. It's an absurd power and impossible to show to second and third parties.

Once—after multiple drinks—he said to an acquaintance: "I have the power to make my dreams not come true." And his friend looked at him the way you look at an idiot and said: "Me too."

So he explained better: he'll never have a heart attack or find himself naked in the bookstore where Ella works or be chased for stealing books or have Ella slap him.

And he'll never discover the formula to cure all the ills of the world and this world won't be saved by the cosmic fondness of lyrical or invasive aliens, the ones who wait until you're asleep to steal your body and replicate and replace you while you dream. He'll never be defeated by the dictatorship that sinks and buries his country.

And the ones he remembers here are just a handful of the dreams he's had. A small sample of variations—hundreds, thousands, there are nights when he dreams up to five of them—where the good news is, again and again, aborted and dead, by the power and volition of a possible new love in a permanent state of gestation and, as far as he knows, with no clear due date.

Then they'll ask him what he dreamed before he met Ella and he'll say he never remembered his dreams before and didn't care to remember them. He's not responsible for everything that could've happened or stopped happening before he started dreaming of Ella. Or he is. But he cares even less about that than he cares about what happened or about what happened in the dreams he does remember, his dreams of Ella.

And he'll add that not a night goes by when the pleasure of dreaming of Ella hasn't signified the death of some good news. Dreams like the one about the heart attack, about stealing books, about finding himself naked, about the slap, are not the most abundant; they are of the more transcendent variety.

And yesterday he dreamed that, while he was in the bookstore, the newspaper vendors hawked bonus issues with information regarding the capture of that serial killer who, he's sorry, because of him, will never be captured.

They'll tell him he's a miserable bastard * (to say he's just a miserable bastard doesn't seem sufficient / find more powerful synonyms) and he'll say, agreed, that's possible. But it's not something he asked for. This power incubated during nine months floating inside his mother, swinging in the hammock of a coma isn't something he's dreamed. He never wanted to be a hero and, much less, a secret hero. It's too great a responsibility (that would force on him the terrible and constant exercise of not dreaming certain good things and thereby aborting the possibility that they happen or the imposition of dreaming terrible things so they never take place) and not something he asked for. Not even in his dreams. Besides, he's certain—were he able to master such discipline—he wouldn't last long. His neurons would resist those chains and before long the blooming party of rebellious and inoperable tumors would take place.

So he opted for something more humble and intimate: to not let Ella love him in his dreams so that, who knows, her love might reach him some waking day while, there outside, everywhere, the world keeps committing suicide in slow motion, unhurriedly yet unceasingly, as his insomniac nightmares come true.


There it is.

He already said it

He already confessed it.

He has the power to make his dreams not come true.

And, yes, all of you do, too.

But no.

It's not the same, not the same thing.

And all that—his dream made of dreams—is what he's on his way to sell, right now, up in the Onirium.


Here it comes, here it is, as if in a dream; passing from one stage to the next, from one sleep stage to the next less-asleep sleep stage, coming up toward the surface and oh so difficult to interpret.

And to him, the interpretation of dreams always seemed as absurd as attempting to weave sheets and blankets out of spider webs. He supposes—it occurs to him now—that one of the most important secret moments in the history of humanity took place when an ancient man proclaimed and convinced his contemporaries that dreams were not another life as real as waking life, but, simply, a delirious catharsis and a necessary shut-eyed purge. But maybe, in attaining such certainty something else was lost, something important, something simultaneously lively and tranquil.

And in the past he laughed at and made fun of those dream dictionaries and books of dreams. And that doesn't mean he hasn't read and studied them in depth, the same way—atheist and agnostic—he has always been interested in religions and sacred texts, as repositories of ideas, as (des)instruction manuals, as places to pause and look up at the stars, head tilted back, reading and not praying. Were sacred texts realistic or fantastic depending on who was reading them and believing or not believing in them? Did that matter? What mattered was that the gods were practical as well as theoretical.

The gods have always used dreams as a direct line for communicating desires, mandates, and omens. Dreams like a telephone ringing in the night; and few things are as frightening as a telephone ringing in the dead of night. Especially when it startles us from our sleep, disguised as an alarm clock, as a machine with a will and disturbing plans of its own * (the invention of, probably, one of the most hated yet unknown men in History: the American clockmaker Levi Hutchins, in 1787, to help wake himself up at four in the morning; though they say Plato already had a clock with a mechanism similar to the water organ, to mark the beginning of the hour of his lectures; and that the Buddhist monk Yi Xing had already designed a device governed by the music of the stars; and that Dante Alighieri, along with his Beatrice is already contemplating, in *Paradiso*, canto 14, verses 10-18, inexplicably enraptured, a kind of infernal cosmic alarm clock made of spheres and wheels and lights).

So, better, dreams like the rungs on the ladder Jacob dreamed, or like the ripe bovine dreams of the Pharaoh Joseph interprets, or the dreamed conversations between Solomon and his Maker, or the Three Kings dreaming it would be best to avoid running into Herod, while another Joseph, unsatisfied, dreams of angels who advise him to flee to Egypt after his, supposedly virginal and immaculate, wife tells him she has something unbelievable yet true to tell him.

Dreams like fractured highways intersecting without stoplights or road signs indicating the answer to that perpetual are we there yet of the most miraculous children, in the backseat, but knowing that, if there's any justice, they'll arrive long before and far ahead of their drivers.

And he has also read dream books and journals, trying to find an explanation for what happened to him. * (But he never found anything resembling his own dreams in the dreams of Emanuel Swedenborg, Franz Kafka [who never got around to telling us what Gregor Samsa's "disturbing" dreams were about before he wakes up and discovers that his life is a nightmare], Graham Green, Jack Kerouac, Federico Fellini, Georges Perec, or Bruno Schulz, where no one ever says it's all just a dream and yet . . . )

His dreams seem, always, suspiciously related to his own and respective books, functioning as a kind of occupational annex or attic. More or less unhinged architecture that, nevertheless, isn't too out of sync with the main floors. Only the words of William S. Burroughs moved him: in an introductory fragment to his book of dreams, *My Education*, where he also offers a recipe for "making botulism" that "was used with conspicuous success by Pancho Villa."

*(Here it is: "For years I have wondered why dreams are often so dull when related, and this morning I find the answer, which is very simple—like most answers you have always known: No context . . . like a stuffed animal set on the floor of a bank.")

No context.

Burroughs was right.

But what Burroughs—who fired his first pistol when he was eight, who was convinced he gave off ultraviolet infrared rays that turned him into *"el hombre invisible"* * (just so, in Spanish); who said he'd crashed a passenger plane with the power of his mind; who with his sharp and jagged cut-ups of words believed he was shaping extra-dimensional and talismanic structures of language; who killed off his enemies in his novels; who was convinced if we didn't dream we would die, because our brains need diversion and get bored of waking life and let go—he didn't or couldn't know that dreams can, if trained and strengthened, first modify their context to later be transformed into the context themselves.

He does know that. And so—his case, his life—hundreds of stuffed animals on the floor of a bank nobody considers a bank anymore, but the maddest warehouse of stuffed animals, where feeding those clawed and fanged mummies isn't permitted.

And he's the guardian of that warehouse of stuffed animals that was never a bank but a bookstore. He strolls through it every night, when nothing is moving, when all the stuffed animals have gone to sleep, and he, asleep, takes aim at one of them * (he feels a special predilection for the elephants, an animal that has always seemed to him the most oneiric of all and he just remembers, dreaming, something he read once in deluded monastery manuals or something like that about elephants disappearing from Europe during the Middle Ages and turning back into fantastical animals) with the beam of his flashlight and moves toward Ella. And his steps are interrupted so that another dream—another version of his dream—starts over and, once again, the speed of things is altered. And so, suddenly, there are too many glass keys and too few steel keys and so little time to try to open that thin yet invulnerable door that separates wakefulness from sleep.

He already said it: his metaphors are few but rustproof.

And, ah, that song, that song . . .

A song that—like a lullaby rocking itself never to sleep but forever awake—seems to go on and on and on, as if you were running shirtless across the rooftop of a hotel in Avignon where you slept with but didn't *sleep* with Ella. A song that seems to always be rising, as if seeking a refrain that's ever higher, higher still.


The long and sinuous climb that leads to the edifice of the Onirium is not exactly a climb. The climb that leads to the edifice of the Onirium * (a chaos of stairways as if bursting out of one of the M. C. Escher prints that tended to adorn the walls of his adolescence, where the steps appear to lead nowhere and everywhere at the same time) is long and tiring, but at no time does it give you the feeling of climbing, but, rather, of ascending. As if you were floating. The way you float in dreams. And he wonders if that might not be the idea: that the journey here is tiring, exhausting, producing the need to sleep and the desire, perchance, to dream.

He's not the only one. There are multitudes here. A long and serpentine line that starts at the edges of the city, passes through the residential neighborhoods, skirts around a ring of barracks whose diameter grows by the day, until at last it reaches the first stairway at the base of the hill.

They are many, yes, but fewer all the time; because those in charge of buying dreams, the Onirium scientists, have gotten better and better at identifying the mythomaniacs and the fraudsters and even those who've convinced themselves they're still dreaming when actually they're just sleeping.

That's not his case.

He is authentic and true and legitimate.

One of the few Morpheus Pluses.

And, of course, what certifies him as such isn't anything as banal as a falsifiable and losable and thievable piece of plastic: it's his palm print when he sets it atop a laser/digital scanner at the gates to the Onirium.

Being a Morpheus Plus gives him the ability to avoid the whole process of the climbing up to the edifice and grants him the privilege of entering through a special door for the chosen few. For the subjects who have special value to the Onirium and to all humanity. The Morpheus Pluses are the select bearers and dreamers of recurrent dreams. The few who remain, the ever fewer, the now you see them, now you don't. The abracadabras! and the prestos! And the thing is that the magic of the recurrent dream—those who run the Onirium have come to understand—is what keeps them dreaming. The recurrent dream that withstands and resists The White Plague. The recurrent dream that immunizes you to the vapors and desert breath of the White Plague that prevent all possibility of precipitations of dreams. The personal and unique and exclusive recurring dream: a recurring dream that has nothing to do and nothing to dream with the recurring dreams everyone has. It's been said, been enumerated before, here are some more: the menacing banality of being hunted by people you don't know or running away from ones you do, your teeth falling out in public (for Sigmund Freud the equivalent of the desire to get pregnant in women or the terror of castration in men), the inability to get your house in order or discovering new rooms inside it or not knowing where the bathroom is or not being able to turn on the lights in the place you live and sleep (the home as the body, Freud again), finding lost objects, losing control of a vehicle, being swept away by a tornado or a huge wave or of drowning. All manifestations of anxiety or posttraumatic stress or some obsessive disorder of neurotic and repetitious compulsions or (Carl Jung now) some other factor contributing to the integration of the psyche. *
(Or, why not, a sleeping form of the constant rewriting writers endure

while awake: a dose/free sample of the torment they all suffer so that those lucky enough to be just readers are given a brief awareness of everything they've saved themselves by being simply devoted to the blessing of reading those letters, recurring but always in a different arrangement, arranged by others who those letters—though they may appear to—never entirely obey.)

None of that applies to him or his thing.

To what is his. To his recurrent dream.

But the truth is he prefers to blend in with that whole ebbing flood of mendacious riffraff, desperate individuals who invent dreams or who're awake and dreaming they're asleep and dreaming. All of them make him feel—for once in his life—like a successful person.

Someone who has succeeded in life.

Someone—never put better—whose dreams have come true and whose personal success has been the unexpected consequence of a cosmic failure.

Someone surrounded by beings whose dreams will never come true because—though they want to convince the authorities of the Onirium to the contrary—they can't and won't ever be able to dream.

Does that make him a mean-spirited person?

Probably.

But he never was, nor claimed, nor pretended to be what's called and known as "a good person."

And the truth is that until the outbreak of The White Plague, he'd been an outcast with no real value. All his endeavors—all his waking dreams—had failed. And the only one of them he could consider a success was the one that led him to meet Ella and . . .


Now—surrounded by losers, many of whom knew success in many fields and professions before The White Plague—he feels like a winner. And it's clear that it's not due to merit. That he did nothing to distinguish himself and to be recognized. And, yes, there are many among those who line up and ascend the hill to the Onirium who recognize him and reach out touch him with the tips of their fingers and worship him with beatific devotion; awake and dreaming that merely coming into contact with him will bring them close to his greatness and maybe he'll infect them and, for a night or two, give them back the ability to dream. Or that, at least, he'll lie and tell them it won't be long now, that soon they'll be able to dream again.

No: all he did to stand out and become one of the select members of Morpheus Plus (the most exclusive club on the planet, the best and greatest accumulators of frequent-dreamer miles; someone in the Onirium said in a very low voice there were barely more than a dozen) was to *not* do something. To not do something not because he didn't want to do it, but because—to go against the grain; because going against the grain was the only triumphant gesture left for a loser like him—there was nothing easier than not doing it.

Like this, to simply close his eyes on everything and everyone.

To deny the real world and affirm the world of dreams.

And to dream.

To be one of the select and exclusive and *very few* who keep on dreaming and on whom depends and in whom resides, they tell him, the increasingly faint hope that the human race will dream again, will have dreams again. And that from that material, the stuff of dreams, they can once again dream realities. And make them reality, make them come true.

And so—he admits, vanity of vanities—though he could utilize the benefit of a direct and exclusive heli-transfer to the Onirium's rooftop, he continues to opt and still enjoys ascending like everyone else. Like the thousands of normal people who come here—never put better, ha ha ha?—in search of a dream.

He could, as he already pointed out, make a triumphal and conquering and almost messianic entrance. Descend from the skies in a helicopter, the reflectors of the Onirium illuminating him like a movie star on opening night, to be worshipped by spectating and expectant mortals, eclipsed and dazzled by his fame's brilliance. Or, at the very least, he could make use of the network of secret tunnels that lead to the Onirium and where the people who work there move, coming and going. Sleepless. The inexact scientists who study the inexact science of dreams. The people who committed the dark error that awoke The White Plague.

And Ella is one of them.

Ella and her recurrent and true dream.

Ella, like another one of those guilty insects that know, if they were identified as such on the surface, they would be squashed like cockroaches.

All of them with their heads bowed except Ella, who, whenever he sees her, retains that same pride she always had and that led them to have long conversations/discussions over breakfast, in a world that no longer exists, a world where the possibility of dreaming of other worlds still fit. A world that more and more resembles a dream and in which the glaciers melt and the honey runs out and sperm move ever slower and ever weaker and ova become increasingly inhospitable and monsters die of starvation. Because nobody dreams of the cold and of bees and of butterflies and of the birth of children and of creatures with hundreds of eyes or a single eye that arrive here through the doors of majestic wardrobes or prefabricated closets in search of fuel, refined from childhood fears, for their city anymore. And what doesn't get dreamed gets turned into a waking dream on this side: into something that ceases to be real because nobody dreams of it anymore. Into something that disappears as if by the art of dreaming.

Now, everything is calculated, everything troubles and disturbs and he supposes his attitude of not worrying about what might happen to him as he climbs the stairs that lead to the Onirium has to do with the immature impulse of not settling for the unpredictable, for the accidental, for letting someone else's dream turn into his nightmare; who knows.

Or maybe it's nothing more than another of his many unseemly and self-destructive characteristics and gestures. A way of flirting with his own suicide, disguised as murder at the hands of others.

Those in charge of the Onirium (concerned that something will happen to him or that the others will attack him and rip his head open with their teeth trying to discover or perhaps even devour the secret mechanism of his secret) have begged him more than once to give up this little farce of ascending alone and of his own accord without any kind of security. Though he could swear there are snipers on the rooftops of the Onirium tracking his movements and incognito bodyguards watching over his passage, ready to open automatic-fire or break bones by hand in the event of the slightest risk to his person. Let them do as they will. Their problem. He, as long as he's able (and, ha, there's *so* little time, almost no time, until he won't be able to;

until the pool from which they extract his dreams dries up completely and he's just one more among those who now venerate him), he prefers to go on like this, here. He prefers to blend in with the starving and desperate and insomniac masses. To ascend with them to this Mecca. To let them think he's one of them, that he's like them and, at the same time, like Jesus entering Jerusalem, irreconcilably different, and denying them the hope of his miracle.

And, of course, to enjoy the landscape and those who inhabit it.

The empty buildings, the full streets. The whispers and the screams and the map-less and plan-less war of those who don't sleep in peace because they can't even dream of things that diffuse and abstract. * (If they were able to dream, they sob, they would like to dream of a favorite picture, of that girl from long ago they never got up the nerve to talk to, of making the decisive move in the decisive game of a sport they never played.)

The bonfires burning not for heat but so they can try to see something in their flames while he watches them burn, feverish, awake and dreaming they're asleep and dreaming.

Here they are, all those who in the first dreamless days, desperate, emerged naked into the streets or plummeted from tall buildings or threw themselves onto the objects and individuals of their desire, trying to bring to the waking side of life something of that sleeping side they no longer had access to.

Here they all are, having made it through that first confusing time, seeking some kind of structure, and dividing themselves up into genres and races and categories and—unlike all the dreams or the lack thereof that confront and unite them—so far removed from any possible interpretation.

Here they are, opposite yet complementary and, beyond all battle and duel, without truce or peace, united by the inability to dream.

Here are the men who're called the Sheep Counters * (who simply count aloud until they collapse, wrecked throats and vacant eyes) who are locked in eternal combat with the women known as the Mares of the Night (who keep nightmares confined to the forest of the nocturnal, when everyone knows that daymares also abound, that, as the years pass, nightmares are becoming increasingly diurnal), their eyelids shut forever, stitched with fishing line; and atop those eyelids there are tattoos of eyes, wide open and blue, in whose center, microscopic, you can perceive ink and multi-color figures: the dreams they long for and the dreams they don't and won't ever have.

Here are the factions of technology facing off: the Cathode Ray Tubes * (who recall having always dreamed in black and white and of primitive images distorted by ghosts and problems of transmission, reception, and antenna) versus the Plasma Screens * (who champion perfect resolution, freeze-frame and fast-forward and rewind, picture-in-picture, and 3-D), but both coinciding on the fact that—as recent studies show—modern man slept and dreamed, when he dreamed and slept, pretty much just like ancient man; and so there's no reason to go around blaming innocent electricity and its multiplicity of applications.

Here are, onomatopoetic, the silent ZZZZs and the snoring JJRRRRRs . . . ! both wearing those absurd and antiquated sleeping caps; and he always wondered why it was that, at some time, people put on hats to sleep * (what was the point? so dreams didn't escape in the same way that, out the top of the head, body heat escapes?).

Here are the Sand Men * (always trying to push the powders of a "new and revolutionary drug," a substance made of light, consumed through increasingly dilated pupils and that today might be called Electron Blue and tomorrow who knows, and that will give you back the innocent dreams of childhood, products of reading fairy tales, witch tales) opposing the naturalist and anti-artificial-substance ART/REMs * (who keep the dream alive that, while dreaming, without chemical additives, profound miracles can be illuminated, like that of Dante Alighieri dreaming his *Divine Comedy* one Good Friday; or that of Samuel Taylor Coleridge dreaming "Kubla Khan" and bringing here a flower from the other side; or that of Robert Louis Stevenson dreaming *The Strange Case of Dr. Jekyll and Mr. Hyde* [and then writing it with the help of his brownies or "little people"]; or that of Mary Shelley dreaming *Frankenstein*; or those of Lewis Carroll inspiring his mathematic and chess-master marvels; or that of Gérard de Nerval dreaming *Aurélia ou le Réve et la Vie*; or that of Stephen King dreaming *Misery*; or that of James Cameron dreaming *Terminator*; but, careful, among sweet dreams spinning round bitter dreams, nightmares like

Richard Bach's *Jonathan Livingston Seagull* or Stephenie Meyer's *Twilight* can also be illuminated).

Here are the **Tense Sheets** * (fundamentalist practitioners of making the bed as the first waking activity, because order is basic and indispensible, and it makes sense to assume that discipline commences upon waking and that the chaos of dreams has been left behind and set aside until the next night) **and the Blanket Kickers** * (who, to the contrary, advocate leaving it all up in the air so the mattress doesn't turn into a stew of microorganism cultivation and who like to read shapes and messages in the forms the cottons and linens acquire after hours in motion but horizontal, like the lines of a hexagram) **and the sort of bastardized mutations of both that are the Nibelung Eiderdowns and the Banzai Futons.**

Here are the **Dreams of Reason** * (always recalling Niels Bohr dreaming the structure of the atom and Elias Howe dreaming up the sewing machine from a dream of getting stabbed in a dark alleyway, the movement of the knife up and down; and Srinivasa Ramanujan dreaming revolutionary theorems under the guidance of goddess Namakkal; and August Kekulé von Stradonitz dreaming up the rings of benzene in the wake of a dream of snakes; and Frederick Banting dreaming of the distillation of insulin and Albert Einstein dreaming up the speed of light and the Theory of Relativity after dreaming of a herd of cows being electrocuted, one after another, hopping back from an electric fence; and Otto Loewi dreaming the frequencies of neurotransmitters and Thomas Jefferson dreaming the first draft of the Declaration of Independence and, oh, in times when dreams were less urgent a subject of study it was known that republicans have more nightmares than democrats; and the insomniac chronicle of Thomas Alva Edison dreaming of electricity and convinced that those responsible for waking memory or the fact that we often forget what we dream are "little people"—the same ones as Stevenson's?—working in shifts inside our brains and that's the reason we remember some and not other things, depending on which shift it is when we ask ourselves something; and René Descartes dreaming up his Method after a dream of hurricane winds and ghosts and watermelons and a bedroom in flames; and Colonel Harold Dickson dreaming of where in Kuwait to drill to find oil; and William Herschel dreaming of what point in the sky he should aim for to hit Uranus; and Dmitri Mendeleyev dreaming of each and every one of the spaces on the periodic table; and Marie-Marie Mantra dreaming the wet Multidimensional Theory of Swimming Pools). All colliding with the Produced Monsters * (inseparable and united by that famous quote etched in a Francisco Goya print of a man collapsing on the hard bed of his desk, dreaming of owls and nightmarish bats flapping around his head, which can only think of things that have gone wrong, that didn't work out).

Here they, and many more besides, are. Whirling like somnambulant dervishes, beating a horse to death on the roadside, beyond all crime and punishment, wearing those surrealist mushroom hats, howling lullabies at the moon, pulled together and apart by the centrifugal force of their desperation.

Should he reproduce here and now the things they say, the sounds they emit, the careful and prolix senselessness of their beliefs?

No.

Better not.

Let others who can still hear and speak to them do it.

He, here and now, has grown tired of hearing them.

Or maybe his lack of interest is, again, a direct result of knowing that soon, very soon, he'll be like just them. He'll be one of them. Bereft of his last dream, his recurrent dream; and he'll have no choice but to join one of its factions, to be part of another feature on the nervous face of those who no longer dream and, as mentioned, only daydream of being able to dream again.

But, warning, above all of them rises his favorite. The sect of a single man, prophetic and deafening, his throat already beyond all tearing. A man strangled by his own vocal cords. A voice that roars and shouldn't exist but never ceases and gives the impression of being heard everywhere, in the farthest reaches of the world, ringing out in multiple languages simultaneously. In both the Latin and Cyrillic letters in which the man thought and spoke and felt, in color.

The man—an old man, yes; but one of those old men with that youthful air and vigor that transforms them into something powerful and unsettling and outside of time—is always dressed in short trousers that come down to his knees and a shirt and light sweater and hiking boots and wearing a hat with the authority of one who wears a crown atop a royal and immense cranium. And in one hand he holds aloft and waves, as if it were a flag all his own, a net for hunting butterflies.

The man—with a patrician face, one of those robust and satisfied faces that barely conceals the past of a gaunt and long-suffering face—reminds him of someone he can't remember.

A writer.

He's almost certain that it's a writer, yes.

And, moreover, that it's a writer who had something to do with him. Better: that he had something to do with that writer. But, of course, having something to do with a writer could mean, no more and no less, having read him, having seen his lectures, and recognizing his face from photographs he once saw. He can see him now, can remember him a little. * (Again that face that seems painted by two portraitists—the greatest portraitists of the last century—at the same time. Lucian Freud for the skin and Francis Bacon for what's beneath the skin. But not an oil painting, no.) In old photographs. Photographs in sepia, which isn't the color of dreams but the color of memory.

And making memory is a little like dreaming with your eyes open, right? Thus, when you are left without dreams, the first thing you lose is your memory. Researchers of the oneiric and custodians of the Onirium discovered it long ago: if you don't dream of things not of this world you end up forgetting things of this world. Likewise if you don't dream of the dead, the dead cannot ascend to the category of ghost, they can never return as waking dreams * (though not long ago he saw a movie about this, he has it on his list: a boy, whose dreams become material, starts to dream of a little brother he never knew, who died before he was born, spurred on by his increasingly nightmarish parents who've never gotten over the death of their firstborn; the premise was formidable, but, as always, it ended up spoiled by the obligatory special effects and lame plot twists). Dreams are like the varnish that fixes and protects paint, both oil and watercolor. Landscapes and portraits. Yes: when you stop dreaming you lose not only the possibility of imagining what never happened and will never happen, but, also, the memory of things that happened to you. And by "memory" he's referring to personal and private memory. To things that did or didn't happen or that you think happened or that should have happened. The rest: the collective memory, secondary things like song names and movie titles and characters in novels (unless they've been particularly important in your own life; all that gets forgotten) remain, almost always, unforgettable though he still remembers them, yes, as insubstantial things. More or less clean money, uncomfortable baggage. But out of context: without a bank or anywhere to go to buy something. Without context. As if in a dream dreamed by someone else. Like shards suspended in air rocked by an explosion. Loose fragments that, really, just upset you and stress you out and force you to think about everything you know and have seen and experienced and enjoyed, or not. But, now, as if memory were one of those gelatinous and invertebrate organisms, like one of those deep-sea phosphorescent fish never exposed to the light of the sun. Remembering yourself on the basis of everything you remember that isn't as important as everything that's forgotten and is, without a doubt, indispensible for you. And making you think that absolute and profound amnesia would be a gesture and symptom and consequence far more pious than this partial and frivolous and pure-surface memory.

All he has left is one dream and almost no memory of his own.

And that's how he recognizes that name (the name of that person who, he thinks, is or was a writer) like a faint taste, on the tip of the tongue. A taste of the water of a long and winding river, flowing past a country house whose name he can't fully or entirely remember either. The name of a river * (the name of a river [Oredezh?], read on a map, on a page at the beginning of a book that opens with a bit about a cradle rocking over an abyss) and the name of a writer that everyone pronounces incorrectly, stressing the wrong syllable, and that the writer never stopped correcting in interviews. But he remembers nothing more than that, nothing more than almost nothing. And within that almost nothing, some details perhaps secondary yet revelatory: like that the writer looked down on science fiction and all that "rocket racket" and "competitive confusion" and "phony gravitation"; though he once fantasized about writing something about an astronaut in love; and was deeply moved when man set foot on the moon (yet he completely dismissed the "utilitarian results" of the achievement as well as "irrelevant matters" like "wasted dollars and power politics"); and he'd written a novel that takes place in an alternate dimension; and that he once described himself as someone who traveled "through life with a space helmet." A writer who considered fantascience boring and pedestrian and overrun with clichés (which is why, most likely, he'd be furious at seeing himself appear here involuntarily in such a future-tech context, the Onirium and all of that) and comparable to those cookies of varying shape but always the same taste of nothing. Beyond all of this, all these loose pieces, it was clear to him that this writer, this *old-fashioned* but ageless writer, has or had something to do with him or he had something to do with that writer. Beyond the simple fact of reading or of reading him. He's almost certain. That's why his name escapes him. Something to do with Switzerland, he thinks. The man who is maybe a writer, feet firmly planted on the ground, leaning onto the back legs of a worn-out chair * (but proudly upright, with the martial air of someone who has conquered a peak in the Alps), repeats something about how reality is overrated. How reality is nothing more than a combination of information and specialization, and how he refuses to let his dreams be interpreted; because his dreams were, for him, always of an absolute clarity. His dreams, he roars, had always been "useful dreams." And he also talks about his desire for "translations with copious footnotes, footnotes reaching up like skyscrapers to the top of this or that page so as to leave only the gleam of a textual line between commentary and eternity" and that "existence is a series of footnotes to a vast, obscure, unfinished masterpiece" and . . .

But his words are overwhelmed by the words of a woman who whirls and whirls and doesn't stop whirling, howling: "Bang, here goes another kanga. Woomera. Ti-Ti-Ti. Me-Me-Me. Sing, O gods, the fury of Morpheus, son of Hypnos and Nyx or Pasithea, it matters not. All springing from the dense seed of Chaos's nocturnal emissions. This one and those others making love in the Erebus underworld, in that dark cave with black curtains, where the sun never shines and through which flows the Lethe, the river of forgetfulness, and from there—remember?—dreams are forgotten or fade so quickly, as soon as you wake. That cave with two doors: true dreams emerge from a door made of horn and bone, false dreams from a door made of marble. That cave which now purports to resemble that cruel and sinful edifice known as the Onirium. That sanctuary of blasphemers, that infernal paradise, that mirage disguised as an oasis . . . Oh, forgive us and forgive them for taking your name in vain, Morpheus, brother of the daemons Icelus and Phobe-tor and Phantasos, who occupy themselves with the dreams of animals and inanimate things. Oh, but you, always first among the thousand Oneiroi and unjustly punished by Zeus, who accused you of inspiring mortal kings when they closed their eyes. You, beating your wings and bringing dreams of almost-immortal glory to those sleeping earthlings, those ancient Greeks, who never said I *had* a dream but rather I *saw* a dream. Not anymore, now we've ruined it all. Unforgivable mortal and sacrilegious sin . . . Forgive us, forgive us . . . Mercy, mercy . . . You who are not satisfied with having sunk the skies and fouled the waters and laid waste to the lands, men have destroyed the land and air and seas of dreams too and now don't even have that anymore and . . ."

And then sparks begin to shoot from her throat and the flames envelop that burning woman who keeps on whirling and now he knows how to go on, how not to end, like in a loop, the way the madwoman's speech starts over without ever having ended. A raving that bites its own tail and the tail of the line that leads to the head of the Onirium grows ever shorter.

And he's already there, here, at the doors to the dreamed and dreamlike Promised Land.


The edifice of the Onirium * (no matter that it's already so well known and so oft seen and reproduced on postcards and miniatures/sou-venirs like the Great Pyramid of Giza or the Eiffel Tower or the Empire State or the Haworth Parsonage) still makes as much or more of an impression than the Empire State or the Eiffel Tower or the Great Pyramid of Giza or the Haworth Parsonage. * (He had already dreamed it and already put it in writing in another invented part of this same dreamed part: he dreamed it as a mutating museum of himself beside whose stairway, under a big sky, a Young Man and a Young Woman met over and over, a Young Man and a Young Woman who were not so young anymore, who'd once been two of his most devout fans, insist-ing on recapturing his absence in a world where he, accelerated and particulate, was contemplating and rewriting everything.) A black and glowing cube with a closed eye on each of its four faces that—due to the disposition of strategically positioned lights, at nightfall—appears to show the rapid movement of the pupil under the lid of always-lowered blinds. On the roof, there's another eye and, he's certain, on the bottom and subterranean face there's another eye, staring into the depths, into the deep longing of dreams.

And inside the edifice, there they are: the guardians of dreams. On each of his visits, he's noticed that there are more and more Asian people among the Onirium's staff * (someone told him the most advanced scientists of the theory and practice of dreams live in and come from China and Japan). And there, among the guardians of dreams, is Ella: the high priestess about whom, here outside, everyone speaks in reverential whispers. They worship her cold beauty and both fear and respect her professional treatment of some and contemptuous and calculating treatment of others. But, oh, what can he say about it, he who—chosen and privileged once again—knew her horizontal and naked and hot between the sheets. In times not so distant but, now, in his ever-briefer memory, seem to have acquired the condition of remote dispatches, as if transmitted from another planet.

Clearly nobody would believe him if he said the two of them were together, in bed, and they made love.

They would, no doubt, tell him he was dreaming and he dreamed her; and they would say it with the unmistakable and blatant envy of those who no longer dream and know he still can. Shutting his eyes, living impossible things, and waking up cleansed and renewed.

It's clear if he told Ella, Ella wouldn't believe him either.


Now he enters.

The lobby of the Onirium is like that of a cathedral, the ceiling so high that, there above, if the climate so chooses, clouds form and, sometimes, it even rains inside, as if in a dream.

First, the guardians divide them into groups based on sex. The men they herd into an enclosure for the examination of all the Little Nemos * (baptized thusly after the comic by Winsor McCay, starring that compulsive and wild dreamer) while the women are led to another chamber where they will proceed to the classification of the Dorothys * (in honor of Dorothy

Gale, the dreamer protagonist of *The Wizard of Oz*, who for him is the successful Americanized plagiarism, but plagiarism all the same, of the original dreamer: little Alice—Dorothy was considered a safer and more predictable name than Alice to assign the female patients—falling down a rabbit hole or passing through a looking glass bound for Wonderland and then waking up wondering who dreamed whom; and, really, truly, who in their right mind could believe for a second that Dorothy wants to go back to Kansas after having been in Oz simply because—in this she *is* right and because for worse or for worse—"there's no place like home"?).

The next stage in the process is quick and cruel * (discovering how with pleasure they submit to it though it isn't necessary and the guardians barely conceal their annoyance at having to be complicit in such a farce: a kind of eye exam like in the beginning of that movie whose title he doesn't remember based on a book by someone whose name he doesn't remember, either, and of which all he remembers is that scene in the first minutes and some questions like "Your little boy shows you his butterfly collection, plus the killing jar. What do you say?"; and he thinks about butterflies and thinks about that man there outside, at the foot of the Onirium, with his net, with his winged and colorful words) and soon eliminates all the imposters who have gotten in by lying that they still dream when, in reality, what they're after is to be given the alms of a dream. To be given a dream like a coin tossed in a beggar's nagging can. Any dream, a silly and banal dream, nothing grand or prolonged or worthy of an Endymion or a Merlin or a Rip Van Winkle. A dream of the kind that everyone has * (a dream that in other times, at one of those parties where a "You'll never guess what I dreamed last night" turned you, for a few minutes, into the irresistible center of the night and into the object of the most varied and absurd interpretations, regarded with an air of faux interest and a look resembling that of those who smoke the green smoke of opium all day long) or a dream so banal and worn out that nobody would have dared recount it in public for fear of playing the fool.

As they say, the impostors—the white plagues, the pale epidemics, those who have arrived there seeking the beneficence of a dream, of anything, even if it only lasts a second—are quickly detected and their information is taken so they won't get past the first checkpoints again. They receive the tattoo of a small and permanent barcode in the center of their foreheads. And they are cordially ushered to the exit. It only takes a few seconds to detect their lie. They are instantly found out: all the symptoms of no-longer-dreaming, of *nondreaming*, are visible, in their gaze. You know: a sound in the eyelids like a poorly oiled door, a faded dryness in the color surrounding the corneas, the impossibility of tears, and pupils almost immobile, fixed, and dilated after so many nights without rapid eye movement. * (As a form of goodbye, like the bag of favors that mobs of hyperactive kids are sent home with after a birthday party, they are given a dream catcher, an *atrapador de sueños*, an *ihánbla gmunka*, an *asabikeshiinh*: one of those pendants designed by the Lakota and Ojibwa tribes in North America and made with string and feathers and beads of various colors and shapes—skeleton, teardrop, turtle, spider—whose purpose is to capture everything that happens when your eyes are closed and thus protect sleepers from nightmares. A net. A filter that only lets good dreams through and that dissolves bad dreams between its strands, in times when there were bad dreams and not, like now, when any dream is good, valuable, indispensible. The person who hands out these magic—trickless but, also, useless—objects is one of the Onirium "professionals." The man has an aboriginal air, a crazed smile, and over his lab coat he wears a faded Confederate Army officer's jacket and, as he distributes the dream catchers he shouts things like "I live in so many different centuries. Everybody is still alive!" and "Sabers, gentlemen, sabers!" He saw him outside once, riding Kawasaki 1500 motorcycles and Kamikaze 666 women, firing a pistol into the air and downing a bottle of bourbon, other models of dream catchers, yes.)

Some resist and, as they're dragged toward the doors and shoved down the hill, they desperately recite rants from dream dictionaries or swear to have received prophetic and dormant symbols that would end up unmaking History. And, oh, how was it there were so many people (many more than the passengers on board) who swore they hadn't boarded the *Titanic* at the last minute because of a warning that'd come to them in a dream. And the same thing happens with that arrogant waking dream of reincarnation: how is it everyone remembers perfectly having been Galileo Galilee in another life, and why was and is and will it be that nobody ever claims to have descended in soul but not body from that anonymous Greek astrologist, expelled by Archimedes from the planetarium for his habit of drawing mice dressed as sorcerers in the margins of his parchment, and whose only particularity worth remembering was that of suffering some cosmically painful αἱμορροΐς in his black hole. And yet, maybe to forget the fleeting and trivial nature of waking life, they insist—like how they claim to have been someone famous in another life—on the certainty, between tragic and comic, of being *someone* when they sleep. A singular receiver of fragments of triumphal or catastrophic warnings. Random pieces of destinies or origins of movements that would change the face of the world with laughter or tears or nervous tics taken from the most well-know plots of sacred texts written by prophetic dreamers. * (Because, hey, if it happened to Nebuchadnezzar and Agamemnon and Julius Caesar and Alexander the Great and Marie Antoinette and Frederick II and Abraham Lincoln and Adolf Hitler and Winston Churchill and J. Robert Oppenheimer and Marilyn Monroe and those three pre-cogs floating in the prediction of crimes yet to be committed, why couldn't it happen to them, right? Why can't they feel historic and hysteric, dreaming of silver and bronze statues that fall before them; of a "pernicious dream" commanding the conquest of Troy; of holding bodies drenched in blood in their arms; of a reverential satyr saying "Tyros is yours"; of walls ablaze in the rising sun and heads severed from bodies; of stars leaping down from the sky and laying waste to the earth all throughout the night of the day of Napoleon Bonaparte's birth; of hallways in the White House adorned with black mourning bows, where the body of the dreamer who walks with somnambulant steps is wide awake; of the deafening voice that tells you "Get up and get out of here" and you wake up and escape that trench seconds before the mortar falls; of sitting and sketching a portrait of your own deceased father who gives you strategic advice from his armchair; of numbers that reveal to you an error in the calculations that days later will be transformed into Shiva the Destroyer of Worlds; of going into a cathedral and walking slowly down the central aisle and feeling how everyone turns to look at you and worship you with toothy smiles; of a hand that points out the book you're looking for on your shelf; and of receiving visions of how the Roman Empire never ended while counting electric sheep to wake yourself up.)

Poor fools.

Is there anything sadder than inventing dreams the way realities were once invented?

He's surprised to discover * (he's not that surprised, it was clear this moment was coming) he's the only person granted access to the second level. He walks down white hallways—ceilings and floors and walls all white, like the air—every now and then interrupted by reproductions of paintings. * (*Sleeping Nude Woman* by Courbet, *The Nightmare* by Fuseli—also the painter of the lesser known *Midnight*, in which two men speak from one bed to another, far from sleep and dreams—which Mary Shelley mentions in *Frankenstein*, Edgar Allan Poe alludes to in "The Fall of the House of Usher," and Sigmund Freud had a reproduction of in his studio in Vienna; *The Knight's Dream* by Antonio de Pereda, *The Dream* by Henri Rousseau, the annunciating and angelic dreams of Giotto di Bondone, and all those diurnal nocturnal paintings by René Magritte.) And he arrives to the elevators that descend to the basements where the dreams are extracted. He gets on the elevator and hears the music. And there's something fun and perverse in the song selection. Anthology of songs for torture by sleep deprivation. Songs about dreaming to keep you awake until you confessed everything you dreamed. * (Dream songs to be listed: the list is the literary genre of not sleeping and not dreaming and he always starts making lists when there's nothing else he can do, when all he can do is enumerate. He knows some of them because he never sang them, some he forgets now, when he thinks of them for the last time. He remembers them because he sang them all the time and now bids them farewell. Songs that might be "Mr. Sandman (Bring Me a Dream)," made popular by The Chordettes and used in many movies, always in supposedly tranquil and sleepy scenes ready for the fury and the nightmare and so here comes "Enter Sandman" by Metallica. Or "I've Got Dreams to Remember" by Otis Redding, or "In Dreams" by Roy Orbison, or "Moonage Daydream" or "When I Live My Dream" by David Bowie, or "Dreamer" by Supertramp, or "All I

Have to Do Is Dream" by the Everly Brothers, or "California Drea-min'" by The Mamas and The Papas, or "The Dreaming" and "Army Dreamers" by Kate Bush, or "Dream Police" by Cheap Trick, or "Run-nin' Down a Dream" by Tom Petty, or "Dreams" by Fleetwood Mac, or "Dreams" by The Cranberries, or "Dreaming of Me" by Depeche Mode, or "Sweet Dreams (Are Made of This)" by Eurythmics, or "Goodbye Sweet Dreams" by Roky Erickson, or "Last Night I Had the Strangest Dream" by Ed McCurdy, or "Last Night I Dreamt that Somebody Loved Me" by The Smiths, or "Last Night I Had a Dream" by Randy Newman, or "I Could Be Dreaming" and "Judy and the Dream of Horses" by Belle And Sebastian, or "I'll See You in My Dreams" in the sonorous voice of Frank Sinatra, or "I Have a Dream" floating in the syrupy voices of ABBA, or "Don't Dream It's Over" and "Recurring Dream" by Crowded House, or "I Often Dream of Trains" by Robyn Hitchcock, or "Sleep, Don't Weep" by Damien Rice, or "Sleepwalker" or "I Go to Sleep" by The Kinks, or "Like Dreamers Do" by The Beatles, or "Stew-art's Coat" by Rickie Lee Jones, or "Lost in the Dream" by The War on Drugs, or "Behold! The Night Mare" by The Smashing Pumpkins. Or "Daysleeper" and "Get Up" and "I Don't Sleep, I Dream" and "We All Go Back Where We Belong," the farewell single [in whose one of two videos John Giorno appears, the sleeping "protagonist" of the five hours and twenty minutes of the somniferous *Sleep* by Andy Warhol] of that oneiric band, R.E.M.—"That was just a dream . . . That was just a dream . . ."—where, as a sort of goodbye, they advise "write about dreams and triumphs." And, also, all those other songs and music not about dreams but dreamed, sung or performed for the first time in dreams: "Yesterday" and "Sun King" by The Beatles, or "(I Can't Get No) Satisfaction" by The Rolling Stones, or "The Man Comes Around" by Johnny Cash, or "Five Years" by David Bowie, or "Here Comes the Flood" and "Red Rain" by Peter Gabriel, or "Infinity" by [again] Rickie Lee Jones, or "Photographs (You Are Taking Now)" by Damon Albarn, or "Purple Haze" by Jimi Hendrix, or "Pesadi ¡Ya!" by La Roca Argen-tina, or "Everybody Understands Me" by Federico Esperanto, or "Il Trillo del Diavolo" dreamed by Giuseppe Tartini—like Beethoven and Stravinsky and Wagner also dreamed sounds—after Mephistopheles appears to him in his dreams, playing violin with a never-before-heard mastery, at the foot of his bed, after making a deal for the soul of the composer who, when he woke up, said he was just copying what he'd heard and it was, he always complained, the best he'd ever turned into a score and, oh, *larghetto affettuoso, allegro moderato* . . . Or, affectionate and moderately happy, the one that, no doubt, is the best song about dreaming in the history of the world, the one that best describes today for nostalgics what it once was to dream, what that was like: that song whose title and voice he can't identify any-more, because he already remembered it for the last time. The song he heard walking to the Onirium and also in that dreamed bookstore where he walks toward Ella and his steps are interrupted, but the song keeps playing and begins like the chug of a distant locomotive approaching. And so, until he reaches the station in flames where that voice—for many, a nightmare voice—does nothing but launch random images at us, slides on a carrousel, of someone who was now "just thinking of a series of dreams" and "I was just thinking of a series of dreams / Where nothing comes up to the top / Everything stays down where it's wounded / And comes to a permanent stop." It's the voice, he remembers, that'd already sung other dreams. A dream where it saw, from a train, reunited with the voices of childhood friends in a cabin by an old wooden stove and laughing and singing old songs while outside a storm raged out of tune; a dream about walking through the organized chaos of a World War Three and ending up proclaim-ing that everyone is having crazy dreams where they see themselves walking around with no one else and offering an "I'll let you be in my dream if I can be in yours"; one of those dreams that make you laugh in your sleep and take you floating to sail aboard the *Mayflower* and to discover America with Captain Ahab at the helm; a dream dreamed by the lookout on the *Titanic* who falls asleep at his post and dreams the *Titanic* sinks; a dream with miserable St. Augustine wearing a coat of solid gold and ordering kings and queens to listen to his sad complaint and ends up waking himself up terrified and bowing his head and crying and looking out a window with a view of nowhere. Here, now, tonight, another voice, that of the oneiric imaginer John

Lennon (he thinks and forgets his name), repeats over and over that senseless thing he heard for the first time in his sleep and that is "Ah! Böwakawa poussé, poussé" in the sensual "#9 Dream," but that, for him, faithfully reproduces the stiff diction of dreams: the turbid and disturbing voice of those who speak so deeply asleep to those who listen, beside them, and so wide awake in that place where they used to go and where now nobody, except him, goes. And, again, he remembers he has to remember to mention to the guardians in charge of the music, those dreamer DJs of the Onirium, to, please, include "City of Dreams" or, better, "Dream Operator" by Talking Heads, his *other* favorite song out of all the songs about dreams, he thinks, he barely remembers it, but he's sure that it reminds him a lot of his sister. So he has made an important effort to hang onto it, to not let it go. A kind of languid waltz, no? yes?)

He's alone in the elevator as it descends.

And then, suddenly, there she is.

He always sees her, like he saw her the first time.

And Ella sees him as if it were the first time, because she can no longer remember the first time she saw him. All that's left of Ella's insomniac memory, in a race against the clock, is now exclusively devoted to the attempt to recover the ability to dream for all humanity, expelled from the Eden of dreams. Ella's mission is to find the pathways and signs that lead back home through a fierce forest, like the forest in those stories that were anything but tranquil and relaxing, and that parents read to their children before surrendering them to the world of dreams, and that function as the inspirational fuel for oneiric adventures and terrors.

Ella looks at him without seeing him. Like how you look not a person but at a specimen. And it's fine. He can't complain. Better this—with Ella—than nothing.

And he looks at Ella and it's not love at first sight, no.

It's love at thousandth sight; but as if it were first.

Every time he sees her, he sees again how he falls in love, how he stays in love, how he'll love her until the end of his dreams, until the end of the last dream he has left.

Every time he sees her, he closes his eyes and sees her with his eyes closed.

And he opens them again.

And—no, it wasn't a dream—there is Ella.

In the corner.

His head full of cables and electrodes, the little nocturnal music of the monitors, "Good Night" by—now he remembers and knows—The Beatles in his ears. His mouth still full of the taste of the psychotropic drug that puts you in an intermediate state between wakefulness and trance. And him on the cot, and Ella on top of him.

But, ah, not on top of him like Ella was on top of him so many times in bed, but, now, rather like someone tending to something with extreme care, with a different form of love; with a love that, perhaps, is somewhere between the love of geishas and the love of beginners of any kind of hobby. A solitary activity where the other is indispensable, but always *the other*. Something outside and to which you devote an absolute yet dispassionate interest and care. Discipline and not sentiment.

But maybe it isn't so.

Maybe the unforgettable memory he's now starting to forget—of how Ella once was with him; of how they were together, the one with the other, the other with the one—obscures and distorts his perception of that other kind of love Ella feels for him now. A love less passionate and physical but far greater and more generous: because through his person, with these electrodes and cables Ella sticks and pins and plants on his head like flowers in a garden, Ella loves the whole human race. And, most loving of lovers, all Ella wants is to give the love of dreams back to humankind.

The lost and, it's known now, essential to life, ability to dream.

Dreams turned out to be the foundation of reality and, though the poets and oracles and mystics have been saying and reciting and prophesying it for millennia, Ella and the brains of the Onirium paid them no mind.

And so it was that they awoke the now-impossible-to-put-back-to-sleep monster. The nightmare of an always-awake monster that you're no longer afraid of dreaming of because it's already here, awake and keeping everyone else awake.

The White Plague.

And that is why Ella, why none of them—shut inside this edifice—sleep anymore, seeking a solution to the problem they created themselves. Yes: those who now desperately seek the solution to the problem were the ones who caused the problem when they were seeking the solution to another problem and . . .

The history of humanity, and even the great scientific advances, is over-run with episodes and errors like this. But none of them was as important and decisive as the one they caused with their triumphant defeat. And unlike what happened on other occasions—no serendipity here—it wasn't by seeking something miraculous they found something else more or less marvelous. Penicillin or LSD or the color magenta or that spring that slinks down stairs or the pacemaker or Post-its or Velcro or Cellophane. No. A dead-end alleyway with no way out. Nothing good—and everything bad, really bad, the worst—came of turning on the lights of The White Plague.

Something horrible was unleashed.

Something was unleashed that could not be put back.

If sleep deprivation is a direct route to psychosis, then dream deprivation . . .

They dreamed of something impossible and the only thing they got was the impossibility of dreaming. They wanted not that dreams might come true but that dreams did come true. They wanted to know everything about dreams—theretofore a subject as inexact as meteorological forecasts or stock market predictions—and they achieved the absolute exactitude of nothingness. And, along with it, the progressive and in the end total disappearance of memory.

And the appearance of desperation and madness and living as if in a trance. All day long. Like in those moments when we wake up or can't fall asleep.

And goodbye to saying that thing about "I had a dream that, I hope, someday will come true."

And the end of that trope that was so infuriating when everyone dreamed: a story being told that, in the end, was revealed to be a dream of the protagonist and, as such, a deception.

Now everyone would give anything for it all to be a dream or for their dreams never to be made reality. Anything would be better than sleepwalking all night long, like balancing on the least tight of ropes, like occupying a borderland that comes from nowhere and leads nowhere, intoning a countdown without bottom or zero, jumping with ever greater effort over a fence, like sheep bound for the slaughterhouse.


He'd come to the Onirium for the first time before it was a cult and pilgrimage site, a magnet for liars and the delusional. Then—not that long ago, but in another age—the Onirium was, merely, an institute devoted to researching the world of dreams. A luxury and latest-generation laboratory funded by a magnate who, in a dream, had been presented with the winning lottery number or with the premonition that an illness was growing in the intestines of his young son, which he was able to eradicate before the doctors could even detect it.

Something like that, something of that style.

He doesn't remember well.

And he'd come to the Onirium not to be treated but to do research.

He was a writer, which is to say, a screenwriter for movies and, as such, now, a screenwriter for TV series in the so-called golden age of television. * (He'd been a writer, but one thing led to another and now it was so easy to describe something in writing so that someone else could film it, so much easier than writing something where the letters themselves had to do the showing, and so much more profitable in every sense. And yet, he always wrote down "writer" when filling out "profession" on forms, because he felt not doing so was a lie.)

And his new project had to do with the world of dreams.

And he'd always been bothered by the issue of filming a sleeping dream, of how to illustrate and represent it to those who are awake.

So he'd come to talk to Ella about it. So Ella could explain it to him. So Ella could provide him with scientific evidence and the latest findings and precise data that later he would betray without guilt and with great pleasure and enthusiasm.

And, of course, he had a dream to tell Ella.

Something to give her, to give the scientists and researchers running the Onirium, in exchange for what Ella and what they would give him.

A dream that'd pursued and caught him for as long as he could remember in which there appeared—at different times and moments—a woman.

The woman of his dreams.

And should he mention now that he was surprised to find that the woman of his dreams was Ella and that Ella was identical to the woman of his dreams?

Yes.

And no.

Because artists—who are nothing but vocational dreamers—are used to the fact that such things, such supposed coincidences, exist. And that they are like the ropes that keep the idea and events of the day-to-day tightly bound together. And their gift is knowing how to see them and detect them and look for them and find them and even domesticate them; while everyone else is limited to experiencing them now and again and being occasionally touched by the wind of wonder.

And so he saw her and he loved her because he already loved her.

And it's easy for him to think—and they talked about this the next morning, at their first breakfast together—Ella felt something *too*. A certain recognition of the unknown. That model of a waking-dream souvenir, like an echo, known as *déjà vu*. Or something like that. He likes to think Ella felt something. And then, in her role as woman of science and hostess, Ella took it upon herself to dissimulate and hide it all. A strange tremor she'd never felt before and, confused, attempted to conceal under mountains of information.

And, oh, Ella spoke to him of so many things and didn't speak of so many others.

She didn't speak to him (a more than telltale omission) or make any allusion to William Shakespeare's *A Midsummer's Night Dream*. But she did tell him about the dense roots of the Latin word *somnus*; about electroencephalograms and about electrooculograms and about electromyograms; about the different stages of sleep; about the encephalon and the hypothalamus and the basal prosencephalon and the mesencephalon and the cholinergic neurons; about the mysteries of the naps of earliest infancy and those you reencounter in late old age; about rapid and slow ocular movements and about the reticular activation system; about sleep spindles; about apnea and insomnia and narcolepsy; about dreams of animals and about cats who spend seventy percent of their lives dreaming (and maybe that's why they regard everything with that air of knowing it all, smiling in the branches of a tree) and about horses who sleep standing up like equestrian statues; about sleep as purge and great eliminator of the brain's "cellular waste" and about sleep as an entity fundamental for fixing knowledge and memory.

But don't fool yourself, quit dreaming: nobody really knew what dreams were for and, maybe, he thought while listening to her, their ultimate and true function is to ask what they're for and how they function and never receive an answer. A mystery. And from this constant questioning of something you don't see because you're asleep spring stories and landscapes and books and paintings and wars and loves on this side, to keep us so awake and alert and dreamers forever.

In the end—because she was a scientist and he a romantic—Ella showed him what he was most interested in: the few worthwhile films they'd been able to make of dreams.

And he pretended to listen to her and to watch them (and Ella lowered her eyes when she saw how he looked at her), but really all he was doing was daydreaming about her. Happy because—unlike his recurrent dream of Ella—nobody and nothing could wake him up now. He would no longer feel that sadness when he opened his eyes. That melancholy of wondering how much time would pass before their next meeting in his dreams.

Now Ella was there, on this side of things, awake and talking nonstop, beside him.

And now the thing—at last, the time had come—was how to keep from falling back asleep.

But the one who is totally and completely and absolutely awake now is Ella.

And, of course, there have been some advances.

The confused filmings of the first dreams (a gray fog that reminded him of the fog that pulsated behind the thick screens of the televisions of his childhood) were now precise and detailed. Sometimes in color and sometimes in black and white, depending on the dreamer.

But also, now it was much sadder to see there, on those almost-liquid plasma screens, how the recently extracted dreams lasted almost no time at all after being excised. Seeing those dreams produced the same stunned sadness as those accelerated filmings of the sun furrowing the sky of one day at top speed, of a flower sprouting and withering with an opening and closing of petals, of an army of worms invading a dead animal until nothing was left but the bones of what it once was.

Yes, the dreams were over far too quickly.

Seconds. A minute, if they were lucky.

With that invertebrate elasticity of dreamed time that never corresponds to real time.

Not enough time to clone them. Or to transplant them, as if the dream were an organ. Or to distill them into the fluid of a magic vaccine that would give the ability to dream back to humanity.

But now his moment had arrived.

The moment to donate his last dream to science, the way one donates a lung so others might breathe.

His Ella dream.

His dream of Ella.

The dream that brought them together and now pushes them apart because, once they remove it, he'll have forgotten her.

But that's what he prefers.

It's not some kind of heroic gesture on his part.

He could care less about everyone else.

The only thing he cares about is Ella and he cares about Ella so much that—tired of so much dreaming and dreaming of her—he would rather forget her the way Ella forgot him. To lose the only dream he has left and thereby to lose her, but to immediately forget he lost her. Better that way, he tells himself. To be like one of those foxes that chew off their own paw to escape the jaws of that snare that's trapped them and won't let go. To get away from there, hobbling, leaving behind a bloody trail.

And now a buzzing in his head and the feeling of someone sucking in the floors of his mind and a vibrating of cables and, suddenly, Ella's face on the screen of the monitor. Perfectly defined. Like when he saw her, in his dreams, for the first time, in that bookstore, walking toward her and his steps being interrupted. And Ella looks at the screen without comprehension and, maybe, as he begins to forget her, Ella begins to remember something.

And the images are downloaded one by one. Precise and gleaming.

And the minutes pass and something happens. Something unexpected. His dream doesn't die. His dream survives and stays alive and dreaming.

And everyone in the laboratory embraces. They embrace him.

They shed all those tears they've not shed for so long.

And he stares at the screen and sees his dream and then, from overhead, from the surface of the Onirium, comes a descending sound. A sound like a single scream made up of many screams, a sound like one of those giant waves everyone has dreamed at one time or another.

* ("To dream of giant waves is a very disturbing thing and is full of meaning. To dream of giant waves that sweep us out and drown us conceals a sense of foreboding, possibly brought on by a change in your daily life . . . To dream of waves that are too big and stormy warns us we are making bad decisions based on our most impulsive instincts—'control yourself!!!' dream dictionaries seem to favor a style of emphatic exclamation and one rarely agrees with another— . . . But if the waves are very calm, the news is worse: you're doing nothing and just letting yourself be rocked, waiting for the miracle of happiness 'that may never come!!!' . . . If you're able to walk on waves, that's an excellent omen: 'we'll become super-powerful and nothing will depress us in the future!!!'." Dream dictionaries said things like that, so badly written, back in days when people dreamed of everything.)

Here and now * (when those dream dictionaries are like compilations of improbable legends!!!), his dream smiles, there, on the screen. His dream has survived and is still dreaming. That cliché with the affectation and solidity of clichés that have to do so, so much work to become clichés again: "A dream of hope."

But now that noise and roar approaches and is already reaching them— curling and liquid and blue and its mouth full of foam—and something tells him they won't be able to surf or walk on that wave.

And everyone comes in, howling their waking and unveiled nightmares. Reclaiming that brand, well-worn yet eternally-new in its contradiction and absurdity, for themselves: dreams of freedom, the freedom to dream again, freedom like something that can only be dreamed, the dream like the thing that frees you from reality, but it's only a dream and all of that.

Like a torrent, dancing that variation of the Watusi that is the tsunami, the Sheep Counters and the Mares of the Night, and the Cathode Ray Tubes and the Plasma Screens, the silent ZZZZs and the snoring JJRRRRRs . . . !, the Tense Sheets and the Blanket Kickers and the Nibelung Eiderdowns and the Banzai Futons, the Sandmen and the ART/REMs, the Dreams of Reason and the Produced Monsters all come in. And with all of them, in the lead, that old man with short pants and hat and butterfly net, howling in multiple languages simultaneously.

And "Molotov!" he remembers him all of a sudden, as if in the center of an explosion. The name of that man with the butterfly net leaps to his mouth and from his mouth. But no, that's not his name exactly. That is, merely, the snoozing sound of the name of that man who once specialized in the playful deformation of words, in the way that always-wide-awake words are deformed when you talk in your sleep, in the language in which always-wide-awake words sleep. And, all of a sudden, an adjective that doesn't appear in any dictionary but comes from somewhere far from there, far away, in the childhood of his waking life: "Everything is so *yuckicky*," he remembers and thinks.

And the sudden memory is like a door slamming shut.

A door that'll never open again.

And the invaders, the barbarians, lay waste to everything in their path.

And they shatter his dream. The dream that could've been for all of them, the seed of future dreams, the chance, now forever lost, to dream again. They pull his dream out by the roots and stomp on it, and everything is sound and fury and short-circuit and he—it'll be a relief to not be able to remember it, it'll be a dream to never dream it again—dreams his recurrent dream, one last time.


Time passes slowly when you're lost in a dream, because the very idea of time has about it something of a dream. In what time do dreams live? In the present, in the past, or in the future? In all times at the same time? Or in a fourth time, a time that belongs to them alone?

"Out of the processes of dreams, man trains for life," wrote someone who wasn't him, and whose name he doesn't remember but is certain wasn't his.

"Night is the factory of tomorrow and the museum of yesterday," someone else wrote, and yes, he does remember that that someone is and was him. The line, that he reaches for as if it were a piece of wood to cling to, as if he were the survivor of a shipwreck at high sea, gives him a strange joy. Yes: it's a good line.

And if museums are the place where infinity goes up on trial and factories the place where the present is continuous and assembled in a line, then dreams—what's produced and revealed in them—are a mixed product: functional works of art difficult to catalogue and classify according to technique and style and school, though in the late days of dreaming there already existed a whole critical school of dreams that calibrated their narrative tempo and flow and symbolic potential and . . .

*Los sueños, sueños son;* but no, dreams are not only dreams, not what they once were.

The thing from before, the thing about the experiment, the thing about the Onirium.

Something went wrong there.

Something was set adrift, floating in the waves, into a nightmare with no land in sight where it could open its eyes.

In any case, everything that has happened or ceased to happen to dreams * (a "universal catastrophe of yet impossible-to-determine consequences," according to the newspapers) doesn't really matter to him. What matters to him, and a great deal, is that, at least, he continues to dream.

Still. For the time being.

Knock on wood. Knock on the headboard with the head.

Strange and complex and restless and flashback and fast-forward dreams that are, for him, now, the closest thing to what it once was to write. The stuff of dreams, they say, tends to produce reasonable, reasoned monsters. Few things are more open to interpretation by self and others when we're awake than dreams. And when we sleep, when we dream the dreams, even more so: because within them we move in both first and third person, we see and see ourselves, we write and write ourselves, we are authors and protagonists, story and novel. All at the same time and in an elastic time where the minutes seem to stretch out and live entire lives. It's in dreams that we're the closest we'll ever be to gods, capable of contemplating and controlling all their creation, or to extraterrestrials who've developed the technology to make all stories happen at the same time.

 * (Again, just in case, is there anybody out there? How many possible readers has he already lost, having written all this like he did back in days when he wrote and slept and dreamed of writing and, each morning, after a cup of coffee, that dream came true? He asks because of that aforementioned rule, "Tell a dream, lose a reader," declaimed by Henry James. And that's all he had to say about that. Henry James considered those words more than sufficient when it came to removing the temptation to put into writing what one cannot read because, supposedly, obviously, one's eyes are shut. But why such a categorical assertion? Other quotes engage the previous quote and might offer some insight. To wit, counting quotes jumping over a fence: "Are not the sane and the insane equal at night as the sane lie a dreaming?," Charles Dickens. And one of his favorite texts by Dickens is titled "Gone Astray," a brief essay, early yet seminal, in which the author recalls a time he got lost as a boy, in the somber and already Dickensian slums of St. Giles. And then, between anguish and wonder, to distract himself from the fact of his being lost, he stopped and sat down to think in a doorway—to daydream like a sane-insane person—about all the possibilities for his life from that moment on, astray. To think about everything he might have ended up becoming and wouldn't become now or maybe he would, who knows. Until, at a certain point, the boy gets bored and stands up decisively and finds his way home, no problem; choosing the fate of becoming Charles Dickens, which is no more than the fate of becoming everything he could become and, becoming a writer, will be to create so many characters. And "The study of dreams presents a special difficulty: the fact that we cannot examine dreams directly. We can only examine or talk about the memory of dreams. And it's possible that the memory of dreams does not correspond directly to the dreams," Jorge Luis Borges, again, maybe because the blind have a special affection for and preoccupation with dreams, when they dream, when they see again. The two quotes point in different directions, but, to tell the truth, they hit the same target: dreams are not to be trusted. Dreams

are a more or less controlled manifestation of the irrational part of us and their story, back in the waking world, is always partial and uncertain. And what happens if—correcting Borges—there's really nothing else to remember but those never-finished sketches? And if dreams are nothing but swirling tatters in the wind of memory? Dreams like those little eddies of dry leaves in the autumn air? Something you remember perfectly but never ends up coming together, and then you invent some partial forgotten thing to endure the lack of connection, the absence of the mechanism's missing gears that were never there and never will be? It's no coincidence that in antiquity dreams were understood as interference from the conversations of the gods or the dead; something off the human frequency, but fragmentarily audible at night. Something like what happened with those primitive telephones, when you picked up the receiver and, wires crossed, heard two strangers having the most absurd and boring and terrifying of conversations. And then people tried to decode all those murmurings, sleeping beside the statues of their divinities or the tombs of their loved ones, so they would function like antennas and reward them with the gift of better reception. True, it's possible dreams are mankind's first aesthetic manifestation, but—as much in Artimodorus of Daldis's *Oneirocritica* as in Aristotle's *Parva Naturalia* or in Sigmund Freud's *The Interpretation of Dreams*—even now there's no certainty as to whether dreams' functioning, dreams' *style*, is abstract or figurative or, merely, surrealist. And, true, something *else* Henry James most certainly didn't like *either* and that lost more than one reader or spectator: that aforementioned and condemned gimmick whereby, right at the end of the story, it's revealed that it was all a dream, that the dead are alive, that the bad guys are good guys, that everything is in order and where it belongs within the supposedly realist logic of reality, but that, as it concerns art, is never plausible. Nothing is less realistic than the clearly marked trajectories of Anna Karenina or Emma Bovary or Jane Eyre. Real life isn't like that. Real life isn't so wide-awake. Real life has an imprecise flow much closer to that of dreams. Much closer to the plausible irrealism of *Tender Is the Night* or *Wuthering Heights* where nothing is fully explained or understood.

Real life is the bud that cocoons around a man who plucks a flower in Heaven to bring it to this side, or around a butterfly and a man wondering who dreams whom. And so—with all of that pretty much cleared up, never trust a dream—it makes sense to move along a bit, as much as we can. And he's never been all that advanced when it comes to technical things. Should a dream be told in first or third person singular? It's clear that, when you tell a dream, you always do so with shock or fear or a smile or a burst of laughter whereby you reclaim the leading role of narrator. You remember everything, everything you can remember, yes, with a constant ". . . and then I . . ." But while the dream is happening—and on those rare occasions when you open your eyes and for a minute or two evoke everything perfectly and you wonder if it might not make sense to turn on a light and write it all down in random scribbles that, in a matter of hours you'll reread and not understand anything of what it says there that was supposedly so clear and precise in the moment you wrote it all down—you feel and seem to be there and, at the same time, not to be. And how to write a dream to later capture it on film? How to combine its disordered but steady pacing? And he—every time he wakes up, every time he emerges from a dream—was always intrigued not by how to tell what he'd just experienced with his eyes closed, but by how to translate it into images and sounds after putting it in words. In color or black and white? How long to make it last? How to turn dreams' liquid structures, which resist any and all storyboard ideas, into something solid? He always had the uncertain certainty that a dream should look and sound like certain music videos from the golden age of MTV. Or something like that. Mixed techniques, diverse photography, sounds and noises. Now, until a short time ago, the advanced technological instrumentation of the burning Onirium had solved the problem and cleared up all doubts. Being able to see his dream—as if it were a TV show—he marveled again at how old dreams look. The image had an astonishing clarity, yes; but the texture was more or less the same as the footage of impossible beings like Yeti or Nessie or Bigfoot and had nothing of the eloquent screenings of Hans Castorp and Humphrey Chimpden Earwicker. And it all had that timeless air, yet at the same time, seemed much older than it was and when it took place. Like footage of World War II, like soccer games from a few years back, and like a fair number of movies filmed in the '70s, where the washed-out colors of American streets give you an automatic desire to return to the black and white of German expressionism, please, right? Dreams—maybe because of their nocturnal and lunatic condition—seem transmitted from the moon. A small step for the unconscious of one man, a great leap for nobody else, in space no one can hear you snore . . . Or maybe someone can.)

In any case, to those in charge of the Onirium, the idea of being able to examine the recurrent dream up close had seemed a good offer. He would arrive there, describe his dream, the possibility of further study of his dream would be calibrated, and, in exchange, they would give him a consult in "oneiric visualization" and the most useful way to "portray" a dream in an episode of the project he was working on.

The idea had come to him after reading a text by another of his favorite writers * (is he still unable or unwilling to remember his name, could it be because he doesn't want to forget it?). A handful of not particularly well-known pages where that writer recalled the recurrence of a dream. A dream about a young woman whose ghost, more and more alive, had followed him since his adolescence. A chance encounter that—like a stone thrown into a pool—kept expanding, in waves, across the years. The girl had appeared to that writer for the first time on a bridge in his dreams, crossing a river. And ever since, she appeared again and again. In different places and under different names. But it was always her.

The text had made an impression because the same thing had happened to him. Once. In his adolescence. At a dance. At one of those dances where he never danced. But that night he did. In the dream, he danced. Because—even though his dreams were never spectacular, their special effects always pretty low budget—the truth is they never disappointed him when it came to correcting and improving on reality.

In reality, he'd arrived to that party uninvited and stayed on the edges of the dance for a while. Watching * (that was him in the corner, "that's me in the corner") everything and everyone as if from the shore of a lake he didn't dare dive into. And Ella was at the center of all of it. Dancing alone.

At those young dances, a boy dancing by himself is a sad and desperate sight. Whereas a girl dancing by herself is a perfect love letter, a seductive neon sign, blinking, beckoning. Seeing a girl dancing by herself always makes you daydream she could be dancing with you, he thought then, as if in a dream. And, there, he couldn't stop reading her, watching her. Ella danced alone, at the edge of a swimming pool, and in a strange moment, as if in a dream, she dove into the pool. More than dive, she did something far more elegant: Ella let herself fall. And then she got out of the pool and kept dancing. Alone. Her wet dream that was his. And was she a succubus * (succubus, from the Latin succuba, from succubare, "lie under"; according to Western medieval legends—in times when it was thought dreams had their origin in the stomach and they rose from there like bewitching gases until they reached, following the dictates of Greek texts, "the most profound regions of the body"—is a demon that takes the form of an attractive woman in order to seduce men, above all adolescents and monks [monks who pray "Deliver me from the dreams and the ghosts of the night"], slipping into their fantasies, more awake than ever, as they sleep. In general they are women of great sensuality and extreme incandescent beauty. The myth of the succubus may have arisen as an explanation of the phenomenon of nocturnal emissions and dream paralysis. Looked at another way, experiences of obvious supernatural visits can take place at night in the form of hypnagogic hallucination). Or was it he who watched her like an incubus (incubus, from the Latin incubo, from incubare, "to lie upon"; is a masculine demon—the opposite sex from the succubus—in the belief and popular mythology of the Middle Ages that, supposedly, settles atop the female victim and has sexual relations with her while she lies there sleeping, according to a broad quantity of mythological and legendary traditions. An incubus might seek to have sex with a woman in order to father a special child, like in the legend of Merlin. Some sources suggest an incubus can be identified by its unnaturally large or frigid penis. Religious tradition maintains that having sexual relations with an incubus or a succubus can cause a decline in health or, even, death. Then, the victims live their dying moments and death as if it were a dream they can't wake up from)? Either way, he watched her. And Ella let him watch and danced hard and fast. And droplets of water flew off her body and her dress like diamonds suspended in the night air; like those diamonds that—he'd read somewhere—certain African deserts were known to perspire, and that people went out to gather by the light of the moon, the way people elsewhere gather strawberries or seashells. Or like what—streaks of water, a multidirectional rain—a wet dog in heat sends flying, centrifuging herself dry. And he doesn't like to think like that: it's not that it really makes him uncomfortable * (OK, yes, it makes him a little uncomfortable) thinking of her as a "dog" * (one of those svelte and languid dogs, dogs with the personality of cats); but that "multidirectional" and that "centrifuging herself" make him grind his teeth, sounding like bad science fiction: futuristic and spatial and operatic science fiction. And he asked himself if he could get up the nerve to approach Ella and answered himself, no, and so he went home.

And that night, he dreamed of Ella for the first time.

That was the first time he had his recurrent dream, which wasn't recurrent until the second and third time he had it.

And on like that ever since and until now.

A recurrent dream that hadn't come true, but that did come, two or three times a week, always the same, so that he saw it, dreamed it. Sometimes, even, interrupting another dream that had nothing to do with that one and coming on, suddenly and without warning, like when you change the channel and find yourself watching the best episode of your favorite show.

A recurrent dream that was much more than a dream: it was the between-fragile-and-invulnerable version of a memory, of something that refused to be forgotten. It was a dream of the *Based-on-a-True-Story* variety and, as such, inspired by something that happened and, at the same time, offering the best version of what'd happened or, better, of what should've happened: a dream come true inside the dream itself.

Those in charge of the Onirium—who delayed their work considering whether or not their salvation might lie in the resistance of recurrent dreams, dreams that in other times were considered symptoms of anxiety or obsession—had been in awe of his recurrent dream. They'd recorded it multiple times. And what made his dream unique was its implacable precision. His recurrent dream—the recurrent dream that always followed that other recurrent dream, always incomplete and variable and always taking place in a bookstore, where a song played that he knew but whose distinguishing features he couldn't and didn't want to remember—was always exactly the same, without any variation in time or density or plot. Nothing about it changed. His dream was like the inalterable record of a historical event. Like the footage of the head of a president riding in a convertible exploding in the air, like airplanes crashing into towers; but with a more intimate tragic element, because the catastrophe was external to the dream: he'd seen her, he'd loved her, he'd stopped seeing her, he kept loving her.

In his dream they danced together, holding each other close, as if to keep from falling. The song they danced to was a modern but heartfelt waltz. He already mentioned it: "Dream Operator" by Talking Heads. With that voice between melancholic and euphoric of David Byrne that in the movie *True Stories*, directed by Byrne himself, was sung, off key but movingly, by a woman, as background music in a sequence at an absurd fashion show, with hallucinated and hallucinatory outfits, like the one Ella was wearing at that party in his dream * ("You wish you were me / I wish I was you / Now don't you wake up / The dream will come true . . . / Every dream has a name / And names tell your story / This song is your dream / You're the dream operator" . . . And what time was it and how long had they been dancing? "Shake-it-up Dream / Hi-di-ho Dream / Fix-it-up Dream / Look at me Dream / I've been waiting so long / Now I am your dream"). And he always had felt an absurd pride that his dreams were so "economical"; that they were not pure "special effect" and impossibility. * ("Hard to forget / Hard to go on / When you fall asleep / You're out on your own.") His dreams had always been, yes, realistic. Only small details—if one looked for and found them carefully—made it apparent that it was a dream at all. * ("It's bigger than life / You know it's all me / My face is a book / But it's not what it seems.") In his dream of Ella at the party, for example, there was little or nothing dreamlike about it. Just the one detail that, as they danced, Ella's dress changed color psychedelically and submarinely. That was it. And it wasn't that disturbing, because there was that great doubt (and that was one of the things he had come to the Onirium to clarify) about whether or not dreams were dreamed in color and, maybe, there was an explanation for that color change: the strobe lights of the dance floor on the white fabric of her dress. And such a dream was simple and easy to interpret. * ("And you dreamed it all / And this is your story / Do you know who you are? / You're the dream operator.") In a way—their own way—his dreams were always dreams-come-true and that was why waking up was sometimes, almost always, so painful.

But the deal was that, first, he had to give so later he could receive.

And so there he was, at the Onirium: riddled with cables, for the first time, ready to dream without his dream being removed. Because it was still a time when everyone dreamed every night, and The White Plague—the real nightmare of living without dreams—had not yet awoken.

So they told him to wait there, and the doctor would be with him shortly. And then Ella came in and * (yes, the not-so-imaginative cliché of pinching yourself to see if you're dreaming, as if you could be dreaming you pinched yourself and you weren't asleep) he knew she was the more-or-less-grownup and equally beautiful version of the girl he'd seen dancing alone that night, but who, for years, had danced so often in his dreams.

His dream operator.

Not the woman of his dreams, but something and someone far more valuable: the woman of his dream.

And he watched her and couldn't stop watching her.

And when Ella looked up to see why he wasn't answering her questions, he couldn't help but recognize in her eyes a recognition similar to his own.

Ella knew who he was. She had to.

And he didn't wonder if he was dreaming, because he knew he was awake.


If midnight is the witching hour and three in the morning is the hour of the dark night of the soul, then breakfast time is the hour of the bewitched and of the luminous day of the body.

The day of the morning-after breakfast at breakfast time.

For him, always, the best place and best time of the day.

The time and place invented so people would wake up ready to recount their dreams from the night before; to make dreamy lists of what they'd dreamed in exquisite notebooks of high-grade paper; or to read what they'd dreamed, like the dreams of a capricious deity, in pages of freshly printed newspapers: baking all night long in a party of inventiveness, news so different from the slower and heavier news of the dwindling afternoon newspapers (which he referred to, a bit humorously he thinks, as "afters") that seem written as if mixed in the drool and sweat of long afternoon naps following heavy lunches.

And that time, breakfast time, on that day, is even better now that he's with Ella.

And the rest of his life, of his previous life, all the past and not future time (he hopes) when Ella wasn't there, now, takes on the vague and solvent texture of a dream.

Breakfast time, on the other hand, is the most real time for him, though it all seems like a dream. *This* breakfast time. The best dream of all, one he doesn't want to wake up from. The dream that follows that other dream, one of the most truly dreamlike and wakeful acts a human being can perform: to penetrate or to be penetrated in the name of something that's so many different things at the same time. And that—lacking a better name to simplify its temporal parameters and spatial coordinates and emotional constants—has come to be known as "love." That love made by making love.

And, ah, few times has he had such conversant conversations at breakfast time, he says to himself. Especially with a woman. Women, in general, when he woke up next to them the morning after, had almost always seemed different to him than how he'd seen and desired them the night before. Not worse, but yes, inevitably, different.

And, though they were there, present and tangible, right away he began to forget them.

And another thing: women aren't that great to talk to when they've just woken up. When just waking up, women barely offer stray syllables, grunts, grimaces, sometimes painfully eloquent silences. But always as if they weren't yet entirely back online.

None of that had happened with Ella.

Ella woke up wide-awake.

Ella was perfectly conscious of everything from the moment she opened her eyes.

And it made no sense for him to remember how there'd been that moment of mutual recognition. Ella remembered him too, yes, of that he was certain.

She *had* to remember him. And after he fell asleep among the machines *
(and after Ella and the Onirium scientists verified, astonished, that
his was the most stable recurrent dream they'd ever seen; and that it
could only be the most significant and auspicious of coincidences that
Ella herself, the doctor and head of the Onirium, appeared, inserted,
so suddenly in his dream, not even suspecting that Ella had been
living in that dream for years, that that dream was as much Ella's as
it was his) what follows is much easier to understand and accept with the
spasmodic ellipses of dreams.

You already know it: he's lying on a gurney while a doctor, Ella, asks him
questions and all of a sudden he's in bed with that doctor who now is simply
Ella and who, undressed, is dressed in nothing but a T-shirt that once was a
man's T-shirt but not anymore.

And then he and Ella are talking about what they'd begun to talk about,
still dressed, in the Onirium, the night before.

And the conversation they have, just emerging from their dreams, is the
one they interrupted yesterday and now take up again.

Nobody talks *like this* when awake, true. More than dialogues, these are
like recitations à deux. A minuet where, alternatingly, they offer bows and
pirouettes. And between one spin and the next, exchange information, like
those dances in Jane Austen novels, where one dances in order to say all
the things frowned upon for men and women to say to each other when
sitting, or standing, or lying down. A space and a time for seeking explanations based on definitions, with true encyclopedist pathology: using the
solidity of the past and historical authentication to support the quicksand of
an unprecedented present with no solid ground in sight.

And this conversation is about dreams.

And, he's already pointed this out, he always looked down on using dialogue as a form and format for introducing great quantities of names and
information. The use of dialogue—written dialogue, in literature—felt to him
like a kind of cowardice elevated by many to the category of heroic achievement. Artificial flavor and coloring permitted. And that's why he was never
all that interested in Anton Chekhov * (though he does remember that
story of his in which a nanny suffocates a child whose crying keeps
her from sleeping), or any of his epigones * (especially those who make

their characters speak with some phonetic particularity as a trait of their personality and even their way of acting in and relating to the world), or film in general, which he hoped to change with his literature * (with those conversations set up, apart from on a few masterful occasions, as calculated choreographies where nobody stepped on anybody else's voice with their voice), or almost any theater * (especially those oh so artificial moments when someone spoke to someone else off stage; and he couldn't help imagining that invisible being as wandering dazed through the ruins of bygone scenographies, responding automatically; while he also thought that the big difference between film and theater actors was that the latter spit when delivering their lines and you could see it even from the cheap seats). For him, dialogue—in those moments when people were speaking supposedly to communicate—was nothing but a stilted and dry interruption of the mysterious and far more fluid and liquid syntax of thought, of imagining symphonies in silence. That act was what distinguished human beings from the bleats and whinnies and barks and buzzings and clucks and lows of animals * (many of them dreaming a great deal, asleep on their feet, Ella would say the platypus was the most REM animal of all) who, every so often, in books and movies, are given the stigma of human voices, with generally disastrous outcomes. There was, yes, one exception. Hemingway before he was Hemingwayesque * (the Hemingway of insomniac and battle-front traumatized stories like "Now I Lay Me," where falling asleep might mean "my soul would go out of my body," where he prays not to fall asleep); and the conversations in the books of some psychopaths of language—generally swampy southerners who would always hold the northern position in his sky—in which the dialogue was like thinking aloud, in an even louder voice. And, yes, again, that writer with the butterfly net whose name he doesn't dare pronounce had something to say about this *too*, something with which he couldn't help but agree. * ("Dialogue can be delightful if dramatically or comically stylized or artistically blended with descriptive prose; in other words, if it is a feature of style and structure in a given work. If not, then it is nothing but automatic typewriting, formless speeches filling page after page, over which the eye skims like a flying saucer over the Dust Bowl.")

But—as a kind of apology for his almost-zombielike artificiality—this is a dream conversation with a high informational content that more than one person will want to jump over, but, if you do so, jump over it the way you jump a fence with the smile of a sheep wearing the hide of a wolf. A conversation bursting with names and titles that he hopes he'll be forgiven for here—could this be his apology and excuse?—by turning it into the longest footnote, scrambling up onto the shoulders of all of this and sitting down and leaning back resting its neck and falling asleep and dreaming.

And you never decide how you dream what you dream. The style of dreams—feature-deformity, lunatic-encyclopedic, referential-maniac, blind-quoting—is never chosen by the dreamer, dreams choose the style of dreams. And so, again, you immediately forget a good part of what you dream, like how you forget a good part of what you see, along the side of the road, on a nighttime ride, out the rolled-up window of a car someone else is driving and . . .

* (—I never really understood that thing about the stages of sleep and how it relates to dreams . . . —he says.

—It's not complicated. When you sleep and when you dream it's like when you travel. You pass through different stages. Take-offs, turbulence, fastening of seatbelts, landings, sometimes emergency ones and sometimes perfect ones . . . —Ella says.

—I hate perfect landings. No, I hate the people who applaud them, inside the airplanes, as if they were waking up relieved from a nightmare at 20,000 feet . . . Let's see . . . Tell me a little. I'll take notes.

—It's a little complicated to understand. And to explain . . . Okay . . . Sleep, the act of sleeping, is comprised of long- and short-wave cycles, and of what is known as paradoxical sleep. And these cycles can occur multiple times throughout one night. Four or five times. Like variations. Each one takes up about ninety minutes. Get it?

—Ah-ha . . . Four or five . . . Ninety minutes . . .

—The first stage might last an hour and a half. And it's short wave. There's somnolence, drowsiness. It's the transition between wakefulness and sleep; so you might even hallucinate things with your eyes still open, going in and out of this stage . . . And, please, stop looking at me like that, okay? You're making me nervous.

—Okay. So, better, I'll listen to you with my eyes closed, ha.

—Yes, better . . . No don't be silly . . . Open your eyes. Stop . . .

—My eyes are open.

—Okay, then, in the second stage, cardiac and respiratory rhythm slows and, as such, there is a shift in blood flow to the brain. And so brain activity increases or decreases with periods of calm or sudden activity. And so also, sometimes, as the brain is disconnected from the body, those sudden movements occur. Hypnic jerk or myoclonic jerk. The sensation of free fall, of letting go of a rope, of leaving the body and going somewhere else. Those kicks in bed are the brain's way of reasserting contact with the body; to let you know that it's still in charge and on top of everything. So you don't forget about it. So the body doesn't stop thinking in the brain.

—Do you kick a lot in bed? I didn't notice last night . . . I know you scream and scratch, but . . . do you kick? [And this type of humor is just what he detests in dialogue; but now that he's here, it can't really be avoided.]

—Very funny . . . And while we're on the subject: there are a lot of people who claim if you go to bed alone you sleep and dream better. And it turns out to be much healthier. Sleeping in pairs is a historic incoherence, a product and bad habit of times when multiple people slept together in the same room. It's unnecessary. It doesn't make sense. And by the way: you *do* kick a lot . . . And, better, let's move on . . . By the way: researchers are postulating that people who kick a lot in bed might be foreshadowing, unconsciously, a preoccupying propensity for developing, over the years, Parkinson's disease.

—Uh . . .

—Should I go on or not?

—Please, Doctor, proceed.

—The third stage is the transition toward deep sleep and not much happens there. It's as if you're moving down a passageway that's two or three minutes long.

—Okay. I get it.

—The fourth stage is slow-wave sleep. Deep sleep. It lasts about twenty minutes and is very hard for us to come out of. When you can't wake someone up, it's because they're in this stage. Really sleeping. Resting. There aren't even dreams in this stage. Or they're very minimal and very short . . . And then comes the REM stage, which was only just discovered in 1953 through the careful observation of the movements of sleeping eyes under the sheets of the eyelids . . . ah, it seems like I woke up a bit metaphoric today . . .

—Or maybe it's my bad influence . . .

—Yes, that's probably it. But as I was saying: the REM stage was "discovered" by those two, unknown to many, heroes and explorers of hitherto virgin territories: Eugene Aserinsky and Nathaniel Kleitman. Eyes moving rapidly. With the brain at maximum sleeping activity and receiving more blood than at any other moment of the day. When you dream the most; but that doesn't mean the sleeper stops taking in information from his or her surroundings. To the contrary: you can incorporate sounds and conversations and music from the world around you into your dreams. And brain activity is just as intense as when we're awake. It's been proven adult humans have REM dreams that last between ninety minutes and one hundred twenty minutes total. These dreams are episodic, starting out short and ending up long. They've also been able to determine that human fetuses have up to fifteen hours of REM sleep that, I suppose, might be like pure light and shadows and sound, as if filtered through very heavy curtains. And that newborn babies have eight hours of REM. Recent studies have suggested a correlation between age and amount of REM sleep, showing decreased quantity and occurrence as we age . . . Could it be that, unlike babies who spend a good part of their time there, old people dream less and more superficially because they have less waking life left to dream about? I suppose that's the stage that interests you most, right? The stage when you dream best the best dreams . . . What's wrong? What're you thinking?

—No, nothing . . . It occurred to me to see if the four stages of sleep aligned somehow with the experience of love. You know, cycles and curves and ups and downs and variations in intensity and ability to create or believe in stories in the name of love. Love, the perception of love, in it's own way, is always a dream and . . .

—Yes, but I'm afraid it's not advisable to mix science and feelings. They're two completely different languages. It doesn't seem right to me to fuse or confuse the theory of one with the practice of the other. I think it would be a failed—not to mention dangerous—experiment and . . .

—Okay, okay . . . But, really, I don't mean to diminish its importance. How much do you all *really* know about what you're claiming to know? Because it seems to me there's something paradoxical in dream research: the more research you do, the less interesting they become, no?

—No.

—Yes, seriously, think about it: dreams were very important when they were magic and intangible objects. And that importance reaches its most profound peak with Freud and the "idea you only have once in your life, if you're lucky" and the division of dreams into prophetic, visionary, or symbolic, and the need to interpret them. Dreaming as a language we all speak, but in which we don't know how to express ourselves clearly. But starting in the 1920s, when it begins to be possible to trace a map of electrical brain activity, with the awakening of neuroscience, dreams lose rank and category and trustworthiness and interpretative exactitude, and Freud's hypotheses fall out of favor and goodbye Oedipus as science and hello Oedipus as, again, a good story told by a good teller of fantastic stories. Dreams start to be understood, or not understood, as simple pollutions and babbling of the brain as it sleeps and not as doors to hysteria or psychosis of the repressed desires of infantilized infants. Dreams as something more or less interesting that happens when we sleep and think without any particular order about uninteresting things. The idea has prevailed that, since we don't understand why we dream, dreams themselves are not worthy of attention. The conclusion has been reached, with a logic as crushing as it is dull, that "we dream because we are tired." And so we think about dreams in the same way that we dream. Without much logical or memorable discourse and . . .

—Thanks a lot . . .

—No, no . . . Okay, from what I saw yesterday you've advanced a great deal with the whole filming of dreams, but . . . isn't it like uncovering pyramids without really knowing how they were built?

—No.

—No?

—No.

—Oops. Are you upset?

—No. It doesn't upset me when someone who knows nothing about something I know a lot about comes and explains to me how I really know nothing about something he knows nothing about and I know a lot about.

—Ah, our first argument . . . Now it's a serious relationship . . .

—Or it was just a one-night stand. A first and only and last one-night stand and . . .

—Is it too late to apologize? Or to blame all of it on one of those incubi or succubi who possess you in your dreams?

—Mmmmpff . . .

—I assume that "Mmmmpff . . ." is the way the natives of the planet of the most beautiful women in the universe forgive you when they wake up and . . .

—Right. Forgiven. But from now on nothing but intelligent questions and silence from you.

—Yes, mistress.

—And regarding how we know nothing about dreams . . . There are some things we *do* know.

—I'm all ears and eyes.

—We know everyone dreams. As I said: at least five dreams a night. Even babies, whose dreams are, it is thought, pure dreams: shapes and colors and sounds aboard cradles in rooms painted with that new unisex and politically and oneirically correct color, half pink and half blue, that is known as *dreamtime* color. Though there are some cases of people who don't dream. Or who have lost the ability to dream. They suffer from something called Charcot-Wilbrand Syndrome. It was first diagnosed in 1880. Not dreaming can be a consequence of serious emotional problems . . . But there's nothing completely proven to that end.

—Noted.

—We also know dreams are forgotten very quickly. And the statistics confirm that more creative people remember their dreams more and better than more rational and pragmatic people. And there are theories that hold that those who never remember their dreams are more likely to end up being, contrary to the depiction of them insisted on in movies, as visionaries, when they close their eyes, dangerous psychopaths, mad scientists, and serial killers, and . . .

—Yes, but why do they forget? Are dreams made of the same stuff as jokes? Are dreams the kind of joke we never really get, but laugh at all the same to not look dumb in front of whoever tells it at a party? Why do we forget dreams and jokes?

—I don't know anything about jokes. Nor do I care.

—Ha.

—Yes, ha.

—I can enlighten you there: I read somewhere we don't remember the best jokes we're told because they're the ones whose punch line surprised us and we didn't see coming. Whereas, because they're predictable, it's much easier to remember bad jokes and . . .

—I said I didn't care. But I *am* interested in the fact that we forget 95 percent of what we dream when we wake up. There are those who claim our most important dreams, the ones that could end up being useful during our conscious lives, are the ones we forget most often and most quickly . . .

—Ah, just like good jokes.

— . . . and maybe that's why they can't survive crossing the border between sleep and wakefulness.

—Or maybe they've been confiscated at customs, right? Like dangerous cargo, like fire—and fury—arms. Anyway, all that hasn't really left all those biblical and pharaonic dreamers and ladders ascended and descended by angels standing, more like knocked down, not to mention the interpretations of Sigmund Freud, right?

—Right. Though you might argue that what Freud was interested in wasn't what we dream, but what we think we remember or choose to remember of our dreams. That what was most interpretable and revealing was precisely that residue or what we wish we'd dreamed, convincing ourselves we have dreamed it.

—But I still don't understand why we forget. Is it a defense mechanism? Maybe, I insist, there's something there, in our dreams, we cannot bring back to this side. Some information that's denied us because it could be the cause of great catastrophes and . . . Good idea for a movie with a lot of special effects. I'm going to write it down to see if I can sell it to someone and . . .

—Hello? Anybody home? Can we continue?

—Yes, sorry. I wrote it down already.

—Perfect. Happy to be so useful . . . Getting back to forgetting . . . One theory ventures that, when we dream, the brain lets the memory-making function rest. Pause. Others say the idea is, simply, not to remember anything. And dreams would be something like a solvent of useless accumulated information. And still others claim if our brain didn't permit itself that kind of crazy truce of dreams, where it never reflects too much on what it does or doesn't do and what it all means or on its almost-immediate and near-total oblivion, it would lose the capacity to faithfully remember what happens to us when we're awake . . . To forget the irrational in order to remember the rational. Survival of the fittest. A Darwinian version of dreams. They also say increased magnetic activity produces more realistic dreams.

—Ah, so dreams as a kind of laxative, for purging, for eliminating constipation . . .

—Mmm . . . That's one way of looking at it, I supposed. But you can also think of dreams as a kind of exaggerated and irreal simulation/training for situations we'll confront in our daily life. Dreams like field tests for our avatar.

—What else?

—The thing about dreams in color and in black and white . . . Until recently it was thought we only dream in black and white. But it turns out that's not the case. There are dreams in color. Almost all of them. We recall dreams in black and white because our memories of them are deficient, but we dream them in color. Not very bright colors.

Pastel tonalities. And this part will interest you. A lot. There is a very recent theory that holds that, in the past, people dreamed only in black and white because the TV they watched was only in black and white. As soon as color arrived to the screen, people began to dream in color.

—Ah, cool. Like an automatic association of film and television with the world of dreams, with what's dreamed and what's not reality. As if when we watch a movie we were dreaming. Hollywood like "The Dream Factory" . . . Fantastic!

—That's right. But that doesn't keep the blind, even those born blind, from dreaming.

—Really?

—Yes. They dream of sounds and textures and smells and tastes . . .

—Ah! So, for the blind, dreams can be truly sweet, right? Sweet dreams . . . Though, it seems to me dreams are never sweet. Because even those dreams that are supposedly sweetest turn bitter when you wake up, when they send us back to reality with a bad taste in our mouths and bad breath. That's why we brush our teeth when we get up and . . .

—Another very interesting thing. Based on surveys, it can now be said that men and women dream in different ways. Men's dreams are more aggressive than women's. Women's are calmer and longer and have more "characters." And men dream more about other men than about women.

—Ah, that explains why those dreams are forgotten. Better, just in case, not to remember them . . .

—While women dream about men as much as they dream about women. And they are better when it comes to remembering what they dream.

—Good for them. And good for you. But I doubt you remember me better from your dreams than I remember you from mine.

—Mmm . . . Another thing: it's probable that animals dream too.

—Was that a veiled insult? A way of calling me an animal? What do animals dream of? Of getting discovered and hired by Disney?

—Now that I think of it: it's lucky that pretty soon I'll forget all these magnificent jokes you're making.

—*Touché.*

—Yes, better if you control yourself a bit. Which brings me to the fact that dreams can be controlled, directed. It takes real practice, of course. It's what lamas and shamans do. "Lucid dreaming": being aware you are dreaming and, based on that awareness, thinking you can do something with all of it. One of the post-Freudian branches of dream interpretation, but already mentioned by Aristotle and Saint Augustine of Hippo and the aristocrat and sinologist Marie-Jean-Léon, Marquis d'Hervey de Saint Denys, in his *Les Rêves et les moyens de les diriger: Observations pratiques.* Not walking in your dreams but making dreams walk in the direction you want them to. Dreaming like writing and reading at the same time; though there are studies that discard the whole notion with a "you aren't dreaming, you're just half-asleep or half-awake." And, though they don't agree on this, researchers say the people who achieve it most easily are those who spend hours awake and plugged into videogames. And anyone, in the middle of a nightmare, takes control and says, "This is a dream and I'm going to wake myself up." And they wake up.

—That's true. I've had that happen.

—Another: negative emotions are more common in dreams. We experience moments of pleasure and happiness and even fear. But anxiety and bad desires take precedence. To kill or have someone die whom we detest. The most interesting thing is that the "heaviest" nightmares take place not in the depths of sleep, but when we're on our way to waking up. So the most terrible thing that happens to us or that we happen to think of when we're asleep, in our imagination, takes place close to reality, much closer than it seems . . . Again, the thing from before, a kind of cleansing.

—But with a vomitive more than a laxative, ha.

—And while we're in the REM stage of sleep, the body reaches a state of complete paralysis. To keep you from acting out your dreams, to keep you from moving. There are times, especially after a very "real" nightmare, when you wake up and feel like you can't move. And that's because you *really* can't. Sleepwalkers, on the other hand, suffer from an overstimulation of neurons. That's why they move when they're asleep or half-asleep, in a hybrid state between sleep and wakefulness. Somnambulism is one of the most interesting forms of parasomnia. The most interesting of all sleep disorders, like night terrors, bed wetting, narcolepsy, teeth grinding, talking and making love and eating and even texting while asleep, . . .

—Really? Seriously? And what do people text? "Guess what I'm dreaming?" Is there an emoticon to indicate you're dreaming? An emoticon of an emoticon dreaming of another emoticon? There probably is, right?

— . . . and even always sleeping in a fetal position, which, according to some, is a way of confronting a daily lack of confidence, which is why they recommend, always, doing a full body stretch before getting up . . . And the so-called Exploding Head Syndrome, which consists of auditory hallucinations. It's more common among children and . . .

—Is it true it's dangerous to wake a sleepwalker?

—Yes and no. There's no clear rule, but it can be risky. There are sleepwalkers who wake up terrified or screaming. Or wanting to throw themselves out a window.

—Never wake up a sleepwalker next to a window.

—The best thing to do is, without waking them, bring them back to bed. And this will *definitely* interest you: in 1996 they recorded for the first time, as a consequence of stress or drugs or alcohol, a form of somnambulism called *sexsomnia*: panting and masturbating while asleep and even raping the person in bed beside you and . . . No, don't even think about it, we're not going back to bed . . .

—Okay: no bed . . . I remember that Lady Macbeth was a sleepwalker. At a certain point two other characters in the play watch her pass by, asleep, and, yes, they decide it's best not to wake her. . . And how right they were, no? I've read about a guy named Ken Parks, who stabbed his mother-in-law while asleep; and he was tried and declared innocent. And about the American editor Hugh Person, who strangled his wife while sleeping: guilty, eight years in prison, insane asylum . . . But enough bloodshed. I don't want to have nightmares tonight . . . Let's talk about more peaceful things . . . Have you recorded baby's dreams? And dreams of sleepwalking parents who can't sleep because of the crying of their kids who wake up crying after dreaming things more abstract than figurative? And back to the thing from before: have you recorded the dreams of sleepwalkers? I guess it wouldn't be easy to record them, right? Really long cables and coming unplugged all the time and . . .

—You're making me sleepy . . . So, to wrap this up, the idea of the universality of certain dreams. Common dreams and dreams in common. To dream of a death or of a house. To dream of being naked, of flying, of falling, of being lost, of feeling like you're being chased, or of running through the halls of your school and arriving late to that important class. Or of Jesus Christ or the divinity of your choice smiling at the foot of your hospital bed. Or of that light at the end of the tunnel which is nothing but a cataclysm in our cerebral chemistry thinking maybe now it's time to bow out . . . But who has determined these to be the hit-single dreams and on what basis? . . . Or who are the people who came to the conclusion that they can dream the dreams of others in certain metal beds or on certain hotel mattresses, surfaces believed to be more prone to receive and transmit a certain type of short longitudinal wave? That's why, they explain and justify, in hotels we always have dreams that are strange, inappropriate, other, dreams that don't correspond to the coordinates of our normal oneiric pathways . . .

—Ah, so in hotels we're tourist dreamers . . .

—There are so many absurd theories . . . There's nothing easier than theorizing about the unknown . . . Is there anything that better combines the idea of the strange with the idea of the familiar than dreams? Anything is valid. From the idea that our life is nothing but the dream of a superior being to the theory that . . . whatever you want. Thus the need to *normalize it*, to shine light on it, to clean it up. To *wake* it all up . . . Like that thing they say about the dreams of cancer patients . . .

—What do they say?

—They say they're spectacular. Pure special effects. Almost lysergic dreams. You no longer dream that you're naked or flying, but that the whole world is flying and has been stripped naked. Optimists claim they're "healing dreams." That it's the mind's way of laying waste to all of reality and, in the process, of distracting you from the bad trance you find yourself in.

—Ah, the chemotherapy version of dreams. Dreams like radiation bombarding nightmare cells . . .

—Or that other one, "in style" a while back: dreaming about that mysterious man people all over the world said they dreamed about, remember? That man with no face. "This man" they said. *This Man.* And there were those who sought an archetypal explanation à la Jung, for whom [unlike Freud, for whom dreams were everything] dreams were *more* than everything. Or the ones who talked about the viral phenomenon of mass hysteria and collective suggestion contracted and propagated by so many others on the Internet. And those inclined toward the idea of the dream-surfer: the meddlesome astral traveler leaving behind his body, someone with the ability to enter the dreams of others and . . .

—Ah, like a Freddy Krueger; but at all ages and with better intentions. Or like the Sandman . . .

—I never said anything about his intentions being good.

—Ah, so what did he do? Why did he appear to people? Did he warn them about accidents? Did he give them the winning lottery numbers?

—Not that I know of . . . And who is Freddy Krueger?

—That guy from the horror movies. With knives in his gloves and a burned face and that striped sweater and that hat. The one who appeared to teenagers in their dreams and killed them while they slept and so they tried not to fall asleep and . . . But you told me you were a cinophile . . . How do you not know who Freddy is?

—I am a cinophile, but of good cinema.

—Ah . . . And regarding what you were saying . . . On your list of universal dreams, you missed one. One of the important ones.

—Which?

—You know . . .

—Which?

—Eh . . . Ah . . . Let's not forget about the universal dream of meeting the woman of your dreams.

—That's not a common or universal dream.

—And meeting the man of your dreams?

—Nope. Meeting the woman of your dreams only in your dreams would be a contradiction and an absurdity. Nobody likes to dream that. And then to wake up. In any case, it's a waking and romantic dream. A daydream. Like in the movies when the colors brighten and the music swells and a man and a woman run toward each other in slow motion.

—Which brings me to what interests me most. The thing that led me to interview the people who run the Onirium and, then, to find you at long last. The woman of my dreams. That girl. Her. And for you to find me and that I had also appeared in your dreams and . . .

—I'd rather not talk about that, okay?

—I get it. I get you. It's like insisting too much on the description of something magical. You always run the risk of discovering the trick and, though it may not be the case, it all turns out to have been just a dream and . . .

—You said, "Which brings me to what interests me most . . ." right?

—Right. Understood. Indirect direct hit and right on target . . . . I was saying, for my next project, I wanted to know how to film dreams. How to show them and make people see them. And I want to be as faithful as possible to what it's like. I'm not interested in being easily dreamlike and taking advantage of that everything-valid in the oneiric imaginary. I have something here Susan Sontag wrote, an introduction to an Icelandic writer, almost the last one she wrote, where she stipulates that "Time and space are mutable in the dream novel, the dream play. Time can always be revoked. Space is multiple."

But that's not what attracts me most, that free will of the sleeper. Just the opposite. I wanted to bring some rigor and discipline to all of that. Impose a few rules on this game . . . I have a few examples I'd like to bring up with you. In fact, when I called the Onirium on the phone, they told me I was lucky because "one of our specialists is a big cinophile." And that's you and . . .

—Get to the point. Stop telling me about your movie.

—Okay, alright. What I was telling you. There are many movies with dream sequences and none of them really do it for me. To begin with, there's *Sherlock Jr.*, with Buster Keaton. And, in literature, there's even a great story, one of Vladimir Nabokov's few favorites [ah!, that was the name he couldn't remember!]. "In Dreams Begin Responsibilities," by the then twenty-something and perfect Delmore Schwartz: everything in that story is a dream turned into a movie . . . I've got a list of them here that, in a way, configure a brief history of the dream on the big screen. Let's see . . . The Coen brothers and the dreams in *Raising Arizona* and *The Big Lebowski* [that are like old dreams, dreams in movies in which dreams *were telling* something] and that other dream told while awake at the end of *No Country for Old Men*. Or the voiceover in the films of Terrence Malick, with the wind whipping the curtains [like the voice of someone talking in their sleep], or in those of Wong Kar-wai [that mood, that almost languid slowness in his oh so romantic films]. And the special cases, the trance films, dreamlike trips, missions like dreams: *2001: A Space Odyssey*, *Apocalypse Now* with Kurtz's recorded voice whispering how he has dreamed of a snail crawling along the edge of a straight razor and surviving and "That's my dream. That's my nightmare." . . . And, then, the classic options . . .

—Yes . . . Go on.

—Well, a classic example is the dream sequence that Salvador Dali designed for Alfred Hitchcock in . . .

—*Spellbound!* Agh! No! Never! Verboten. Redundant. The best dreamed parts in Hitchcock are the waking parts: those close-ups of objects, all that irreal backprojecting, those sets, those slow kisses, his speed of things . . . The same is true of the first Buñuel. There's nothing less dreamlike than surrealism, though André Breton considered dreams a fundamental part of his credo, "communicating vessels." The dream as surrealism is a cliché and banal and easy. Dreams are never surrealistic. We don't think, "Wow, this is so surrealistic" while experiencing a dream. Dreams are a kind of alternative realism where, unlike waking realism, anything can happen. It's realism without rules, without limits. But it is *not* surrealism.

—Tarkovsky.

—Tarkovsky makes me sleepy. He doesn't make dreams.

—Fellini.

—Not him either. Almost for the same reasons. And it's too personal and recognizable. One doesn't have Fellinian dreams. One does not have Fellini dreams because one is not Fellini. Even though personal and individual and private elements appear in them, dreams are never entirely our own. They don't have an aesthetic or a particularly marked style. Dreams have the style of dreams with the addition of some trace of whoever is dreaming them. But you couldn't say that we put our own stamp on our dreams.

—And yet, I feel that my dreams are mine alone. That nobody else can dream or direct them like me. In fact, I have dreams in which I only appear at the beginning and the end, like a host, like the one who opens the door or the box. A little bit like Rod Serling's role in *The Twilight Zone*, in those episodes of *The Twilight Zone* where life and death depend on dreaming or not dreaming or on reading or not reading. Or like in that great episode of Louie with the recurrent nightmare as a consequence of having refused to help someone. Or like the Man from Another Place, that dancing dwarf, in the "waiting room" in *Twin Peaks*.

—There we are in agreement. Above all in *Mulholland Dr.*, which Lynch described as "a love story in the city of dreams" and the abbreviation Dr. as being as much of *Drive* as of *Dream*. The dream like a lost highway with confusing road signs and unexpected intersections. Things occur in David Lynch in a dreamlike way. As if in dreams. But they are dreams in which we never see the dreamer. The dreamer is outside. And the dreams seem, all the time, to be searching for

him or waiting for him to wake up and try to wake them up. So you
don't watch David Lynch's films, you dream them, better in the dark.
That's why what David Lynch does always has something of an opiatic
quality, and on more than one occasion, produces in the spectator a
fear that's the same fear you feel confronting the unknown, in the
face of not having the slightest idea what might happen next. Like
in dreams, where we never know and struggle to have some control
over the twists and turns of the plot . . . Yes, David Lynch is a case to
pay attention to and consider with great care. The way time passes or
doesn't pass in David Lynch. And the constant allusions to dreams, to
that obsession with thinking that "the dream is a code waiting to be
deciphered." But I think there's someone who goes even further.

—Who?

—Ah . . . Robert Altman in *3 Women*, a film almost nobody remembers that emerged from a dream its director had . . . And, of course,
Stanley Kubrick in *Eyes Wide Shut*. The most dreamlike film ever
filmed. What Kubrick does is very interesting and far more faithful
to the feeling of a dream. Something similar happens in *Casablanca*.
Not so much in strictly oneiric films, which are garbage though they
mean well, like Richard Linklater's *Waking Life* . . . Or a certain ingen-
uous romanticism, like the addicts of recording and watching their
dreams over and over again on small screens in Wim Wenders's *Until
the End of the World* . . . Or like *Abre los ojos* and its separated Siamese
twin *Vanilla Sky* . . . Or those dreams in the narcoleptic clouds of *My
Own Private Idaho* . . . Or like the overwhelming stupidity of *Incep-
tion* . . . That one is definitely completely absurd in its pretension
that dreams can be something so rigorously narrative and linear and
shared. That dreams have such a clear desire to dream and to be
dreamed. Accustomed to them telling us something and to telling
it all, we furnish and give the lie to our dreams in a successive and
organized way when really everything in them happens in a multiple
and simultaneous way. We intervene in them and correct them as
if they were a text, a text that we are reading or writing quickly in
that notebook we have beside our bed. And then we proceed to decode
them with those absurd dream dictionaries that claim to explain all

possible meanings except for what it means to dream of a dream dictionary . . . We, here in the Onirium, are trying to do something about it and believe me . . .

—Do something?

—Yes . . . But . . .

—But . . .

—But I'm not really supposed to talk about it. It's a confidential, revolutionary project. Something that, if achieved, would change the history of humanity . . .

—Ah . . .

—Ah, what?

—No, nothing . . .

—I don't like that little smile of yours. What's that little smile about?

—I can't help it. When a scientist says that thing about "changing the history of humanity," I always have the reflex of grabbing onto my chair and thinking "Here comes trouble." That's always how it goes in the movies and . . .

—Yes, we already know you've seen too many movies.

—No, seriously, please, don't get mad. But it seems to me the majority of scientists only develop the theory after the practice. I'm not saying they don't get results and illuminate wonders. But I always have the impression that in the majority of cases they arrive to them purely by chance. Like Viagra, remember? They were trying to develop something to make hair grow and, well, they found they could make something else grow . . .

—Yeah, I remember . . . But it wasn't for growing hair. It was a medication for arterial hypertension and angina pectoris. You're confusing it with minoxidil, which was a vasodilator, and then they discovered that it had very interesting side effects in what it did for capillary growth . . .

—There it is! You just said it! Side effects!

—What? What're you talking about?

—That terminology: side effects. More words that make me shudder. "Side effects" is like "friendly fire" or "collateral damage" . . . I'm sorry, I can't help it, but . . .

—Okay. I get it now.

—That's why I can't help feeling a certain pleasure every time it's "discovered" that the universe is much bigger or older than was previously thought. Or when a supposedly infertile couple, after having passed through all the Stations of the Cross of those treatments and having given up, defeated, end up getting pregnant days after having adopted a faraway and probably intolerable baby. I love the way the professionals, confronted with "new evidence," try to find explanations to keep from looking bad. They look like kids caught by their teachers making mischief and trying to blame the classmate at the next desk.

—I see . . .

—I see that it would be best to change the subject. Let's see, I know. Scientists from the University of Oxford with too much time on their hands and yet ever so well remunerated have reached the conclusion that counting sheep doesn't do any good at all and that, besides, "it's too boring." The best thing, apparently, what they recommend, is to imagine self-hypnotizing landscapes, relaxing and tranquil places. But to me, when it comes to postulating such things, I like what writers and poets, with more caution and less arrogance, propose better. The other day, I read one who ventured that in our dreams we assume the heavenly God gaze. Seeing everything at once and not occurring in succession. And in nightmares we are given a sort of preview of hell, like drops of liquid magma seeping through the cracks and rising to our surface. But could there be anything more hellish than the gift of seeing everything at once? Maybe that's why we wake up. And, when we wake up, we forget almost everything we saw or experienced, and we struggle to give it some kind of narrative structure so we can pay exorbitant sums to recount it for our beloved psychologist. Or for our supposedly-more-beloved loved one sleeping beside us. You see, more assumptions . . .

—Ah, I get it. All of this is your way of forcing me to defend myself. And to end up telling you what it is we do in the Onirium. And why we're so interested in your recurrent dream where I, a me from years ago, appears and . . .

—Yes; and getting really paranoid now, why they made you pretend you remembered me too and that you've been looking for me ever since, in order to seduce me and get me to voluntarily submit myself to an experiment that, supposedly, "will change the history of humanity" but whose unexpected and impossible-to-prevent "side effects" will . . .

—I don't find what you're saying the least bit funny.

—Which part? The thing about the side effects? Or that you were pretending to feel something for me?

—All of it.

—Ah, all of it.

—Yes.

—Oh. We're having our *second* fight.

—Indeed. Better not go there.

—Better, indeed.

— . . .

— . . .

— . . .

— . . .

— . . .

—A cure for insomnia? Is that what you're working on? The other day I learned that the *Guinness Book of World Records* has stopped accepting submissions for days without sleeping [eleven is the number to beat, apparently, a student in 1966], considering it too unhealthy. As if holding your breath in a bathtub full of spaghetti or jumping off a skyscraper astride a killer whale or trying to memorize the equally soporific and rousing *Finnegans Wake* and reading it aloud in reverse and without vowels weren't unhealthy and . . . Ah, good, you're smiling again. For a second there I thought the side effects of our fight had atrophied all the many muscles needed to achieve a smile and . . .

—Stop.

— . . . that it was my fault, and so I'd always be remembered as the man who forever deprived all humanity of such a heavenly vision and . . .

—Stop! I know I'm laughing, but seriously . . .

— . . . and I'd wander the world like a pariah. Stoned by men when I happened upon their town, spit on by women, mocked by children, and bitten by dogs, and . . .

—Stop. I get it. You win. I'm going to tell you about what we're working on . . . You'll have to find out sooner or later anyway and sign some forms and . . .

— . . . so I don't guess at the malicious intentions of your superiors who want only to take my dream and . . .

—I already told you not to go there.

—Oops. Sorry. You're right.

—I mean it . . . Why are you smiling?

—It's just makes me smile the way you say, "I mean it." But it's not a mocking smile. It's adorable.

—You want me to tell you or not?

—Go for it, please.

—Well . . . You know, you've probably heard it a time or two, the thing about how we spend a third of our lives sleeping.

—Uh-huh . . .

—And how, of that third of our lives, it is about nine years that we spend dreaming.

—That I didn't know. I'd not made the calculation.

—We don't think of it as some big waste of time, but we do think it's something we could take better advantage of.

—I don't get it.

—What we want is to take advantage of our sleep and our dreams. Not to stop sleeping or dreaming. But for all that time to be more beneficial.

—I still don't get it.

—What we're after, what we're seeking, is for our dreams to become practical and useful and, in a way, rational. So we could keep working in our dreams, so we could find practical and logical solutions in them. So, in a way, our dreams could be made reality because they are reality, they're realistic. Logical. Going from A to B and not from

C to X. And, of course, so we could remember them in their entirety upon waking. Down to the smallest details. And, yes, so we don't wake up right at the best part. We've already made some advances.

—. . .

—What's wrong now?

—. . .

—Right. You don't like it . . .

—It's not that I don't like it. But it seems to me some apparently irrational things are the foundations atop which reason is held up and erected and fortified. Maybe, as they say, when we dream, we let ourselves go mad for a while and that's how we're able to tolerate seeing ourselves forced to be sane so much of the time, the other two-thirds of our lives, right? I don't know, I'm not really compelled by the idea of dreams being like domestic animals, like useless pets we force to be useful. I like wild dreams more than dreams in captivity. Dreams that run free in the open field and don't stop to think about whether or not they're dreams, lacking any of those tricks for figuring out if *los sueños, sueños son*, if it's all just a dream. A dream that's not even aware it's dreaming.

—What tricks?

—The most popular is trying to count the fingers on your hand and not being able to do it. Or to read something somewhere and look away and then read it again only to discover what you read has changed . . . To realize what you read isn't what you're reading . . . To read that what you read no longer has anything to do or to read with what . . .

—Okay. But your way of thinking isn't very scientific.

—No, agreed. It's a post-scientific way of thinking. Like I said, it's what scientists always think after an experiment comes out wrong or different and they wake up from their dream and discover that, indeed, "The Sleep of Reason Produces Monsters."

—Ah, I see: the person talking now is the artist concerned with such transcendent issues as how best to film a dream . . .

—No: the person talking now is the human being concerned

because, when you wake up, the person you love says "Bet you don't know what I dreamed last night" and you, automatically, say something like "I dreamed you had to take the car in for its annual checkup and, while you were there, you found out there's a better priced insurance policy than the one we have" and . . .

—Ah, I see . . .

—You see.

— . . .

—And on the other hand . . . What makes you think people would like that? Why do you think people would sign up for such an experiment?

—People will sign up for anything, will buy anything. People are addicted to the idea of the latest model, of novelty. People will even pay a great deal for it. The constantly unsatisfied desire for always-changing mobile phones has blazed the trail for any new idea, imposed or not. It'll be like giving them a new app, a new fashion, a new function. They'll be oh so happy . . .

— . . .

—So this is the moment when, so we can stop fighting, I have to ask you what you dreamed last night.

—Correct.

—Okay. What did you dream last night?

—I dreamed something crazy, complete nonsense . . .

—I can't wait for you to tell me.

—Well, in the dream I was ascending a slope toward a very strange edifice. With two immense eyes on its façade. The edifice was surrounded by screaming people. And then I was inside. And you appeared and you didn't recognize me and they strapped me to a bed and connected me to cables and electrodes and after that I don't really remember . . .

—And then?

—Then, luckily, as you know: suddenly, again, like so many other times, I was at a party, years ago, and I saw you dancing, and your dress changed colors, and I danced all night and I, knowing it was a dream, said to myself, "I hope this dream lasts forever and I never wake up." And then I saw you in a bookstore where another song was playing, one of my favorites songs, that one called . . .

—And then?

—And then I woke up, then you woke me up.)


Heraclitus postulated that the waking world was common to everyone while, in our dreams, we travel to our own nocturnal world in order to, there, work on understanding our diurnal life. Cervantes, to the contrary, thought we're all the same when we sleep.

In his dream, he's not the one thing or the other. He advances as if balancing on a taught steel cable, as if the aisles between the rows of bookshelves were a high wire he's walking, one foot in front of the other, an open umbrella to help keep him from falling into the void.

He walks toward Ella and his steps are interrupted and Manga Boy and Freak Batman pull out pistols and tell Ella to give them all the money in the bookstore cash register. To one side, visible behind the counter, in a pool of blood, Homero's legs protrude. He doesn't know why, but the only thing he can focus on—the only thing that matters to him—is that the laces of his left shoe are untied—something there to be interpreted, no doubt * (dreaming of your shoelaces signifies you're not ready to face a transcendent event. "Possible mishaps and unexpected risks!!!").

Ella trembles and he throws himself at them and a bullet pierces Ella's heart.

Ella trembles and he throws himself at them and gets a bullet in the brain and is left in a coma. And he stays like that until he dies a few days later without even getting to enjoy that right or privilege of seeing your whole life pass before your eyes in a matter of seconds. To fall into a coma is, also, to fall into the elastic time of dreams. And then he dreams—he remembers it—what his comatose mother dreamed, a series of dreams.

Ella trembles and he throws himself at them and takes them down and the police arrive and then Ella comes up to him and puts her hand on his shoulder and he, like a sleepwalker, puts his hands around her throat and squeezes and squeezes until he feels something inside break.

And he wakes up thinking he would like it if his dreams—the power of his dreams—could, just once, be narrated not as they're narrated here, but with the precision and economy of one of those old and immortal moral tales, introduced, on the television of his childhood, by one Rod Serling, that ectoplasmatic host. Stories that, a little more than twenty minutes later, show us how, even within the strangest and most dreamlike plot, nests the seed of order and logic and true morality.

Rod Serling saying something like, "Here we have a man with the power to make his dreams never come true."

And, then, his life story.

In black and white.

And waiting to find out—you don't have to wait long, just over twenty minutes—if his story has a happy or a sad ending.

Because in the twilight zone you can have sad endings or happy endings, but never an open ending—a sleeping ending—like this one . . .

* ( . . . after this quick commercial break, this message from our sponsor, this confession of a crime and admission of guilt: he doesn't like any of this. Or, better, he likes it as scattered fragments, as pieces of a dream—dreams never work as a whole and only their best plots are remembered—as the debris of a shipwreck without bottom or shore, like footnotes leaving footprints where the sand ends and the water begins, where the sea ends so the forest can begin. Liquid ideas, somewhere to get lost. But it is what it is, what remains, what will last; what he can tell and share after so much time here inside, dreaming. Like what you retain when sand or water runs through your hands. Not much. And what's left isn't necessarily what's important, what's indispensable. What's left is just what was left. A frustrated desire, knowing every dream is the paradox of something that only accepts itself as such once you wake up: every dream is the frustration of that same dream. The broken and not-entirely-rewritable formula of a failed experiment that ended up spawning a monster made of random and poorly put-together parts. The dreamed part, which is nothing without the part of those who dream it and without the part of the one

who only dreams of dreaming and can no longer do it.

We return now to central laboratories, where we continue our broadcast.)

Yesterday, before closing his eyes to open them again—after the weatherman communicated the signs and symbols of that variation of a waking-dream diagnosis known as the "meteorological forecast," which is nothing but the examination and symptomology of the brain waves of the climate across the crust of the skull of the planet—he heard that song again.

It came from the open window of the guesthouse, on the other side of the garden. He stayed there, in his bed, until the song finished with an "I've already gone the distance / Just thinking of a series of dreams."

He copied down the verses on a piece of paper. Maybe he could find them floating in the collective and always-awake unconscious of the internet. Maybe finding them and identifying them would bring him face to face with the reality that that song changes nothing. Maybe better to keep believing in what he doesn't know; to maintain the same illusion that's worked so well for all the great religions for millennia.

Tomorrow.

Better tomorrow.

When he wakes up.

There's time.

There's too much time.

Then—context, at last—he closed the windows and lowered the blinds with the remote control, and turned off the light.

And he walked toward Ella and nothing interrupted his steps and he lay down beside her and she was already sleeping, she always goes to sleep before him and always wakes up after him. Ella, like everyone, no longer dreams, no longer remembers, no longer remembers him or how he once dreamed her.

And—having already gone the distance, thinking of a series of dreams—he closed his eyes and prepared himself, once again, for the joyous waking dream of thinking Ella hated him, only to realize it was all just a dream. And waking up, happy, just before Ella began to love him. To dream it, so that, please, one day or one night Ella might love him again as much as she once loved him and how once—with that voice only used to say things like that—she said she would love him forever, the way she loved him in the dreams she no longer has because she no longer dreams.

Dreams in which Ella walks toward him.

Dreams in which Ella approaches him, and comes close, and stops a step away from her mouth touching his, and—with one of those smiles that means just the opposite of what she says—smiles and says: "Don't even dream of it."

# THE OTHER NIGHT
## (IRRATIONAL CATALOG FOR AN EXHIBITION OF RESTLESS SHADOWS)

I have dreamt in my life, dreams that have stayed with me ever
after, and changed my ideas; they have gone through and through
me, like wine through water, and altered the color of my mind.
—EMILY BRONTË
*Wuthering Heights*

A ruffled mind makes a restless pillow.
—CHARLOTTE BRONTË
*The Professor*

I love the silent hour of the night,
For blissful dreams may then arise,
Revealing to my charmed sight
What may not bless my waking eyes.
—ANNE BRONTË
"Poem 14 / Night"

The night is cold and loud the blast.
—PATRICK BRANWELL BRONTË
"Winter-Night Meditations"

I have no objection whatever to your representing me as a little eccentric,
since you and your learned friends would have it so . . . Had I been
numbered among the calm, concentric men of the world, I should not
have been as I now am, and I should in all probability never have had
such children as mine have been . . . Their fun knew no bounds.
—REVEREND PATRICK BRONTË
Letter to Elizabeth Gaskell, July 30th, 1857

More than anything else, however, they had each other.
—JULIET BARKER
*The Brontës*

# I

Let there be light, yes; but only so, in the next instant, the light can be snuffed out by the darkness.

Here it comes again.

What?

"The darkness!" exclaims the auditorium, ecstatic.

The darkness arrives ready to drown it.

What?

"The light!" everyone celebrates together in the auditorium of this melancholic and toxic "sanatorium."

There, mad with pure joy and the fury of sleepless nights; healthy patients jumping and invoking, *invocatio musarum*, exalted and wuthering, atop their seats, not one free or empty, fists aloft holding fists aloft holding fists. So ready (here, only the red fire of raised torches is authorized to splash across the dark night) for the thrill of burning with the spontaneous combustion of speaking in tongues. You can't understand anything they say, but nothing is easier to comprehend than the sound and noise of unbridled joy, escaping their mouths, like teeth gnashing the air.

The light made now unmade by the darkness, oh, yes.

The light leveled like a sand castle, lovingly and patiently begun and built by small hands throughout the suntanned day; that castle that ends up taken by storm and dissolved in the grips of the crashing and rising tide of the night.

Or the light silenced with the kiss of a soft wind slipping between lips to extinguish the gleaming ruby of the candle flame.

Or the light turned off with the *click* of the little lever of the light switch being lowered. And, oh, that intimate triumphal march ("Soldiers are dreamers," wrote a poet of the trenches while all around him shells fell and gases rose) the unknown and secret soldier imagines, alone, as he advances along the battlefront as if it were the rearguard of the hallways of a house; turning off the lights in room after room, one to the next, as if he were counting down the chapters of a novel until he comes to the darkness of a beginning where nothing is known and anything is possible.

Or the light surging through and pulling on a cable until it rips it out of the two sparking holes, like the electric bite mark of the most energized vampire on the lower neck of the wall.

Or the light throwing a stone that was once the point of an arrow to strike the glowing target of the last lamp of winter.

Or the light projecting the softness of the fade to black of darkness falling across the seats of a movie theater so the show can begin: always *noir* films where the night is an American night; films with titles like *Nightfall* or *Twilight Rendezvous* or *A Sleepwalker Sleeps, Finally* or *Soursweet Dreams*: all with an untrustworthy femme fatal heroine singing expressively expressionistically on the stage of a chiaroscuro nightclub that could well be called Bad Country.

Or, after all the foregoing, she finally sets aside that recurrent and oh so fraternal (her bad brother's bad influence) mania of turning everything into part of an enumerative list, when there's nothing left to stain black; and so the light resorts to the most time-honored and easy and personal and primitive way of unmaking the light to let there be darkness: closing its eyes.

And thereby learning to see the invisible.

Close your eyes.

See.


Here comes the darkness; here overhead, falling, the night.

And with the darkness and with the night, she lights up.


Here, her dream is life, Stella D'Or shines: splendid terrorist, immortal dead star. Her black light reaching us so many years after being snuffed out. Her resplendent voice still audible, like an echo reverberating across galaxies, saying things like:


"You may say I'm a dreamer, but I'm not the only one, I hope one day you'll join us and, oh, imagine: once upon a time the night was full of stars. And so many falling stars, seen so clearly, that people didn't have enough wishes to justify that level of cosmic exaltation and to honor their kamikaze trajectory with impossible waking dreams. Wishing on a star for things like happiness and health and money. Attributing to the stars the pale pulse of the dead, raised up into the heavens. And they're up there still, of course. The living stars and the dead. They haven't gone anywhere. They come and go. But it's impossible to see them now. The color of the night, once an oceanic blue—ultrasky, not ultramarine—is now a dirty gray, electrified by the static of all those artificial lights down on Earth that make it restless, into a kind of insomniac sleepwalker. The faithful and virtuoso night, with eyes shut tight, yet unable to sleep. The night like a vaguely darker part of the day . . . Stop already! . . . Enough! . . . No more! . . . Never again! . . . We'll go back to when the nights were nocturnal. Nights that struck fear into mortals, falling over them like a curtain not to end a show, but to begin a new one: the best and most entertaining of all. The night when things forbidden by day are permitted. The night without all that light containing it. The 'dark and stormy night' that opens that purple and Victorian novel by Edward Bulwer-Lytton—who also postulated that 'the pen is mightier than the sword'—in its first line that so many people mock because they actually admire and envy it . . . And I want to be like that opening line. I want to be like the black hole that swallows all that light and spits out its bones. I want to be the voice singing that lullaby beside the cradle shaped like a coffin—a coffin like a music box; because coffins always seem much smaller than the person who rests inside them—in which to put to bed that false and tiring day, tired of working all those extra but never extraordinary hours. I want the night that no longer is what it once was and now has so little to tell and to be again what it once was: a bottomless sky, a deep pool from which to extract stories and in which to weave the plot of the constellations, a house of extraterrestrial gods and alien divinities. I want for the night to be the novel that follows the bedtime story your parents read to you and, after, you live throughout the long night—though your eyes are shut, so far yet so near—reading it, though you don't know how to read yet. I want for the night not to be just another hour on the clock but another time altogether, elsewhere. The location of the night like that place where we are how we really are and, at the same time, where it is much harder to see ourselves, snugly tucked into the sheets of our dreams . . . Thus all notes of an obscurist noctographer (of a biographer of the night and student of the many things that happen there and the kinds of shadows that fall then) should, to have anything to offer in terms of story, by obligation and strategy, go way back. To the beginning of time, to the first darkness from which light originates . . . And I have a dream . . . I *also* have a dream . . . And it's a waking dream. A dream made reality. A dream in which night will fall so day never rises and the words of that monastic and almost-black-as-midnight pianist come true: 'It's always night, or we wouldn't need the light' . . . But in order for that to be possible, for that to *occur*, first we need to reinvent the night . . . Reestablish it . . . Return the darkness to the night, return the night to the darkness. Dark matter! . . . To be done with easy and automatic superstitions like God is *Lux Mundi* and the Devil, Lucifer, the most brilliant angel fallen and transformed into the obscurantist Prince of Darkness, governing from a 'visible obscurity.' All that nonsense to dazzle the dupes, like '3—Then God said: Let there be light. And there was light. 4—And God saw that the light *was* good; and God separated the light from the darkness. 5—And God called the light day, and the darkness he called night. And there was evening and there was morning, one day' . . . Nah . . . *Nacht* . . . Nonsense, not to mention the small but definitive problem of editing and narrative logic in the Bible where it's never explained how there's light in the first instant of Creation when God only creates the Sun on the fourth day . . . And don't give me that absurdity of God himself being pure and shadowless light, please . . . Because then what need would there be *to make it* when those shadows already existed, created previously by Him and where He, supposedly, resided, tripping over all the furniture in the darkness . . . The light is not good and the dark is not bad. Enough of these easy and half-baked beliefs. Wars have been fought and pacifists imprisoned by the light of day too . . . And don't ever forget that the Quran is revealed during the Night of Power, the most significant night according to Islam, for it's the night when Mohammad makes his journey from Jerusalem to Mecca, and from there, to Heaven, under cover of the most sacred darkness . . . And it's by night and not during the day that Abraham becomes aware of the existence of a supreme and absolute being, the one who commands, let there be light . . . And we all spring from the darkness of our fathers to be conceived in the darkness of our mothers . . . How'd it go? What was the line? Ah, yes . . . But now, changing one key word, to give it a new meaning . . . How's it go now? . . . It goes like this: 'Rage, rage, against the dying of the dark.' Here comes the night. The Night."


And Stella D'Or's words always glowed. Whenever Stella D'Or spoke, whoever was listening *saw* her words. As if, fluorescent and synesthetic, in strange neon colors. First their straight lines and curves, but, then, what those written words were describing. As if written in flames on a stone wall as old as stone itself. אנמ, אנגמ, לקת, ויסרפו or *Porpozec ciebie nie prosze dorzanin albo zylopocz ciwego*. Her words and deeds following, as Stella D'Or told it, "the system developed by Charles Barbier de la Serre, captain of the French army, at the request of Napoleon Bonaparte: a secret code dubbed *ecriture nocturne*. A cardboard grid with six by six squares and a series of points in relief that correspond to letters and sounds and can be read in the dark, with the fingertips. And, of course, it wasn't easy to use amid the trembling and the shock of the battlefield; which is why it wasn't put into practice until Barbier de la Serre was invited by the Institut National des Jeunes Aveugles, in whose classrooms studied a precocious and blind student named Louis Braille and . . ."

Or when Stella D'Or referred to other wars, to terrible and luminous wars: to the reflectors of "artificial moonlight that the Nazi army used to drive crazy the sleepless and dreamless nights of American soldiers, daydreaming they were back on their parents' farm in Iowa, on a tractor setting the course of the crops, and not inside a blind and armored tank, blindly wandering aimlessly through the forests of Schnee Eifel, in the Ardennes, being massacred and taken prisoner and driven all the way to Dresden which, blazing, would burn for two whole nights, in a storm of bombs and fire ascending into the heavens."

Or when she invoked "the already ancient night of those ancient people who then, thinking themselves so modern, stacked up pyramids or erected columns or learned to fly or split the atom."

But did Stella D'Or say all those things?

And did she say them with those exact words?

Does it matter?

Who can be sure that the things supposedly said by Yahweh or his son Yeshua of Nazareth actually came out of their mouths? Words that, among other things, supposedly created the entire universe, proved that a second part can be better or at least as good as the first, and proposed the idea that if you suffer now while you're alive, don't worry: because you'll have a great time after you die if you prayed to the Masters, to the Holy Ghost and his ever growing family (that reminds her, the historian of Stella D'Or, so much of that family with whom she spent part of her past life). Holy words their disciples later preached and rewrote with the automatic obedience of ecstatic ventriloquist dolls. It doesn't matter . . . Does it make any difference that at some point we stopped believing in those terrifying stories that, supposedly, help you sleep well and that, with loving sadism, your parents repeated to you over and over, so you had sweet nightmares? The same phrases, hypnotic with their "Once upon a time . . ." and their "ever after." Does it change anything whether or not there is any truth to the parchment-scrolled or bronze-cast speeches of the founding fathers of the nation, memorized by children in schools bearing their names or in parks where their statues are always pointing somewhere else, far away, farther still? Does it alter the landscape in any way that it's acceptable to pledge and repeat—on the surface of parties, to break the ice—all those immortal and famous last words or last breaths (yes, she's *also* writing, a writer)? Is there anybody out there or in here who doesn't write?

And, yes, again (another of her bad brother's bad influences), quoted phrases that Stella D'Or is compiling for her in-progress *A Brief History of Darkness*. Pronouncements like "I see a light" or that one "Light! More light!" by Johann Wolfgang von Goethe, conveniently and transcendently edited by his biographers from the by comparison far more banal "Open the second shutter so that more light may come in." Or in the case of Victor Hugo, "I see black light." To recount the last and always-dubious and unforgettable and in-memoriam living words of an almost-forthwith dead man (though probably, in more than one case, well thought-out and rehearsed in front of the mirror for years). Words spilling out like vapor from the depths of a body already beginning to cool, to be breathed in by and to inspire an always-nearby and -providential listener, notebook in hand, whom posterity never manages to clearly identify. Are we really to take Thomas Alva Edison (so hated by Stella D'Or, who considers him responsible for the phenomenon where children, frightened by the warm and inspiring darkness, suddenly start asking to sleep with a lame and predictable and expensive night light that never gets turned off) seriously, saying goodbye with an "It's very beautiful over there." Or should we just write it off as the last words of a man who wanted to be annoying to the last second of his biography? Or the "Mozart!" of Gustav Mahler? Or the impossible "Get my swan costume ready" of prima ballerina Anna Pavlova.

Again, as Karl Marx had it: "Last words are for fools who haven't said enough." Last words are like a tweet that reveals nothing but the brevity of the act of dying relative to a long life or to the immensity of life. Last words are like wanting to resolve everything quickly and at the last moment.

Again: does it matter whether she, Stella D'Or, said this or that? Does it make sense to put down here that the best last words Stella D'Or never read are the most prosaic and etched in marble or cast in bronze—she finds it consoling that at the hour of death one thinks of little things and not great matters—"Put on your white dress. I like it," which prince Nikolai Bolkonski says to his mistreated daughter Marya Bolkonskaya in *War and Peace* at a pause in their flight before the advance of Napoleon and his troops? (And Stella D'Or's biographer tells herself she gets it, in that book and based on her own experience in the hard and immense heart of a vintage family, the inexorable need for all the men to run to the battlefront, far more terrified of the battles being fought in the rearguard of the family, without truce or possibility of surrender, among all those parents and fiancés and lovers and future spinsters.) And is it worthwhile to dwell on the fact that, in the realm of non-fiction, the goodbye Stella D'Or admires most is that of the almost-pleading Pancho Villa, concerned with his place in History, begging, "Don't let it end like this. Tell them I said something"?

But no.

No.

No no no.

*That* isn't the tone she wants for *this*.

That tone is already known, already been heard, this sister tells her three other sisters with, yes, an accusatory tone. A tone that reminds her, the chronicler of the comings and goings of Stella D'Or, of the grim and grating tone of her grim and grating bad older brother. The tone of one who sees his style and rhythm altered according to the medication of Mondays or the medication of Fridays. A tone at turns depressed and exalted. A tone that is accelerated by the electricity that enters your head or decelerated by bathing in cold water. A tone like that of a telephone of bygone days. Telephones with operators to whom you had to recite a number so they could weave it in for you as if on a loom of plugs and cables.

Thus, a tone transmitted, in a low voice, crackling with static and white noise, as if piped-in through the microphones and speakers of another book already read and written. With another strange girl. That of her bad brother. Falling into a swimming pool or ascending into the skies. And, true, maybe it's always the same girl, but isn't there another language, a different phrasing and tune, to tell and sing her in? Isn't night the time and aren't dreams the vehicle that allow us to change and to be other people?

Every story can be rewritten in the dark.

Thus, the desired tone for all of this is not *like that*. The abandoned speech—a call to arms that isn't answered, that nobody answers—of a landowner dispossessed of his soul and with words as the only inoffensive ammunition he has left. Nobody listens to him. Firing blanks, bleating sheep that refuse to jump over the fence of insomnia. A rant to be delivered, if possible, in a kind of aristocratic and decadent and swampy *lingua* with bourbon or vodka or chewing tobacco or snuff on the breath. And the buzz of mosquitos and the green kudzu covering gravestones in a gothic and vegetal shroud, yet, *also*, with a counterpoint replicating a lysergic seism and a jam session for attracting hurricanes named for an accursed and cursing woman, and here she comes again. And, oh, the juvenile desire to set the world spinning so, along the way, you attain the maturity of understanding you wanted to go so far away just so you could return to the point of departure. To the veranda of that swamp dacha; so the comprehension and compression of the universe wind up making us ever so regional. And once there (wrinkled suit of white linen, that skeletal washed-out white, gray moustaches, red eyes, yellow livers, black of soul and enslaved and bound by the loving chains by our mistress and madam and drinking and downing shots to the health of Stella D'Or) discovering that, after all, it doesn't matter if what you say was said was indeed said. It's not what is left behind that matters but what is yet to come: the nearly ritual repetition of those sayings, though they seem improbable and riddled with errors not orthographical but chronological and geographical. To believe in them like fixed mottos. To perfect their modulation and phrasing. To enunciate them ceaselessly until the words stick to each other and turn into one long and *ommm*inous sound that we hear inside ourselves, like a mantra of gut and muscle, until the end of time, for centuries and centuries, etcetera.

To say them over and over with the techno-disco-voice of a rolling little robot and vocoder: the voice of Stephen Hawking, Oscar for Best Disease. (Will there be a film about Stella D'Or's disease? Tricky, if not impossible: because it would have to be a film of total darkness in which not even the projector beam would light up.) Hawking, whom nobody would take seriously (does anyone really understand that stuff about black holes and temporal wormholes and alternate dimensions; things all directly responsible for the fact that increasingly incomprehensible yet successful television series are written all the time in whose plots anything can happen?) if he didn't have and couldn't count on that degenerative disorder that, if you think about it a little, might just be pure and hard dissimulation. The exact equation for a precise performance. An origami man. A contortionist act, long and difficult to memorize with all those digits entering his eyes; but an act in the end. Because, hey, statistically speaking, if he really were sick, Stephen Hawking would've died years ago if what ails him is actually that particular kind of motoneuronal disease. A disease originally categorized—again, more names named in the night—by the Frenchman Jean-Martin Charcot (1825-1893). A disease related to amyotrophic lateral sclerosis, otherwise known as ALS. A disease that, for reasons impossible to clarify (this is true, seriously), has impacted, among many, groups of people that tend to include, again, statistically speaking, a worryingly high number of Italian soccer players, veterans of the Gulf War, and inhabitants of the island of Guam (and she remembers, sounding so much like him, like her useless and complicator-of-all-things-in-this-world bad brother, once in love with someone whom he referred to as Ella, and whom with time and resentment, in public, he had nicknamed ELA—the Spanish acronym for ALS—because, another of his overabundant bad jokes, "She atrophies and paralyzes me and renders me speechless." And she, not Ella, but the bad brother's sister, has to make an effort to keep these intrusions of his from happening; and it's not easy; and it's something that upsets her and makes her dizzy with vertigo and fevers and . . . ).

Which, inevitably, because speaking of diseases is a bit contagious, brings us to another disease.

Stella D'Or's disease. To the grand mal exotic Stella D'Or referred to as if it were a work of art, a true miracle, an inheritance inherited, a gift given.

Like this:


"Ain't it just like the night to play tricks when you're trying to be so quiet, sitting here stranded, though we all do our best to deny it, steam in the heating pipes and 'Last Night I Dreamed of Heaven' on the radio, tuned to a station that plays nothing but starry-skied country, the volume down low. If so, silence and say its name aloud. I say its name in the dead yet serpentine tongue used to classify incurable diseases. The language of a fallen but unforgettable empire, far more sonorous and poetic than those modern ailments, oh so nouveau riche and designated by the double surname of their 'discoverer.' My disease is old as time, the disease that led innocent men and women and children to be burned at the stake or have a stake driven through their hearts or to became oracular visionaries, capable of seeing in the dark and reading the stars. 'The children of the night,' they were called in true legends . . . For they existed . . . For I exist . . . I'm living proof of the evidence of their dying. My disease is that of superheroes entranced with their own power and, yes, getting marvelously Marvel Comics here, you can call me Eclipsa. Or Nocturna. Or Morphea. Or thorny and flowery and pointy and spiky and colorful soprana and sovereign Queen of the Night. Or, better yet, *nom de guerre*: Capitana Nyx ('Nyx or Nicte being the name of the Greek goddess of the night; rival of Aether and feared even by Zeus, according to Homer; consort of Erebus and mother of Hypnos, the god of sleep, brother of Thanatos who kills you slowly while you sleep and husband of Pasithea, goddess of hallucination; all of them happily dwelling in the darkness of their cave/adyton, and as their divine skins touched, "they awake from their daydream and set all the peoples of Earth in motion,"' writes Stella D'Or in her *A Brief History of Darkness*) . . . And here we go, all together now, the magic words: *Xeroderma pigmentosum* . . . Or *XP*, for addicts of top-secret resonance . . . If so, mine is an *XL XP*. The most chronic and extreme form of *XP*. For me, unlike those Mexicans, tanned by the glow of UFOs like in that one movie, the sun doesn't come out and I don't sing; because for me, the sun is just another actor: because I can only see its exits and entrances from the stage on large or small screens . . . And I don't emerge for the sun . . . For me, emerging and being touched by the sunlight is an absolute impossibility, because, were I exposed to its rays, my skin, ravaged by the pincers of cancer, would fall from my bones. My pupils would turn white and blind. And as the days passed, my nervous system would be like a seism of irreconcilable-polarity electricity, until I turned into the madwoman in the attic singing the ultraviolet blues, there above, alongside that other woman who is writing me . . . And locking me up and throwing the key into a lake so nobody can find it . . . I, the one and only among two hundred and fifty thousand people and not even able to resort to blaming it on my parents being the children of consanguineous marriages . . . No, my parents had nothing at all to do with it, mine is a rare disease and it's not hard to believe that it begins with me . . . I am the Patient Zero, I am Alpha, I am *In the beginning* . . . I am something and someone much closer to the folkloric than to the scientific and pathologic explanation, leaning on crutches of 'damaged DNA,' 'nucleotides,' 'melanoma,' '(6-4) pyrimidine photoproducts,' 'cellular mutations' . . . XP-Men-Women don't tend to live past twenty. And their bodies end up crisscrossed with marks and ulcers, as if they were brought up under invisible lashes tracing a map that doesn't lead to any treasure. And I don't have a single freckle or mole anywhere on my skin . . . Which doesn't stop me, of course, from being the most impassioned of all racists. I believe and am convinced that black people are the superior race and chosen tribe. Why? Easy: because they're black, black like the night. I'm black too. I'm the negative of a black woman. I am white like the moon in the blackest night."

And then, having said that—as the zombies and devils and muzhik ghosts, hanging from trees like Christmas decorations or burned beside burning crosses, dance atop the crossroads of their own tombs—Stella D'Or untied the one or two or three ties that keep her black diamond-studded top up.

And, naked and white, she revealed herself to those who watched with kaleidoscopic eyes and telescopic sexes, repeating her name and the name of her disease. Tattooing the verses of future ballads across the skin of her legend. Swearing to her, swearing they're ready to do anything in the name of her face and her bones where the ghost of electricity and the radiation she's been submitted to howls. Proclaiming themselves ready for her glory, leaping from the ledges of her cheekbones and coming down singing, like prisoners enchanted to be free from enchantment.

Falling just there.

The place Stella D'Or is from is the same place as always; but, like her, here and now, its name and situation are delicately yet definitively manipulated.

It's enough to brush a chromosome with your fingertips to make a Y into an X and everything changes and nothing will be how it once was: Somber Hymns is the name of that place, not where Stella D'Or was born, but where she was taken as a newborn.

A small city—really barely a villa that once was barely a castle surrounded by the dwellings of its serfs as caramel-colored as Oompa Loompas, as garish as Munchkins—now on the outskirts of another city and barely separated by a forest and a sea and a bridge and high walls.

There, and hence its name, for centuries a noble insomniac had convened musicians to compose soporific music. Arias and variations so, when their fingers hammered away at the clavichord, they dreamed of the secret melody the wings of the tsetse fly sing as they rub together.

Now, since not that long ago, all of that—though the scene hasn't lost a certain ferocity, like that of a Britannia recently abandoned by the Romans and their gods and ready to embrace the sleeping dragons and wizards and swords in stones and Knights-errant on horseback—was acquired by a foundation. And it functions as a top-secret-campus for advanced researchers in all the sciences, in numbers and letters, and in those ever so interesting blank spaces that separate the ones from the others.

In that South where Stella D'Or's father is born (more details coming up), which is the North for the one who dreams.

Stella D'Or's father is a linguist of international fame. Someone who believes in the power of words with the same intensity with which others believe in the fragile power of weapons or in the cowardly valor and value of money. Stella D'Or's father is, in his own way, a warrior. His face has the patrician nobility that's found in some frescos or mosaics or amphoras. His air and figure are the same that, one night in Casablanca, made Captain Louis Renault laugh, that "Rick is the kind of man that . . . well, if I were a woman, and I were not around, I should be in love with Rick." Stella D'Or's father isn't named Rick and his name doesn't matter here; but it's clear women fall in love when he comes by without even thinking twice: all it takes is seeing him. And they are not to blame and he is not to blame. And even other men understand him and comprehend women's reactions to him. All of them, compared to the aerodynamic and speedy father of Stella D'Or, are small Renaults more than ready to move out of his way and even sneak him complicit winks. The men fall in love a little bit with Stella D'Or's father without having to imagine themselves as women: because Stella D'Or's father is how they want all women to see them; and how, if you're a real man, can you not fall authentically in love with such a vision?

And so, Stella D'Or's father is a unisex fantasy, international, multilingual, addictive. His books and lectures are always successes that transcend the merely academic. His name is known and uttered with a "There he is, here he comes" at vertiginous jet-setter parties. And Stella D'Or's father often appears on TV shows and participates in documentaries and, miraculously, his profile has never crashed head-on into the frivolous, the banal, the ridiculous. His most transgressive and risqué move was having, on one occasion, hosted *Saturday Night Live*. And his monologue was masterful and his surprising sense of comedic timing got big laughs from the live studio audience and from the audience at home when he assumed the personality of the forever-foiled Dr. Wong X. Periment, explaining his "methods" with quotes from George Bernard Shaw ("Science never solves a problem without creating ten more") and of the compulsive, illuminated illuminator Thomas Alva Edison who, as mentioned, would become one of the historical figures that Stella D'Or hated most ("I have not failed. I have just found 10,000 ways that won't work"). And, of course, Stella D'Or's father had the where-withal, despite the requests of Lorne Michaels and cast, to not go back for an encore performance of the character who (prophetic glimmer foretelling the coming of his photon-allergic daughter?) brought about, at the end of the sketch, when he tried to fix a flashlight, the definitive blackout and end of electricity in the world.

And so, Stella D'Or's father had achieved with linguistic studies what Carl Sagan had achieved with the cosmos. Something cool. Someone described him in the press as "a Marlboro Man who smokes a pipe." Someone on TV dubbed him "the Indiana Jones of languages." And the nickname infiltrated public opinion and that's how they introduced him, here and there. And he put up with the humor with resignation and gratitude. It's a small price to pay if it helped him secure funds for his research. And in that way popularize a strange art and a preoccupation few had and, it never gets old to repeat, everyone should; joking seriously that "if because we understand don't trouble we are in each other, right?"

And so, Stella D'Or's father like a cross between a babelic and esperantic evangelist transporting the solidity of the exact sciences to the fluid territory of sounds and to the construction and structure of sentences.

Stella D'Or's father speaks twenty languages perfectly and can more than hold his own in another ten. And, after so many trips on which he has collected vocables and inflexions—in Amazon jungles, racing and stumbling over Celtic roots, and revivals where the spinning enraptured speak in tongues—Stella D'Or's father attains something akin to an ultimate destiny, a precise goal, an irrefutable certainty.

Stella D'Or's father (who isn't yet Stella D'Or's father; who has yet to meet Stella D'Or's mother; and to whom it hasn't even occurred, in the first place, the possibility of loving a woman and, in the second place, another woman who would come out of that woman; because his love is for words and, always, for the way in which the names of absolutely all the women far and wide across the world are written and rewritten; and to love only the names of two women above all others, there being so many and such lovely ones, would be as unjust as it is senseless) discovers something.

Stella D'Or's father reaches a zenith.

He comes to the certain conclusion—though he'd already been theorizing about it—that the conjunction of the words *cellar* and *door* is, from a semantic and sonic perspective, the most beautiful phrase in the English language. The, yes, door in the cellar that leads to the loftiest of rooftops. A place that leads—more names, more information, more sleepless lists—to a place of linguistic dreams that could be called Wonderland or Narnia or the alternate reality dreamed by the nocturnal walker Donnie Darko, who reads "Cellar Door" on a chalkboard in his low-intensity high school. *Cellar Door* were the letters of Edgar Allan Poe's favorite words, which he paid homage to, in a distorted yet recognizable echo, with the "The Raven"'s repetitive *Nevermore*. J. R. R Tolkien, Dorothy Parker, and Norman Mailer also defended that intuition and sentiment. But Stella D'Or's father proves and verifies it with the help of a latest-generation computer, elevating the hypothesis into a law that, in addition, now encompasses all the living languages and dead tongues of this world. And amid the applause, the man—who has never thought of becoming a husband much less a father—thinks: "If I were ever to have a daughter, I would name her Stella D'Or. *Estrella de oro*. Star of Gold. Light in the darkness."

And few moments are of greater transcendence than the moments when, for the first time, a mortal names something divine. Giving a name to an ancient and forgotten god on the basis of a broken statue's arm (or, in this case, a goddess yet to be born, and who will be unforgettable and indestructible) might be the gesture closest to immortality. So, the man who will be Stella D'Or's father creates a secret story (the name of his yet-to-be-born daughter) beneath the folds of a public story (Cellar Door). And the idea makes him debut a different and faraway smile for the flashing cameras that his feminine fans find "irresistible." His masculine fans devote themselves to practicing it, in vain, in front of bathroom mirrors, behind doors locked so as not to be surprised there, doing that.

And the next (and tragically last) mission of the future yet ever-nearer present father of Stella D'Or is to strike out for the North Pole: rumors have reached him that in an Inuit village a new word that, also, means "snow" has been born. Another word. A new word that surpasses the fifty other proverbial and celebrated and melted-from-overhandling words (some people say there are as many as one hundred; others consider the whole thing nothing more and nothing less than a lurid academic farce of the kind that sound good to uninformed laymen, but are never entirely accepted by serious scholars) the Inuit have for "snow" based on the tiny yet decisive differences in quality and density and texture and shape. Brief words to differentiate the immensity of the falling snow from the immensity of the fallen snow. Words more or less the same in appearance, but, as with snowflakes, no two are identical. This word, this new-yet-always-there word—they tell the man who is not yet, but is now closer than ever to becoming, Stella D'Or's father—will be the definitive word. The sound of snow falling never to rise again, the sound that will elevate and make the linguist able to capture it ascend to the greatest heights, opening his mouth, sticking out his tongue to catch it the way you catch the snowflakes the sky brushes off its shoulders.

The expedition party of one man in search of a solitary word regains— according to the newspapers and news broadcasts of the time—the enthusiasm for adventure that once drove Jules Verne's explorers in a world whose maps were still being traced in the half light.

But also, inevitable, data of the moment and sign of the times: the voyage of Stella D'Or's future-father is sponsored not by a club of aristocrats or a society of scientists, but by a brand of ice cream whose flavors are ever so complex linguistically (combining typography of multiple alphabets); and there goes our hero, amid the satisfied moans of women and the frustrated sighs of men. And, in retrospect, Stella D'Or will always look down on her father's gift for self-promotion; for demonstrating that even the most cryptic science can be transformed into a product desired by the simplest and most manipulable minds. The immemorial phrase and piece of history repurposed as hysterical and irresistible slogan. "Eureka!" and all of that. But it's well known—myths abound across all cultures repeating this story for millennia—the person for whom things always go well, sooner or later, tumbles from the heights of their triumphs into the underworld of a single yet definitive failure.

And what follows, once more but not as a part of Stella D'Or's father's plans, seems again to take on the nineteenth-century chiaroscuros of those serialized novels, with the end of each chapter left hanging from the edge of a bottomless cliff and (*to be continued . . .* ). A cliffhanger as narrative as it is geographic. Illustrations instead of photographs so you can visualize the invisible, the so remote, the almost impossible to imagine; because that black winter sky and that austral white down below are like a landscape where nothing seems to happen, but, at the same time, that void is so tempting to smudge, mixing the white and the black until the perfect gray tonality of catastrophe is achieved.

Lost signals, artic storms, ice mirages, and the voice of the man who already is—though nobody suspects it—Stella D'Or's father, appearing and disappearing on the other side of receivers, like an aurora borealis of words. His voice, all of a sudden, interrupting the programming not to offer his latitude and longitude, but to describe gigantic birds that shriek "Tekeli-li! Tekeli-li!"

A year and a half after going missing, the man is found.

They find him floating on a small ice floe, out of his mind, clutching something that turns out to be a newborn girl. An infant—an illness more miraculous than any cure—who, they realize right away, smiles in the darkness and cries under even the weakest light, which burns and blisters her skin. Stella D'Or's father manages to tell them—the only words he says that seem to make any sense, his last words—the name she should be given and registered under. And he goes mute. And he returns to Somber Hymns. And he shuts himself away never to come out or make another sound, because—as someone argues with a truly absurd but subsequently so quotable lyricism— "now he ceaselessly speaks the perfect language of absolute silence."

At last, it was time, it all arrived, an innovation in the familiar landscape of mists and mansions and curses, a delayed but sorely-missed variation in the genre: a gothic madman, a delusional masculine figure shut away in the attic of the mansion.

Anyway, apart from what's already more or less known based on what happens in those serialized melodramatic novels, there are more alluring mysteries. Like that of the origin of the girl: a blood test reveals that, yes, she is her father's daughter.

Her mother's identity is never known; there are traces of Inuit in her chromosome strand and her almond-shaped eyes, but, also, spirals of something not of this world in the double helix of her DNA. And Stella D'Or (who imagines her mother as an Amazon in a palace with the shape of a colossal igloo, empress of the eternal snows and ices amid bipolar bears and unctuous whales and sarc*arctic* sharks, all of them white) will always like the idea, *also* her father's daughter after all, that "Inuit" is written and sounds so similar to "*minuit*."

And soon (in the care of governesses with top-model profiles sponsored by companies once linked to her father, and whose marketing consultants have determined there's nothing more attractive than Stella D'Or's story) she rejects all those children's stories that terrify with black nights and dark places. And Stella D'Or opts for the luminosity of the Inuit legends. Stories far more intriguing than those tales of princes and princesses who see vanquishing witches and dragons as a necessary formality to be able to attain the triumph of marriage. Stella D'Or prefers tales told on those long and strange nights (nights that are really pure dusk and dawn with nothing between the one and the other) when the sky seems dazzled by the light of the moon (Taqiq) reflecting off the snow blanketing the Earth (Nunarjuaq). That glow like a gag and a blindfold that keeps the stars from helping you figure out where you are and how not to get lost. There, in a landscape where little or nothing happens. A landscape where, with the arrival of the long polar day and of the sun (Siqniq), everything looks even more like a frightening impossible-to-fill blank page. And so (contrary to what's repeated over and over, the arctic nights do not last six months, but four and a half months; the rest of the year everything is white or gray) the Inuit have, really, only two and a half months of authentically nocturnal and black sky when they can learn to read it and later to retrace it from memory. And so they've been forced to simplify and synthesize and abbreviate. To impose limits on the sky. For the Inuit it's enough to name thirty-three principal stars. And to divide all the rest into sixteen constellations, with a little story attributed to each one. You remember a story faster and better than a name or a bright spot twinkling through light pollution and atmospheric disturbance and, better, why seek a scientific explanation when you've got emotional motivations, for the unstable moods and concentration of those who inhabit the celestial firmament. And so a Man in the Moon disinterestedly harpooning sperm whales; and hunters chasing a bear that escapes with the help of the aurora borealis ascending high overhead; and foxes who turn the Northern Lights on or off at will. Stories her father cannot tell her because her father no longer speaks and only emits a low and deep sound like the sound of the wind. Stories Stella D'Or carefully compiles in a succession of notebooks that'll end up becoming the too many volumes of her *A Brief History of Darkness* and that, later on, will be studied as credo and dogma and manifesto by her followers. Notebooks where Stella D'Or not only writes down the mythic origins of the night according to Inuit beliefs (Malina, sun goddess, coexisting with Annigan, her divine and lunatic brother and the terrible fight they have and Malina runs away and Annigan chases her and the centrifugal force of the one racing after the other gives rise to the spinning of the Earth and the impossibility of them ever being together), but, also, those of so many other races and nations and religions.

But the different branches of what those stories tell—beyond whether their deities are wielding katanas of cosmic samurais or are decked out in feathered headdresses with names of pure pre-Columbian consonants or are ascending, always in profile, into pyramidal desert netherworlds or are riding in chariots drawn by the Mediterranean sun—always have a single root: the night being pursued by the day for a crime it never committed.

And it ends up being impossible for Stella D'Or—her phosphorescent skin lashed by ultraviolet whips, her life of lowered blinds and drawn curtains and the hours of a vampire who doesn't bite—not to identify with all of that and not to feel the need to alter the polarized plotline of the pursuer and pursued. Vengeance and revenge and—also there, in those notebooks, in minuscule script and florescent ink—astrological alchemy and quantum physics. And the perfectly calibrated recipe for the composition of the night, the ingredients that illuminate the darkness: zodiacal light (a diffuse glow that extends like space dust from the vicinity of the Sun); *gegenschein* (that soft shimmer in the area of the antisolar point glimpsed for the first time by a Jesuit astronomer, but only later named by a German explorer wandering through South American jungles); bioluminescence (all its light emitted by a living organism, though it be the microscopic incandescence of mortal bacteria, or the contagious glimmer of love in the eyes of the suddenly in-love, or the plasmatic pollutions of the newly-invented body part that is the immobilizing mobile phone); and the airglow or nightglow (which is nothing but the restructuring of atoms that've been irradiated throughout the day and that, suddenly, when night falls, seem to burn).

And that, when the exact configuration of dusk has dawned, is when the trouble begins, when discussions light up about what to do with sleepless nights or the dreams of Stella D'Or.

What to do with her, what to make her do.

What she will or won't be.

Should Stella D'Or be a devout luminescent scientist; warning humanity about the psychological-spiritual-physiological damage of living in cities that are so bright at night, streetlights reducing the body's production of melatonin, the "hormone of the night and sleep," and where it's no longer possible to stare up at the healing light of the soothing stars?

Or, better, an urban warrior battling neon lights around the world, causing blackouts on The Strip and on Broadway and darkening forever the Eiffel Tower, which you can photograph for free by day, but, when the sun goes down, if you want its portrait, you have to pay the company that makes the lights that illuminate it?

Or to go even further and turn Stella D'Or into a terrifying character feared by children and adults and guilty of "invading" their little teddy bears and giving them a voice that keeps the children from falling asleep?

Or maybe, better, make her an artist? An intellectual rocker—first a writer and then a songwriter—fronting a band called Nocturnal Habits of the Army Dreamers, albums with titles like *The Sleep Disorders* or *Lights Out!* or *Black to Fade* on which they put lyrics to W. A. Mozart's *Eine kleine Nachtmusic* or music to F. Nietzsche's *Das Nachtlied* or do a happy-aching-voiced version of "Nightime" by Big Star or "The Night" by Morphine or "Tonight, Tonight" by Smashing Pumpkins or "Well . . . All Right" by Buddy Holly where you hear, in a sweet and perverse voice, that thing about dreams and desires you desire at night when the lights are low?

Or turn her into someone who died suddenly in her sleep: a tragic and romantic and spiteful nymph, victim of Ondine Syndrome, saying farewell with a "Darkness is not the absence of light, light is the absence of darkness"?

And once her fate is chosen, how to tell it, what form should it take?

Long or almost monosyllabic phrases? Free stream of consciousness in the first person? Or classical third person, watching her from outside and starting with something like "In the early years of the twenty-first century, when the Reign of X was approaching the end of a long decline, the art of turning off the lights became first a twinkling hobby and then a burning fever and . . ."?

Now, the three of them argue and fight over her (and she hears them and writes down what they say).

The three sisters locked in combat over the combative Stella D'Or, to settle who thought of her first, to whom she belongs more, though they all know that Stella D'Or belongs to all of them. That they couldn't live without her. That she wouldn't exist if not for their different yet complimentary gazes (all of which are her own gaze, the one who watches the three of them watch Stella D'Or) that now, as always, stare down at her. And they write her with conviction so thousands of kilometers away millions of people can hear them read her aloud and, without yet knowing what will happen to her in the coming chapters, imagine her like this: whirling in the darkness, looking up at the night sky, Stella D'Or, asking herself what will become of me and answering what will be will be and asking again who it is who's writing me.

# II

Who wrote that and who is writing this, now, in the place where, once again, all three of them come out and raise their eyes and look at the Earth.

And they go leaping through the air and return to the place with the footprints and the flags.

The footprints that are still there, as if those steps had just been taken, fossils in soft yet motionless dust. The old but brilliant flags—stars and stripes and hammers and sickles—taut in the windless air.

The meteorites—large and small—seem to have reached an agreement not to touch them, not to unmake the History made by those who walked there and raised those flags in ever more remote times when arriving here still meant something.

And the three of them have taken great care—since arriving on the Moon, so many years ago—not to touch anything and not to break something. Back when they were so young and didn't yet know how to read or write, but—with the help of some little wind-up tin astronauts that they were given during the farewell ceremony, in front of the TV cameras, beside the space shuttle—were already imagining and coming up with stories. Stories that they said, as soon as they were able, they would transform into letters and words and sentences.

They are the three Tulpa sisters.

Alex and Charley and Eddie Tulpa.

Unisex names.

Reversible names that are not their true names, but the ones they chose as *noms de plume* and are now known by the world over. That other world where they were born, but remember little or nothing about (the faces of their mother and their two older sisters who died when the other space shuttle that was to bring them here crashed during takeoff are, merely, shadows); because they were so young when they arrived to the moon with their father and their brother.

Their brother who has also adopted a sexually ambiguous alias: Bertie.

It has been a long time since Bertie has played or written with them.

Bertie is going mad or, really, he always was. And now he is not going mad, rather he is going back to being mad after a brief interval of calm and reason. Bertie is returning to his madness.

Alex and Charley and Eddie don't know if they are a little afraid of him or just lack patience. In any case, they leave him alone. And they no longer include him in their writing sessions and in their transmissions when they read what they write. Reading what they wrote so that down below or there above (hard to say exactly, and they're not really that interested in knowing clearly where things are for fear that would influence or limit their imagination) people listen and tremble and sigh along with the lives and exploits of the pale Stella D'Or, or of her glowing extraterrestrial son dAlien, or of all the things that take place in their imaginary and luminous Kingdom of Drakadia, on the ever so imaginative dark side of the moon.

Bertie listens to them tell their stories too, the three of them alternating voices, which all sound like just one, in front of the microphone. And he just snorts with disdain. And keeps on drinking that moon-man vodka he distills from the juice of green potatoes. And sighing for the lost love of a starlet/journalist who came to the moon to interview "The Legendary Tulpas," just so, with capital letters, a few months ago. And—refusing to let Alex and Charley and Eddie make any kind of statement—the girl slept with Bertie to mine him for information, and all she managed to tear out of him was his heart. Now, Bertie is a tragic and inspiring figure for his sisters. But he's also an inconvenience and a hazard, because Bertie is always having issues with hatches and seals. And Bertie has gotten addicted to snorting lines of moon dust (which, he informs them, "doesn't smell like Swiss cheese but like burnt gunpowder after it has put some holes in something or, better, someone"). And Bertie is determined to be the champion and lone player of a "sport" he himself invented (this has been his most recent and perhaps definitive creative gesture) and has named "Russian-American Roulette" in honor of the two protagonists of that first vertical race into the heavens. And Bertie adds with ethylic diction and phrasing: "I didn't include the names of the Chinese or the Indians, who just landed on the moon not long ago, and showed up like those tourists only interested in crossing a place off a list, never to return . . . Begone from here, intruders and laggards! . . . My actions honor the memory of all those great men from one side and the other who arrived to this fucking rock who knows why or what for . . . Unless it was just because they wanted to take some good pictures of Earth and deliver some well-rehearsed phrase and take a few little leaps and, hey, time to go home now so they can applaud us first and ignore us later and we can go a little crazy believing we saw the Creator or become serious alcoholics and pack on that muscular fat, but fat all the same, and develop heart conditions as a result of all the weightless exploits we had up here and so, retaining only these short and almost-sculpted haircuts, we grow old leaning on the bartop and harassing the clientele with an 'I'm sure you couldn't even imagine it looking at me now, but can you guess where I went once upon a time? A clue: it's very far away yet seems so near. Look up.'"

The "sport" Bertie created (ever since Bertie learned human beings can survive up to ninety seconds without a helmet in atmosphere zero, fifteen of those seconds perfectly conscious that whenever they stop holding their breath their lungs will collapse) consists of staying outside as long as possible, without oxygen or spacesuit, looking up at the stars and interrogating them in silence, until they answer and tell him when his love will return.

So far, the stars haven't answered, but, Bertie insists, they've told him that they'll reveal something soon, that they're thinking it over, that he be patient, that he not lose hope.


The Tulpa sisters' father, Pat Tulpa (not his real name either, but his daughters pinned it on him, and he indulged them because the pleasures he can give them are so few), is a believer in the faith that claims to worship the deity iGod. iGod being a carefully balanced combination of all the divine thoughts that brought about the end of religious conflicts around the middle of the twenty-first century. iGod as the application that homogenized and overcame the economic crises of all the churches by rebranding them as an universal gadget under a single brand, sponsored by a data empire and the immortal memory and infinite capacity of its creator. A man who—after all, he'd erected an entire model of faith as if atop the pillar of the unquestionable faith in the product he sold—had the guile and the resignation to end up providing that thing all religions demand: to die in order to be resurrected as myth. And Pat Tulpa arrived to the moon on the dime of one of his many disciples. Another digital magnate who'd hired him to found, in his name and with his money, the First Orbital Church. Pat Tulpa signed a lifetime contract with excessive fine print and clauses of the "Under no circumstances shall it be demanded of the employer to take responsibility for the return trip of the employee" variety. And it's not like Pat Tulpa had an abundance of work opportunities on Earth either.

Yes: when it was clear governments had no interest in the moon, it was decided to privatize and divide it up. And, beginning in 2017, individuals with too much free time and bulging bank accounts started to go up and come back down. To take things up and bring back things. But, mostly, to take things up. The moon turned into a kind of chaotic attic where they transported theoretically important things (ashes of family members) or practically trivial things (ashes of family members). And to and from there embarked all those echo-space-drones, which had to be guided with skill and precision (in the end, and in exchange for considerable compensation, all those talentless kids with deformed thumbs who in their youth had done nothing but live and kill on the screens of videogames found their calling) to avoid crashing while passing through the ever longer and wider belt of space trash with ever fewer holes wherein to adjust its buckle. Obese tons of satellite and module debris. Metallic cholesterol in the arteries of space. The stratospheric equivalent of things tossed out the car window. The splinters of unforeseen accidents or the calculated entropy of machines in motion. Soon they managed to open gaps and channels through all that floating alloy and (because they couldn't come up with anything else and because nobody thought of anything better, when it was emotionally and scientifically proven that the moon was a piece of the Earth that broke off after a cosmic collision) they thought again of the moon as it'd once been thought of. But without the sense of adventure or the senselessness of romanticism. Now, pure functionality: the moon as a possible vacation resort, as launchpad/layover for longer, future voyages, as a site for escaped passions (after millennia of staring up at it in the name of love, promising to deliver it but never coming through), like a gallery seat for contemplating the instantly-antiquated novelty of Earth's eclipses, like a stage for future reality shows and Olympics and movies that take place on the moon and, then, with special effects, movies that take place on Earth. Yes, the advantage of empty spaces where nothing happens: everything fits and anything can happen. And, of course, right away, the most obvious and immediate aspect of the thing, the inevitable idea of being transported to a place once considered an all-powerful deity—Our Lady of the Changing Phases of Powerful Tides and Menstrual Cycles—and, from there, to ask spiritual questions and hope for divine answers, gets worn out. The moon like a "We've already taken the first step in your direction. Where are you, Creator? Show us your face. At least one side of it, the dark side, if possible."

But it's known the enthusiasm of magnates is an unstable thing, and their mystical discipline is never that firm or constant. And so it is that, now, the Tulpas are there: on the moon and—as she often tells herself, but in a manner more appropriate to her situation—in God's hands.

Just a few buildings resembling Inuit igloos, a preacher-father without a parish who rarely leaves his chamber, writer sisters, a distressed and distressing brother who's no longer good for anything but inspiring his sisters to come up with alternate and epic versions of his sorrowful sorrow.

And all the time not in the world, but, yes, all the time on the moon to tell stories.

"I have something new to read," announces Eddie, the middle Tulpa sister. And Alex, the youngest, and Charley, the oldest, sigh and look at each other out of the corners of their eyes, their pupils rolling up like those of some virgins. They're worried about her, about Eddie's imagination that's no longer all of theirs, and that seems to be wandering alone across the moors where it's so hard to insert the figures of Stella D'Or or the little dAlien.

The things that occur to Eddie are stranger all the time and, they're sure, cannot be to the liking of the earthlings who prefer adventures and romances and doors that creak and lightning that thunders. And yet they let her do it and let her read; because Eddie eats little and sleeps not at all and says she hears voices not her own, now, over the microphone, sounding like the voice of someone talking in their sleep, of someone reading with their eyes closed, like this:

In the desert, the days are very hot and, at night, the temperature plummets from vertiginous heights—like that Coyote betrayed time and again by some ACME-brand product, in his eternal, never-ending pursuit of that Roadrunner—and crashes into the rocks and sand.

Beep Beep.

The sound inside his spacesuit.

A call from the base.

Technical jargon oh so specialized and precise, but, at the same time, so absurd and so out of time and place.

Simulating he's somewhere else.

The base.

Wanting to make him think he's not where he is, but somewhere far away.

Him.

Very far away.

Farther still.

There.

You can point at it with your fingers but can't touch it. You can imagine it because there's so much information about it. Postcards from bygone travelers who went and came back and lived to tell the tale, to tell its tale. All of them smiling, though you can't see their smiles behind the thick plastic of their visors. Saying "cheese," thinking at one time they'd thought everything surrounding them now was cheese. There, on the rocky moor where the wind doesn't blow and where the footprints of footprints are left behind forever.

There above and then.

The moon.

They were on the moon and they were so happy to be there.

And they're not so happy now, here below.

Like him. Unhappy. A fraud.

The command base not thousands of kilometers but just a few meters away. Behind all those cacti he is approaching, taking small steps for man that'll never be giant leaps for mankind.

Here he is.

In the Sonoran Desert, the hottest desert in the United States. A desert so hot its tongue lolls out all the way to Sinaloa, in Mexico.

Two hundred and sixty thousand square kilometers of border/ hinge desert divided into an atemporal puzzle—the image to be assembled is that of an hourglass—of desert sub-ecoregions composed and decomposed of irregular pieces, but, even still, of diffuse edges, difficult to differentiate the ones from the others. How to tell where one part of the desert ends so another part can begin? In any case, someone whose name he doesn't know named them: Colorado Desert, Altar Desert, Lechugilla Desert, Tenopah Desert, Yuha Desert, and Yuma Desert, if anybody out there is interested in such things. Desert pieces, yes, but oh so populated and inhabited: sixty species of mammals, three hundred and fifty of birds, twenty of amphibians, more than a hundred of reptiles, a thousand of bees, thirty of fish in the few streams that escape while they can from the Colorado River, and two thousand of plants you'd never put in your living room unless they were painted by Georgia O'Keefe (and thanks to Wikipedia for all this information, that he uses to flesh out and expand the increasingly synthetic and dehydrated emails he sends to his small and increasingly distant son; and more about all of this coming up).

A desert where there's no sound but that deafening sound of absolute silence. A sound that, every so often, makes even more obvious and oppressive its operatic and unfathomable voice, mute and broken, with the click of some kangaroo-rat's teeth or the flapping wings of some Chihuahua-crow (in the Sonoran Desert names of species melt together and combine, like those ancient bestiaries illuminated in monasteries and so, yes, he would become something like a castaway-astronaut) or, when you've already been there for a few hours, the leonine roar of the sun filling your helmet and shaking and shaking your head.

And, true, the thing about the heat by day and the cold at night can sound—though we're talking about the singular Sonoran Desert—like pluralistic obviousness. All deserts are really temperamental and bipolar and change mood depending on the time of day.

But that's the way things are here.

Nothing new and the sparkling novelty of the oh-so-easy-to-memorize nothing to see here. The desert is unforgettable because there's nothing all that memorable in it. The desert is like an unforgettable dream. The desert is the land of the instant déjà vu. Of something already seen that presents no difficulty when it comes to evoking with precision where you saw it. Where? Easy, simple: what you see right now you saw right here, in the desert, about four or five minutes ago.

Or two.

Or one.

Or zero.

Which leads him to admit here—to count down—what's so hard for his young son to accept: his father is an astronaut, yes, gee whiz what pride.

But it's more than likely, not to say certain (his father is separating from his mother; and the young son floats now in an atmosphere where, to keep breathing in that zero gravity, it turns out to be vital to believe nothing is definitively ending: neither the possibility of the voyage nor the permanence of love), that he'll never get to go float in space and much less to bounce off the surface of the moon. His father, for the young son, is like an actor, but his little friends can't see any of the movies he acts in and, for that reason, they don't believe him. And, if they do believe you, it's even worse.

And for him it's not something easy to explain to his son.

Though the reasons for not venturing into space are really easy to understand.

NASA isn't what it once was. Drastic budget cuts, it's true. But the real problem is something else.

Space is no longer what we wanted it to be. Or it is. It's still the same space as always: infinite and full of stars and all of that. But the men who stare up at it now regard it in a different way. Men regard space the way one regards a desert. With true resignation, because there's nothing new to see there. They regard it the same way he regards his wife now (for whom love began as an oasis and ended up a mirage), who's in the process of detaching from him, as if he were one of those sections the rocket leaves behind as it moves away, bound for the unknown but, nevertheless, the oh so predictable.

So it is. For a while now, there's been little desire to, like in *Star Trek*, think of space as "the final frontier" and there's less and less enthusiasm for "exploring strange and new worlds and for seeking out new life and new civilizations" and for "boldly going where no man has gone before!"

It's all too many gloomy light years away.

The supposed exoplanets (a few new ones appear every week) that, supposedly, meet the conditions for life like those on Earth are there, yes, but they take on the gaseous substance of myths. Hard to believe in them from here. They're so far away and *no future*.

Like his wife with respect to their marriage. Antimatter and black hole. Little enthusiasm for seeking a higher intelligence and possible savior. No solution appears—like the moon appears overhead, and he blocks it out with his hermetically-gloved hand—to all the planet's problems or, even, to the problems of his home. A home that's so far away, thinking about it from here, but feels just as far away when he's in it.

And the few meters separating the living room sofa where he sleeps from the master bedroom cannot be crossed even with the help of the *beam me up* or the *warp speed* Captain James Tiberius "Jim" Kirk commands from Montgomery "Scotty" Scott or Mr. Zulu during the comings and goings of the USS *Enterprise*.

No.

All of that is already gone.

Déjà vu again, yes.

Now, the man has turned into his own alien: cosmic outer space has been replaced by genetic interior space. And the species itself is the voyage, manipulated and modified and conditioned and, if possible, evolved.

Yes: there isn't anybody out there.

Or no: there are many, but we don't interest them anymore ever since they heard the artistic-geologic-existential synthesis sent (as if it were one of those half-sordid and half-desperate profiles in those sections or sites for, never put better, "making contact") on one of those golden records, aboard the *Voyager* space probes. "Is that really all they've got to offer?" they might wonder. "And how did they end up picking something by Chuck Berry and not The Beatles or Bob Dylan or by the far-more-astral Pink Floyd? Clearly they're a doomed species, better to leave them be and let them wipe themselves out," they'll reason, clicking telepathic tentacles and all of that.

And yet, every so often and as the rules stipulated, he and his coworkers are sent back to the Sonoran Desert.

Where at one time the astronauts who really *were* astronauts trained.

The "true" astronauts of the *Apollo* missions.

The missions aborted at the last minute or already in the air or, perhaps, falsified in a top-secret film studio (which for him and, probably for his son, would be better than anything) though, to tell the truth, if you're going to lie, lie better and in a more exciting and dramatic way. And the truth is nobody could really think something as visually dull as that first moon landing was faked or simulated.

And the missions of the astronauts who went and came back (and who, probably, smuggled small samples of moon to give to their kids).

And even the missions of astronauts who died in the moment of the launch (which, he thinks on some long nights, would be better than nothing and better, just in case, not to know what his son would think of such a possibility).

Here they are now where once all those unforgettable and legendary names were.

The savage astronauts.

Their names—if you were to look for them or find them as soon as you stopped looking—etched into the rock of the Sonoran Desert, which doesn't even offer the comfort of that soundless desert from where you can look down at the noisy Earth. He's here, but he doesn't like it: in a landscape more lunatic than lunar and where, at one point, they created craters with the help of (ACME brand?) explosives, to increase its resemblance to the surface of the Moon.

And here, so much time later, they put on suits whose design and comfort have improved greatly but pointlessly.

And they go here and there, "enduring extreme conditions." Even more extreme than those prevailing in that Mare Intranquillitatis above which orbits the Mother-Wife Ship, with a tendency to undergo turbulences and lurches: like the ones in those cheap sci-fi scenes where the whole crew slides from one side to the other, rolling across the floors of the control room.

So better to stay here for a few more days and a few more nights.

Better—he thinks and tells himself and convinces himself—the burning days of frustrated terranaut than those of failed crewmember about to be shot off to some kind of hotel beyond Jupiter. Growing old and dying and, in his case, never being resuscitated and never returning home corrected and enhanced and reborn.

Better—he convinces himself and thinks and tells himself—the sunsets of sharp shadows and the sunrises dancing across the rusted and poetic skeleton of a Chevrolet Impala or a Camaro.

Better—he tells himself and convinces himself and thinks—the freezing nights under a sky with so many more stars than the skies of cities, but where, at the same time, it's harder to believe those stars will ever grant you a fleeting wish.

In the desert, the stars don't look at you. In the desert, the stars turn their backs.

And who knows: maybe his fate will be the same as that Mexican, face tanned by UFOs, in the opening scene of that movie, right here and not so long ago, repeating over and over, like a mariachi mantra, that thing about how: "The sun came out last night and sang to me." With the difference that he would beg the extraterrestrials to, please, not sing to him so much in the beginning and, like at the end of that same movie and without waiting so long, to take him with them. That they do with him as they please. That they study him from top to bottom and inside and out. The only thing he would ask them in return—at some point, between one invading and invasive test and the next—is that they let him speak to and see his son.

And that his son see him and hear him on a liquid screen and, at last and forever, that he feel unconditionally proud of him.

A brief communication in which he would tell him that he was there, floating in a place without map or sounds, lost in space, but having found himself at last.

And that he's seen things his son wouldn't believe and that he'll never let them be lost, like tears in rain.

But, again, he doesn't think he'll ever see anything like that or have anything like that happen to him.

Or that it'll ever rain.

The desert is the desert.

The desert is deserted, with everything in view and nothing hiding.

The desert is the most exhibitionist of all landscapes though it has the least to show off. "This is what there is, I never lied to you," the desert seems to say; and that's why few are those who fall in love with the desert, with its stark and dry sincerity, forever and ever.

The desert doesn't deceive.

The desert stretches out as far as the eye can see, to the horizon, which begins much closer than in other places; because the desert— beyond the irregularities of the terrain—is horizontal. Horizontal above and beyond all those things that are not many, though what few things there are are vertical. Like all those tumultuous tumulus of tall and narrow stones with another flat stone atop them, as if a giant hand had gotten bored of playing with them, millennia ago, and hadn't picked up the pieces before being sent to bed, punished and without dessert, never to wake up again.

And, in addition, this is a desert with very little history or epic.

No rebel T. S. Lawrence here saying he likes this desert because "it is clean"; no philosophical Wittgenstein thinking now that "I can well understand why children love sand"; no replicant bidding farewell with an "I've . . . seen things you people wouldn't believe. Attack ships on fire off the shoulder of Orion. I watched C-beams glitter in the dark near the Tannhäuser Gate. I've seen sand storms whipping through the Sonoran Desert . . . All those moments will be lost . . . in time . . ."

The Sonoran Desert is a desert unfit for minors and it's blurry and dirty and full of emptiness. A nothing replete with everything. With so many things he pretends to ignore to keep from losing hope, which is the last thing you lose. And it's so easy to lose things in a desert. All you have to do is drop them anywhere and the desert swallows them and then they become part of the desert.

And so that's why he kneels down now and, pretending to collect samples, etches his initials into a rock. And why he then walks slowly, as if in slow motion, trying to look as little as possible where he is stepping (any lizard or any of those rolling balls of straw, tumbleweeds, they're called; and his son calls them something very funny, but he can't remember what it is right now, and that makes him feel a sadness like he never felt before). Or why he avoids looking up at the night sky that begins to spread out from overhead on down. And to look up at the moon from somewhere on Earth; that moon that doesn't even have a name, that's named nothing more and nothing less than what it is, as if all dogs were called Dog and all cats were called Cat. And it's so easy to lie to a dog and it's impossible to lie to a cat and that's why parents, in general, choose dogs and not cats as pets for their children: because parents lie a lot to their children and, then, children lie to their parents.

And a dog fits much better in that irreal yet authentic landscape.

A dog helps you not see.

And he wouldn't mind having a dog right now.

One of those dogs that—unlike those seeing eye dogs—help you not to see. Because to do so, to *see* everything that surrounds him, would ruin all possibility of believing that what he believes will never come to pass might indeed happen.

Hard to believe in anything in the desert.

There's no context in the desert for him to hold onto as if it were an escape hatch. His surroundings are not a landscape. They're a living-dead nature. A still life in suspension, in suspended animation.

And he's tired of all of it, tired of all that nothing.

Tired of pretending. Here and in front of his young son.

So he brings his hands to his head and starts to unfasten the seals of his spacesuit helmet.

One by one.

From the base they transmit that he shouldn't, that he shouldn't be crazy, that he's going to ruin everything, that he'll put the whole "mission" in jeopardy, and that he will lose "everything he has heretofore accomplished."

He doesn't care.

Better that way.

He takes off his helmet and imagines his young son, at home, receiving the delivery of a medal and a flag.

And his wife, full and growing, with that pale and eclipsing beauty that never wanes from the widows of astronauts.

And his own face smiling in old but impeccable photographs on the evening news while the host says his name in a deep voice.

And he takes a deep breath and looks up at the moon.

And—though in the space of the desert nobody can hear you scream—he howls.


Eddie finishes reading her bit and Alex and Charley don't say anything and—they can perceive a mild discomfort on the other end of the waves, back on Earth—say goodbye to their listeners because better not to add anything. Better to leave the new installments of Stella D'Or and dAlien for next week.

And, yes, their decision was a good one. Because as soon as the transmission is cut, Bertie shows up, absolutely and lunatically drunk, scream-singing that same thing he always sings. That "The lunatic is on the grass . . . The lunatic is on the grass" and then fading it into another song in another language with a *"Qué lejos que estoy del suelo donde he nacido . . . Inmensa nostalgia invade mi pensamiento"* and *"Prefiero estar dormido que despierto"* and then, swiping the microphone away from them with a "calling all of my fans, my planetary babies, with love from your favorite satellite boy—fortunately they have already cut the connection with the studios back on Earth—I also have something very interesting to share with you, my dear listeners."

And, with liquid diction and floating words, Bertie begins:

"They say that this isn't true. That it's an urban and moon-man legend. That they have studied in detail the recordings and transcript of that unforgettable July 20th, 1969 down to the last recorded sound. But I don't care. I do believe it's true, because that's what myths are for: to doubt them at first in public in order to, later, be able to remain convinced of their veracity in private. First the undeniable, the confirmed: the first lunar meal consisted of bacon, cookies, coffee, peaches, and grapefruit juice. But before that, the oh so religious Buzz Aldrin chewed up and slugged down, on the sly, a communion wafer and little bit of wine, blessed by the Presbyterian reverend of his parish. And he says the prayer they didn't let him say aloud at NASA, so he wouldn't offend the other Christians there who believe in other far more fun versions of the same thing and with many more gods. Not content with this, Aldrin was also the first man to piss on the moon, inside his spacesuit, and, hey, I know that feeling. I won't be the first, but I can guarantee, esteemed listeners, I am the man who has pissed on and inside his spacesuit the most on the moon, where, one thing we do have too much of is water. But getting back to where I wanted to go . . . Ah . . . Eh . . . Uh . . . Yes, then Neil Armstrong saying (and the truth is, he doesn't say it very well, his diction is imprecise, a little bit like mine) that "One small step for man, one giant leap for mankind." They forced him to memorize it. And he practiced it a lot, but didn't understand it all that well . . . Oof, Neil Armstrong, stepping hard and for the first time on the surface of the moon. And I already said it and I'll say it again: *true story* for some, sonic hallucination for others, thunderous rumor for all. A great story in any case: Armstrong says his celebrated and official little words and, then, almost in a whisper, he adds, on his own account: "Congratulations, Mr. Gorsky." That phrase sent the CIA, FBI, and NASA, and all the acronyms of the day into a frenzy. Who was Gorsky? Was it possibly a coded message for the Russians? Had Armstrong suffered a burst of lunacy? And when he returns to Earth and is interrogated, Armstrong says nothing. He just clarified and promised it wasn't anything that put the national security of the United States at risk and, over the years, Armstrong changes the subject every time the issue comes up in interviews. Many years later, in a report, Armstrong finally tells the tale and the story behind the story: 'Now that Mr. Gorsky has died . . .' Armstrong begins. And he clears up the dark side of what he said or didn't say on the moon. To wit: one day, when he was a boy, little Neil's ball landed in the yard of the next-door neighbor, one Mr. Gorsky. When he went to retrieve it, the boy clearly heard the voice of Mrs. Gorsky, coming out from a window, saying and laughing with one of those laughs that cause shame and pain and even fear: 'Oral sex? Don't even dream of it, Gorsky. You'll get oral sex the day that Armstrong boy steps foot on the moon.' Rest in peace, Mr. Armstrong, Mr. Gorsky, and Mrs. Gorsky. And congratulations to all of us who remain. And good night to all of you, including my love, wherever she may be . . . Fog: thy will be done . . . This is my last transmission from the planet of the monsters."

Then Bertie stands up and struggles into his spacesuit, as if he were unleashing a battle against his own skin, and says to his three sisters that "I have received information about how there were chimpanzees that survived up to three minutes in the absolute void" and that "I'm taking a walk with my little shovel out to the Tycho Crater to see if I can find that fucking black monolith that sings so beautifully."

And that's the last time Alex and Charley and Eddie see and will see Bertie. And they don't see him disappear on the dark side of the moon (the cameras distributed across the colony are few and they don't record footage of that blind spot), but they do imagine him disappearing, walking into the shadows like someone exiting the stage.

And nobody, none of them, dares say it aloud, but they do imagine it in low voices. Better that way. Better that Bertie goes and doesn't return. That he be gone because Bertie has already been gone for a long time now.

And Alex and Charley and Eddie remain silent and feel as if the silence is making itself, as if the pieces of the silence are putting themselves together, the ones with the others. A silence like the one you hear when there's no sound, out there.

And without saying a word (they only need a look to comprehend; so well do the three of them know and understand and intuit each other; nothing transmits ideas and thoughts better than the oxygen-less air of the small and concentrated and intense company on the infinite edge of that immense solitude) they tell each other there will be plenty of time to decide which one of them, and with what style and what form, will get to tell all of that and put it all in writing first so they can read it later.

# III

Last night she dreamed she returned to Mount Karma. And then she woke up, immediately, to write it down. To write, to put it in writing; because for Penelope, to write is the only thing left for her to write.

To write that she writes, that she is writing.

To write in notebooks and on the walls of her cell/study and, sometimes, even on the sheets of her bed.

To write in the air, in the dark, her hand moving like that of the conductor of an invisible orchestra. Nothing of *allegro*, all *adagissimo* and *dolente* and *lacrimoso*, and yet, *agitato* and *obbligato* and *risoluto* and, above all, *con fuoco*.

To write, now, the overture to how last night she dreamed she returned to Mount Karma.

Penelope writes her dreams.

Not to keep from forgetting them (supposedly that's why people write them down, but, really, they're almost always forgotten in the act itself of putting them on the page and what's left is like the impression of a thing already gone), but (and supposedly this is another reason people write dreams down) so they aren't repeated.

Or, which would be even worse, so they don't come true.

Especially that dream that once was true and that she returns to again and again and to which, she's sure, she couldn't bear returning to awake, as if in a nightmare.

Penelope thinks that first sentence—Last night she dreamed she returned to Mount Karma—and remembers that other first sentence. Sentences in which someone arrives to a place they don't know or returns to a place they thought they did.

And she also remembers (she doesn't remember well, she's going to remember now) what her bad older brother once told her on one of his, fortunately for her, increasingly sporadic visits. Better that way. It's not like she misses him, or that she's happy to see him. Her bad brother who always shows up with an air that's like a combination of asking forgiveness and an expectation of gratitude. Yes: her own private Branwell Brontë. A useless man with multiple applications who, after believing he was great for so long, now thinks the rest of the world should believe it too. And—sometimes, many times, it happens—he can't believe the world doesn't believe it. And, of course, it hasn't been easy for him to accept that she has succeeded as a writer; no matter how much he looks down on what she writes. And yet, he is always suggesting "possible collaborations" because "it would be interesting to see what came of it, right?"

And no: the truth is that, for Penelope, it wouldn't be interesting to see what came of it, because she's already seen what she would see, what would come of it. Penelope has read her bad brother's books. Including the one on commission in which her bad brother had the audacity and lack of respect to appropriate the Karmas (the Karmas who, if they belonged to anyone, belonged to her) transplanting them from Abracadabra to Mexico City.

And yet—Saint Penelope of All the Guilt—she continues to listen patiently to what her bad brother continues to propose.

And she—not to love him a little, but yes to forgive him a lot—wants to think her brother proposes all that to fill the silence with noise. That silence so wide and yet so uncomfortable where—as if in outer space—no one makes a sound about their disappeared parents or her lost little son who was (or so he says, said, does not say anymore, because the doctors have forbidden him to do so in front of her) like a little son to him, her bad brother.

So, her bad brother, hands waving around and pupils dilated, like someone selling hair tonic or machines to make it rain in the desert, his, his own. There, dehydrating, her bad brother's ideas (in her bad brother's almost-hairless head) to "be incorporated into the Tulpa Universe," he reasons.

That thing about the never-finished project by his beloved Vladimir Nabokov for Alfred Hitchcock: "A love story between an astronaut and a starlet that'll be developed by one of your little Tulpa sisters, right? Throw in a little wink for connoisseurs and all of that, right? I can take care of the purple Nabokovian prose and you who're so good at coming up with plots with a hook . . ."

And that thing about the Onirium, which her brother has reentered, amid dreams of Bob Dylan and Vladimir Nabokov and that girl who falls into swimming pools in all his books, and that's the only thing of her bad brother's she envies: that love. For that girl. She remembers little to nothing about her, except one unforgettable detail: she didn't like The Beatles, which, for Penelope, was like saying you don't like oxygen and, for their Uncle Hey Walrus, would have meant, if he'd ever met her, one/another of his mental breakdowns. But, in any case, envy. A lot of it. For that love, yes. A kind of love she never felt. A victorious love, Victorian in its loss. Her bad brother like the paladin of unconsummated love and her like the priestess of all-consuming love. Her bad brother who'd begun falling in love early. First, with that middle-school teacher who'd supported his literary vocation and all that. Her brother, it seemed, had the need to fall in love over and over again in order not to love anybody but his impossible love. Whereas she never had anybody. There'd been that boy they met at the movie theater, when they went to see *2001: A Space Odyssey* and who became their friend and with whom they hung out and listened to Pink Floyd. But really it wasn't him she was attracted to, it was the fact that he was so attracted to her and, yes, she was like a Catherine Earnshaw awaiting a Healthcliff who never appeared and who never would because, maybe, he'd already appeared in a book, in her book.

And there are long and waking nights when Penelope touches herself down below, in the Antarctic to the south of her shriveled heart and her polar brain, to see if it exists, if there's still any life down there.

And she wonders if her favorite book might not be partly to blame: a book so passionate and at the same time so chaste, without sex, pure desire, like something that could only be written by a burning virgin. Sublimated theory before realist practice in nineteenth-century days when opposites never touched: dandy and exotic degeneration or husbands collapsing on their wedding nights when they discover their wives—unlike the Greek statues in the British Museum—have pubic hair and even bleed from between their legs several days a month. And, in the center—between the freak and the meek—the sex act like nothing but a mechanism to produce children for manual labor, children who labor manually as soon and as quickly as possible.

And Penelope tells herself she never fell in love with anybody because she never met anybody capable of falling in love with her the way her hero fell in love with her heroine. Or the way her heroine fell in love with her heroine.

And then Penelope remembers Lina in Abracadabra and . . .

But, ah, the so many pages of the "treatment"—another treatment, as if there weren't enough treatments in her life—that her brother put her through and that are almost illegible. And that, besides, as if it weren't enough that he'd stolen the Karmas for his little mercenary and Mexican novel, he keeps appropriating and altering what doesn't belong to him and what belongs to her.

And, there, a comatose woman inspired by Maxi who gives birth to a son possessed by recurrent dreams. And, there, all those quotes from different places. And all those different names. And the conciliatory and evidently servile gesture of including Talking Heads in the mix to ingratiate himself to her, though it was more than clear he preferred cooler and more cult bands like Lloyd Cole and The Commotions (Lloyd Cole had a case of referential mania almost as acute as his and Vladimir Nabokov's and Bob Dylan's); not bands you get high to, but bands whose songs about getting high, when you listened to them, were better than any high on any drug. And, oof, it must be hard to live in her bad brother's head. It can't be easy to be interested in so many things, to have to remember so any things, and to have to think about so many things, Penelope says to herself. So many songs and so many movies and so many novels. And to remain not so young but so *juvenile* with so many years atop and to the sides and under him.

And so she gives thanks—many thanks, all the thanks necessary—because hers has been a fixed idea, a single and immoveable idea, bolted down like the chairs and tables on ship decks. Something unsinkable and basic and primordial that doesn't resist all change, but resists all change of trajectory.

A book.

That book.

For Penelope one book is enough and more than enough so long as it's *that* book.

And, again, Penelope does remember now that her bad brother once told her something about a writer insisting—with that oh so childish certainty that uncertain adult writers, even the great ones, tend to have—that all stories could be boiled down and synthesized into two, going in two directions: someone leaves home or someone arrives somewhere they've never been.

In Penelope's favorite novel—her only favorite novel—both things happen.

And if it were true—though Penelope is certain it's *not*—hers, her own case, presents a third possible story: that of someone who doesn't leave and doesn't arrive anywhere, and who's never entirely sure where she is.

She is—Penelope *does* know this for sure, on a physical and geographical plane that does not include the mental—in a religious monastery where they welcome people who feel they have lost their place in the world, who no longer know how to be anywhere. So, a retreat for a not-necessarily-*happy few.* The monastery-convent-retreat-deluxe asylum is called Our Lady of Our Lady of Our Lady of . . . And (when Penelope's lawyers presented it to her as an elegant-reclusive option if she wanted to avoid other more severe options and locations after what happened at the Brontë Parsonage Museum, in Haworth, in West Yorkshire; at the place where Penelope *had* wanted to shut herself in forever and never come out again) here Penelope came. To a place she didn't know, from a home—hers—that no longer existed. And from that other foreign home she knew everything about, from which she was removed by force and restrained and left floating in a chemical fog, so different from the fog surrounding that house that couldn't be bought with all the money in the world.

And the truth is Penelope liked the concentric name of that place—Our Lady of Our Lady of Our lady of . . . —that, consciously or unconsciously, was mocking the cloning of the Virgin Mary carried out by a Vatican that condemns cloning. And Penelope—a writer in the end and after all—appreciated the orthographic detail of that ellipsis that, they explained to her, corresponded to the faith of believing that one is master of oneself, but, at the same time, master of nothing.

Our Lady of Our Lady of Our Lady of . . . like the architectural-existential antithesis of Mount Karma: architecture of simple lines, almost absent decoration (compared to the indecorous psychotic clutter of Mount Karma), and the near impossibility of running into anybody in its corridors (on Mount Karma you were never alone); with the exception of that nun who always frightened Penelope a little, who stared at her, who had a face that was like several faces at the same time. A long-suffering face made to suffer. A face that was a cross. A crusade face. A face that seemed to be looking up at itself from below. One of those reconstructions after a car crash or, maybe, a deconstruction after too many cosmetic surgeries, whose maintenance had been let go and now were stacked one atop the next, like heavy geologic layers, like mudslides provoked by the aftershocks of ancient earthquakes, plastic and melted. Penelope heard about how that nun was something like the great resident theologian of the place, and that she had arrived here from a cloistered monastery. Someone who'd achieved certain renown with the functional miracle of a theory that, they explained, reconciled Darwinians and Creationists and everybody happy and she'd even been nominated for the Nobel Peace Prize: man is not descended from apes, rather apes are the first study/sketch of man that God, in his infinite mercy, decided to toss into the trash can. And there they both are, looking at each other from opposite sides of the same cage. Something like that.

Whereas Penelope has more or less a clear idea of where she comes from (from what heights she has fallen), but she can't be sure where she's going or in what place she'll wind up. Maybe, she likes to say to herself with a shred of humor, she's no longer going. She, just, bah.

So, Our Lady of Our Lady of Our Lady of . . . like a parenthesis in the lives overly laden with question marks and exclamations points of its residents (a set of parenthesis like those parenthesis that, one facing the other, remind Penelope of the basic contour of two hands coming together in the gesture of prayer); a place to reflect on everything that happened in a context where nothing would happen to you anymore. A space to reread, without hurry and word for word, your own life as if it were one of those voluminous nineteenth-century novels with the name of a place or person on the cover. To see yourself from outside and, after a while, to tell yourself you might have done it differently, you might have written it *like this* and not *like this*. And, arriving to this point that's not the end but is a period and new paragraph, supposedly, you're cured. Or, at least, you'll have time and space to get sick from one thing or another that's not desperation about the mystery of how did I get here and the panic in the face of what's yet to come. What good readers feel when they read a good book, though not of someone else's paper and ink but of their own flesh and blood.

And, yes, Penelope sounding now like the nameless heroine of *that* novel that could never have been written if it hadn't first read *this* novel.

Her novel.

Not hers, not one of the ones she has written. One of the now many books with bright covers and letters in relief and explosive illustrations. Covers where you see above the title and author's name (an apparent pseudonym everyone understands as real; without her photograph at her express request) "International Bestseller" beside a number of copies sold with so many zeros you have to think the number over before saying it aloud with a whistle of admiration.

No: the other novel.

The other novel that's hers but not one of hers.

The novel of another that possessed her so she could possess it.

A singular novel and the one and only novel its author wrote, a novel without which she would've never written anything, something, everything she's written.

A novel that cannot be improved because it's perfect, despite its imperfections.

A novel whose imperfections are perfect and are what make it a perfect novel.

One of those novels everyone should read, but, really, is written with only one person in mind, its singular and ideal recipient. That reader who would read it as if she were writing it, the way Penelope read it.

The novel that, when she read it for the first time, when she was a girl, woke Penelope up forever, transforming her into the most alive of zombies, into the suddenly imprisoned subject of a book and the story of that book.

The novel with the name of a house. A novel like a house: opening it like opening a door (the same mechanism, yes) and Penelope entered and the cover closed behind her with a slam warning you it's easy to enter and hard to leave. As hard as leaving behind certain vices one can fall into with such ease.

The novel to go live inside of until death do you part from that house. And yet: because, like so many old houses, at that house, the garden melts into a small family cemetery where the headstones stretch out in the shade of trees or are covered by undergrowth and moss; as if firmly insinuating you, so that you don't ever forget it, that your future is present and you're aware that this place where today you run and grow tomorrow will be where you fall and turn to dust. In times when you died in the same place you lived, yes. So, your eternal death taking place in the same space as your brief life; and the errant and erratic Penelope always yearned for that possibility, so far removed from the serial moves of her childhood; from the comings and goings and the now never-returnings of her distant parents (parents who sometimes felt so far away she wanted to think of them as adoptive and to think of herself as orphan and alien and, with time, to feel and convince herself she belonged, like Heathcliff, to the honorable and turbulent lineage of children who're never entirely children and never will be because they're only children, children of themselves); from the enchanted-compass wandering of her youth and adulthood; to feel like you're moving and yet to be standing perfectly still at the site of the confluence of all things in the world.

Penelope tells herself that she would've given anything to have a house like that, that she would've offered whatever she had for a home forever.


A house that isn't called Manderley or Mount Karma, but that—smaller and older—has found a way to devour them all with a wild and youthful appetite.

A carnivorous house.

Wuthering Heights is the name of that house, is the name of that book.

A name Penelope came to for the first time via the inspired translation of *Cumbres Borrascosas*.

Though first there was that TV adaptation, a Venezuelan telenovela, on a black and white screen. Telenovela on the television that a six- or seven-year-old Penelope (Penelope's chronology, like that of Emily Brontë and, even more, like that of *Wuthering Heights*, is a bit diffuse, as if veiled in a blanket of fog) stared at, every afternoon from Monday to Friday, in the company of the girl who "took care" of her and her bad brother. One of the many "Rosalitas" hired by her parents to watch them and bathe them and feed them and take them to school during their prolonged absences; when they went abroad to film those *bon vivant* ad spots that had made them stars.

Her parents were two golden models in the golden age of advertising in their country. And one day her parents had a great idea. To sell to an international brand of whiskey with the never-ending campaign of a couple of young and beautiful adventurers (themselves) traveling the world aboard a sailboat, the *Diver*, dropping anchor in the world's most glamorous ports and (super low costs) starring in and filming and assembling the material they subsequently mailed in to be broadcast on the screens of televisions and movie theaters. Their proposal was accepted and the adventure not only won many national and international prizes, but, being advertisements without dialogue, just background music, they had the added appeal of a universal language, one that everyone everywhere got, how the good life is understood and envied and desired in all places. Those images and those inaccessible though plausible and verifiable paradises and those songs that always became fashionable and whose composers were more than happy to share royalties with Penelope's parents. Anything in exchange for having their music play alongside the long legs and just-the-right-size breasts of her mother and the full-toothed smile and long hair of her father. Spots that could air without any kind of post-production or adaptation the world over, and that made her parents into characters, if not famous then at least well-know at all the parties, on all the television and movie theater screens. And so, her parents leaning in front of the Tower of Pisa and adoring each other on Juliet's balcony in Verona. Or dancing with Cossacks in Moscow. Or riding camels in the Sahara or rappelling down glaciers in Patagonia. Or crossing the London Bridge or going up to the top of the Empire State Building. Or pretending to draw a heart with their initials on one side of the Great Wall of China. Or in the still-primitive and gangsterish and Sinatra-esque Sands Hotel where her mother looks like a backup singer and her father like an Elvis impersonator. Or who knows where next time, but always here and there and everywhere. And, in spite of herself, Penelope actually likes one of those spots: her father as an arctic explorer and her mother as a sexy snow queen. Her bad brother's favorite—more than anything because it makes him very popular among his little friends at school—features her father at the controls in Cape Canaveral and her mother floating in a space simulator, weightless, clothes so tight she appears to be naked, oh so Barbarella. Yes, her parents on the screen of that TV where Penelope *sees* her novel for the first time.

Penelope sits down holding a plate with a hamburger and mashed potatoes in one hand and a glass of Coca-Cola in the other (the basic diet in her home). And, coming back from a commercial break, there are her mother and father, the *Diver* anchored on the edge of Seine, the two of them running through the Louvre and her mother's smile imitating, quite well, that of the Mona Lisa, before bursting into soundless laughter, because what you hear is "a very lovely song by a very ugly person named Serge Gainsbourg," her parents explained. And they showed her a photograph and he didn't look ugly to Penelope and, with time, even made her think a little of Heathcliff. And sitting beside her, the Rosalita of the moment, as if in a trance, saying in a low voice "Those two are so crazy," staring at the TV where something very strange is happening; and, no, Rosalita isn't referring to her parents. Penelope looks at Rosalita and looks at what Rosalita is looking at and what she sees is a location covered in that fake smoke of dry ice. Rocks that, it's easy to see, are made of light papier-mâché. A backdrop showing a bleak and fleeting landscape that just reaffirms the fact that it's all taking place on a set of no more than four square meters. Suddenly, a young man with an unbuttoned shirt and exceedingly wrinkled pants enters the frame shouting "Catherine! Catherine!" He exits the frame, his voice not growing more distant but growing quieter in an attempt, ingenuously, to give the impression of distance; and a few seconds pass and now what appears before the spectators is a girl, in wide skirts and a corset tight across breasts that want nothing but to escape, wailing "Heathcliff! Heathcliff!" And she exits and then he comes back and "Catherine!" and exits and she enters and "Heathcliff!" And so it goes for that entire segment of telenovela. Until—break—they're back, but so far from home, Penelope's parents (now, magically, in Mozambique, her mother in a metallic bikini surrounded by black boys who look at her wondering if it might not be a good idea to revise the whole goodbye to cannibalism). But Penelope forgets about her parents, wherever they are, and can't stop thinking about that place. And about that fog. And about those two (they seem so much unhappier yet also much more real than her happy parents). And about those two names that, more than names, are like magic words, spells, conjurations of conjurers. Penelope waits for them to come back on and in the next scene they're no longer there (now appear some servants talking in a kitchen, a drink, and someone listening to a story told beside the fire in the fireplace), but they all keep repeating those names as if they were nouns and verbs and predicates. Heathcliff's Catherine catherinian heathcliffically by the heathcliffs and among the catherines. They don't seem able to talk about anything that isn't Heathcliff and Catherine. And Penelope watches all of that and all of them until the end. And she doesn't understand any of it, but she waits until the final credits. And there she reads "Based on the immortal classic by Emily Brontë" and, ah, so all of that is a book . . . And it's the first time Penelope experiences that great pleasure: discovering that something she likes a lot is not the original, but comes from somewhere else, from something that's probably much better than the thing you already like.

And that afternoon, Uncle Hey Walrus comes to visit and takes Penelope and her brother on a walk. Her uncle, it's known (since he was sent back exquisitely wrapped, like a gift nobody really wanted, in a straight jacket, after his brief yet powerful stay in Pepperland, London), isn't who he once was. And sometimes he barks like a dog or like a walrus; but he hasn't lost the ability to feel an invulnerable tenderness for Penelope and her bad older brother whom he refers to as "my little orphans of living parents."

Her Uncle Hey Walrus is for Penelope—in a hypothetical catalogue of novelesque categories of the nineteenth century—what's known as "a benefactor." A secondary character, yes, but of the first order. Someone indispensable and decisive when it comes to attaining a more or less happy ending. Or an ending of any kind.

So the three of them go out and enter a bookstore (the sun already went down and went quiet, but the bookstores stay open, as the local legends say) and Uncle Hey Walrus buys her bad brother *Dracula* and wants to buy Penelope *Little Women*. But she—with the certainty and assuredness with which other kids select ice cream flavors out of so many colors—asks the bookseller, "Please, *Cumbres Borrascosas*, the immortal classic by Emily Brontë." And she carries it home with her, never suspecting it's really the book that's carrying her, the book that will read her over and over again throughout the novel of her life.

That night, under the covers, with a flashlight, Penelope begins her never-ending relationship with that book and, when the sun rises, she has reached the last page with a feeling of triumph she has never experienced before. Penelope reads it and has read all of it. From the name and address of the publisher to the name of the translator who took it by the hand and led it from another language and taught it how to speak in that of Penelope. Penelope returns again and again to paragraphs she has marked with a pencil, convinced that, yes, anyone can read *Wuthering Heights*; but that it was written for her and her alone. And Penelope suspects, without understanding very well why she suspects it, that every human being has a book *like this*, a book that is their destiny. A book by someone else but all *theirs*. And most everyone passes it by, though it's right there throughout their lives, or never finds it. And they die having never read it. Or they only find it in the last days of their life and wonder, through tears, a mix of joy and sorrow (as if they were, again, flavors of ice cream, irreconcilable yet eaten together all the same), where that book was all this time, where they were that this book wasn't.

Whereas Penelope has been lucky and chosen: she has discovered it very early, the book found her almost right away. And she has her whole life in front of her to reread it as if—even by the end of that first opening night, together—as if she were already a quiet octogenarian returning to the books of her impetuous youth.

Penelope, over the years, will learn everything there is to know about *Wuthering Heights*, though the version she gets to know first speaks a different tongue, her own. Translation by one Cebrià de Montoliu, urban planner and social reformer and proselytizer of Anglo-Saxon culture in Cataluña, dead in Albuquerque; great name, his, like that of a swashbuckling womanizer, says Penelope; and for that alone, for his inspiration when it came to importing that title into Spanish, Penelope counts him among her favorite writers. And it was under the influence of Cebrià de Montoliu that—when she had to choose a city in which to lose herself in order to find herself—Penelope traveled to Barcelona. A city where, also, José Bardina, her first Heathcliff, the one from the Venezuelan telenovela, son of a Barça soccer player, had been born. Yes, *Wuthering Borrascosas* there as well, influencing that, influencing everything.

And, when it comes to remembering and organizing everything that happened, for reasons of physical and mental health (so the religious psychologists of Our Lady of Our Lady of Our Lady of . . . have suggested to her), it's best to do it quickly, without pausing too long on the details. Like the recaps of previous installments in those Victorian true-crime penny dreadfuls, like the one about Bernadette Dawn, who locked up her own daughters, or in the serialization of *Great Expectations*, with its manipulative masculine version of Heathcliff and that demented and ruinous bride; both, the real and the imagined, so heavily influenced by the foggy radiations of *Wuthering Heights*.

And so, Penelope in Barcelona where she first encountered the project, with no possible practical application for a writer, of Maximiliano "Maxi" Karma; whom at first she mistook for a Heathcliff, but soon realized was nothing but an Edgar Linton. And, then, overdose and deep coma for the young dynastic heir of a family from a place known as Abracadabra. And there Penelope went, accompanying her deeply sleeping beauty. And there Hiriz and Mamagrandma and Lina were waiting for her. And Penelope, rechristened Penita, fled that place on the morning of her wedding day, crossing a desert riddled with diamonds, riding on the back of a gigantic and mutant and telepathic green cow and drinking its strange and intoxicating milk to then, her wedding dress in tatters, enter the clinic where the comatose Maxi lay and climb atop him, and suffocate him, and get impregnated by him, and continue on her way, fearing the Karmas would come to reclaim her soon-to-be-born son.

And it's then—after opening their arms and bending their knees and breathing deeply and taking their mark and leaping from on high—that events *really* precipitate. And when everything ceases to have the robust texture of a serialized novel, where too many things are happening so, suddenly, the plot fills up with ellipses, with avant-garde tics, with experimental poses.

All of a sudden, for Penelope everything happens suddenly, as if she'd landed in the middle of a party where everyone is talking about the same thing at the same time but telling different parts of the story: her bad brother has a kind a psychotic break in a particle accelerator near Montreux, she burns down a house and flees and later—still reeking of smoke—is detained at the Brontë Parsonage Museum for "attempted robbery of public and private property, and for disturbing the peace." And Penelope is dragged out of there the way her brother is dragged out of the Swiss hadron collider (now a family tradition, it seems; this thing of being removed by force from sensible buildings for inappropriate behavior). And the lawyers at her publishing house pull strings (though the whole episode is still a great publicity stunt; our misanthropic star author, adored by children and young adults and adults, victim of a "literary crisis from which, we're certain, great things will emerge"). And they agree to make a generous donation to the museum in honor of the Brontës' memory and they plan and announce her stay at Our Lady of Our Lady of Our Lady of . . .

And above and beyond all of that, the one thing that happened but never stops happening. The lightning bolt that never ceases to split the sky. The expansive wave that keeps expanding and perhaps someday, after washing over everything, will return to the point of departure to explain everything. Meanwhile and in the meantime, that inexplicable and unforgivable thing, that thing Penelope cannot comprehend, because Penelope can't remember almost anything of what happened.

Penelope remembers her feet in the sand, the moon in the sky, the trees in the forest, and the water where the river mouth opened into the sea. And, later, the beams of flashlights and that, for her, unnamable name in the mouths of everyone searching for and not finding that name's small yet immense owner. Penelope remembers all of that, but doesn't remember the most important thing, the most important part.

Oft-recapped recap of the event: one night, at her house on the beach, Penelope went out on a walk with her little son and Penelope returned to the beach house alone, without him.

And Penelope doesn't want to think about that, Penelope doesn't think she wants to think about that ever again and, yes, that's the reason for not giving interviews; because there's always somebody who connects the loss of her son with the discovery of one of her more celebrated creations: dAlien, the extraterrestrial boy who, unlike so many other sidereal travelers, never wants to return home, because he can't stand his parents. dAlien would rather get lost in space. No "phone home" for dAlien. And no: no easy symbolism there. No fictional boy more solid now than that real boy, standing in for that real boy who seems ever more invented; because before you saw him and now you don't, but, nevertheless, he's still there. What's never found is always in view, everywhere. It's enough and more than enough to think you see it to see it. It's so much easier to see what is not there than to stop seeing what is there . . .

The problem—if you are a writer, if you devote yourself to recounting something that doesn't exist so it will exist for others—is that's where the lines get a little blurred.

For Penelope it's clear there are millions of people out there who believe more in Stella D'Or or in dAlien or in the Tulpa sisters than in Penelope herself, their creator. Which to her, doesn't seem like a bad thing; because for Penelope, the Tulpa sisters and dAlien and Stella D'Or are steel-plated doors, soldered locks, deep firewalls to keep her from ever being reached unless it is she—for whom there are no limitations—who is chasing herself. Hermetic compartments, but, at the same time, communicating vessels. Inevitable cracks and leaks between one wall and another, this house and that one, as if in the reflexive and absorbing structure of *Wuthering Heights*.

And now she's here.

Alone.

Penelope. Not the most epic name, as her parents had given it to her not in honor of the original Odyssian wife, but as a derivative stemming from that popular song with, yes, more than a little Catalan perfume in it.

Penelope, all alone and nobody asking her that whole "Tell me, Muse, of the woman of many ways . . ."

Penelope, unable to see herself in her mirror-less cell/study, but staring at herself all the time.

Penelope, surrounded by all those who hold the always-unsteady beam of her past over her head. All it takes is one of them to let their arms drop for events, once again, to precipitate.

Down on top of her. All of them.

Their names clear, their faces out of focus, like the illustrations in a book that never coincide with the idea you make of them reading the adjoining page; and so Penelope has always avoided editions of *Wuthering Heights* with supposed portraits of Heathcliff or Catherine on their covers, opting instead for editions that favor desolate landscapes. Covers with painted or photographed postcards of Yorkshire that, if you bring them close to your ear, you can almost hear the embowered conversation between a limited number of trees and innumerable rocks.

And no: Penelope doesn't have a copy of *Wuthering Heights* with her now, in her cell/study of Our Lady of Our Lady of Our Lady of . . .

Neither in English nor in Spanish.

Not one of the many editions she'd gone around buying over the years (she'd get a new one every time she reread the novel, and she'd reread it so many times) including that treasured first edition, bought at an auction with her first, but already quite substantial, royalties payment, payments which have just kept on increasing. An antique in a perfect state of conservation that, when she touched and worshiped it, Penelope put on gloves and knelt down: one of the first editions in three volumes of *Wuthering Heights*. Written by Emily Brontë between October 1845 and June of 1846; written at that speed of days when there was little to do but read and write. Published when she was twenty-nine years old, just before she died. Signed by her androgynous *nom de plume* Ellis Bell and edited in a trio of small volumes riddled with errors and sloppiness by Thomas Newby along with, in the last of the three little books, *Agnes Grey* by Anne "Acton Bell" Brontë.

At Our Lady of Our Lady of Our Lady of . . . Penelope has been forbidden to get anywhere near *Wuthering Heights*. They have forbidden it "for her own good," they explained. And she tries, wants to understand the value of such treatment, really; but she can't wrap her head around how someone could come to the conclusion that, therapeutically, the thing that makes you happiest could end up causing you harm.

And, true, *Wuthering Heights* is a toxic book with a highly contagious power. A book that transcends borders and languages because what it sets out and carries along and pushes through to end of the road is a universal feeling: to have once felt a love *like that*, to feel a love *like that*, to know you'll never feel a love *like that*. But don't get confused, she explains it *like this*: for Penelope, *Wuthering Heights* was never a recreational drug of the kind that distracts you from the woes of the world. No, for her, *Wuthering Heights* was always her reality, clouded by the fog and wind of everyone else's reality, so much less entertaining and passionate, so much more poorly written, and so plagued with orthographical errors.

But it doesn't matter, she doesn't miss it, she doesn't need it.

She doesn't need the object.

She knows the novel by heart.

And now Penelope is like one of those human-books wandering the woods like in that other novel in which all ink-marked paper was burned for fun. Penelope can recite *Wuthering Heights* from beginning to end. From that opening where Lockwood enters the scene and stage with an "1801. —I have just returned from a visit to my landlord—the solitary neighbour that I shall be troubled with. This is certainly, a beautiful country! In all England, I do not believe that I could have fixed on a situation so completely removed from the stir of society. A perfect misanthropist's Heaven—and Mr Heathcliff and I are such a suitable pair to divide the desolation between us"; to that closing, when all of them are already in their graves and Lockwood departs with a "My walk home was lengthened by a diversion in the direction of the kirk. When beneath its walls, I perceived decay had made progress, even in seven months—many a window showed black gaps deprived of glass; and the slates jutted off, here and there, beyond the right line of the roof, to be gradually worked off in coming autumn storms. I sought, and soon discovered, the three head-stones on the slope next the moor—the middle one, grey, and half buried in heath—Edgar Linton's only harmonized by the turf and moss, creeping up its foot—Heathcliff's still bare. I lingered round them, under that benign sky; watched the moths fluttering among the heath and hare-bells; listened to the soft wind breathing through the grass; and wondered how anyone could ever imagine unquiet slumbers, for the sleepers in that quiet earth."

Yes.

Word for word.

Line for line.

All off the cuff and with no respect for paragraph breaks or page order. Penelope pushing paragraphs together, mixing voices, blending views and landscapes and times and, every so often, inserting herself; as if piercing a membrane, as if lifting a veil to see better and closer up. As if the text of the novel were like that informational ticker at the bottom of the screen on the evening news. Live extras and the latest breaking news, which Penelope knew and anticipated to perfection, and yet never failing to surprise and move her. *Wuthering Heights* rising in the chasms of her brain, changing from the language she read it in for the first time to the language she read it in later and forever (with the help of a dictionary, that's how Penelope learned English) leaping from the *heights* to the *cumbres* and back from the *borrascoso* to the *wuthering*; running through the fog and the wind and the rain of those pages and discovering that the rain and the wind and the fog always speak the same language. A language everyone understands. And there, in the middle of the storm, all those words. Arranging and disarranging themselves like spiraling gyres of fog that, sometimes, slip away from Penelope like smoke between her fingers. But she chases them down and traps them and wraps them around her again, there, where she always wanted to be and will never want to leave. Lines she returns to again and again when she feels everything is falling apart, immovable feelings that transcend time and death and to which she clings with the same tenacity others cling to psalms and verses; despite the fact that, in the moment of its publication, various horrified critics might have described *Wuthering Heights* as "a Bible of the infernos" and would've wondered how it was possible its author hadn't succumbed to the consoling temptation of suicide, after birthing such a somber aberration.

What do they all know, what does anybody know.

And the only thing Penelope knows for sure—when she feels a black wind lashing her or the sun of injustice shining in the sky; when others resort to reciting a long credo or repeating a brief mantra—is that she sits down in a corner and in a low voice, lips moving, repeats, with variations, more or less this:

"Winter 1801 and a man named Lockwood arrives to Wuthering Heights to arrange with the owner, one Heathcliff, to rent a neighboring house, Thrushcross Grange, and, yes, here we go with these oh so strange yet unforgettable names, and Heathcliff is likely the meanest man that Lockwood has ever met, but provokes in him certain curiosity, and then a snowstorm, and Lockwood finds himself obliged to spend the night at Wuthering Heights, and his room comes with a ghost who asks to be let in because she is lost on the moor, the ghost of Catherine Linton or whatever surname she prefers among her various surnames, and Lockwood screams and everyone screams and when that awful night is over, Lockwood sits down to talk with a full-service housekeeper Ellen 'Nelly' Dean, a woman whose raison d'être and purpose in life is that of awaiting the arrival of some stranger to whom she can tell everything that happened in that house with the same precision we never entirely trust in tourism guides, and what she has to tell is the bellicose and shadowy saga of the Earnshaws and the Lintons, and Nelly, war correspondent always moving from one battlefront to another, from one house to another, has spent years reporting the hostilities, ever since Mr. Earnshaw brought home the seven-year-old orphan, Heathcliff, who is immediately hated by the young Hindley and adored by the young six-year-old Catherine, and soon the girl and the boy are inseparable and go running around together across the wuthering heights, but years later, when Mr. Earnshaw dies, Hindley returns from college with his brand-new wife, Frances, and turns Heathcliff into a servant to be tortured, but Heathcliff doesn't mind the humiliation and mistreatment so long as he can keep running off with Catherine, wearing boots or barefoot, races without starting or finish line, up and down, between rock and heath, and one night they arrive to Thrushcross Grange and, through the window, they spy on the precious and far-better-dressed-and-combed young Lintons, Edgar and Isabella, and the guard dog bites Catherine, and Catherine finds herself obliged to convalesce there for some five weeks, a little too long, if you ask me, more than enough time for the young Catherine to fascinate the young Linton while, alone, Heathcliff is having a harder time than ever at Wuthering Heights where Frances dies giving birth to Hareton, and Hindley, turning to drink, behaves more and more despotically with Heathcliff and Catherine who confesses to Nelly that, though the love of her life is Heathcliff, better that she marry Edgar, which sometimes happens, and a destroyed Heathcliff departs Wuthering Heights forever, but, as also sometimes happens, he returns stronger and transformed into a rich man of eighteen years, an adolescent magnate, and offers no explanation regarding where his fortune comes from, but soon reveals where it's all going and what he'll devote it to with enthusiasm and Hamlet-esque calculations, (Heathcliff, revenge!), in order to take over Wuthering Heights, winning it in a game of cards against Hindley, who is castaway with too many bottles and no message, and then Thrushcross Grange by marrying Isabella, Edgar's sister, and thereby found a sort of Heathcliffland he'll reign over with Catherine when she realizes once and for all they were born apart only to die together, but, after intense arguments—because here, unlike in other novels of the period, people argue and don't dance and definitely don't drop hints with word games and veiled comments—Catherine falls ill, and never really gets better, though just before dying and accusing Heathcliff of killing her, she gives birth to a daughter whom, to complicate already exceedingly complicated matters, she names Catherine, and the crying of the newborn mingle with the living-dead wailing of Heathcliff, calling out to the ghost of Catherine who haunts and curses and torments him, just as she did when she was alive, behavior which ends up being too much for the already excessively punished Isabella who flees to London and there gives birth to Linton Heathcliff and, suddenly, it's as if everything is starting over again and, through the next thirteen years, Nelly Dean becomes the tutor of the young and happy Catherine II at Thrushcross Grange where her father takes very special care to make sure the young girl knows little or nothing about Wuthering Heights and about the ogre residing there, but, her mother's daughter, Catherine II escapes on expeditions up the cliffs and arrives to Wuthering Heights just as her mother once arrived to Thrushcross Grange, and there she meets Hareton, the son of Hindley, but, really, a kind of weathered and half-wild Heathcliff II, and in London Isabella dies and the young and mentally and physically ill Linton is brought to Thrushcross Grange by his uncle Edgar, but Heathcliff demands his son live with him, perhaps so he can detest him from closer range the way he already detests Hareton and, on one of her wild rambles, Catherine II encounters Heathcliff and later Linton with whom, using the complicit milkman as messenger, she initiates an amorous correspondence and, when Edgar and Nelly go to bed, Catherine II escapes to Wuthering Heights to visit Linton whom Heathcliff wants to marry to Catherine II and thus make him the owner of Thrushcross Grange, apparently convinced that everyone will die before him and he'll survive even the extinction of the sun and the stars, master of the universe, and Heathcliff convinces Nelly and Catherine to move to Wuthering Heights where he keeps them prisoner and forces Catherine II to marry Linton in a marriage that, though its author doesn't care, is completely illegal and without any validity in terms of property, but those details don't apply in the entirely extralegal environment of Wuthering Heights, and soon Edgar dies and Linton dies, and Heathcliff now has everything he wanted, including his daughter-in-law as a slave and now Lockwood has arrived to rent Thrushcross Grange, but, after hearing everything Nelly has told him, he decides having a landlord like Heathcliff might not be the ideal and maybe it would be best to move along and he returns to London, though everything seems to indicate he too has become an addict of wutheringheightina, and six months later he's back to visit Nelly who catches him up on everything that happened in the episodes he missed, she tells Lockwood what he has missed and, yes, Catherine II has taught Hareton to read, like Jane taught Tarzan, while Heathcliff, *last man standing*, as often happens, now can only think of the dead, of those who, he realizes, beat him by setting the trap of having ended their lives before him, and they are many and so many and, above all the others, the hysterical Catherine I, whose ghost has even rejected him, and Heathcliff dies, and it's hard to say if he dies happy or if he's happy to die, and Catherine II and Hareton inherit both houses and plan a wedding for New Years Day and, before leaving, Lockwood takes a stroll through the cemetery and visits three tombs, in order of appearance, Catherine I, dead at eighteen, and Edgar, dead at thirty-nine, and Heathcliff, dead at thirty-seven, and maybe amid such epiphanic-farewell thinking, he says to himself that there's something strange in all that Nelly has told him, that there's something in her story that doesn't entirely come together, that it's all very imprecise, and that, if he were up to him, the first thing he would do is convince Hareton to dismiss her and then tell him to go see the world before getting married and, with the young man far away, court Catherine II and live happily with her until Hareton returns and here we go again, amen and ommm and hare hare and a great peace descends from Heaven, life, abundance, salvation, comfort, liberation, health, surrender, redemption, forgiveness, atonement, openness, and freedom, shalom."

And, for now, the storm has passed until the next storm comes. Penelope has managed to distract the *cafard*. And it has already passed and it won't be long before Penelope has to think that, with the exception of *Wuthering Heights*, she doesn't want to think about anything anymore; and that there's only one way to achieve this, but many ways to make it happen.


Penelope had attempted suicide multiple times and, long before reaching its twelfth chapter, *Wuthering Heights* had distracted her from that idea, just so she could see and reread what happened next, unconcerned with knowing it to perfection. Every time Penelope had felt the impulse to let herself slide toward death, the words and dialogues of Heathcliff and Catherine had kept her on this side, clinging to the edge of the abyss, because, she thought, nobody was worthy of ending their own life if they hadn't lived a love and a hate and a *lovehate* like that of Heathcliff and Catherine, of those two adding up to one.

And so, then, she evoked and cited them blindly, but knowing them down to the last and slightest of their features, now without a page on which to rest her eyes, but moving the tips of her fingers, as if she were reading both of them in the braille of the air. Their two voices one, their two sexes one; until not caring where the ghost of the dead woman ends so the possessed dying man can begin. Their lines of dialogue becoming the hook of a monologue Penelope recites in the solitude of her convent-asylum cell/study.

Asking herself and answering, in Catherine's voice, "Whatever our souls are made of, his and mine are the same; and Linton's is as different as a moonbeam from lightning, or frost from fire . . . What were the use of my creation, if I were entirely contained here? My great miseries in this world have been Heathcliff's miseries, and I watched and felt each from the beginning; my great thought in living is himself. If all else perished, and *he* remained, I should still continue to be; and if all else remained, and he were annihilated, the universe would turn into a mighty stranger: I should not seem a part of it. My love for Linton is like the foliage in the woods: time will change it, I'm well aware, as winter changes the trees. My love for Heathcliff resembles the eternal rocks beneath—a source of little visible delight, but necessary. Nelly, I *am* Heathcliff—He's always, always in my mind—not as a pleasure, any more than I am always a pleasure to myself—but as my own being—so, don't talk of our separation again—it is impracticable; and—"

And again answering herself and accusing and asking herself again, now with the voice of Heathcliff, with a "You teach me now how cruel you've been—cruel and false. *Why* did you despise me? *Why* did you betray your own heart, Cathy? I have not one word of comfort—you deserve this. You have killed yourself. Yes, you may kiss me, and cry; and wring out my kisses and tears. They'll blight you—they'll damn you. You loved me—then what *right* had you to leave me? What right—answer me—for the poor fancy you felt for Linton? Because misery, and degradation, and death, and nothing that God or Satan could inflict would have parted us, *you*, of your own will, did it. I have not broken your heart—*you* have broken it—and in breaking it, you have broken mine. So much the worse for me, that I am strong. Do I want to live? What kind of living will it be when you—oh, God! would *you* like to live with your soul in the grave? . . . May she wake in torment! . . .

Why, she's a liar to the end! Where is she? Not *there*—not in heaven—not perished—where? Oh! you said you cared nothing for my sufferings! And I pray one prayer—I repeat it till my tongue stiffens—Catherine Earnshaw, may you not rest, as long as I am living! You said I killed you—haunt me then! The murdered *do* haunt their murderers. I believe—I know that ghosts *have* wandered on the earth. Be with me always—take any form—drive me mad! only *do* not leave me in this abyss, where I cannot find you! Oh God! it is unutterable! I *cannot* live without my life! I *cannot* live without my soul!"

To all the foregoing—from the one and the other—listens, always obliging and attentive, Nelly Dean who, as she remembers it, tells how Catherine clasped her hands together and brought them to her breast and how Heathcliff "dashed his head against the knotted trunk; and, lifting up his eyes, howled, not like a man, but like a savage beast getting goaded to death with knives and spears."

And so, Catherine dies accusing Heathcliff with a "You have killed me—and thriven on it, I think" and Heathcliff says to her "Don't torture me till I'm as mad as yourself . . . Are you possessed with a devil to talk in that manner to me, when you are dying? Do you reflect that all those words will be branded in my memory, and eating deeper eternally, after you have left me? You know you lie to say I have killed you; and, Catherine, you know that I could as soon forget you, as my existence! Is it not sufficient for your infernal selfishness, that while you are at peace I shall writhe in the torments of hell?" And she responds, "I shall not be at peace" and doesn't deny herself the chance to comment to Nelly Dean, there present, "Oh, you see, Nelly! he would not relent a moment to keep me out of the grave! *That* is how I'm loved! Well, never mind! That is not *my* Heathcliff. I shall love mine yet; and take him with me—he's in my soul." And Catherine seems to lose consciousness and, as Nelly tells it, Heathcliff "flung himself into the nearest seat, and on my approaching hurriedly to ascertain if she had fainted, he gnashed at me, and foamed like a mad dog, and gathered her to him with greedy jealousy. I did not feel as if I were in the company of a creature of my own species."

And Penelope knows what they're talking about and has been there, foam in her mouth, but accusing herself, in the two languages she drives at top speed and without fastening her seatbelt. First, once more and always, the

Spanish in which she read the novel for the first time when she was around seven years old; second, again, in the English she learned reading it, line by line, with the help of a bilingual dictionary.

"Él es más myself than I am y no puedo vivir sin my life," Penelope recites.

And no, hers, her *other* novel, the novel of her life, doesn't begin with someone remembering a dream that leads her back to a mansion or with a traveler arriving to a kind of farm on the moors. But it doesn't matter. Those are little details that will be resolved in the final montage, she tells herself now, remembering then. There, in her increasingly distant and remote yet, again, always shiny and new past. And she already remembered it a few minutes—a few pages—ago; a past she'll think of again as if she were a nineteenth-century heroine, a minimal landscape, where every day you think the same thing.

There it stays so she will open it: the iron gate and the path that leads to the cluster of houses of that family of lunatics, the Karmas, from which she'd fled, so long ago, decked out in her wedding dress and crossing a diamond-speckled desert on the back of a gigantic and mutant and telepathic green cow. But now all of that, suddenly, Brontëified by Penelope: the desert is a highland moor, the crazy cow is a colossal mastiff, and, in the sky, just above her head, glow asteroids #39427, #39428, and #39429 christened respectively Charlottebrontë, Emilybrontë, and Annebrontë. And it's their twinkling brilliance that makes the diamonds sparkle (the diamonds always were and always will be diamonds, the diamonds don't change from one version to the next) and Penelope picks them up, not thinking of making herself rich, but thinking that, while there are diamonds to be picked up, and there are so many, she won't die, out there, all alone.

And, suddenly, in her mind, the tribal architecture of Mount Karma (multiple medium-sized houses surrounding one massive house, as if paying tribute and honoring, relatives of the Karma surname orbiting around the queen sun that is Mamagrandma, totem and chieftess of the tribe) melting into that of her other house beside the river mouth opening onto the sea. The house she set ablaze before they brought her here, thinking they were locking her up when, in reality, she'd done all of it to find sanctuary behind these other bars. They think those bars keep her from getting out when the truth is: these bars keep them from getting in. Mamagrandma and the Karmas and even her bad brother, who's only admitted if she authorizes it and she no longer does.

Everyone outside.

The only ones authorized to come in and visit her from now on have to meet a condition, they have to bear the surname Brontë and be direct descendants of the Brontë sisters, and there aren't any, there never were.


What's in a name? What's in a surname? Many things if that surname is Brontë. More a registered trademark than anything. Pronounce it / *brontiz* / or / *bronteiz*. Drag it here pulling it by the hair, up the stairs, moving away from the original sound of an Irish clan, that of the Ó Pronntaigh or Sons of Pronntach, Anglicized as Prunty or Brunty; until the always unpredictable Reverend Patrick Brontë—father of the sisters and the brother—rewrote it definitively as Brontë, who knows why. Perhaps to move it up in the hierarchy, latching onto the honorable Admiral Horatio Nelson, Duke of Bronte. Perhaps to associate it with the Greek and divine echoes of the roaring Greek word βροντή, which means "thunder." Perhaps for both reasons or perhaps for none of them except the clear nonsense of those two little dots above the ë, which, typographically, alert you to the fact that the surname is comprised of two syllables; but which always remind Penelope of the bite mark of a vampire on the neck of the young immaculate virgin with—the damsel in distress discovers in that exact instant—previously inconceivable longings to cease being impurely innocent in order to feel so immaculately sinful.


Penelope, yes, has spent so many years being brontëified. The surname like an action to react to. Penelope has gone along crossing out everything else until they're all she has left, those who bear that name.

Sometimes Penelope thinks of her bad brother, writer and exwriter, poor little thing: his mind overpopulated and Vonnegutified and Cheeverified and Bobdylanized and Proustified and Nabokovified and . . . Her bad brother's head is like the name of this convent/asylum, its battery never dies: "It keeps going . . . and going . . ."

Or she thinks of her Uncle Hey Walrus, madly Beatleified (if you asked and supplied him with the pertinent information, her uncle would've answered that "Charlotte Brontë and her *Jane Eyre* are definitely the romantic Paul McCartney advising 'When I find myself in times of trouble ... Let it be'; while Emily Brontë and her *Wuthering Heights* are unequivocally the hallucinatory John Lennon, disorienting everyone with a 'Let me take you down 'cause I'm going to . . . Nothing is real'; and Anne Brontë would be George Harrison and Branwell Brontë would be Ringo Starr").

Or she thinks of her parents, disappeared, now and so, yes, feeling so fulfilled, a true orphan; joining that race for whom the only surname to answer to—beginning and ending in themselves—is their own: that name like the solipsistic sun that, in their flight, her progenitors flew too close to. And, from there, someone gave them a little push. And Penelope doesn't really want to think about that, because it'd be easy to say it was there and then (if you were to look at Penelope from outside, never understanding her, the way many tried in vain in their time to understand Emily Brontë) the process began, a process without a clear end that's known, conveniently yet imprecisely, as "going mad." The madness where you go and never ever leave.

And so, the "experts" didn't hesitate to diagnose Penelope with a "pathological obsession with the Brontë family and a special fixation on the sister Emily."

But they don't understand anything.

The Brontës and Emily, for Penelope, are not an illness: they are, if not the cure, at least the medicine that slows down the poison circulating insider her organism. The antidote expanding the distance and slowing down the speed between the heart and the head or between the head and the heart.

Penelope has discovered with no need for college or diploma or years of psychoanalysis that—when trying by any means not to think about your own family—the best way to do it is not to blink and to focus all your attention on another family.

Thus the Brontës.

The most functional of dysfunctional families.

A father.

Three sisters and one brother.

The ghost of a dead mother and two dead sisters.

An unmarried aunt and two servants.

The landscape of their myth and their reality as landscape.

And, there inside, all of them writing; because there's little to read in the world of minimal lines that surrounds them. A world that's like a blank page that doesn't provoke fear but produces that form of oh so nineteenth-century boredom that, almost immediately, is translated into boundless creativity. Into black ink full of letters.

Penelope enumerates names and counts dates and Charlotte Brontë (1816-1855) and Emily Brontë (1818-1848) and Anne Brontë (1820-1849).

All three of them assuming masculine pseudonyms, because, as a woman, that whole writing stories thing isn't something you do (before them, Jane Austen, who already mocked the gothic cosmogony the Brontës worshipped in *Northanger Abbey*, began signing her books as "A Lady"; and after them Mary Anne Evans disguised herself as George Eliot).

And, thus, the brothers Bell: Currer, Ellis, and Acton Bell.

To whom is added the real and authentic brother, Patrick "Branwell" Brontë (1817-1848), who doesn't deserve a tolling pseudonym because the truth is, upon reaching adolescence, he begins to distance himself from his sisters' increasingly realistic and sublime fantasies.

Free verse and imperfect rhyme, the poor Branwell, the unbearable Branwell, the Branwell who supposedly was going to be a multifaceted artist and all-terrain genius. Branwell who doesn't take long to become someone—in the first translations that Penelope reads as a girl—frequently described with words already brittle from lack of use. Words like "dandy" and "spendthrift" and more or less pious forms of saying very cruel things like "good for nothing" or, in the British parlance of the day, "casual worker." Those who have tried to heighten the mythic and supposedly Byronian air of Branwell, beyond his hysteric outbursts and bratty tantrums and unfounded egocentrism, despite being repeatedly rejected by all (there's a biography by Daphne du Maurier, Manderley again, that refers, almost breathlessly, to his "infernal world"; and Matthew Arnold included him in several lines of his poem "Haworth Churchyard"), only to end up increasing the shame that this man produces in a world of men, but eclipsed by three mad sisters. An ink self-portrait (where he reminds Penelope a great deal of the actor Paul Dano) shows him with the characteristic defiant profile of the ever so insecure.

And so, Branwell, who soon is swept away in a torrent of opium and booze and laudanum and impossible-to-pay debts and dismissals from jobs for stealing money and smoldering yet inevitably unrequited infatuations with a married woman. Branwell works as a tutor for her family and—pioneering attitude that, looking back, makes him quite predictable and unoriginal—the woman is named Mrs. Robinson. And Branwell is fired from his position by the husband and is continually rejected by Mrs. Robinson even when she is widowed. And one night, Branwell lights his bed on fire and is rescued by Emily, and after that he is obliged to suffer the humiliation of sleeping with his father. And Branwell dies an early death of the damned leaving behind a few middling poems, a few paintings of poor quality but great historical and anecdotal value (like that one of his three sisters, in no way resembling how they actually looked, they say, and where he effaces himself and thus disappears, appearing as an kind of ectoplasmic yellowish pillar), and maybe most important of all: his sisters' need to console him and rewrite him and improve him and turn him into a masculine paradigm and archetype in their novels.

Before all of that, in the beginning was the other Word. That of the wordy father and reverend Patrick Brontë (1777-1861), the head of that household, a household that was parochial and rural and traditional yet with unorthodox and modern customs. Patrick Brontë let his daughters and son run free, without limits or schedule, amid the rocks and winds and to the despair of his unmarried sister-in-law Elizabeth Branwell (1776-1842) and the servants Tabitha Ayckroyd and Martha Brown (little trace of them remains, gravestones with limited information, dates of departure but not arrival), who are there to help the motherless family, who adore children, and whom the children adore.

Patrick Brontë is also an aspiring poet and polemicist who takes pride in certain peculiarities (though perhaps they aren't entirely certain), like modifying women's dresses in unorthodox fashion, his propensity to send his progeny to infernal "charity" schools riddled with tuberculosis and malnutrition and infested with rats the size of cats (true: more out of economic necessity than conviction), firing his pistol into the air when in a bad mood or to end an argument, removing the backs of chairs, dining alone; though he doesn't do the latter in order to sink into profound reveries, but to hide (not entirely, because they could be heard from any corner of the house) the deafening blasts of flatulence he suffers, but, also, enjoys releasing like the groans of a personal domestic demon who watches over all of them.

Patrick Brontë—who'll end up surviving his whole family and, octogenarian, profiting and benefitting off their legends—buys his daughters all the books they ask for and is in possession of a well-stocked but somewhat antiquated though exceedingly classic library. William Shakespeare, Miguel de Cervantes, Lord Byron, John Milton, Walter Scott, John Bunyan, Daniel Defoe, the Bible and collections of condemnatory sermons, *One Thousand and One Nights*, a variety of gothic fantasies, and folders with illustrations of the imaginary architectures of John Martin. And he has subscriptions to all the weekly and monthly publications of the day, which his daughters and son devour with an insatiable hunger for everything that happens outside and far away. So, a curious mix of the vintage and the contemporary. Lost ancient mythologies melting into the modern news of the latest discoveries of explorers of the Empire in exotic lands, immediately annexable in the name of Queen Victoria. Back then, you read to know you were alive, to live more. Long dresses, heavy cloths, the light of candles, which is the light of the happily awake who make letters dance across pages, as if they were alive and exhaling their breath in the faces of those who inhale them and read them. Is that a happy childhood or a terrible childhood? It depends on the eyes with which you look at and read it. Penelope, she's certain, would have lived it in a levitating ecstasy while any Karma girl would've asked to be sacrificed to save herself from further suffering. Sisters are, for the Karmas, figures to train with in preparation for the inevitable combat and competition against female cousins and friends and girlfriends and wives of brothers and male cousins. Sisters aren't allies, they're rivals. Sisters aren't playmates. Sisters are toys to be broken.

And, returning from a trip, on the 5th of June of 1826 (historic day duly recorded, the day of the Big Bang, the day of let there be light and let there be darkness), Patrick Brontë brings his son Branwell the gift of twelve toy soldiers. Little wooden soldiers. Little soldiers made of wood and not of lead;

and this material detail seems more than pertinent to Penelope: little soldiers made not of the lead from which bullets are fabricated and the dead made, but of the wood from which books are assembled and lives created. Little wooden soldiers Branwell distributes without hesitation among his sisters. Three for each of them and three for him. At first, those little soldiers are Napoleon Bonaparte or the Duke of Wellington and his deputies and troops. But then they get bored of real history and, playing with them, setting off sparks, is no longer enough for the small yet immense Brontës and their imaginary friends. Because it can't contain them: they need imaginary planets. And so it is that the flames of their invented yet ever so real worlds are ignited: the African kingdom of Glass Town, The Angria Empire, the island of Gondal, located in a secret fold in the Pacific Ocean, to the north of the island of Gaaldine and sheltering in turn the kingdoms Gondal and Angora and Exina and Alcona. One kingdom for each sibling. Imaginary lives, role-playing games. Names and personalities like those of Julius Brenzaida, of the Duke of Zamorna, of Geraldine Sidonia, of Augusta Almeda, of Rosno, of Alexander de Elbë. Also, the radical reformulation of the characters of others recreated at will. Rob Roy is no longer Rob Roy when he wakes up on the shores of Verdopolis.

Then, the need for what's told to be written, for the voice to become letters and, so, they turn into writing machines. And, thus, minuscule books, the size of a matchbox, bound with string. "Bed-plays," the Brontës call them, because they write them in bed, at night. There inside, primitive science fiction, fan fiction, anything goes, in microscopic uppercase script without clear punctuation, accompanied by maps, landscapes, drawings. The idea, they say, is that the books be just the right size and weight to be enjoyed by those little wooden soldiers to whom they owe so much, to whom they owe everything. So they write and write. They write much more then than they'll write as adults.

And soon—playtime is over—the sisters go out into the world.

To work as teachers in schools or as governesses for families, jobs where they often experience romantic passions for the master of the house or the smartest teacher at the school, passions that never amount to anything, but find a way into their most important novels. But it doesn't take long for all three to return home, to Haworth and to Glass Town and to Gondal and to Angria. Homes, sweet homes where all rational bitterness is reprocessed as delirious fiction. Better like that. Back in Haworth, Aunt Elizabeth has died and Father Patrick is going blind, and Brother Branwell howls in streets and in pubs, and his bad reputation sinks a local school project to be directed by the madman's three sisters.

And they have no option but to become professional writers.

The idea is to always stay together, to publish as a trio.

They don't say anything to their dearest Branwell—who makes them feel something unconfessable yet closely akin to vicarious shame—so he won't feel left out. Though Branwell is already far away, in his own realm, drifting through the opium vapors. And one night in 1848 he falls into bed and closes his eyes never to rise again; though there are witnesses who claim that, in a final demonstration of stoicism, Branwell gets to his feet and dies standing up and "chronic bronchitis-marasmus," concludes his death certificate, diagnosing something that seems to his three sisters like a tropical and Gondalian malady that, in truth, is nothing but a broken heart.

And the self-publication of a first volume of melancholic poems from three sisters transformed into three brothers goes unnoticed (they sell just two copies; a critic highlights the poems of Ellis, of Emily) and their first manuscripts are rejected by editors who don't even feel the slightest curiosity about finding out who's hiding behind those strange aliases (more than one thinks they're all the same person) that change sex as if it were a mask, but underneath retain the initials of their feminine faces.

But in 1847, with the success of *Jane Eyre* by Currer Bell, everything changes. The manuscript arrives to its editor with a letter in which its author claims he'll be "remembered forever."

And so it will be and so it is and, for the time being, nobody can forget that heroine, forever in distress yet forever overcoming all adversity. *Jane Eyre* is followed by—in a single volume, after many rejections, but its publication justified now because of the success of the eldest sister—the publication of the, at the time, less successful *Wuthering Heights* by Ellis Bell and *Agnes Grey* by Acton Bell.

Currer Bell's novel is celebrated for its structure and its reformulation of classic motifs.

Ellis Bell's novel, on the other hand, frightens the people who read it; some condemn its pages as giving off a whiff of sulfur, others enjoy it almost in secret.

Acton Bell's novel is considered lesser (like Anne herself, its author, less attractive and less spectacular, with a stutter and a desire to never inconvenience anyone; to the extent that her not-so-far-off tombstone gets her age wrong, and her ghost never returned to demand the error be corrected). But, like her subsequent *The Tenant of Wildfell Hall*—also not appreciated by critics upon publication—it's now understood as a proto-feminist text, denouncing the injustices suffered by working women or the enslaved housewives of despotic husbands. Beings in whose face—as can be read and heard there for the first time, with the force of a slap—the bedroom door can be slammed and locked. Charlotte Brontë, always judgmental of her sisters, does not—the same, of course, goes for *Wuthering Heights*—like it. And "At this I cannot wonder. The choice of subject was an entire mistake. Nothing less congruous with the writer's nature could be conceived. The motives which dictated this choice were pure, but, I think, slightly morbid. She had, in the course of her life, been called on to contemplate, near at hand, and for a long time, the terrible effects of talents misused and faculties abused: hers was naturally a sensitive, reserved, and dejected nature; what she saw sank very deeply into her mind; it did her harm. She brooded over it till she believed it to be a duty to reproduce every detail (of course with fictitious characters, incidents, and situations) as a warning to others. She hated her work, but would pursue it."

(The Karma women and girls don't like it either. They don't like anything to do with the Brontës; except Charlotte Brontë, in *Jane Eyre*. They find that ending with the tamed man moving. And it's not like they read the novels, rather that Penelope tells them about them. Upon request yet obligatorily. It occurs to one of the Karmas—whichever, it doesn't matter—that "Penita should do a literary workshop for us, like one of those book clubs, like the one that one black millionaire has." Really, what the Karmas actually want is for Penelope to spend less time reading alone—which makes them very nervous; nothing unnerves a Karma more than solitude, not being seen by and not seeing everyone else—and for her to be with them all the time and talking more. Nothing upsets or unsettles someone who doesn't read more than the happiness of someone reading. Also, of course, as always: the gratifying feeling of having someone, someone else, at their service. That there be someone for them. So Penelope—with all the enthusiasm she can muster, as if describing colors to someone blind from birth—tells them the plots of the novels. And the Karmas, immediately, yawn and deem Anne Brontë's heroines "dummies" and, more than precursors, "really old school." Because, for the Karmas, the truest and most triumphal feminism is not to go on the attack, rather to pretend to be obedient, but actually to do whatever they want, to get their way. When it comes to the shivers and fevers of Catherine Earnshaw, they judge them too complicated and arduous and counterproductive. Besides, *Wuthering Heights* is the great family-unplanning—tribal-deconstruction—novel. And that, for all of them, inseparable at any cost, is like an incomprehensible language and, "of course, Penita must like all of that so much because she doesn't have any family except for that writer brother and that crazy uncle and those dead parents and . . ." And some Karmas are indignant because "that book is a rip-off of that telenovela I saw a long time ago." Why such public scandal, why go around switching houses, when you can always have a hysteric and never-consummated and vacuum-sealed and fantasy tryst with your tennis or riding or hip new jazzercise coach? they wonder. For the Karmas—supreme queens in the art of mental masturbation—there's no sense or benefit in being on everyone's lips. The important thing, on Mount Karma, is to not have people talking about you and to fill that silence talking about someone else, about what this or that so-and-so did, about what they really wanted to say when they said nothing, about what is behind the secret of a secret of a secret that everybody knows because it is a secret. And secrets do not exist if they are not told and cease to be skeletons in the closet in order to become incorruptible living dead or hairy monsters of the kind that feed off the fear of childish adults, hanging in the darkness like genuine fur coats; coats they can't display as trophies out of discourtesy to the tropical climate of Abracadabra, and so they languish there, addicted to naphthalene, and are taken out only every so often to be worn with a sweaty forehead and profile.)

Soon, the secret is recognized as such—look: there goes a secret—because the secret of the true names and sexes of the shadowy sisters Brontë comes to light. And the sisters are a topic of conversation and curiosity in London.

The three become fascinating, like everything that comes in trios: The Holy Trinity and The Three Graces and the Three Furies and the three fairies and the three witches of Macbeth and the three daughters of Lear and the Three Stooges and the three knocks of the ghosts on the table of the medium and the three verbal tenses and three possible answers to the same question and three wishes to be granted.

Everyone wants to meet them and some (like William Makepeace Thackeray) achieve it and get past the walls of their almost-autistic shyness. Charlotte Brontë is, of the three, the most sociable (and spends a good part of her *Jane Eyre* royalties fixing her teeth). Anne Brontë ventures out occasionally just so she can come back in. But they can't rely on Emily Brontë for anything or anyone and she feels betrayed by her sisters' public personalities' betrayal of their private personas.

And Charlotte Brontë will end up getting married against the wishes of her father, who refuses to preside over the nuptial mass (and Charlotte Brontë will die before giving birth, beset by nausea and dehydrated from incessant vomiting). And her sisters die first (they die young, but all surpassing 28.5 years, the average life expectancy of the time, in harsh Haworth, where 42 percent of children don't make it past six years). But first, Currer and Ellis and Acton Bell die.

And it's here that Penelope begins to hate Charlotte Brontë (despite admiring her *Villette* far and away above *Jane Eyre*) and the way in which—with prefaces and postscripts—she manipulates and administers and manages her sisters' ghosts at her pleasure and convenience.

Charlotte Brontë has the forethought to become friends with the writer Elizabeth Gaskell, who later the Brontës' father entrusts to write a posthumous biography, which turned out masterful (and which they publish to great and already-fetishistic-and-freak-fan success, two years after the death of the author of *Jane Eyre*), but not especially reliable. A biography—maybe the first in which someone writes about someone who writes—in which the parameters of the imminent myth of the sisters had already been demarcated in long conversations by the very selective memory of Charlotte Brontë.

There, first Charlotte Brontë invents her sisters and then Elizabeth Gaskell invents Charlotte Brontë in what turns out to be, barely subliminally, a/

another—the first of many—novel about the sisters Brontë, written by one of their fans. Starting with Elizabeth Gaskell, the sisters Brontë are perceived by their increasingly numerous readers and critics as literature's first writer-characters, the sisters Brontë as characters who write, immersed in the atmosphere of the life of a novel.

There, oppressive moors and closed environments and houses taken over and all of that with three girls holding candelabras and speaking in whispers when, really, they had a great time, laughing nonstop, somewhat mad laughter, but laughter all the same. And for Elizabeth Gaskell's book—as well as for postmortem editions of *Wuthering Heights*—Charlotte Brontë has specially devoted herself to the customized (to suit her own ends) re-creation of Emily Brontë and her *Wuthering Heights*. A book that—you don't need to be a Sherlock Holmes or a Sigmund Freud to realize—Charlotte Brontë admires and hates and praises and condemns in supposedly clarifying yet murky "biographical notes," masterpieces of passive aggression, penned by "the editor Currer Bell."

There—with manners resembling those of Ernest Hemingway when, some time later, he conveniently "adapted" the figure more than the genius of Francis Scott Fitzgerald—she judges *Wuthering Heights* with malicious innocence as "rustic, wild, and crude" and "hewn in a wild workshop, with simple tools, out of homely materials." Something like the fascinating offspring of a savant and self-destructive creature and—shamelessly lying—little read and not at all refined. Someone—and Penelope read between the lines—"Stronger than a man, simpler than a child, her nature stood alone. The awful point was that while full of ruth for others, on herself she had no pity; the spirit was inexorable to the flesh; from the trembling hands, the unnerved limbs, the fading eyes, the same service was exacted as they had rendered in health. To stand by and witness this, and not dare to remonstrate, was a pain no words can render . . . In Emily's nature the extremes of vigour and simplicity seemed to meet. Under an unsophisticated culture, inartificial tastes, and an unpretending outside, lay a secret power and fire that might have informed the brain and kindled the veins of the hero; but she had no worldly wisdom; her powers were unadapted to the practical business of life: she would fail to defend her most manifest rights, to consult her most legitimate advantage. An interpreter ought always to have stood between her and the world."

Emily Brontë, for Charlotte Brontë, like someone who, almost blind-folded, steps up and hits the bull's-eye, but who—give it a rest, already, right? Lightning doesn't strike the same place twice and the next time an arrow fired by that archer, lucky in the first place, good or ill, might end up killing someone.

Which, before dying, didn't keep Charlotte Brontë—who, as if in passing, happily mentioned that there were critics who, at first, thought *Wuthering Heights* was a juvenile and immature manuscript of hers and not her sister's—from concerning herself with sweetening her sister's nature into the heroine of her novel *Shirley* (her worst book) and even imitating Emily Brontë in a final inconclusive fragment entitled *Emma* ("The Story of Willie Ellin," featuring an exceedingly mistreated boy à la Heathcliff).

Or even from being accused of throwing an endless continuation to *Wuthering Heights* into the fire, because she considered it too bestial (though *Wuthering Heights*, like the Bible, has the great audacity of including its own sequel/deforming mirror; the first section of *Wuthering Heights* can be under-stood as the book of a writer and the second section as the book of a reader, Penelope says to herself).

"Whether it is right or advisable to create beings like Heathcliff, I do not know: I scarcely think it is," the surviving older sister advised. And, true, hers is the great foundational idea of the madwoman in the attic and the thence-forth cliché of the seduced servant seducing her lord and master. Hers was also, in *Jane Eyre*, to end up offering and delivering that revolutionary line, looking the reader in the eyes, "Reader, I married him" (and not "Reader, he married me" or "Reader, we got married"). There, headed for a horrifying altar, Rochester blind and invalid and dependent on the heroine has learned to wait, patient and complaisant and humiliated, for the hero's inevitable fall. Perfect. Formidable. Congratulations.

But, for Penelope (no matter that almost all contemporary writers rate the formal perfection and subtlety of *Jane Eyre* above the volcanic chaos of *Wuthering Heights*), Emily Brontë went much further. Emily Brontë, unlike her sister, didn't limit herself to locking the mad and flaming Bertha Mason in the flammable heights of Thornfield Hall. Emily Brontë opted to cre-ate the heights of a world where everyone is mad and running wild. Yes, a mad world where Penelope feels she can live not happily (because she'll never be happy, except when she thinks and recites select sections of *Wuthering Heights*) but, yes, madly. A world where—unlike what happens in the majority of books—nobody felt obligated to justify their actions.

Once, Penelope had read the difference between fiction and reality was that a novel explained that "she did this because" while life limited itself to saying that "she did this"; that books are the place where everything was clarified, while in life little or nothing wound up comprehensible. That was why people preferred books. That was also why *Wuthering Heights* was the exception to that rule and why it so resembled Penelope's inexplicable life, where little or nothing was entirely visible.

The blindness of critics regarding *Wuthering Heights* is, maybe, not an attitude to be unexpected, confronted with a work of such brilliant and disturbing power, sending tremors through such a tranquil and bucolic landscape. Penelope always thought one of the unmistakable features of a work of genius is that, at first, it always appears as something nobody expects or thinks they need. Something abnormal and, at first, uncomfortable and out of place. Something that doesn't come with an instruction manual or tool kit. Something that has to sit down and wait for everyone else to get it or catch up to it or learn how to use it.

The perception of a work of genius becomes even more complicated when it is delivered by the hand of a genius who, to top it off, doesn't correspond to the conventional idea of a genius or of how a genius should be and behave.

And so, at first, nobody can see Emily Brontë.

The only person who really saw her and couldn't stop staring at her—her sister and administrator of her unforgettable memory—proceeded to set the first stone, with the posthumous edition of *Wuthering Heights*, of her construction by demolition.

There it reads and is told, settling scores with a love bordering on the most sensitive of reproaches: "Her will was not very flexible, and it generally opposed her interest. Her temper was magnanimous, but warm and sudden; her spirit altogether unbending. Doubtless, had her lot been cast in a town, her writings, if she had written at all, would've possessed another character. Even had chance or taste led her to choose a similar subject, she would have treated it otherwise. Had Ellis Bell been a lady or a gentleman accustomed to what is called 'the world,' her view of the remote and unclaimed region, as well as of the dwellers therein, would have differed greatly from that actually taken by the home-bred country girl. Doubtless, it would have been wider— more comprehensive: whether it would have been more original or more truthful is not so certain. As far as the scenery and locality are concerned, it could scarcely have been so sympathetic: Ellis Bell did not describe as one whose eye and taste alone found pleasure in the prospect; her native hills were far more to her than spectacle; they were what she lived in, and by, as much as the wild birds, their tenants, or as the heather, their produce. Her descriptions, then, of natural scenery are what they should be, and all they should be. Where delineation of human character is concerned, the case is different. I am bound to avow that she had scarcely more practical knowledge of the peasantry among whom she lived, than a nun has of the country people who sometimes pass her convent gates. My sister's disposition was not naturally gregarious; circumstances favoured and fostered her tendency to seclusion; except to go to church or take a walk on the hills, she rarely crossed the threshold of home. Though her feeling for the people round was benevolent, intercourse with them she never sought; nor, with very few exceptions, ever experienced. And yet she knew them: knew their ways, their language, their family histories; she could hear of them with interest, and talk of them with detail, minute, graphic, and accurate; but with them, she rarely exchanged a word. Hence it ensued that what her mind had gathered of the real concerning them, was too exclusively confined to those tragic and terrible traits of which, in listening to the secret annals of every rude vicinage, the memory is sometimes compelled to receive the impress. Her imagination, which was a spirit more sombre than sunny, more powerful than sportive, found in such traits material whence it wrought creations like Heathcliff, like Earnshaw, like Catherine. Having formed these beings, she did not know what she had done. If the auditor of her work, when read in manuscript, shuddered under the grinding influence of natures so relentless and implacable, of spirits so lost and fallen; if it was complained that the mere hearing of certain vivid and fearful scenes banished sleep by night, and disturbed mental peace by day, Ellis Bell would wonder what was meant, and suspect the complainant of affection. Had she but lived, her mind would of itself have grown like a strong tree, loftier, straighter, wider—spreading, and its matured fruits would have attained a mellower ripeness and sunnier bloom; but on that mind time and experience alone could work: to the influence of other intellects it was not amenable."

There, in that territory that's hers and hers alone, according to Charlotte Brontë, are buried the roots of the good depressive wild-woman and of the recluse who stalks the moors. The volatile substance that should never be shaken before use and that moves in a matter of seconds from being sunk in deep wells of melancholy to flying through the skies in ecstasy. That goes from secret tears as she revises her nocturnal verses (those that say things like "I am the only being," "The night is darkening round me," like "Shall earth no more inspire thee," and speak of the imagination as a "Benignant Power" to be worshipped and feared) to the screams of fury when Charlotte Brontë goes through her desk and finds them and proposes publishing them and, later commits the definitive and unforgivable error of revealing the name behind her alias to her new literary friends in London.

The anecdotes abound, yes; because the anecdotes are, to begin with, the boards holding up an as-yet unrecognized genius. She's not considered a genius, no; but she is, yes, without a doubt, *different*.

And Emily Brontë has a great deal of material to offer up when it comes to her primary designation as enigma and, according to one critic, "sphinx of English literature" and "author of the most treacherous of English classics."

Emily Brontë is the one who, unlike her sisters, doesn't want to be "educated," who doesn't need to leave home, and who, when she is obliged to do so, returns soon thereafter on the brink of dying from homesickness, having rejected all pedagogical methods during her stint in Brussels.

Emily Brontë who doesn't speak to acquaintances but speaks to birds.

Emily Brontë who has an extreme relationship with dogs: when one bites her, she says nothing and cauterizes her lacerated flesh to the bone in secret with a red-hot poker so the dog won't be put down; when another dog attacks her, she punches it and kicks it down the stairs, and nobody dares intervene, for it was better not to go near her "when her eyes shone in that way in her pale face and her lips pressed together into a stony line" or something like that. And, yes, Miss Hyde in action who, subsequently, turns back into

Doctor Jekyll and heals the dog that would love her "with the love of a slave" until the end of her days.

Emily Brontë who would rather cough and die than visit a doctor and be cured.

Emily Brontë who, at first, still fresh and not having settled into the dirt of her tomb, is remembered by those who knew her as, merely, "dull" and "intractable" and "always wearing those old-fashioned, ill-fitting dresses and moving clumsily, always stooping," to, then, the engines of immortality kicked into gear, beginning to correct her version of the subject with increasing and increasingly impassioned loquacity. With elegiac imagery that, at times, sounds like involuntarily parody of *Wuthering Heights*: "hers was a mix of extreme timidity with Spartan airs," "she should have been a man—a great navigator. Her powerful reason would have deduced new spheres of discovery from the knowledge of the old," "She had a head for logic, and a capability of argument unusual in a man and rarer indeed in a woman," "she was a wild, original, and striking creature," "she possessed a lovable personality and a very personal elegance and moved with a wild free grace," "mistress of a defiant humor," "a pianist of wonderful fire and brilliancy who, besides, did willingly and untiringly the heaviest household drudgery," "she was the most enigmatic and mysterious of the three Brontë sisters."

The work of genius produced by the genius undergoes a similar process. *Wuthering Heights*, which—contrary to what Charlotte Brontë insists on stating and making us believe—was not unanimously condemned in the beginning, though it did suffer the lashes of critics who seem suddenly abducted by the punishing spirit of Heathcliff, ever since and until not long ago. Renowned academics like F. R. Leavis didn't include it in his *The Great Tradition*, claiming it was "a kind of sport" (adding that the rest of the sisters' work was nothing more than "a permanent interest of a minor kind" and, hey, pins to stick in a little Leavis doll or, better, strangle that little dog he surely has around or, if he's dead, to profane his tomb and dance on his bones; Penelope promises herself she'll do this and, also, promises herself not to mention it to her doctors); and people continue to pop up every so often who don't hesitate to write off *Wuthering Heights* as "a romance novel of certain prestige."

Before, in the beginning, *Wuthering Heights* was: "a disagreeable story," "a strange, inartistic story" seemingly only interested in "painful and exceptional subjects," "We know nothing in the whole range of our fictitious literature which presents such shocking pictures of the worst forms of humanity . . . There is not in the entire *dramatis persona*, a single character which is not utterly hateful or thoroughly contemptible . . . Even the female characters excite something of loathing and much of contempt," "How a human being could have attempted such a book as the present without committing suicide before he had finished a dozen chapters, is a mystery," "It is a compound of vulgar depravity and unnatural horrors," "There seems to be great power in this book but a purposeless power," and "It could be that this book was written by a woman, but it was not written by a lady."

And yet, in breaking storm, amid so much outcry, there are moved and admiring voices that, even from the beginning, start to put *Wuthering Heights* in its rightful place: "Respecting a book so original as this, and written with so much power of imagination, it is natural that there should be many opinions. Indeed, its power is so predominant that it is not easy after a hasty reading to analyze one's impressions so as to speak of its merits and demerits with confidence. We have been taken and carried through a new region, a melancholy waste, with here and there patches of beauty," "Yes, as Lockwood describes in its opening pages: a perfect misanthrope's heaven," "This novel contains undoubtedly powerful writing, and yet it seems to be thrown away. Mr. Ellis Bell, before constructing the novel, should have known that forced marriages, under threats and in confinement are illegal, and parties instrumental thereto can be punished. And second, that wills made by young ladies' minors are invalid. The volumes are powerfully-written records of wickedness, and they have a moral—they show what Satan could do with the law of Entail," "This is a strange book and the people who make up the drama are savages ruder than those who lived before the days of Homer," "It is humanity in this wild state that the author of *Wuthering Heights* essays to depict," "In the whole story not a single trait of character is elicited which can command our admiration, not one of the fine feelings of our nature seems to have formed a part in the composition of its principal actors. In spite of the disgusting coarseness of much of the dialogue, and the improbabilities of much of the plot, we are spellbound," "*Wuthering Heights* is a strange sort of book—baffling all regular criticism; yet, it is impossible to begin and not finish it; and quite as impossible to lay it aside afterward and say nothing about it. In *Wuthering Heights* the reader is shocked, disgusted, almost sickened by the details of cruelty, inhumanity, and the most diabolical hate and vengeance, and anon come passages of powerful testimony to the supreme power of love—even over demons in the human form. The women in the book are of a strange fiendish-angelic nature, tantalizing, and terrible, and the men are indescribable out of the book itself. Yet, toward the close of the story occurs the following pretty, soft picture, which comes like the rainbow after a storm . . . We strongly recommend all our readers who love novelty to get this story, for we can promise them that they never have read anything like it before," "The author only had three ideas: but those ideas are nothing more and nothing less than life and love and death," "The nightmare of a superheated imagination," "Its characters do not resemble any others in our reading experience, so we must leave it to our readers to decide what sort of book it is."

And the readers decide.

And soon *Wuthering Heights* turns into a fetish object of the sighing and moaning schoolgirls of the end of that century who sleep with it and delve into its ardors under boarding-school pillows. Algernon Charles Swinburne admires "the dark unconscious" of its author. Dante Gabriel Rossetti refers to *Wuthering Heights* as "A fiend of a book—an incredible monster [. . .] The action is laid in hell—only it seems places and people have English names there." And a short time later, the philosopher May Sinclair inaugurates the idea of Emily Brontë as mystic-proto-ecologist. Someone points out that *"Wuthering Heights* is a more difficult book to understand than *Jane Eyre*, because Emily was a greater poet than Charlotte" and someone elevates it to the heights of "a kind of prose *Kubla Khan*." The languid feminists and the muscular feminists and lesbians of action and the passive lesbians hoist it aloft like a standard and the suicide poets Anne Sexton and Sylvia Plath (driven mad by that Heathcliff Ted Hughes) dedicate their own crepuscular poems to it. And *Breakfast at Tiffany*'s Holly Golightly recommends to the writer that he write "something like *Wuthering Heights*." And Yoko Ono (telephonic typer of aphorisms like "If you can't sleep, visualize your friends and enemies being happy. Go to sleep thinking about that") screeched in "You're the One" that she is Cathy and John is Heathcliff. And mentions of the novel in *An American Werewolf in London* and *The Simpsons* and in *Mad Men* and in an interview with the actor Johnny Depp where he asks and answers "Am I a romantic? I have seen *Wuthering Heights* ten times. I'm a romantic."

And Penelope—who can't help but wonder if Johnny Depp has *read* *Wuthering Heights* at least once in addition to having seen it ten times—cuts out and compiles and stores all this information in scrapbooks and on hard disks. Everything Penelope knows about just one thing. Information now deposited, along with all the rest—shall we say Brontë-esquely—of her "earthly possessions," in a basement in the gothic mansion where, now, her bad brother lives, guardian of her memory, of the memory of her, she who can't forget anything and can't remember *that*. And Penelope agrees: there's nothing worse than older siblings who say they're protecting you and who, so you don't fall down, chain your foot to the wall and, yes, can even end up burning inside your head the second novel you never managed to write. And nothing bothers Penelope more than those interpretations that claim Catherine and Heathcliff are stepsiblings, daughter and son of the same father. And that their passion feeds on something so crude as second-rate incest, when, actually, it is a love beyond love. A love for which love is nothing more than the entryway to a straight-lined labyrinth, or the elevator to a launch tower to the stars, or the ladder of the tallest diving board off which to plunge to the bottom of all things.

"You have killed me," says Catherine, more alive than ever and on the brink of death, to a dying Heathcliff who will live on after her for many long years.

Here inside, as it relates to feelings, for Penelope, everything is much more clumsy and mild and fleeting and as if anesthetized.

Common love is, in the words of Catherine, "like the foliage in the woods: time will change it, I'm well aware, as winter changes the trees" and it looks nothing like "the eternal rocks" beneath the roots.

Here, in Our Lady of Our Lady of Our Lady of . . . Penelope likes to tell herself that "if the heart could think like the brain, the heart would stop immediately." Voluntary victim of sudden cardiac arrest. Ripping open its shirt, sending all its buttons flying, to flip the secret switch that marks the end of all heartbeats and the immediate echo of the next heartbeat.

Heartbeats like footsteps up a ramp that climbs and climbs and climbs only to reach a wall with no way out. A wall that, the effort of trying unsuccessfully to tear it down, ends up breaking your heart in a thousand pieces.

Emily Brontë (unlike her two sisters, who write about society's external forces) becomes the first great explorer of the tyrannical internal forces (in *Wuthering Heights*, novel-of-homes, the domestic is elevated to the Olympic) and thus the psychoanalysts have new archetypes to assist in their diagnoses.

And the legend continues and grows until it reaches Penelope when she's going through puberty.

And Penelope reads *Wuthering Heights* and she can't believe what she's reading, but, from then on, she believes in nothing else. *Wuthering Heights* as religion and state of mind and way of life.

A book that, as much in the moment of its publication as right now, is simultaneously old-fashioned and avant-garde.

A book that's mad and wise. A book that's imperfectly perfect and perfectly imperfect.

A brilliant book, both idiot and savant.

A book where, yes, everything is love and hate and life and death, but that's really all you need.

And it's not that such things don't happen outside books: it's that such things don't happen in any other book that's not *Wuthering Heights*, whose only defect is coming to an end and being unique—being one of a kind.

So, Penelope keeps reading everything else, everything that comes with it. Penelope reads everything the sisters Brontë ever wrote and even what the brother Brontë wrote, and a good part of what has been written about them and him; but she always goes back to the beginning, to all those copies in all those languages and with all those different covers for the same book that, as there's only one, she bought whenever possible so she could begin it again from the beginning. And reread it as if it were the first time, unforgettable and with the uncertain texture of a fever dream and immoveable structure of the most precise insomnia. All those copies of *Wuthering Heights* lying there, underground, with her bad brother as gravedigger, whistling amid the headstones, like in that movie they saw when they were kids in which the protagonist lived obsessed with being buried alive. His whole life in all those boxes, long and skinny like coffins.

History of a coffin. An open coffin, like one of those cases that's never entirely closed and one—maybe the most disturbing of all—of the many mysteries around and on all sides and above and below *Wuthering Heights*.

A unique case because, yes, there abound optical illusions and visual mirages; but Penelope knows of no other case of hallucination that doesn't just generate images but imagined letters.

So, that thing that does or doesn't happen with the corpse of Catherine Earnshaw in *Wuthering Heights*.

Does Heathcliff embrace death? Does he dance with death?

Everyone has seen it and swears they read it, but nobody can find that moment in the book when they look for it.

Yes: in chapter XVI, Heathcliff pays his respects to Catherine's still-warm body in her chambers in Thrushcross Grange and inside a locket, after removing Linton's, inserts a lock of his own.

And in chapter XXIX, Heathcliff tells Nelly Dean that, while they were digging Linton's grave, he told the sexton "to remove the earth off her coffin lid, and I opened it. I thought, once, I would have stayed there, when I saw her face again—it is hers yet—he had hard work to stir me; but he said it would change, if the air blew on it, and so I struck one side of the coffin loose—and covered it up—not Linton's side, damn him! I wish he'd been soldered in lead—and I bribed the sexton to pull it away, when I'm laid there, and slide mine out too. I'll have it made so, and then, by the time Linton gets to us, he'll not know which is which!" Nelly Dean is horrified hearing these words and she gets indignant because it's not good to disturb the dead (but she's also already licking her lips with the pleasure she'll get from telling something so twisted and insane); and Heathcliff tells her he hasn't disturbed anybody and he feels quite relieved. "Disturbed her? No! She has disturbed me, night and day, through eighteen years—incessantly— remorselessly—till yesternight—and yesternight I was tranquil. I dreamt I was sleeping the last sleep, by that sleeper, with my heart stopped, and my cheek frozen against hers." And then Heathcliff, as if in a trance and with the voice of a sleepwalker, recalls what happened almost two decades before, during the burial of his beloved. "In the evening I went to the churchyard. It blew bleak as winter—all round was solitary: I didn't fear that her fool of a husband would wander up the den so late—and no one else had business to bring them there. Being alone, and conscious two yards of loose earth was the sole barrier between us, I said to myself—'I'll have her in my arms again! If she be cold, I'll think it is this north wind that chills me; and if she be motionless, it is sleep.' I got a spade from the toolhouse, and began to delve with all my might—it scraped the coffin; I fell to work with my hands; the wood commenced cracking about the screws, I was on the point of attaining my object, when it seemed that I heard a sigh from some one above, close at the edge of the grave, and bending down. 'If I can only get this off,' I muttered, 'I wish they may shovel in the earth over us both!' and I wrenched more desperately still. There was another sigh, close at my ear. I appeared to feel the warm breath of it displacing the sleet-laden wind. I knew no living thing in flesh and blood was by—but, as certainly as you perceive the approach to some substantial body in the dark, though it cannot be discerned, so certainly I felt that Cathy was there, not under me, but on the earth. A sudden sense of relief flowed, from my heart, through every limb. I relinquished my labour of agony, and turned consoled at once, unspeakably consoled. Her presence was with me: it remained while I re-filled the grave, and led me home. You may laugh, if you will, but I was sure I should see her there. I was sure she was with me, and I could not help talking to her."

In short: Heathcliff never removes the body from the coffin.

Nor does he dance with it.

Though it's not entirely clear (like so many things are unclear regarding Penelope and her parents and her son) if he does, at least, touch it; because Nelly Dean guesses that, during the wake, Heathcliff takes advantage of a moment when the body is alone: "He did not omit to avail himself of the opportunity, cautiously and briefly; too cautiously to betray his presence by the slightest noise; indeed, I shouldn't have discovered that he had been there, except for the disarrangement of the drapery about the corpse's face, and for the observing on the floor a curl of light hair, fastened with a silver thread, which, on examination, I ascertained to have been taken from the locket hung round Catherine's neck. Heathcliff had opened the trinket and cast out its contents, replacing them by a black lock of his own. I twisted the two, and enclosed them together."

History of another coffin: Emily Brontë, depressed in the wake of her brother's death (many speak of incestuous passion, others say he was the one who wrote *Wuthering Heights* not her), falls ill and wastes away. They fear it's the flu she contracted at Branwell's burial, contaminated water is considered, and that nineteenth-century and oh so functional ailment, consumption, is blamed. And Emily Brontë stops eating (in recent years, it has been reconsidered and re-diagnosed as the first case of celebrity anorexia) and proceeds to vanish like a shadow. And Emily Brontë dies, like Catherine Earnshaw, not in a bed, but on a sofa. Or perhaps this isn't true *either* and it's another of the licenses Charlotte Brontë (who reports in a letter that she was "in Eternity—yes, there is no Emily in Time or on Earth now . . . I will only say, sweet is rest after labour and calm after tempest, and repeat again and again that Emily knows that now" and doesn't miss the chance to quickly compose the lacrimonious poem "On the Death of Emily Jane Brontë" reproaching her, on this occasion, for the pain her death produces) when it came to novelizing their lives. And, according to Elizabeth Gaskell, that night, Charlotte Brontë walks around and around that round table hundreds of times until she collapses.

But this is true: the carpenter hired to make Emily Brontë's casket commented that never in all his experience had he "made so narrow a shell for an adult. Barely sixteen inches."

Keeper, Emily Brontë's dog, the one she once almost beat to death and whose injuries she healed, came to the burial and, witnesses there claim, howled inconsolably.

More names, another surname. Penelope's conversion of Brontë into Tulpa. A name she owes to Lina Liberman, possibly the only person Penelope ever loved and whom she still loves, and whose adventurous and subversive face and profile she honors with the invented figure of Stella D'Or.

Lina, though adopted by a couple of Jews beyond orthodox—and oh how Penelope envies her for being adopted, for not knowing where she comes from and, as such, coming from everywhere—is a polymorphous and perverse mystic and she gives Penelope the gift of a ring with the Buddhist and Tibetan symbol of the Tulpa. A sound and word that means "to construct" and "to create," Lina tells her. The ability to invoke a solid entity with the power of your mind. To fill the sky with astral bodies, to cover it with living beings. "Like Gautama Buddha did in the *Divyavadana*," she explains to Penelope. And Lina details the process by which to achieve this miracle. And Penelope thinks it's not all that different from creating a literary character. Layer by layer. Detail by detail. Physical contexture, voice, eye color, clothes, abilities, name. As if being dressed up from the most absolute nakedness. The last thing added to a Tulpa is its memory, its story. A story that you must take great care, Lina warns, not to make too similar to your own, because then the Tulpa might feel the irresistible temptation to replace its author. And the author—as has so often happened in the history of literature, the first person for the third—will allow and even encourage that replacement, until death do them vanquish but never does them part.


And—this is true but seems a lie—the morning of Penelope's wedding to the comatose Maxi Karma, Hiriz orders Lina killed because, she claims, she "mistook her for a thief or a sniper" when she saw her up there, in a tree, not sharp shooting, but filming the delirium of that wedding. Lina dying of laughter, laughing at everyone and everything. And that's why Hiriz gives the order to have her executed. A single shot. Rifle with a silencer. Nobody hears anything or—much better and so much easier than not hearing—pretends not to hear anything: a sport within the Karma family that, along with pretending not to see and pretending not to speak, configures the existential triathlon of the clan. And Lina makes almost no sound when she falls and disappears into a huge rose bush. Lina sinks into the flowers and thorns with a surprised smile. And the whole scene is like an old silent movie with that simple and efficient and primitive special effect. Cutting a few meters of celluloid. And sticking it back together. And what was there is no longer there. And Lina is no longer there. Her body will immediately and discretely be removed by servants who attend to what nobody wants to attend to and abandoned alongside a back road. And, when it is found several days later, swollen by the sun and the heat, it will be written off as just another victim of the violence between Abracadabra's rival narco gangs. And, yes, the autopsy will reveal traces of illegal substances floating in Lina's blood; thus: "the girl was a drug addict and degenerate and delinquent, indeed," no need for any follow-up investigation. And, outside of all the preceding, to what just happened, to what and whom (the life of Lina, the life, Lina) has just come to an end forever so eternity can begin (the immortal death of Lina Liberman like the immortal death of Catherine Earnshaw), Penelope arrives to the altar repeating over and over, as if she were praying, in the lowest yet most deafening voice of thought, something she once read in a book. Not in her favorite book, *Wuthering Heights*, but yes in a book very close to that one, a direct relative of her favorite book. She already quoted it. "Reader, I married him." But in that moment, Penelope is not thinking about *Jane Eyre* but about *Wuthering Heights*, about the book to which she has wedded herself until the end of time so, once there, she can return to the first page and start to read it all over again, as if it were the first time, as if it were the last time, as if it were the first and last wedding night.

Lina's death—change of relationship status—turns Penelope into a writer. Not right away. A little time has yet to pass. A few years that seem centuries. Meanwhile and in the meantime then—"in the dark night of the soul," as her parents used to say all the time, busting out laughing who knows why but probably at everyone and everything—Penelope asks herself questions without answer. Questions of the kind that don't expect an answer and, at some point, she decides the way to answer them and to answer herself is to write them down in books.

In the books the Tulpa sisters write, high in the sky, about Stella D'Or and little dAlien down on Earth.

She's going to write those novels as if they were, all of them, mutant variations of Emily Brontë's second novel that may never have existed, it doesn't matter.

"The Brontë sisters on the Moon!" thought Penelope, thinking this is the kind of loony thinking only a lunatic can think.

And then, following the instructions of the immortal dead Lina, she set about creating tulpas and sisters.

The reader is a robber of tulpas. Someone who uses and abuses bodies and souls created by others and incorporates them into that other life within life, that life that takes place inside books. Letting someone else do the hard and dirty work first and only then, at the end, with the table set and guests at the ready, does the reader show up. And only having to sit down beside them and stare at them (of all gazes, reading is most like staring, though the pupils never stop moving and contracting and expanding depending on the situation) and to make very personal modifications to them, so they become unique and nontransferable.

Thus Penelope cannot conceive of the existence of a Heathcliff or a Cathy not her own, the ones she didn't make but did finish to suit her needs and taste.

And so, in the solitude of her cell/study, Penelope toys with the cast of *Wuthering Heights*, handing out roles and speeches written by Emily Brontë, sure; but at the same convinced she wrote them doubtlessly suspecting that, sooner or later, she—Penelope—would arrive to recount them, to count on them.

And, it's true, it's a somewhat kitsch and somewhat cliché and somewhat cheesy device: the shadows of your creatures passing through walls to evolve around the bed of the one who evokes and invokes them. There are various biopics that end like this. And many are the people moved by those farewell scenes: the communion between creator and creation and all of that.

The unsolvable problem for Penelope is that, after her stint in Abraca-dabra, the cast of her favorite book gives her a bit of a headache, because they have, for her, been *karmatized*.

She finds herself constantly drawing equivalences between the characters in *Wuthering Heights* and her one-time, now distant in-laws who, though they've been left so far away and so far behind, are always at her side. Not all of them all at once; just a few at a time; as if taking shifts and poking out their heads, heads she tries to cut off, but really, what's the point, one always escapes.

And something seems to have gone wrong with all of them, something that weighs on her: like the Karmas, the characters in *Wuthering Heights* only have each other to feed on and feed off of, to devour and spit out, to chew up and digest and eliminate with no chance of escape. The Karmas only think of the Karmas and yet, when saying goodbye for but a few hours or even a few minutes—always afraid of being the first to leave a gathering and that everyone will start talking about them as soon as they depart—they don't say "We'll see you soon" but "We'll look you up soon," because they think fixing their eyes on something is bad manners. To look is elegant and aristocratic, to see is vulgar and plebeian. The rich look and the poor see. You look at the surface whereas you see into the depths. To look the way you look at a sunrise and say, "How pretty" and that a sunrise be exactly like a sunset: there are no shades, there are no senses. Long live indifference and glory to uniformity. Superficial gamma rays instead of penetrating X-rays. Not to see yourself but yes to look at yourself and better to half-close your eyes and use your tongue to stab people in the back and talk behind their backs, the tongue like a stinger.

And the Karmas, in their way, are very *Wuthering Heights*: because they never do what they say they're going to do. They do something else. Or they do something else even though they think they're doing what they said they were going to do. And that gives them a sense of zombie accomplishment and empty plenitude. To be thinking all the time about what they would do or what they should do or what they would like to do to and, once all those possibilities are considered, to opt for nothing, or that form of nothing that's doing the same thing as always or what everyone else would do. The Karmas, like characters from *Wuthering Heights*, but in a bastardized version, prisoners of a private loop where the rest of the world doesn't exist.

Just in case.

Better like this.

And—for once it is going to be Penelope who steals something from her bad brother, that symbol he uses to separate paragraphs in his notebooks— here they come and here they are, and she looks at them and sees them:


† *Heathcliff* / It's enough and more than enough, because hurricanes are named pure first name and no last name. What's known is he's named in memory of someone who lived briefly and died soon thereafter. A phantom child of Mr. Earnshaw, a dead son. And so, a stigma from the beginning. The obligation to be someone who never was and thus Heathcliff sets out to

be someone like never before and to become unforgettable so everyone forgets that other Heathcliff who was but a quick sketch. And, sure, Heathcliff
is one of the most romantic and impassioned characters in all the history of
literature. But he's also a psychopathic sociopath, a control freak, a possessive
obsessive, a superb bad guy, a dangerous bipolar whose ferocity is even more
frightening than that of those hunting dogs that lap at your ankles and are
always ready to go bite whatever they're told to, after watching their master
strangle a puppy with a wicked smile, one of those smiles that bares teeth
and fangs. And no: being an orphan discovered in and taken off the streets
of the Liverpool port doesn't justify Heathcliff or his wrathful nature. Or,
later, being abused by his stepbrother or driven mad by his hysteric stepsister.
Because, in the words of Nelly Dean, "from the very beginning, Heathcliff bred bad feeling in the house." And, on the heels of such certainty, so
many questions. Is Heathcliff Arabic, or is he a gypsy, or is he black, or is
he the bastard and unacknowledged son of Mr. Earnshaw? Does Heathcliff
get rich trading slaves in The New World or did he distinguish himself in
the early wars in the Colonies? Might Heathcliff have been in the Carib-
bean and encountered *Jane Eyre*'s Edward Fairfax Rochester in Jamaica?
Or might Heathcliff be, perhaps, the abandoned son of those two, though
the dates don't align and match up? (I'm the only person who thinks about
these things, I, who am madder than Bertha Mason, Penelope thinks.) Or,
as is hinted at here and there, did Heathcliff make a pact with the devil?
Might Heathcliff be the true father of Catherine's daughter? Is Heathcliff
a sublimated version of the unspeakable incestuous love—consummated or
not—that Emily Brontë feels for her dissolute brother in the process of dis-
solution? Did Heathcliff beat Hindley to death? Is Heathcliff based on that
dark-skinned orphan Emily Brontë's great-great-grandfather brought home
from Liverpool? Or is Heathcliff—as Nelly Dean wonders—"a ghoul or a
vampire?" Or might he be a changeling, one of those children kidnapped by
fairies and returned as monstrous beings or peter-panic entities who torment
mortals with their actions? (And Penelope prefers not to consider this possibility, not to continue that line of thinking: not to travel down the path,
without map or compass, of lost children, disappeared to never reappear, as if
by the art of magic, the blackest of magic.)

Nothing is clear in and about and with Heathcliff.

Nothing beyond his skin tone and his gothic and vengeful personality, foreshadowing those of Edmund Dantès and Bruce Wayne.

Heathcliff is a hermetic character, sealed of his own volition in the absolute void, but to whom—as tends to happen with the best mysteries to be solved—you can attribute anything. "A riddle wrapped in a mystery inside an enigma," as Winston Churchill said of Russia, and might Heathcliff have been born of the union of a Siberian father and a prostitute from the taverns along the River Mersey?

Anything is possible.

And for that reason, Sigmund Freud doesn't hesitate to analyze him mythologically and Karl Marx to consider him the embodiment of the New Man and Albert Camus to take him as the inspiration for his Man in Revolt.

And, oh, the many Heathcliffs in other books by other authors. Pastiches that, in general, tell what Emily Brontë never told (generally what happened in his three missing years and how Heathcliff made his fortune) with titles as imaginative as *Return to Wuthering Heights*, *Heathcliff* or *Heathcliff: The Return to Wuthering Heights*. Or mash-ups that make him a wolf man or vampire or zombie or a sex addict (or as a wolf-sex addict vampire-zombie man). Or as an unsurpassable and insatiable lover who enjoys innovative positions and is able to prolong his pleasure beyond even the tantric (tricks learned, perhaps, during his absence abroad). Or novelized biographies of the Brontës. Or even detective novels in which he lives and dies to find and hold onto the manuscript of Emily Brontë's second novel that in the end Charlotte Brontë didn't destroy but that . . . Or to reencounter him, more or less unconsciously, under other names like Jay "Gatz" Gatsby or Lázló "English Patient" Almásy. (And Penelope finds it amusing that the protagonists of the film adaptation of that last novel, *The English Patient*, have since been reunited in a version of *Wuthering Heights* that, though it costs Penelope to admit it, wasn't all that bad and at least, for once, didn't overlook the detail of telling the plot of Emily Brontë's novel in its entirety; though Wuthering Heights, as in the majority of adaptations, is depicted there, architecturally, more like a photogenic haunted mansion than like the rather dilapidated and possessed estate described in the novel.) In any case, no derivative is on a level with the original and no antecedent, not even that Greco-Shakespearean, is, for

Penelope on a level with her Heathcliff. With the Heathcliff whom she read for the first time when she was a girl after seeing him on television. For Penelope, Heathcliff is like a black hole that devours and expels all light; like an expelled and fallen Luciferian angel; like a devil ascending to reconquer the heavens only believing in thunder and lightning, declaiming things like "I have no pity! I have no pity! The more the worms writhe, the more I yearn to crush out their entrails! It is a moral teething; and I grind with greater energy in proportion to the increase of pain." Heathcliff forgives no one and loves no one (not even his wife Isabella or his son Linton, whom he tortures with care and devotion) other than his completely irreal idea of the dead Catherine Earnshaw, of his Cathy. His rage, at last, near his end, is extinguished with an almost existentialist sigh and with a sincere confession to his housekeeper Nelly Dean, always all ears and blabbing mouth: "It is a poor conclusion, is it not . . . an absurd termination to my violent exertions? I get levers and mattocks to demolish the two houses, and train myself to be capable of working like Hercules, and when everything is ready and in my power, I find the will to lift a slate off either roof has vanished! My old enemies have not beaten me; now would be the precise time to revenge myself on their representatives: I could do it; and none could hinder me. But where is the use? I don't care for striking: I can't take the trouble to raise my hand! That sounds as if I had been labouring the whole time only to exhibit a fine trait of magnanimity. It is far from being the case: I have lost the faculty of enjoying their destruction, and I am too idle to destroy for nothing. Nelly, there is a strange change approaching—I'm in its shadow at present—I take so little interest in my daily life, that I hardly remember to eat and drink . . . . The entire world is a dreadful collection of memoranda that she did exist, and that I have lost her! . . . I have neither a fear, nor a presentiment, nor a hope of death—Why should I? With my hard constitution, and temperate mode of living, and unperilous occupations, I ought to, and probably *shall* remain above ground, till there is scarcely a black hair on my head—And yet I cannot continue in this condition!—I have to remind myself to breathe— almost remind my heart to beat! And it is like bending back a stiff spring . . . it is by compulsion, that I do the slightest act, not prompted by one thought, and by compulsion, that I notice anything alive or dead, which is not associated with one universal idea . . . I have a single wish, and my whole being and faculties are yearning to attain it. They have yearned toward it so long, and so unwaveringly, that I'm convinced it *will* be reached—and *soon*— because it has devoured my existence—I am swallowed in the anticipation of its fulfilment. My confessions have not relieved me—but, they may account for some otherwise unaccountable phases of humour which I show. O, God! It is a long fight, I wish it were over!"

And the problem with wishes is that sometimes they come true, but, a few mornings later, Heathcliff doesn't seem all that upset being discovered by Nelly Dean, in his rain-soaked bed, the window open, and his hand resting on the windowsill, as if waiting to be held by another hand. There is the master, loveless, but at last at peace, "laid on his back. His eyes met mine so keen, so fierce, I started; and then he seemed to smile . . . I hasped the window; I combed his black long hair from his forehead; I tried to close his eyes—to extinguish, if possible, that frightful, lifelike gaze of exultation, before anyone else beheld it. They would not shut—they seemed to sneer at my attempts, and his parted lips, and sharp, white teeth sneered too! Taken with another fit of cowardice, I cried for Joseph. Joseph shuffled up, and made a noise, but resolutely refused to meddle with him. 'Th' divil's harried off his soul,' he cried, 'and he muh hev his carcass intuh t' bargain, for ow't Aw care! Ech! what a wicked un he looks girnning at death!'"

Then, a few hours later, a boy claims to have seen the ghost of "Heath-cliff, and a woman," among the crags, revealing themselves to mortals and making them realize how lucky they are, because, as someone once sang in a song Penelope once heard, "If you have ghosts then you have everything."

And no, it's not true: there's nobody like Heathcliff among the Karmas; but Penelope can't help but connect the man's fits of rage and despotism to the dictatorial character of Mamagrandma (here another sex change, but male to female) reigning over the fates of her entire clan ever since the death/ disappearance of Papagrandpa of whom nobody speaks. Mamagrandma like the woman who takes up arms and bites bullets; playing chess with the pieces of her family on the board of Mount Karma and always winning; getting her way and deciding who gets in and who's left out and who'll be expelled never to return. With Mamagrandma on the command bridge and at the helm and with her thumb always hovering over the red button, it's not that nobody does what they want and only does what Mamagrandma wants. No, it's something far more disturbing: Mamagrandma makes you do what she wants you to do while simultaneously convincing you you're doing exactly what you want to do. Mamagrandma has the gift of all great political dictators and the most powerful religious leaders. That of, in her name and image, making you march toward the conquest of the Promised Land, without giving it a second thought, drink that cup of poison in order to ascend to that comet that'll take you back to Heaven. The difference is that Heaven and the Promised Land are already at and on Mount Karma. And if you go, you'll soon return asking, please, that they let you back in, like the spectral Cathy, lost and roaming the moors, asking Lockwood, "Let me in—let me in!"

Once, before disappearing from the "literary circuit," on the only tour she ever did, in New York and for one of those festivals, Penelope ended up sharing a roundtable with an important writer, prestigious, serious. She assumes someone thought it a good joke: bring together the éminence grise (but really cool and millennial and de luxe countercultural) with the colorful superstar of the youth who were suddenly reading as if possessed, but reading only her. The evening didn't begin very well (the huge auditorium full to overflowing was composed of an audience eight to two in her favor); but the writer, no doubt accustomed to such things, was kind to her, and told her when he'd started writing "it didn't occur to anybody you should go out on tour to appear and present and to sign and to *get to know* your readers so they can *know* you. You wrote and that was it. The end. The book. Now, the book is almost what matters least . . . Now, writing seems to be merely the prologue and they want you to be like a politician or a preacher and for you to offer an opinion about everything and I wonder if we aren't betraying the basic idea of the whole thing: the mystery of creating an object that contains all the explanations for those individuals who know how to read them on their own, without needing us to go around from one auditorium to the next pointing them out, ringing our little bells, like leprous visionaries of the end of the world . . . And, seeing ourselves fade away, so much easier and quicker when we're judged and condemned. Because it's much easier to read a writer than a piece of writing, right?" And the writer cleverly suggested to her that, to avoid falling into clichés, he read something of hers and she read something of his. She can't remember what he read of hers (maybe a fragment where a rocketless astronaut wanders across the sands of the Sonora Desert, maybe that invocation of the spirit of Stella D'Or); but she remembers perfectly what she read of his. And that she read it in a faltering voice, more broken than fragile, wondering how and why it was the writer had ended up choosing precisely those brutal and illuminating pages for her to read. Something about the family as "the cradle of the disinformation of the world" and that there must be something in the idea of the family that generates constant error. Something that is due perhaps to the excessive closeness and the heat of being near one another, and thus that the family process was always working toward being sealed off and isolated from the outside world. Something about how that was why the strongest families with the tightest bonds tend to be produced in less developed societies, where not knowing, or, even better, not wanting to know or acknowledge, becomes a weapon of survival. Something about the family as a sanctuary where magic and superstition blend together like clan orthodoxy. And that the family, as an entity, tends to be more powerful in places where reality is more powerfully misinterpreted. And Penelope read that and thought, "This man is a sage." Penelope read that and said to herself that yes, that just so, that exactly: that the Karmas were the least bookish people she'd ever known. The highest concentration of nonreaders per square meter; creatures that asked themselves and asked you if you were okay or bored or depressed anytime they saw you reading, by yourself. But, also—as her own damned and thieving and bad brother tested and verified—the Karmas as the easiest creatures to introduce as characters in any book. They are so classic and nineteenth-century in their depths and their forms and Penelope envies them so much for that. Family as subject is one of the two pillars of the novelistic genre. The other pillar is the solitary journey. And the Karmas are always traveling en masse away from and toward themselves, asking to be let in without ever leaving, so alone on the inside, so accompanied on the outside.

And Penelope traveled toward them. And it was one of those journeys some would designate a *bad trip*, others an odyssey, and everyone as unforgettable.

And it's known that the nature of memories with respect to persistence is good or bad or more or less ambiguous.

† *Catherine Earnshaw Linton* / The dead woman calling outside the window-panes to be let in. Again, forever: "Let me in—let me in!" And, before, alive and capering about, impassioned romantic temperament, with a tendency to run across the moors with the lower classes without that, when the time comes, keeping her from also running off toward a well-to-do marriage. Thus, Catherine Earnshaw the dreamer for whom Heathcliff turns into the nightmare of all those around him and the Catherine Earnshaw who marries Edgar Linton, young sir and master of Thrushcross Grange, without really knowing what she's getting into. Like when someone goes swimming in the sea with a hangover and gets swept out too far by the undertow. And Penelope always liked that Edgar Linton succumbed to her charms after Catherine Earnshaw gave him a good ear-boxing. Which, Penelope thinks, no doubt establishes a pattern of behavior for what will be their brief but intense married life. Edgar Linton idolizes Catherine Earnshaw and Catherine Earnshaw is at her best when she's being idolized. As tends to happen with such specimens, on her deathbed, with Edgar Linton at her side, the volatile Catherine Earnshaw Linton only recalls the idyllic moments of her youth with Heathcliff, while her husband looks on, thinking he'd much rather move to a Jane Austen novel. One of those novels the Brontë sisters didn't like at all and in which there was nothing they cared for besides their revolutionary use of free indirect style and masterful dialogue. Novels the Brontë sisters looked down on, considering them too polite and lacking passion. Novels whose heroines—unlike the high-velocity and vertiginous and marathonic and careening Catherine Earnshaw—are, merely, "good walkers," moving from one house to another across landscapes of meadows and hedges, perfectly maintained by an army of gardeners, concerned with trees if and only if they're of the family-tree variety, appraising the branches of possible marriages and, most important of all, trimming the hedges of perfect matrimonies to suit their needs.

And, yes, there's something of Catherine Earnshaw in Hiriz, Maxi's sister and Penelope's sister-in-law; but there's a lot more of Emma Woodhouse.

Hiriz, capricious and calculating, but exceedingly preoccupied that nobody miss out on her marvelous person, someone she loves so much and who, if she loves herself so much, there must be a reason, deserves to be so beloved by so many.

† *Nelly Dean* / If she had lived during the Cold War, Nelly Dean would've been the greatest double agent ever, Penelope thinks. She also knows how to tell a good story, because Nelly Dean is a sharp-eyed voyeur and powerful-eared listener. Penelope read, once, in one of the best pastiches of *Wuthering Heights*, Nelly Dean communicating one last time with Lockwood. Sending him a letter and summoning him so she can, yes and for real this time, tell him everything she never told him, everything she left out. And it wasn't bad as a novel, but Penelope didn't like it as a gesture: the whole pointing out inconsistencies in the plot of *Wuthering Heights*, when actually those inconsistencies are not defects. No. They are the dynamic constants of a race apart, of beings not exactly human, castaways on dry and lonely land. Like Mount Karma. Everyone is a little bit Nelly Dean on Mount Karma. Everyone talks among themselves about everyone else, but never asks each other direct questions face to face. They all make sound but never converse. Everyone knows everything about everyone, but never via a straight line and from the mouth of the one who supposedly knows it all. Everyone interprets and theorizes and makes claims, but never asks. They whisper, they gossip, they talk about everyone else to fill up that silence that, if left empty, others would fill talking about them. And, yes, they would say really bad things. And it doesn't surprise Penelope that the always false and supposedly well-meaning Charlotte Brontë rescues Nelly Dean from all the novel's monsters as "a specimen of true benevolence and homely fidelity." Right, of course, whatever you say, Charlotte . . .

† *Lockwood* / Just a first name, like Heathcliff. Penelope's favorite; because Lockwood is the traveler who arrives one stormy night and to whom a story is told. Don't forget, always keep in mind: *Wuthering Heights* is not a novel that "happens," but the more-than-subjective tale of a woman put into writing

in the diary of someone who is passing through and doesn't seem in full possession of his faculties. True, Lockwood says he listens and takes detailed notes. But even still, he doesn't seem like someone to be trusted in days when it didn't occur to lie in writing, because it was much better and easier to lie with a living voice. So, the written word is indisputable and the voice dubious. And *Wuthering Heights* is voices made written words. In this sense— Penelope thinks that her bad brother would think—Lockwood is the missing link between faithful narrator and the unreliable narrator of modernism à la Henry James and Joseph Conrad and Ford Madox Ford and anticipating Nick Carraway of *The Great Gatsby*. To which Penelope would respond that *The Great Gatsby* is inspired by *Wuthering Heights*: the arrival of a new neighbor, a romantic obsession, a farewell in a cemetery and . . . But Lockwood is an even more fragile person than Carraway. To begin with, Lockwood seems to have a somewhat strange notion of romance, and he confides without giving much detail that he has just left behind an unrequited love at a seaside resort. And he says he always feels "out of place" and always has the impulse to shrink "icily into myself, like a snail" faced with any uncomfortable situation. Which doesn't prevent the oddity, in the first pages, when confronting the specter of Catherine Earnshaw Linton or whatever it is, Lockwood didn't hesitate and "pulled its wrist on to the broken pane, and rubbed it to and fro till the blood ran down and soaked the bedclothes: still it wailed, 'Let me in!' and maintained its tenacious gripe, almost maddening me with fear." Even still, supposedly terrified, Lockwood (perhaps avenging himself on the memory of that young woman who ignored him on the seaside) kept at hurting that arm, so pale as to be transparent, on the sharp edges protruding from that win-dowsill, where all those names had been carved into the wood as the years passed and feelings changed: Catherine Earnshaw, Catherine Heathcliff, Catherine Linton. Also, at some point, the naïve Lockwood comes to believe he has some kind of chance with the young daughter of Catherine Earnshaw, who can't stop looking at him or ignoring him with something quite akin to disgust and disdain. Lockwood is outside reality, yes, and at a certain point, frozen and terrible, it dawns on Penelope: "Lockwood, *c'est moi*," she says to herself and hears herself and thinks that, like in her own, there's something secret and guilty in Lockwood's past. Something even Emily Brontë doesn't know because Emily Brontë doesn't want it to be known.

† *Catherine Linton Heathcliff Earnshaw* / Or "Young Catherine" or "Cathy." Her mother's daughter and born of her death. Capricious as the original yet, consciously or unconsciously, resolved not to repeat her mistakes. Penelope, to tell the truth, was never that interested in her and second parts are never good. The same thing happens to her with the Karma daughters: they're just like their mothers and the only revenge they get is that their daughters will be just like them. For thus it is said and written.

† *Hareton Earnshaw* / More or less the same. But à la Heathcliff though in a docile way.

† *Hindley Earnshaw* / Wicked like Heathcliff, but banal and nothing epic about him. Dies a drunk. Thirty-seven years old. There've been and are and will be so many like him on Mount Karma, thinks Penelope. For centuries and centuries. They all think they're a big deal and can only feel secure when they're taking somebody else down, because their strength and well-being depend on the debilities of others, on things going badly for others. Timeless. Boat shoes and Lacoste polos and hair slicked back with gel and their glasses always full. Glasses that, miraculously, are never empty and there they go, obese and flushed and eyes always moist, saying incomprehensible things and sometimes breaking into song for no reason at all, while their wives (trained at religious schools in the mornings, stuffed into spandex for the gym in the afternoon, electrifying themselves with online geisha-porno forums at night; so much like their husbands but with a malevolence that's more sinuous yet equally banal and predictable) watch them with a smile on their lips, calculating how much longer it will be before they fall down to never get up again. And, oh, the evolutionary cycle of the Karma wives is decidedly insectivorous, Penelope catalogues and sticks in pins: they all begin as enticing dead mosquitos, develop into striking butterflies, transform into devouring praying mantises, and end up sated black widows, poisoning and weaving suffocating webs for all their daughters, all those dead mosquitos.

And the circle of life continues.

Hakuna matata to the death.

† *Edgar Linton* / A good guy surrounded by psychopaths, his wife included. A little boring, sure. And a bit hypersensitive. And putting on certain airs. But, in the end, a good person. Which, in the eyes of his wife and compared to Heathcliff, turns him into something like one of those elegant pieces of furniture that, as time passes, you stop seeing even though you sit on it every day. Dead weight under living weight. Ricky, Hiriz's husband, was a little Edgar Linton, with the addition of being a repressed homosexual, thinks Penelope. A gay man who'll never be happy because on Mount Karma such things are never admitted. On Mount Karma, if you're gay, what you do instead of coming out of the closet is build yourself a dressing room with enough space for a resigned and permissive wife and four or five kids who, over the years, realize something strange happens to Dad at the country club when he has one too many drinks and his voice changes and he starts to dance differently and better to take him home and undress him in his closet. There inside, a limbo replete with drawers and mirrors, with dark corners and secret niches, like in those convent catacombs where the bones of fetuses or newly-dead newborns bloom. And there he remains and there they remain, forever: until death do them part but never do them divorce. Dead.

† *Isabella Linton* / Poor thing, the product of having read too many novels of the kind the Brontë sisters read, but, unlike the Brontës, Isabella Linton doesn't do anything with them apart from thinking they can be lived. The non-protagonist version of Anna Karenina and Emma Bovary. And, yes, the grave error of falling in love with Heathcliff, taking him for the primitive archetype of the "boy on the motorcycle" or the proverbial tall dark and handsome man. More than one Karma girl succumbs, for a while, to that temptation. Some even lose their virginity to him and to them and, later, have it gynecologically reconstructed, so as not to disappoint come their wedding night. But in general it doesn't go that far and they get over it and get engaged and married to men who're a combination of who their fathers are and who their sons will be. Or of who their mothers are and who their daughters will be. People nobody would marry in real life. And even better if they're cousins or more or less close/distant relatives so that, in the face of any conflict, everything is resolved or carried out within the family, behind

closed doors. There they go, down the aisle toward the alter of sacramental sacrifices: the women with hairstyles based on blonde appliques in the style of Helen of Troy-Lady Godiva-Rapunzel (as the years pass, they'll be able, courtesy of Photoshop, to correct and modernize the photographs of that day); the men like a somewhat zigzagging version of that little man atop the wedding cake; the women and the men both with the disconcerting detail of dressing up their eyes in blue contact lenses. And there they are, dancing to the childish songs of their childhoods (the same childhood and the same songs, Anorexia y sus Flaquitas, yes) as if not wanting to let go of something that has let go of them in order to attach itself more powerfully than ever. The honeymoon already on the wane in Las Vegas: the Karmas preferred destination whenever—only in the controlled and group environment of cruises and excursions—they leave Mount Karma. And if they travel to Europe, they go to the Louvre and stand in front of the *Mona Lisa* and say and think "What a mysterious smile" and then leave right away and head over to the Champs-Élysées. In Rome, stopping off for a spell at the Vatican, because they've paid a small fortune for an audience with the Pope that includes a photograph and certificate. And in Spain, dedicating themselves to eating and drinking and to bulls and horses. That's why, for them, Las Vegas is the perfect place to go and to come back from: boutiques for the women, tits and asses for the men, shows for both—Celine Dion is the great Karmatic crooner—and most important of all: all those scale replicas of landmarks from around the world that now you never have to visit. Everything shrunk down and all close together and within claws' reach, and, oh, the joy of vacationing amid falsifications for those who live amid falseness. To look at all that and—satisfactorily unsatisfied—to say: "I thought it was bigger." They arrive as newlyweds, with hangovers and jetlag and no idea how to go on with the rest of their lives, in sickness and in health, till death do them part. Yes, the Karmas get married thinking it's going to be like playing house and before long find themselves lost in a haunted house. Wuthering Heights, indeed, and better to come back from the honeymoon already knocked up in order to gain a little time with breathing classes and gynecological checkups and baby showers and baptisms. And then, the rest of their lives. So, the best way to hide the vertigo of all the days is to deny it all and get together often with friends (always the men separate from the women) and to sing and to weep and to swallow pills as blue as those contact lenses and to try to ask themselves as infrequently as possible how they ended up there and where they parked the car, and to not be surprised that that isn't their beautiful wife or husband or their beautiful house, and letting the days go by, and here comes the twister. When it comes to Isabella Linton succumbing to Heathcliff, in her defense, you have to say that, where she lives, there aren't many options, but it's still a mistake. And yet who can undo what's already been done, thinks Penelope. And so Heathcliff confides in Catherine Earnshaw that: "I like her too ill to attempt it, except in a very ghoulish fashion. You'd hear of odd things if I lived alone with that mawkish, waxen face: the most ordinary would be painting on its white the colours of the rainbow, and turning the blue eyes black, every day or two: they detestably resemble Linton's." Another death. At thirty-one.

† *Linton Heathcliff* / The son of Heathcliff and Isabella, briefly husband—as ordered by Heathcliff—to Catherine Linton Heathcliff Earnshaw. Totally worthless. He lasts but a sigh. Or, better, a pant. Dead at eighteen.

† *Frances Earnshaw* / Little to nothing is known of her past and she arrives to Wuthering Heights and contributes to Heathcliff's abuse, and her main achievement is conceiving and giving birth to Hareton. She coughs a lot and, as tends to happen to everyone who passes through Wuthering Heights, soon dies, also at eighteen.

† *Joseph* / Servant who speaks the Yorkshire dialect with a marked accent and a lot of exclamation points. He makes Penelope really nervous and puts her in a really bad mood. Not Hiriz, definitely not; because for Hiriz and women like Hiriz, servants are silent and invisible. And they don't speak. They just listen to orders and assent and walk backward out of rooms. Joseph—noisy— is like an impotent and deflated and onomatopoeic version of Nelly Dean and it wouldn't take him long to be let go/ejected from Mount Karma or confined to the stables. Joseph is always in the vicinity, but all he does is release creaks

and groans. He doesn't count and doesn't like to recount. Charlotte Brontë took the liberty of rewriting him a little for the rerelease of the book, slightly softening his provincial and local speech so all readers could understand it or because to her it seemed a bit extreme or disrespectful, or something like that. Which leads Penelope to think about the Karmas' speech. About that strange and personal idiom in which they communicate among themselves rarely hearing each other. Fixed phrases. Pretentious sayings. Constant repetition of their own names (Penelope has heard long sentences composed exclusively of surnames), always the same, generation after generation and death after death to keep their lives from getting complicated. Automatic and easy nicknames (if your name is José, you'll be Pepe or, in a fit of audacity, Pepé; if your name is Rosario, you'll be Charo; if you were a boy born in France or a girl in the United States, you can only be El Francés or La Gringa). Insignificant monosyllables that signify nothing more than a "Here I am" (the Karmas make sounds; they have no qualms when it comes to squandering small fortunes on enormous trifles, but it seems like each word cost them its letters in gold). Constant and automatic fits of laughter like the sound of the dentures of those mechanical skeletons (the Karmas laugh incessantly with that type of laugh that seems to ask itself what it's laughing at, but laughing all the same, just in case). Occasional torrential and compulsive and cathartic sobbing (at funerals and during mass). Exclamations of the religious variety to fill uncomfortable silences (because nothing discomfits and disturbs a Karma more than silence; silence is a result of bad manners and means that someone might be thinking of something related to you and thinking is dangerous and so "Glory to God on high" making all of that explode in the heavens). The micro-nuclear and macro-expansive and multifunctional particle of *"posí"* (contraction of *"pues sí,"* meaning "yes" or "well yes," which, Penelope thinks, is the root of a philosophical-familial movement known as "posí-tivism": to say *"posí"* isn't to say "yes" or "no," it's not to choose between this and that, it's not to commit to anyone or anything). And the very particular use they make of diminutives, thinking in the reduction resides the inoffensive, the comprehensible, the forgivable, the affectionate.

And so, on Mount Karma, nobody is a bad person, rather that "we've noticed lately he's having a little problem, *un problemita*." The diminutive deactivates, but, also, underlines and allows you to comment on something that's making, the way certain automobiles do at some point in their lives, "an irritating or little noise, *un ruidito.*" Yes: Penelope has never encountered a higher concentration of people "*con problemitas*" in a space that's so teeny-tiny, so *pequeñito.* The negation or distortion of the symptom resulting in the transmission and expansion of the syndrome. The Karmas and Mount Karma like the home of an environmental catastrophe or of an atomic accident of the kind whose importance corporations and governments tend to downplay and, yes, diminish its size and intensity. Contamination and toxicity of small and numerous miseries punctuated every so often by a devastating plague that always leaves someone by the wayside. Most horrifying and fascinating of all: all of them, the Karmas, are convinced they're excellent people, great human beings, the best of the best. Chosen and, above all, deserving of that choice no matter their level of academic preparation or natural ability. And, of course, they're never put to the test outside Mount Karma. Why bother? Why do they need to be compared with outsiders? They're all great for each other and among themselves and so they only need one another to verify all their benevolences and talents. Thus, regardless of committing the most reproachable and incomprehensible of atrocities, a Karma—Hiriz, for exemplary example—will never be entirely bad in the mind of another Karma. The bad people are the people who are not Karmas. Outsiders. People who have big and wide and deep and acute problems. People who are, and will always be, bad because they're not Karmas and who help the Karmas live in a sort of ecstatic certainty: because if they do something bad or are bad it's because they're not like them; or if they do something good and are good, though they don't bear that surname, it's by virtue of proximity, of having been improved by their mere presence and treatment and unquestionable benevolence, which leads the Karmas to sign up for any kind of philanthropic activity and thereby paper and carpet over and mask the fact that they don't work or produce anything beyond a certain dynastic inertia in and with which they're always "oh so very busy."

And, yes, Penelope—who isn't exactly a Karma, who has many problems, who is very bad—was always fascinated by that lack of generosity of well-to-do clans toward the bad. The Bad like a relative and fleeting form of bad upbringing and not what it actually is: a vital and important and, yes, ever so valiant decision. You have to be very good to be very bad. Penelope always maintained that choosing to be bad is like reaching a sainthood of inverse, negative polarity; it's like being touched not by God's palm but by the back of His hand, by the part used to deliver a slap. That's why, sometimes, Penelope thinks Hiriz was so unbalanced, because nobody acknowledged the achievements and advances of her vileness. Nothing could be more frustrating than having better bad people not recognizing the goodness of your badness, so superior to their own, that they don't admit the transcendence of such a premeditated life choice like that of being bad. Nothing more disconcerting and, immediately thereafter, disorienting. Hiriz like a misunderstood artist who, of course, had thus committed that oh so common error among bad people: believing she was good because nobody—to avoid sounding rude—ever told her she was perfectly cretinous. And thus renouncing her greatness and destiny. Penelope always thought if Adolf Hitler hadn't gotten distracted with that nonsense of bringing justice to Germany and reinstating his honor by setting up an Aryan nation and, from the get-go, accepted responsibility as a straight-up, hard and fast psychopath, nothing would've stopped him from winning World War Two. Penelope, on the other hand, has never had that problem, those *problemitas*: it's perfectly clear to Penelope that she became an un-attenuated bad person when she was about eight years old, shortly after reading *Wuthering Heights* for the ninth or tenth time.

† *Mr. Green* / Edgar Linton's lawyer, but—you never fully trust his kind— who actually manages to turn Heathcliff into a sort of Charles Foster Kane of the moors. There are few lawyers on Mount Karma; because Mamagrandma is the one who resolves all legal-familial problems. Her word is law and punishment and the first and last unbreakable commandment is "Though you hate that you seem to love each other; openly hating is for all those outsiders who don't bear the name Karma." And, in the end, Karmatic conflicts are easy to understand and correct: all problems and their solution (it's enough to go up and down; to get extra by taking away and redistributing) pass through the selling and buying and inheritance and addition and subtraction of the shares of that family company/factory. All the Karmas, even of the "in-law" married-in/second class variety, work there. Though Penelope has never heard anybody say, "I'm going to work" or "I'm coming from work" or "I'm

working." Any undertaking—always fleeting—outside the company/factory setting tends to have the lightness of a pastime and is forever destined for failure or more or less direct or indirect sabotage by relatives urged on silently (silence spells consent) by Mamagrandma. Ventures such as sailing schools for Karma kids on a lake that's dry a good part of the year or volatile thematic restaurants. Casual workers, indeed. The important thing is to fail successfully and to be sure you won't be the last one to fail and, Penelope thinks, to wind up understanding that less money is wasted by investing in doing nothing or concocting unfeasible slow-motion plans. Through all those ventures, if losing money were a profession, the Karmas would be millionaires. But no: sooner or later they return to the fold, blaming their setbacks, always, on "the political situation in the country" or some other convenient fantasy like that. And Penelope never was able to figure out what it is the Karma factory produces. Clothespins? Toothpicks? Shoeshine? Those little bathroom mats where you put your bare and sleepless feet, sitting on the toilet in the predawn hours, thinking privately of all the things the Karmas don't dare think in public or, better, among Karmas? Of one thing Penelope is almost certain: the Karmas do not fabricate—*cannot* fabricate—little wooden soldiers.

Maybe, who knows, sacred and bleeding and weeping images of the most gore-slasher-splatter variety with nails and arrows and thorns of the kind that, supposedly, it's a sin to worship through your tears and on your knees. There abound on Mount Karma, in place of lawyers, a staggering number of salaried priests. The bulk of the Karmas' social activity is taken up with baptisms and weddings and funerals and memorial masses, and saints' days (the ephemeris like a scheduleable form of automatic affection), where they all rotate from Saturday to Saturday and Sunday to Sunday. There isn't much else to do. And so it is that the Karmas spend their time getting hitched and giving birth and dying. Like rabbits and like rabbits and like rabbits. Sudden loves and rapid impregnation and—most disturbing of all—lighting up sudden and fatal tumors at very young ages. When none of this is happening—during the rare dry spell—somebody will make the sacrifice of killing himself or herself in a car or horse or private jet accident or as an extra in some international cataclysm. Suicide—though, in a way, a good part of the Catholic faith is built atop the suicide of Jesus, king of the passive aggressives, and passive aggression is one of the most common Karma attitudes of all—is frowned on. Out of place. It's taken as "a misunderstanding" and "an inconvenience" and they never mention the possible suicide notes left by the one "who had a serious accident." And thus all the "family" priests. To be there with them for all of this, but whose primordial labor is that of guaranteeing perpetual divine forgiveness, charging by the kilo of sins to be absolved without delay and *vaya usted con Dios*. Aha!: Jesus Christ—who said that thing about "Let the little children come to me"—washing away your sins via an intermediary you've known since you were a little girl, an intermediary who, probably, fancies children a fair bit more than is appropriate. The understanding of faith and of the divine by the Karmas is as if it were a contracted service combining the best/worst of Catholicism with the Hebrew: the inquisitional with victimism. Divine functionality, prayers answered, cleansable sins. Like that app on their phones with the triangular logo with an open eye inside it (that one that allows them to confess in gusts of one hundred and forty characters and endure the penitence of not being able to send selfies for fifteen minutes if the sin is very grave). God like something that confirms for them that God believes in them: that's the only way they can understand living with such absolute focus on themselves. To be Alpha and Omega. To, in the beginning, be the Verb and, at the end, the principal Subjects. Penelope doesn't remember having ever heard the Karmas talk about anything but themselves, saying things like "I swear on my soul" before dishing out a lie or insult or rumor about another Karma. And Penelope wonders if, when they fill out forms, the Karmas put "judging others" or "lying about others" in the box for occupation or hobby. Because she's sure they must mention or acknowledge it; but she doesn't know if that reflex is vocation or pastime. Or both at the same time and with the whole soul. Their own.

Penelope thinks "soul" is one of the words that appears most and is uttered most in *Wuthering Heights*, almost always shouted, with fury and passion and desire and with a fist held aloft or a stroke of loftiness.

Penelope thinks the Karmas are the most soulless people she's ever known (not because they're malevolent, but because they lack soul, because they're automatic and robotic and as if in a trance and following not the orders they're told but the orders of what they'll tell); and, maybe for that reason, the Karmas believe like nobody else in the idea of that soul, not the one they were born with, but the one—they pray and pray and pray for it—they'll be reborn with beyond death, improved so as to be even worse. The soul not as something you sell, but yes as something you buy and the more expensive the better.

† *Dr. Kenneth* / Penelope imagines him, in his youth, saying to himself: "I'll be a rural doctor, far from the big city, and I will live a peaceful life without too much work." Wrong. On Mount Karma, yes, many hypochondriacs: when one of them gets bored, when one of them has nothing to do, an illness is an almost sporting distraction and even a gift and a privilege. The Karmas compare illnesses the way others compare automobiles (the Karmas *also* compare automobiles). And, oh, it's such a delight to be admitted to the suites in those clinics/high-tech body shops where everyone visits you and are at your service and gets together to play cards and place bets, unconfessable, on how long it'll be before the next and never-ending sequence of funeral masses and who they'll be praying for.

† *Zillah* / "Stout housewife" and Nelly Dean's forewoman. Now you see her, now you don't.

† *Various dogs* / The "hairy monsters" that guard Heathcliff (Gnasher and Wolf) and that leap for Lockwood's throat; the dog that bites Catherine and forces her to stay at Thrushcross Grange (the bulldog Skulker); Isabella's springer spaniel (Fanny, the only one with a docile and inoffensive name), strangled with a handkerchief by Heathcliff. And there are so many dogs on Mount Karma. Purebred. Contestants competing against each other (like illnesses, like automobiles, like wives and husbands and boyfriends and girlfriends) by edict of their ever-competitive masters. Every so often, they manage to break their chains and flee and are never found, winding up far away, mating with anything that gets near them, and remembering their past on Mount Karma as if it were something that happened to some other dog, to dogs that bark but do not bite.

Penelope remembers that she met Lina Liberman in Abracadabra, on one of her few successful escapes from Mount Karma. Getting out of there on her own (without some Karma hanging around her neck, without the ever-vigilant Hiriz, without the Sauronic eye of Mamagrandma controlling everything) was no mean feat, and Penelope went into a jewelry store called The Lady of the Rings, specializing in rings with runic and druidic symbols.

And there was Lina behind the counter. Lina smiling a smile that, for Penelope, is a weapon of mass reconstruction. And they become friends right away, with that speed with which certain women become friends when they meet and, upon meeting each other, are fully aware they've been always been looking for each other, though they never knew or suspected it.

Lina has taken over running the store from her adoptive mother (it used to be called La Señora de los Anillos and specialized in the always fertile selling of wedding rings; because in Abracadabra, you're nobody until you get married and hunt down a new surname); but her primary occupation seems to be that of laughing and laughing and to not stop laughing. An animal and contagious laugh that, really, is the funniest thing in her monologues as a stand-up comedian at a bar (a "bohemian bar," the Karmas would say, wrinkling their noses like someone smelling something odd) called Carpe Noctem. A bar where Lina, when its owners (two Argentines: one skinny and sad and one immense and ferocious) allow or are distracted fighting among themselves, has been mutating into a sit-down tragedian, starring in the dead yet lively monologue of Joan Vollmer, that wife of William S. Burroughs. The wife of the writer who put a bullet in her temple and soon thereafter, he recalled years later, became a writer, pasting and cutting and pasting again.

But when Lina isn't Joan and is Lina . . . And Lina can't stop laughing and making people laugh. And Penelope laughs so much with her. And Penelope falls in love with that laugh, which is a tremendous laugh. A laugh of the "Huahuahua" variety that would embarrass anyone else who released it, who would cover it up with a hand and turn down the volume. But not Lina. Lina laughs that laugh as if it were the first and last time. And Penelope, who hasn't laughed in so long, who never laughed *like that*, wants that laugh so badly and knows it'll never be hers, but, maybe, she can possess it a little bit if she kisses that mouth and then that body. And Penelope falls in love with that laugh (with that happiness) and with Lina and they make love, the one laughing and the other hearing that laugh and smiling like she never smiled before.

One night, Lina takes Penelope to a movie theater in Abracadabra. Penelope has succeeded in escaping Mount Karma without being seen, without anybody offering to go with her, not even asking where she's going first because it doesn't matter. The important thing is that she not be alone, because to be alone is to be sad and to be with anybody not a Karma, they think, is a sadness. The important thing for them is to be all together and to go everywhere all together and for nobody to do anything without everybody else. But Penelope succeeds. At dinner, she excuses herself on the pretext of a headache and slips out a window and there goes Penelope and there is Lina, waiting for her. At the door to one of those huge movie theaters that no longer exist or that have been wrecked by the developer voracity of the multiplex concept, chewing them up into multiple smaller theaters. Into the architectural-cinema equivalent of tweets, showing movies that are sequels or prequels or adaptations or remakes, where the only thing that has improved— and sometimes not even this—is the technical quality of the special effects of Superman flying or Spider-Man swinging. All of them with ever-spiffier uniforms and fluctuating faces and ages (ever younger actors to win over the young audience with ever greater consumptive capacity, financed as they are by their parents) exhibiting the true superpower everybody dreams of. A superpower that's far more useful than running at the speed of light or being able to breathe under water or to pass through interdimensional portals or to change color and grow considerably larger: the ability to start over. Over and over again. However many times is necessary until the thing comes out right or better or even worse; but it doesn't matter, because you can always start over and try again and the mistakes of the last time will be corrected in the next screenplay with a new yet minimal twist to a plot you already know by heart in the same way you know all the open-secret personalities.

And now, years after going to that movie theater, Penelope thinks about all of this. And she feels a little guilt and a little shame, because, after all, her

Tulpa sisters are a fine-tuned version of the Brontë sisters. A sci-fi remake in which they appear transformed into something they never were, but without ceasing to be and to conjure their phantasmal figures in 3D and Dolby Atmos surround sound.

But the movie Lina invited her to isn't one of those.

It's an old movie in black and white and spoken and acted in Spanish. And, right, it's another version—but very different from all the ones Penelope has previously seen—of *Wuthering Heights*. In fact, Penelope didn't even know it existed and maybe it'd escaped her because its title wasn't *Cumbres borrascosas* but *Abismos de pasión*. In any case, Penelope gave up on any movie based on *Wuthering Heights* a long time ago. It can't be done, impossible, doesn't work. And all of them always stray into an irredeemable and unconsciously *machista* error: in the films, Heathcliff is always the dominant figure, while in the book Heathcliff is dominated by Catherine; and, yes, in more than one, though never described, S&M reigns supreme.

Penelope remembers, yes, that telenovela adaptation with a great deal of affection and infinite gratitude for opening the door to let her come out to play; but, disappointed so many times, she prefers not to accept new invitations. And so she hasn't seen the supposedly faithful or respectful or innovative (the constant redos by the BBC & Co. or the novelty of Heathcliff being black) versions; not the Indian or Philippine or French or Japanese (a country where, with so many suicides and self-destructives of varying caliber and voltage, *Wuthering Heights* is considered a seminal text) versions either; and definitely not that MTV-produced version or the one taking place at a high school in Malibu Beach and that other one in a web series format set at a college and everyone talking to the cameras on their computers and, no doubt, sending SMS with furious or sobbing or shocked emoticons. She hasn't risked the operas or ballets or comics either (though she always liked the studies to illustrate it by Balthus—studies Penelope bought—who said, "I'm a very emotional man, perhaps too much so . . . My youth was an absolute whirlwind of Feelings, exactly like Emily Brontë's *Wuthering Heights*, which I illustrated. I was completely at home in this novel. It described my youth perfectly. I was in love with Antoinette de Watteville—what a Brontësque name, thought Penelope—and I was determined to win her. But

Antionette, on top of being a difficult girl, was already engaged to someone else. I reread her letters every evening. I think that, like Heathcliff, I didn't want to leave adolescence"). Or the biopics of the Brontës with languid actresses of the kind who later lead wuthering lives in heights from which to throw themselves (Isabelle Adjani and Sinead O'Connor were Emily Brontë and there they are; Ida Lupino, with a very gondalian surname, did better and, as her bad brother told her once with a reverent voice, was the only woman who ever directed an episode of *The Twilight Zone*). And Penelope never understood that appearance, as sudden as it was gratuitous, of Emily Brontë in Jean-Luc Godard's *Weekend*. And nothing unnerves her more than the name *Wuthering Heights* being taken in vain elsewhere; like how the sales of the novel quadrupled after it was mentioned as the favorite book of the girlfriend of a vampire, condemned to attend high school for all eternity in a YA romance series. (Penelope can't stand that franchise; but she also knows she has inherited a good chunk of its addict readers, who—when the saga concluded, listless and in need of a new passion, perhaps not to consume them, but, most important of all, that could be consumed—leapt ravenously on the Tulpas and their environs.) Or when a British prime minister described himself as "an older Heathcliff, a wiser Heathcliff" (achieving, immediately, that his rivals in Parliament asked him whether someone given to domestic violence and kidnapping and torturing and possibly digging up the body of his beloved, not to mention going around in a bad mood all the time, was a good role model as a ruler). Though Penelope has to admit she got a kick out of the Monty Python sketch with Catherine Earnshaw and Heathcliff communicating with flags and standing atop rocks; that comic strip of Tom Gauld's proposing a Brontë sisters videogame was funny too (Level 2: The Moors); and that "Wuthering Heights," the great hit-single of the debuting Kate Bush bothered her for all the wrong reasons: the song was really good and the oh so gyratory and, yes, adolescent Kate Bush (the little harlot had also been born the same day as Emily Brontë: July 30th) resembled Catherine Earnshaw more than Penelope ever would.

But, this film, now, is different, because she's going to see it with Lina. And, right away, entering the foyer, as magnificent as it was dilapidated, of that theater (one of those theaters with all-powerful names like Olympia or

Atlas or Majestic or Alhambra or Rex), she liked that title, *Abismos de pasión*, that switched polarity and flipped circuit, making the heights descend into the abyss so the wuthering would become impassioned.

Lina tells her that a friend of hers inherited that theater, and that he has turned it into a film club, and that the film is directed by the Spaniard, Luis Buñuel, and that it was filmed not far from Abracadabra, just across the border in a neighboring country. Penelope reads the program, its text typewritten and photocopied, and remembers those movie theaters in the heights where she went with her bad brother when she was a kid. And she reads there that "Emily Brontë's book always fascinated the surrealists as they loved *amour fou* above all things in this world" (then Penelope makes the connection and, of course, this is the same Buñuel of *The Exterminating Angel*, that film where everyone is mysteriously shut inside a house and unable to leave, which reminds her so much of the Karmas). And at first, Penelope struggles with the fact that Heathcliff is named Alejandro and Catherine is Catalina and Isabella is Isabel and Hindley is Ricardo. And she is unsettled by the transformation of the English moorland to a Mexican paramo, of cold and damp to dry and hot, of farmhouse to ramshackle country mansion, of Wuthering Heights to El Robledal.

But the truth is it's not bad at all.

Above all him: the leading man, Jorge Mistral, is a much more powerful and savage Heathcliff than the one from the telenovela or the one played by Laurence Olivier who, for Penelope, is insufferable in Wuthering Heights and in Manderley and in Elsinore and everywhere. And, true, Buñuel made a lot of changes from the novel, but he did so with a curious form of disrespectful respect. And Penelope liked that—"due to the censorship of the time," the program explained—the cursed lovers couldn't kiss on the mouth but only on the neck, as if Alejandro were giving vampire bites to Catalina and Isabel. And that's really well done, thinks Penelope, they have turned a negative into a positive: because *Wuthering Heights* is not a novel of vampires. No. It's something far more interesting. *Wuthering Heights* is a novel of the vampirized. A novel where the vampire has already come and gone, already moved on, already bitten all of them—they're all victims, even the victimizers—and left them alone to bleed and drink each others' blood, to fix themselves the best and worst they can. And, in the end—when Alejandro is gunned down, oh so Mexicanly, in a hail of bullets, because nobody can bear that son of a bitch, that *hijo de la chingada*, who doesn't care about anything and to whom all of them *le valen madre*, mean nothing—when the music of the final credits (so quick and expeditious if you compare them with those eternities of rolling lines of present-day films, with million-dollar budgets and that multitudinous volume of technical titles, which you have to sit there and watch and read, because there could always be a brief and revealing coda after that avalanche of letters leaves you wondering what a *gaffer* or a *key grip* is), swells, Penelope doesn't feel betrayed at all, despite the fact that with *Abismos de pasión*, Buñuel has inserted more of a meddling hand into her book than Lina is inserting into her right now, in the abyssal yet impassioned darkness of the movie theater. That darkness where, in *Wuthering Heights*, Heathcliff, though surrounded by people, is always talking to himself.

The monologue, it's well known, is a gift and privilege of the powerful and the mad, of the madly powerful, and of the powerfully mad.


One of the things Heathcliff might say if Heathcliff were one who theorized and not just one who practiced, if Heathcliff had some capacity for reflection beyond his impure pure action. Or one of the things Nelly Dean might say if Nelly Dean were to finally assume her role as manipulative cerebral schemer.

One of the things the so powerful and so deluded Mamagrandma *did* say to her—emerging from a corner of a room full of monitors, like a specter—on her last night in Abracadabra, after Penelope crossed the diamond desert, losing her mind, on a jade-green cow, and arrived to the clinic where the comatose Maxi lay, and climbed atop him, and ended up impregnated by him after suffocating him with a pillow in the moment of his orgasm, and fled from there to only ever return her in dreams, the way she returns to Wuthering Heights or Manderlay or Mount Karma, towering on the deep REM horizon.

And so—with eloquence heretofore unknown to Penelope—Mamagrandma spoke then, in that room in that clinic in Abracadabra, and Penelope remembers her and remembers her voice as if in a dream, like in a scene from a movie that might be called *Depths of Evil*:

"Ah, here you are . . . The fugitive bride going back not to the scene of the crime, but to that scene without a crime. Poor Penelope. Poor Maxi. But I suppose what you've just done was inevitable . . . The imminence of the ending—not of my work but of your participation in it—demands this kind of gesture, these kinds of actions, slight pushes at the edge of the abyss to precipitate events. Offerings and sacrifices and exchanges so everything stays the same, with the exception of those offered and sacrificed . . . Poor Maxi. And poor Hiriz. She reminds me of a fox I hunted once, when I was just a girl. That damn fox that was eating all my chickens. So I covered the blade of a knife with honey and left it like that, standing there, the handle buried, beside the chicken coop. The fox came one night and began to lick the honey and cut her tongue, and so greedy and insatiable was she that the fox continued to lick her own blood, down to the last drop, until she bled out entirely. The next morning I found her there, dead, but smiling. And that's the key to surviving, Penelope: keep in mind that underneath the honey, a knife could always be lying in wait. Hiriz is not like that. Hiriz—like the fox—doesn't know when to hold back, she doesn't know how to stop. She loves the taste of herself. And I wonder if that might have been the reason for all those yoga classes: to make herself flexible enough to run her own tongue around down under. In the end . . . Hiriz can't comprehend that the Karmas are a closed-circle, a movie with clear and fixed roles where no spectators are admitted but us. We love and hate among ourselves, we betray and steal and even kill among ourselves. Our crimes are only punished by our justice. There is no room for improvisations or departures from script. But Hiriz doesn't think before she acts, and that's how she's always been, and at last she's gone too far and has put us in danger. And it's not even that Hiriz is an idiot. It's much worse: she's someone who thinks she's very intelligent, though all the evidence indicates the opposite. And what do people who are not intelligent do to convince themselves that they are? Easy: they convince themselves that nobody, except them, is intelligent. So, the difference that actually makes them idiots makes itself, for them, into the difference that makes them very very smart. Once the idiots manage to convince themselves of something like this, there's no going back. All that's left is to put up with them with patience or with love, which is the same thing, because love always ends up being one of the many kinds of patience, Penelope . . . What's going to be complicated indeed is how Hiriz will go on after that little scene at your wedding, after ordering your little lesbian friend killed. Now Hiriz is like one of those wild animals that grew up in captivity, supposedly domesticated and harmless, and one day draws blood and . . . There's nothing to do but eliminate her. Or perhaps, better, as I already said, force her to lick her own blood, down to the last drop. Hiriz . . . Hiriz . . . Hiriz was an unresolved issue for me: Hiriz could not remain among us, because Hiriz is a starving time bomb with a thirst for vengeance. She's not the first: there have been spoiled Karmas and crazy Karmas. But Hiriz is spoiled *and* crazy. The whole thing about how people can change is a lie, Penelope. People never change; they just get better or worse when it comes time to be who they always were and are and will be. And it's quite clear that Hiriz is going to get worse. Her evil is no longer the banal and predictable evil of her relatives, so easy to anticipate, as is the case with almost everything arising from being convinced you are the center of the world. Her evil is banal and predictable but, also, different. Any one of these nights Hiriz would burn Mount Karma to the ground just to get us to listen to her sing. Hiriz, sooner or later, would end up disrupting the delicate balance that sustains and keeps the Karmas together. And you cannot imagine what it takes to maintain the balance of something that's half tightrope half hangman's noose. And, on their own, the Karmas are nothing—easy prey for the masses of non-Karmas. So bye-bye, Hiriz, I wish you well. With any luck, if it occurs to her—and *I* will make sure that there is luck and that it does, in fact, occur to her—tomorrow Hiriz will get it into her head, her crazy little head, the possibility of becoming a saint, of being beatified and canonized, and she'll enter a cloistered convent. Forever. After all, our family lacks a saint just like it lacks a writer. Yes, yes, in that way and to that end, Hiriz will go—cloistered order and vow of silence. Poor little nuns. But, after all, who told them to call themselves Humble Sisters of the Pricked and Suffering Martyr Heart of Our Poor Little Abandoned Jesus Bleeding Out Slowly on the Cross with No Right to Resurrection. With a name like that, they deserve Hiriz. And Hiriz deserves them too. So ugly. Nuns are so ugly, Penelope . . . Maybe that's why they are always so pretty and delicate and high-voiced and ballerina-bodied in movies: to compensate a little for so much facial and anatomical deformity, right? Hiriz will be happy among them, because at last she'll be the most beautiful beast. End of her projects, end of her journey. But first things first. And the saint doesn't come first . . . Which brings me to the sinner. And the sinner is you, Penelope. Mortal sinner. But even so, as if blessed. The kind of sinner who can end up being an object of adoration. A threat to the established order. And I am the established order. Which doesn't keep me from knowing how to recognize someone powerful when I see them. And you are powerful. Like I am, but in a different way. A free spirit who could end up becoming a leader. There's no space for both of us here, Penelope. So I'm going to let you go. Nothing to see here. You killed Maximiliano the way I killed Papa-grandpa. You and I are different yet the same. We operate on our own. Papagrandpa—who was raised in the macho patriarchy without ever figuring out that it's the woman behind him who pulls the strings and draws the reins—couldn't understand it. And I made him understand. And there he is: stuck inside a wall in Mount Karma, behind his portrait, may he rest in peace. And your thing with Maxi, killing him—I don't get it. Was it out of love or pity, out of interest or strategy? I don't understand the first one, the second one either; because you won't get any inheritance. You signed documents of separation of assets and the religious ceremony never concluded. I thank you for it: Maxi, always and forever in a coma, he would've turned into a, into another, short-term complication in the financial-familial hierarchy, in terms of shares and allotments. And we, for religious reasons, so convenient on other occasions, could never unplug him. And because of the thing with Papagrandpa, my dance card is already full in that area. I'll confess my mortal sin on my deathbed (which, as its name indicates, is where and when you have to confess your mortal sins) and I'll be forgiven, yes; but best not to exaggerate too much, right? So, better this way, thank you for everything, Penelope, and may Maxi sleep with the angels. And getting back to the religious stuff . . . I really liked that thing you said once about the foolishness of wasting time praying for God to change his designs. You said it was . . . a contradiction, right? Because you can't ask God, in his infinite wisdom, to alter his actions. Even less if you're one of God's little creatures. And you're right. That's why, when I go to mass, I never ask for anything and I always give thanks. I thank God that He's allowed me to have my way, that my will be done and that my will, always, be His. I thank God, as I told you once, for the fact that He's helped me understand that though life is, in fact, very short, life is *also* very wide. And God says to me you're welcome, and what's more, Mamagrandma, I'm the grateful one. What's the voice of God like? The voice of God is the silence of God. And ye who are silent shall receive. And it's of my will and my will alone that I let you go now, Penelope, that I won't say anything about what I just saw, that I leave you free to do anything except come back here, where it's not that you're not understood, but it's impossible for you to understand our kind of happiness. It might be true that it's a hard happiness to assimilate, but that doesn't mean it's not a happiness that makes us happy. What you have, on the other hand, is pure and absolute sadness and dissatisfaction. A *profound* sadness that you give such importance to that you laugh at our superficial happiness. You like to think that the problem is our family, when the problem is the family that you never had and will never have. Here I could get really annoying and witch-like and tell you that I curse you so you'll never know the joy of family. But there's no need. You've cursed yourself. You've condemned yourself to wander, lost. Safe travels, yours shall be a very long trip. And lonely. We don't love you, we can't love you, because you don't love you—you consider yourself cursed by everyone else, but actually you've cursed yourself. Nobody would tell your story because it's sad and boring. Only the part that overlaps with ours will be somewhat amusing. And that part, so entertaining that many will say it must be the invented part, ends here. Good luck, Penelope. You're going to need it. I won't ask you to go with God because you don't believe in Him and because not even He would be able to accompany you. Because He'd get bored after five minutes in your company and would start in with the floods and the plagues. Goodnight, sweet princess."

And then Penelope tells herself she must flee and the fear helps keep her from weeping for Lina and that pain from paralyzing her. Penelope thinks if Mamagrandma found out she'd been impregnated by Maxi and was going to have a boy (because Penelope is sure she has, even though her ovum was fertilized barely five minutes before), she wouldn't rest until she reclaimed that little Karma boy and took him back to Mount Karma.

And now Penelope wakes up in Our Lady of Our Lady of Our Lady of . . . —from that replay and that rewind and that "Previously on . . ."—and realizes she's not alone. Sitting in a chair, staring at her, the scars on her face giving off a phosphorescence like those toys that glow in the dark, is that nun who inspires such fear in her and who now says: "I heard you scream and came to see if you were okay. It looks like you were having a nightmare. But, relax, it's over, it's over . . ." The nun leaves the room with a smile of the kind that's only smiled because smiling is the only more or less socially acceptable way of baring your teeth.

And—nothing happened, everything keeps happening—then Penelope thinks nobody lies more than nuns and priests; because the only thing they talk about is a God with whom they claim to have more or less direct communication. A God who answers them and listens to them and visits them in their dreams, after they say that prayer that goes if I die before I wake.


And it's been said and written many times and Penelope is not going to contradict it: the world where *Wuthering Heights* takes place is constructed of the stuff of dreams.

Everything there seems to happen at the same time and in all places.

Everything—beds, windows, ghosts, animals, and houses—is allegorical and symbolic and worthy of being interpreted.

And everyone dreams there and Penelope wonders what the suspensive dreams of the comatose and profoundly yet so superficially suspended Maxi might have been.

Are the dreams of those whose dreaming has no clear expiration date different? Are they clear and linear dreams that seek the comfort of imitating waking life as best as possible? Or are they more experimental than ever: pure colors and sounds, like, they say, the dreams of newborns and those about to be born? Are they perfectly memorable dreams or are they a bit like the reading of *Wuthering Heights*? Something imprecise and vague yet impressive and unforgettable (again: did Heathcliff dance with the dead Catherine Earnshaw? Did he pull her out of her grave? Or did he dive headfirst into the coffin to love her, possessive and wanting to possess her?) that encourages successive rereading to discover new and decisive details.

In any case, everyone dreams in *Wuthering Heights*.

Lockwood dreams (or hallucinates or sees) he is visited by Catherine Earnshaw and dreams he's in a chapel.

Catherine Earnshaw dreams she chooses the site of her tomb and dreams dreams that have altered "the colour of my mind" and she dreams she's already in Heaven and that, to her great sorrow, it bears no resemblance to Wuthering Heights; and, luckily, her prayers are answered and a squadron of angels returns her to her Eden on Earth, buried in the earth.

Heathcliff dreams of Catherine Earnshaw every time he shuts or opens his eyes.

And, when Heathcliff dies, all the inhabitants of the surrounding area begin to dream of the two of them, reunited beyond the grave, strolling like lovers through the final paragraphs of a happy ending, while Lockwood—who, without a doubt, dreamed of them for the rest of his days and nights—stopped by on his way out and bade farewell to all of it and all of them and "watched the moths fluttering among the heath and hare-bells; listened to the soft wind breathing through the grass; and wondered how anyone could ever imagine unquiet slumbers, for the sleepers in that quiet earth."

That, of course, is not Penelope's case.

Lockwood would never admit his quietude (though Penelope's cell/study is always, yes, like that so-oft invoked Victorian simile, "quiet as a grave"); because Penelope's quietude is that of a dormant though never entirely dead volcano.

And Penelope knows well you can choose your dreams, but your nightmares choose you.

Penelope knows ghosts don't exist, but the dead do exist.

Penelope knows writing yes-fictions is the best way to keep from thinking of your own non-fiction.

But that approach doesn't always work and the trick isn't always pulled off and now neither Stella D'Or nor dAlien nor the Tulpa sisters are there to help her.

And the Brontë sisters betray her, they tell her to come by and visit and, when she does, Penelope discovers other phantasmagoric dead there waiting for her.


Last night Penelope dreamed she went back to Haworth Parsonage, to the Brontë Parsonage Museum.

And Penelope dreams it—like the reverse of a prophetic dream—not exactly as if it were going to happen but as if it already happened. Not a divinatory dream, but a dream that, though unresolved, already came true on this side of things.

Penelope returns to the place she didn't want to go that night. To the goal. To the moment in the adventure when the adventure finally makes sense and embraces its final destination.

Penelope arrives to the Brontë Parsonage Museum.

To the place where the Brontës lived and wrote. To the scene of the crimes solved in books. To Haworth, in West Yorkshire.

Penelope is neither the first nor the last visitor to that place because this—according to the sponsors of the Brontë Society, one of the oldest literary societies in the world, operating and charging admission here since 1893—is the most visited "literary destination" in the world.

This is where the first great literary family industry was created (promoted by the Brontës' father, by Charlotte's widower, and by the great success of the Elizabeth Gaskell biography) along with marketing and merchandising that included the sale of lines Patrick Brontë cut out of the letters of his ever-more-alive dead daughters.

Then, in the beginning of the trend that never ends, with the three sisters gone, hundreds of young girls were already coming, week after week, and throwing themselves on the old and blind and terrorized pastor, in order to touch the man who fathered those daughters. Some shriek that Emily has possessed them or that Emily is alive and lives in their homes. And the truth is they all have present-day incarnations, shut away in their houses, in front of the pale glow of bulimic screens and blogs with titles like *Wuthering High* or *The Heat Cliff,* suggesting candidates past and present for the starring role, giving him the faces of Brad Pitt or Vigo Mortensen or Clive Owen, without comprehending that Heathcliff was so much younger than all of them, though—Penelope thinks—Owen, who knows . . . Brontëmania, indeed. They were here, almost from the start of the myth, already in 1860, all the readers of the sisters Brontë.

G. K. Chesterton passes through and rightly thinks that "It would not matter a single straw if a Brontë story were a hundred times more moonstruck and improbable than *Jane Eyre* or a hundred times more moonstruck and improbable than *Wuthering Heights* . . . The emotions with which they dealt were universal emotions, emotions of the morning of existence, the springtide joy and the springtide terror. Every one of us as a boy or girl has had some midnight dream of nameless obstacle and unutterable menace, in which there was, under whatever imbecile forms, all the deadly stress and panic of *Wuthering Heights*. Every one of us has had a day-dream of our own potential destiny not one atom more reasonable than *Jane Eyre* . . . Yet, despite this vast nightmare of illusion and morbidity and ignorance of the world, those are perhaps the truest books that were ever written. Their essential truth to life sometimes makes one catch one's breath. For it is not true to the manners, which are constantly false, or to facts, which are almost always false; it is true to the only existing thing which is true, emotion, the irreducible minimum, the indestructible germ."

A very young Virginia Woolf came here—she admired the Brontës the way she admired everything: at a safe distance and without demonstrating great enthusiasm—to report on the phenomenon in her first article (unsigned) in *The Guardian* and where it says that "Haworth expresses the Brontës; the Brontës express Haworth; they fit like a snail to its shell" and where she recounts how she paused in front of their graves, which "seem to start out of the ground at you in tall, upright lines, like an army of silent soldiers," maybe already anticipating her own oh so Brontëian end: stones in jacket pockets, sinking below, and down the river, hearing voices even underwater.

A Henry James strolled through here with a Henryjamesian face of disgust at the extra-literary phenomenon (this "beguiling infatuation" with "their tragic history"; save me the "fantastic" and the "sentimental" and "the ecstasies" of "our wonderful public"), which, for him, obscured the achievements of their work, and yet, no doubt, he was deeply breathing in the air of the place and the scent of besotted specters like those in *The Turn of the Screw* and "Maud-Evelyn" as well as the suffering and epiphanic and infirm men like Ralph Touchett and Milly Theale, while, at all cost, he tries to forget how his own sister, the mad Alice, so closely resembles a Brontë character.

And Penelope arrived there, driving always at night, naively thinking in that way nobody would see her; but looking at herself in the rearview mirror and saying: "I don't look like a deer blinded by the headlights, but like a blinding deer behind the steering wheel."

Penelope arrived in a brand new rental car that after a few miles (miles wear more than kilometers; miles pass more slowly) already looked like one of those vehicles worn out from robbing banks and making prison escapes.

Penelope drove through Keethly, where the sisters went to buy what little clothes they had, stopped off to pee along the side of the road in Top Whitens (a ruinous property which may or may not have inspired Wuthering Heights) and to vomit in Ponden Hall (which may or may not have inspired Thrushcross Grange), and then passed a small forest.

And suddenly there, on the other side (luckily it's a small forest; Penelope is afraid of forests), was the church where the three girls prayed. And the school where Charlotte Brontë taught (and where the children gave her bouts of "nausea" and to Emily seemed "less intelligent than any dog"). And the pub where Branwell drank everything in reach of hand and gullet while reciting grand plans impossible to put into practice, trying to forget his Mrs. Robinson and—on top of it all, without them knowing, but, probably, suspecting it—having discovered his sisters were writing on the sly and didn't want to play with him anymore. And there were all those Brontëified businesses (including an Indian restaurant that served spicy dishes with allusive names like Chicken Heathcliff Very Spicy).

And, at last, the parochial house canonized as museum.

Penelope entered it the way one enters a dream, the way one returns to a place from their childhood and finds it smaller than they remembered, but, also, more important in relation to all the other places that came after.

Everything begins here, including me, thought Penelope. And I've ended up here, to make an offering of myself and to see if they have something to offer me. To see if I receive some clear instruction and some saving advice, she said to herself.

And there amid the manuscript pages in glass cases and the locks of hair and the small portable desks of polished wood and the dog collars and the tiny adult shoes that looked like those of children and the son's paintings and the father's pistol.

And the small beds/chambers in the small rooms with sliding doors (they reminded Penelope of the sleeping modules on space shuttles and stations). And the round table where all three of them wrote at the same time, feeling they had all the time in the world as long as they didn't stop writing. The table around which they paced circles until they fell down exhausted when they couldn't shed the spider webs of insomnia (Penelope walked several circles around it, in both directions).

And, of course, the gift shop. There, as if in passing, books, the books, the life's work. Pocket, Trade, Hardback. Cheap and limited editions. But the main and most and best-selling items are teapots, key chains, coasters, refrigerator magnets. And prints of those portraits signed by Branwell Brontë and that flattering drawing of Charlotte Brontë (who drew a lot and more and better than her brother) that George Richmond did for her. And those photographs of trios of women who might be them though nobody's entirely sure. (Blurry photographs and so different from those retouched photographs of the Karmas, omnipresent on Mount Karma, on bookshelves sans books, on bookshelves made photoshelves, in living rooms and bedrooms and bathrooms and kitchens, massive group pictures, with everyone perfectly positioned according to their power in the family pyramid, but, in the end, all of them there, prisoners not of a golden cage but of so many silver frames. Photographs that, Penelope thinks, are the family version of fast-food restaurant billboards: where everything looks so perfect and tasty, but, ah, the cruel reality when you arrive to your table and you open the little cardboard box and what's there inside has little or nothing to do with what those magnificent vistas sold you.) All that's missing is the Haworth Parsonage Lego set (little figures of the family included; Branwell's with a bottle in hand), thinks Penelope.

And then—is it possible that even here, even now she can't stop thinking about the Karmas?—Penelope feels strange and crazier than ever. Penelope feels again like she did that morning at the wedding and that night on the beach. Penelope realizes she's in trouble, that she doesn't know where she is, just that it's a place called trouble.

But it's called Haworth.

It's not even called Wuthering Heights.

Or Cumbres Borrascosas.

And Penelope thinks the world would be a better place, a more comprehensible place, if all the names of towns and cities and countries were descriptive and emotional. Wouldn't it be better if Barcelona were called Touristic Inferno and Rome Vocational Averno? There are half-assed attempts, faint glimmers, that aren't, in the end, effective, because they're overly concerned with the aesthetic or the style: New York as Gotham, Paris as Ville Lumière. And there are disorienting errors: Buenos Aires, or Piedras Negras, or Sad Songs (where Penelope was happier than anywhere else, when she was a girl, high up on those ever so gothic and windy and nineteenth-century cliffs). There are functional cases, but cases that, really, aren't names: El Paso, the pass to cross, or Death Valley, where you go to die, or the Puerto Escondido, where you go to hide. But, though there are many, they are not sufficient, they do not attain the climatic and topographical but also spiritual and temperamental perfection of Cumbres Borrascosas or Wuthering Heights.

And, here, Penelope feels like this: high and turbulent and a little like Alice Liddell plummeting toward Wonderland or Dorothy Gale spun away by an Oz-bound twister. She's at the X on the map and at the precise and real place that, nevertheless, feels irreal and disorienting, it feels just how she feels. Like a dislocated location, like a depersonalized person.

It took her so many years to get here and now that she's here Penelope wonders why she came, what did she think was going to happen, how did she imagine that things could ever change. That this Haworth could alter or correct or erase what she did, so long ago, when she was eight years old, on behalf of this Haworth but from so far away.

And everything gets worse when, in the souvenir shop, she sees the prints of the Fritz Eichenberg and Clare Leighton woodcuts, used to illustrate respective editions of *Wuthering Heights*. And, of course, it's known, Penelope detests when Heathcliff and Catherine Earnshaw are *shown*. She hates that they get drawn and put in front of you and ask if you recognize them, as if they were robot portraits of two fugitives like her and who knows what they've done or whom they've done it to.

The answer, of course, is no. She has never seen them. She has never read them. That version of them. They're not hers. They bear no resemblance whatever to the ones who're everything to her.

But in the case of Eichenberg and Leighton, Penelope has to acknowledge that there's something there; that the artists knew how to produce a kind of rare alchemy where the writing itself was transformed into the lines they carved. There, Catherine Earnshaw with one foot on a rock, posing like a defiant explorer, birds seeming to burst from her windblown hair. And Heathcliff at her feet, almost worshiping her, in happy times. It's not bad at all. But the effect and the achievement are intensified even more in the three prints of Heathcliff alone.

One of them shows him moving through the snow, heavy footsteps, under a stormy sky, like an explorer of the known and not the unknown: someone who knows perfectly well what he wants to rediscover and to recover in order to plant his flag right there.

And the best of all are the other two, one by Eichenberg and another by Leighton, but both focusing on the same abyssal and tormented moment of *Wuthering Heights*: the scene in which the always helpful Nelly Dean, never one to miss out on a big moment, tells Heathcliff—who's waiting for her outside, in the park that surrounds Thrushcross Grange—the news that Catherine Earnshaw has died.

Then Nelly Dean tells Lockwood that Heathcliff "was there—at least, a few yards further in the park; leant against an old ash-tree, his hat off, and his hair soaked with the dew that had gathered on the budded branches, and fell pattering round him. He had been standing a long time in that position, for I saw a pair of ouzels passing and repassing scarcely three feet from him, busy in building their nest, and regarding his proximity no more than that of a piece of timber. They flew off at my approach, and he raised his eyes and spoke: 'She's dead!' he said; 'I've not waited for you to learn that. Put your handkerchief away—don't snivel before me. Damn you all! she wants none of *your* tears!'" Then Heathcliff fires off his instantly famous and quotable curse and Penelope recites it again now, in her cell/study, remembering her time in Haworth: "Catherine Earnshaw, may you not rest, as long as I am living! You said I killed you—haunt me then! The murdered *do* haunt their murderers. I believe—I know that ghosts *have* wandered on earth. Be with me always—take any form—drive me mad! only *do* not leave me in this abyss, where I cannot find you! Oh God! it is unutterable! I *cannot* live without my life! I *cannot* live without my soul!" And Heathcliff begins to beat his head against the tree trunk and releases the howl of a wounded wolf and Nelly Dean, though moved and frightened, cannot help but analyze the scene with a forensic obsession that promises not to miss the slightest detail; or, perhaps, inventing the best way to tell all of it, because she owes her audience: "I observed several splashes of blood on the bark of the tree, and his hands and forehead were both stained; probably the scene I witnessed was a repetition of others acted during the night. It hardly moved my compassion—it appalled me; still I felt reluctant to quit him so. But the moment he recollected himself enough to notice me watching, he thundered a command for me to go, and I obeyed. He was beyond my skill to quiet or console!"

And, yes, another exceedingly Karmatic quality in Nelly Dean: the way she's always saying that she is helping and supporting, but is only doing so in appearance. A lot of talk, not much action. And so, nobody does anything, because they're too busy talking about what they would do and what others don't do if they weren't talking all the time. All blah-blah and no do-do. Hiriz in particular and the Karma females in general were like this, Penelope recalls: adding up all their theoretical undertakings, but subtracting themselves when it comes to putting them in practice and leaving you all alone and on your own. Like how Nelly Dean abandons Heathcliff, who, again, in the prints of Eichenberg and Leighton, looks so much like Penelope's Heathcliff.

In the first, Heathcliff leaning his back against the tree, its branches like bolts of lightning, cursing the heavens. In the second, Heathcliff with his face in shadow, pressing it against the trunk, as if wanting to fell it with nothing but the pressure of his forehead. In one and the other, Heathcliff has an air similar to that of the heroes of independence of Penelope's home country. Titans with long sideburns and names like those of the country's secondary schools who cross cordilleras and soar through the air on their steeds—even behind enemy lines—and die in the solitude of exile. And Penelope wonders if the fact that she likes those prints so much and that they seem appropriate and that their perspective corresponds a great deal to her own might not be because they were done not long after *Wuthering Heights* was published. Not yet considered "a period"—and, as such, an irreal—piece. Maybe that's why they feel so believable and true to her. Prints with no motivation but the powerful and imaginative radiation of the book's pages. There being, at that time, neither movies nor actors' faces.

It's not the first time Penelope has seen those prints and she remembers the first time she saw them.

She can't forget it.

She was still a girl, but was already, also, a veteran worshipper of all things *Wuthering Heights* with all the same passion her few friendly little friends at school had for collecting dolls and little houses to put them in, resplendent little houses that had nothing to do with the dark architecture of Wuthering Heights.

And her parents laughed at Penelope and made fun of her "madness." And told her Emily Brontë's novel was a "minor" work. And if she was interested in star-crossed love, then she was old enough to read *Tender Is the Night*, their favorite book. And that's the way her parents acted and how they raised her: through opposition and option. It was enough for you to say you wanted a cat for them to bring you a dog (and Penelope always thought, like Heathcliff, the only use for those animals was to be able to command them to "Attack!" or to help you strengthen your hand muscles when you strangle them); or to say you wanted to learn to play the saxophone (long before Lisa Simpson, that *saxualized* girl, would become the paradigm for the family-problem-solving daughter) for them to toss you an acoustic guitar.

And Penelope—just to be able to argue with the authority of knowledge—reads the Fitzgerald novel right away (she never understood that idea that you have to "be old enough" for a book or that once you have learned to read and understood that all books, beyond what they tell, are read according to the same system). And the truth is, *Tender Is the Night* doesn't seem that special to her, because—to begin and to end with—*Tender Is the Night* is not *Wuthering Heights*. And the woes of Nicole and Dick are so sordid and domestic and maybe that's what appeals so much to her parents, who always go around looking for themselves in everything. Maybe that's the origin of that "great idea" of theirs, so Fitzgeraldian and so marketable ("Fitzgerald began in advertising," her father always recalled, as if he were just starting out), to travel the world filming themselves and promoting a brand of whiskey. The perfect crime: they make money and get famous (the kind of fame almost all the Scotts and Zeldas who don't write will attain in the twenty-first century, with their compulsive exhibition on social media) and spend little time at home with their children.

On one of their trips, Penelope's parents arrive to England, tie off the *Diver* on the bank of the Thames and, there, her parents playing dirty tricks on the Royal guards at the doors to Buckingham Palace and disguised as John Steed and Emma Peel and walking across Abbey Road.

And when they come home from that trip—as a conciliatory gesture—they bring Penelope the two prints of Heathcliff by Eichenberg & Leighton. Penelope asks to have them framed (none of that sticking them to the wall with thumbtacks) and hangs them beside her bed at eye-level when lying down. And she talks to them every night. And tells the two Heathcliffs that, without a doubt, it won't be long now before they meet.

And her parents tell her they have another surprise for her. "Another *Wuthering Heights* surprise," they warn; but they aren't going to give her any kind of preview, they prefer she see it for herself when the moment arrives.

And weeks later, they turn on the TV and Penelope sees it.

And what Penelope sees is something she never wanted to see.

And it's then Penelope decides she's going to stop being Lockwood (the one who listens and takes note of everything everyone does and he would never do) and is going to enter the fray.

Penelope is going to be Heathcliff, Penelope thinks then, as a girl, seeing her parents on TV, while her parents watch her watch them, there inside, on the TV screen, in the black and white of sweet dreams, in the black and white of bitter nightmares suddenly come true.


When she was a girl, Penelope didn't know where her parents ended and the TV began. Her parents were tuned in and broadcast every so often in the house where they lived or, rather, passed through a few days a year. But her parents were on TV all the time and at every hour.

Appearing suddenly, like a holiday spot, between one block and the next of more dramatic shows and afternoon telenovelas and evening procedurals and even the misty chapters of *Cumbres Borrascosas* or the crepuscular episodes of *The Twilight Zone.*

There.

In front of her.

Much closer than they tended to be in person.

Her parents interspersed with other ads for cigarettes or sodas or laundry detergent.

Her parents making their way between other stranger and more disconcerting spots. Ad spots selling no consumer product but the one that consumes you: fear and guilt. Spots of the "public service" variety. Spots showing the perspective of a man drowning in the ocean for having failed to take the necessary precautions or soliciting money for children (depicted like little Heathcliffs, a keening song as background music) who live in the streets and were born, also, because someone failed to take the necessary precautions. And that other spot asking for "the collaboration of all citizens" if they see "any suspicious or subversive activity" and where a telephone number is provided to call and "denounce controversial elements and enemies of the state."

All those spots like stains, there, on those apparatuses with antennas to manipulate, without remote control, and "ghostly" images and sudden spasmodic fits "from the vertical and the horizontal."

And also, suddenly—not technical imperfections but historical imperfections—interrupting the transmission of national comedies or foreign series to break the news of new terrorist attacks and counterattacks by the brand new military government.

And during one of those commercial breaks, Penelope sees her parents for the last time: on the Christmas morning of 1977 following Christmas Eve 1977 (when Penelope and her bad brother and Uncle Hey Walrus went out looking for them all over the city). And there they are, and there the news is delivered that "the onetime models and beautiful people were captured by the toxic ideology of the Marxist apparatus." And no, that's not quite right. The hosts on the news program got it wrong: her parents' relationship with the urban guerilla is as close (equally thin and fragile and, given a little time, equally dismissed) as the ones they had with Zen Buddhism or vegetarianism or folkloric dance lessons.

And, true, her parents *did* film that ad on the beaches of Cuba: her mother crammed into some camo mini-shorts and shirt knotted up around her waist with a gun belt and machine gun, and her father with a fake beard and a hat and smoking a cigar.

And sure: her parents *did* start a sort of urban commando; but they treated it like another game to be played with their friends, models and plastic artists and publicists and even the occasional writer.

And their takeover of a prestigious department store on December 24th (an "operation" that Penelope overheard them plan amid fits of laughter over the course of weeks) was nothing but a "performance" and a "happening" and a "participatory and ephemeral work of art" and "a joke" that later they would explain to journalists and then their hostages, who would be there buying last-minute Christmas gifts and, suddenly, would feel more surprised than scared at being taken hostage by that "couple from that sailboat."

And, OK, nobody will be able to help admiring the perfect cut and tailoring of their guerilla-chic style uniforms. And one of the hostages will ask for an autograph and to take a picture with them.

And her parents, of course, will comply.

And they'll smile for the camera.

And Penelope doesn't smile.

But, of course, Penelope is just as mad about that "other *Wuthering Heights* surprise" that her parents had prepared for her and that they'd shown her on TV earlier that December.

"Here it comes . . . You won't believe it," they said.

And Penelope couldn't believe what came next.

And then, after that unbelievable thing appeared and she witnessed it, Penelope turned into Heathcliff, indeed.

And Penelope took her revenge.

Like Heathcliff, yes.

And Penelope—the last day she spent at her grandparents' house, in Sad Songs, before boarding the train to head back home, on Christmas Eve— called that telephone number that appeared on the screen and they answered and she revealed to that voice on the other end of the line what her parents were going to do that night.

And Penelope said she didn't know if they were "enemies of the state," but she was sure they were "controversial elements."

And Penelope described in detail what her parents would be undertaking in a few hours. Their performance and their happening at that department store.

And it's the end of the year.

And it's a good moment for the forces of order to strike a warning blow, to make an impression, and they surround the building and ignore the shouts from inside alerting them "it's all a performance."

And they are "subdued by the forces of order." And "subdued by the forces of order" means the army comes in with tanks and bazookas and many people die, among them several customers there buying Christmas presents.

And the attack is filmed by the news channel cameras and broadcast at midday, between ad spots of her parents sailing, happy, voyaging.

And during one pause in the special coverage of that "regrettable and tragic episode, product of minds alienated by alien ideologies that have nothing to do with our more deeply-rooted customs and more sensible beliefs," there it is, yes, once again, the "other *Wuthering Heights* surprise."

The spark of death that set Penelope ablaze and made her do what she did then and what she'll keep on doing. Because what Penelope does then is of those acts that never stops being done, that is and will forever be there: its expansive wave like a window opened so a hand can reach inside accompanied by wailing voice begging to be let in.

That strange and sacred and dark motivation.

Which leads you to see, though it's not there, someone opening a coffin and lifting a dead woman in his arms and dancing with her.

Which led Penelope to suffocate a comatose husband and to lose a son and to write all those books. If William S. Burroughs became a writer "thanks to the accident" of killing his wife with a bullet to the head, Penelope became what she is thanks to the surprise her parents gave her and the surprise she subsequently gave them.


Surprise!: when Penelope's parents were in England, they filmed the obligatory pop-Londoner spot; but they also made time and space to film second one.

Her parents went to West Yorkshire, to Haworth, to the Brontë Parsonage Museum.

And there they set up the cameras and rented period costumes and dressed up as Heathcliff and Catherine Earnshaw.

And that's how the little, belittled, Penelope saw them, unable to believe what she was seeing.

Ghosts on TV. Her father and mother running through the mist and rocks, shouting names not their own (names Penelope felt were hers), calling at windows and beating on trees and, all the time, laughing uproariously, maniacally, laughing at her, at their daughter, no doubt about it.

Her parents who'd never filmed an ad in the south of France depicting—like in *Tender Is the Night*—a couple enduring and suffering a traumatic and never-entirely-explained episode in a bathroom.

Her parents who now were making fun of her book instead of bringing it to life with their own, Penelope thought then, with the implacable and precise logic of children.

Yes: her parents had done to her something even worse than parents did to children in children's stories. They hadn't killed or eaten her; but they had taken the thing she loved most and profaned it.

And Penelope asked herself what Heathcliff would've done in this situation.

And she knew the answer.

And she did it.

And all it took was dialing six numbers, her tiny finger turning that telephone dial that spun back and forth with the same sound, clack-clack-clack, as the teeth of those mechanical skulls.

And so it was that Penelope—now you see them and now you don't, nothing here and nothing there—made her parents disappear, transforming them into *desaparecidos*.

And so, ever since, Penelope has been wandering the moors of her dying life, talking to herself, reciting and rewriting:

"You teach me how cruel you've been—cruel and false. *Why* did you despise me? I have not one word of comfort for you—you deserve this. You have killed yourselves . . . May you wake in torment! . . . May you not rest as long as I'm living! You say I killed you—haunt me, then! The murdered do haunt their murderers, I believe. I know that ghosts *have* wandered the earth. Be with me always—take any form—drive me mad! only do not leave me in this abyss, where I cannot find you!"

And no: her parents' ghost did not visit Penelope just as Catherine's ghost doesn't answer Heathcliff's calls, except maybe at the very end, who knows; because Nelly Dean wasn't there to tell it and had to settle for a dead man with open eyes and a frozen smile.

And, now, at some point during the night in her cell/study at Our Lady of Our Lady of Our Lady of . . . , Penelope decides the time has come to turn the page and it's the last page.

She's so tired of writing and living as if she were reading.

As if her life were a novel with too many ellipses.

The death of Lina and the death of Maxi.

The green and enlightening milk she drank that night in the desert and the impossible to illuminate black hole of that night when she went out walking on the beach with her young son and "Reader, I lost him." And—contrary to what's recommended in such situations—she didn't stay in place, to wait for him to appear, clapping so he would hear and find her, rather, since that moment, Penelope hasn't stopped moving and cursing herself. Everywhere. Until she achieved her fade to white going madder than ever before, at the Brontë Parsonage Museum, where something clicked and something snapped; and suddenly she was beating on the walls of the museum with one of those jacks for changing tires that she grabbed out of the trunk of her rental car.

Penelope wrecking everything.

Penelope like Heathcliff beside Catherine Earnshaw's coffin.

Penelope howling "The Brontës' little wooden soldiers are hidden somewhere around here! Buried alive! *Desaparecidos*! And I am going dig them up and free them from their chains and torment!" and thinking that if she found them and played with them, if she gave them roles and names, she could rewrite the past, her past, her parents' past.

All their dirty pasts.

Revise them. And that—erasing the whole dirty war—all of them could live happily in the perfectly conjugated past in a castle in Glass Town or Angria or Gondal.

But she can't.

Real lives don't allow for the chronological spasms of true fictions.

And now Penelope, in her cell/studio at Our Lady of Our Lady of Our Lady of . . . can only look ahead and think of what's to come, and pray that it not be too much, and that it'll all be over soon.

And that's how Penelope comes to imagine purifying flames.

Thornfield Hall and Satis House and Manderley (and, why not, the

Overlook Hotel; because Penelope always thinks a version of *The Shining* where it was the mother and not the father who went mad would be much more logical and coherent) and her, in all places, like the underground madman at the heights of his delirium.

Like Bertha Mason in the attic of Thornfield Hall.

Like Miss Havisham in the decayed hall of the never consumed nuptial banquet of the never consummated wedding at Satis House.

Like Mrs. Danvers beside the window of Manderley.

Like Wendy Torrance in the boiler room of the Overlook Hotel.

And like, yes, Zelda Fitzgerald, Cinderella turned to cinders, in the blazing Highland Hospital, only identified by her slippers. Burning buildings, burning women.

Her love under lock and key and her love's keymaster and the key to her love and a son to save from all those ghost parties, from all those haunted bedrooms.

And Penelope imagines herself in flames, but no longer burning as she's been burning all these years. Penelope all along thinking only about what her bad brother once said about one of his many favorite writers. Something about a writing program whose final and decisive step/assignment ("an exercise that never fails," that writer explained) was to write a love letter from inside a burning building. Like those buildings that burned in those songs she liked so much and, she supposes, still likes, though it's been so long since she listened to them.

Talking Heads. *Cabezas parlantes.* TV newscasters. Voices in her head. A band that, in the last years of her adolescence, Penelope imposed on herself almost as a therapeutic gesture: liking something not of the nineteenth century and *so* modern and *so* in fashion. Maybe—it would've been more logical—to choose something more languid and gothic. The Cure. But no. Penelope was far from logical and had always felt a deep distaste for obvious choices. And, festive but as if possessed, Talking Heads always struck her as far more impassioned than The Cure and their derivatives with midnight-scarecrow hairdos. Penelope danced to those songs—songs about serial killers and electric guitars and cities and drugs and animals and about "The book I read was in your eyes because you wrote it" or something like that—with her bad brother at Coliseum.

It's possible they were never closer than they were at that moment. It's also true they were high. Up to their noses. And drugs make you close, stick you together. "Happy noses," her bad brother said while they jumped and shouted, his physical body ever so chemical. And her, there, who more than dancing was running around the dance floor (à la the living Catherine Earnshaw) or playing dead (à la the corpse of Catherine Earnshaw) so her bad brother picked her up à la Heathcliff and danced with her. Profaning her or not. It didn't matter. Amid the artificial fog and flashing strobes.

And after—at Coliseum there were successive live numbers throughout the night—and Penelope even went up on the stage to sing, with a group of friends. In a band who called themselves The Showers (Lina laughed a big huahuahua when she told her about it years later in Abracadabra), because they were really off key, because they sang versions of popular songs as if singing in the shower. Including by the Talking Heads. That wailing voice and those tribal drums and those sparkling and flamboyant verses that she remembers now to, right away, find nexuses and connections between the here and the there. Some songs are like that. Some books are like that. Waiting to make total and absolute sense and to turn into a "They're playing our song," into an "I'm rereading my book" and suddenly and without warning . . . Sounds, written or sung, that possess you when you think you possess them, but no. And, sometimes, unexpectedly, and even though at first the one thing doesn't seem to have any relation to the other, they become the perfect soundtrack for the ideal typography.

Everything was connected and everything is connected, thinks Penelope, yes, "When my love / Stands next to your love, / I can't define love / When it's not love / It's not love / It's not love / It's not love / Which is my face / Which is a building / Which is on fire" and "There has got to be a way / Burning down the house / Close enough but not too far, / Maybe you know where you are / Fightin' fire with fire" and "All wet / Hey you might need a raincoat / Shake-down / Dreams walking in broad daylight / Three hundred six-ty five de-grees / Burning down the house" and "My house's / Out of the ordinary / That's right / Don't want to hurt nobody / Some things sure can sweep me off my feet / Burning down the house" and "No visible means of support and you have not seen nuthin' yet / Everything's stuck together / I don't know what you expect staring into the TV set / Fighting fire with fire" and "Goes on and the heat goes on / Goes on and the heat goes on / Goes on and the heat goes on / Goes where the hand has been / Goes on and the heat goes on."

Now, for the first time in so many years, Penelope, scream-singing in her cell/study.

Wuthering Heights like her own ever so out-of-the-ordinary house, yes.

Her face, pure open mouth and soaked with the kind of tears no raincoat can protect you from. Her dreams walking by the light not of the day but of the night, losing footing and finding it, without means of survival, but, even still, her love arriving to a burning building, burning down the house, not wanting to hurt nobody but having done so much damage to so many, fighting fire with fire, fire that connects and holds everything together, staring into the TV set when you haven't seen nothing yet, seeing it like seeing a fire, close enough but not that far. Seeing it like seeing yourself from outside: Penelope becoming panoramic and bursting into flames along with Stella D'Or and the Tulpa sisters and dAlien.

Penelope writing her love letter from inside a burning building that is this building.

A letter that cannot be deactivated or corrected—there's no red wire or blue wire here; there's no red pen or blue pen either—and that Penelope finishes and sends and says goodbye to with nocturnal tenderness, with an "I always loved you so much" and "Forgive me for everything."

A letter to herself to be received elsewhere, under the moon or on Earth, where the "entire world" is no longer "a dreadful collection of memoranda," a better place, memorizing herself, making memory of everything she'll at last let herself forget.

Penelope will receive it and tear it open and read it beside her own tomb. The paper and ink burning her fingertips, her body underground, unrecognizable but at least recovered. Happy to be a skeleton free from the obligation or responsibility of sustaining her skin and her features and her guilt and her sins.

Reading and reading her and reading herself.

And amazed someone could attribute such restless dreams to her.

To someone who now lies, resting and at peace, read by everyone forever, in a tomb so new and so quiet.

# TONIGHT
## (MANUAL OF LAST RITES FOR WAKING DREAMERS)

Many years have passed since that night.
—MARCEL PROUST
*Du côté de chez Swann*


There's too much on my mind
There's too much on my mind
And I can't sleep at night thinking about it
—RAY DAVIES
"Too Much on My Mind"


Don't start me talking
I could talk all night
My mind goes sleepwalking
While I'm putting the world to right
—ELVIS COSTELLO
"Oliver's Army"


Real things in the darkness seem no realer than dreams.
—MURASAKI SHIKIBU
*The Tale of Genji*


There are truths which one can see only when it's dark.
—ISAAC BASHEVIS SINGER
"Teibele and Her Demon"


Many years have passed since that night.
—MARCEL PROUST
*Jean Santeuil*

At night, the past blows more powerfully.

The ruinous past that passes, without ever passing completely, or in its entirety, or all the way to the end.

The past laying waste to everything in its path and yet, in its way, preserving it; wrapping it up like a gift that nobody wants to open yet can't stop thinking about. And that, when thinking about it, pops open and springs out, as if from inside one of those so-called Jack-in-the-boxes, containing a supposed surprise though one everybody's anticipating, so they hold it with a mix of fear and pleasure, like one of those flowers that never loses its leaves, with carnivorous blooms and an asphyxiating perfume.

The past like the predictable surprise, slow yet incessant, of a jungle swallowing cities we once knew how to build.

The past climbing green up the sides of abandoned and ruined buildings, returning the civilized remnants of parks and plazas to wilderness, reminding us on our sleepless nights that every city is really an island. A desert island. There, the past and its roots strangling and ripping down the solitary palm tree of a present that lacks a treasure map and where—surrounded by all those people—we're always alone: standing atop the X that marks the spot where everything that happened and won't happen again is buried.

The past not passing away but twisting and turning through its own limbless leaves. The past like the hoot of plucked and hopeless owls; like a cat that smiles overhead, inviting us to eat and drink it; like the fruit of a wisdom that many prefer never to taste at all, not even a little nibble, for fear that the knowledge will do them harm and be too heavy, grave and gravitational, like a divine condemnation from the voices in their heads to the mouths of their stomachs.

The past like that dawning realization in their minds and that taste on their tongues (a taste like the taste of figurative words or abstract thoughts breaking down, which, as someone once said in a letter, is the taste of moldy mushrooms) that forces them to reconsider each and every law of their increasingly contracted and opaque universes.

The past that—as the Arabic or Chinese proverb warns—no god can change. So the gods get even, orchestrating increasingly unharmonious and terrible things. Present and future things and, thus, mosques aflame, cathedrals collapsing, pyramids devoured by waters or swallowed by the desert. Divine punishments for those who, in the past, had the audacity to invent them and put them in writing with clauses as immoveable and unchangeable as the above. Clauses that teach us the past is the religion nobody can help but believe in, on their knees and begging forgiveness for sins committed, always, some unforgivable yesterday. Because, yes, when it comes not to the History of all people but the histories of each individual person, the web of the present shrinks and compresses and fades away, and becomes impossible to bear. The future is modern and ephemeral and, suddenly, unattainable. The future is no longer science fiction and dreaming of marvels yet to come in our lifetime, but, merely, not risking going beyond the unknown of what tomorrow's or, at most, next week's, weather will bring. While the past is classic and never goes out of style and is always returned to. And, going around all feline and fierce (as if across a catwalk decorated like a forest in whose center shines the bright window of a dark house), the past files by again; amid *haute couture* and *prêt-à-porter*, reminding us, unforgettable, what we'll never be, what we wished we could've been. The past walks all over us, stabbing us with high heels and voodoo pins and vampire fangs, draining us of ourselves through those small holes and filling us back up with itself.

And suddenly, when we take it into account, the past is the only thing that counts, all we've got left: things pass and keep passing all the time in the past. "I am the past and I passed by in order to stay," exhales the past, in ecstasy, vapor roiling out of its mouth, a smoke with an ancient scent. The wintery past, cloaked in furs and doffing in greeting, with the most irreverent of reverence, a hat that, regardless of any wind, never flies off and always tops its unimaginable head of uncontrollable hair, like braids whipping about in a gale, ensnaring everything. Knots tied when the past makes memory and corrects and changes something that happened or never happened; but that happens now, altered and altering the one who remembers, so long after, like someone recounting a dreamless dream, a dream with nobody to dream it.

The past revising, passing through again to clean up or mess up what can never be fully expurgated.

The past that's always returning from exile only to, straight away, exile itself again.

The past—nothing to be done, nothing to do about it—that never asks permission to come in, because you already inhabit it; because it's you who enters it never to escape and to watch, impotent, as rooms and corridors and staircases are added to its impossible-to-trace blueprint.

The past that's full of windows that you don't know if they open in or out, but from which you can always perceive your arrival or your departure.

The past that is heavy air in the light air. "Here I am and I am not going to leave," exhales that wind, spiraling in from so far away. Changing dates, rearranging furniture, driving curtains wild, forcing you to cling to banisters, to tie yourself to masts, to blow out candles of ever-fewer birthdays, to go down and take refuge in basements out of which, after the tornado doesn't stop but takes a break to recharge its energies, you come up to discover that nothing—in B&W or in Technicolor—is as you remembered it; that it no longer resembles the past Kansas of our lives where, invariably, after so much adventure and misadventure, we all wish to return.

The past like time and timepest. Yes, as the years pass (more and more all the time, it's easier to remember better what's remote while what's close appears as if enveloped in fog), the present seems to barely sustain the vertigo of that circular cyclone circling in reverse, coming from everywhere and moving in all directions, constant and consonant and chorusing and "ZZZZZ," the cavorting current of electric air sounding comical and comedic, as if mocking the wakeful, drifting those empty and blank bubbles over their heads in which they neither saws nor logs are depicted.

The past like a giant wave crashing against the highest cliff or someone quietly waving hello from on top of it. A sudden shift of atmospheric pressure and the past laughing at your surfboard, your umbrella, your dock or your jetty, your always-soaked raincoat, your sandcastle or your lightning rod, your boat and your lifejacket and your lifeboat, your meteorological oracle who trembles, under the sun, delivering a "deteriorating toward nightfall" or a "the fury of the titans is drawing nigh" or a "producing powerful precipitation." So, events that once precipitated begin to precipitate again. Yes, tonight's wind is a tormenting wind that brings down the circus tent of your life, scattering its three rings, where, without a net, a trapezing tempest swings. Lightning bolts that frighten the animals in their cages. Rolling thunder drawing ever nearer, like the drumroll anticipating the magician's trick or the clown's tumble or écuyère's smile or the tamer's whip.

The past that's a domesticated but never-entirely domestic animal (not to be trusted, don't lower your guard: no feeding the animals through the bars) that, suddenly, remembers its wild yesterday and bares its claws and fangs and rips your hand off instead of shaking it. And then the night is filled with screams and people run through the streets shouting, "Take cover! The past has been unleashed and it's hungry for justice and thirsty for vengeance!" And, in the stampede, the clown seizes the moment to rape the écuyère, and to steal the whip from the tamer to whip the magician, while the audience, hypnotized, discovers that the present is a flaming circus with neither future nor safety net.

The past that destroys everything, but that, at the same time, does so by constructing, clarifying or correcting, making memory or unmaking history while everything flies through the air, hanging in suspense. And there, the suspended loose pieces of the past's scattered rooms, making up the whole that he assembles now, remembering one of the few poems he ever memorized. A poem in one of those pale and slender collections of poetry that look so fragile compared to those thick novels with broad backs and dangerous smiles. Poetry was never his thing, poetry always frightened him in the same way—now, after everything with Penelope, more than ever—that nuns or riding horses frightened him: he never understood how someone could wed themselves to a god or entrust their body to that of an animal or arrive at the certainty that a poem was bad or good or perfect. Poets—sometimes washed up, sometimes fucked up, always clever—were, for him, writers wired in a different way, writers who were able, in just a few lines, to illuminate the mystery of how your parents had screwed you up or the irrational reasons behind the suicides of your wives or daughters or the way in which your kids would end up screwing you up, and that leads him to fantasize about the idea of reinventing himself as a poet: he said once that writing long was like reading and writing short was like writing and, yes, maybe composing those marginal and irregular lines . . . But no. It wasn't for him. Or, better, he wasn't for it. He could appreciate but not apprehend it. That poem in its craft or sullen art and when only the moon rages and ha ha ha, while everything is falling apparently out of place but, in the end, right where it belongs. The false order of all these years submitted now to a new perspective. Almost out the door, a new way of looking at that which, from the outset and after so much seeing, was almost invisible, and that now makes sense in a new way and takes on new meaning.

The past that never lets us leave it.

The past that always includes us on the guest list for a party we're not allowed to miss. Though we neither dance nor drink nor flirt, though we limit ourselves just to watching and following the rhythm with a foot and an empty cup. There we are and there we'll be because there we were.

The past that does what it wants with us and—though we might think we mount and master it, drawing on its reins—takes us where it wants and to its own beat, to the most unexpected places, down wide and well-lit avenues or along shadowy shortcuts and byways. In the past we are always and forever. We are even in the past that precedes our own past. In the past of our past that we can consider and learn from and visit in books and films and paintings and songs.

The past is a museum where we always have a room reserved and a key that allows us to open it and not to touch it, that's forbidden, but to look as long as we like—even with our eyes shut, when we sleep—until closing time, the time to close ourselves in and, sometimes, to stay shut away, there inside, flipping through the most irrational *catalogue raisonné*. Goodbye to all of that and hello to what the past tells him so he can note it down according to time and place and position it in the right room in the retrospective exhibition of his life. Minor sketches and great canvases. Title or no title. And dimensions and technique and, sometimes, the doubt of whether or not he actually painted something in all of that. *"That Night, Tonight (1977), mixed technique, varying dimensions."* Surrounded by a red rope that forces you to keep a certain distance, and gives a "no touching" order he—who after all is the author, its author—will disobey. He killed time in the bathroom, waited until everyone left and all the doors were locked. And so, now, alone with his own past. Face to face. Facing the profile of that past that tends to turn its back on you, but that, in his case, always looks him dead in the eye as it recedes.

The past as epigraph/footnote taking up more and more space than the dead body of the text it detaches from as if it were its soul. Everything that already was, but now coming after that *, sometimes between parenthesis. Like this: (*). As if inserted between two taught springs that have just been set, compressed for instant distension, given all the strangling length they need, with the touch of a minute mechanism within the immense clockwork. And, then, the movement; like that toy from his childhood, a childhood when most toys were still so primitive: unplugged and corporeal, without clicks or spaces where the heat of a fingertip sliding across the black ice of a screen sets things in motion. His favorite toy from that time. A little man made of tin with a jacket and hat, carrying a suitcase covered with stickers from the places he'd visited. A toy like that one that appears in line 143 of the poem "Pale Fire," and that John Shade shows to Charles Kinbote in the book by Vladimir Nabokov, explaining to him that "he kept it as a kind of *memento mori*—he'd had a strange fainting fit one day in his childhood while playing with that toy." A toy that (his parents offered to exchange it for another, but he decided to keep as it was, strange, different, unique) only moved backward, because of a defect/improvement in its manufacturing. A broken toy is a toy with a story. A toy that stands out from all other toys. A seasoned toy. Mr. Trip, he called and named him. And Mr. Trip obeyed by disobeying: he moved, backward, watching him watch him. Mr. Trip, who at the time was already anticipating for him the retro idea that the past never ceases to spin and to expand and to take up space until the past is everything and everything passes through it.

And, ah, how to forget that first movement—that succession of instants— when the flashbacks in movies began to take place no longer in prehistoric caves or ancient Roman temples or in the trenches of First and Second World Wars, but in places and times in which you'd lived and remembered living: in pasts where you'd been and that remained in your mind to be discovered, without warning, as something that, for so many young people, was part of a distant age. Suddenly you were "of a period": the past, there, in the darkness of movie theaters, was no longer something foreign and immemorial but, merely, a prior stop along the way. A landscape out a window that, though blurry and fleeting, was remembered with ever more clarity. A landscape that could already be studied and evoked in documentaries (documentaries no longer like they once were; documentaries full of tricks where every so often they inserted colorful sequences of animation to keep the infantilized viewer alert and to distract him from the idea that his own life being filmed and packaged and broadcast didn't turn him into a documentarian, at least not until he learned how to draw and animate his photographs). A starting line that was, suddenly, the finish line. Moving backward like a disoriented toy, yes, until the past not only *has been* but also *is* and *will be*.

And there he was again, sleepless, enumerating possible present definitions of the past.

The past like the indispensible foundations of what is happening and what will happen.

The past slipping in through windows of today that we forgot to shut before going to sleep and running through the straight corridors of a tomorrow through which we'll no longer be able to circulate. And, ah, that terrible moment when you discover all your wishes are no longer in the future but in the past. That burning icy instant when it dawns on you—a phrase in three times, all times in one line—that *what will be is no longer what you thought it would be*. And where, you realize, that supposed looking to the future is nothing but trying not to look at the past but being unable to avoid it. There, then, a melancholic futurism in which all we have left is remembering how we imagined everything to come would be when we had everything before and not behind us. The same way you try to ignore an accident on the side of the road (the twisted metal, that arm poking out of a window in an impossible position) that, nevertheless, is impossible not to register down to the last detail, thinking, "Poor people," thinking "How lucky that it wasn't me." But the past always touches you, strikes you, runs you over, crashes into you. And so, you say to yourself, looking, better not to look. And you make an effort to think of any other thing while focusing on the voice of the bus driver suggesting and commanding and instructing that "There's more space behind you . . . Let's see . . . Everyone move back."

Behind you.

Move back.

Everything is there now.

In the darkness.

In the night.

Back in the dark night.

Even—and this is disturbing—sexual fantasies. Suddenly—like a blow to the jaw—you fantasize about what could've been and not about what will be. Those names, those eyes, those voices forming always-improvable conversations underlined with intention and a bit affected in the italics memory gives them. And those bodies, those body parts, your body how it once was and, broken, no longer is. Situations are revisited, invited home, caressed, and improved until they come true. Unmaking memory in order to remake it.

The past—its most muscular musculature, its most agile agility—that moves better all the time, yes. The future no longer serves, doesn't work, it tripped and fell and was broken. Now the future is that too-near yet unreachable workday on a calendar where all days are marked not in holiday-red but in danger-red. *Danger. Warning. Alert.* Any day now could be the last or the beginning of the end. Everything comes so clear (though you see less and less of what you want to see) that from there, so close, you can easily glimpse life's farewell looking you right in the eyes. That's why, reaching a *certain point*, you look back, and never glimpse the border or horizon.

The past that might be a foreign country where things are done in a different way, yes; but it's a foreign country that's always at war. Without truce or peace. And it proceeds to invade the whole map, covering all the colors one by one (those colors on maps that help distinguish one country from another) with its own. It's one uniform color, a grayish-blue mixed with sepia. An attacking color with shades of take-no-prisoners and that leaves him alive only so he can keep asking and answering himself what shade and color they might be; and then to appreciate the devastation of the conquered landscape and—surrendered and color coordinated—to offer testimony and tell the tale.

And he, there, who can do nothing to stop it. He can't look elsewhere. He can't even close his eyes and, much less, sleep, stay asleep, sending to bed without dessert everything that knocks on the door of his eyelids, kicking them open.

The past that's a mirror, but a rearview mirror. One of those mirrors that warns you "objects in mirror are closer than they appear" just before you crash into what's yet to come, but what, right away, has already passed by.

The past that's always making you think of the past and is like a *Peanuts* comic strip (where the kids are nothing but old people dressed up as kids) in which (panel 1) Linus asked Charlie Brown: "Charlie Brown, you know that there's one day in your life that will always be the best compared to all the other days?"; And Charlie Brown (panel 2) answers asking: "Of course, why do you ask?"; so that Linus (panel 3) answers: "Well . . . And what happens if that day already passed?" And what happens if that night already passed *too*?

The past that's like one of those children with the illness that makes them age rapidly and ceaselessly, but without that preventing them from still being children. The past like a childish creaking of bones and gurgling stomachs that sound like onomatopoetic conversations between roadrunners and coyotes. Long and wailing sounds. Sounds that are only made when you fall as if shot from the highest heights of a canyon/cannon and, once you've crashed, into the deep target of a returnless abyss that you only climb out of so you can fall again, when you think you're poking your head over the edge, a rock falls on you, and clouds and dark spots on the mental X-ray of everything you thought you'd memorized and had under control. Lesson well learned, yes. And, suddenly, it's the past that pushes you back, from behind, as if the past were that XL-bodied and Medium-brained boy who waits for you at recess to settle scores and exact tribute. There, the past, in the middle of the playground, with crossed arms and clenched fists and saying, "Where do you think you're going?" and then making you remember with a beating everything that wanted to not be remembered: everything that wanted to be but in the end never was and never will be because there's not enough time or strength left. There, on the ground, the present that fears the past with all its future, but that—as in the perverse and pathological playground hierarchies—only wants to please it and be recognized and enslaved.

Yes, the past that grows as time contracts, and the past that catches up though the present takes off running (the past is retro *but also* avant-garde). And that's why, he thinks, the true tragedy of people like Lord Jim or Jay Gatsby: bastards who insist on going back into the past to alter the present, not knowing that such a senseless and logicless colossal effort will end up breaking them beyond all repair. Wiser on his part, he says to himself, would have been to sit down and await the slow yet inevitable return of that boomerang through the years. Getting old. To recapitulate revising and rewriting with the help of what was thought to be oblivion, but, really, was understanding.

And, ah, many years had to pass before they would discover all those degenerative mental illnesses to which they attributed the gradual yet incessant destruction of the more or less recent memory (like waves lapping at the foundation of a castle) were just the opposite: they were the ever healthier past eating the weak and sickly present and spitting it up all over the future. Chewing it unhurriedly but unceasingly to thereby attain the privilege of not recognizing anything or anyone who hadn't been around or passed through on that ever greater and longer yesterday. In that landscape full of details they didn't know how to see or decode in their moment. Having the past present, yes, was nothing more than, finally, understanding *everything* that'd happened. Understanding it too late, when there was no tomorrow left and—tomorrow never knows—everything was the certainty of the pure dark night.

Like him and where he is now: being the light with the lights out; because there's no desire left to read others and you read yourself better in the dark, blindly, without being able to see the enormity of what's crashing down on top of you.

Here it comes

*Look out! . . . 'Cause here she comes . . .*

Here it is.

*She's coming down fast . . . Yes she is . . . Yes she is . . .*

The night.

The night that, in an ideal order of things, you shouldn't know but only imagine. Having never been there, because at night you were sleeping.

Another night that's the same night as always, barely interrupted by those diurnal and blank pages that separate the chapters of a book.

And who was it who wrote that night is always a giant? Probably his favorite writer. Or one of them. Or one that once had been his favorite but not anymore. He has and had so many . . . The same thing happens with favorite authors as with girlfriends: at first, you want them to be identical to you, you want to write like them; then you come to understand, maybe when it's already too late, that what most and best suits you isn't an opposite but, yes, a complement (and so, sometimes, as a reader, you ended up getting married to and living happily ever after with books that, as a writer, you hated and only dreamed of leaving or murdering or being unfaithful to until death do you part). Someone who wasn't an implacable mirror of your own defects but a container of strange virtues that could end up saving your life, distancing you from faults and vices and tics, completing you. When you're no longer young, on the other hand, you fall in love with the books of others you realize you'll never be able to write. An unrequited love and yet, even still, a warm-hearted love. A good friendship. A mature or resigned love that has already learned that a favorite writer always arises from the distant or nearby echo of other writers who were once or continue to be or—though he hasn't read them yet, though he may never read them—will never now be but might have been his favorites. It's all the same. For good or ill, writers on their own are never really alone: they're accompanied by other writers who are also on their own. In the harsh dark, immersed in the impassioned and faltering and so-oft cited madness of art of the Henry-James variety. Another favorite of his, one who was and remains and will remain a favorite. A creator of great sleepless characters (those professional witnesses, those "reverberant" beings, who seem to absorb everything around them) and of long sentences that wake you up though some people said they put them to sleep. Either way: some and others working, doing what they can and giving what they have and all of that. Occupying small rooms in an immense tower. Looking out from one window to the next, waving to each other with a sad and complicit smile. Passing like ships in the night and . . .

In any case, if it were so, if that were true, once more, another model of the past to add to his list.

Another past to which now, as he writes it, he adds a † in the margin. The symbol that always precedes each of the entrances with no exit.

There inside.

In biji notebooks.

Many. Too many.

All devoted to sketches and never-developed plans.

He had notebooks devoted to the project of a novel about Gerald and Sara Murphy, the people who inspired the characters in Francis Scott Fitzgerald's *Tender Is the Night*, his own parents' favorite novel. Photographs of the ones (the Murphys) and the others (his parents). The ones and the others stuffed into those robotic/automobilistic get-ups/costumes. The Murphys at a ball in Côte d'Azur; his parents, decades later in one of their nomadic ad spots with the Festival de Cannes as backdrop. Calling each other—like the Fitzgeralds—"Goofo." Thinking, like the Fitzgeralds, that maybe it would be better to be siblings before being lovers and envying their children without having the slightest idea what it meant to be siblings, because his parents were both the kind of only-child who can't accept competition or sharing. His parents fell in love with each other because, at last, they'd found someone else who loved themselves as much as they did.

He had so many notebooks about his sister Penelope and about the things that'd happened to her and about the things that she'd made happen to him. And, yes, Penelope was a great character, his best character. And she'd always hated him for it, because that's what she was for him. And that was why Penelope had done something so terrible, so that, for once, not even he would dare put it in writing and tell others about it. Something that snatched sleep away from her forever and went running off with it, hooting with laughter, into the night, along a beach where a river ended so a sea could begin.

He had the inevitable notebook/chronogram containing his romantic history. Names and phone numbers (from the times when telephone numbers were written down) and places, starting out with the mystery of that girl who let herself fall into swimming pools and wrapping up with X throwing himself out a window. (X, who'd been the closest he'd ever come to a homosexual or bisexual experience or whatever it was: they got along well, they had a great time, they happened to be on one of those writers' trips together and discovered they no longer believed in love, for that reason, they took on the role of the perfect and asexual couple, with the exception of one night when they were a bit drunk and tried something, but it turned out so choreographically awkward they decided not to repeat it. But they kept traveling together and saving money by sleeping in double rooms together, until one night X woke up and said, "I can't take this anymore" and went over to the window with two, admirably graceful, little hops and a third hop that was slightly longer and definitive. X was a poet. Quite a good one, according to people who understood such things.)

He had a notebook dedicated to the attempt, as vain as it was in-vain, of transcribing a dream where, in a time when almost everyone had lost the ability to dream (an obvious expression of desire, a longing for everyone to suffer what he suffered), a kind of futuristic delirium melted into the memory of a brief yet (something he only came to understand years later) transcendent love episode with, in the background, one of his favorite Bob Dylan songs playing the whole time. He'd taken a lot of notes on that dream, rehearsed different variations of its trajectory (somewhere he'd read you can control your dreams if you put them in writing first and read them while falling asleep and thereby crossed a threshold, like someone passing from one room to another). The idea, he thought then, making use of the diffuse memory that ended up being the last of his waking dreams (he didn't know it yet; but, yes, it'd been a dream about the end of dreams), was that of trying to write something in the International Language of Dreams, like a dialectical variation of something he'd once written about the International Language of the Dead:

† I.L.D. (International Language of the Dead) Short sentences. Referential mania. Selective memory. Words other people said so you repeat them later. Parentheses like the echo of something that happened or could've happened. Many Capital Letters. Footnotes like the part underneath, what gets packed away first. Stickers on the suitcases of celebrity tourists. Stamps on passports. Swimming pools of memory. Ellipses (three or more than three dots). Chemical syntax. Cut-up. We interrupt this program. Short Attention Span. Zapping. Kamikaze. Heil. Loops and Samplers. Volare. The suddenly comprehensible language of airports. Osmosis. What happens to

people who don't speak English when they listen to Bob Dylan or to those who don't speak French when they listen to Serge Gainsbourg: somehow you understand them, as if the words were signals, like the mute eloquence of the signpost on the side of the road. The drawing of a rolling stone, the drawing of a made bed. Next exit. Emergency exit. Kilometers. Miles. Frequent flyer. Turbulence coming up. We'll keep reporting. Back in our studios. Last minute: it has been proven that human beings keep functioning for an indeterminate amount of time after the death of the heart. The brain stops receiving blood, but it doesn't know it, nobody tells it anything, it keeps thinking, dreaming it's still alive.

Question: What're the post-mortem thoughts of a brain like?

Answer: They're *like this*:

He had other even more personal notebooks that recorded an accelerated and particular excursion of his to Switzerland, theoretically in name and memory of Vladimir Nabokov (including fragments of his books, reflections about the author, and the latecomer journal of another and again-frustrated attempt at reading, for the tenth or hundredth time, *Ada, or Ardor*, the only book of Nabokov's that'd resisted him). Journey and journal justified by the celebration of a conference on Nabokov and an article about a particle accelerator for an airline magazine. Trajectory that, in reality, (im)practically, had ended up configuring the secret and crazed itinerary with the more unstable than stable objective and intention of destroying the entire planet.

He, also, had a desperate notebook where he collected the never-realized book projects of others, and whose authors included authorities from David Copperfield and T. S. Garp, to George Steiner, or to that loon Maximiliano Karma, the onetime comatose fiancé of his sister Penelope. And from this last one, fan of the *noveau roman* (that maneuver only for geniuses but so often poorly executed by those without talent), he'd stolen an idea he'd found interesting, enticing. And out of which he'd been able to squeeze a few pages. Scribbling them with handwriting that went up and down, throughout a couple hours, sitting in and never leaving the car of the Territet-Glion funicular, in the outskirts of Montreux. In that funicular that appeared in the plot of *Tender Is the Night* by Francis Scott Fitzgerald and that, inevitably (that book and that author were his favorites), had been used by his parents as the stage for one of their many traveling ad spots.

Something, once again, with Vladimir Nabokov (and along the way rescuing the Russian from the clumsy and unworthy-of-his-person claws of "Maxi," that loony and comatose and one-time husband of Penelope) and his relationship with an FBI agent. Really, about the relationship of the agent with the writer.

And he looks for it at the foot of his bed and finds it and reads his notes:

† He can see him because he can imagine him. He imagines he sees him: lying in his motel bed, awake and unable to sleep because of the hoarse, rasping voice of the air conditioner, so sick and tired of trailing VN and VN2.

Here it comes again, like a movie revealed by the camera obscura of his mind, projecting itself in the darkness, passing through those transparent things that are time and space. And, his eyes wide open and as if lidless, the blinds lowered, outside a dog is barking; in the next room, walls wallpapered with a harlequin motif, he feels and hears VN's fierce and luminous peals of laughter and VN2's dark and delicate chuckle and, at times, it's as if they're laughing at him, damn them.

Thus, then, his need not to hear them and to deny the present and to throw the whole thing in reverse. The past that doesn't pass: the history of his ancestors arriving and founding Russian America (Русская Америка, trans. *Russkaya Amerika*, and, oh, how he savors the character of those Cyrillic characters, like a taste at once exotic and all his own) in the name and by the will of Peter the Great (Пётр Великий, trans. *Pyotr Velikiy*), settling there from the beginning of the eighteenth century until the middle of the nineteenth century, places later known as Alaska and Hawaii and California, acquired in 1867 by the United States government, paying the colonists seven million dollars or what would be about one hundred and twenty-six million dollars today. All of them, corpulent men swathed in XL animal skins, guided by the pioneering star of Semyon Dezhnev and his drifting voyage and, later, the course set by the sails, crisp with frost, of the *Sv Petr* and the *Sv Pavel*, bows facing what for them was East and what would soon be the Far West for so many. The frozen vapor of those blazing men billowing from the small volcanoes of their bearded and orthodox mouths, letters catching like hooks in their throats, harpoons and seals and whales and bears of polar white.

Ivan Nijinski—renamed and translated as Johnny Dancer by his coworkers at the Bureau—counts and recounts all those snowy and frozen things while others count the warm whiteness of sheep, to shelter himself from the lupine and steppe-ish winds of insomnia. It does no good, of course; and yet he likes to imagine them anyway. To bolster himself with their bygone heroism and convince himself that his present mission—though not so epic—shares something of the grandeur of his ancestors' trajectory.

Ivan Nijinski (a.k.a Johnny Dancer, agent 0471 of the Federal Bureau of Investigation, FBI) following and observing the writer and professor Vladimir Vladimirovich Nabokov (Влади́мир Влади́мирович Набо́ков, C-File 6556567, error of agent John F. Noonan to be fixed in the file: *Vladimar* in place of *Vladimir*) and his wife Véra Yevesyevna Nabokov (Ве́ра Евсе́евна Набо́кова, C-File 6556566).

Why him? Because he is a descendent of Russians and because he speaks Russian and—above all—because of his perfect student aspect. Johnny Dancer doesn't stand out among the other attendees of seminars in Russian Literature (Lit 311) at Cornell University, Ivy League, East Hill, Ithaca, New York (climate like that of the Yalta summers and Siberian winters).

Plus, Johnny Dancer likes to read and now, since he's been going to the Russian's classes, he likes it more and more; though not as much as that oh so nerdy roommate of his (Thomas Ruggles Pynchon) and his friends on whom a file should be opened immediately (David W. Shetzline and Richard George Fariña; check the latter's Cuban connection).

That previous agent sent to this university by the FBI, on the other hand, had the unmistakable aspect of a not-so-secret or open-secret bureaucrat; he hadn't the slightest idea who Vronski or Doctor Henry Jekyll were; and he was immediately unmasked by Vladimir Nabokov (VN from here onward) and invited to tea by Véra Nabokov (VN2 from here onward); both ending up asking him (as a joke? in earnest?) what the chances were of their son Dmitri (Дми́трий Влади́мирович Набо́ков, as yet without a case file, young man of a perpetually bored air) joining the Bureau in order to combat those "ever so shoddily written soviets and, along the way, those ever so shoddy soviet writers."

Johnny Dancer, on the other hand, has had no direct contact with VN or VN2; but there are moments when he feels they know everything about him and, like right now, in the next room, they're making fun of him (days before, the couple was conversing animatedly at a table in a highway café in very loud voices and, he's sure he's not imagining it, giving him sidelong glances and smiling mischievously and making comments about how much they'd someday like to travel to Machu Picchu so that, it scares him to think that's what they're plotting, he'll be forced to follow them astride the backs of llamas). Beyond all of this, there's something that intrigues or, rather, fascinates him about the two of them: VN and VN2 seem to be a single entity split into two people (might that be true love, Johnny Dancer wonders, or a form of romantic psychosis? his parents never *felt* like that with each other), so happy to be together all the time. And he, Johnny Dancer, darting after them like one of those fish feeding off of what's tossed overboard from those perfect and unsinkable vessels. VN and VN2 forcing him to follow them along the highways and byways of California and Oregon and Montana and Wyoming and Utah and Colorado and Nevada and Arizona and New Mexico. VN2 at the wheel of various automobiles (the only time VN, following VN2's instructions, tries to drive that Buick or that Chevrolet Impala or that Plymouth in the wide open parking lot of a shopping mall, the Russian takes aim and fires and hits the only other automobile parked in the lot) along the chasms and plateaus of the Grand Canyon, of Oak Creek Canyon, of Palo Alto, of Estes Park, of Ardis Heights, of Longs Peak, of Rollinsville, of Telluride, of Glacier National Park, of West Yellowstone, of Taos, of Ashland, of Lone Peak, of New Zembla, of Mt. Carmel, of Afton, of Dubois, of Jackson, of Riverside.

And Johnny Dancer has no space left in his pupils to store the colors of all those CinemaScope sunrises and nights with too many stars. And cactus (what's the plural of cactus?) and coyotes and lizards and stores with indigenous souvenirs attended by natives who already resemble totems, petrified, skin like wood turned to stone. And all of it hurts Johnny Dancer from the outside in (the kind of hurt the wind produces in those stone walls over the centuries, he thinks; and it surprises him to be thinking *like this*, thinking not in the precise terms of the law, but with images and sensations difficult to transcribe in reports to his superiors who, no doubt, are already wondering what's going on with him, if something strange is happening to him, if the sun shinning down from that desert that is the sky, might not be striking him a little hard there above, on the terrestrial crust covering his brain). And Johnny Dancer wonders time and again why he couldn't have been assigned to surveil Yul Brynner (parties in Hollywood and on Broadway) while he follows these two who, he's sure, pose zero threat to the nation: few are the times he's seen two émigrés more white and pure and besotted with the American way of life and haters of all things communist. VN has lost everything he had in Russia and ceaselessly introduces himself as an American writer and doesn't even write in his native language anymore (Johnny Dancer has read everything of his, what was signed by V. Sirin and what was published in the pages of the *New Yorker* and has even been moved by his eloquent and selective memoir) and he sees him as ecstatic, climbing among the crags and wearing short pants and with a hat on his head and a net aloft in his hand on the hunt for his beloved butterflies. In the beginning, at the Bureau, someone had the idea that—availing himself of fluttering and antenna-ish technical jargon—VN was sending information to other nets, networks of red spies, via the pages of publications specializing in lepidoperology. But Johnny Dancer is certain that's not the case: because he's never seen someone so happy to be pursuing an insect with colorful wings. VN's joy when he traps and snatches one of those ever-so coveted prizes from the air cannot be faked (on one occasion, at one of those faculty parties, he heard him say that, if the revolution hadn't happened, he would've devoted himself to insects and not to characters) and transcends all political ideology or patriotic longing. VN is a citizen of a world all his own, unique, his and only his. A world where he postulated, "a writer should have the precision of a poet and the imagination of a scientist."

The specialists—from what he thinks he understands, from what he's read—reject his theories, as imaginative as they are precise, regarding the genetic and evolutionary cycle of the brand of butterfly known as *Polyommatus blues* of the family *Lycaenidae* or just *blues*, but VN doesn't seem to care. And he doesn't care because—as with so many other things, the same as when, from his podium in the great lecture hall, he tears down Dostoevsky or Faulkner or Freud—he's completely and absolutely certain he's right. According to VN, these butterflies arrived—like ancient Russians—in five waves from Siberia, crossing the Bering Strait and settling from Alaska to Chile. And, true, his written postulation (composed in 1945, before what will come to be known as molecular genetics, with the help of only a microscope and his own penetrating eyes, and that included the portrait and the point of view of "a modern taxonomist straddling a Wellesian time machine" to witness the crossing) wasn't considered particularly rigorous by scientists. Johnny Dancer doesn't care. Johnny Dancer doesn't care *either.* Johnny Dancer—after following him far and wide over several summers—believes in VN. He believes in everything about him. And it's that new faith—no longer his love for the United States of America—that leads Johnny Dancer to note down everything in the minutest detail, as if it were the curve of small antennas or the pattern of pigmentation on little wings. And yet, yes, the assignment remains and for a few months he was worried that Lolita, whom VN and VN2 spoke of so much, was a seductive femme fatal (but later he understands she's a twelve-year-old girl) and he investigates everything and checks everything in libraries (it doesn't take him long to discover that the variety of butterfly the Russian refers to as *Chuangtzutiana blues* and that "has the particularity of believing itself a butterfly that dreams it's a man or vice versa" can only be a joke VN2 celebrates with a crystalline laugh). A laugh that can turn into something terrible when VN2 gets angry: Johnny Dancer hears her Russian shouts, one afternoon in Cornell, when VN2 and VN fight about what appears to be a stack of pages VN is trying to throw into the fire he's lit in a metal cube on their back patio (classified information?). But the thing from before, the same one as always, everything turns to nothing, to smoke, to ash. Everything is snuffed out like a flame or melts like the snow. Everything but the will of Johnny Dancer who, at some point, realizes he's been possessed. That he's been transformed—the way a caterpillar mutates into a butterfly—into one of the oh so many footnotes to the legend of VN and VN2.

And now Johnny Dancer can't stop following them (VN wound up calculating that, between 1949 and 1959, he and VN2 traversed some 150,000 North American miles tracking the flight of the butterflies) though his superiors inform him that the case file has been closed, that enough already, that he should return home, to central command, to be debriefed and assigned another mission. And Johnny Dancer trembles thinking that the next one will be to find the proof needed to take down one of those bad Hollywood actors who once slept with an idealist more redheaded than red.

And so Johnny Dancer doesn't go back. Johnny Dancer receives his university diploma (he has become an expert in the insect of Kafka and his postgraduate thesis is published and praised) and, on the heels of VN and VN2, he strikes out for the Old World.

Return trip: Johnny Dancer is now a reverse pilgrim, an adventurer who severs all ties with his family and country. A foreigner. An émigré.

His handle on English and Russian, his air of terminal efficiency, his profile that combines traces of telenovela heartthrob and those of perfect son and implacable soldier, get him a job in reception at the Montreux Palace Hotel, where the couple installs themselves, because, they understand, it's now impossible for them to reproduce the accommodating world of their childhood; they don't have enough time left to properly train servants to meet their needs and, so, a hotel is the first consolation prize, plan B. And from there, he watches them. He keeps track of them. He attends to them. He wouldn't dare say he's happy like that, but he's privileged because, in a way, he's become part of VN's oeuvre, and one morning he thinks he detects and reads himself, between the lines, veiled, in a line of *Ada, or Ardor.* One day, VN and VN2 ask him to bring a television up for them, they're going to rent it for a few hours, they specify, and after they want it out of there, they don't want to see it again. He takes charge of bringing them the apparatus. One of those early models more or less but not entirely portable. More plastic than wood but, even still, weighing its weight. The couple are waiting at the door to their room, as if he were bringing them something somewhat important that might or might not be marvelous, as if he were the bearer of tidings and omens. And so it is. VN explains to him—with something resembling an apology and a command—that "I must see the moon landing" because "they are going ask me to offer an opinion about it; they are always asking my opinions about the strangest things, as if they think that writers are oracles or they can see reality better than anybody when, in truth, the only thing they want is not to see it or, better, to see it the way nobody has seen it before . . . Please, if you like, stay with us to watch this monumental event. We're absolutely useless when it comes to handling these inventions and it would be good for us to have somebody in the vicinity to take charge of the controls." And, of course, he asks permission from his superior and, of course, again, permission granted. And they serve him a little glass of liquor and he sits down with them. And there's that faraway image, transmitted through space, the moon landing on Earth, there in front of them and the symmetric smiles on VN and VN2's faces. And VN standing up and going to the reading desk by the window and speaking aloud while simultaneously taking notes: "Treading the soil of the Moon, the strange sensual exhilaration of palpating its precious pebbles, the absolutely overwhelming excitement of the adventure, feeling in the pit of the stomach the separation from Earth, hanging there like a marble globe in the black sky . . . The most romantic thrill ever experienced in the history of discovery . . . Ah, that gentle little minuet that despite their awkward suits the two men danced with such grace to the tune of lunar gravity was a lovely sight . . . feeling along one's spine the shiver and wonder of it . . . I would never drag in such irrelevant matters as wasted dollars and power politics." The three of them listen to the words of Neil Armstrong there above. The thing about the small step and the great leap that everyone remembers (and he said it wrong, because he said "man" in place of "a man") and what came next, the bit that goes "And the—the surface is fine and powdery. I can—I can pick it up loosely with my toe. It does adhere in fine layers like powdered charcoal to the sole and sides of my boots . . ." which everyone forgets right away and that provokes a grimace of pain on VN's face, a "Couldn't you have said something better and more inspired?" in his thoughts. Obviously rejoicing that the Americans made it before the Soviets, but also resignedly admitting that any third-class Russian poet would have demonstrated greater inspiration and loftiness than all those NASA scriptwriters put together.

Broadcast concluded, while offering views of scientists hugging and people crying in the street, everyone with a sore neck from looking up to see what they cannot see but there it is, VN and VN2 tell him that's enough, to "deactivate the apparatus" and "many thanks for your collaboration in this enterprise."

VN keeps hunting butterflies (Johnny Dancer will never forgive himself for not having followed him to Davos, where VN falls down a slope and nobody comes to his rescue until two hours later; he would've liked to have helped him and for VN to have thanked him with a "Thank you, Ivan," which would make evident the plotline that the writer always knew everything about him and that he'd been hunting him for years with his net). VN couldn't stop smiling when he reads of himself as a writer who "occupies a strange position in the Alps of contemporary literature, at once admired and forgotten," because, after all, that's the limbo where the true classics go to reside. And he's also tickled at the rage he arouses in certain feminist writers. In life and near death, Nabokov is like a writer of the nineteenth century and the twenty-first century. His present can't and has no idea how to contain him. And yet, Nabokov is subject to certain laws that transcend literature, though they imitate it with bad manners and even worse writing.

Before long comes the season of mysterious and incomprehensible fevers, comings and goings from the hospital with no precise diagnosis, a window left ajar by a daft nurse, and the final sneezes, an increasingly unfocused VN losing his first games of Scrabble, and the last details of the falling night. And Johnny Dancer is always there. His disguise as a nurse allowing him to come and go from the Nestlé Hospital of Lausanne. One afternoon he enters the room, sees him there sleeping, and reads what VN has written in his journal, lying open on the floor where it fell: "Slight fever. 37.7 degrees. Is it possible that everything starts over again?"

In any case, everything or something comes to an end and Johnny Dancer watches—from the respectful distance of the room's doorway—a wife and a son beside the bed where there lies a freshly minted corpse. It's the 2nd of July of 1977, and Johnny Dancer hears VN2 say to Dmitri: "Let's rent an airplane and crash."

"I volunteer to be pilot," thinks Johnny Dancer.

He imagines he sees him.

He can see him because he can imagine him.

It's easily done.

Easy, you know, does it, son.


And no, that wasn't so bad. It was even better than how bad he remembered it; but it wasn't good enough to make it grow, to turn it from a caterpillar into a butterfly, and let it spread its wings. To hear these pages buzz as if they were a fly and slam them shut as if to squash a mosquito and, ah, he had so many notebooks and, inside of them, so much nothing. The kind of thing that resembled the sound one makes when talking to one's self or talking to a cat: a cat he never had but, if he'd had it, he'd have called (bad joke, the kind of joke that cracks him up most) The Great Catsby. There, paragraphs like meows or likes those hairballs that, every so often, felicitous felines hack up and spit out. With handwriting recalling insect legs fixed in place. Pinned. Crucified by a little cross or run through by what looks like a sword in a stone, a sword whose name, contrary to what most everyone believes (and this is the kind of item/note he scribbles all throughout wide nights in his thin notebooks), is not Excalibur. Because Excalibur (he wrote this information down, thinking he could someday unsheathe it somewhere) isn't the name of the sword Arthur pulls from the stone, it's the name of the other sword he's given by The Lady of the Lake.

Or a †, like the one that's laid atop a tomb or sunk into the body of those asterisks buried at the foot of a note. A † at the beginning of each good or bad idea or, not even that, each almost immediate and instantaneously forgettable idea.

Things like this:

† The past is a broken toy that everyone fixes in his own way.

Or

† The past is an elderly child. Obedient and misbehaving at the same time. Someone who wakes up on time, but always wakes up crying and waking up those who are still sleeping and who, then, night after night, only thinks about killing or dying; about anything that isolates him from everyone and everything that will come to pass and that is coming to pass and that did come to pass. But it is still there. Because the past—like radioactive material—takes so long to die out.

Or

† The past passing in the night like the footsteps of that dark giant who shatters everything. Here and now, boots on, stomping heavily down on the wood floor of a wood forest.

And, ah, will he ever be able to silence that kind of metaphorical enumerative cadence of variations around a single aria of air? Lips moving in the dark, threading together incredulous pagan prayers he'll no longer write while so many others recite sacred prayers composed by a small number of people so everyone else would kneel down and give thanks and beg forgiveness before receiving the blessing of a baby's sweet sleep, of dreaming *con los angelitos*. Will he ever be able to kick the habit that no longer does him any good, like someone kicking off a blanket, heavy with years and perspiration and rough drafts? When it came time for an evasive maneuver, he remembers, the best thing to do was to cut the reel by telling a joke. A bad joke. Again: really bad jokes always seemed really good to him and (again the challenge, as happens with dreams or the faces of the dead, was not to forget them) just now, he remembers one. And who it was who told it to him. Decades ago. In another millennium, which is like saying on another planet.

He was on tour presenting one of his books. And he'd gone into a university bar, carrying a copy of *Three Tenses*, the famous novella by R., in his hand. And he recalls perfectly having encountered there, at the bar, an immense writer who was sweating profusely, sweating more than a sauna inside a sauna. A writer who wore a handkerchief tied around his head, so the multiplicity of long-winded and serpentine ideas he kept there inside didn't escape him. A writer who was about to publish a book that was huge in every sense; and who, years later, diminished with depression, committed suicide. He hung himself from a rafter like a dream catcher, and immediately thereafter everyone rushed to hang their lamentations all over the Web, in times when everybody needed to be part of everything, to comment on it, to leave their mark in the void. And he also remembers his voice, the voice of the writer so alive then and now so dead. That writer seeing first, in his hand, resting on the bar, the cover of *Three Tenses* (nothing interests a writer more than finding out what another writer is reading; their eyes always darting away from faces to scan covers or bookshelves) and then telling him (ho-ho-ho and laughing last) that joke where "The Past and The Present and The Future walk into a bar . . ."

And he remembers that the punch line didn't translate.

It went "It was tense." (In Spanish, where verbal "tense" translates as "tiempo"—also meaning "time"—not "tenso," even though "tenso" does mean "tense" in the other sense of the English word, the joke loses the double meaning, is no longer a joke, bad or otherwise.)

But he also remembers that, when it came to retelling it in his own language (for once that joke hadn't dissolved into oblivion; it was as if he'd wrapped that joke around a finger or tied it around his head), he'd figured out how to translate/betray it with a trio of ridiculous punch-line options to be chosen from depending on the mood and situation.

To wit:

† "El Pasado y El Presente y El Futuro entran en un bar . . ." and *(a) No tenían tiempo que perder (They had no time/tense to lose); or (b) Tenían todo el tiempo del mundo (They had all the time/tenses in the world); or <<¿Que hora es?>>, preguntaron todos al mismo tiempo respondiéndose la misma hora pero en distintos días ("What time is it?" they all asked at the same time, answering with the same hour but on different days).*

Now, later, he chooses all three options. He has time. He has tenses. He has all the tenses, all the time. He himself, the same him, at the same time. He has that clock there, glowing with the same glow as those Aurora-brand monsters from his childhood. That clock that was given to him years ago. A funny clock and specially designed for insomniacs. A nocturnal and phosphorescent clock. A clock with that green glow in its numerals and hands (Open-eyed Fluo-Green, the color of insomnia in the Pantone Matching System) that on occasion you see floating above tombs and that many mistook for ghosts; but really it was just the gaseous chemistry of the bodies rotting underground rising up to the surface. A clock on whose face the 12 and the 6 as well as the 3 and the 9 switched positions. It's funny. It has time and it has tenses and nothing has more tenses and time than he has now, a now that seems like an always and a forever.

So—*(a)* and *(b)* and *(c)*: he has no time to lose, having all the time in the world whatever time it might be—now is then and whatever will be will be—as that saccharine song says.

But the song isn't the same song, the song is another song.

And now the other song sings:

"Same as it ever was . . . Time isn't holding up . . . Time is an asterisk . . . Same as it ever was . . . Same as it ever was . . . Same as it ever was . . . Same as it ever was . . . Same as it ever was . . . Same as it ever was . . . Same as it ever was . . . Yeah, the twister comes . . . Here comes the twister . . . Same as it ever was . . ."

Lyrics and music that arrive to him from a nearby house, while he tries not to hear them, distracting himself with multiple approximations of the idea of the past.

But it's hard for him not to hear it because he recognizes it, remembers it, sings it between his teeth.

A kind of invocation.

An almost tribal litany, enumerative and *muy lista*, ever so clever.

A song of his and Penelope's youth.

A song by Penelope's favorite band, but a band he liked a lot too, really, truly. And also, for its time, a great music video (one of the first great songs to watch) that sang of letting yourself go, floating in the inertia of not thinking too much until one day, as if waking up from a long dream, you may ask yourself how did you get here: to a beautiful house with a beautiful wife, neither of which you recognize, what have you done, how do you work this, while you let the days go by like silent water flowing underground and under the rocks and stones and into the blue again.

A spasmodic song of the kind that in his youth—after years of those, for him, prohibitive, due to lack of coordination, disco-choreographies of fevered Saturdays—finally allowed him to dance spasmodically, to dance like the singer who sang that song.

A song that was and is almost a march to the battlefront and that looks and sounds nothing of the tenderness of what, again, is broadcast out in the night by the country-music stations, accompanied by the vaporous cough of the hot water shooting up with a wild and high-pitched and mercurial sound through the heating pipes.

And, right, yes, as the song sings, will they not even let him forget it now?: this is not *your* beautiful house.

This is Penelope's beautiful house where he may wonder how did he get there without needing an answer: because he knows perfectly how he got there.

He came with nothing and no one.

Like an orphan.

In any case, now, all of a sudden hearing this song, like a thing of the past that distracts him from the present. And, in the present, this convulsive refrain reaching him from the nearby home of that family of monsters, of incessantly talking heads, he's come to call "The Intruders." Epithet referencing those science-fiction movies or series from his childhood, produced during the smoldering Cold War, where the extraterrestrials adopted and usurped human bodies and they could only be identified with the help of some special glasses or by slight anatomical particularities or manufacturing defects like the inability to flex their pinky fingers or something like that. Days when science fiction was the literature of dreamers and, if you stayed asleep, while you were sleeping, the extraterrestrial spores enveloped you in a membrane and duplicated your body. And replaced you (or, even worse, replaced the adults, replaced your parents, who'd always been pretty Martian, you've got to admit) and "They're here already! You're next!"

And, oh, what he wouldn't give to be replaced and invaded with the ability to sleep a little, when not sleeping turns you into some increasingly unrecognizable and alien and foreign and faraway thing. And especially fragile confronted by the activity of The Intruders whom he also calls "The Motherfuckers Who Never Let Me Sleep Though, True Enough, I Must Admit, To Be Fair, I Barely Slept Before."

But it would be most accurate to call them "The Guests."

A tribe of performance artists he'd like to blame for his present situation, except for the fact that they weren't to blame. But, even still, so conveniently at hand and eye and ear when someone needed to be blamed: because they're there, in the vicinity, on his property, which is, actually, technically not his property. Both he and The Intruders are there (he in the main mansion; they in a house across the road, where the forest ends so the sea can begin; where there once was a house where a little boy vanished, a house that burned in the night) by the good will and memory and patronage of Penelope, his lost and missing sister, now turned to ashes in the wind.

So he's not an intruder, but he's not a lord and master either. He lives off a loan he'll never be asked to pay back and never even a hint he'll ever have to leave.

He lives here—paradox, irony—thanks to the books Penelope wrote. Those sagas with neo-gothic lunatics who replaced the child wizards and witches and teenage vampires and young rebels and post-apocalyptics, competing with and combating the tyranny of adults with strange hairdos and imperial get-ups. Books that seduced millions of readers in hundreds of languages (how many languages were there?), and had made Penelope into a sort of perfect poster-woman for all tribes. Sects running the gamut from wowed little girls to veteran feminists with stops at all stations in between.

Yes, he was now "the brother of."

And, he supposes, having moved past all gestures of uncertain pride and false dignity a while ago, the truth is he can't complain.

And his only gesture of self-esteem had been, on repeated occasions, to refuse to write a biographic memoir about Penelope. It was one thing to live off of what she'd written and another to live off writing about her. For the moment, he set certain limits though he often stared at them fixedly, like someone staring at a border that might be crossed should the situation so require. The public explanation he'd given for refusing had been that he had nothing to add to her myth. The real reason was that—in the eventual case that he might put something in writing—what he had to tell, if he were honest, was too terrible to be true.

Nobody would want to believe him.

And not to mention that to do so would've been to push himself over the edge into a bottomless abyss.

So, better not to.

Better to stay how and where he was.

And yet (few things are more unsettling than a comfortable situation with neither rules to abide by nor directions to follow, but, also, coming to its end, without rights to invoke or protections to demand) there's no waking night when he doesn't take five minutes to imagine the possibility, oh so nineteenth-century and Penelopean, of, any day now, a lawyer knocking on his door that's not entirely his. A lawyer informing him that, at 00:00 hours of the next day, a posthumous clause in his sister's last will and testament would take effect, specifying the expiration date and immediate end of the armistice and the commencement of hostilities, which is why . . .

And to tell the truth, again: it's not The Intruders' activities that keep him from sleep. If they weren't there next door, he would still lie awake and settle for blaming, though it wasn't their fault either, the incessant conversation of bacteria and microbes nesting in his ears. But it's true that their familiar and noisy presence makes him more aware of his lack of sleep, of the solitude of someone who no longer wakes up because he no longer sleeps.

There they are.

Come from a nearby kingdom to the north, probably, he thinks.

And, like so many of their compatriots, convinced that here, by the sea and in the sun and to the south, they can do anything they so desire and everything they're not allowed to do back home. They—though he's not seen them up close yet—are definitely always soused in alcohol. Cheeks red and swollen, shrinking their eyes, bellies rising with yeast, arms always at a right angle with hands always half-closed, clutching or not a can of beer. And their wild children (an older boy and a younger girl; he's identified the always pressured and pressuring timbre of their tremendous little voices). All of them and all of it coming together now. He doesn't even need to see them to know what they're like. He knows them by heart, and not having had children of his own has made him an expert in everyone else's children. And so, he knows it, the adults will play at growling at the children (to scare them) and the children will play at screaming at the adults (to scare themselves) and, yes, that's the standard dynamic of parents and children who have little or nothing to say to each other. Fright like a dense language of shared blood. Mutual fear like a bond. So some of them growl and some of them scream, and the years go by, he says to himself, until at some point the roles are inverted and it's the children who frighten and the parents who're frightened.

He's watched it more or less close up—but always at a distance—with friends of his he hasn't seen now for such a long time. And at that time he said to himself that never, that he was never going to trip or stumble into that.

He would be an orphan in both directions: he no longer had parents, and he was never going to have children who would have him as parent.

He'd previously celebrated every anti-conceptive advance and—as soon as he heard *that* rumor—he started writing lying on his back and with his laptop balanced atop his lower belly to facilitate the radioactive frying and clean sterilization of his spermatozoids.

He'd been great and lots of fun (in brief and homeopathic doses) with the children of others (not so much with the parents of those children, disturbed as they were by his comments like, "Why do you have to undergo so many tests to adopt a child and none to have one of your own?") and, above all, with Penelope's son (whose name should not be mentioned; his name is like brambles in his mouth), whom he doesn't dare think of as entirely gone though he no longer has him.

And he thinks about that and about that unnamable boy (who gave names to so many things he later wrote down in his books; like that thing about the "floating doll," that spectral figure that frightened him at night, hanging from the ceiling; or Camilo Camito Camoncio, that horizontal boy controlling the entire world from his bed) and changes the subject like someone changing the channel. Tuning in the image of that boy—ghosted, with issues adjusting the verticals and the horizontals, with antennas constantly needing reorientation, like those enormous cubic televisions from his childhood— hurts so much.

So he focuses on these intruder children.

And, every so often, he watches them at a distance, just in case, in their comings and goings through the branches and bushes. Like zoetropic stains, like flies in the eyes: like the spasms of those minuscule drawings in the upper-right-hand corner of the pages of small books that give the impression of movement as they're flipped through, high speed, with the tip of a thumb. Digital technology, indeed; but with traction and blood. Or like how you see something when you blink your eyelids open and closed quickly and repeatedly. Or the way people run and fall and get back up in silent movies. But here in colorful octophonic sound. Music and screams and cries and the piano recently added to the mix, a piano the Mother Intruder plays as if she were playing it to death: an occasional and never-predictable faltering fingering of the most basic scales that are cut off and dropped with a clumsiness that doesn't even reach an infantile level, with an *infra*ntile clumsiness (his own mother once got excited for five minutes about the idea of learning to play the piano and those were the most terrible five minutes ever, he remembers). Now, again, those melodies of unlearning, all the time: The Intruders with that ever so flexible but never so muscular schedule that's the schedule of alcoholics and the children of alcoholics who, when they grow up, will also become alcoholics and alcoholic parents and grandparents.

Fucking performance artists, he thinks, considering performance art the most convenient and easiest art form. Especially now that everyone's life has been uploaded to the lowest of all places, online, and everyone's convinced anyone can be an artist and the act of looking was part of being looked at. Like that woman who got rich by starting to cry in front of (and making cry) whoever sat down facing her in the halls of museums. What was *that*? Is *that* art? Is *that* what we've come to after millennia, from the Altamira Cathedral to the Rothko Chapel? And that's what The Intruders are into. The exhibition of exhibitionism and more details about this and them coming up, he supposes.

But not yet.

There are many things to hang onto tonight. Many things to hang up, like paintings in a gallery, paintings looked at one by one, but that, at the same time, will no doubt end up telling a single story, a work: life.

Life, which is written moving forward but read in reverse.

And, looking back over it, rereading what was written, remembering this or that, somewhere in there, that paragraph that unfurls like one of those paper mandalas that open and flower when submerged in the water of memory.

That night.

This night, tonight, when he, suddenly, remembers that night; and now he can't stop remembering, thinking about that, about *that* night on *this* night. And he wonders if that night will, tonight, this night, merit a new biji notebook to fill with crosses, like those burning crosses illuminating that night.

That night that was the first night in his life he lived awake and not asleep and when he felt, walking through a wide-awake city, he was discovering the dreams of that hero that was him.

That night when, remembering it, he is who he is now but, also, who he was.

The Boy.

The Boy, on that long and waking and as-if-dreamed night, trailing along behind his Uncle Hey Walrus through avenues and parks, searching for his parents, and at first leading his little sister by the hand and later carrying her on his shoulders.

The Boy walking through a city that no longer exists.

A city that's been laid to rest beneath the waters, and where—in his precise memory—all those people they crossed paths with that night are dead. (And he always liked that thing about *being* dead; as if death were an occupation and being a dead person was like practicing a profession, like being a lawyer or doctor; as if you could be dead for a while and later stop, or retire from, being dead; as if having died were the same as having completed a very difficult task, your own life, with great success: "I'm dead now, but at least I was able to finish what came before.")

Being dead, yes, like being awake or being asleep.

Some of the people The Boy and his sister and Uncle Hey Walrus are about to cross paths with are going to die very soon.

It's a dangerous time; "The lively Age of Aquarius is already giving way to the metastasis of the Age of Cancer," foretells Uncle Hey Walrus, who not long ago had come back and been sent back from London. And those who survive, inevitably, will die over the years, incredulous, confronting the reality of having grown old, having believed they'd stay forever young. They'll die from what's known, perversely, as a "natural death." In three movements/chapters: the moment their body ceases to function, the moment their body is disposed of according to their preferred method (earth, fire, air, water), and the truly mortal moment when, in the future, their name is uttered for the last time or the last living person who remembers them dies too. And again, he thinks: natural death. As if there were something natural in death, as if there were another variety known as *artificial* death, encompassing, presumably, all other forms of death. And he always remembers the conclusion in the forensic report of the volcanic Malcolm Lowry: "Death by misadventure," the doctor wrote there. Death due to accidental bad luck, passing away from pure misfortune, or something like that. Did his parents and Penelope die and he survive them all by misadventure? Who is the truly misfortunate one in this story: those who no longer count or the one who recounts it all?

In any case, in his memory, then, all those soon-to-be or on-the-point-of-being dead people now occupy a legendary space and, before long, become the fodder and fertilizer of mythology: the place where he was born, but that, for a long time now, is for him *El Extranjero*. A place that he no longer visits—in the absence of dreams—except in his mind. A territory that's always outside and remote physically and inside and nearby mentally.

There, in *El Extranjero*, in the past, a city that never sleeps and the impossibility of bookstores staying open all night that everyone has decided to believe in. The myth of people who wake up at three in the morning with an irrepressible need for a dose of Raymond Chandler or Gabriel García Márquez and there they go, with a robe over their pajamas, to the bookstore around the corner from their homes, because, in addition, as legend has it, there were bookstores on every block. And now, yes, all those people are dead and all those bookstores closed. And he remembers that, they say, those who're dying or have little time left to live—defense mechanism on this side or *coming soon* from the other side?—tend to dream more and more frequently of their own dead. Or, he's heard this too, that the dead stop being merely the stuff of dreams and start showing up throughout the day, like waking thoughts.

And he remembers too—remembering that night from his childhood—a novel that at the time hadn't yet been written. A novel by someone who, with time, would become one of his other many and multiple favorite writers. Better: he would become one of his favorite favorites. Top Five. A writer named Kurt Vonnegut whose work he would hear about for the first time that same night. That night that he's now beginning to reconstruct (actually what he would hear and what he heard about was and would be a movie based on Vonnegut's most famous novel). A writer who would be and remains very important to him and, over the years, he would read all his books; and who, many years later, he would finally meet, on a snow-covered street in Iowa City; and with whom he would have a brief and disconcerting conversation. But it's not Kurt Vonnegut's voice, under the snow, that he remembers that night.

It's the voice of Uncle Hey Walrus that he remembers.

A voice that manages—across the wide and long years—to reach him, as if crossing an avenue of absurd physiognomy.

There it was, there it goes, there it goes again.

† Uncle Hey Walrus runs into a friend in the very center of "The Widest Avenue in the World," on one of those "islands" between one lane and the next where cars fly by like arrows with no memory of the archer who fired them. In those days—before social media—everyone ran into everyone on the street, all the time. In person. Flesh and bone. Live and direct. In bars or in bookstores or at movie theaters or on corners or, like now, in the middle of the avenue. There they are, on a platform covered with grass, with an obelisk in the background and, beyond, the silhouette of his school rising solitary amid rubble and bulldozers. His school, which soon will disappear as if by the art of magic. And, yes, that was the Age of Disappearances. Uncle Hey Walrus and his friend exchange bills and small envelopes. Uncle Hey Walrus gives the bills. His friend passes him the small envelopes. They contain pills of far brighter colors than those Sugus chewy candies. Uncle Hey Walrus's friend—with a slow voice and spinning pupils—says: "I just saw the craziest movie I've ever seen. The hero lives in all times at the same time. As a young and fairly useless soldier in a firebombed city during WWII, in a house in the United States when he's older, and on another planet and under observation by some extraterrestrials who keep him inside a kind of geodesic cage, where they make him mate with a porn star and . . ." Uncle Hey Walrus interrupts his friend and says: "Say no more. Nothing new for me. I've always felt just like that, without even needing to take any of your pills." And Uncle Hey Walrus removes two pills from one of the envelopes and tosses them up in the air and opens his mouth and catches them as they fall. As if Uncle Hey Walrus were a dog being thrown a bone or a walrus being thrown a fish.

And, yes, he, here and now, *also* feels exactly like that. The way his Uncle Hey Walrus felt and the way the space-time traveler Billy Pilgrim, hero of that novel and that movie called *Slaughterhouse-Five*, lived. Like this. Neither now nor then but both at the same time. Neither what was nor what is but a mix of both: seeing yourself there with the eyes of here. In that place but from this spot. Rereading yourself as if reading something for the first time, but knowing perfectly what's going to happen; but noticing things that, then, when he was someone much shorter, went right over his head.

And before long—he was growing and not, like now, shrinking—he saw that movie. And later he read the novel. *Slaughterhouse-Five*.

Many times.

And he liked it every time and he keeps liking it more and more, like he likes the act of rereading more and more. Something you do a lot during childhood (until you know those first stories and latest comics by heart) and do again when you start getting older: when, tired of so many risky undertakings and increasing frustrations, you return to particular classics like someone returning home and asking for forgiveness. With a combination of conclusive sadness and the fantasy that you're starting over again with an enthusiasm like you've never felt before or that left you long ago. (Recently he'd returned full-on to Vladimir Nabokov, who postulated on various occasions that "Curiously enough, one cannot read a book; one can only reread it. A good reader, a major reader, an active and creative reader is a rereader.") When you reread, you don't just read again—and like new—something you already read, rather that new reading includes a new character in the plot: the reader. And who we were, and perhaps no longer are, when we first read it so long ago. When we reread we already know what's going to happen, but we're not entirely clear what's happened to us in the intervening years. And rereading other people's work we become aware of our own. What the radiation of *Tender Is the Night*—to bring close a book even closer to him—produces is very different when you're single or married or divorced or broken from having already passed through all those states. It's not the same to read *The Catcher in the Rye* when you're ten years old (pre Holden Caulfield) as it is when you're seventeen (during Holden Caulfield) or to reread it when you're fifty (so long after Holden Caulfield).

What's the sound of one hand clapping? Easy: the sound one hand makes while clapping is the imperceptible yet deafening sound we make when we read. And that sound is even more powerful and intimidating when you reread, when with one hand you hold up the book and with the other you clap. Rereading something unalterable shows us how we change, like a mirror. Rereading is one of the manifestations of what physicists know as "ambidextrous universe." Thus, we begin reading as children to get to know the world down to the slightest detail (and by heart, without exchanging even a word) and we end up rereading as adults to check whether that world still recognizes us and to understand what, in the end, we prefer or find ourselves obliged not to know (to cross out, skip over, forget) about it. When we reread, we regress only to what made us happy and to what made us feel eternal and, yes, in all parts and ages at the same time and place.

Rereading is like seeing real ghosts.

Generous ghosts who believe in us.


† Perfectly clever answer to the question what's the sound of one hand clapping: "I'll show you," Ella said. And Ella raised her hand. And Ella slapped him. "That's the sound one hand clapping," Ella smiled.

And then Ella let herself fall, fully clothed, into the swimming pool.


† Perfect excuse while you lift your hand to your smarting cheek: "Don't bother me with that again: I'm rereading."

As far as the ducks in Central Park: who cares where they go in the winter? The important thing is whether one shows up alive in the spring.


But, returning to death and the close or distant dead, in another novel called *Galápagos*—one he also liked a lot, but hadn't read as many times as *Slaughterhouse-Five*—Kurt Vonnegut proposed the following maneuver: put an asterisk—"time is an asterisk," spinning like a twister—before the name of the character who is going to die next, to warn the reader that something dreadful is about to happen to that man or woman. The really dreadful thing that happened in that novel (in several novels by that author, this being his specialty) was nothing more and nothing less than the end of the world. Over and over again. Ends of the world that combine the catastrophism of special effects with the profound melancholy of the survivor.

He thinks now that, when it comes to the representation of the end of the world, as the years pass by, you go along changing tastes and appetites. When you're little, you might enjoy the movies of Irwin Allen or Roland Emmerich or anything from Marvel Comics: those movies that, when they were over, you had to stay there and wait for the names and numbers and the final technical credits to scroll by to receive the last homeopathic dose of one brief scene minimally previewing what was to come in the next Marvel release, and so on over and over until Galactus devours us all. Bang. Crash. Kaboom. The end of the world increasingly accomplished and spectacular on a technical level. The apocalypse as spectacular choreography. But, as you grow up and move forward, you begin prefer the more deliberate and thoughtful ends of the world.

The end of the world like in "The Great Seraphim," by Adolfo Bioy Casares. Or the end of the world like a long and drawn-out entropy in the novels of J. G. Ballard or Philip K. Dick.

Or the end of the world almost like something intimist and domestic in Lars Von Trier's *Melancholia*.

Maybe, now that he thinks of it, those are ends of the world he hopes his own singular end will resemble: to die very old and in good physical condition, lucid and, if possible, while we sleep. That the end of the world and of your world finds you and takes you when your eyes are closed, so you don't see it, being elsewhere, maybe, dreaming about the end of the world. The end of the world like a sleeping dream and not a waking nightmare and, if you're lucky, winding up like that sleeper on Pompeii's Via Stabiana, covered and molded by volcanic ash, antiquity with futurity, preserved forever and sunk in a sleep so deep not even the snoring of Vesuvius could interrupt it.

But now the end of the world takes up a mere one hundred and forty ephemeral characters. An end of the world written quickly and read even more quickly. And lasting until the next idiotic SMS arrives, while awaiting the creation of an emoticon that signifies "end of the world."

Which would be very Vonnegutian. Vonnegut, also, often drew an asterisk and inserted it between paragraphs in his novels, explaining that it was the drawing of an asshole, his anal orifice, the ass of his world.

Now, that world has come to an end.

And that world no longer exists except in his thoughts.

Now, the dead appear before him.

His dead.

The dead you possess so they possess you.

The dead like mirrors.

The dead like open books.

So he rereads them and is reflected in them.

And it's the dead who bear not the fatal asterisk of that writer but the asterisk of footnotes. Asterisks like the keyholes. Asterisks marking the expanse of their lives reexamined from the end, with the exhaustive and almost unblinking gaze of a boy who wants to miss nothing and take everything in with his eyes.

And remembering it from here and now, he thinks—in his way and without The Boy he was then suspecting it though probably intuiting it—that night would mark the end of a world.

The end of the world as that boy had hitherto known it.

The end of the world in a night full of asterisks, like stars, like those stars—they try to convince children—that the dead become.

The dead who remember everything in silence and strangely depressed and almost ashamed for having died and for shining there above, with the most hubristic discretion.

The dead who now live in the sky like dead stars. Stars that—then, that night, in the middle of The Widest Avenue in the World—The Boy looks up at and wonders which of them would correspond to the little poet and his rival and friend from school (see: † Nicolasito Pertusato) who died in front of his eyes, in an accident, weeks before. There and then, a few meters away, his first dead contemporary. Pertusato, Nicolasito as the first dead person he saw in his life and, in addition, the first living person he saw die (he saw him transform into a dead person, to mortify), in front of him and on the ground, at his feet. Could Pertusato, Nicolasito be that star? Or that other one? Or did it take longer to climb up there and starify? The Boy wonders. The Boy who at that point is a little—not much—bigger than The Boy he was when he almost drowned one summer, on vacation with his parents. But with a decisive difference from his previous incarnation: now, then, he could read and, though he doesn't yet write professionally, he does describe and reread and *compose* (the verb used for the compositions he composes in class).

So The Boy knows, when he grows up, he wants to be a writer, because he already feels he is a writer. Because he'd already written about that school (he doesn't know it then, when he goes there every morning, but that school will be the closest thing to an alma mater he'll ever have, in his brief and diffuse academic trajectory).

He wrote about that school, in one of his books, which he reads select paragraphs of now, and which, while transcribing it into his biji notebook, inevitably, he rewrites, corrects, maybe improves, maybe not.


† Nicolasito Pertusato / 1. First rival in the alternative sport (for those who "are no good" at soccer) that takes place not on the playground but in the hallways and classrooms of their school. Competitive writing. Fixed- or open-subject composition. Today the assignment is something about a hero and tomorrow we'll let you write something about Martians or dinosaurs. A public but particular school. That glorious and legendary school christened with the name of a patriotic foreigner, a Mexican who, perhaps disoriented, ended up fighting in the independence wars of the southern continent: the post-mortem general and independentist Gervasio Vicario Cabrera, immortal and befuddled, hero of the Battle of Sad Songs. In the beginning, a back-of-the-line solider nicknamed "The Mad Aztec," Cabrera—result of an explosion of gunpowder—flew, astride his horse, over enemy lines, landing right next to the tent housing the high command, whom he subdued without difficulty (they were unarmed and drinking wine in the midst of their maps) and, upon returning to his troops, seeing him return from the front suspiciously intact, he was immediately deemed a traitor and summarily shot by a firing squad. And so, by the time they learned of his bizarre feat, it was already too late, but there's always time for posthumous laurels and for your face to ascend to grace stamps and currency. The interpretation of Cabrera's story offers up—for students at the educational institution honoring his memory—multiple possibilities: you can ascend pretty high and not be recognized or resign yourself already to the idea of a world where exceedingly bizarre things happen and idiots, who don't know how to interpret and honor them appropriately, abound.

The n.°1 school of the First School District (so many number 1s produce in the school's students, of course, a kind of stupid pride) was famous for its advanced and progressive education. Which didn't keep—being an establishment subject to state rules—the students from having to attend dressed in a shirt and tie and white pinafore and with a haircut whose length was never to exceed that of The Beatles from the beginning. A school where the more or less illustrious names of the intelligentsia of the day sent—from eight in the morning until five in the afternoon, lunch at noon—their male children, with inclinations that could be nothing but artistic, though, it also offered refuge and sanctuary to those who preferred sports, provided that they knew how to pick out and appreciate the narrative threads that also ran through any activity more physical than mental. And so, there, soccer teams with names like The Little Tigers of Mompracem or The Invisible Men or The Bats of Krypton or—direct allusion to the school, and the team that the cracks who traveled to interschool tournaments played on—The Flying Patriots.

Gervasio Vicario Cabrera, n.°1 school of the First School District. The French-style building was situated amid the ruins of other French-style buildings. A window that opened to nowhere, a stairway climbing toward the bottomless void of the sky, like the paintings by the then very popular painter of posters, René Magritte, an artist who coincides with the acidic psychedelia of Peter Max and with the visions of Bosch and with the Brueghels that, on their bedroom walls, children sense in the darkness, feeling their figures move around and merge together, the ones with the others. But Magritte surpassed all of them with his paintings of diurnal nights and shadowy sombrero-wearing men and his certainty that it's dreams that dream life: *La nuit de Pise*, *La belle de nuit*, *Les chasseurs de la nuit*, *Gaspard de la nuit*, and *Les figures de nuit* and *Le sens de la nuit* and *L'heureux donateur* and *L'empire des lumières* and *La clef des songes* and the last one Magritte paints before dying: *La page blanche*. And it can't be a coincidence that all those children seek (irresponsibly overfed on surrealism at an age when everything is surreal), when they grow up, to hang on their adult walls the clear and melancholic realism of Edward Hopper and thereby conjure the memory of those childhood rooms in houses where everything hovered in the air and came crashing down. Like, again, his old school, surreal under the light of the moon. Like in a Magritte painting. Or a Pink Floyd album cover. Sometimes its students pass by—coming or going like sleepwalkers from one of those hallucinogenic all-night parties their very young parents drag them to, feeling oh so innovative—and see it as something impossible but real. There's nothing more unsettling than a school by night and that school is doubly or triply unsettling. The children see it there, their pupils shrunken with sleepiness, wondering what they're doing out there at that time, awake, when they should be in bed, dreaming, perhaps, that it's the middle of the wide-open night and they're sleepwalking past their shuttered school. There it is, like a funereal monument where what's dead and monumentalized is the monument itself. A patient, terminally ill and in suspended animation, waiting for the plug to be pulled. A school already ready to be demolished by the municipal authorities, insistent on extending the trajectory of what, they repeated over and over with a kind of primitive pride, again, once more, was "The Widest Avenue in the World," so they could thus make it, also, "The Longest Avenue in the World." And it's not true that it's the widest; it's a trick, the width of the multi-lane avenue actually incorporates and phagocytes (a verb that the *cabrerista* kids have recently learned in biology class and use whenever they can) other older streets along it's periphery that at first glance appear to be lanes, but no. (And yet one thing is true for him: ever since that night when he crossed that avenue with Uncle Hey Walrus and heard him recount the plot of that movie based on that novel, good ideas for stories and novels always come to him whenever he crosses wide avenues. Once he heard a writer say, "Writing a novel is like driving a car at night. You can see only as far as your headlights, but you can make the whole trip that way." He'd never learned to drive; and so, for him, writing a novel was like crossing a street without being entirely certain the stoplights were in your favor, your shoelaces were snugly tied, or the puddle in front of you wasn't really a pothole several meters deep.) Yes: the municipal authorities had consented to respect the educational nature of the building and hold off its inevitable end until after the 1977 school year. And meanwhile, during that year, the students played amid the rubble and bulldozers, pretending it was planet Earth after an atomic blast, after so many atomic blasts, like in those B movies, like *The Planet of the Apes*, like in the best episodes of *The Twilight Zone*.

The *cabrerista* students pretend they're the lone survivors of a cataclysm and there they go, out into that mutating landscape, running around releasing the wild shrieks of earthly science fiction after nonfiction science class.

As mentioned: these kids are different. They read a lot and write a fair amount; they worship their school pens (Insert: "303 brand pens typical of the working class; Shaeffers, distinctive of the intellectual middle class; Parkers, sign of the bourgeoisie. Some and others were thrown like knives at the wood floors, the Styrofoam ceilings, the backs of an enemy, to see if they stuck in. Some and others get their butt ends bitten during exam nerves and when, after excess chewing, teeth perforated the ink cartridge, the mouth flooded with a rush of that metallic and washable navy-blue taste. A taste they imagined must be what death tastes like and they played at being struck down by an internal hemorrhage of ink and surprise. Mouths erupting with a vomit of real blue blood"); they don't watch much television because there isn't much to watch ("*En su corcel, cuando sale la luna . . .*," "Space, the final frontier . . . ," "There is a fifth dimension beyond that which is known to man . . . This is the dimension of the imagination."); and at night they dream they're given an encyclopedia. Twelve volumes with Roman numerals on the spines and, yes, there was a not-so-remote yet irrecoverable time when childish longing passed through books. *Lo Sé Todo* [*I know It All*] was the name of that—megalomaniacal and messianic—encyclopedia. It contains neither batteries nor electricity. Paper and ink. *Lo Sé Todo* (ambitious project by the publisher Larousse; from whom they already all had acquired, by scholastic mandate, the dictionary *Pequeño Larousse Ilustrado*, which came with little drawings in the margins, but wasn't small, and made them feel its weight in their book bags) promised with its hubristic title to put the sum of all knowledge in the universe within reach of their little hands. And all that accompanied by full-color drawings emulating the aesthetic of trading card and action figure albums of the day, and composed in the style of the student who draws better than the rest of the class: detailed and, at the same time, simple and easy to imitate or trace in their notebooks. Everyone's favorite volume of *Lo Sé Todo* was number V; because it included the material referencing pre-Columbian civilizations whose ruins (the little *cabreristas* jumping around amid the brand new ruins surrounding their school to the point of strangling it) they profoundly envied, being from a country where the indigenous peoples had ridden horses a lot and had settled down very little and never managed to attain the dialectical wisdom of, for example, the Mayans when it came to greeting. *Lo Sé Todo* knew this and demonstrated it with an I-bet-you-didn't-know-this face: when two Mayans met they greeted one another like this. One said "In lak' ech" ("I am another you") and the other answered: "Hala ken" ("You are another me"). And, oh, those consonant and tongue-twisting names of plumed and serpentine Aztec gods. And pyramids atop of which to rip out hearts and cities in the Andean mountains where, they said, Pink Floyd would soon land (years before creating that insomniac man, walled inside a hotel room and dismantling everything in front of the television of his memory) to play their long and hypnotic songs live. All these years later, there are no young boys left who, today, would wish for something so great that takes up so much space. Now, the cosmic wish is for everything to fit in the palm of a hand and to be no more than a couple thumb-lengths and thumb-swipes away. The utopia of the micro and invisible and infinite, of everything in reach for everyone, futurism made present. And everyone plays not at being apprentices but Deus Ex Machinas running across pixelated meadows. Not them. They still run around outside and sit down inside to read and it doesn't occur to them to wonder if they're the last normal children or the first strange children.

In one of his biji notebooks (which one?) he has a photograph of all of them, all together, last names first and first names last.

He saved that photograph of his class the way others saved supposed pieces of the supposed cross on which Jesus Christ was supposedly crucified. A cross—to judge by the quantity of wood splinters that adorned it—taller than the Empire State building and wider than The Widest Avenue in the World. He saves that photograph, he supposes, because he needs to believe in something. He finds it easy to believe in that photograph because, appropriately, it's hard to believe in. All of them together and wearing uniforms of a blinding white, which makes the contrast between the grays and blacks of the photograph still more supernatural. A photograph of a group of ghosts—because when you're shorter and newer you're nothing but a ghost of yourself—where the most authentic and verifiable specter of all is the absence of Pertusato, Nicolasito. The empty space radiating his presence. His last name always preceding his first name. Like when attendance was taken every morning at the foot of a twisted flagpole where a dirty-colored flag barely waved. Or like when they went out in single file, after eating lunch and assuming that digestive "resting position" (head between arms, resting on the cafeteria table, speaking in whispers, sometimes someone fell asleep, which was almost considered a show of cowardice), for the longest recess of the day, while, there outside, the rumble of the bulldozers and the rat-tat-tat of the jackhammers reminded them that The Widest Avenue in the World was hungry and it wasn't resting and time was running out before it would eat all of them. The Widest Avenue in the World wanted blood as if it were one of those Aztec deities thirsting for sacrifice.

And Pertusato, Nicolasito was the offering. Though Pertusato, Nicolasito hadn't been his real name. The alias came from (he'd given it to him, many years later) the name of that harmoniously proportioned dwarf that seems to be sneaking in, in motion and slightly out of focus, in that scene where everyone else is motionless and in focus, on one side of Diego Velázquez's painting *Las Meninas* (one of the works he always visited whenever he went to the Prado, the other is that dog of Goya's) and that reminded him so much of the names of the hero-dreamers of the most hilariously demented novels and stories by Adolfo Bioy Casares. Nicolasito Pertusato had been a palace dwarf come from Italy, first to the court of Felipe IV and later that of Carlos II. A small social climber who, they say, climbed to great heights (and, no doubt about it, a dwarf who figured out how to pass from one court to the next had to know how to play his cards and graces just right). A character of the most colorful kind who outlived all the other figures who appear in *Las Meninas*, including its painter. He'd given his first rival in the literary arts that name, first, because it sounded like his real name. And second, because he liked seeing him as a dwarf. His Pertusato, Nicolasito was small and pale and of diminutive aspect and asthmatic respiration; but he seemed to grow every time he fought a "composition duel" (an idea of that woman who was so much younger than the rest of the teachers, that entrancing woman who taught "artistic activities" and who, under her pinafore, wore really tight blue jeans instead of a skirt) against him, his primary rival. In front of all their classmates and even students from classrooms of older classes, who were given the power to judge and vote (democratic activity that was regaining popularity around that time, after many years of not existing, in his now nonexistent country of origin) for the person who wrote "best and most interestingly." It's not easy for him to admit and remember that Pertusato, Nicolasito almost always beat him for reasons inexplicable to him at the time, but that he now understands with perfect clarity: Pertusato, Nicolasito wrote what others wanted to read and hear, in a flowery and purple prose and a precise and functional narrative sensibility. But (only recently could he admit it, remembering many of his compositions word for word, with that memory children have for remembering forever and never forgetting something that they hate or that makes them feel bad) the brief stories of Pertusato, Nicolasito already breathed with a certain precocious brilliance. Turns of phrase, a strange way of adjectivizing, long sentences. Features of a style he began to study and imitate. And very soon it was difficult to distinguish the one from the other. And his teacher had reproached him with a smile and he'd acted like he hadn't heard her, but soon he knew—no longer able to tell where Pertusato, Nicolasito's thing began and his thing ended—that there wasn't room for two writers in that same class and classroom.

One night he saw a horror movie on television, the kind his classmates couldn't watch for the simple reason that—unlike his—their parents were home at night. It was called *Tales from the Crypt*, starring his favorite actor: Peter Cushing, the best Van Helsing in history, a remarkable Sherlock Holmes, and a Victor Frankenstein who wasn't half bad. And it was one of those movies in episodes, telling various stories, like episodes of *The Twilight Zone*, but with much bloodier modalities. But Peter Cushing was not in the segment that most impressed him. It was the penultimate episode and it was titled "Wish You Were Here," like that album he listened to over and over, and—with time he realized—whose plot was an adaptation of a classic story of the genre, one of the most terrifying tales in the history of literature: "The Monkey's Paw" by W. W. Jacobs. In that episode, a Chinese statue replaced the monkey's paw of Jacobs's original, but the plot device was the same: the figure grants three wishes that come true in ever more terrifying ways that the movie exaggerated to grotesque effect, concluding with the wish that someone be brought back from the dead, failing to remember that person had been embalmed. He had difficulty sleeping that night, but finally fell asleep wishing Pertusato, Nicolasito wouldn't participate in the grand finale of the composition competition that would take place the next week.

And, yes, Pertusato, Nicolasito isn't in that photograph, because by the time it's taken Pertusato, Nicolasito is no longer alive and is already dead. He and his friends managed, for once, to convince Pertusato, Nicolasito, when school was dismissed, to come out and play in the ruins surrounding it, which they imagine and believe are pre-Columbian; and they all go down into a crater and in its bottom they see what appears to be an extraterrestrial hand protruding out of the rubble. At the time, the alien-archeological theories of Erich von Däniken—in books and magazines and documentaries—are very popular. And they all shriek with excitement and tell and order Pertusato, Nicolasito, as he himself is a newbie in that landscape, that he has the honor and duty to welcome that god from beyond the stars. So Pertusato, Nicolasito shakes the hand which is nothing but a high voltage cable that one of the workers forgot to disconnect and what all of them see then is something the best special effects in movies still haven't achieved: Pertusato, Nicolasito's hair begins to smoke and his eyes pop out and sparks shoot from those holes (Pertusato, Nicolasito seems to have emerged from or entered one of those animated drawings where everyone dies so they can be resuscitated and die again) and, oh, that horrible smell that'll keep them from eating baked chicken for months without feeling nauseated and running to the bathroom. And, yes, as already mentioned: Pertusato, Nicolasito is his first dead person. The first of various, of many. But he's more than that, he's more than a simple and common dead person: Pertusato Nicolasito is a *live* dead person, a dead person seen in the very moment of dying, in the precise instant when a living person begins their life as a dead person. And he sees him again very soon, one last time, there inside, looking over the edge of the coffin, like someone peering into an abyss. An unscheduled field trip to the wake and burial and all of them walking through that cemetery where the tombs resemble small houses. His first dead person at his first funeral. His first dead colleague. And, of course, not his last. There were many more to come. Writers were fragile machines. They broke down easily. Ever more quickly and more frequently. And from a very young age he spent time going to authors' funerals. His black suit and white face always at the ready. The heavy, unbearable, lightness of the dead. The coffin full of an empty body. (Readers clapping for the coffin with the same emphasis, between frightened and victorious, with which they clap when the airplanes they're traveling in land or, best not to think of it, the way they clap when a boy is separated from his parents on a beach.) Funerals like those sites that always change location but maintain their climate and geography: you travel there to look at yourself in the mirror of your own future death that—still, for the moment, who knows how long—reflects back a different face, that's not ours, but that we know better than our own face, because we looked at it more often, for more time.

And seven days after his funereal debut, he reads his composition (which is a kind of hypocritical but heartfelt elegy-homage to Pertusato, Nicolasito in which he appears as a close friend and literary guide) and draws tears and applause from the auditorium and for the first time he feels a strange feeling. A feeling he doesn't understand very well, but knows it's what really ends up turning him into a real writer. On the one hand, discovering the possibilities the real can offer when passed through the filters of reality. One the other, experiencing for the first time that happiness so unique and particular to writers: that joy a writer feels not when something goes well for him, but when something goes badly for another writer.

A joy running hand-in-hand with the joy of writing a good sentence or of reading an excellent page.

What's known as—for lack of a better designation—the literary vocation.

Random notes from his biji notebooks:

† He was always a writer. Even before he knew how to write. Before being a writer he was already a writer-to-be: a nextwriter.

† And over the years they will ask you, over and over again, that question of "As a writer, where do you get your ideas?" And, wearing that parentheses face, that writer who will always be that boy will wonder why it is that they never ask him something far more important, or, at least, more interesting, than "As a writer, where do you get your ideas?"

Why do they never ask: "What made you want to be a writer?"

† Though less and less, it still works: an atavistic reflex, an ancient instinct. They ask him what he does, he answers "I am a writer." And then something happens to the expression of those asking. A film forms over the eyes of

his interlocutors; as if they were overcome with emotion, as if suddenly they were evoking an imaginary kingdom from their childhood they hadn't heard mentioned and hadn't traveled to for so long. Some of them, even, catch a glimpse of a very distant past in which they *too* wanted to be *that*.

Then, right away, it left them and leaves them now.

And everything returns to normality.

And they no longer think about any of that.

† Each of the many times they ask how you become a writer, save some time and gain some truth, and always give the same answer: "But the thing is we're all born writers. We all have that need to tell something. And all of us, around more or less five years old, have the tools (very inexpensive) and the faculties (very sophisticated) to be and do it. The trouble comes with the added need to tell it better and better. Better and better and better and even better and better still and just a little bit more to be a little bit better and . . . So, the majority of writers die very young. Of exhaustion or heartbreak. Many commit suicide. And they're reborn as something else, with another profession, with another vocation. And, sometimes, on nights of insomnia (the world is full of writers' ghosts, of bewitched people), they say: "Once upon a time I was a writer" or "I could have been a writer." If there's any luck, all those people will receive the better-than-consolation prize of turning into great readers. The closest thing to being a writer. But without the invented part, without the part of having to go around inventing all the time.

† The true mystery doesn't pass through how one became a writer (there's nothing too strange about that first lightning bolt, about that need to put something in writing that beats inside everyone at some point early on in life and that in the majority of cases flashes out after toppling a tree or electrocuting some passerby), but through why one continues to be one after already having been one, which has been proven to be a desperate, when not demented, gesture and that—unlike what happens with other forms of madness—doesn't disturb two or three or ten or a thousand or a million

others and make them worry about our mental health. For them, we're not mad (madness *does* arouse certain curiosity and interest), we're just fools (and there's nothing less interesting than a fool insisting on his foolishness). The answer to the enigma, in any case, is not at all surprising. One keeps on writing because—like what happens with those bomber pilots who discover they no longer have enough fuel to make it back to base—they can't do anything but keep on flying and dropping bombs from on high, hoping that they hit the right target, that they finish off the bad guys and help the good guys, before coming down and crashing into the sea or the forest. Quoting that William Gaddis quote about how the idea of "leaving it all behind" seems quite tempting, but then he understands that "it's too God damned late now even to be any of the things I never wanted to be."

† Shamanstvo (шама́нство) / According to Vladimir Nabokov, shamanstvo—a sound that contains the word "shaman"—was the most important gift a writer could have. "The enchanter quality," he explained. Generating in the reader the irrepressible need to keep reading. Shamanstvo applied to the use and calibration of the two narrative elements according to the Russian formalists: the *fabula* (the story as a sum total of interconnected events) and the *syuzhet* (the ordered and managed plotting of those events). One and the other defining and deciding the best way to tell something. To show and to hide and to insinuate and Vladimir Nabokov raises this tension to the max in stories like "The Vane Sisters" and "Signs and Symbols" and in novels like *Transparent Things*.

The Canadian writer Robertson Davies also invoked that Russian word— "shamanstvo"—and compared it "to the silk-spinning and web-casting gift of the spider" and the writer who makes use of it "must not only have something to say, some story to tell or some wisdom to impart, but he must have a characteristic way of doing it . . . A true writer is descended from those story-tellers many hundreds of years ago who spread a mat in the marketplace, sat on it, placed their collection bowl well forward and cried: 'Give me a copper coin, and I will tell you a golden tale.' If the story-teller was good, a small crowd gathered around, to whom he told his tale until he arrived to the most interesting part; then, he paused and passed around the collection bowl again. That's how he earned a living; if he didn't retain an audience, he had to devote himself to something else. That is what a writer should do."

And in one of his most recent notebooks:

† The end of the literary vocation like experiencing something akin to the difference between going bald (horror) and the strange gratification of already being bald (miracle) and wondering why you spent so much time caring about and maintaining so much demanding and useless hair (when you could've been enjoying full justification for using fetching caps and elegant hats, helping to keep the warmth from escaping your head, the place where the most body heat is lost).

† Enough supposedly epiphanic idiocies, enough lyrical-vocational illuminations: is there anybody out there with an antidote or even a magic potion that removes the desire to be a writer? Something that immunizes or cures you from such a calling? Something that turns you into *something else*? Into a lawyer or programmer or odontologist or scientist or, at least, a writer of really badly written bestsellers? (The doctor who discovers the vaccine for the literary vocation will receive the Nobel Prize in Medicine *and* in Literature, for services rendered to the art, thereby eliminating so many random toxins and viruses.)

† And when the Nobel in Literature gets privatized (something that'll inevitably happen), they'll give out two per year: the same one as always and the one that never was. A second redeeming and righteous Nobel for all those who never won it and should have won it and, among them, almost everyone: James, Proust, Fitzgerald, Vonnegut, Salinger, Borges & Bioy Casares, Nabokov . . .

† Ages/Times/States in the life of a writer: nextwriter, writer, exwriter.


But he was no longer thinking about "writer" things. White flag and hands up and emerging from the trenches and retreating. He'd already surrendered, asking for mercy and forgiveness, when nothing occurred to him anymore. The end of what Franz Kafka in his *Diaries* called "the essence of magic." Something only comes and arrives if it's called with the precise word and by the right name. Something that "does not create but summons." Something that ceased to create when no one summoned it. When he experienced that terrible relief of there being nothing left, of being dried up, of the Hemingwayian it just won't come anymore. Was he like that war correspondent who, having survived everything, winds up slipping in the shower and breaking is neck once he's home? *Musa musa, lama shavaktani? Hineni Hineni?* The End. No more. Over and out. Something he thought would never happen; but it was also true that the voyage of the literary vocation, from the beginning, led not to the fear of the blank page, rather to the resignation of the completely black page (letters on top of letters on top of letters until they rendered the ones indistinguishable from the others) where nothing more would fit. Maybe, he consoled himself in vain, his was not a nothing occurs to me anymore but an everything occurs to me. Who knows. Again: he was no longer interested in the results of his own autopsy. He was no longer interested in understanding if, when the finale finally came . . .


† . . . the literary vocation was something that would die from an accumulation and avalanche of ideas, asphyxiated. Or if the literary vocation was nothing more than . . .


† . . . a progressive loss of irrecoverable skins. Skins more of serpentine cellophane streamers than of snakes where, at first, there was the desire to be one-of-them, then there was the ecstasy of placing your first book on the shelf with all the others, and, after, a Sisyphus-brand perpetual starting over.

A strange uphill inertia where you drag—who was it who said this?—the kind of deformed and demanding child, clinging to your knees, drooling and making incomprehensible sounds, that was the book you were working on and that, it didn't take long for you to realize, was the same book as always: a book made of books that hated its creator for having given it this awful life always at the front, in front of him, fighting for a lost cause. A reenlisting in another tour of Vietnam; because civilian life is not for you anymore; because there's no space left for another vocation out there other than the lecture hall or the editorial office or trying to sell that capillary tonic that, in addition, magically teaches people to write. Something, whatever it may be and whatever the cost, to help you avoid the fact that it's not that you're nobody's hair-losing fool, rather that you've already lost all your hair, period. Inspiration and "only connect" turned into total disconnection. No cables sparking in your brain. A hairless scalp. Like his and like him now (or like he would like to be or seem): contemplating with satisfaction an immemorial and ageless skull, a skull half newborn baby and half ancient mummy, a skull like David Bowman's just before he mutates into Star Baby in the final stretch of *2001: A Space Odyssey*, a movie among his favorites that he—increasingly resembling that disconnected computer and that wrinkled astronaut at the end—had a copy of at hand, next to his slippers.

† *2001: A Space Odyssey* like an instruction manual and method of composition and astral chart. A timeless masterpiece that doesn't age and whose only "defect" is its title, situating it at a fixed and passing and passed date (the year by which it was assumed, in 1968, humankind would make contact with an extraterrestrial intelligence, traveling in spaceships, but, in the end, that only collided with terrestrial lack-of-intelligence in the form of airplanes crashing into towers). There, Stanley Kubrick puts into practice his system of writing that was non-narrative and non-linear, but firmly guided by "seven non-submersible units" connected, one to the next, by submarine chains. If you deploy these seven key points, Kubrick insisted, everything would end up making sense and paying off with interest. To wit: 1) The monolith visits humankind in its infancy, 2) A hominid discovers technology, 3) The monolith is dug up on the moon and sends a message to Jupiter, 4) A mission is

sent to Jupiter to investigate the destination of that message, 5) Advanced technology ("I'm sorry, Dave . . . I'm afraid I can't do that") endangers the mission, 6) Technology is defeated ("I'm afraid . . . I'm afraid, Dave . . . Dave, my mind is going . . . I can feel it . . . I can feel it . . . My mind is going . . . There is no questions about it . . . I can feel it . . . I can feel it . . . I can feel it . . . I'm a . . . fraid") and the surviving astronaut is welcomed by the extraterrestrials, 7) The Star Child is born.

There are also seven (though some, like the expansive reductionist Tolstoy—who, don't forget, came up with "The Death of Ivan Ilyich" after, merely, passing by a very sick man, being told he'd spent the last days of his life screaming nonstop; Tolstoy who hurried out of his house to go and die in a train station—reduce them to two: a man goes on a journey or a stranger comes to town), according to some who have studied the subject, basic plots. To wit: 1) defeating the monster, 2) going from poor to rich, 3) the search, 4) the comedy, 5) the tragedy, 6) the rebirth, and 7) the journey from dark to light. And that's all folks. Seven days, indeed. A final book—a novel in seven freewheeling yet connected parts—written following this trajectory.

A book, hard but soft.

A book, freezing hands and burning eyes.

A book half *Titanic* and half iceberg. Sinking and floating.

Zero gravity. Total emptiness full of stars. *This is hardcore.* Constructive self-destruction. A book in which he was trying to bring about the end of the world.

Here it is.

There.


Now when someone—someone he didn't know who knew who he was and wanted to get to know him—asked if he was a writer, he never said yes.

First, because he wasn't sure he still was.

And, second, because—unlike the pride and the lack of awareness with which he answered affirmatively in his youth—he'd learned, over the years, saying he was rarely brought any gratification.

To say, "Yes, I am," often led to an "Oh, my life would make a great novel, got five minutes?" or a "Coincidentally, I have the manuscript of my magnum opus right here" or that "Really? Have I read anything you've written? What's your name?"

So, for a while now, whenever somebody sniffed him out the way you catch the scent of possible prey or a hunter to hunt, he slipped away with a "No . . . Absolutely not. Why would you think that?" And he'd identify himself with an absurd and uninteresting profession like "balanced-diet certifier for dream-activity-simulating sheep" or something like that. Something that would make it hard to prolong any kind of conversation.

But the man who sat down that morning at his table on the terrace of the Montreux Palace without even asking permission, launches in with a categorical "I see you're a writer," which gives him no chance of escape.

Because the stranger points at the book he's reading, rereading (yes, he's failed again in another attempt to dive into William Faulkner; so he stays afloat with the style he knows and loves most and best of all): his heavily underlined copy of *Transparent Things* by Vladimir Nabokov.

And then the stranger adds:

"Few ever read that book. At most, *Lolita* and *Ada* (which they read because they read *Lolita* and because of the misunderstanding of it bearing the name of another nymphet on its cover). And after, if they're very brave, *Pale Fire* and *Pnin*. But almost nobody reads *Transparent Things*. And many of the people who do read it consider it a minor work. Because it's so deceptively brief and light—only in appearance (one of those books that's so much bigger inside than outside, ideal for trips around the continent, fitting inside a pocket, and to be knocked out on the flight there and back)—and because, of course, it's one of those writer-books for writers, right? So you, sir, because I see your copy has been read and reread, must be a writer . . . If you've noticed, and you probably have, *Transparent Things* has one of the strangest combinations of beginning and ending in all of Nabokov. In all literature, really . . . After giving it a lot of thought, I've come to the conclusion that that master-of-ceremonies voice, as if floating above the anguished editor and the sleepwalking assassin Hugh Person, can only be the singularly plural voice of the dead . . . Sometimes it's an *I*, other times a *one*, and others still a *we* or a *you* . . . Among them, I think, the ghost of the writer R. Who, we're told, suffers the hounding of 'Insomnia and her sister Nocturia.' And whom Person edits. One of the only protagonist editors I can remember. There are many as secondary characters, but starring roles for editors don't abound and I wonder if that might not be a subliminal way writers have of taking revenge . . . Anyway, Person, 'a singularly inept anthropoid,' jumping from place to place and time to time. Person understanding dreams as 'anagrams of diurnal reality,' until that final fire in that hotel . . . 'The dead are good mixers, that's quite certain, at least,' I love that line. And the things those supposedly dead people say! . . . The dead like 'intervening auras' in our affairs! . . . May I?"—The man takes a deep breath and announces and recites from memory—"Here I go: 'Direct interference in a person's life does not enter our scope of activity, nor, on the other hand, tralatitiously speaking, hand, is his destiny a chain of predeterminate links: some "future" events may be likelier than others, O.K., but all are chimeric, and every cause-and-effect sequence is always a hit-and-miss affair, even if the lunette has actually closed around your neck, and the cretinous crowd holds its breath . . . Another thing we are not supposed to do is explain the inexplicable. Men have learned to live with a black burden, a huge aching hump: the supposition that "reality" may only be a "dream." How much more dreadful it would be if the very awareness of your being aware of reality's dreamlike nature were also a dream, a built-in hallucination! One should bear in mind, however, that there is no mirage without a vanishing point, just as there is no lake without a closed circle of reliable land.' . . . Marvelous . . . And it's great you're rereading it here. It's a very Swiss novel, no? Very Montreux, very hotel, very border, very liminal, as if transpiring in a ghost zone and taking up little physical space, but filling up mental immensities. Perfect size for a trip: weighs nothing, brief on the outside, immense on the inside. And it never ends. You can always start it over, right? And, beyond its very clever plot, if *Transparent Things* is about something, it's the murky yet shimmering relationship between writer, character, and reader."

The man smiles a smile of yellow and twisted teeth. A worn-out smile, almost as worn-out as his copy of *Transparent Things*. The man has the aspect of someone walking the fine line that separates the bohemian from the *charme* of the so-called "ne'er-do-well," of the amiable yet ever-volatile variety.

And then the man—maybe sensing that his attention was beginning to wane—delivers the coup de grâce: "My father was a friend of Monsieur Vladimir. My father was of Russian descent and followed Nabokov here, from Ithaca. And he got a job at the Montreux Palace. And my father and Monsieur Vladimir became friends. And I played with Monsieur Vladimir and Madame Vera when I was a kid . . . I went with them to catch butterflies . . . Near here . . . Monsieur Vladimir told me that I brought him luck. That I attracted the best specimens . . . Something to do with the sugar in my blood or something like that . . . Not much sweet left at this point, I suppose . . . Ah, if it doesn't bother you, I'll have a bullshot: one quarter vodka and three quarters beef broth, lime juice, and a few splashes of Worcestershire sauce, ground pepper and celery salt, chilled for twenty seconds . . . Have you ever heard of anything better *composed* and written?"

After all that, there was nothing he could do but order him a bullshot, and then another one.

And to say that yes, he was a writer. And that he would be participating in a modest local literary festival, at a round table on "Literature and New Technologies." Where, on his own, he would deliver a talk on Vladimir Nabokov and dreams or something like that; but the truth was he was there as a journalist to write an article for an airline magazine on the CERN particle accelerator, and to listen to it and . . .

The man interrupts him again: "Ah, that glorious monster collider of all things in the universe . . . The keyhole in the eye of God . . . Once, at this same table, I asked Monsieur Vladimir, during an interview, if he believed in God. And I never forgot Monsieur Vladimir's response, which, as he said it, he wrote it down and corrected it: 'To be quite candid—and what I am going to say now is something I never said before, and I hope it provokes a salutary little chill—I know more about that than I can express in words, and the little that I can express would not have been expressed, had I not known more.' Don't you think that's a great answer? It's the answer of someone who knows they're different, divine. The answer of a chosen one . . . And Monsieur Vladimir and Madame Vera chose me. They even invited me to watch the moon landing with them, in their room, on a television they rented especially for that occasion . . . Do you believe in God? I do. But with a notable difference in the shape and unpinning of how He tends to be believed in. I believe in God only after taking a spin around the world and His Creation. I believe in God only after having believed in everything that denied His existence . . . Once I was that type of individual who, looking at a rainbow, said to myself some people see God in it, others the harmony of form and color, and others a phenomenon caused by the refraction of light and the deflection caused by waves of varying longitude intersecting, or something like that . . . And I thought those three options were applicable to everything that surrounded us, that those three options always coexisted when we look at something. And that the first of them was nothing but a way of distracting us and giving a more or less human face, a face in our image and semblance, to what we do not understand, to the fear of death and to the unknown and to our absolute solitude in the universe . . . But one morning I felt my bed moving, I sensed a presence not of this world and yet part of it. And then my telephone rang and I answered it and I heard a voice saying my name and . . . Did I tell you my name yet? . . . I don't think it matters who I am . . . It matters what I am . . . What I was . . . A physicist and mathematician and cosmologist . . . It's not a simple occupation. And it's well known that a good number of the members of my 'race' reach their peak between twenty and thirty years old. After that, only exceptional beings achieve anything with formulas and equations and theorems . . . Writers, I've read, last a bit longer, right? I read that, statistically, they're more likely to hit their high point around forty-five . . . But there are always isolated cases, of course . . . You can always find the hidden path to the fountain of eternal youth and . . . Oh, speaking of miraculous concoctions: here comes that magnificent bullshot, still more of the abundant proof that God loves His children. A love far greater than the love He, apparently, felt for that son He sent to Earth on a suicide mission, right? Jesus, who—being a writer maybe you've already noticed this—only writes once throughout all the Gospels. In John 8:7, when he says that thing about 'Let he who is without sin cast the first stone.' Around him everyone is going mad and Jesus bends down and writes something in the dirt with his finger. But we're never told what he writes. It's clear he writes something brief. But that something *must* be transcendent. Or maybe it was just an X. Not the X people who don't know how to read or write use to sign their name, rather, the X of someone crossing himself out, of someone who decides not to write about himself so that, better, others can write about him. To be a great character in the hands of people who'll end up making you think that thing about forgive them, Father, for they know not what they write or that thing about, Father, why have you redacted me . . . But I don't think it's a text, I think it's a formula. The formula for the experiment he'll soon be submitted to by his father . . . Yes: Jesus as Patient Zero, as test pilot for that thing I've devoted myself to researching: departing in order to return and, listen up, never departing again. Shake all that up and serve it and . . . I . . . well . . . My idea was to be something like the Steve Jobs of the resurrection. Not an inventor, but yes a 'populizer.' An . . . never put better . . . evangelist: to bring the Good News to everyone. To make it so that 'cocktail' was in reach of all the regulars at the bar . . . Bullshots *also* are *good mixers* . . . Where did you say you lived again? . . . Ah, wonderful! . . . That's the city where you can get the best bullshots I've ever had. At the Belvedere . . . But let's get back to our—to my thing. To what I was: a scientist . . . Well-recognized and admired . . . Widely published . . . Until one night of insomnia I had an idea. One of *those* ideas that wakes you up when the rest of humanity appears to be sleeping . . . It was a dark and stormy night, indeed . . . The Lazarus Equation and, yes, mea culpa: it sounds a bit like Robert Ludlum and Dan Brown. But when it comes to these things you have to find names with a hook, because otherwise . . . I'd already postulated the possibility of traveling in time using an extremely heavy cylinder of infinite longitude, spinning around its own axis at a speed approaching the speed of light, creating an extreme gravitational pull and generating a closed loop and . . . But I won't bore you with the details . . . Suffice to say that my 'reputation' among my colleagues was of the 'let's-see-what-he-brings-us-this-time' variety . . . Would obtaining another bullshot be inordinately complicated? . . . . I always make the same mistake: I drink the first one in two or three gulps. The need to believe, again, that something so perfect can exist makes one anxious, thirsty for miracles and . . . Would it be possible? . . . Yes? . . . Many thanks . . . And, well, the following was nothing more and nothing less than the illumination of the exact formula proving the existence of life and death on the basis of an artificial intelligence, something I named, as I said, the Lazarus Equation. And that I identified with the Judeo-Christian idea of God. The idea, my idea, was that sooner rather than later humanity would end up attaining such great computational speed and storage capacity that all of that, all of that very big data, would be transformed into an entity capable of generating an infinite virtual time, which would allow the invocation of and communication and consultation with every being that's ever lived . . . And in light of such power and such a challenge, enticing Him and tempting Him, God would have no choice but to reappear. And to take control of that knowledge. Not to deny it, but to make clear who the owner of the brand and manager of the thing was . . . you follow me?"

And, yes, he followed.

And he finally came up with the answer to the question he'd been pondering while following along: who did that man remind him of? He reminds him of a character from a Kurt Vonnegut book, one of those enlightened lunatics. Better: he reminds him of a character from a book by the writer Kurt Vonnegut in a book by the writer Kilgore Trout. Those synthetic-capsules that summarize the plots of science-fiction stories down to the slightest expression, taking shelter in the certainty that the genre doesn't produce novels of ideas but novels of an idea. Just one. So it was best to relate that idea in few words and move on to the next one, in the next nebula.

"And, of course, many, almost everybody, laughed at me. They accused me of propagating pollutions and baseless pseudoscience, denying the Copernican Principal . . . My idea of Christianity as an exact science is too revolutionary. And my suggestion that miracles aren't just supernatural events violating the laws of science but highly improbable events carried out by God without violating any natural law is . . . how to put it . . . a bit extreme. For example: the so-called Star of Bethlehem was not a conjunction of Jupiter, but a supernova exploding in the Andromeda Galaxy. But, attention, a supernova perfectly calculated by God to announce the Singularity of the birth of His son . . . The virginity of Mary: parthenogenesis! Something common among snakes and lizards and turkeys and that could be tested if they were to grant my request to analyze the DNA of the blood of Jesus on the holy Shroud of Turin and thereby prove that it doesn't contain the gene of original sin but does contain the reverted neutrinos and antineutrinos that made his resurrection possible, when he materialized in a second body . . . a spare body . . . A Jesus Reloaded . . . Once this is proven, and it won't take much, it will produce en-masse conversions of Jews and Muslims and

Buddhists to Catholicism. And the first Jewish Pope will be crowned and, as I said, God will be pure and hard artificial intelligence. God will take charge of our advances and setbacks. And God will take responsibility of being . . . God . . . God will return. How to accelerate that encounter? How to hurry along His manifestation? . . . Easy: attract his attention. Smoke signals. Start fires. Awaken Him up from His dreaming the way Merlin is awoken . . . 'Great novels are all great fairy tales,' Monsieur Vladimir would say. But Creation is a witch tale. A script where everything is predetermined. Even our encounter here. Nothing is coincidental, no . . . And what you were saying about that article you've come to write . . . Your access to the particle accelerator puts you in an enviable position to call upon God. I can't get in there anymore. They've got me well marked. But you, yes . . . And all you'd have to do is lock yourself in the control room and press the buttons I tell you and that I'll write down for you here, with these instructions . . . It won't take you more than a couple minutes to kick off the end of the world and the long night and the awakening from dreams and the end of God's insomnia . . . You can't deny it. You deny that you're drawn to the possibility of being part of God and bringing back all your own dead, can you? . . . Another bullshot? . . . Yes? . . . Perfect . . . Now, if you want, I can tell you a bunch of entertaining first-hand anecdotes about Monsieur Vladimir . . . Although what pleasure or interest could they really hold for you when, by pressing *here* and *here* and *here*, you can converse with him directly. And ask him who is or who are the true and elusive and omnipresent narrators or narrator of *Transparent Things*."

And he wanted to be a narrator *like that*. Ambiguous. Diffuse. Divine. But, of course, it was already too late to be different. And nothing is more difficult—nothing is less productive—to question only at the end what you were so sure of in the beginning. Sure: there are great novels on the subject and with the believer-protagonist who ceases to believe. But a farewell like that really isn't all that interesting. Or, at least, he's never been interested in writing it. He never had any desire to put how he stopped writing in writing. On the other hand, he wrote about the opposite so many times: about the Alpha of the matter. He analyzed and reinvented it from all possible angles. And the thing is, so long ago, it felt to him like a mandate and a mission and a destiny. So he never hesitated. He was sure. He would be *that* and wouldn't be anything else, because there was no way he could be. He wasn't about to change direction or goal along that trajectory, because, defeated on various sports fields (he hadn't made the slightest attempt to kick the ball toward the goal, knowing it would fire off in any other direction and, probably, break a window or end up in his own net) or confronting the exactitude of equations (commas and letters mixed with numbers? who came up with such non-sense?), he understood that he would be perfectly useless at any other activity or in any other profession. And such certainty made his parents nervous. Very nervous. They looked at him strangely. They referred to him, with apparent affection, as The Mole. They shut up and kept quiet (or communicated with each other in a supposedly secret language that'd only taken him one after-noon to decode) every time they sensed him come into the room, always with a little notebook in his hand and a little pen behind his ear, trailed by his little sister who, he announced, was his secretary. They watched him sidelong with a fear as childish as he was. Not because they were worried about how he would make a living doing that (it'd never been easy to access the grand prize and just desserts receiving 10 percent of the cover price of each copy sold signified), but because, narcissistic and self-absorbed and devotees and fans of themselves, his parents were disturbed that, in the future, he would offer his version of them. And others, not them, would read it. A vain and in-vain worry: because by the time he—as they feared—put them in writing, his parents had already been crossed out and ripped from the pages of History to enter the pages of his stories. And he remembers them and remembers himself, as if he were reading them, as if reading himself. He remembers the quaking in their eyes when he told them officially not that he wanted to be a writer when he grew up, but that he already was a writer, that he was already writing. He remembers, also, that someone said: "When a writer is born into a family, the family is finished." Or, really, that family starts over and is retold. Corrected and rewritten and . . . Now, he doesn't write anymore, all he can do is remember his own, the ones he appropriated. Direct relatives or close acquaintances. And remember himself and remember them. And read what happened and what happened to him and what happened to them. Inventing them and dreaming them. The closest thing to writing, to writing himself. Consolation prize or punishment, who knows.


Years later he would learn that reading and writing take an enormous physical toll, as much on the muscular tissue as on the nervous system. That several hours of sitting and typing was the same as running up the street. That illiterate people who were taught to read start needing more hours of sleep to restore their energy. But that's not his case now, back then: reading and writing made him stronger. A double superpower. And one he'd have forever (or that's what The Boy thinks) and not just a few minutes, like at the mouth of that river on that beach after almost drowning and living to tell the tale.

Now, afterward, back then, The Boy can read all the time.

He already has a library all his own and growing, finding itself unexpectedly added to when Pertusato, Nicolasito's parents—moved by his ode to their dead little boy at the memorial service held at the school—insisted on bequeathing him the books of his ex-competitor. Now, without a rival, The Boy feels he reads better and faster and as if the novels burned up in his hands and turned into dense smoke his eyes absorbed. He needs more and more, and there is less and less space and time for all of them.

Superman was, he remembers, the first great casualty of his reading life. Another death. There was a moment when he felt he had to choose—a time when there was only room for one superhero—and he didn't hesitate even for a second: Batman. One and the other—Superman and Batman—shared with The Boy the tragic and violent death of their parents. But Batman's get-up was so much better than Superman's jingoistic pajamas with the underwear on the outside (the only thing that still interested him about Kal-El, son of Krypton, was his allergy, kryptonitic and shared, to all matter from his home planet turned to stardust). And—he intuited it all along, but only recently rationalized and theorized it—Superman came already made, ready for use, instructed by his father who, yes, had had the oh so saturnine character to send him to a world with a perpetual propensity for the catastrophic.

Whereas Bruce Wayne—Dickensian yet millionaire orphan—had made and invented and written himself. Bati-I Literature. When he was The Boy, very little of Marvel made it to his now nonexistent country of origin, and so he never wondered until he was already an adult why the X-Men are called X-Men when there are so many women among them, in that little, perpetually demolished school, where no halfway-responsible parent would enroll their children, mutants or otherwise and . . .

OK, sure: like all writers, he never really grew up.

Writers are bonsais who dream they are oaks.

Writers are fragile and delicate and fade away so easily and what looks so easy from outside turns out to be so difficult to maintain with internal harmony. It's not enough to be cultured to be able to cultivate and germinate and harvest something. And he was never great when it came to pruning. He was always more inclusive than exclusive.

And so he always pretended to let leaves fall, while filling coffers he'll keep on filling and filling throughout his life and his library.


† To the Titans of the Inclusive (like Laurence Sterne and Herman Melville) and to the XL-Men and the Baggy Monsters of overflowing pockets and flashing zippers and to those Divine Devourers of Entire Worlds (remembering with special affection and respect—he'll come back to them later—that bicephalous and bisexual and bi-ethnic entity composed of Iris Murdoch and Saul Bellow, two so imperfectly perfect writers). And also to all those *riff writers* (Thomas Wolfe and Henry Miller and Malcolm Lowry and Jack Kerouac and Ralph Ellison and Harold Brodkey and Richard Brautigan and Frederick Exley and Barry Hannah, to mention only a few who write in English) who produced that joy of watching somebody run and at the same time, reading them, to feel you were running with them, alongside them, not really comprehending why and not really understanding what they're trying to tell us there, in that deafening wind, hands and arms and legs in ceaseless motion. Almost nobody read those writers anymore; almost nobody dared feel that kind of euphoria or had the energy to run like that. There were almost no writers who wanted to be like them anymore; because, near the end

of literature, writers began to say things like "When I write I think about the reader" and "What I'm concerned with are the problems of the people" and a Nobel Prize winner had even stated that "Many writers have distanced themselves from public life and even feel a certain disdain for politics. But I think the writer should always be in that sphere, he cannot be isolated like Proust, who ordered his walls lined with cork so no outside sound would reach him. That image terrifies me." And he said it perfectly and gloatingly unaware of the other terror he was producing by saying such things and, while he was at it, failing to recall the pages upon pages upon pages the Frenchman devoted to the Dreyfus Affair in the life of his novel.

And thinking it wouldn't be too bad—in the face of such nonsense—for what's given to also be able to be taken away. And so everybody would have to be a little more careful about what they say and what they write. And would read again those who did their thing in small spaces, invoking immensities, giving life to brooms, provoking floods.


† But also—with time, perhaps because the brain increasingly resembled the prostate and the lines came out like ever more sporadic drops—you have to know how to learn to prostrate yourself before those magicians of that deceptive brevity that contains everything. Not the iceberg of Hemingway but the icicle of, for example, Penelope Fitzgerald. Another form of running or, better, more than running, of skating. As if sliding on sharp steel blades across ice that might break at any moment, but doesn't. That kind of absolute lucidity that delivers the straight-line speed and precision you—after years of so many elaborate spins and baroque pirouettes and falls—crave in your own life.

But no.

There are some wishes that never come true.


† In the same way, you learn to be more courteous with all those very unsuccessful yet, also, very ambitious and triumphantly failed books (helping them cross the street the way you help a blind man, far more sensitive and

interesting than all those wary youths with perfect eyesight, calculating each and every movement, worried first and foremost and when all is said and done, about never falling down in public. But, sooner or later, if there's any justice, they do fall).

But it's a long time before he'll think or write *like that*. Back then he's new and happy: he reads without thinking about writing or, at least, about what writing will mean. He's pure and innocent and he is The Boy. And then, *Treasure Island*, which is, probably, the best first book (and the best written) that a boy who already wants and needs to be a writer can read and that, in its way and subliminally, functions as the best possible metaphor/symbolism for the reader for whom it's no longer enough just to read: because if the pirates kidnap you, then you join the pirates. And—after passing quickly through the trio of Jules Verne & Emilio Salgari & Alexandre Dumas, through voyages and wars and friendships and betrayals—he's already on to other things. To "real" books and "original versions." He was already on to Frankenstein (which has nothing to do with the movie and whose monster, whom almost everybody calls Frankenstein, as if his creator had, also, sewn his own last name onto him, drags around his backpack of select books to educate himself, like those of Plutarch and Milton and Goethe). And to the insomniac Dracula (a gift from Uncle Hey Walrus, with the monster that barely makes an appearance in the book, but seems to be there all the time, reading over your shoulder and the shoulders of those who write and describe him without seeing him). And to the *Fellowship of the Ring* (is it just him or is there something sadistic about Gandalf, who always seems to wait until the last minute in battles or adventures, first allowing hundreds of men or elves or dwarves to die, only to intervene at the end and save Frodo and his friends? And wouldn't it have been much faster and more practical to climb aboard those giant eagles that show up at the end and, from the beginning, fly directly and without delay, from the Shire to Mordor and throw the fucking ring from the air into Mount Doom and save themselves all that walking and all those battles and all that death?). And, also, to the occasional aberration; like that book full of photographs of a seagull that believed it was Jesus

Christ or something like that. And he mixes all of that together and invents characters like D'Arktagnan, the undead musketeer descending to the center of the Earth to recover the ring (and not the necklace) from the Kingdom of Darkness. And then *Martín Eden* (where he read for the first time about the effect of the hurricane of literature entering into a life and how it's possible that, after experiencing something like that, the hero ends up committing suicide); and *David Copperfield* (where it's not very clear where the character ends and the author begins). And soon flying and teleporting with all those science-fiction novels that begin to land in all the bookstores along with entire collections of noir novels. And, yes, it's the beginning of the days of lead bullets and laser beams and people thrown from the heights or vanishing into thin air above his city.

And The Boy already intuits that his next vital leap as a reader will be like moving from a bathtub to a river. One of those rivers with views out to sea. And no: his episode at the mouth of that river and the entrance to that sea where he almost goes under never to float again hasn't left him traumatized. Just the opposite: he dreams only of feeling *that* again. When he could read without having yet learned to read. When he realized that there was something more than reading and that other thing was another form of reading, a way of reading what isn't there but should be: writing.

Now, back then, when he isn't reading he goes along daydreaming all the time about writing when he grows up; when he'll still be The Boy, yes, but in a larger and perhaps more respectable container for containing the most childish of vocations. Something you tend to decide as a kid, without thinking about it too much and is there anything more basic and intrinsically childish than the idea of working to make come true things that are not? It's a vocation even more childish—though just as sacrificing and long-suffering—than that other one that drags so many who are unaware of having decided, at the irrational age of three or four or five years old, into wanting to live for and through ballet. But his thing will involve leaping and pirouetting and crying and cramping and enduring sleepless nights for so many more years on the stage of battle than a ballerina: the literary vocation. Working not with swans and fauns but with eagles and chained Titans whose guts are eaten by the eagles. Unhurried and unceasingly. And now he has time and has times.

And nothing—in a now that seems an always-has-been and always-will-be—has more times and time than he has now.

He has insomnia.


Or insomnia has him, either way.

He has—or is contained—by that word that evokes for him the name of a Greco-Roman god and that was cribbed from the Latin *in* ("not") and *somnia* ("sleep"): not a negation of sleep but something different.

An *is not asleep*, yes. Neither is it being awake.

It's something else and located at that location where the three times coexist at all times, the night (the A-Side of insomnia) and the next day and the day before (the B-Side that, sometimes, includes the best and most daring tracks).

Insomnia like something as enumerable and *listifying* as the past (and as difficult to leap over; the first is very long the second is so high) and here he goes again, recounting and writing in a biji notebook, saying hello when he would rather say goodbye.

The interpretation of insomnia as something far more unforgettable and precise and revelatory and personal and faithful and original than the interpretation of dreams. Something far more interpretable.


† Insomnia that says goodbye to sleep like in one of those old movies. On the train station platform. Insomnia that says goodbye to sleep the way you say goodbye to so many things. The way you say goodbye to the romanticism of running alongside that train car as it pulls away, taking with it your closer-than-ever beloved whose love, nevertheless, is already beginning to feel like some faraway thing. The way you say goodbye to daydreaming.


† Insomnia that, also, opens the train car door and throws sleep off as the train travels ever faster and ever further. And sleep lands badly and breaks all its bones as if they were glass.

† Insomnia that's more black and white than any dream. The black and white of insomnia is so expressionist.


† Insomnia like that shared code, that complicit wink, that recognizable handshake that—sooner or later, later or sooner, it doesn't matter what hour or moment, with insomnia it's always the time of insomnia—all writers share. List within a list. Everyone was, is, or will be there. Insomnia like Vietnam (the only narcoleptic he knows: Henry David Thoreau, maybe because he spent the whole day running around). Poets abound perhaps because the exact rhyme stays wider-awake than *le mot juste*. And Franz Kafka ("During last night's insomnia, as these thoughts came and went between my aching temples . . .") dreaming he wakes up every fifteen minutes and jumps out the window to land in the street and the trains run him over again and again and, then, he decides it's better not to sleep than to dream he wakes up and commits suicide. And Charles Dickens (who always slept facing north, because he thought it increased his creativity and kept the insomnia, which forced him out on long nocturnal walks, in its place). And Sylvia Plath ("My mother told me I must have slept, it was impossible not to sleep in all that time, but if I slept, it was with my eyes wide open, for I had followed the green and luminous course of the second hand and the minute hand and the hour hand of the bedside clock through their circles and semi-circles, every night for seven nights, without missing a second, or a minute, or an hour"). And Emily Dickinson and Elizabeth Hardwick. And William Wordsworth and Walt Whitman (who both went out walking at night). And the Brontë sisters (who paced around a table to wear out the energies that kept them awake) and Dorothy Parker, at the table of the Algonquin Hotel ("How do people go to sleep? I'm afraid I've lost the knack"). And Thomas de Quincey and Percy Bysshe Shelley (who got addicted to opium to escape that place). And Alfred Tennyson and Francis Scott Fitzgerald (to alcohol and barbiturates). And John Updike and Haruki Murakami ("It was literally true: I was going through life asleep. My body had no more feeling than a drowned corpse. My very existence, my life in the world, seemed like a hallucination"). And W. B. Yeats and Joseph Conrad and Edith Wharton. And Joan Didion ("To live without self-respect is to lie awake some night,

beyond the reach of warm milk, the Phenobarbital, and the sleeping hand on the coverlet, counting up the sins of commissions and omission, the trusts betrayed, the promises subtly broken, the gifts irrevocably wasted through sloth or cowardice, or carelessness. However long we postpone it, we eventually lie down alone in that notoriously uncomfortable bed, the one we make ourselves. Whether or not we sleep in it depends, of course, on whether or not we respect ourselves"). And George Eliot ("In bed our yesterdays are too oppressive").

They cannot sleep and so they invent not to remember and they write not to dream.

Studies on the subject theorize that what keeps so many writers awake is the anguish and fury confronting such a poorly written world. Then, tossing and turning in bed or making their chairs spin, they rewrite it, they correct it, not always for the better. And, then, adding and throwing into the witches' brew the Macbethian guilt: the king who bids farewell to all "innocent sleep" insisting in the third person of the sleepless who "'Sleep no more! Macbeth is murdering sleep . . .' Sleep that soothes away all our worries. Sleep that puts each day to rest" sounding almost as if the name, Macbeth, were a brand of powerful amphetamines.

† Insomnia like a dislocated location where you think about what comes to pass and what came to pass and what will come to pass.

† Insomnia like—great expression, as precise as it is inaccurate—being *passed sleep*: sleep like something that came to pass but no longer comes to pass.

† Insomnia like the impossibility of getting (that terrible verb often used to affirm in the negative: no agreement was reached, *he couldn't get to sleep*) to sleep.

† Insomnia that teaches you quickly and efficiently—and makes you learn by

heart and from memory—that daydreaming and insomniac-dreaming are not at all the same thing.


† Insomnia that is the shadow of sleep, its negative, its dark side. Paradoxical-idiomatic-semantic-signification oddity: to say I *am* sleepy does not mean *to possess* sleep. *To be* sleepy, with any luck, is nothing more than the preliminary movement in having sleep possess us, consume us, devour us, dream us (sleep does dream) making us dream of it. When we're sleepy but sleep decides not to take us, to reject us, to abandon us, what we end up having is insomnia. Insomnia lets us have it. It's all ours, "I'm all yours, I belong to you," it says, with a yawn and a smile.

When we have insomnia, we are indeed masters of something that's nothing other than the inability to be asleep, the ability to not sleep.

Trying to connect all the foregoing with another lexical rarity that's intrigued him since childhood: when you stayed awake (and it wasn't easy not to fall asleep) to watch a late-night movie; when you said "to watch television" when you looked at the screen of the TV. As if the television were something inside the TV. The genie in the bottle, the ghost in the machine. As if the television were a dream dreamed by the TV that, when it was turned off—another paradox—remained awake, insomniac, nothing to see, without anyone to look at it. That white point in the center of the black screen that took forever to disappear.


† Insomnia like something that seems mean-spirited. They say it steals sleep, but that's not true; what steals sleep from us isn't insomnia, it's something prior to insomnia. Insomnia is, in its essence, quite generous: something *gives* us insomnia first so *we have* insomnia later. The same thing happens with that close and rather histrionic sibling of the rather laconic insomnia: fear. The fear fear gives us so, then, we're fearful. And often that fear—which comes in a variety of exceedingly personal flavors—is the fear of insomnia.


† Insomnia is like the Hound of the Baskervilles while sleep is like the

Cheshire Cat. Insomnia never stops barking for no reason, while sleep meows occasionally and only approaches you when you pretend to ignore it, though you're thinking about it all the time.


† Insomnia like a symptom/sign of the times that some people associate with the uncontainable tsunami of freewheeling capitalism, which will do everything possible to keep you from sleeping. Because when you sleep you're not spending and, as such, you don't count. You can't type or input your password or credit card number on the screens of those phones that glow in the dark. When you sleep you neither consume nor consult and don't contribute to the growth and perfection of your personal algorithm/robot portrait that needs to be monitored more or less periodically by databases of security agencies and stock exchange. And so, late capitalism like the only economic system that never sleeps. Like sharks. More information in *24/7: Late Capitalism and the Ends of Sleep* by Jonathan Crary. Crary explains: "The huge portion of our lives that we spend asleep, freed from a morass of stimulated needs, subsists as one of the great human affronts to the voraciousness of contemporary capitalism . . . within the globalist neoliberal paradigm, sleeping is for losers." Thus, a new physical-existential concept, already acknowledged in the pages of the *Oxford Dictionary*, known as *lifehacking* (or "a strategy or technique adopted to manage your time and daily activities in a more efficient way"). The idea, in the beginning, is good, or beneficial for someone: to better diagram your life, to squeeze every drop out of it. But—as happens with Frankenstein's monster—the best inventions have their dark flipside. And not in vain has man always required doses of something called nothing, of the *dolce far niente* from which on more than one occasion springs the spark of genius. Now no: now rest is beginning to be understood as "dead time." Thus, the sadism of TV channels scheduling multiple-episodes of a series to play late into the night. Thus, the young German banking intern collapsing in London City after working seventy-two hours without sleeping in order to earn bonus points, to retain his spot on the eternally flat starting-line with no way out. Thus, the Pentagon research aimed at creating victorious soldiers who no longer need to sleep. Then, you know the story, friendly fire and collateral damage and side effects, and a/another young

veteran who—unable to distinguish between waking and dreaming—walks into a shopping mall armed to the teeth, pupils dilated, time for sales and discounts and total liquidation.

† Insomnia where everyone is equal but each in his own way. And where there's no value to the consolation of learning that in the nineteenth century, when the darkness was more difficult to penetrate and fell so much earlier, it was common to sleep twice in a night with a period of activity between the one and the other: a space, in the first place, to check if the predatory beasts had gotten too close, and, later, an interval when it was accepted and acceptable to converse or talk to yourself or to make love or to compose sonnets or even to go out and visit some future friend or to fight a duel with some ex-friend. An intermission between dreams in which to waking dream. A time between times. Times of going to bed much earlier because there was very little to do. The world had shut down with the setting of the sun. And so, then, understanding it as the most normal thing in the world (because it happened to everyone in the world), to lie there: in the darkness, for two or three waking hours, and stare up at the ceiling and think about everything and nothing. Back then, insomnia was part of sleep. It was its obligatory and waking non-fiction prologue you had to pass through first in order to subsequently be able to understand and enjoy the fictions of sleep. Insomnia was the hypnotic countdown before launching on the long voyage through the space of the night.

Insomnia was a giant step before that small leap.

† Insomnia arrives doing little hops, down the hill, hand in hand with depression and challenging us—what came first: the chicken or the egg?—to guess which of the two is the older sibling. And to pick either the One who gets depressed and has insomnia or the One who has insomnia and gets depressed.

† Insomnia that ends up translating into the thinness of a condemned and

infirm man who has lost the fatty stuff of dreams and the musculature of wishful thinking. And no: it's not that he loses weight, rather that, not sleeping, he loses the heaviness of dreams, heavy dreams.

† Insomnia that spells the end (maybe as a result of a redistribution of blood flow, flowing from the genitals to the brain) of all those formidable erections he used to wake up with, like a flagpole whereon to raise the flag of a new day. Now, not so much. Now, at most, half-mast, distress signal, but never resting in peace.

† Insomnia that's the most *minimal* and most economical form of the nightmare you end up missing the way, they say, the prisoners of Auschwitz and its subsidiaries missed their nightmares: because no sleeping nightmare could ever be worse than that waking nightmare. So you would never wake up the people who were having nightmares in the concentration camps, but allow them to enjoy them, de-concentrated, until the sun rose on that blinding and re-concentrated reality.

† Insomnia that's solid while dreams are liquid.

† Insomnia that expands as sleep contracts.

† Insomnia that—unlike dreams—is unforgettable.

† Insomnia—transparent opaque thing—that abides no interpretation. Nobody will ever write a book entitled *The Interpretation of Insomnia* because there are no two insomniacs alike or systemizable. Nobody will ever tell their insomnias nor will they say, "you'll never guess what or whom I *insomniated*

last night." Nobody thinks their insomnia holds any interest for anyone else and, besides, it's embarrassing to bring it up: having insomnia is the closest thing to making that dream of discovering you're naked or your teeth are falling out in public come true, with the particularity that, there and then, the only audience is yourself. There's no more extreme way of looking at yourself than with the look of insomnia.

† Insomnia that has no eyelids and whose pupils are like stones.

† Insomnia so difficult to track (Pliny tells us that the Thracians had the custom of placing black or white pebbles in an urn for each good or bad day; and thus, reaching the end of their lives, they knew if they'd been happy or not; but Pliny says nothing about how the Thracians had explained what to do and how to calculate the black-white nights of insomnia)
    Find gray stones.

† Insomnia is a terrible and absolutely realist thing. Thus—during its somber reign—it forces spasms of thought, and fluxes of consciousness, and fixed ideas floating through the air to thereby become more bearable.

† Insomnia that speaks not the language of the free association of ideas but that of the imprisoning association of ideas: dragging steel balls and chains, like those ghosts (ghosts more frightened than frightening, with those *booos* closer to wailing with sadness than fear) who no longer remember who they'd been when they were alive.

† Insomnia that's avant-garde prose (without punctuation or capitals and all in one single long sentence for pages and pages) while sleep is free yet rigorous verse.

† Insomnia that, when it comes to being creative, so unjustly, has so much less glamour and cachet than sleep.

† Insomnia that, the legend tells, is the result of you appearing, awake, in the dream of some other, sleeping, person. If this is true, recurrent insomnia would be the consequence of being very present in the thoughts of others (of Ella?). For good or ill. For sweet dreams or bitter nightmares. (Doubt/ possibility/terror: that the dreams of people in comas are one, single dream that repeats over and over on a loop / Penelope's husband / Maxi Karma / fly-by-night encounter in a bar in B. / Maxi Karma wanted to be a writer / that love-hate look of aspirants at those whom they aspire to be / Maybe Maxi Karma, in a coma, dreams all the time of who he wanted to be and never was.)

† Insomnia like irrefutable proof that not sleeping doesn't mean not having nightmares.

† Insomnia like that nightmare you can't wake up from.

† Insomnia that—like certain dangerous liquors and certain volatile explosives—isn't safe or advisable to shake or stir.

† Insomnia where and when you feel drunk, dizzy like on the deck of one of those ships inside a bottle, message-less, adrift, and more alive than ever, raising a glass to the health of all your dead.

But, ever more explosive and shaking and bubbling, not sleeping was now, for him, like a concentration camp, of maximum concentration, on himself:

being there, eyes open and bags of such density under them they could harbor entire civilizations, thinking of a thousand things and of none. Thinking in the language of insomnia, which is the language of deafening silence, the oh so eloquent muteness of the dead. The sound of insomnia like the sound you hear inside a seashell, that sound that's not the sound of the sea but the sound of something that, like the sea, never sleeps and is never entirely still. Insomnia like being underwater and, at the same time and in the same place, where everything seems as if suspended in the air. Where everything took a long time to get started and nothing was ever entirely finished. And, sometimes, feeling how his mind seemed to be on the point of melting down from the pressure, ready to be blown to bits so all those things he'd seen there would be lost, like rain in the tears or something like that (yes, he was recalling that movie and bad joke and bad play on the words from that final monologue where the android finally shuts his eyes, and from there who knows where, from there to . . . ).

But with insomnia—unlike what happens with dreams—there are no special effects. There are no living who depart or dead who return or omnipresent spirits. The only particularity, in his case, is the sporadic shift in the tone of his mute voice. A voice he imagines with a switch of typography, with the character and characters (American Typewriter) of an old typewriter. The same font as the first typewriter he ever had. That one he struck at top speed and ceaselessly until he erased the letters from the keys and the fingerprints from his fingers. A device—that font, always preceded by an asterisk—that he once imagined as his deus-ex-machina voice. His words and commandments floating above everything and everyone, above the wakeful and the sleeping. His voice inserting itself effortlessly into their lives, after having fantasized about taking a Swiss particle accelerator by force and there disintegrating in order to be reintegrated into space. To be the most singular of Singularities. To bring an end to, without delay, with absolute certainty, the Uncertainty Principle. To pass from one state to another like what they call (he loves the name, sometimes the sciences hit the mark in such an enviably literary way) exotic matter. From solid to gas. From visible and minuscule to invisible and infinite. A having returned after having departed. A coming back transformed into a triumphal entity and delighting in taking the revenge—after years of not being read—of rewriting everything in his image and semblance and style and syntax and, ha ha ha, submitting everything to the torture of thinking like writers think, of dreaming like writers dream, of not sleeping like writers, and—damn you all, don't even think about blinking, lightning and thunder and seven plagues on all your houses!—of falling asleep listening to him or reading him.

But that all-powerful and messianic illusion doesn't last long.

And the plain old insomnia remains; something that for him has been expanding and reducing his sleep and his dreams from vast and successful fantasy sagas in which he roared like a capricious and destructive deity to terse chamber *nouvelles* with a little man nobody believes in.

From miniatures where his figure is more reminiscent of those little figures drawn by Franz Kafka, of supposedly ingenious microstories and, in the end, of random lines and more or less connected observations, of unconscious or entranced nonsense.

From the irrefutable truth of insomnia nothing seemed certain or verifiable or credible. So, to keep from killing himself, he killed time unmasking everything, down to the unattractive fertilizer of all seductive flowers. To the point of even delving into the origin of counting sheep jumping over a fence. An activity he saw for the first time in comics and cartoons from his ever so remote childhood where—the day-to-day of childhood was a little like this— with each new adventure, everything seemed to start over, as if the characters were waking up from a succession of dreams, one inside another inside yet another. An activity, since it didn't work for him at all, whose origin he had time (he had so much time, the elastic time of the night) to research. And it didn't take him long to find it. Because since the beginning of the new millennium, it was so easy to track down the roots of everything. And thus he discovered—with a quick dance of his fingers across the convoluted keys, where each matter had multiple *raisons d'être*—that the whole thing had to do with boredom. That boredom supposedly makes you sleepy and there are few things supposedly more boring than counting sheep. That, probably, the similarity between the sound of *sheep* and *sleep*—the electricity in the letters connecting one word to the other—was related to the supposed ease and rather relative effectiveness of such an activity. And that, of course, there was also the inevitable, more *legendary* version: Morpheus losing the ability to make the mortals fall asleep and going down to Earth and discovering nobody was sleeping because everyone was too worried about their waking lives, always being shaken by the capriciousness of the gods. And Morpheus setting out in search of a solution. Morpheus trying everything—white magic and black magic—to no avail. Until one morning, desperate, he lies down on the side of a road and watches a shepherd counting his sheep as they leapt over a fence. One by one. And there are many. And, bored, Morpheus's eyes close. When he wakes up from a deep sleep, Morpheus understands he's been given a solution. If you can't sleep, you should convince yourself the world is boring and dreams can be so much more exciting than a life counting sheep. In your dreams, the sheep can even count you. And leaping over that same fence, also, somewhere, he'd read that the ancient Greek root of the word "tragedy" came from the word *tragos* whose meaning is "sheep" (or was it "goat"?) and that it gained its dramatic meaning when that animal, preferably one with black wool, was sacrificed to appease the wrath or whims of the always-drowsy-after-all-that-orgy Dionysus. But the method transcended the English or the Greek language. And *Don Quixote* (in which, near the end, the hero finally falls asleep and when he wakes up, resting and having regained lucidity, he keeps his eyes open and reasonable only long enough to write his will and to die) also alluded to counting (not sheep but goats) based on certain Islamic texts. And as you can see: the truth is that nothing makes him more awake or more alert than feeling bored. Counting (numbers) was for him the admission that there was nothing left to recount (letters). So, then, after a brief countdown, the yawn like a voice. Hazards and shades of his ex-occupation. Uneventful boredom was the place where so many things always, eventually, occurred to him.

So many things that might work for him somehow or in something, he thought, while, in the background, the *Aria mit verschiedenen Veränderungen vors Clavicimbal mit 2 Manualen*, better know as the *Goldberg Variations*, played, over and over.

He'd heard them so many times—he's counted them on so many nights— that he no longer needs them to play to hear them inside the musical chamber of his head.

† Music supposedly composed by Johann Sebastian Bach (a composer who, for a time, during the time of The Boy, was very popular after getting run through the filters of a Moog synthesizer) and at the supposedly magnanimous request of a supposed noble who had problems falling asleep (and who liked to have his lead organist play it extremely softly). Centuries later, music popularized by the performance of a verified and true insomniac Canadian pianist, addict of all kinds of pills. Music that was later repurposed as soundtrack or background music—as once had been the case with the slow concertos of Tomaso Albinoni or the counterpoints of Johann Pachelbel or the miniatures of Erik Satie—for almost everything and everyone: accompanying the orbits of interplanetary and multitemporal pilgrim veterans (*Slaughterhouse-Five* again, indeed), to the crimes of exquisite serial killers, and the melancholy of misanthropic magnates.

It's true that piano didn't help him sleep (ironically and paradoxically, decades before, it'd been one of the sounds that most and best helped him type, wide awake, on his keyboard and screen, along with Pink Floyd's *Wish You Were Here* and the mercurial verse of Bob Dylan circa '65-'66), but it did, apart from reminding him of times of creative fertility, conceal now the distant yet immediate tinkling, like ice cubes in a marble cup, of The Intruders' piano, in the house next door. And it was music that made him breathe in quick breaths and sharp words. Words in his voice, but immediately implanted like elephant tusks in the little mouths of others, of his characters. Little good it did now; because long ago it'd been proven that dreaming was an aid to creation. And that not sleeping hindered all inspiration, provoking only the exhalation of almost empty sighs. And he was the most wide-awake of sighers. True, there were the defenders of creative insomnia, the self-styled "owls" standing in opposition to the "larks." Like Wolfgang Amadeus Mozart, who claimed to reach peaks of creativity "When I am . . . say, traveling in a carriage, or during the night when I cannot sleep; it is on such occasions that my ideas flow best and most abundantly." Like Fran Lebowitz, who coined the aphorism "Life is something that happens when you can't get to sleep" (but who spends decades trying write a novel). Like Virginia Woolf (who was mad). Like some of his friends (writers who broke themselves) who loved to write at night and went to bed at dawn and didn't get up until after midday (and who died so young, their organisms aged from all those nights of staying awake). Like when Leonardo da Vinci points out in his notebooks that "I myself have proved it to be of no small use, when in bed in the dark, to recall in fancy the external details of forms previously studied, or other noteworthy things conceived by subtle speculation." But Leonardo was, it's known, a race apart. And, no doubt, Leonardo even built his own mechanical sheep to count: sheep that spit flames or flowers from their mouths or that flew over fences. And Leonardo wouldn't even pause to consider arguments about how the idea that you can come to understand foreign languages or mathematic formulas while sleeping by wearing headphones has already been shown to be a fallacy. And much less to think about the idea that, when you sleep badly or don't sleep well, it's been proven that the brain begins to create false memories. Cryptomnesia, they call it: the paradox that the impossibility of dreaming leads you to invent yourself a dreamed life, a waking-dream past that ends up swallowing the nightmare of the real. Or that while sleeping, everything that really happened is fixed for your preservation and consultation. And he remembers that epidemic of insomnia that strikes and shakes all the residents of Macondo and forces them to label everything around them to keep from forgetting the names of things. There is nothing more admirable artistically than the recreation of memory, insisted the *sleepless*. There they are, so content in their torment. And, yes, he thought, not in vain did the visionary William Blake recommend, "Think in the morning. Act in the noon. Eat in the evening. Sleep in the night." And that Leonard Cohen was right when he claimed that "The last refuge of the insomniac is a sense of superiority to the sleeping world." That was not his case, that was not his thing, he wasn't so good at convincing himself of a bad thing. No pride. His memories were forever faithful and never promiscuous and much less cryptomnesiac.

But such an idea—the faith of the waking illuminators, in what they wanted to vainly believe in—provided him in its moment with another list in the dark, another flock of sheep to count off. The list is the favorite sport of those who neither sleep nor dream of being an athlete. But who nevertheless can, for a while, become obsessive and controlling champions at raising the exemplary banners of participants in the sport of not sleeping. It's already known: you always go looking for some external glamour to make up for your own internal disgrace. Saying the same thing happened to *him* or to *her* that happened to you. Feeling kindred in the worst possible way, but, in the end, kindred all the same. To get in line, but far behind, farther still, of . . .


† Renowned insomniacs / Abraham Lincoln (who took long waking and sleepless walks around a sleeping White House). Bill Clinton. Winston Churchill (last words: "I'm bored with it all"). Margaret Thatcher (who claimed that "sleep is for wimps"). Queens and kings, too many. The King of Rock 'n' Roll Elvis Presley (in one of his final notes, in big and childish handwriting, surrounded by his collection of teddy bears, the performer of the hit "[Let Me Be Your] Teddy Bear" writes: "I feel so alone sometimes. The night is quiet for me. I'd love to be able to sleep. I'll probably not rest. I have no need for all this. Help me Lord"; his last words are the first words so well known for any insomniac: "I'm going to the bathroom to read," and the book Elvis takes to his final throne is a manual of astrological signs in conjunction with sex positions; his fiancée, Ginger Alden, says "Don't fall asleep in there," Elvis responds with a curled lip: "Okay, I won't"). The King of Pop Michael Jackson (who, at the end, paranoid and unable to remember the words to songs or to memorize dance moves, spends sixty days without reaching the depths of REM sleep, due to liters and liters of Propofol producing an artificial sleep that wasn't regenerative for cellular and muscle tissue). Madonna and Britney Spears and Lady Gaga and Miley Cyrus and Penny Pop and Anorexia y sus Flaquitas (all of them, together, really? is insomnia an endemic malady for this kind of artist?). Albert Einstein (who postulated that everyone knows how to kill time but nobody how to resuscitate it; above all in *the dead of night*). Jimi Hendrix and Prince (they say that the morning he died he'd gone six nights without sleeping, that he died in an elevator in his house/studio/world; wondering if the autopsy report included the datum of whether that elevator was going up or coming down in the moment of his death). Eminem. Dylan Thomas (on the rocks) and Lord Byron (his last words were "Now I shall go to sleep. Goodnight"), Ludwig Wittgenstein (last words: "Tell them I have had a wonderful life"). James Matthew "Peter

Pan" Barrie (his last words were "I can't sleep") and Peter "Jim Yang" Hook (who, he just now realizes, in his insomnia, correcting the books of others, really should have been named Hooked and not Hook) and Ray Davies (great writer of insomniac songs for interminable and sleepless nights like "All Night Stand," "There's Too Much on My Mind" and that hymn fearful of thinking too much about the darkness that, paradoxically or not, bears the title "Days"). Vincent van Gogh (who brushed his pillow with camphor as a kind of sleeping pill). Judy Garland and Marilyn Monroe (pills and more pills and a 1961 letter to her therapist: "Last night I was awake all night again. Sometimes I wonder what the night time is for. It almost doesn't exist for me. It all seems like one long, long horrible day"). Tallulah Bankhead. George Clooney. Groucho Marx (who, when he couldn't sleep, called strangers on the phone to insult them) and Karl Marx ("author of *Das Capital*, the fruit of insomnia and migraine," according to the insomniac Vladimir Nabokov who, interviewed by Bernard Pivot for French television at an hour when "I am usually already under the eiderdown with three pillows tucked beneath my head," explained that it's then that "the inner debate begins: to take or not to take a sleeping pill? How delicious is the affirmative decision!"). Oscar Wilde ("Life is a nightmare that prevents one from sleeping"). The race of insomniac philosophers: Plato ("When a man is asleep, it's no better than if he were dead") and Clement of Alexandria ("For there is no use of a sleeping man, as there is not of a dead man") and Georg Wilhelm Friedrich Hegel (who claimed that the wise owl of the wise Minerva never flies by day) and Friedrich Nietzsche ("The need to sleep does not dwell in the spirit, because the spirit knows no rest") and Emmanuel Levinas ("Philosophy is nothing more than a call to infinite responsibility, to an untiring wakefulness, to a total insomnia") and Maurice Blanchot ("In the night, insomnia is discussion").

† A new paragraph for the Transylvanian (nocturnal nationality if ever there was one) E. M. Cioran, who, they say, didn't sleep for fifty years. When he turned twenty, Cioran stopped sleeping "and I consider it the grandest tragedy that could occur . . . Insomnia is a vertiginous lucidity that can convert paradise itself into a place of torture . . . At all hours I walked the streets like

some kind of phantom. All that I have written much later has been worked out during those nights . . . When you came, Insomnia, to shake my flesh and my pride, you who transform the childish brute, give nuance to the instincts, focus to dream, you who in a single night grant more knowledge than days spent in repose, and to the reddened eyelids, reveal yourself a more important event than the nameless diseases or the disaster of time! . . . What strangely enchanted tunes gush forth during those sleepless nights! What rich or strange idea was ever the work of a sleeper? The importance of insomnia is so colossal that I am tempted to define man as the animal who cannot sleep."

But, once all of them were counted, he wasn't that impressed. That is to say: none of them (apart from the philosophers who theorized about it) had done anything particularly practical with their insomnia, through their insomnia, for their insomnia. For him, all of them were, simply, celebrities who had trouble sleeping, shutting down. The majority of them, probably, had limited themselves to turning on the TV or drinking or taking drugs or updating their social media profiles or inviting over some professional companion to put pressure on certain pleasure centers, the exact location of which only certain gurus and shamans from Alhambra, California, or from Patagonia, Arizona know.

None of them having anything to do with what his sister Penelope (writing as one possessed all through the night, as if possessed by the ghost of her beloved Emily Brontë, carving her oeuvre out of insomnia) and two of his idols had achieved.

One of them was Vladimir Nabokov, who understood insomnia as a positive or at least powerful influence on his work (and on the work of some of his creatures like the King of Zembla or John Shade in his "Pale Fire," feeling dead one open-eyed night—tormented because his daughter who committed suicide isn't tormenting him—and remembering his "demented youth," when he suspected "a great conspiracy of books and people" was hiding an absolute truth from him. The knowledge of a secret he wasn't privy to, the key to survival after death, and the instructions to call those back who live there, and he was going to recite it here just to bother all the botherable, the truly bothersome: "And finally there was the sleepless night / When I decided to explore and fight / The foul, the inadmissible abyss, / Devoting all my twisted life to this"; "Instead of poetry divinely terse, / Disjointed notes, Insomnia's mean verse!"; "Life is a message scribbled in the dark"; "But all at once it dawned on me that *this* / Was the real point, the contrapuntal theme; / Just this: not text, but texture; not the dream"; "It isn't that we dream too wild a dream: / The trouble is we do not make it seem / Sufficiently unlikely; for the most / We can think up is a domestic ghost," etcetera).

Another of his pro-insomnia heroes was Marcel Proust (what would've become of Marcel in the days of Twitter and selfies? Would he ever have written anything or would he have limited himself to telling what he had to tell in short sentences and little photographs and to wasting time spying on the *profil social* of his acquaintances?), who suggested that "a little insomnia is not without its value in making us appreciate sleep, in throwing a ray of light upon that darkness" and who accused all those who, night after night, let themselves fall unconscious and like a ton of lead into their beds, of not daring to daydream of great discoveries or small observations.

But it was clear to him that those two—the Frenchman and the Russian—were exceptional beings whose experience was nontransferable. Two Leonardos of writing. The cork panels lining the walls of Proust's bedroom to isolate him from the outside world that he put into writing were, in his case, the cork panels lining the walls of his brain into which ideas no longer entered. And the resplendent and inspiring butterflies of Nabokov were the opaque and bumbling blowflies buzzing around behind the half-closed curtains of his eyelids. According to Plato (all he could do now was quote and quote and quote), "when the eyelids, which the gods invented for the preservation of sight, are closed, they keep in the internal fire; and the power of the fire diffuses and equalizes the inward motions . . . But when night comes on and the external and kindred fire departs, then the stream of vision is cut off; for going forth to an unlike element it is changed and extinguished . . . The eye no longer sees, and we feel disposed to sleep . . . sleep comes over us scarce disturbed by dreams; but where the greater motions still remain, of whatever nature and in whatever locality, they engender corresponding visions in dreams, which are remembered by us when we are awake and in the external world."

All that come to him now are embryos of plots and aborted storylines: nothing but a character's style of dress that will never be his own, just the title of a never-filmed movie to be shown in a film club in some story, everready enumerative lists never settling for the white monotony of sheep when they could count and recount so many other things of so many colors: waking lists that kept him from sleep until it was already too late for him or too early for the rest of the world. Or distant memories, tears in the rain (now, *yes*, he was quoting it correctly; for he'd already quoted it incorrectly) or threads of a mind that was going. Then he felt a little like HAL 9000, a little like Nexus 6. A sensitive and lyrical machine. An ingenious calculator, not counting to exhaust himself with an answer, but enumerating and adding figures as a way to remain alert in an attempt to systematize the world. In the darkness, recounting random verses or evoking far off landscapes that had taken on the tenuous quality of a scene or of a paragraph read or witnessed by a person he no longer was. By person who, yes, he'd once been, but whose DNA had been modified by time and by the more or less failed act of remembering and (he already thought it and already conjugated that verb; nothing more repetitive than insomnia) *unmaking* memory. An act that had nothing to do with that other verbal act: *memorizing*.

An example to ponder and bleat and add now: Uncle Hey Walrus shouting "As I'm the black sheep of the family, I count sheep black as night to fall asleep! Goo Goo G'Joob!"

Uncle Hey Walrus. The voice of Uncle Hey Walrus. Uncle Hey Walrus whispering "I never gave you my pillow . . ." and ". . . and I will sing a lullaby," Uncle Hey Walrus asking and bellowing "Oh yeah . . . All right . . . Are you gonna be in my dreams . . . tonight?"

And, ah, even dreaming of Uncle Hey Walrus would be better than thinking of Uncle Hey Walrus while awake . . .

† Uncle Hey Walrus's many notebooks / Incorporating them as appended material. Uncle Hey Walrus's journal. His notes and sketches as the basis for a novella about Uncle Hey Walrus's stay at Apple on Abbey Road to be titled *The Beatles* (like that, with the s crossed out, singularizing the plural), telling of his trip to London and his nights and days in the life among The Beatles,

who appear in his pages first as Lennon, McCartney, Harrison, and Starr; later as John, Paul, George, and Ringo; and finally as J., P., G., and R. As if they were dissolving in his mind as they are disintegrating as a band. Telegraphic prose but a lot of information to make use of, to cannibalize. And again: his nutritious family had for him always turned out to be exceedingly rich in protein, painfully entertaining. And he'd always counted on that pain that was always so easy for him to chew up and digest.

There's a lot of material there.

There are many guest stars.

At one point, Pink Floyd appears, to record in one of the Abbey Road studios.

They invite Uncle Hey Walrus to bark on their album.

† Songs by The Beatles that drive Uncle Hey Walrus crazy (and from which his alias comes).

The free stream of (un)consciousness of "I Am the Walrus": childish lines from J.'s childhood (that candidly uncouth "umpa, umpa, stick it up your jumpa" ascended and ascending into a Sioux-Tibetan chant), Lewis Carroll, Edward Lear, and J.'s desire to confuse and repel and also feed the compulsive and pathological interpreters of songs. But, in truth, it's the most lysergic and playful protest song ever composed, featuring a J. who is already beginning to throw back his head and release his primal scream.

The same thing with "Hey Bulldog," with its winks at T. S. Eliot and already veiled accusations from J. to P. Walrus barks and dog barks and Uncle Hey Walrus barking when he hears them and winding up in an insane asylum ("family tradition," comments Penelope) the day The Beatles break up and—highs and lows and highs and lows—escaping it forever the night John Lennon is assassinated.

And this is true though it seems a lie: at a birthday party, when he's about ten years old, Uncle Hey Walrus is hypnotized by one of the guests and made to run through the most obvious routine of the (in)voluntary participant in the performance, responding to that "for my next trick, I'll need a volunteer." And so, he orders little Uncle Hey Walrus to keep his hand raised, convinces him that it's very hot (and he starts to strip off his clothes to the panic and delight of his little girl friends), makes him believe he's a dog. And just then, the hypnotist suffers a heart attack and dies right there in front of everyone. And he never dehypnotizes the little Uncle Hey Walrus, who only comes out of the trance with the force of three or four or five or six slaps from his father. But, in short order, little Uncle Hey Walrus realizes that somewhere in his mind, he's still a dog: fits of moon howling, lifting a leg to piss on a tree, lapping at his food. And, most disconcerting of all: already an adolescent, Uncle Hey Walrus loses his mind every time he listens to *Sgt. Pepper's Lonely Hearts Club Band*, at the end, after "A Day in the Life." And soon thereafter, reading an interview with P., the mystery is explained: The Beatles slipped a 15-kilocycle sound, only audible to dogs, into that song. And every time he hears it, Uncle Hey Walrus gets down on all fours (hands and knees) and begins to spin around, as if trying to bite an invisible tail, when it reaches that part of the album (and those who know him stop him and remove the LP from the record player before that drawn-out note of multiple funereal pianos ends, when the last song has concluded).

Uncle Hey Walrus travels to London and stands guard in front of the door of Abbey Road Studios and one morning intercepts P. and tells him his story and P. laughs a lot and feels somewhat responsible and offers him a job doing "something."

And so it was that Uncle Hey Walrus became The Beatles' mascot.

(A joke, whose wordplay—*dog* in place of *God*—doesn't translate into Spanish, included in a novel by that same author who had told him that other joke—which he was able to translate, in several ways—about the past and the present and the future walking into a bar: "what do you get when you cross an insomniac, an unwilling agnostic, and a dyslexic? . . . You get somebody who stays up all night torturing himself mentally over the question of whether or not there's a dog.")

† Holy relics that Uncle Hey Walrus brought back (stole?) from the altars of Apple. The original manuscripts of "I'm Only Sleeping" (handwritten by J. on the back of a mail receipt informing him he owes twelve pounds for a radio/telephone for his Rolls-Royce) and "I'm So Tired," with more prolix writing and which lacks the "stupid git" line. Both of them folded in quarters

("like the painting of the Brontës that Branwell painted and erased himself from and that they found in the upper reaches of his wardrobe," commented Penelope) under Uncle Hey Walrus's bed, on top of which rested the dead body of Uncle Hey Walrus—heart broken over The Beatles breakup and the assassination of one of them—when he finally realized all you need is love, but money can't buy it.

† Another example: a while back now, he'd opted for counting beds, which, in a way, have about them a kind of onomatopoeic bleating (*baaaaah . . .* ): of the shrieks sheep release as they're sheared and from whose wool are woven the sometimes light and almost always stifling blankets of the past you hide under, with a small flashlight, to read, while rewriting, the pages of the novel of your life.

The bed is always the scene of the crime, of the crimes.

You were born there. You reproduce there. You die (if you're lucky and after catching a glimpse in one corner of the room the hallucination of a "horrible big fat woman dressed in black," or of that hallucinatory "distinguished thing," or of "a certain butterfly already on the wing," or of an indefinite "What's that? Does my face look strange?": Proust, James, Nabokov, Stevenson) there.

There—like he is now—you are, alone and staring at the ceiling. Often the ceilings over hospitable yet restless hotel beds (even if it's one of those luxury hotels that includes a menu of pillows of varying taste and texture) where you never sleep all that well. Because it's been discovered, based on neurological readings, that, between unfamiliar sheets, the left hemisphere remains alert and atavistic in the face of the unknown.

There, if possible, you await sleep, lying on your side (because they claim that this position helps to frighten off neurodegenerative diseases) in the fetal position from which, they recommend, we should stretch ourselves out forcefully and enthusiastically when we rise, so our day expands with health and doesn't stagnate in a passive and embryonic and even aborted attitude.

There you end up understanding that it's far healthier and better to sleep alone than in more or less good or bad company (the statistics reveal men sleep better with company and women sleep better alone).

And, in the end, there you lie, thinking of being born and of multiplying yourself and (Exit King, king-sized bed) and of dying, already almost outside of space and time; like Lear on that bed in the twilight of midday after dining in the morning.

It's no coincidence that the majority of people, when asked how they would like to die, answer: "In my sleep." In bed. A living death like the last and oh so lucid dream. A final dose of Dimethyltryptamine (note the participle phonetically equivalent to "trip" in the middle of the name) stored in the pineal gland, provoking that ultimate vertigo of "your whole life passing before your eyes in a matter of seconds" or of "opening the third eye" to a view of the Great Beyond. A *summary of publications* with no (*to be continued* . . . ), maybe dreaming you die and never wake up to say, "It was all just a dream." If the orgasm is *le petite mort*, then death is the eternal sleep, the rest in peace, the end of the war. That devout "If I die before I wake . . ." that many take for a fearful prayer is, in truth, an expression of desire: that death be a dream and dreams be death and goodnight for the last time.


† Death. Death—the act of putting into practice all that theory, memorized throughout a whole life of waiting around for that final exam—that lasts barely a second. Death like a dark punch-line to a blackly-humorous and sad joke. Death like an unfinished assignment that always gets turned in and always receives a passing grade. Death like an easy final exam. Impossible to give the wrong answer to the question. The question is "What's going to happen to me?" and the answer is "Precisely this." And on to something else and next in line. And yet, it's so easy to fail the lesson of how to anticipate and bear the idea of your death. A death that can ask at any moment for you to come up front, though you haven't raised your hand and you're retracting your head between your shoulders, like a turtle, begging not to be chosen. A way to find consolation and some peace (never enough) is to remember that opening of Nabokov's in *Speak, Memory*: "The cradle rocks above an abyss, and common sense tells us that our existence is but a brief crack of light between two eternities of darkness. Although the two are identical twins, man, as a rule, views the prenatal abyss with more calm than the one he is headed for (at some forty-five hundred heartbeats an hour)." And so, facing

this final abyss, saying to ourselves we were already there, at the beginning of everything, in an initial abyss. Repeating to ourselves that we were already dead, that we're returning to the place where we came from, and that our passage here has been but that of a tightrope walker on a high wire. (Having been born dead should be of some added utility in all of this.)


† When you're young, death always comes from far away, from outside, from on high: like that meteor that, they say, wiped out the dinosaurs and almost all other life on the planet, but allowed for the appearance of the evolution- ary mechanism that would culminate in the human being (though it's always preferable to imagine and rewrite big reptiles and humans coexisting and killing one another, like in some kind of primitive theme park, because that keeps it all much more entertaining and turns out to be much more interest- ing). Anyway, at the beginning of our lives, death is always something that happens to others. And every so often, it happens to those young people who, with perspective, when everything has been consummated and they've been consumed, are remembered in a grave voice and saying things like "There was something in them that made you think they wouldn't live that long . . . Like a kind of sadness . . . Like a melancholy not for what they had lived, but for what they would never live." On the other hand, when you're no longer young (when you start to be seen by newer and carnivorous specimens of boys and girls as a dinosaur that can only feed off of bland herbs) death seems to burst forth from the insides of the Earth. Death is like the fiery yawn of a volcano, death is the earthquake of tossing and turning in bed, awake and alert, knowing half of your life has already slipped away and all that's left in front of you are shudders, shaking, the incessant aftershocks of bad news.

Here comes another one.


† While romantic love helps you believe the lie that you're immortal, because you need to and do convince yourself that love will last forever, the truth of constant and eternal love for your children produces the paradox of all the time thinking you might die at any moment. (Note: there're no beings more aware of time and its passing than pregnant women or the dying.)

† The terrible paradox that, as less and less time is left in life, the days pass more and more quickly; and that, when we're children and we have everything in front of us, time seems to crawl, slowly, or to waste its own time, lying on its back and looking up at the tempera painting of the lights and shadows dancing across on the ceiling. There's—as for almost everything—a more or less scientific explanation for the phenomenon. What slows down or speeds up time, they say, is either lack or excess of experience. During childhood, everything is new, everything requires analysis and study and assimilation. When you pay more attention to something, the brain works more and annuls and slows down everything around us to prevent distractions. Thus the occasional zombie-Zen focus of some children. As we grow up, things surprise us less, situations repeat, and—with the exception of those catastrophes that freeze us where we stand or pin us to the ground like the electrified nail of a lightning bolt—events precipitate more automatically. And we do things almost without noticing what we're doing, including making declarations of the "I love you" or the "I'm going home" variety.

† The time of children—for whom the past is so brief and the future so immense—is the time of pure present. This is the time that some old people return to (being pushed around in little chairs with wheels once again, crying at the slightest provocation, uttering words incomprehensible to everyone, and having true difficulty controlling their bodily functions) knowing that the future is no longer inviting them to its party. And that the celebrations that the past puts on are attended by ever more dead people or the memory of too many others that it's better not to think about it. And so, stay and recover, one last time, an absolute now. A day by day and a night by night. A don't make too many plans for tomorrow because you never know and, so, sleep less and never dream again.

† Suddenly understood, just once, watching *The Time Machine* on television with Penelope's son: the time machine has already been invented. The machine that makes you go back to the future or into the past. The time machine is called *Son*.

† Models of Fathers/Writers:

The one who, in a house fire, rescues his son.

The one who, in a house fire, rescues the manuscript of his novel.

The one who, in a house fire, rescues his son, gets him to safety, and goes back into the flames to rescue the manuscript of his novel and dies in the attempt and leaves his son an orphan.

Place your bets, don't give it too much thought, quickly now.

† The accelerating time of adults (the accelerating particles of adult-time, which makes them think and feel time is flying by and burning up and consuming itself faster and faster all the time) is, paradoxically, the promising and slow and leisurely time of children. The time of kids-children is what makes the journey of adults-parents so vertiginous. For people who haven't had children, time passes more slowly, and they never get to experience the wild panting of watching, immobile, how children grow and grow with each passing day. Those who haven't had children (those who've never gotten addicted to that *substance* of children, which makes you see so many things you've never seen and wouldn't ever see if you hadn't first been devoured by them, because best make clear: it's Saturn's own children who devour him) will never bear witness to that terrible sight that suddenly makes the Theory of Relativity so easy to understand. See it: there's a boy of about six venturing into the cave of the open door of the wardrobe of his bedroom, to explore the prehistory of old toys (some broken but impossible to dispel to oblivion) while his father watches, trembling, the artifacts his son is unearthing and he bought what feels like yesterday or, at most, last week. Or they'll never have the experience of watching a movie alone and having it seem dreadful and watching it later with their child and, commenting on it aloud while chewing popcorn, having it transform into something ingenious, into one of the best movies in the cinema of life. Also, all of them, childrenless children, are far more childish creatures than those who have children in the vicinity: they're more afraid of the dark, the shadows that move, the death that approaches. And they end up wondering—like when they were little—where all those children who fill the streets and come out of schools with uniforms

and barbaric manners come from. And, of course, children without children sleep much worse; because they've never helped anyone sleep better.

But he did. He was of some help. He helped put Penelope's son to sleep while struggling not to fall asleep himself. He sang stories and told songs to that little boy who wasn't his son, but who was the closest thing to having a son there was, the closest thing to having a son he had. But that was a period in his life (a thousandth of a second in cosmological terms) that didn't last long. A time that no longer is and that he remembers less and less; that has forced him to live forgetting, because it hurts and frightens him and because it makes him think that, if he ever sleeps again, maybe it'll be to dream of the little boy. Penelope's son appearing to him as something immense, like the sun and, at the same time, like a gray cloud obscuring the sun; like the light and the black hole that devours everything and transforms it into the most alive of dead energies, into the most solid of antimatter. Lost in space. But it's an unfounded fear: his very occasional sleep—a verb in his case, lacking verbosity—isn't long or deep enough to generate dreams. Now, for too long, his sleep has been reduced to sudden and brief and sporadic naps (interrupted with a start, with a whimper, as if afraid of themselves) during the days and nights, sighs in which nothing thinks or happens. Assorted dreams that remind him of those double or triple or even quadruple features at the movie theaters and on TV channels of his childhood. Extended sessions, they were called: you could enter any time, the show already underway, and imagine everything you'd missed while trying to wrap your head around why that blonde had just slapped that man with the twisted smile or wondering whether the man who'd just died was good or bad or just passing through like an extra, like a bit player with no role left to play. Movies of multiple or mixed genres, like dreams: westerns, biblical peplums, comedies, mysteries, horror, children's (or horror with background music with the voice of little girl humming), some documentary that postulated the extraterrestrial origin of gods and pyramids, and those science fictions of the Cold War where everything ran through atomic energy and the imminent end of the world. Movies, often in lousy condition (depending on the honesty of the theater, a little poster at the box office warning of possible mishaps), cutting off, with scenes missing, subliminally teaching him the art of the ellipsis. And, sometimes, the movie continuing after the lights came up (after he wakes up) and after he falls back asleep (after the lights go out) to keep watching. What was showing? *The Black Cat*? *Puss in Boots*? *When the Cat Comes*? *Cat on a Hot Tin Roof*? *The Aristocats*? *The Shadow of the Cat*? *The Cat That Couldn't Sleep*? To think of it in a blink of the eyes and what's it called when you slept a little and nothing and something? Ah, yes. *Catnaps*: a feline sleeping. But, in his case, not the slumbers of those agile and aerodynamic cats, but the unsatisfying spells of round and heavy cats always on the laps of queens and fairies. Now he's almost always awake to daydream and to watch new movies in perfect condition where the mutations aren't a product of radiation but—like the one he saw a few nights ago—a result of the dumping of ultra-hormonized chicken shit into the waters of a bay where people go diving never surface again. All that empty time to fill with imaginary fears to cover up the true fear; with everything that already happened, with the little that might still happen, at the moment of nothing is happening or of, calm down, it already happened. That ocean full of sharks. Those fish that move even in their sleep, they say, and among them the one called *Somniosus microcephalus* and that, apparently, can live for more than three centuries (and he feels like that, so long-livingly somniosus, nothing makes you feel more anxiously long-living than the eternal nights of insomnia). Sharks he's been evading, but can't stop thinking about and pondering and attracting with the color of his bad blood. Moving from one wave to the next, the free association of ideas, thinking of everything and nothing and swimming from one small island to another, clinging to a piece of driftwood.

And, he always remembers, how when they began to talk about surfing the Internet, how the novelty of the reflex wasn't at all surprising to him.

He'd always done it, that, always.

He'd never thought or moved in a different way and, probably, all writers moved like that, from one thing to another, finding not what they were look-ing for but what, even still, would work for something, clinging to a piece of wood that once belonged to a shipwrecked bed.

The bed is also a whole made of pieces, each of them, indispensable.

The pillows that start a fight or are used to silence a scream or hide a smile or suffocate a dream.

The mattress beneath which is hidden the fondled money or nudie magazines or secret letters (letters that for a while now aren't written with good handwriting, with written handwriting, with ideas considered deliberately and at almost the same speed that it took letters to reach their recipient, always with a trace of the sender's DNA in the saliva that moistened the backs of the stamps).

The sheets that function as well at the hour of escaping as at that of hanging yourself and that are the stitched shroud and raw husk of a ghost (it was never clear to him if sheets are the underground fabric that the ghost slips into to acquire shape and solidity or if sheets are, also, phantasmagoric and were sewn on looms of air).

And so many things fit under the bed: monsters and lovers and the dust that we came from and the dust to which we return.

And the idea of counting beds—like a historic encyclopedia of the horizontal—is, if you can't get to sleep, at least a way of reaching the sanctuary of your own bed, at the end of all those other beds. Like on the good cover of that bad Pink Floyd album, for many (not for him, that title was taken by, yes, Yes) the greatest band of somniferous music in history.

Draw me a sheep!

No!

What do you want a sheep for (or was it a lamb)?

Draw me a bed!

A bed in which—puny yet princely—to sleep thinking what's essential is invisible to closed eyes. And nothing matters to you less than that they draw you a lamb.

What could you want a lamb for?

What you need is for them to take all those thousands of unconscious pieces of meat covered in wool to the slaughterhouse so you never have to count them again.

What you need is a bed that sleeps across its entire surface and that dreams deeply.

What you need is a bed in which to fall asleep counting beds.

† And so, from the depths of millennia (like in those increasingly erect graphics showing the evolution of the sleeper) beginning with the straight and horizontal line where somebody collapses with sleepiness. Anywhere at all and the ground is hard. And next a stack of straw and palm fronds beside a wall where painted buffalo graze (imagine primitive peoples falling asleep and looking up at that the way now, during childhood, children fall asleep looking up at the childish figures on the wallpapered walls). And moving on to the hides of animals killed while they slept. To Moses's basket floating on the water. To the stiff beds of the Egyptian pharaohs lying in profile (a copy close at hand of *The Book of the Dead*: that instruction manual for getting back to the eternal dream that taught them how not to go underground face down or how to adopt the head of a crocodile and how to not be decapitated by the guardians of the Underworld). To smooth stones, Odysseus's charpoy of taught rope in *The Odyssey*, there dreaming of the faraway nuptial bed he carved for his wife, now besieged by suitors. To the first headboards made of turtle shells and the arrival of pillows and pillowcases as luxury items and status symbols on Roman mattresses (already back then and even now the absurd and disproportionate prices of mattresses as "inventions" designed to last ten years if used with restraint and courtesy). To mattresses stuffed with feathers and *lectus cubicularis* (for sleeping alone) and *lectus genialis* (to go to bed and not sleep with another person) and *lectus discubitorius* (where the revolutionary custom of eating in bed is premièred) and *lectus lucubratorius* (for studying) and *lectus funebris* or *lectus emortualis* (for displaying the lifeless body and it occurs to him now that his current bed is all of these beds minus *genialis* and not yet *funebris*). To the heavy and immobile medieval beds with posts and canopies, incorporating the little bedside table with reading material and candle. To the magnificent Renaissance beds. To the four hundred and thirteen beds (and the courtesans who played in them) of Louis XIV, especially that one in Versailles with *The Triumph of Venus* embroidered in gold thread on its curtains. To the "bed of justice" from which the kings of France ruled their court and parliament (the princes were sitting, high ranking officials standing, low ranking ones kneeling) and the most relaxed *chambre de parade* for receiving ambassadors and artists, like the first version of TV in the bedroom. To "my second best bed" that Shakespeare bequeaths to his wife, without specifying to whom he is leaving the first and best one.

To the iron beds cast in the eighteenth century (free at last from the insects and termites in the wood). To the beds whose measurements are defined as King or Queen. To the beds on display in the Victoria and Albert Museum. To the silver bed of a maharaja and the Spartan futons of samurais and the minimalist ottoman sommiers. To the novelty of convertible beds (there is one that turned into a piano or was it a piano that turned into a bed) and to the modern air mattresses and waterbeds (which are like rafts containing oceans and many associate with shipwreck-like orgasms) and to the hammocks on ships cast off for dreamed-of lands. To the psychotic sofa beds and with the shy beds named Murphy that lift up and turn into wall and to beds that vibrate if you feed them coins. To beds in flames (not because you fall asleep smoking, but because you've fallen into the vice of sleeping with your mobile phone under the pillow and the device heats up and explodes; in that place where once rested a tooth, a photograph, a cross, a perfumed letter, or even the dose of an addiction far more interesting and creative than those little marooned messages without a bottle). To hospital beds that can end up being deathbeds and where many—like a few bull fighters—say goodbye with a "Mommy" or a "Mamita."

And from there to his own beds, the beds that are his. To his parents' bed, to his cradle (that cradle that, yes, "rocked above an abyss"), to the little bed in the shape of a rocket and the trundle bed (him on top and Penelope below), and his first bed away from home, accompanying him up and down in various apartments, and the hotel beds and the beds at some literary foundation, and the beds where he stayed a few nights (never a thousand and one), and the ones in which, the next day, he woke up thinking "How did I end up in this bed and what is the name of its owner, there beside him, sleeping or pretending to sleep?" and praying that she not wake up before he leaves, because the truth is she talks nonstop and what she has to tell isn't on a level with what Scheherazade told.

There he is now.

In bed.

Inside it.

But knowing where he is and how he got there and what his own name is.

Alone. And he can't even pretend to sleep, because he has already forgotten what it was like to be able to pretend to sleep.

His definitive bed.

His noble, end-of-the-road model bed.

The bed he imagines now in bed, a waking dream, trying to silence the attack of the past by playing at futurism, but an antiquated futurism, a steampunk futurism.

The bed—like the planet where that bed lies down to go to bed—that has been modified with the passing of the pillows and mattresses.

The bed that began being meteoric in the late-decadent Des Esseintes style on Sunday morning after an agitated Saturday night.

The bed with Finnegans pillow and blankets with Oblomov print.

The bed to which he has been adding pieces and appendices and even a ladder to access its height (the height of one of those lofted beds of his childhood, bunk beds they're called, command bridges, off of which to jump or up which to climb) making it something unmistakably his, a unique specimen. Almost a living and fluctuating organism. Or a kind of exoskeleton that defines and contains him. The furniture version—a bed that you don't take off even to go to bed—of that second skin that's the ruinous wedding dress in flames of Miss Havisham or something like that. But in perfect shape and perfectly maintained.

His bed like a cathedral, like a site of worship and pilgrimage.

His bed like a dream made reality.

Or is it an irreality made dream?

Or a †?

Does it matter?

His bed is, yes, much more than a bed. This bed is a normal bed like a black marble mausoleum with angels and gargoyles is a simple tomb in the earth with two pieces of wood forming a cross.

His bed is a colossal structure—ebony with inlaid mirrors and precious stones—that seems to rock, like a ship, on the waves of his memories and on the rails by which he moves far and wide throughout his house. He has ordered (the royalties that ceaselessly pour in courtesy of the gothic fantasies of his flamboyant sister have allowed him this and so many other whims) walls torn down and hallways fit with rails and stairways turned to ramps and a complex invention woven with steel cables and pulleys that carries him here and there without ever needing to get up. Like in the old comics about the sleepyhead Little Nemo.

His bed moves.

His bed travels.

The sheets like sails, the pillows like clouds where gulls get tangled and can only escape by leaving behind their feather suits, and his memories like a voyage across mutinous waves that he shouts at from the command bridge. And they pretend to obey him. From his bed, the world is horizontal, like a beach where, lying down, he walks in reverse, backward, burying his feet again in the sandy echo of his own footsteps. Some of them still appear clearly defined, others have almost been erased by the tide. But even still, he can see them with his eyes closed, he can feel them still fresh, easy to trace and to be used like the dotted lines on those maps that lead you to the site of the original treasure.

And this is the moment when he would be forced to offer some specifics. The latitude and longitude from where he thinks all of this, for example. But, sorry, he never liked that almost reflexive gesture of the supposedly realist novels of his childhood. The almost obligatory need to situate everything (to plant and germinate the stage of a world) before the characters can begin to play their parts. Because reality isn't like that; it doesn't obey such strict orders or fall in, disciplined, like battalions preparing for the attack of the plot and the story.

Vladimir Nabokov thinks the same thing as he does or, better, Nabokov thought it first so that, later, when he read it, he could think, so excited and pleased: "Hey, but if I think the same thing as Nabokov . . ."


† Vladimir Nabokov / Interview: "Reality is neither the subject nor the object of true art which creates its own special reality having nothing to do with the average 'reality' perceived by the communal eye. [. . .] You can get nearer and nearer, so to speak, to reality; but you never get near enough because reality is an infinite succession of steps, levels of perception, false bottoms, and

hence unquenchable, unattainable. You can know more and more about one thing but you can never know everything about one thing: it's hopeless. So that we live surrounded by more or less ghostly objects—that machine, there (the recorder?), for instance. It's a complete ghost to me—I don't understand a thing about it and, well, it's a mystery to me, as much of a mystery as it would be to Lord Byron [. . .]. We speak of one thing as being like some other thing, when what we are really craving to do is to describe something that is like nothing on earth."

He read that in the night, with a little blanket around his shoulders, at a time when he didn't yet dare consider himself an insomniac, but someone who "worked better when everyone else is asleep." And he looked at his computer and his computer looked back with a circular and red and HAL-9000 screensaver and transported part of the best day into part of the best book and "Do you read me, HAL?"

And no: nobody read him.

The laptop computer like a medium between his dead-living ideas and a living-dead book and the more than probable possibility that he'd already written the best thing he would ever write without being fully aware of it, but suspecting it all the same.

And he wondered if he shouldn't also blame his machine, programed with something whose name was as absurd as it is intimidating and, in the end, deceitful (WordPerfect), and include it along with mobile phones and "smart" watches and tablets in his luddite diatribes. That ghost-time invention in whose memory past and dead books reappeared in new circumstances. But it was also clear to him that without the help of the *search* and the *cut and paste* he would never have been able to write the books he wrote. Especially the last one, with all its echoes and all those reflections between some pages and others. If he had to use a normal typewriter, like from back when he was starting out, when his stories were so much easier to read aloud (and, he had to acknowledge it, his sentences sounded so much more marmoreal and immovable and *finished*), he would've never dared to use the liquid structures of his last book, of—if he could keep from getting worn out and think with greater optimism—his last book so far.

The question, of course, was whether or not a book *like that* would've happened without such technical assistance; the enigma was whether the book's form was more a product of the tool than of his head. Should he try to find out? Should he look for and find *that* book in the library of his bed and spend his insomniac night like that? No, sir! Reading yourself is difficult, hard, and even dangerous. It's like going back to the old neighborhood and going up to that house where you once lived and putting your face up to the window and looking inside and discovering that the furnishings are different (really they aren't different, but they've been rearranged, and the kitchen is now the bathroom); that other people live there now, that none of it is yours anymore and that, if you don't leave soon, someone (who looks a lot like you or, better, looks like you once looked, and yet . . . ) could come out with a rifle and mistake you for a psychopath and shoot first and only ask what you're doing there after. And so you flee.

And it's so dark.

And it's raining.

And all the dogs on that street bite your name and gnaw on your signature.

His own books were not there, under his body. To the contrary: he had them in the most remote and frozen regions of his library, several rooms to the south, in the never-now-explored Antarctic of his readings. His books were now for him like the point at the center of the Pole: he knew of their existence, he'd seen photographs of their creaking and breakable flags waving in a cold so cold it no longer gave you time to feel the cold, it just froze you instantly; but he had no need to revisit them.

Similarly, another unrealizable fantasy, decades ago he'd given up in defeat when it came to the chimerical promise and impossible desire to put his library in some kind of order. So he let it run wild and free throughout the rooms and the kitchen and the bathrooms. Once he'd dreamed of a possible system of classification for his always-nightmarish bookshelves, scaling to the tops and ends of the walls and filling up all the *jolly corners*. Wanting a criterion that would bring them closer, at least for a while, to his sister's best and most maniacal crowds, stretching out and encompassing entire buildings. To wit: alphabetical order by author, nationality, century, subject and genre, publisher, date of publication or, even, the color of their spines, until they composed one of those horizontal and panoramic bookshelves like the most vivid of *tableaux vivants*, just the opposite of dead nature. But then he'd failed. And, so, ever since, that incomprehensible secret classification where the books change places when you're not looking and provoke that terrible joy of—just as in life outside of books—finding *this* when you were looking for *that*.

Magic.

Presto!

Now you see it, now you don't just see it but so much more than it.

Everything here and everything there.

Miracle.

And on more than one occasion he wondered if, maybe, the most perfect—and, of course, impossible—classification system for personal and domestic yet wild libraries would not be to have a lifetime of books, from first to last, arranged in the order they were read. Thus—like those concentric circles that tell the age of a tree when it's chopped down—from the wood the paper's made of we come and to the wood and paper we return. And you could—following titles and authors, high and low, clear sequences and untimely detours, that put Mary Shelley next to Charles Bukowski next to Ford Madox Ford next to Juan Carlos Onetti next to Cervantes—read the novel of your own existence, punctuated every so often by the parentheses of your own books that were written, from "Once upon a time . . ." to "And they died happy." The library as *liferary*. Like an alternate but parallel form of the biography. A personal bibliography. The library is the mirror of the soul you sold to the Devil or God or both; because, after all, if they exist, they're the same person. The person who enjoys writing us so much, complete with errors and moments of absolute genius, but who later leaves, and there they both go, going and going and gone.

And they haven't the slightest interest in reading us.


And he—like one of those messianic and satanic mad scientists—has achieved the impossible. That his library flows—like that river flowing into the sea there outside— right into his bed.

His bed that reminds him that, back when he was designing it, he remembered that dream once dreamed and put in writing by Leo Tolstoy. That dream much admired by Vladimir Nabokov in *Anna Karenina* (one of his favorite-favorite books), to which he devoted multiple pages of his lectures on literature, and described as "the double nightmare." A nightmare dreamed by Tolstoy on the heels of the "triple dream" of that poem with concentric dreamers by Mikhaíl Lermontov. And where, in a few very perturbing lines, Tolstoy makes Anna Karenina and Vronsky dream simultaneously. The same dream, at the same time, like an unmistakable sign of the synchronicity of their love, but a dream not romantic in the least. Anna and Vronsky dream of a Russian peasant babbling in French. And Tolstoy dreams of himself in a kind of gadget-bed assembled with springs, suspended between an abyss below his feet and an abyss above his head. "The immensity below repels and frightens me; the immensity above attracts and strengthens me," Tolstoy specified, making quite clear which of those paths most interested him. And suddenly and just before waking (and returning to his desk to punish his character, the ceaselessly afflicted Pierre in *War and Peace*, with a dream in which he was pursued and caught by dogs, attractive and fierce, as he pounded at the doors of the "temple of virtue"), Tolstoy hears a thundering and sweet and illuminating voice that orders him: "Pay attention! This is what it's all about!"

That hasn't been his case, of course.

He still doesn't have the slightest idea about the story of his days and much less about the plotline of all Creation. He paid attention and yet no attention was paid to him. He gets into his bed not to drift over an abyss, but to keep his feet off the ground. The bed like a magic carpet. And that's how he wound up deciding to go even further and not just to dream of but to build a bed *en abyme*. Neither war nor peace but bipolar armistice, between pacific and belligerent. A restless dream, a placid insomnia to be deposited just there. The bed like a vanishing point and him like a fugitive.

And that's how he conceives and imagines it.

Like that, awake, he dreams it.

His bed with the Victorian aesthetic of inventions he'd seen for the first time in movies of his childhood: *The Time Machine*, one of his mother's favorites, and *Chitty Chitty Bang Bang*, among those his father liked best.

His bed with four posts that don't hold up curtains or canopies but are topped with four votive lanterns, their flames burning ceaselessly beneath a ceiling onto which they project galaxies and constellations.

His bed to which he has added a receptacle for his bottles of Coca-Cola (the little vintage ones, emptied in just three big gulps), which he's been drinking forever, as far back as he can remember, since back when he already wanted to be a writer, before he knew how to write. And he kept on drinking it when he was writing. And he keeps drinking it now that he's not writing anymore. The spark of his life, indeed. And there are nights he wonders if the residual accumulation of this caffeinated beverage over so many years in his organism might not be the root of his insomnia. And there are nights he thinks the famous and never-entirely-identified-with-absolute-certainty secret ingredient in Coca-Cola could only be him.

And next to that always-full-to-be-emptied bottle, an empty telephone. A hollow telephone he'd emptied out. A telephone like the ones of his childhood: black, heavy, a numbered dial where you inserted your finger to turn and dial it, the way secret codes were decoded in those venerable spy movies. A telephone with a spiraling cord connecting the receiver to the dark Bakelite body that, in more than one thriller (and, yes, there was a whole subgenre of mysteries with insomniac detectives or killers), was utilized to bash heads or murder heroes and villains. A telephone of antique design, with features resembling those of—again—that time machine in that film about a time machine in which the only good thing was the time machine. One of those telephones with which, too often, it took so much work just to make brief and synthetic calls, saying only what was necessary and on to something else. One of those telephones that rang deep in the night and was so frightening. Fear itself was a telephone ringing in the dead of night, speaking in the universal language of bad news. An ominous device that, all of a sudden, took on the voice of a loved one, telling us another loved one no longer was or no longer loved us. A telephone that—in this case, with this specimen—would never ring again. Because he'd sent it to be eviscerated like a deposed king's body, and he's got it there as an adornment and, almost, an object of adoration, evoking times when phones didn't go with you everywhere you went but stayed at home, like a bird in its cage, and were only used for making phone calls. The kind of device that, telephonically, was the equivalent of the monocle: nobody used it anymore and they couldn't even remember anybody who'd once used it other than in those black and white movies where everyone speaks very quickly and hangs up even more quickly. The kind of device that—because it can't ring—distracts him from the idea that, even if it could, nobody, on the other end of the twisted and scratchy line, would make it ring. There's no busy signal when nobody's picking up a phone nobody calls.

His bed, including, also, a small retractable desk that folds out from the joint of a titanium arm, with a space for an inkwell, pens, paper, magnifying glass, and that antique toy, that little wind-up man made of tin, already mentioned back when it was new, in its youth.

Mr. Trip.

Here he comes again: he never functioned properly or, perhaps, always functioned perfectly; walking only backward, carrying a suitcase. It's been years since he set that toy in motion for fear its key might break. But it doesn't matter. It's not necessary. Mr. Trip now fulfills the relaxing function served for many by a teddy bear or a little blanket faded after so many washings or any other comfort object of the kind used in various therapies and even seized by police and paramedics from those who end up surviving an accident or a murder.


† Random notes for *something* about stuffed bears / otherwise known as teddy bears, iconic toy that owes its name to the American president Theodore "Teddy" Roosevelt, who hated that nickname, which he was given on a hunt in 1902, by some rather sadistic companions who tied a bear to a tree. And, the story goes, when Roosevelt saw that, he ordered them to finish off the animal quickly and mercifully. The newspapers published a caricature of the incident in which the bear was dubbed Teddy. Seeing it, the son of the founder of the Ideal Toy Company has an idea, a good idea. And he sends a prototype to Roosevelt and asks permission to use his name. Instant global success (at the same time, synchronicity, a toymaker in Germany launches his own line of little stuffed bears) that soon incorporate that exceedingly creepy mechanism of eyes that shut when you lie the bear down and open when you sit it up. And children's books (*Winnie-the-Pooh*) and songs and movies (that run the gamut from childish innocence to adolescent transgression

to hardcore yet fluffy porn) and novels (the little bear Aloysius, belonging to Lord Sebastian Flyte in *Brideshead Revisited* by Evelyn Waugh) and the dreaming soldiers who bring their little bears along with them to the nightmare of war.

And possible plotlines: terrorists place bombs inside teddy bears; or they kidnap the teddy bear of a magnate and demand a ransom in the millions; or the rumor gets spread that Rosebud wasn't a sled but a teddy bear.

And the adults save all their teddy bears and continue to sleep with them (it's estimated that 35 percent of the grown-up global population keeps doing so until the day they die) and the men and women pass on, but the teddy bears remain. And hotel managers are always receiving anguished calls from the far reaches of the world, people sobbing that they can't sleep without them, that they never meant to leave them behind, begging the managers to send their little bears that have been but will never be forgotten back to them. Supposedly they are "transitional objects" that help young children to detach from their mothers and confront the long road of life alone. Alone but with a stuffed little bear. An animal that—unlike stuffed monkeys and dolphins and elephants and dogs and tigers and cats—seems to guarantee greater security and comfort and protection. Questioned for a study looking at the reason for that unconditional and never-ending love, all the subjects, invariably, gave the same answer: "It knows all my secrets." And some have ventured even further never to return. There's a documentary about them. They transform themselves into *furries*, into human stuffed animals, into people who live inside teddy-bear costumes, and who, no doubt, dream the sweetest and deepest dreams of all.


And again, coming back, here once more. He never had a teddy bear *like that* (and much less did he turn himself into a giant stuffed bear). But he still has *this*, his little tin traveling man. Mr. Trip. With its, for him, always noteworthy particularity, a reversed polarity: though there was a time when he even tried using it as a substitute for counting sheep (he imagined it always retroceding, moving backward toward the interior of airplanes, always flying in reverse, so the point of departure become the destination), that tin toy is now a mascot for not sleeping. A mechanism that makes him think of all the time behind him, that forces him to reread everything that happened and happens again every time he remembers it, though he doesn't wind it up and let whatever happens happen, which is what happened, yes.

And, next to Mr. Trip, there's even a special spot for that invention that'd been developed for all those increasingly numerous writers and was petrifying their cerebral innervation, whose function was to appreciate reality as they became more and more creative. More fictitious in times when the confessional and the testimonial had taken over. A small terminal loaded with autobiographical fragments and revising all of it, inserting it into the context of current events: cleaning it like a fish of its scales, removing all imaginative gestures to serve it up as pure-boiled or steamed chronicle without added ingredients of any kind. He tried it a couple of times; but he wasn't at all interested in that clear linearity, that lack of style as style, that "commitment" to the real world. But many people plugged in, delighted to be there, to be guests on more and more TV talk shows and to write more and more newspaper columns where they opined about their first love or the recent elections. And to write a lot about themselves. A wish granted. A blessed curse. Like that horrifying story he read and got scared by for the first time when he was a kid. Again: "The Monkey's Paw" by W. W. Jacobs. Soon all of them, wrung out, began to die off because they had nothing left to tell, to tell about themselves. He never contracted that disease that came to be known as Qwerty's Malady. Or that he named thusly, in one of his many waking dreams and he no longer knows if he remembers it as a nightmare or as a dream he hopes will come true. That defense mechanism against not dreaming: waking dreaming, waking up dreaming, dreaming dreams with eyes wide open. And so, anyway, Qwerty's Malady: the virus that attacked and struck down writers by the hundreds, all at once, no-names and celebrities alike, whose bodies had to be quickly incinerated for fear of contagion.

And so, no more epic funerals like those of insomniacs Charles Dickens (last words: "On the ground!") and Victor Hugo (last words: "This is the fight of day and night. I see black light") and Leo Tolstoy (last words, depending on the version you prefer: "But the peasants, how do they die?" or "Run! Run!").

Just, a special and increasingly robust and healthy section in the newspapers: cultural obituaries. And—if there were any and if anybody spoke them—those firsthand last words are always suspect. And he remembers that his mother and his father once fantasized about growing old and, when they were old (something that, they were certain, would never happen because someone would discover the elixir of eternal youth), setting up an "agency of last words . . . slogans for the dying, custom-made for imminent death . . . the spark of death and the rest, not refreshing but embalming and . . ."

There it is. It's over.

That waking dream.

It doesn't last long, it fades quickly, like one of those effervescent pills to assist digestion after a heavy meal. Short-lived relief to hide his own ailment, the impossibility of falling asleep, like a screen hiding another impossibility: the impossibility of that form of dreaming that is writing. Which, for him and inside him, isn't even pure laziness or the law of minimal effort or having enough money to spend on anything he wants. His thing is impotence and drought. He put his last words in writing, but he's gone on living. Anticlimax, lengthy coda, an ending so open it seems like a beginning. So, once in a while (once in a great while) he winks an eye (the latest computers no longer require typing fingers) and there, on the almost-organic plasma of the screen, he reads "zzzzzzz." And he must stay awake and horizontal.

In his bed. It's not bad. It could be worse. He could be standing up and unable to sleep. Or upside down. Or walking. Besides, he likes that his bed buzzes and vibrates. He likes to feel like part of a machine that achieves its goal to perfection (and that, though shame keeps him from even thinking of it, includes the vanity of a sophisticated mechanism of pipes and swirling waters enabling him to carry out both physiological functions without needing to get up). The bed is, after and above all, a machine for lying down and he *can* do *that*. Lying down is the consolation prize (or punishment, depending on the day, depending on the night) for one who doesn't sleep.

Plus, the sparking scent of electricity (the invisible scent of something invisible) covers up the swampy smell of his own acoustic (but rusting, that rust that never rests) body and makes the metal in the molars of his childhood flash, a metal (a toxic amalgam of silver, tin, aluminum, copper, and mercury) that, so long ago, a dentist explained to him should be replaced with one of those new artisanal plastic or ceramic substances. A dentist whose office he never returned to, because her knowledge was insufficient when it came to clarifying his great dental question: how was it that those multicolor stripes of toothpaste emerged from their tubes so straight and well separated and didn't get mixed together when you squeezed them, there inside, where it was incomprehensible how they were able to get them inside without twisting them together, eh? The dentist (one of the many who throughout his life looked at his teeth with a combination of horror and pity) pretended not to hear him, probably attributing his curiosity to the effect of the anesthesia. And she opted to return to one of the favorite territories of dentists in particular and deliverers of healthcare in general: terror, the *terrortory*, all the frightening things that can happen to you there, always your own fault, for not having visited the given arcanist more often. And the dentist went on telling him that the most fundamentalist practitioners of her trade insisted the slow yet constant flow of mercurial vapors from the teeth to the brain were responsible for all the mysterious and inexplicable diseases, for those fires in the mind that every so often bring down their thinkers, accused of seeking refuge in the psychosomatic until it's already too late and the fire makes it impossible to see the forest. The metal in those molars, the woman went on, could be the cause of other annoyances: sometimes it allowed you to tune in radio broadcasts, songs and voices, and ever more telephonic videos that could be mistaken for the stuff of dreams and cause sudden waking and insomnia. Who knows . . . That would explain his present condition: he doesn't sleep because actually everything he thinks he's thinking might be nothing more than a random collection of rants and sounds piped in from far away. His head like the last radio, playing shooting stars, waiting for the last fire truck from hell. Live and direct. That would, also, he tells himself, be of some comfort; but he's not kidding himself: there are too many personal details in those ethereal-cerebral waves. Too many names belonging to others, yet his, and too many actions unlike him but that he has to own in his monologue, more that of lay-down tragedian than a stand-up comedian. More laughing with tears than crying with laughter. The finite but increasingly-long-to-tell jest of his past repassing and revising itself, yes, from the here and now to the there and then, when, if there's something of which he's certain, it's that, in bed, everyone, in a way, turns back into children of impossible-to-measure dimensions. The size of that head they've had since so early on and with which the body only attains harmony when they're about twelve years old. A body whose—like now—length or height turn out to be difficult to specify under sheets and blankets. The only thing he doesn't doubt is that there—body on mattress and not on earth—everyone, in a way, regained the condition of those feverish children who stay in bed, reading all throughout eternal and elastic days when school seems to acquire the contours of a mythic land.

And—healthily infirm—floating in the darkness, the bed like a raft or an island, like him now, someone no school would accept as teacher or student.

In this bed.

And, between the legs of this bed, almost as tall as those of a giraffe, multiple bookcases. Arranged there—down below, like cats of ink and paper—the first editions of his favorite books; some signed and dedicated to him or to strangers whose descendants (the books of the dead are the first thing processed by their living survivors, the paper alongside the ashes) dumped all of that on second-hand bookstores, never suspecting what it was they were virtually giving away.

And his unpublished journals and his photo albums from times when photographs still had to be developed and you had to wait and they never came out entirely how you imagined when you'd framed them.

And his notebooks—one for each of his published books—that every so often he flips through and eyes as if they were family records and in which, passing through, he's moved to find how each of them begins with slow and deliberate handwriting, more time given to the notes themselves than on what he'll do with those notes. And how, as time passed, he spent less time on them and more on the manuscript. And his handwriting became crazier and wilder, almost illegible, like a Hyde imposing himself on a Jekyll, anxious to get out of there only to come back and realize the best moment of his life is the brief moment of transformation and not the more-or-less-drawn-out moment of being transformed.

And all his many biji notebooks. Notebooks with broken lines and inopportune quotations (visionary quotations of others blindly quoted; but the idea was, always, that those lines from other writers operated as part of the action, almost like characters).

And random and somnambulant photographs and ideas that, they say, it was better not to awaken from their trance for fear they would lose their reason or their reasons for coming into being.

And his collection of writer biographies from which he extracted famous lines and oft-cited pronouncements that he clung to to keep from being pulled under with the shipwreck of the night. And so, big names and marmoreal quotes and him spinning through all of it: like a Forest Gump launching forward, magnetized by celebrities sighted in various sites, citing them, so the night would pass more quickly.

Thus, and therein, the lie of the present as something clever and current (when really it's just something instantaneous, an instant, something that, right away, *already happened*) and of the future as something splendid, a time when everything would be better except for the fatal clause, the fine print, that you won't be part of it.

Again, once more, as always, forever returning to the same thing, the thing you can always return to: the past, of course, that equally placid and unstable parasite, feeding off the substance of everything yet to come. And the terrible paradox we opt to think about as little as possible: many, too many times, only in the distant morning or the morning after, do we attain the certainties and reasons for something we did yesterday. Everything that, suddenly, we recall as if it were an old photograph we rediscover stuck inside a book. But, even still, for that reason, we prefer to contemplate the future like a light at the end of the tunnel, a tunnel full of intestinal byways. What, they say, we see before us when we come to our own THE END. Something that, confronting the inevitable, we choose to think of as wondrous in the true sense of the word wonder. Thinking that, if you think about it a little, the future, right now, already contains us, he thinks. And so, overcoming that small and agonizing pain caused by being aware that everything will go on after we're gone, the wonder and relief of believing, he believes, in something we won't be part of, imagining it without any kind of passion or commitment. A perfect place, because it no longer makes the mistake or error of including us, or of considering the possibility of us figuring in the plot, or of thinking of us so we think of it. Looking at it from outside, from overhead, and from a distance, from that privileged perspective only possessed by divine immortals in ancient times and the gods of not-so-ancient times, the gods of his childhood.

And the last song has given way to the next song.

And now, from the house on the other side of the garden, someone who he's heard scream many times, with all the power in his lungs, "When I get to the bottom I go back to the top of the slide. Where I stop and I turn and I go for a ride. Till I get to the bottom and I see you again. Yeah yeah yeah hey."

Yes, you can climb up and go down and slide to the bottom, but you always end up seeing it all again.

Yeah yeah yeah hey.

To go and to come back.

To turn around and to do it again.

Another song of *his*, of his songs, but anterior to another song he heard before, that one that goes "Same as it ever was . . . Time isn't holding up," that drifted in to him, when night was falling, from the house where The Intruders reside and, supposedly, create. And it unsettles him a bit that The Intruders are turning into some sort of DJs of his past; that The Intruders are playing the soundtrack of his nights in reverse, as if they were approaching him from the other side of the street, crossing through the forest, coming ever closer to where he was, to where he felt so far away.

To that night, without going any farther.

He thinks "that night" and he's moved by the possibilities those words offer him. A concept of going and coming, yin and yang, right and left, front and back: because "that night" sounds to him like a tempting beginning (with "That night . . ." functioning as a substitute for "Once upon a time . . . ") or an ending without extenuating circumstances (with a " . . . that night." And that's it, over and out, end of the world news).

Here and now, tonight, that other night comes back.

And it doesn't come back alone.

It comes back with so many other things.

For example: "There is always one moment in childhood when the door opens and lets the future in." He suddenly remembers that line. From Graham Greene.

And yet another from Flannery O'Connor: "Anyone who survived child-hood has enough material to write for the rest of his life."

He remembers, too, that years ago he copied them down in a biji note-book, because he was sure someday they would be useful to him.

But no. The lines remained random and he never inserted them (he forgot to) in his novel about childhood and its myths and not—the one from Greene coming from *The Power and the Glory*—in his Mexican novel either.

Maybe because they were oft-quoted quotations.

But he's using them now. Not in his writing, but aloud, and rewriting them in his own way: "There is always one moment in the old age of a survi-vor of childhood when the door closes and shuts in the past."

And, yes, contrary to what people say, it's not that you're always going back to childhood, rather, it's childhood that's always crashing back down on top of you. Childhood like one of those waves that seems to come out of nowhere and flatten us and—laughing and swallowing water—makes us think about the eddy it once was and, in the blink of an eye, is again. As if naked but clothed in darkness, stuck—again, sci-fi—inside pajamas of an athletic cut, woven with an organic fabric of antigravity plasma-steel (pre-venting those falls of old age where the earth seems to begin to reclaim your body and death is, always, slipping in via a broken hip and hello crack-up and goodbye hula-hoop and welcome to the limbo-world) and that, when he walks, keeps him always about five centimeters above the ground (like some characters at the ends of some stories, like being always in love without needing to fall in love) and makes his body almost cubical and disproportion-ate and, oh, the things that occur to him. A body, now that he thinks it and remembers it, again, like that singer of spastic phrasing and movements, singing that thing about, again, "Time is an asterisk . . . Same as it ever was . . ." in that song in that film of that concert of that band that Penelope loved so much and that he listened to and, he already remembered, even danced to, quite a bit in fact. A model of pajamas—he invents, he imagines—first designed for people struck with mysterious paralyzing illnesses, but adopted in the end by almost everyone, no longer with any desire to move or make the slightest effort. And, hey, is he hallucinating all this due to lack of sleep? These floating pajamas and this moveable bed? This démodé and ever so stale version of futurism? So much living to come to this, to the beginning of the idea of the future, without it having undergone a single evolution? Not even that previous and at-some-point-novel and already-antiquated variant where it's always raining and the robots function worse than his own Mr. Trip? Could it be possible that such a thing might be possible? The future as it was understood and anticipated in the days of his childhood? In the sixties, in the last authentically sci-fi decade, before the future (with cities of glass and light and those superior beings arriving from tomorrow to warn of an imminent holocaust and *Klattu barada nikto*) took off from the tomorrow and leapt over the today and the now and proved itself to be far more banal? Or in his adolescence of predator and replicant and terminator and alien?

If so, he—who in the past read many novels of anticipation and always wanted to write something in it—never liked the technical part of the genre. Not now not then. Nothing matters less to him. And the books of science fiction he enjoyed most were the ones that ended up being books *with* science fiction and not *of* science fiction. Books in which every marvelous and imagined datum was but a faint fragrance or an uninteresting part of the scenography. And he liked those books from his past that took place in the future, yes, but whose protagonists lived and even suffered as if in a present where nothing worked all that well: androids disobeyed, nuclear cells inside rockets were left stranded in orbit, presidents pressed the wrong button, home computers got blocked because somebody sent a computer virus via email, social networks where people went around insulting each other under aliases or stole each other's identities, things like that.

So he won't say anything else about pajamas (probably inspired by the cuts and confections of elastic miniskirts and tight and instantly-out-of-style-but-eternally-arousing get-ups from those photographic productions his parents shot in front of backdrops with tons of acrylic and neon and monoliths for those ever-so *in* magazines with names like *Astro* or *Tesla* or *Moloko Plus*). Or about what did or didn't happen in these last few years (is anyone interested in the thing about three great Islamic wars, that thing about the kamikaze bees, that thing about space-time distortions as a result of the decodification of all those prehistoric gravitational waves, that thing about the shift in the orbit of the moon and the colonists abandoned there to their fate, that thing about coastal cities underwater, that thing about the end of fertility and the death of sperm, the thing about himself as a frustrated master of the end of the world inside that Swiss hadron collider?); and he'll concentrate on his thing. On the lack of sleep and the increasing abundance of waking dreams and in tracing the latest straight lines of his horizontal trajectory, as if running a blind race. Breathing deeply to fantasize about obtaining, at least, the consolation prize of being able to, at last, close his eyes. But no. No such luck. All that's left for him is to lose time, trusting that time is falling out of his pockets, to beg for it to stop passing or for it to pass a bit faster, composing— could he go any lower?—mental *chansons de geste* to his high-tech organic pajamas. Pajamas that, at times, if you don't inspect them carefully and just touch them, running a hand over his body, actually seem like normal, everyday pajamas. As normal as that real bed beneath his imagined bed. Flannel pajamas with a red and black plaid pattern, only different in their size from the ones he wore to sleep (and not to imagine luminous mutant pajamas in the darkness) when he was a kid. When sleep came like a cyclone, sweeping away everything, taking him by surprise, holding a great book about and with extinct extraterrestrials in his little hands. When he would never have thought to imagine that in the future he would spend hours (all times at the same time) imagining a futuristic garment specially recommended for those who had spent at least a third of their lives sitting and typing (reading and writing is another form of dreaming, another third of life) like immovable Sitting Bulls dreaming they were galloping Crazy Horses, with spinal columns that once were straight like an exclamation point now twisted like a question mark. And with no answer as to why they can no longer escape to that other third part of life: the part of sleeping and of dreaming and not of reading or writing or daydreaming about what they'll never write or read.

The part where he didn't think about what he was writing, but where, even still, something could always happen to him or he could always happen to think of something worthy of putting in writing.

Without excuses. Without alibis.

Because, of course, it's true, though for him it doesn't suffice as an explanation or feel like a justification: as people age they sleep less and sleep worse. Which (unlike the thing about the fragility of bones, which have been reinforced with graceful application of titanium coating) the specialists still haven't been able to remedy. In the beginning, it was thought—the difficulty of keeping eyes closed—to be due to a kind of physical-psychological shift.

That, having less time left in life, those who have been alive longer decided their days would begin earlier. In the dark (soon there would be more than enough time to sleep deeply and not wake up).

And in that way they could witness the birth of the light of day and accept what that light has to offer before those younger than them. A dirty and tremulous light. A light not yet transparent, but one you see and can almost touch, rubbing off on the tips of your fingers. A light with the color of the screens of the childish televisions of his childhood. Televisions that made him so happy whenever the people in charge of programming those non-stop cycles of multi-genre movies on Saturdays—him on the couch, cradling a bottle of Coca-Cola—decided it was time, once again, to broadcast *Mr. Sardonicus* or *The Baron Sardonicus* (he'd even gotten a DVD where they'd given it the title *The Baron Mr. Sardonicus*). A movie that his sister Penelope, of course, and she wasn't wrong, had accused of stealing "parts and senti-ments" from *Wuthering Heights*. But that was, nevertheless, his favorite movie to watch "at home" (*2001: A Space Odyssey* was his favorite to watch "on the big screen"); and oh how he savored that moment where, almost at the end, William Castle, the movie's director, interrupted the action and asked the viewers if they would rather forgive or punish the monstrous mister/baron. And, of course, they say, they never found footage of the supposedly merciful option, but it wasn't necessary: because everybody wanted the bad guy to meet a bad end. The petrified smile of Sardonicus (the state of Sardonicus's teeth was even worse than his own as a kid, maybe that's why he liked that movie so much) on a television on which you changed the channel by hand and with movements like those of turning the little dial to open a safe. Back then the channels stopped broadcasting around three in the morning, offer-ing the last viewers that gray and staticky vibration where, if you stared at it, you started to feel you could see things and you ended up seeing visions there, in the ether behind the glass.

Pure illusion, of course. Impractical theories that, as always, don't take long to be torn down, so that atop their happy ruins can be constructed spec-tacular certainties supported by scientific truths.

To wit: the elderly sleep less because they lose a certain type of neuron. He didn't know it then, but knows it now. They told him about it at the Onirium where he goes two days a week. Or so he believes. He believes in that place that only exists in his mind, but, in any case, such a belief isn't that different from that of all those people who prostrate themselves in churches, convinced they're houses of God. He goes to the Onirium, it's understood, with his imagination, in his waking dreams. He arrives to that place that's his version of the Institute of Preparation for the Hereafter from Vladimir Nabokov's *Pale Fire*, where the dead are catalogued as if they were dreams, understanding and calibrating the dead as dreams that once came true. He looks it, ghostly, from under a sheet with two eyeholes. The actual place isn't even called the Onirium, nor does it possess the messianic-architectural lines he attributed to it in . . . in something. In some vague, stray idea he once offered to Penelope, wanting it to be an apology when actually it was an entreaty. An opportunity to "collaborate on something." Something in which he had attributed to that most late-night and vintage-sci-fi of places an entire mythology and planetary catastrophe and even the possibility of a great love that he surrenders to, like when he was young and surrendered to that great love. Something that's come to him as if in broken pieces, as if in the random scenes of a dream he no longer has. Something he's never able to grasp or tie down in letters and words. Something that, when he wrote it and when he rereads it now, he made as if it were happening many years ago but in the future, in an alternate present ten or fifteen minutes from now. Something with mechanical dialogues (reference to movies and songs) inserted in an apparently romantic atmosphere (the activity of having breakfast the morning after) that does nothing but demonstrate his complete and absolute lack of knowledge about such a situation. It's clear that, if he ever really fell in love, it was always unrequited. Reading it now, it's obvious he composed that whole choreography with the inexpert and adolescent bumblings of someone who, in addition, never *fell out of love*: he never knew what it was to stop being in love, to just be there, passing time, waiting to see what happens now that everything has stopped happening.

He had, yes, read and heard people talk about it. With good prose and bad words. But as it concerned him, love (a hormonal alteration, a chemical imbalance, and neurological aberration, in the end) was always getting closer to being declared an epidemic by the World Health Organization or by one of those organisms that patented plagues in order to, subsequently, sell pleasant placebos or miraculous cures to the world.

In his case, when it came to love—beyond a succession of more or less interchangeable names and bodies—nothing of any importance beyond that first time ever came to pass. A succession of women like gifts from a less-than-generous melodrama. Until one day—or one night—there were no new gifts. Goodbye to the dream of giving himself to someone and of that someone giving herself to him and of dreaming happily and waking up together and of feeling as if they were running along a beach in slow motion, hand in hand. And everything spins around as they pause to kiss with their eyes closed and that first girl, who kissed him just once so he would "remember that kiss above and beyond any kisses that would come after," and then let herself fall into the swimming pool.

Here and now, he goes to that place—a laboratory where they're trying to solve the mystery of insomnia—to see if they can give him back the lost desire to dream. And extract the bitter impossibility of dreaming sweet dreams. And wake him up from this horror of nights as long as days. And it's the neurons in the intermediate lateral nuclear group of the brain, in the area of the brain designated the ventrolateral preoptic nucleus, that are to blame, they informed him, a female doctor who seems fascinated by the fact that he is or was a writer informed him. First, of course, they experimented on rats. And then on people. The doctor tells nonstop stories, spurred on, perhaps, by that wandering and aimless idea that clinical cases can make good stories, good literature, being backed up by statistical data like "A person who lives to be seventy-eight years old, for example, will have spent nine of those years watching television, four of them driving, ninety-two days in the bathroom, and forty-eight days maintaining sexual relations, and, of course, twenty-five years sleeping" or that "The world record for not sleeping is held by a student who, for a school science project, kept his eyes open for eleven days." But the doctor—like so many others—seems ignorant of the most basic fact: nothing interests a writer less than having stories—apart from the stories he reads—told to him.

It's a common error: someone finds out you're a writer and they start telling you something, anything, whatever.

And so, the doctor tells him—and he listens with the annoyance of a sultan ready to decapitate her that the night, night number one that'll never be one thousand—scientific facts about insomnia as if they were good ideas for future fictions.

Some of them were interesting (like the case of that genetically insomniac Venetian family, afflicted with something called "fatal familial insomnia," who generation after generation, die from sleep, from lack of sleep).

But the truth is he's not really interested in insomnia as something that knows how to open the door so Parkinson's disease (and various viruses and mood swings and cardiac arrhythmias and a propensity for accidents and the acceleration of the engines of aging and the cutting off years of life and the reduction of his body of work) can come in to play.

Or that thing about infectious and protein-based prions that keep you from sleeping by making you hear, all night long, their little feet dancing in pointy stilettos across the spongy surface of your brain until they turn it into something akin to the carnivorous minds of those mad cows.

Or that thing about the elderly losing an hour of sleep. An hour that the present takes from that strange version of the past that are dreams; an hour of life, that's all they earn, all they get, for their many unimaginative or well-imagined years of life, he commented, feeling like a centenarian, when they told him the thing about the neurons.

Having crossed the threshold of a century of living (or at least feeling that way, like a relic, insomnia distorts times and spaces and he lets it take him, because rewriting yourself is the closest thing to writing), he's not a simple old man. He's a complex old man. A very old old man. An ancient old man. So he sleeps less than a young old man; taking a young old man to be someone who crosses the fifty-year line and heads out onto one of those beaches where the sea remains quite distant yet sometimes experiences sudden and devastating swells capable of sweeping you away in a matter of minutes. Thus, in the ocean of the night, he sleeps many hours less than those less old. One of the great paradoxes of such an old old-age is that he doesn't have much time left to live, but all the time he has is free time. A minimum infinitude. A brief eternity where the minutes are long as days and an entire glacial age fits in a week. And all the time thinking. Thinking about things like the paradox of his present without much future. Thoughts that come to him as if between parentheses, yes. Parentheses that, when he was a boy, were always tomorrow and now are always yesterday. Parentheses that yesterday were a pause in the today and today are an intermission in the yesterday.

And, there, not just what happened, but, also, what could've happened, what should've happened, what he would've liked to have had happen and to have had happen to him. The yesterday multiplying in variations and models. And thinking about all of that, as if replacing the dreams he no longer has, because in order to dream you have to be able to sleep. John Banville, another of *his* writers, had postulated something about that. Something about the need to dream first to remember later. But what happened if you couldn't sleep? If the past passed through sleep to an insomnia that never passed. To dream of what he would dream if he could dream, like a placebo, until he attained a kind of timeless limbo. And the future or the futuristic no longer included him, though he may have something left there, awake, to live.

And he no longer sleeps.

He, merely, goes to bed, lies down. But he never reaches that place where he falls asleep. And the "experts" at the Onirium aren't fooling him: they care less about "curing him" than about "studying him." About discovering how the people who don't sleep at night think. The way they order their ideas out of the disorder of their thoughts. Free stream of consciousness and all of that. And at one point, from behind a door, he heard them whispering about how he might be the first person impacted by an imminent epidemic. Patient Zero in the Ground Zero of his bed.

It doesn't matter. What does it matter?

He's elsewhere. Above them.

Above the ground and looking at the roof where it's so easy for the blades of the ventilators to sound like the blades of helicopters when you haven't slept in so long and, yes, shit, you're still in Zzzaigon, and bad joke, indeed. Insomniac joke, joke not of a zombie but yes—bad joke n.°2—of a zzzombie. But there and then very little seems funny, so better not waste funny things: nobody hears you when you laugh alone. And nobody can ask what you're laughing at. And nobody, lying beside you, can reproach you with a how can you laugh at that??

And—from the other side of the trees, from Penelope's house where The Intruders reside—the harmoniously noisy music, a tumult of electric guitars and screams and helter skelter. And the drummer—after eighteen brutal takes—throwing his almost-flaming drumsticks and howling that he has blisters on his fingers while the guitarist runs in circles around the studio with a flaming ashtray on his head.

Uncle Hey Walrus told him about that.

Uncle Hey Walrus was there, in person, when The Beatles recorded that song.

And now he, though alone and safe, takes advantage of that "I've got blisters on my fingers!" to release one of those gaseous accumulations that accumulate in his body, when he horizontalizes it every night, as if the stillness inflated him slowly, like a balloon. And, again, he's shaken by that thunder of those intestines, his, so different from the sounds those same intestines released when he was a boy. New organs then, more onomatopoetic than noisy and more playful than broken, with the scent of animated drawings (ACME n.°5?), half gunpowder, half candy.

Now, to the contrary, what he hears is like an airplane plummeting out of the sky to crash in a desert. Something unequivocally beaten, expired. He heard similar things bursting from the maws of whales beached on the beaches of his childhood or trumpets calling retreat in low-budget and high-drama movies. And all of it accompanied by the unbreathable stench that, he's sure, is the same as the stench released every time they discover one of those tombs of unknown and pyramidless pharaohs. And he (though he read once that the old smell better than the young; the Japanese, who have names for everything, call it *kaireshu* or "smell of the elderly," that mature and soft fragrance) takes a deep breath and reabsorbs with a scrunched up nose that scent of living mummy. That essence of a dead thing inside his body, where his organs, which should've been dust for decades, keep creaking on, thanks to the advances of science, advances with no clear aim. But he's not complaining. It all could've been worse corporally.

In his youth he was—as advertising for the Charles Atlas method on the backs of the comics he read as a kid warned and accused—one of those "44-kilogram weaklings" who got sand thrown in their faces at the beach. And yet, as time passed, he hadn't turned out that badly. And around middle age, his body acquired a kind of martial *bearing* (of a hibernating bear) it still retains. Or maybe he's still only in his fifth decade, who knows (and he tells himself that, whatever it is and whatever age he is, his skeleton is experiencing something similar to what Vladimir Nabokov experienced in that space between those slender youthful photographs at Yale and those other corpulent and old-age photographs in Ithaca). And, again, that whole thing of being an Onirium-centenarian might be nothing but a hallucination, resulting from insomnia, from inhabiting that territory that's the most post-apocalyptic of all.

Another of his waking dreams.

Few things make you feel older and more outside of time than insomnia.

In insomnia—this is the only way to bear such punishment—you can't help but think of all the lucky sleepers as dead and think of yourself as the lone survivor living to tell the tale.

In any case, whatever age he is, he's already an *elderly man* who retains certain physical authority but, also, an illusion verging on a mirage. Because his brain, against all visual and palpable evidence, keeps fooling him into thinking of himself as if he were twenty-some years old. Lying to himself in the same way that, as long as you don't get the diagnosis/diploma from the hands of an expert, it's possible that you're dying without being aware of it. When do you know that you're old? Easy: when you no longer know how old young people are and all of them seem to be moving through some imprecise time between fifteen and twenty-five years old and between twenty-five and thirty-five years old and between fifteen and thirty-five years old.

In any case, he's not complaining, with perspective, he's come out on top, he's laughing last: his great decline has given him an authority he never had in his short-lived glory. To the contrary, the svelte and toned athletes of his adolescence (some of whom even ended up becoming writers) collapsed like the slow and controlled explosions of those outmoded gangster hotels in Las Vegas, built at a time when stubborn atomic bombs were being tested in the nearby desert. Structures that sighed as they fell, like cheap miracles, watched by openmouthed spectators on the artificial slopes of Centennial Hills. Buildings that come crashing down, down from above, like faces folding in on themselves, like what *had* happened to his face, which is now like an accordion in repose that nobody touches or plays anymore.

Ah, the problem—the boomerang curse—of possessing true elegance and good posture too early and too intensely: the heartbreak of the breakdown is so long and so captivating in the worst and most perverse possible way for everyone else. Each successive downgrade in rank becomes more apparent; as if medals were being torn one by one from your once firm chest. And all of it happens as if in slow motion and in descending order. Enveloped in a dust cloud in front of spectators who will always remember (and remind you of) what you once were and no longer are and won't ever be again.

Again, that wasn't his case: he always knew, from early on, he wasn't that attractive, nothing concerned him less, and this ended up making him into an "interesting" person.

And you can be interesting for more years than you can be attractive.

And being nothing more than interesting had led him to cultivate a real sense of humor (it's true, that thing about how women want, as they respond on romantic surveys, "someone who makes me laugh") and to harvest a couple always-useful tantric tricks (because women *also* want someone who can make them moan amid all that laughter). Poses and positions picked up from volumes in the meditative and transcendental library of his parents who, in one very evanescent Zen moment (the different aesthetic-spiritual incarnations of his parents lasted as long as a seasonal product and sometimes not even that long), bought a *chacra*—or country house—in the outskirts of the city that they (with characteristic advertising wit) christened Chakra.

A place that, after a brief period of running it as a "*de luxe* hedonistic religious center for beautiful people," was converted by his parents into a training camp for their fashionista-terrorist cell (really it's not that they changed it much in form or function; more than holding machine guns, his parents seemed to pose with them, swathed in bandoliers and camouflage-print bathing suits and smoking Cuban cigars, for a revolutionary centerfold) from where they designed "cosmetic-guerilla performances" preordained by consultations with the I Ching and . . .

But, now, the evocation of those past and passing victories is a relief that doesn't calm him but keeps him alert. Remembering is the same as continuing to play. And nothing succeeds at getting his body—much less his mind, which keeps dealing cards like a mad croupier—to sleep. No thing or substance has been discovered that could take him back to the deep sleep, without untimely visions, of those first nights in a cradle, nights that span almost whole days. When there isn't yet any dreamable material, or memories to remember, or reality to distort, or fear to sublimate, or longing to lift you up among the clouds, or terror of finding yourself naked in the streets. But even that would be preferable: he would give anything for the most absurd or terrifying of nightmares and the exquisite relief of waking up. Anything would be better than this uninterrupted projection of a waking film with serious structural issues. A film where all the lines seem improvised or barely written (and that's the paradox of improvisation: it doesn't work unless you know perfectly what you're improvising; and nobody knows anything about insomnia except that they don't know where it's going). Insomnia where there's no precise plot, and where everything seems avant-garde; but really it's so easy to understand. The shared desire for the wish that time pass be granted. And that the lights of day be switched on and, already awake, to feel normal among the waking and to no longer be a solo pariah.

That's what it is, that's what it's all about.

But we've got a long way to go before that.

In fact, it's even possible that ending hasn't been filmed yet.

And there he is, unable to even call out "Action!" and finally bring it all to an end. He can't look elsewhere, he can't even shut his eyes and, much less sleep, fall asleep, send to bed without dessert everything knocking at the door of his eyelids, trying to kick them open, misbehaving.

He's tried it all.

Nothing worked, nothing works.

All the chemical variations and all the forms of mental relaxation or religious meditation or agnostic hypnosis. But—again, once more—nothing had worked. He thought, even, of converting to some religion in order to be able to pray to some god and ask him for the blessing of sleep and that he grant it and thereby prove his existence and power. But God didn't exist or, at least, he was never given His phone number. Which didn't keep him from believing he believed unbelievable things. Like—for a few nights—the hallucinated thesis of an acquaintance, also an insomniac, who'd confided in him that he'd been the happiest person in the world ever since he'd stopped being able to sleep. His reasoning was that daily life was unbearable. And that not sleeping at night amounted to the blessing of enjoying with full and even enhanced consciousness that handful of delicious hours in which you were alone and there was nobody to pester you with their spite or stupidity (the conversation had taken place many years before the new insomniacs took the Earth, those voluntary auto-insomniacs fixated on their telephones). The world was in suspension and you orbited around it, far away and outside it all, free of gravity and all things grave, his acquaintance rhapsodized. He listened to all of it amiably and, as tends to happen, remembered something when he was already back home: he told himself the next time he saw that man he would tell him about the happy dreamers of nightmares in Auschwitz. And, as also tends to happen, he never got the chance. The fact that that person was run over and killed by a car (witnesses of the accident stated the victim was singing, screaming, stuffed into an incandescent Hawaiian shirt, fruit and feathers and volcanoes and surfboards, on an afternoon of stoplights whose colors his pupils were no longer able to distinguish) didn't give him a happy ending to all that sleepless ecstasy. In any case, at that point, it didn't strike him that the irrational dead man had been right, of sound mind: just that he had lost it.

And the possibility of sleep continued to be an impossible dream and, when it came to convincing himself of the existence of paradises, he sought artificial paradises with a bit of chemical backup. Causes that produced effects. Ambien and Damixan and Stilnoct and Norkotral and Halcion and Electron Blue, drugs that sounded like DC & Marvel superheroes (he chose them for the sound of their names; his favorites: Beneficat, Sucedal, Maleficet, Hypnogen, Sonata, Desirel, Circex, Stillyet) and that, in many cases, were just placebos. Bad idea, of course. He'd read their informational printouts as if they were horror novels that warned of possible hallucinations, paranoia, suicidal impulses, amnesia, criminal somnambulism (which, inevitably, led him to reread Vladimir Nabokov's *Transparent Things*) and, perhaps, the performance of embarrassing acts, like regaining consciousness far from home, in a karaoke bar, surrounded by Japanese people who were applauding and even weeping at his rendition of that unsinkable Celine Dion song. But no, nothing so creative as all that. Consulting testimonies regarding the side effects of various hypnotics and sleeping pills on the web—yes, the Internet was useful for that: for capturing the twists and turns of the ways the masses express themselves—revealed, in most cases, everyone had the same chilling experience: obliviously sending (and not remembering doing so) text messages from their phones, that made barely less sense and might have had fewer orthographical and syntactical errors than the ones they wrote when they were supposedly lucid and conscious of doing it. Sign of bad times, indeed: human beings once drugged themselves to get closer to the gods, or to compose symphonies of ice or to set pages alight or to illuminate starry landscapes and cosmic horrors. Now, merely, under the influence, they devoted their trances to typing brief lines about longed-for meals or imaginary lovers or selfies with a pillow in the background, instead of great circumstantial works of art. Yes, pills like potions you swallow to be inhabited by your ghosts. But, at least in his case, they had little or no effect—no redactable impulse—with the exception that the dark of night took on a touch of gray and, once, there was the sound of a voice that asked him over and over "Are you asleep?" and that, no doubt, was his own.

And, later, he downed liquors of varying density and proof and color and format in shiny bottles that—those who design and bottle them know it well, it's all calculated—turn the bewitching and possessive spirits into an imminently collectable item and the liver into an album of trading cards to be completed (but alcohol had never been his thing, his resistance to intoxication was almost legendary, and the only thing he received in exchange for all that fiery liquor was a headache and shaky hands). And marijuana, which, in his case, only intensified his hunger for sleep and increased his visits to the frigid light of refrigerators in the middle of the night. And the exotic opium, chasing dragons that ate all those sheep. And he returned to the drugs of his youth when he'd been on the high wire and the hard line (luckily, at that point, cable TV had arrived to accompany him during all those white nights, because, if not, what would he have done, there, awake, like right now) to thereby feel, at least, that *that* was the reason he couldn't sleep. He remembered with a little laugh (back then he had a mechanical typewriter, and he rewarded the nose of his brain with a line every time he reached the bottom of a page and after half a page and, one terrible and fantastic night, every time that little bell rang, as if for the end of a round or like a rifle reloading, when he came to the end of a line and oh, how fast he wrote back then and there was no blank page he didn't make himself the center of) that someone, concerned about his addict-level consumption of cocaine, had even considered staging one of those interventions. But the idea was dismissed when it was discovered he didn't have enough family or friends to attend it. He returned to those rousing powders that turned body and mind into something like an overly starched shirt, activating dormant areas in the gray matter (the so-called "reward centers") and making you fantasize, with almost magical hope, that in the extreme of sleeplessness you would reach the edge of a cliff of fatigue off of which you could let yourself fall into unconsciousness. That didn't work either. In the end, the obvious, the minimalist, the only thing left on the other side of everything. The natural way. So, saying good-bye to coffee and hello to chamomile tea and a glass of warm milk and the ommmm of burning lavender-scented incense, which many insomniacs, he was sure, had traded in for the not-at-all meditative commmment (another bad joke), for the sleepless impulse to have to say something. Not talking in their sleep, but, like somnambulists, writing directly online whatever came to mind. To emphatically state they dislike something they know nothing about or to post an automatic "RIP" at the end of any obituary, like those automatic weepers or cathartic drinkers slipping into the wakes of strangers always giving a thumbs-up.

Actually, he envied them for being able to be *like that*. To fall asleep under the blue light of the screen and no more special mattresses and eyemasks and earplugs. But that wasn't his case. His insomnia was a primitive, ata-vistic insomnia, more of the Age of the Rock-Hard Pillow than the Age of Silicon. So he'd sought intermediate solutions: the unplugged yet electronic, watching, along with millions of other non-sleepers, that, in its moment, quite popular too-many-hour-long video of the Bonet River in Ireland flow-ing under a wooden bridge. Or that website that offered the re-creation of the sinking of the *Titanic* in real time, which seemed like slow motion. Or the late nights of the History Channel, which he'd renamed the Hitlery Channel, with all those perfectly synchronized marches and oh so elegant uniforms and operatic torches in the Aryan night, which, actually, woke him up and made him wonder how it was he never knew or allowed himself the sweet tribal relief of surrendering to a mass passion, political or sports or religious, to hide out there, to put himself to sleep, to close his eyes, to go through life as if asleep. And, later, those new-age recordings of hushed ancestral winds and whales singing in bubbling rushes and even those classic subliminal-Hollywood-sex images: a DVD with the sound and the image of logs crackling in a fireplace and of waves crashing into the rocks at the base of a cliff. He'd also listened to the somniferous CDs of the actor Jeff Bridges. An actor who had one of his favorite voices and, on those recordings, recited brief episodes, sixteen tracks of contemplative ambient-drone, while the actor strolled through Temescal Canyon under the light of a coyote moon, with an occasional drifting piano—nothing at all to do with the noise of The Intruders—or the sound of children at breakfast or the gurgling of the toilet tank refilling or the groan of Mrs. Bridges who seemed exceedingly tired of her husband not letting her get any sleep. And a closing moral/message, after forty-three minutes: "We're all in this together and, well, maybe you've reached the end of this album and, hey, you're not asleep yet. Well, what the hell, fire the thing up again." And also the albums of the "post-minimalist" composer Max Richter (who, hence his initial distrust, had previously composed a series of ringtones and recomposed Vivaldi) and his eight-hour long opus called *Sleep*, composed with the help of neuroscientists so its sound synchronized with the different stages of sleep, resulting in a "personal lullaby for a frenetic world" and an "invitation to dream." He'd liked *Sleep* a lot, but it'd had an undesired effect: not only had it not made him fall asleep, but, with its liquid beats and ascending and descending rhythmic sequences, it'd made him remember with perfect clarity everything that'd seemed lost forever. "Ah, yes: that's what someone who dreams sounds like," he said to himself, looking back, to the most distant past and beyond, moving out from the shoreline, ever further out to sea. Hearing it, he felt like one of those once-original science-fiction clichés: the lyrical-epiphanic extraterrestrial touched by the earthlings, by their feelings and their coffee makers and the shape of a table leg or a tree's leaf or a bird's feather, and saying things like "Ah, the dreams of you humans who sleep . . . On our planet we don't sleep and, oh, how I would like to be able to sleep, just for a few minutes, to thereby be able to dream what you all dream." Listening to that thing of Max Richter's all throughout one night, he felt like, they say, those old Japanese men feel when they go lie down beside geishas without touching them, because it no longer makes any sense to do so.

From there he traveled to the other extreme, to the beginning, to the childish "Once upon a time . . . ": he recorded himself reading (to listen to later, the way children once listened to their parents reading to them, with a voice between mellifluous and accelerated to bring the process to an end as quickly as possible) that book about that little bunny that wants to fall asleep, patented by a Swede, which proved to be a multimillion-dollar bestseller and successful tool for progenitors driven to desperation by their insomniac progeny. A little book in which the words "dream" and "sleep" are repeated over and over and that—its maker instructed—should be read aloud, punctuated by overly exaggerated yawns, huge and warm-hearted yawns, like when you do the voice of a fierce wolf or a fairy godmother. Nothing.

He'd even wound up taking—before they were commercialized, for obvious reasons, and soon thereafter turned into a new form of E at clubs where they played music known as *freeze-beat* to stop people from dancing—pills containing splinters of the parasitic and African virus that caused encephalitis lethargica: something all the rage in the World War One trenches, where Siegfried Sassoon penned that poem with the line "Soldiers are dreamers," and that, they say, turned you into something like those statues stretched out atop the slabs of Victorian and Edwardian tombs. And yet, again, nothing. The only thing he'd achieved, oh so awake, was an additional form of torment: a perfect evocation of past dreams but now with eyes open. Knowing perfectly well they were dreams, the majority neither fun nor interesting, until he reached the one he considered the first dream he could remember, his original dream: a nightmare with chimney sweeps chasing him, a three-year-old boy, across the rooftops of a city with a pop-gothic aesthetic and with vertiginous camera angles he would only encounter again many years later in the best and most personal of Tim Burton's movies. After that primeval dream, even earlier on, the torment of self-induced regression became even more torturing: his recovered dreams ceased being figurative and became pure form and sound and the liquid abstraction of something that felt like sinking without drowning, like being a wordless message floating in the amniotic soup inside a bottle shaped like his mother, an exceedingly unstable bottle at that. A bottle (it was clear his mother hadn't given up any of her recreational activities during pregnancy, he'd seen multiple photographs of her, belly out in the air and painted with psychedelic mandalas and third eyes, in the middle of parties and festivals) of the variety that never stops being shaken, as if full of champagne about to be uncorked and bathe everyone in the bubbles of its nights.

Seeking to recover that sanctuary of restless calm, so close and so far from everything, advised by a known addict of said activity, he'd gotten up the nerve to go into one of those isolation tanks to float in faux salt water: there he would bob in the darkness of a saline solution until he lost all notion of above or below and, supposedly, feel again the nothingness a hypersensitive fetus feels. But the only thing he'd achieved had been to think, more awake than ever, during a very long hour, "I am a fetus . . . I am a fetus . . . I am a fetus." And on like that until he attained the suspicious conspiranoid certainty that, in truth, all the things you dreamed and thought and forgot before age three were absolutely logical and realistic visions. That we never "sound" more lucid and reasonable than at that time. That, if we so desired, at that point we could already speak and even write our best pages: but, out of pity and a dash of sadism (because it would be terrible to be fully conscious of all the stupidity and senselessness that awaits us), something makes us forget. And unlearn all of it. And concentrate on the lack of control of our most basic bodily functions. And so, as babies, we're reduced to unconsciousness and to sleeping almost all the time (when we're not crying and keeping everyone awake with voices like a flock of restless sheep) while rocked to the voices of fragile giants, terrified something will happen to us. Something like what, quite specifically, with our arrival, has happened to them.

And, of course, already on the subject and situation, so diminished, he'd submitted himself to constantly listening to the repetitive structures (which help to domesticate the breathing rhythm and heartbeat of babies and the development of their nervous system, studies claim) of rockabye lullabies. The ones that, supposedly, strengthen the bond between mother and child. The ones that his mother had never sung to him because to her they seemed "so boring they make me sleepy." The ones that the expert on the matter Federico García Lorca—whose skeleton did not rest in peace—had considered fundamental because "various crucial elements are involved in lulling the child to sleep, including, of course, the consent of the fairies. The fairies bring the windflowers and the right climate. The mother and the song supply the rest." It sounded good, but was improbable. It doesn't matter. He knows all of them now. And they all sound as if performed by an electronica and new-age band that might well have been called Nessun Dorma. The classic children's songs ("Duérmete, niño . . . "). Or the children's classics (Brahms,

Chopin, Ravel, Stravinsky, Gershwin). And the pop versions weighed down by jangling instrumentation (*Cry Baby Cry: The Beatles Go to Sleep*; whose title song, according to John Lennon, was inspired by a verse from the classic nursery rhyme "Sing a Song of Sixpence" and the headlines of an advertising magazine). And the immemorial and folkloric songs from all around the world, about the night that advances—that opens and closes, like a curtain—from right to left across the map with that gear-driven diction of the insides of music boxes. His favorite of all was the Danish "Elefantens vuggevise" or "Elephants Lullaby," because nothing seemed less sleep-inducing to him than an always potentially raucous elephant singing and swaying: because the elephant was his favorite animal; and because it reminded him of something he'd read a long time ago and had never forgotten or one of those characteristic things you swept out from under the rug or blankets whenever you couldn't sleep. Something about the disappearance of elephants on the European continent with the retreat of the ancient Romans, who'd used them as a kind of military tank in barbaric battles. Elephants that, after centuries of absence, when represented in medieval bestiaries and no faithful testimonies of their composition and anatomy remained, were deformed by their illustrators, bringing them closer to dragons and sirens (in the same way that manuscript copiers of the time mutated from readers into writers, going along correcting and amplifying the text as they transcribed it). There, in convent cloisters and cells, with very few hours of sleep, monks giving elephants trumpet-shaped snouts and dog ears and horse bodies and fangs on the lower maxillar, like those of a wild boar. They also claimed elephants hated ogres and prayed to the moon with admirable eloquence and were capable of carrying towers of sixty soldiers on their backs. He liked the idea, old as the world, which, in a way, was the fuel of all stories: that of an absence modifying a presence; that of inventing a visible reality from something that's no longer there, sculpting in marble what will become false history and, then, true fiction. And so, when he ran out of sheep (very quickly), he counted elephants. He filled the dark of his night with elephants ridden by golden-robed kings across icy mountains. Thinking he had almost nothing left and imagining himself wrapped in cloaks, climbing up to the attic of a glacier to, regal, lie down, so the circulation of his blood would freeze and the power of his battery would fade and he would attain the welcoming cold of falling asleep never to wake again. But even that was no guarantee: there was the terrible possibility that he would freeze with his eyes open and thousands of years later be unearthed, in a state of perfect preservation, his pupils still open to the air: eternal insomnia instead of eternal sleep.

In a dream or in something that now, in his memory, took on the texture of something dreamed—in one of his last dreams before the insomnia—he arrived to the site that'd inspired the Onirium to document it for his project.

And Ella was there.

As if waiting for him.

Ella had been, without knowing it, the inspiration for his project. A project that wasn't his but that of someone known professionally as ScreaMime or The Mime Who Screams. An individual with avant-garde pretensions who'd started out as a street artist, then got picked up by one of those incomprehensibly popular and supposedly cutting-edge end-of-the-millennium midnight TV shows (hidden cameras, improvised improvisations, tits and asses, cokehead-college-student tone), and was subsequently featured on an album of silent rap music, by a band named Los Autistas Chocadores, and later he made a small fortune creating a ringtone that, without emitting a sound, mimed the ringing of a telephone. The type of individual troubled now by the need to be recognized as a serious artist (he had the idea of exploring the condition of speaking through dreams, another form of the speaking mime, he claimed) and who, on one blank and white and powder-fueled night, had come across one of his books. And he believed he'd found his soul mate and perfect partner and sharer of visions: the book's author, him. And he'd agreed to do whatever, of course. It's not like he was particularly busy. And the extra money could always be turned into the perfect way to make some impossible whim come true (the key to entering into these pacts of more or less Faustian vulgarity had to do with attempting to do what you always wanted to do at the expense of whatever mediocre individual was passing through).

And at that time, he—already come to the idea and the age of rereading—had returned to Vladimir Nabokov. He hadn't revisited Nabokov since his proto-writer adolescence and only now did he discover, between amazed and proud and a little unsettled, the radioactive influence of the Russian throughout all these years on his own work. As if Nabokov's thing had been like the prompting voice of someone whispering vital instructions to you, barely hidden behind the curtain just offstage. And, with his rereading, he'd also achieved, unwittingly, one of the most overused customs of writers at the beginning of the twenty-first century: to write a medium-sized book more or less one's own at the expense of the extra-large work of another. To scramble, with auto-fictional agility, up onto the shoulders of some giant and benefit from their long and powerful shadow, like those small parasitic fish that stick with sucker mouths to the backs of leviathans and feed off their excretions.

And he wasn't the only one; and more than one of the most popular and best-selling and well-regarded names of the contemporary literary panorama availed themselves of that strategy. A serious model of a not-so-serious writer with the ability to satisfy readers who them made feel far more intelligent than they actually were. Readers who'd already passed—obedient and evangelized and ever so anxious to be enlightened and to receive their next dose of revelations—through professionals like Milan Kundera and W. G. Sebald and Paul Auster and Emmanuel Carrère and somebody else, and one more. The fault, it'd almost always been clear to him, wasn't so much of these writers as it was of the kind of reader they attracted: a reader with an almost compulsive need to have them read to him first and explain to him after and, in the end, make him feel so *well read*. The reader like one of those tourists who learns guidebooks by heart and rarely takes the risk of leaving the routes pre-established by his or her host country.

Apart from all of them he set—placing him an immeasurable distance from that lot—the Spaniard Enrique Vila-Matas. A writer whom he envied down to that hyphen-bridge in his surname. Vila-Matas was the only one who seemed to him authentic and honest in what he felt when it came to reading and writing and writing about what he was reading. An obvious ecstasy that sent him turning and revolving like a centrifugal evangelist indifferent to all issues of so-called "reality" (oh so different from his contemporary and conational colleagues, always so "committed"), matters to which he almost never devoted public words or columns in periodicals. Vila-Matas lived off and for and with and through literature. Vila-Matas, who'd attained that privilege of transforming himself into one of his own influences. Vila-Matas, whom he ran into every so often in one of the bookstores of that city, a city that not only believed itself to be, but also proclaimed to the four winds that it was, welcoming to writers of the world (in addition to feeling itself directly responsible for the genesis of great books and the pistol shot inaugurating long and lauded careers). A city that, when it came right down to it, only paraded out those foreign writers as a kind of folk troupe or as prestigious finalists for awards that always ended up being given to the local fauna. To tell the truth, the only real and irrefutable literary virtue of that city for those who wrote was that of having on its shores and in its heights a placid sea and low mountains; which freed writers of a sedentary nature from thinking they should leave and go to the mountains or the sea. Besides, the city had a handful of good bookstores. And there, in one of them, every so often, he and Vila-Matas ran into each other, never exchanging a word, just a conspiratorial glance, like members of a masonic secret society. Though he wasn't kidding himself, their difference of rank was quite clear to him: Vila-Matas was Supreme Master Inspector General of the Order, 33rd Degree. And he, at most, Private Secretary (6th Degree) or—those mornings when he woke up in an absurdly good mood—Prince of Mercy (26th Degree). Vila-Matas, who'd fought in the shadows for years before finally being recognized, was for him an exceptional writer in ever sense. And, as such, he was also aware of the fact that, as it relates to that exception, the Spaniard had received, deservedly, the singular and only available seat of honor he'd once dreamed of for himself. A place that, as such, he would never now access (in his most cerebral and disheartened moments, he couldn't help but think Vila-Matas was the evidence that the good guys could win and, for writers like him, lay waste to the comfortable perspective of convincing themselves only the bad writers were victorious). But that was a unique place, for one person alone. And so he'd opted not to approach him except in his books and in bookstores where he sometimes saw him conversing with that other referential-maniac writer. That guy who he often saw at the supermarket with his young son and wife. That guy who looked like a Ringo Starr impersonator who'd been left outside overnight, but who, nevertheless, always appeared and seemed to feel so happy and satisfied; and the truth is things weren't going too bad for that guy or, at least, better than they were for him (and he spied on them from behind a column, a family, could *that* be the key, the secret? Could you write better being a husband and father or, at least, write something?). There he was: another foreigner. A foreigner like him and one who was born in the same place he was and who seemed to be everywhere writing about everything he was interested in and about which he no longer wrote: another form of torture, another deforming-for-the-better reflection of himself, another perfected clone.

That was why he preferred to never make contact, no matter how much he thought he was receiving sympathetic signals, with Vila-Matas. Because—aware that no beneficial contagion was possible—he couldn't risk that a writer of such enormous curatorial power might wind up with the few microorganisms he had left, barely alive and wriggling, of his literary vocation. Of that home forever, yes; but, in his case, a home falling to pieces under the roof of his head, riddled with cracks and leaks.

Also, his young and perpetual nemesis had made a successful career for himself among that collection of *inteligentista* writers in just that way: the younger and far more ambitious writer he'd supported when he was starting out. IKEA. A writer who now was succeeding here and there and everywhere with truly absurd and supposedly transcendent books, with "good ideas" that seemed to him almost unthinkable.

But the difference between IKEA's thing and that other guy's thing and so many other people's thing was that he never came up with that kind of awful excellent idea. No: he was like one of those spectators who has perfect knowledge of the truth behind the illusion and, for that reason, could never feel magical or like a magician. The trick of those products was perfectly clear to him and maybe that's why he couldn't create them with enough conviction to convince the reading public. And so, maybe, that was why nothing came to him and his prayers—begging for a lightning bolt of inspiration to strike (the miracle in two movements that Nabokov had divided into the initial *vorstog* or initial rapture, the "hot and brief" but not entirely clear movement in which time seems to dissolve, and the subsequent "cool and sustained" *vdokhnovenie* in which you understand how to recapture that fleeting instant and turn it into something that endures) and allow him to, over one week-end, bang out something quite noble and dignified yet simultaneously very commercial and easy to digest—went nowhere. Something like, for example, *Silk* by Alessandro Baricco. The literary equivalent of a fortifying or rejuvenating tonic. A miracle that would let him start over, to be someone else without ceasing to be himself: ancient history, passionate love, subtle metafiction, but all of it made entirely suitable for all audiences.

And thereby set aside so many preoccupations and occupations. But it was more than clear that, in the religious and *sanjuanina* and crucified dark night of his soul—a time the martyr-writer Francis Scott Fitzgerald located at three o'clock in the morning—nobody is listening to his prayers. And the thing is, between three and five in the morning-night/predawn, when there's neither forgiveness nor apology, all these unthinkable things are thought. Before two and after five it's licit to be still awake or already waking up. But at three, there's no going back and nothing to be done; and an old friend of his sang once that *"Los que no podemos dormir de noche siempre vamos de a dos por la vida,"* in other words, "Those of us who can't sleep at night always go through life as two people," but he'd never made clear those two people could turn out to be you and your shadow.

So, in the dark, once, the idea came to him there and from there, then, thinking of whatever thing, to write a Nabokovian and experimental and, of course, oneiric short film.

Something that, right off the bat, ScreaMime found impractical and not "cool" or "trendy" or "hip" enough and abandoned it to its ill fate. But he'd grown fond of his project: to put images and precision to that never-entirely-written-and-described murky waking dream that came at the end of a story in its day inexplicably rejected by the *New Yorker* and ultimately accepted by the *Hudson Review*.

One of his two favorite stories (along with its twin opposite and other favorite, "Signs and Symbols," both originally written in English) by Vladimir Nabokov. Not a ghost story, but something far stranger: a ghostly story. A story whose own plot and writing were bewitched by the actions of two very vivid dead women.

The Nabokov story was titled "The Vane Sisters" (the subject of sisters, yes, always arousing in him a strange but inevitable hypersensitivity to straight and curving lines in letters that always appeared to him in the florescent colors of guilt and synesthesia). And it was, for him, perfect and spectral (the only story that was at the level of his other favorite in the genre, "Los milagros no se recuperan" by Adolfo Bioy Casares, almost its accidental and distant twin). And the story closed wide-openly with an acrostic awakening in the final paragraph. There, at the end of the story, the narrator refers to two types of darkness (that of the solitude of absence and that of the solitude of sleep) and confesses that he cannot "duplicate" the second in writing and settles for making a list (like someone counting translucent sheep) of treacherous ectoplasmic phenomenology. Until, at dawn (he'd always liked that, in the precise poetics of the English language, the noun "dawn" was also a verb used to mean "to realize, to understand, to be enlightened"), the man at last manages to close his eyes and enter into "a dream that somehow was full of Cynthia," one of the Vane sisters. A "disappointing" dream he analyzes in all possible ways and from all possible directions to end up confessing his failure in a couple of final sentences where the first letter of each of the words ends up forming a coded message sent by the dead sisters from the other side, from the so-called eternal sleep. And thus reveals that they'd been the true "authors" of the story, narrating their deaths and lives after death by putting into practice a "theory of intervening auras." Thus, the living not only remember the dead: the living *also* read the dead, the dead writing so the living can read them. Thus, putting into practice and putting in a story the immortality of literature: not only does the work outlive the life, but it comes back from the dead again and again. The reconfirmation that death is but a second, life is long, the work of art is eternal.

The last paragraph of "The Vane Sisters" reads: "I could isolate, consciously, little. Everything seemed blurred, yellow-clouded, yielding nothing tangible. Her inept acrostics, maudlin evasions, theopathies—every recollection formed ripples of mysterious meaning. Everything seemed yellowy blurred, illusive, lost." And when you extract the initials of each one of the words, with Ouija voice and cadence, you discover: ICICLES BY CYNTHIA. METER FROM ME, SYBIL.

Nabokov would build on all this—the whole supernatural maneuver—even more in the subsequent and brief yet immense *Transparent Things*: his own copy autographed by the author's trembling and pale signature beneath the opening credits and, perhaps, his favorite of all his favorite Nabokovs; because it was the most functionally *re-readable* and dream-like of Nabokov's books.

*Transparent Things*, which opens with a condemnation of the future as a figure of speech and a eulogy of the past, as a tool to concentrate on multiple variations of what could or could not have been, and, paradoxically and playfully, interrupts this hypothesis with a, coming up, "More in a moment."

*Transparent Things*, where the Past is defined as "revelatory" and "sans-gêne," and the murky narrator or opaque narrators, similar to those Nabokov had already attempted, preliminary close-ups, in the brief novel *The Eye* (Соглядатай) as well as in stories like "The Visit to the Museum," is/are never defined. Narrator(s) who seem to tell everything from outside time and space and beyond all things of this world. All of them transparently affirming the darkness by saying things (yes, it'd been Nabokov all along, now he remembers it was Nabokov whom he couldn't remember at the beginning of this microscopic night) like "Night is always a giant." And crowning ghosts (the dead were "good mixers," quite social, and blended in better with the whole from the dust and to dust thing) as redactors and editors and first readers and critics of everything the living live.

And he wanted to write it and dream it and make it into images and project it.

He felt doing that was like a form of atonement.

To ask forgiveness for what'd happened with his sister and his sister's little son, who was maybe dead or maybe not. Penelope's little son was now like that "floating boy" he'd been afraid of when they turned off the light in his room, at bedtime. A kind of child-like specter that appeared, hanging in the corners of his bedroom, and motioned for him to follow, and he'd incorporated that "floating boy" into a story, as he'd done with so many things Penelope's son said. Someone who was no longer there, but who now seemed to be floating everywhere. A little boy, taking up more and more space. And whose figure appeared to him, translucent, as if wrapped in a chrysalis, between dreams and awakenings, in the most unexpected places, making frenetic gestures to him, as if wanting to communicate something of extreme importance, as if he were a little brother of the Vane sisters.

Letter by letter so he could put them in order and make sense of them. But Penelope's little son had vanished before learning to read and write.

And with his disappearance, he'd begun to unlearn how to do so many things: to sleep, to write. All he had left was the gift of being able to read others and the curse of being able to write only about them, fewer all the time, closer and closer to being only one.


† Nabokov like the Grand Central Eccentric. An eccentric (Bob Dylan was another) was someone who didn't settle for occupying a central position for everyone, but moved out to the peripheries to establish his or her own center, certain that, sooner or later, everyone would be pulled into orbit around it. Nabokov had been an eccentric writer who'd become centric thanks to a great eccentric and central book, *Lolita*, with which and from there, he gave himself the luxury and pleasure of being more eccentric than ever in *Pale Fire* or *Ada, or Ardor* or *Transparent Things* or *Look at the Harlequins!* Nabokov as someone who'd come up with his own thing (including, at least from outside, an enviable marriage and an excellent relationship with his son of rather perversely polymorphous vocation, capable of bringing together tragic opera arias with treacherous race cars) without fitting any preconceived mold. A universal foreigner who felt his homeland was everywhere ("I am an American writer, born in Russia, educated in England, where I studied French literature before moving to Germany for fifteen years . . . My head speaks English, my heart speaks Russian and my ear speaks French," he said); and all others were his subjects, there down below, lower still, at his feet. A polymorphous and polyphonic and perverse wordplayer who always came out on top in any language. Nabokov was, also, a way of clinging to a he-who-laughs-last-laughs-best; dreaming his exception that proved the rule might someday be repeated; the closest thing to believing God is an atheist. The greatest example to follow, yes, if it weren't impossible to catch him and ask his advice; because Nabokov began and ended in himself, he'd disoriented his biographers and fans, and he'd burned, with the fire of a mischievous prose, all the bridges behind him, including the one that could end up leading to the Nobel committee, which, many years later, had the delicacy to rebuild

them and cross back over them in order to, in Nabokov's absence, give the Nobel to Bob Dylan. (Search for possible mentions from Nabokov of Bob Dylan and from Bob Dylan of Nabokov and, yes, there are stanzas from the poem *Pale Fire* that could work on *Blonde on Blonde*; but there probably aren't any, because practitioners of the same method of appropriation/re-creation/geniusification—a system that dates back to the beginning of time and finds among its practitioners Homer and William Shakespeare, both more than once invoked by Nabokov and Dylan—tend to avoid one another. And, oh, here I have a perfect specimen and example of the kind of logical thought and senseless idea that tends to grow out on the barren moors of insomnia.)

† Warning: Nabokov—like Dylan—can also be a bad influence. He can abduct you like an alien that rips your chest open, intoxicate you with his manners, turn you into a parodic zombie, transform you into a seduced Humbert Humbert or an obese Charles Kinbote whirling around him, advancing and retreating in exaggerated circles, devoured the way a black hole devours you until it is all that's left. Nabokov, like one of those Chaplinesque millionaires who one night invites you over and showers you with attentions and pleasures and the next morning boots you out onto the street to leave you feeling poorer than ever, and yet, even still, addicted forever to the most exquisite and hardest to obtain drug. To be Nabokovian was not to be like Nabokov—or to try to be like Nabokov, at the risk of ending up a sad, involuntary parody—but to have been chewed up and swallowed and finally spit out by Nabokov. To be Nabokovian was to reach the absolute certainty—while unable to stop rereading him—of knowing you'll never be like Nabokov.

† Can you guess who I'm talking about? And, in the most terrible moments of fever, to soothe yourself merely by thinking something similar happened to Nabokov as happened to Marcel Proust whom—opining bluntly and Nabokovianly—he considered not his better but yes his equal. Which was already saying a lot. (Very fun anecdote: Bob Dylan and Leonard Cohen have a conversation. Cohen says: "Okay, Bob: you're Number One, but I'm

Number Two." Dylan smiles and says: "No, Leonard: you're number one," he pauses, and adds: "I'm Number Zero.")

So he was left with—taking ever fewer precautions, embracing his influence—the comfort of worshipping the Absolute Zero that was Nabokov. And, perhaps, the slightly rebellious gesture of not forgiving him (let's not exaggerate, of barely reproaching him) his one sin: having posed for those photographs in pensive and Rodinesque poses, alongside problematic chessboards, which, ever since, had exerted a bad influence on all those writers idiotic enough get photographed in the same pose, thinking if they pulled that off well, they'd automatically write well. (And the closest he'd ever been to Nabokov—with the exception of falling to his knees before his tomb—had been that photograph. Many years ago, a very prestigious French publisher had decided to translate his first book, *National Industry*. And the policy of the publishing house was, in the gallery of the venerable building the imprint with a surname as its name had occupied for more than a century on a curving side-street in Paris, to hang the photographs of the people they were publishing each month. And he'd wound up, by one of those space-time aberrations, being published the same month they were also publishing commemorative and comprehensive complete oeuvres for the centennials of Jorge Luis Borges, Ernest Hemingway and, yes, Vladimir Nabokov. So there he was—traveling uncomfortably and sticking out like a sore thumb—on the heels of the blind man, the psychopath, and the Russian, occupying the ever so sketchy seat of honor of who-the-hell-is-this-guy for all the many passersby.

And he'd *also* come to Geneva for that. He was going to overcome the panic he'd felt regarding the French language (the only two phrases he knew beyond the "good morning"s and the "please"s and the "thank you"s were "Longtemps je me suis couché de bonne heure" and "Voulez-vous coucher avec moi [ce soir]?") ever since, when he was a kid, he'd been attacked by a French waiter in Paris, convinced he'd stolen the tip off the table.

He was going to stay in the Montreux Palace Hotel (actually, he was *not* going to *stay* at the Montreux Palace Hotel; insufficient budget and malice on the part of his boss: booking a reservation at the Markson Hotel, an hourly hotel that allowed weekly booking of rooms between whose walls and sheets resounded the echo of too many past voices). But he was going to pay it a visit and ask—avoiding the suites dedicated to Freddy Mercury and Quincy Jones—to be shown the sanctuary/suite, on the sixth floor of the Montreux Palace, in the right-wing called Le Cynge, a commemorative plaque decorated with reliefs of lilies next to door number 65. The space resulting from the combination of rooms numbered 60, 62, and 64, where, between 1962 and 1977, Nabokov had lived with his wife and son (could one stay *there*, sleep in *that* bed?) after moving from the third floor, where he was annoyed by the emphatic footsteps of the actor Peter Ustinov, rehearsing on the floor above. The longest stay of any guest in the entire history of the Montreux Palace, from which the reigning widow, Vera, like a deposed empress, was evicted, years later, when they began remodeling the hotel. He was going to take a photograph of himself (not a selfie) inside that room. He was going to ask someone to take a photograph of him with his camera (not with his phone, which, moreover, lacked that function and capability) beside the statue of the man sitting in a kind of spread-legged position. The statue of the man who wrote standing up, the statue that he'd seen in photographs, sometimes adorned with bronze sunglasses sometimes not; as if sometimes the statue had forgotten to put them on. He was going to visit his grave (and that of his wife) in the Clarens cemetery where the names and dates and the word "ECRIVAIN" are barely legible. And there he would leave a . . .


† Lily / The flower plucked by Nabokov, in that interview, as an example of how "reality is a very subjective affair" and how "I can only define it as a kind of gradual accumulation of information; and as specialization." How reality is nothing but "an infinite succession of steps, levels of perception, false bottoms." And how, sure, there's a neutral reality that includes and involves all of us; but then, immediately, each of us has our own reality and our own very personal perception of that flower. And how not even "everyday reality"—something "utterly static as it presupposes a situation that is permanently observable, essentially objective, and universally known"—can be said to exist.

"'Reality' (one of the few words that means nothing without quotes)," he concludes in the afterword to *Lolita*.

"The most we can do when steering a favorite in the best direction, in circumstances not involving injury to others, is to act as a breath of wind and to apply the lightest, the most indirect pressure such as *trying* to induce a dream that we *hope* our favorite will recall as prophetic if a likely event does actually happen. And on the printed page the words 'likely' and 'actually' should be italicized too at least *slightly*, to indicate a *slight* breath of wind inclining those characters (in the sense of both signs and personae)," he points out as a kind of editorial advice in *Transparent Things*. "I am no more guilty of imitating 'real life' than 'real life' is responsible for plagiarizing me," he explains in the preface to his collected stories, *Nabokov's Dozen*.


And now he considers the consequence of excess information impeding all specialization courtesy of peoples' addiction to the internet and drowning in Goo-goo-google: an effect similar to eating fruit salad without ever having tried the different fruits separately, without ever having known how they taste individually, or palpated their original shape and consistency. And so, all that nothing, all together and all at once and all diced up into small uniform cubes.

He thought about that in Montreux and in Montreux he did everything he planned to do and so much more.

And he'd even met, under rather bizarre circumstances, someone who, as a child, had known Nabokov: the man who'd once been in charge of the control room at the particle accelerator, the son of an American ex-employee of the Montreux Palace, and based on him and on that, he'd invented an entire story filling multiple biji pages.

Yes, he'd planned a quasi-mystical Nabokov Pilgrimage—Geneva like Mecca and like Lourdes and like Kathmandu—because he needed to commend himself to a higher and benevolent power. Nobody could help him now; so why not Nabokov, eh? he said to himself. The second- and third-level excuses were, of course, more comprehensible: fetishism and mythomania. And a little bit of money in exchange for a magazine article and Nabokovist talk about dreams at the book fair and, while he was at it, taking a photograph in front of *that* hotel, ingeniously famous through association with *that* genius.

A while back, he'd once again reread all of Nabokov, including letters and interviews and plays and university lectures. But, even still, possessed of a full-on fever (that made him pay an inhuman price for a rare first-edition copy of *Conclusive Evidence*), he kept failing, after multiple tries, whenever he attempted to cross the thresholds of Ardis Hall and Van Veen. He felt that same thing that, he supposed, was felt by everyone who was unable to read anything long and drawn out, because they were so accustomed to and hooked on the brief and the horizontal and the vertical of emoticons (defended as a new form of language by those who still didn't know that "are" is spelled with an *a* and an *e*, "you" with a *yo*, and "texting" with an *e*) on increasingly small and multifunctional screens.

As an apology to the specter of his idol, he'd procured all the material available about *Ada, or Ardor*. And he was aware that, wrapped in an incestuous but happy family saga (maybe it was that family happiness, so foreign to him, that repelled him as a reader), Nabokov theorized about the texture of time and alternate dimensions. About an Antiterra where there were no smartphones that idiotized their users (which he'd come to call "thumbies," always plural and lowercase and diminutive) with thumbs deformed like geisha feet and even more deformed syntax. Phones that standardized and uniformized and made everyone the same and on the same level—the famous and the anonymous—because everyone's attitude was the same. Sending and receiving on that small device. And always being there, waiting.

And not long ago he'd heard two ten-year-old boys, coming out of school, acting all grown up with their friends, and saying "Oh, I'm old enough now to have my own mobile phone."

And he'd stood there, trembling: boys no longer dreamed of growing up so they could stay up late and go out with girls or discover the not-so-mysterious mysteries of adult life. Boys, now, only wanted to stare at and text on phones.

The world was shit, indeed.

And he didn't want that.

He wanted to change all of it. To change himself. To mutate into a god capable of imposing his phrasing, his long sentences, his parentheses and dashes, onto the script of all other mortals.

To force the world to adopt his language, comprised of various languages, and his style and his speed and his time.

And, it wasn't hard to see, those dreams of solipsistic grandeur hadn't come true as he'd planned. And he'd returned home, beaten and humiliated.

But out of that defeat, already considering himself finished, he'd managed to create a new book that he'd written as if underwater and holding his breath (as all good writing should be done, according to the recommendation of Francis Scott Fitzgerald, the hero of his parents who'd disappeared so long ago, in another millennium).

He'd written it almost drowning and coming up to the surface only to trap a little bit of oxygen that would allow him to go on a few pages more, down below.

And without meaning to, he'd shut the mouths of those who'd considered him washed up, expended, and opened the eyes of those who still retained a little affection for what he did and they celebrated it like a miracle.

Really, at that time he wasn't—nothing like he felt now—*that* worn out. Nor did he want to be compared to some kind of evangelical resurrection. At that time, he still slept more or less well and liked to think, on the other hand, that his thing had something of the never-equaled performance put on by James Brown who, like him, had been born clinically dead and, to the astonishment of the doctors in the delivery room, just after the declaration of RIP—"get up, get on up, stay on the scene, you gotta have feeling, sure as you born, right on, right on . . ."—he began to breathe and whimper and cry.

His favorite variation of the performance of the unriveled Brown was the one in the 1964 documentary film, *The T.A.M.I Show*. There, along with his centrifugal The Famous Flames (indignant at not being given the closing number, because, they explained to him, that privilege corresponded to, novel and hip at the time, The Rolling Stones), Brown decided to go out and kill it and kill them, entering next-to-last from the right and dancing on just one foot. And the little English boys knew that the worst thing that could happen to them had happened: to have to perform after eighteen black and white minutes of James Brown on fire. There and then and always—it was his never-routine routine—after howling "Please . . . Please . . . Please . . . Please . . . Please . . . Please . . . Please . . . ," Brown fell to his knees, he was covered with a cape by one of the backups, who kept giving him consoling little pats on the back and he was almost dragged, stumbling, to one side of the stage with his face strangled by his own vocal cords, bathed in tears and sweat and disfigured by the agony only to, suddenly, throw off the cape like someone dispelling a curse and return to the microphone, burning with renewed energy and, again, "Please . . . Please . . . Please . . . Don't go."

No.

He hadn't gone.

Please.

But, yes, there abounded in his vicinity numerous specimens who were like the writer versions of The Rolling Stones. And to him, The Rolling Stones had always seemed like a bunch of phony *pasticheurs* who were lucky The Beatles had broken up and they stayed together. The Beatles had invented breaking up and The Rolling Stones staying together. His parents, before vanishing (and his Uncle Hey Walrus would have loved this idea, no doubt), had invented a cross of both things. His parents were The Rolling Beatles: a marriage that broke up just so it could get back together and then break up again and get back together one more time.

And only History's bullets could end that cycle.

And how did that joke/old-yet-still-functional adage go?: love is a sweet dream and marriage an alarm clock?

And that other one?: men get married hoping their wives never change, while women get married hoping to change their husbands?

If that's the case, the romantic combo his deceased parents composed was most similar to a snoozing alarm clock, changing all the time in order to stay the same. A device from which, in days when he still slept, he'd always snatched those zigzagging nine and never-round ten minutes of reprieve and truce (a length of time implanted in the fifties, but that, by tradition, was transported and inserted into the alarm clocks on mobile phones) you're allowed before it goes off again and interrupts your light and poor quality and ever so unsatisfactory sleep, which, like fleeting and ephemeral love affairs, helps you stop dreaming and get out of bed.

In any case, that romantic landscape had immunized him for life from any temptation toward rings and vows, but not from the temptation to put his parents in writing.

And please, please, please, please, going back to the thing from before and the thing from after: his already-mentioned *out of sight / get back / start me up* book became incredibly popular. The printers couldn't produce enough copies (he'd stipulated that it not be sold in any electronic format or medium; the book took a stand against all of that), and people signed up for waiting lists in bookstores and in all the languages of the world while sociologists and critics discussed his unexpected appeal and he said things like "If my work seems really difficult, then don't read it; not reading is even easier than not writing . . . Pass it on to someone else the way you pass to pharmacists—so they can read and explain them—those unintelligible prescriptions doctors write, right?" But not even with that was he able to convince the masses not to bother with those hermetic and personal pages. And the psychologists tried to explain this phenomenon/transfer of unprecedented sales that, obviously, took place (you believed it?, ha ha, ha?) in a parallel/alternate dimension, not this one, not his. A Brigadoon/Shangri-La where, before going to sleep, people read far more than successions of one hundred and forty characters (a format whose recent expansion of spaces was celebrated with a combination of joy and curiosity in the face of the new challenge and not harshly criticized for the effort it required, like what actually happened, causing a global depression over no longer having any excuse to type "r" instead of "are"); and in a book and not on a screen (it'd been proven that reading on a tablet or phone was harmful for sleep; because the artificial light disturbed the internal clock of the circadian rhythm). Yes, in that utopia made and dreamed up by him in his insomnia, everyone read again, like in ancient times, some number of pages of something that didn't have anything to do with them or their lives, but that, nevertheless, made them better. Something that completed them, becoming an inseparable part of their lives and even their deaths and, meanwhile and in the meantime, helped them traverse the blooming deserts of the night.

But no.

Of course not.

In short: he wrote the book and the book left him written.

The coup de grâce in the last breath of the funeral song of the black swan. After that, the desperate conviction, the farthest fall from the highest heights: the certainty he was *living* a book no prose could do justice to, and thereby hide the blinding white. The clean and well-lighted and suicidal and Hemingwayian nothing. How'd it go? Ah, yes: "Our nada who art in nada, nada by thy name thy kingdom nada thy will be nada in nada as it is in nada. Give is this nada our daily nada and nada us our nada as we nada our nadas and nada us not into nada but deliver us from nada; pues nada. Hail nothing full of nothing, nothing is with thee."

Maybe, he thought now, he'd gone beyond his saturation point.

He'd read too much and thought too much and had gotten too tangled up in himself, in all that nothing full of nothing.

"Just another crackpot," indeed.

In any case, more Fitzgeraldian than Hemingwayian, less *nothing* and more *dark night of the soul* (again, that hour when, according to the author of *Tender Is the Night*, "a forgotten package has the same tragic importance as a death sentence"), in the end the book had been published.

A book closer to the one authorized by Fitzgerald's failure. Fitzgerald who always "slept on the heart side" to tire himself out more quickly and, quoting in his *Notebooks* an improbable Egyptian proverb, he moaned "The worst thing in the world is to try to sleep and not to," and "It appears that every man's insomnia is as different from his neighbor's as are their daytime hopes and aspirations" in his essay "Sleeping and Waking," where he writes as if tormented by a mosquito that won't let him sleep.

A book further from the one authorized by Hemingway's success, Hemingway, who didn't hesitate to bellow "I love sleep. My life has the tendency to fall apart when I'm awake, you know?"; but who, also, was a chronic insomniac from early on, you know?

Not much had happened with the book (or absolutely everything that could possibly happen with a book of those characteristics had happened).

Something *had* happened with him: he'd come out of the writing of that book changed, different, as if battered by a brutal wind. That elegant and more or less noble decline (goals unaccomplished, promises broken, desires frustrated) you see in the faces and gaits of certain more or less well-meaning presidents after four or eight years installed in the impotence of power. Luckily, at least, in his line of work you didn't have to go around kissing random babies, though—again, which writer said it?—each book you wrote was like dragging all over the house, from bed to desk and back again, a drooling and guttural child "with problems." One of those babies who from the moment of their birth look so old, so wizened. A needy creature, always clinging to your leg, demanding your attention with its bumbling and its drool.

Or something like that.

That last book of his had been like a six-foot-tall, forty-pound baby whose voice and tears were of proportional power. And it was a strange voice. A voice that even in third person singular sounded so much like first person. A voice, he thought, as if arriving from outside, from on high, but as assimilated as the voice of parents reading their children a bedtime story. A voice that awoke and woke him up in the middle of the night, demanding more, asking for everything, keeping him from sleep, improving his insomnia (which he'd been dragging around since the time of the eternal night-watches of his military service, on the immediately rusted edges of an absurd war, not coincidentally referred to as "*imaginarias*"; when it was a blessing not to sleep, to stretch out the night and thereby put off the curse of a new day of nightmares where infrahuman creatures in uniforms screamed and forced you to drag yourself along the ground and clean bathrooms covered with shit and eat food that wasn't all that different from what they cleaned in those latrines) until he reached the peak: the perfection of not sleeping and of the night as blank as a blank page.

Writing that book had been like letting the currents pull him out to try to rescue an immense little boy from drowning and to do it, yes. And to collapse on the sand of the shore like a Robinson who, suddenly, understood that now, supposedly saved, the truly dangerous part was just beginning. Because now he'd earned the title of castaway.

The book had gotten good (some very good) but slightly disconcerted reviews. And, for once, his habitual nemeses (reviewers trained in universities who considered him just less than the Antichrist or who availed themselves of him, praising him in opposition to other authors and constructing academic theories slightly less than demented) had opted to call themselves to silence.

The book had been considered "excessive."

The book had been qualified as "transgressive" and had overly emphasized his luddite and anti-technological side.

And—his favorite reproach/praise among all the praise/reproaches it was given—the book had been apprised as something "whose reading demanded a true effort."

And, yes, of course, that had been and was the idea: that the book was work, a labor, a challenge parallel to that of writing it. That his book couldn't just be *looked at* and that it demanded awareness of each and every one of its letters from the reader. Reading had to be different than just *looking*, looking at letters, right? You had to *read* first to *see* later.

But none of his most devoted defenders had realized that behind his supposedly experimental pose (he had to be honest: he, the author, hadn't been aware of it *either* until after the book was already in bookstores) there was nothing but the reinterpretation of other books. "Subconscious plagiarism"? Like what happened, according to a judge, to George Harrison with "My Sweet Lord"? That thing that, in a way, is the symptom that feeds off and off which feeds all artistic manifestation, where nothing begins in itself or ends in everyone else? "Really want to see you, really want to know you, really want to go with you"? The vampiric take-me-while-I-take-you? The contagious influenza of the influence contagion?

No or yes.

His book, the product of the confluence of two books he'd read so long ago and created by—here he comes again, once more, with you all—his sweet lord: Vladimir Nabokov.

Books that functioned like farewells to, first, a body of work (the one Nabokov had written in Russian) and, later, to a life (the one Nabokov, at the end of his career, had rewritten to fit his surname turned adjective).

Both books functioning as encrypted or—to use a term chosen by their creator—"oblique" autobiographies.

The first one, Дар (published in installments between 1935 and 1937, and that he had read in English as *The Gift*, from 1963), was a goodbye to his past (his native tongue and literature; including a long biographical-encyclopedic insert) from someone who was already preparing to reinvent the English language and, while he was at it, the entire planet, with the name/species of Lolita and the creation of an Antiterra a.k.a Demonia (a kind of R.U.S.A., a cross between The United States and Russia, to which, again, he'd only traveled between lines and hearsay). Along the way, there, he postulated that all books could be divided into two classes: books for the nightstand and books for the trash can.

The second one, *Look at the Harlequins!*, from 1974, was a never-before-seen kind of autobiography with the modalities of a blurry photograph and a clear-eyed rewrite (in it, *The Gift* mutated into *The Dare*, whose original and Russian title, *Podarok Otchizne*, was the equivalent of a "A Gift to the Fatherland"), commanding "Play! Invent! Invent the world! Invent reality!" *Look at the Harlequins!*, the last of Nabokov's novels published while he was alive (an inspired offshoot of a tense duel with his biographer, the possessed Andrew Field, who'd overstepped in his role and interpretations of the Nabokovian universe), was not an alternate self-portrait but something far more interesting: a kind of catalogue of all the mistaken reasoning and preconceived notions ever attributed to Nabokov. There, a transparent/murky alter ego of the author with the physical/mental particularity of not being able to trace his steps back in his memory. Or something like that. Another kind of Mr. Trip. The fact that this final book was considered "minor" by scholars and fans and even "awkwardly written" as well as "the product of an aging writer trapped inside his own literary personage" concealed, for him (for whom the only thing he had to criticize, and only in a low voice, was the exclamation point in the title), a final and ingenious joke on Nabokov's part: having to retell and correct and rarefy himself in the first person (and along the way prove that he'd achieved the definitive achievement: that the novel of a writer resemble his or her life without falling into that compulsive banality that the life of a writer has to resemble his or her novels), Nabokov had settled the fact that, in reality, nobody was at his level. Nobody was worthy of telling him. And so, the protagonist writer had to be, necessarily, a worse writer than he was. Someone who wouldn't be Nabokov but, merely, Nabokovian. Someone with the imperfections of an imitator, but—inexact on innumerable key details—suffering, to cite just two examples, from a couple defects unforgivable to his author. To wit: the degrading deficiency of having learned to drive automobiles and driving them instead of being driven (only someone who doesn't know how to drive could let himself take such automobilist photographs, so aware of being in a car, like the ones Nabokov took for *Life* magazine) and, the most serious of all, lowering himself to that indignity there was no coming back from and that his creator would never have allowed himself. The indignity of returning to Mother Russia, besmirched by communism, in an airplane with broken air conditioning and crammed with sweaty and lugubrious bureaucrats and fat, bare-armed stewardesses.

Also, important detail, in addition to all the foregoing, that of their coinciding on the perfect imperfection of being unable to sleep: debating and wringing "my four limbs, yes, in an agony of insomnia, trying to find some combination between pillow and back, sheet and shoulder, linen and leg, to help me, oh help me to reach the Eden of a rainy dawn."

Like him now.

And he, then, didn't say, as he said already, any of this.

Moreover, so satisfied with his theory regarding the lesser writer as a tool to narrate the unsurpassable writer, he'd gone back and flipped through/skimmed the book again. And, around chapter three of the second part, he'd read: "I now confess that I was bothered that night, and the next and some time before, by a dream feeling that my life was the non-identical twin, a parody, an inferior variant of another man's life, somewhere on this or another earth. A demon, I felt, was forcing me to impersonate that other man, that other writer who was and would always be incomparably greater, healthier, and crueler than your obedient servant."

Ah, the same thing always happened: every time he was sure he'd gotten ahead, abuzz, of Nabokov's intentions; it didn't take him long to discover that Nabokov was always ahead, waiting for him at the next stop along the trajectory. With his net aloft ready to go hunting butterflies. Or to squash him with a swat, like a somnolent tsetse fly; or to stomp on him firmly, like a cockroach or bug or whatever it was that woke up one day and discovered something strange had happened to it during the night.

And he—*Shut the Fuck up, Memory!*—didn't say anything about that either. He didn't reveal anything. Writers (and especially the writers of his now nonexistent country of origin, from the very totemic to the totem worshippers) were always fine cultivators, not of occulting the figure in the rug, but of sweeping it under it.

And pointing all that out would've probably been too complex (and so easy to misinterpret and question as pedantry) for those who devote themselves to reviewing writers and interviewing writings. Pearls lost in the mud.

And only one of them had noticed the possibly elegiac and last breath of his book and diagnosed and concluded his lines with a "And if it's always an interesting exercise—cruel, of course, but interesting in the end—to think of the most recent book of an author as if it were the last he has decided to write, it's hard not to wonder where this author would fit in the national tradition if he decided never to publish another word after the final period of this novel."

And he'd been moved when he read that. He'd been moved a little, but, as tends to happen to him, that little had meant a lot.

And then he'd worried like when a doctor studies an X-ray and lets slip an "Uh-oh." Or when someone pokes his head inside a half-open door to say: "Hey, the building's on fire. Now we must all calmly proceed to the exit and go down the stairs and nobody will be scared, okay?"

But he swears that, at the time, he tried to keep his spirits high and a spring in his step.

Though the truth is that (something his publisher had been resigned to for a while) he hadn't made things easy or helped all that much when it came to the promotion of the monster. It wasn't ill will on his part. It's just that easy things (among them easy reading and easy writing) easily bored him.

And so—while the noble and mature and well-read professionals languished, recalling the good old days or were retired for having too little online life—young journalists (fellows and interns, fanciful categories that made him think of the ethnicities of the fantasy genre) were asking him with a combination of disdain and "help me, help me!" if he could summarize "his subject," to help them do their job, and keep them from having to read the book. Or, better, get him to write a piece for free so they didn't have to write it for almost-free, let alone see themselves obliged to subtract his words. "It's an 'opinion' piece; and opinions don't pay," they claimed with the precise diction of crooked accountants. "Even when I wasn't thinking of offering an opinion and they ask me to?" he countered in vain, as if haggling over trinkets at an increasingly vacant market. Goodbye to the hypothesis/criticism of Virginia Woolf about how a woman has a right to "money and a room of her own if she is to write fiction." And if you're a man, same thing. Now there wasn't even that once "social" space, like a country club, that shared room that'd once been the editorial department at newspapers and magazines: places where you had to go to turn in an article in person and while there—or at the indispensable annex that was the bar on the corner—mingle with friends and enemies and learn about things, about everything that was happening throughout the cosmos. Now, editorial departments were virtual, places in the air and always on the verge of crashing, you connected to via cables and antennas. And journalism was virtual too. For a while now, the fixed or to-be-fixed idea that writing was done with no hope for remuneration beyond the one-off mention and the fleeting attention. Editorial strategy where the work of the cultural editors consisted of, basically, receiving spiels and responses via email. Bombarding you as if you were a family member when Kurt Vonnegut died or when they gave Bob Dylan the Nobel (to get him to recount his encounters with both; to his bewilderment, he'd received more congratulations for the latter's recent award than for any of his own books or achievements). Or when, spurred on by the global psychosis caused by so many confessional blogs and comments where nobody showed their face but just their alias (more and more of them abandoned by their onetime proud owners, rusting in the air like those cars on the side of the road), that subject of fiction versus reality (what was true and what false in stories and novels)—oh so scandalously new and modern for so many, and as old as humanity for him—became "hip." Or—after that episode, his and only his, with him and only him as indisputable and shooting and fallen dwarf star—when a video-gag faking a human sacrifice next to that statue of Shiva at the facilities of the particle accelerator and hadron collider at CERN in Geneva. And they asked him between chuckles if, after his . . . uh . . . performance?, he'd had anything to do with *that*. Quotes they later blindly cut according to the space available in pages ten or twenty names competed for, to see who was the most ingenious when it came to opining about matters that had less and less to do with noble fiction and more and more with the damned and implausible real. A challenge he no longer accepted (just as he avoided sending all his "unpublished texts" when they were solicited for group anthologies and other people's "projects") because he could still remember times when the designers of those projects tried to raise money to finance their projects and to pay their collaborators first, unlike now where it was the collaborators who worked for free on the thing that would later be sold and wind up financing the project.

He'd also lost any hope when it came to interviews conducted by beings little prepared in the art of more or less intelligent conversation, but only in the transcription of voice to text.

Every so often he flipped through *Strong Opinions*—the anthology of interviews of Vladimir Nabokov, interviews carefully revised and rewritten by Vladimir Nabokov—and he said to himself that, if he were alive and responding here and now, the Russian would've lost his mind. There was no rigor or care. And they could attribute anything to you. He remembered how once, explaining that his first contact with the English language had been the lyrics on the back cover of *Sgt. Pepper's Lonely Hearts Club Band*, his interviewer had opted to type that "I remember learning English reading the booklet *Farmer Peppermint*."

And there it was and there it remained, floating like space trash in the orbits of the web.

And that's why he (following the lessons of the evasive and sinuous Robert Strange McNamara, onetime president of the Ford Motor Company, directly responsible for its sweeping success across many latitudes, including in its infancy, with the infamous model Ford Falcon, later the U.S. Secretary of Defense from 1961 to 1968, and after that the president of the World Bank Club until 1981) applied his "Answer the question you wish they'd asked."

And agree to everything with a polite smile to then respond to/edit things that're a bit out of time and place.

Things impossible to transcribe into letters or fit in the body of a note.

Things like "What's my area of interest, my territory as a writer, my style, my subject? . . . I could offer a brief answer: what interests me is texture. The texture of the text. But that wouldn't be an entirely correct or precise answer . . . Mmm . . . I like to think my thing is something like an airplane in flight contemplated from the window of another airplane in flight . . . Something apparently normal that, suddenly, doesn't seem so normal, right?, no? Is there anything stranger than flying while seeing yourself fly? That space/nothingness between one aircraft and another like my blank page or screen . . . Though now, aboard airplanes, inside airplanes, stranger and stranger things happen. Stranger things than all the things that happened inside airplanes for decades. Like the absurd and useless six rows for smokers or non-smokers on flights of more than fourteen hours, with all the smoke spreading throughout all the non-smoking rows. And it's all good, everything in order. And the terminally ill with their lives in the air and their deaths dragging them toward the most firma of terra; thinking about whether the machine might not be moving too much; about whether that position with head between knees in case of an emergency landing does any good; about whether seatbelts might not actually be there so bodies don't scatter all over the place during a crash, because, after all, what logic is there in having seats for smokers and non-smokers . . . Now, even stranger strange things. Like how there were still ashtrays on the armrests to torture those who would give anything for a little bit of tobacco. Or like that application on the screen that before only showed airplane movies. Movies with airplanes of nonexistent airlines, because, of course, something horrible is going to happen in and with those airplanes that're like the equivalent of those photographs of the betrothed on their wedding day. Light and floating and flying movies in air-planes where now they offer the service and the app, for the addict passengers going through withdrawals, that allows you to send and receive messages from strangers, also in need of their fix, in other seats on the same airplane . . . And, of course, there are always the classics: the nauseated baby that pukes on you, the consparanoic who starts to tell you how the white lines that airplanes leave in the sky are 'chemical agents,' the one who, to break the ice, asks you 'Want to know how many spiders we swallow without knowing it every year while we sleep? Four!' and, every so often, the also-nauseated young, aspiring writer who recognizes you and doesn't hesitate, right there, to puke up on you a copy of his toxic and arachnid unpublished novel . . . And, ha ha ha, now you see, now you hear: concerning what intrigues you or what you don't understand about my digressive style and psychotic theme . . . Allow me to quote for you from memory a brief fragment from a letter of Virginia Reed, survivor of the cannibalistic Donner Expedition, trapped in the Sierra Nevada during the winter of 1846-1847, that seems to perfectly define what I've done and what my novel is about. Virginia says there: 'I have not wrote you half of the trouble we've had, but I have wrote you enough to let you know what trouble is' . . . Or, if you prefer, that thing T. S. Eliot said:

'We shall not cease from exploration, and the end of all our exploring will be to arrive where we started and know the place for the first time' . . . Like that tired but seasoned and wise voice in 'Nettie Moore' . . . When it comes to seeing the airplane from another airplane, it's clear that from that airplane we're seeing ourselves when we see it . . . Next question."

This kind of elastic almost trancelike speech—the idea, as he said, was to make a cleaning up/assembling of the interview as difficult as possible—had replaced his one-time much-remarked-upon one-liners.

He'd ditched that kind of oh so characteristic *boutade* when he realized, maybe too late, the expansive toxic power they had. The way in which they were perpetuated and lost his original and fleeting and quickly expired intention when, living-dead, they were perpetuated in the mouths of epigones or fans or enemies looking for ways to trash him and trafficking in the uncontrolled substance for social-networks addicts with the insatiable need to share, repeat, and post until everything became not a bad but a mean joke.

What a writer says—like what he or she writes—should be, by law, impossible for second and third and thousandth parties to reproduce, he thought. He also refused to obey the requests of photographers to adopt that pose as common as it was absurd: appearing with his face so concentrated on reading his own book. A pose that wasn't just very sad, but where, besides, the writer invariably, upon opening the book randomly and pretending to read some passage, discovered, always, some improvable term, some adjective twice repeated, some typo in a name, some doubt (was it McNamara or Mc Namara or MacNamara?).

And, true, yes, he was a really annoying guy.

And being annoying for everyone else tends to be, many times, like patriotism for the rabble: the last refuge for someone who no longer really matters to almost anyone.

A way of attracting attention without having to sob a "Why don't they pay attention to me?" while simultaneously fantasizing about bombing and spraying them all with napalm and Agent Orange.

And his was—OK, sure, yes—an annoying book: it didn't contain military coups or brutal narcotraffickers or stoic republicans. No sadomasochistic sex, either.

And it's not that he hadn't tried at some point.

The whole, being *hip* thing.

His first book—*National Industry*, his most successful book—had fed off a certain historical-situational potency.

*National Industry* had been the perfect product: a book written by the son of a somewhat famous couple who'd been disappeared. *Desaparecidos* more freak than political. *Desaparecidos* who some people didn't even consider *desaparecidos* but, really, "snobs who didn't know what they were getting into" and "weekend activists" (definitions and accusations also translatable, he thought, to many of the committed and venerated factions of the armed conflict).

A book not laughing at itself, but yes (despite him being who he was and looking down on all long-suffering and opportunistic poses) refusing to turn itself into an epic elegy for the victims of a dictatorship. Which—refusing to cry, he didn't know it then, he soon learned—was almost worse than laughing at the victims.

Well, really, the book (and by extension and association he did, too) smiled to itself a little, but with one of *those* smiles. The kind of smile one sees at baptisms or funerals. The smile of knowing his parents' death had signified (not for him, who'd felt he was a writer for so long, but yes for everyone else) his birth as a writer.

He would never have been able to write *National Industry*, that book would never have appeared, without the prior disappearance of his parents. William S. Burroughs had referred to the "accident" of killing his wife, under the influence and possessed by an "Ugly Spirit," in the same way. And yes, maybe, probably without knowing it or being all that clear on who Burroughs was, one of the most offended critics of *National Industry* (a kind of miserable Javert who would thereafter follow him throughout all his future books) accused it of being "something with an ugly spirit" that "mocks our most precious thing: our *desaparecidos*."

And in one of the stories in *National Industry*, "Children of the Revolution," he told the story of a group of ten year olds—fed up with their transgressive and undisciplined and oh so childish parents—who plan to kidnap their adored arts and crafts teacher and hold her for ransom. The story ended very badly.

In "Love Story," a man who could no longer stand his wife, but doesn't dare divorce her, joined a "clandestine Marxist liberation" cell so he could "get out of the house" and there he discovered an inconceivable talent for urban guerilla warfare and was transformed into "a mythic figure on the level of Lawrence of Arabia."

In "Seeking," a casting agency for mediocre actors—with the slogan "We bring them back to life"—hired the children of *desaparecidos* to liven up parties and dinners.

And in "My Unforgettable Night"—which was perhaps the best of all the stories, also the one least shaded with black humor—he created a portrait of a man who, one night, wakes up his young son get him to help burn, in their backyard, his entire library, because it contained too many "banned" books. As they were throwing the books into the fire, the boy tried to read them as fast as he could, to store them in his head in brief fragments, glimmers of plotlines and shots in the dark, and to invent, on the basis of those random pieces and in the act itself of destroying them, how they began and ended. And, right there and then, the boy began to be transformed into a writer when, really, "he was going to be a veterinarian or Formula 1 racer."

Things like that.

And it sold well and was read even more via hearsay (*National Industry* had attained that curious literary category of "topic of conversation" where you don't need to have read it first to subsequently offer an opinion about it).

And the "intellectual sphere" developed complex theories to discredit it as "writing for the market."

And more than one almost-*desaparecido* (curious category that included those who had been saved by miracle or coincidence or because, actually, they were never that dangerous for or in danger from their repressors though they insisted just the opposite) took issue with him and called him a "literary torturer" and said his parents would be ashamed of him.

Though, to tell the truth, his parents weren't held in high regard *either* (his disappeared parents were, also, politically and ideologically troublesome: a subversive aberration as much for the far right as for the far left).

And so the book, suddenly polemical, sold even more (and he never reread it or those that followed; because his past books were like past lovers, seen from the remove of new love: curious and often inexplicable phenomena exhibited in the display cases of a kind of museum of sentiments that, just in case, he was better off not visiting that often for fear one of them would distract him and, ignoring closing time, he'd stay there, locked inside, not knowing how to get out).

And he was named person of the year and posed on that magazine cover where his disappeared parents had once appeared. A cover that assembled all the people of the year (him there, in that freshly inaugurated democracy *de rigueur*, with a bad TV comedian and an average tennis player and a superb starlet, holding a sign that read "Do you know where your parents are tonight?").

And many people, of course, hated him automatically; because his now nonexistent country of origin was characterized by being a place where anyone for whom things went more or less well had to explain themselves to hundreds of people for whom things went more or less poorly.

And he went to many parties of the kind where you knew what time they started but not what day they ended.

And at one of those parties—something that did nothing to help his profile, the profile of an increasingly more- and better-powdered nose—he met Pétalo: artistic name of Anita Soldán, the sexy director of one of the first music-video TV shows and the supposed daughter (though not really) of one of the most rabid and flamboyant and messianic repressors of the Dictatorship. A colonel considered directly responsible for the final assault on the department store his parents had taken over. The department store that years before—still working for an ad agency and not yet having met his mother at a casting call—his father had gift-wrapped, like a giant package, for Christmas. (When somebody reminded his father that Christo, a Bulgarian plastics artist, had already, on numerous occasions, done something similar with famous buildings and monuments, his father responded: "True, but he didn't do it as *advertising*. And that's what advertising is: the refined and more precise translation into the language of commerce of something that theretofore has only been done for the love of art and without any logic. That's why a good slogan or good headline on the cover of a magazine is better than a good novel.")

Before long, the coronel in question would be assassinated at a discoteca by a schizoid rock musician, or something like that. Gunned down for the love of art. "Big Bang-Bang" read the headline of a more or less countercultural monthly of the day. And his father would've loved it. His father and mother were mentioned in the article several times and it even included a photo of his whole family in which he and Penelope appeared posing aboard the deck of the *Diver*, holding a sign that read: "Special Offer: Kids Included."

Parents and children and children and parents, yes: together in that place where some go in so others come out.

Everything seemed to depart from there in order to return there.

And at some point, a number of books later, he lost track of so many things.

And what disappeared was the desire to keep telling the tale.

That tale.

Let others tell it, he told himself.

And it didn't take long for them to do so, claiming they were doing it *like this*, with reverent irreverence, for the first time; not as if *National Industry* had disappeared (because it was still there and was even reissued every so often), but as if it'd never existed.

And every so often he did go back and write about what happened in his now nonexistent country of origin, yes. But he did so as if the whole country were actually his childhood, the territory of his childhood: a combination of enchanted castle and mad-scientist laboratory that wasn't even acknowledged by its name (that of the country) but by his name (that of the boy who, looking back at it from the future, put it together and took it apart like a Meccano model made up of hazardous and rusted pieces, that could cut you and cause an infection).

He even wrote a novel about it, as a kind of farewell, in a single week. A kind of national and commercial thriller. *Samizdat*, it was called (the title was the last name of its protagonist) and it came to him as if fallen from the sky, in the wake of a dream. A dream whose beginning was the only thing he remembered clearly, two men, aboard a sailboat, one fat and one skinny, conversing. He had that dream while on vacation, at a Mime Union hotel (yes, really, such place did exist), where, in a mountainous region barely connected with noisy civilizations, the guests were banned from pretending to be swept away by the wind or from pressing their hands against the glass of an invisible window pane. And there was pure silence, at a time when telephones didn't yet go on vacation with their owners, because telephones couldn't leave home. And that's where he typed up the novel as if it were being dictated to him, in seven days, thinking it would make him rich. It was an *easy* and clever book. And commercial and smart (the first impulse of setting it in the Paris of Russian émigrés had been aborted by setting it all in the here and now of *militares* and *desaparecidos*). A lot happened in that book and it even included dialogue (for once, his characters displayed an ease in talking at length among themselves and thinking very little). It was sure to be made into a movie. Or a seven-episode miniseries, one episode for each chapter of the novel, which, in turn, unfolded between one Sunday and the next. It was perfect, everything fit. But perfection in private frequently fails to translate to perfection in public and the book faded embarrassingly away without glory.

And so, after it was published, from there, from that twilight zone, he attempted to change subject, change style.

To be less gratuitously funny and more graceful. Besides, before long, all of that went out of style and became something like the legends of lost second-rate civilizations. Not the Incas or the Egyptians. More like the Muiscas or the Akkadians. Military dictatorships and their victims couldn't compete with the history of (*dixit* IKEA, more details coming up) Nazis and Jews.

And what came into style was, in any case, being a writer left widowed and childless by an Islamic bomb (IKEA often traveled giving talks in Arabic countries and in Paris, no doubt toying with the possibility that something might blow up somewhere not too close so he could then exploit it by recounting it as if it'd happened centimeters away from him).

Another possibility had been to somehow make a name for yourself doing something that wasn't strictly literary (to become a champion skateboarder, for example) and to write a memoir where, in addition to your spins and flips, you reveal that your parents had prostituted you out, between the ages of six and thirteen, to their bourgeoisie friends who, in that way, were able to avoid those trips to Indonesia, which had become too risky and too terroristic. Compared to parents like that, his parents were, now, reevaluated as, merely, confused victims of confused times and little more. Amateurs who put their foot in it and let things get out of hand. Little more and nothing less than that. And so he knew too soon that the distance between a *de moda*, or hip, pop writer and a démodé plop writer wasn't great. And that there's nothing more treacherous and boomeranging than a first and precocious success. The reckless and terrifying Orson Welles syndrome. All the lucky novices his weighty shadow, half sultan and half buffoon. But nobody was as immense as he was; because Welles had been like the Oedipus of the complex: the original. And all those who'd followed his bad example were nothing more than early successes who'd subsequently experienced a drawn out loss, only resuscitated, terrible ultimate paradox, as more or less revealing details when the time came for obituaries and epitaphs and revising decades of leftovers and remnants and ill-fated opportunities and failed projects.

He, of course, had never been compared to the director of *Citizen Kane*; but he had experienced his own meager yet indigestible serving of the same thing: the ambiguous sensation that something he'd done a long time ago always came back, again and again, to bite the hand that wrote it. Debut as coda. To leave by way of the entrance, passing right through the closed door. Exit Ghost.

And like what (ah, again, the dumb comfort of taking shelter behind the names of titans) Ernest Hemingway moaned between one round of electroshock and the next. Hemingway after trying to throw himself into the moving blades of an airplane turbine (an airplane that could suddenly be seen from an airplane in flight, yes). Hemingway days before what might have been his last photograph, walking alone and kicking a can high into the air, as if that can were everything that was and would no longer be and that now could only be kicked skyward. Hemingway on that last morning putting on his "Emperor's robe" and resting his forehead on the barrel of a shotgun and endeavoring to hunt himself and hitting the target. There and then, Hemingway came to the conclusion that everything concluded when he did. "Nothing comes anymore," he'd sobbed.

He limited himself to sobbing.

It wasn't like him to off himself in the middle of life to get to the end of life. He had neither the lion-hearted grace under pressure nor rifle at hand nor trigger at finger. He wouldn't know what to do with a rifle anyway; except look at it or let it drop from his hands and go off when it hit the ground and kill some passerby (if he had to imagine an end with bullets, his would have been something closer to the "Let me finish my work" of Isaac Babel in front of the firing squad, but, he thinks, in his case, adding in a low voice an unconfessable and not-at-all heroic "What work?").

But he knew then that he was wounded by gravity, falling.

The descending wound of a dull sword.

Who was it who said that thing about "I hate writing, I love having written"? Ingenious, but, in his case, imprecise: he liked having written, but he didn't like no longer writing, no longer liking to write. Having written was nothing but a permanent reminder that he wasn't writing anymore. Something like an art gallery that's been robbed: silent walls where before hung eloquent paintings, the paint on the walls slightly discolored, outlining empty squares and rectangles where once had been faces and landscapes and shapes and colors and no, no, that thing about how you never forget how to ride a bicycle wasn't true.

You could lose your balance and fall down and never get up again.

You could forget how to write, how to swim, how to sleep, how to dream.


† More or less waking notes for a talk on Vladimir Nabokov and dreams or lack of dreams and his psychoanalytic (non) treatment / Vladimir Nabokov had, also, had a more than interesting relationship with the insomnia that pursued him and caught him and made him suffer throughout his entire life. "I suffocate in uninterrupted, unbearable darkness. The marvelous terror of consciousness rocks my soul in emptiness" with "intervals of hopelessness and nervous urination," he said. But he also considered the act of sleep to be "the most moronic fraternity in the world, with the heaviest dues and the crudest rituals. It is a mental torture I find debasing . . . I simply cannot get used to the nightly betrayal of reason, humanity, genius. No matter how great my weariness, the wrench of parting with consciousness is unspeakably repulsive to me. I loathe Somnus, that black-masked headsman binding me to the block." Which didn't keep him from doting on the great value of the "white birds of dreams" and nightmares "full of wanderings and escapes, and desolate station platforms."

Nabokov dreamed, consciously eschewing any possible interpretation of the Freudian ("that Viennese quack") variety, founded on the symbolic and interpretable at one's will and pleasure: "I think he's crude. I think he's medieval and I don't want an elderly gentleman from Vienna with an umbrella inflicting his dreams upon me. I don't have the dreams that he discusses in his books. I don't see umbrellas in my dreams, or balloons."

"Another thing we are not supposed to do is to explain the inexplicable. Men have learned to live with a black burden, a huge aching hump: the supposition that 'reality' may be only a 'dream.' How much more dreadful it would be if the very awareness of your being aware of reality's dreamlike nature were also a dream, a built-in hallucination! One should bear in mind, however, that there is no mirage without a vanishing point, just as there is no lake without a closed circle of reliable land . . . How can one treat dreams, unless one is a quack?" he wonders in *Transparent Things*.

And Nabokov claimed all dreams were clear and diaphanous in their intentions and meaning. And each vision could be instantaneously narrated and understood in its context: "I cannot conceive how anybody in his right mind should go to a psychoanalyst, but of course if one's mind is deranged one might try anything: after all, quacks and cranks, shamans and holy men, kings and hypnotists have cured people—especially hysterical people. Our grandsons no doubt will regard today's psychoanalysts with the same amused contempt as we do astrology and phrenology. One of the greatest pieces of charlatanic, and satanic, nonsense imposed on a gullible public is the Freudian interpretation of dreams. I take gleeful pleasure every morning in refuting the Viennese quack by recalling and explaining the details of my dreams without using one single reference to sexual symbols or mythical complexes. I urge my patients to do likewise."

And, pressed by journalists on the subject, he ends up casting all Freud's descendants ("I may have aired this before but I'd like to repeat that I detest not one but four doctors: Dr. Freud, Dr. Zhivago, Dr. Schweitzer, and Dr. Castro") and their worshippers by the wayside with a "Let the credulous and the vulgar continue to believe that all mental woes can be cured by the daily application of old Greek myths to their private parts. I really do not care."

Nabokov preferred to understand the dreamed world through of a combination of good bad jokes and good aphorisms ("Youth dreams: forgot pants; old man dreams: forgot dentures" and "Genius is an African who dreams up snow" or "Images are the dreams of language"). And his interest went in the direction of understanding them as transparent narrations, like addenda to his waking work: "When about to fall asleep after a good deal of writing or reading, I often enjoy, if that is the right word, what some drug addicts experience—a continuous series of extraordinary bright, fluidly changing pictures. Their type is different nightly, but on a given night it remains the same: one night it may be a banal kaleidoscope of endlessly recombined and reshaped stained-window designs; next time comes a subhuman or superhuman face with a formidably growing blue eye; or—and this is the most striking type—I see in realistic detail a long-dead friend turning toward me and melting into another remembered figure against the black velvet of my eyelids' inner side. As to voices, I have described in *Speak, Memory* the snatches of telephone talk which now and then vibrate in my pillowed ear. Reports on those enigmatic phenomena can be found in the case histories collected by psychiatrists but no satisfying interpretation has come my way. Freudians, keep out, please! [. . .] About twice a week I have a good long nightmare with unpleasant characters imported from earlier dreams, appearing in more or less iterative surroundings—kaleidoscopic arrangements of broken impressions, fragments of day thoughts, and irresponsible mechanical images, utterly lacking any possible Freudian implication or explication, but singularly akin to the procession of changing figures that one usually sees on the inner palpebral screen with closing one's weary eyes"; to those "so-called *muscae volitantes*—shadows cast upon the retinal rods by motes in the vitreous humor, which are seen as transparent threads drifting across the visual field" and whose flitting and buzzing increases as the years pass by across that gelatinous material on the inside of the eyeball (scientific name: miodesopsias).

For Nabokov, this artistic/literary appreciation of the dreamed world did not, on the other hand, keep him from sensing and researching the possibility that dreams might have a "precognitive flavor" and might let you "catch sight of the lining of time." Time that—in dreams—can go back or forward and so sometimes you can divine the future by going back. And thus, for the composition of the section "The Texture of Time" in *Ada, or Ardor*, Nabokov studied with the passion of a convert the works of Gerald Whitrow and J. W. Dunne and established a classification of his own dreams into categories like professional and vocational; memories of the remote past; influences of present interests or current events; "of erotic tenderness" (which didn't exclude the occasional dispassionate and brutal coitus with a fat old woman); and "very clear and logical," like losing the notes for a novel, or suffering a heart attack during a lecture, or that his hotel caught fire and he saved, in order, his wife Vera, the manuscript of his novel in progress, his dentures, and his passport.

Dreams that Nabokov dreams and writes down between October 1964 and January 1965: he dreams he's listening to his father deliver a speech and he clears his throat too forcefully and noisily and his father reproaches him saying, "Even if you are bored you might have the decency to sit quietly"; he dreams he's dancing with "Ve" (Vera) and a stranger walks by and kisses her and he stops him and, with ecstatic fury, smashes his head, beating it against the walls of the ballroom; he dreams a stranger in a taxi criticizes, in Russian or German, the state of his clothes, and he makes excuses saying he sullied them by absentmindedly stepping in a puddle.

Near death, Nabokov began to dream of guillotines.

From *Invitation to a Beheading* (Приглашение на казнь): ". . . in my dreams the world would come alive, becoming so captivatingly majestic, free and ethereal, that afterward it would be oppressive to breathe the dust of this painted life."

"Why not leave their private sorrows to people? Is sorrow not, one asks, the only thing in the world people really possess?" wonders, suffering, sleepless, Timofei Pnin in *Pnin*.

There, Pnin (though he'd carefully planned it out, and considered his characters "galley slaves," in the end Nabokov didn't have the courage to kill him off), sleep-deprived professor skeptical of any psychoanalytic school (his ex-wife, Liza Wind, is a successful psychoanalyst), praying for the possible existence of a third side in his body after being unable to sleep on his left or his right side.

He would never see a psychoanalyst to have his sorrows interpreted, because they're perfectly clear to him.

His nocturnal terrors have the clarity of sunrises.

† A stellar moment (and not strictly literary, though very nabokovian) in

the history of literature / In 1995, in a car parked on Sunset Boulevard, the actor Hugh Grant is surprised by police in a "compromising situation" with the head of prostitute named Divine Brown in his lap. It's a major scandal: Grant—at the time—is the Americans' favorite Englishman and a charming boy and ever so amusing for daughters and mothers and aunts alike. So Grant finds himself obligated to do a tour/Via Crucis of all the many morning and evening U.S. talk shows to demonstrate his contrition and that he was as charming and stammering as always. The strategy works, but, in addition, it leads to a perfect, historical moment: when one of the TV hosts asks the actor if he's considered getting "psychological help," Grant seems surprised by the question and asks what for. The host explains "to help with your issues." To which Grant smiles one of those Hugh smiles and diagnoses: "Ah . . . But in Great Britain, we have novels for that kind of thing . . . Seriously."

Once, so long or not so long ago, either way, a young publisher had suggested he open one of his books with the following *Author's Note*: "All of this is true."

And he (who always remembered those ironic quotes from Mark Twain, already suffering these tensions between fiction and nonfiction regarding the perception of his work, when he stated that "Truth is the most valuable thing we have. Let us economize it" and that "The only difference between reality and fiction is that fiction needs to be credible" and that "When in doubt tell the truth" and that "When I was younger I could remember anything, whether it happened or not; but my faculties are decaying, now, and soon I shall be so I cannot remember any but the latter") had thought about it, but clearly understanding and clearly reading the fine print in the clause. What untrained eyes, even those of his editor, didn't know how to perceive: that something was *true* didn't necessarily imply that it was something *real*. It was true because, simply, that particular fiction was now an inseparable part of a reality that, on the other hand and according to the latest research, wasn't all that real itself; because it was the brain that was in charge of editing it and intuiting it and completing it when data and details were missing).

That fiction existed and projected itself into the future and would be true every time someone read it and it operated like a bomb of profundity, sending the solid structure of the present flying through the air.

But, of course, there are two kinds of liars: writers and publishers.

The former emit lies, the latter omit truths. Beyond the chosen model, sooner rather than later, more before than after, we all turn into true liars. Into redactors or crosser-outers. We lie to everyone else, to ourselves. We lie first to be able to believe in something after, whatever it is. And thus, when we believe the lies of others, we finally gain access to that consoling privilege of being the best we could ever be: we leave behind the hell or purgatory of being writers or publishers to ascend to the heaven of being readers.


And, yes, those were times when *what was true* had been elevated to the genre of fiction. And when everyone—readers and writers and critics—went around fascinated by the idea of the autobiographical as added value and commercial attraction and topic of conversation in literary supplements and on late-night talk shows.

The young publisher had proposed—once more—that he "do something with his parents . . . but you have to show yourself as being more traumatized than how you've shown yourself so far. Maybe you should start out by saying you've only recently felt the impact of all of that and, along the way, tie it together with what happened with your nephew and your sister and . . ."

To which he'd made the counteroffer of a "story of my life vis-à-vis my library, that place where a writer is born and lives and writes." An exposition of the character of literature as a feature of the characters of literature. He'd even had a title that seemed to him quite good: *Something of that Style*.

But no.

That wasn't interesting. The book market wasn't interested in a book about books.

It asked for something else: written life but not the life of a writer.

Literature of the I, metafiction, *based on a true story* (that notice that often flashed at the beginning of certain sickening movies starring sick people, always up for an Oscar), jumping to the first pages of the "Int. Book. Night: We see somebody open a novel and sigh and smile with satisfaction. And close it never to open it again because they'll be too busy living." What were the precise dimensions? Where was the appropriate border? He thought there was only one: that the irreal reality of a novel surpass the irreal reality of life. That the "Once upon a time . . ." win out over the "There was a time . . ." and turn it into an eternal "This time . . ." every time you entered into that book. Therefore and for that reason, today you never forget the characters who occupied the salons Marcel Proust and Henry James passed through and you have no idea who inspired them. But, of course, such an effect wasn't so easily achieved. The wrapping paper was more important than the gift. Yes: fiction was of increasingly less interest if it didn't come backed by the autobiographical, by that virus incubated on so many blogs and social networks that it'd leapt into literature—or what was called literature—to submit it to its will with the kind of affection used to command a dog to fetch a stick. Over and over again. Recounting, then, the lives of dogs, chewed on by the kind of puppies that bark but do not bite; by domestic dachshunds that dream of being palace mastiffs. Why force yourself to be a writer when it's so much easier to be a character? Thus, always, like in those fictions: choose your own adventure; choose yourself above all and all others; be your own adventure, brave adventurer.

Ah-ha: so the phenomenon of current sales was just another installment in the epic—common and banal but detailed down to the absurdly microscopic—of the life of a Norwegian or German author (in his day it'd been the frigid fever for those Scandinavian thrillers, where everyone is always taking pills to sleep or commit suicide and the grandfather was always an ex-collaborator with the Third Reich who, though he was loving with his grandchildren, continued worshipping swastika flags on the sly, in his secret basement, behind the Finnish sauna) whose name he could never type right because he never knew which *ctrl/alt* corresponded to that small accent in the shape of a circle that goes above the vowels of icy surnames or brands of ice cream. The bestseller of the moment by Sieg or by Heil was exclusively devoted—after telling everything there was to tell about his exterior—to narrating the interior of the body of the author in the parasitic voice of *Taenia saginata* (a.k.a) Tapeworm, eighteen meters long and placidly and reflexively installed in the small intestine of Jussi or Inger, who did nothing but watch TV series, attributing to them almost mystical properties. The opening sentence of the novel was "You can call me Wörm." And the novel—1,001 pages—was titled *Here Inside*. And it'd been described as "a collaboration between Melville, Proust, and Joyce, but under the supervision of Tolstoy, James, and Mann. And also Kafka" in the blurb on its cover.

The one responsible for such praise had been none other than the courtly and scheming writer whom he'd rechristened with the name of a popular global Swedish corporation that sold furniture and decorative objects to be, DIY, assembled and disassembled with names even more ridiculous than Cirque du Soleil spectacles.

IKEA: his forever-young golem whom, early on, he'd launched into the world with an absurdly generous blurb (that had nothing to do with the word, אמת, *truth*, which that Rabbi had written on the clay forehead of that creature) and that now he couldn't erase from the forehead of the monster to deactivate it. Someone—a critic of certain renown whose only strategic error (it tends to happen to the best of his species) had been to publish an atrocious novel that ran contrary to all his prior opinions—had commented to him that IKEA "was to the office of writer what someone had said Ronald Reagan was to the art of politics: 'He is the most profoundly superficial man I have ever met.'" (Similarly, to tell the truth, that same critic had written about him that "Reading him, I'm never entirely sure if what I'm dealing with is the stupidest genius or the most ingenious stupidity. Probably both.")

IKEA would never be a *writer's writer* because he was a *reader's writer*: he fascinated and seduced his followers and made them feel intelligent and refined and sensitive and like such . . . *readers*. He was sure IKEA had never inspired anyone to be a writer, but many to want to produce in others that feeling IKEA made them feel: that he was talking to them and showing them the path of the most commonplace clichés. Them and only them. Like someone offering a magic slap or a pinch with a trick: you think I'm only thinking of you, but I only want you not to think that I think that the only thing that interests me is that you only think of me.

IKEA was succeeding again—a now automatic success, no matter what he offered up—with a collection of superegotistical stories where, in each and every one of them, he claimed to recall what, swathed in his naked-emperor suit, he thought during the brief trajectory from seat and/or table to stage/lectern. The podium where he accepted each and every one of his international awards, in memory of his maestros, in general, titans of the nineteenth and first half of the twentieth century.

The book had one of those superb titles that IKEA was so good at coming up with and that so pleased his medium-rare readers, prostrate and kneeling before his writing by letters, the equivalent of drawing by numbers: *Gifts Received*. To which IKEA had already announced—awards and speeches and reflections would surely not be lacking—the follow-ups *Gifts Returned* and *Gifts Lost*, because he was interested in "the broad concept of the panoramic trilogy."

Another of his novels/museums that'd convinced itself—and was so convincing to simple souls—it was the Louvre or the Hermitage, but really was nothing more than a provincial museum in the hands of a guide with a memorized but never memorable speech, so anxious to be reclassified from servile employee to serviceable work of art.

Even IKEA's book he liked best—or felt the most affection for, no need to exaggerate—had been a product of that ambition of wanting everything for himself and nothing for anyone else. Indignant at not having an exploitable ancestor who'd suffered the torments of a concentration camp, amid a burst of successful Nazi-themed nonfiction novels at the beginning of the millennium by writers of his generation, IKEA had delivered a masterstroke: to write a Nazi novel set in a concentration camp, telling of the misery of his hypothetical *descendent*. Lacking a grandfather, a great-grandson would do; and what'd been denied him yesterday, IKEA would uproot tomorrow. In the novel, everything took place in a future world that—as a result of a never-entirely-explained entropic cataclysm—had gone back, from a technological perspective, to the middle of the twentieth century. Ergo, *Renaizzance* (for once an austere and even somewhat ingenious title) was a "historical novel of anticipation." A book that—to his astonishment and horror, as a first-hand and incredulous witness; it was clear that IKEA was a blessed being for whom everything he did so badly turned out so well—had gained IKEA the theretofore inconceivable affection of the fans of Philip K. Dick and the acquisition of the film rights by a disciple of Steven Spielberg.

And at one of those parties where he always operated in the modality of Birdie Num Num, the far more functional and impeccable IKEA, for once having had a few too many, had given him advice and he'd listened with that courtesy that's nothing but a kind of masochism: "Why don't you write something with the SS? It never goes out of style, man . . . Their uniforms are perfect. The Nazi thing shelters you. And the critics love it. They have to. If you feel like you're missing something, add a Jew, if possible a Cabbalist, weeping in the snow. And a young, blonde-haired, blue-eyed Jewish girl; if she's a librarian, all the better. It helps if the Nazi officer is sensitive and a lover of art and knows how to play the piano that he always finds, intact, in a bombed-out house. And that solves everything, man. Though I am already imagining that you wouldn't be able to control yourself, obviously; and that you would end up devoting pages and pages to musing about the difference between the Nazi salute with the whole arm straight and extended and that other Nazi salute, as if less formal and in passing and slightly apathetic and brief and flexing the arm and . . ."

And in this—at the moment of truth and above and beyond any talent or nonsense, plot over style, for IKEA writing was the craft of telling, whereas he thought writing was what he was telling—he was right.

Nights before, in a hotel bed, a random sentence had occurred to him. A few lines where he began talking about the nature of secrets; he compared them to skeletons in the closet, and from there, they mutated into fur coats nobody used for climatic reasons, but, all the same, you had to show off and sweat in in order to be somebody. He didn't know what to do with that, he wasn't even sure he would ever use it. But he'd been happy thinking about it. He'd experienced a kind of happiness that IKEA would never experience and that, if he did, for IKEA would be something like the saddest of horrors. In IKEA's novels, secrets were kept or told and coats were worn and skeletons were the bones of History's martyrs to be unearthed and done right by. In IKEA's novels, closets only served to store jackets that a hero "pulled on in a flash" to then "turned on his heel" and went out into the street to confront "reality."

Yes, reality—what was real—had turned into a *per se* currency he couldn't trade in; because he'd always understood that, in literature, it didn't matter what was real and what was not and that it did matter what was well written and what was not. And, for him, that went beyond all formats and styles and subjects.

But, oh, not only did he know IKEA.

IKEA *also* knew *him* perfectly, he had to admit it.

IKEA—by opposition—was aware of each and every one of his flaws. And so he let out an almost-admiring little laugh as IKEA continued: "For a while now, there's also the whole Muslim and fundamentalist thing. But better, just in case, to wait a while: it's still somewhat dangerous and better for others to risk themselves first. And, if they get killed, then yes, something very you, very much your style: to write about them, about the martyrs. Something choral, symphonic, and polyphonic, with the voices of the victims of an attack intermingling, one of those voices like that of a boy who goes to an expensive school, and another that of a Latin American immigrant, and another that of a countercultural film director nobody ever contradicts, things like that. And have it all be one very long sentence without periods or capital letters. I'm sure it would go well—I leave it to you . . . And, if all that fails, you could always say the magic word: 'soccer.' Nothing pleases readers of one book per year more than when writers talk and write and theorize about soccer. It brings them closer, makes you feel closer to them. And I know: you're not interested in soccer, of course. But you should get interested in something besides literature if you want to be a well-known and successful writer, man. Writing is not the most important thing. The important thing is *to be* a writer . . . Or put better: *to play a writer* . . . There you have the case of your little sister . . . But enough sermons, let's talk about important things, and, ha, I forgot to warn you: in my next book, I'm going to use all those lists of yours about the past, okay? . . . And since we're talking about my books: what did you think of my latest?"

What did he think of it? Good question. But a better and more intriguing question was, why couldn't he stop reading them? Could it be because it *seemed* to him, yes, that they were a monstrous and far better-known appendix of his own increasingly secret body of work? The supposedly presentable and popular part of that gelatinous thing in the attic with tentacles and many eyes that was his body of work. Because it was clear that, in a way, he felt responsible and guilty for and about IKEA. After all, he'd acted as his introducer, he'd brought him into the world, he'd dropped him like a blessed curse into bookstores.

There were nights when—back when he still slept—he dreamed that he killed him. That he put an end to his life and his work and that—this was the sweetest part of that sleeping fantasy—IKEA didn't leave behind any unpublished or unfinished manuscripts. Nothing. IKEA was finished. IKEA did not continue. The surprises and constants were done. Because *Renaizzance*—and the possibility that IKEA would be transformed into a guru of alternate history—had been an unforeseen hiatus in what'd subsequently returned to normality.

And so, *ritornello* karaoke-clon-bim-bam-boom of the always ravishing and prize-winnable and ready-for-export latinolympic novel with the family saga of political convulsions and sensitive protagonist narrator, tortured by the spasms of his homeland. "My mission as a writer is to explore the most unfrequented folds of the evanescent history of my country and how they come together in my own painful personal experience," IKEA often repeated in articles and presentations, pupils rolled to the heavens like a saint. Never clarifying what it was that was "painful" about his life, but evoking all of it, if possible, from the distance of some comfortable *hôtel particulier* (adjective that reflects and automatically makes him think of that particular accelerator he wanted to make particularly his) in some comfortable European town, between literary festivals.

And, yes, that was the heart of the matter for him: IKEA wrote for *several* hours *every* day without rest. IKEA was a perpetual motion motor, a machine fine-tuned to produce atrocious novels, in days when quantity was part of quality and a continuous presence in the media (if possible photographing yourself in the company of authorities of varying nature and polarity) guaranteed you the respect and admiration of those who didn't read but did buy books and had your name always on the tips of their tongues in case someone were to ask them what the most unforgettable read on their last vacation had been.

And maybe, who knows, IKEA had been a great narrator before being a great writer: someone who didn't know how to write but did know how to narrate, who knows, who was he—someone with books that narrated less and less—to say.

Thus, IKEA, shipping express and certified. *The Benefits of Evil, The Law of the Stage* (collected plays), *Sedentary Movement, Charon's Bribe, Substantive*

*Verbs* (compilation of his "interventions" in the press), *Configuration of Lives,
Stadiums of Rage* (his inevitable soccer novel) and the, for him, undisputed
favorite when it came to marbled-bronzed nonsense: *Crepuscular Pendulum.*

And yes, once—bowled over by IKEA's commercial success and critical
acclaim—he'd even tried to write a novel *like that.*

To write from memory and making memory.

To cling to the warmth of an up-and-running and assimilated tradition.

To be an authentically *traditional* writer and to amble along atop all the
clichés. To be the equivalent of those first black actors in white people's
films: a black man in blackface, all the time chewing fried chicken and spitting watermelon seeds and all the time saying *mistah mistah* and hooting
with goofy laughs and dancing with curly-haired girls, while the plantation
mistresses look on with feverish and sinful eyes. To be a slave, happy to be
exploited and to give thanks to your masters.

To write a book that—as Henry James had written in a disconsolate letter—set out to put the intentions of someone pure and starving for the love
of art in their marble tower in communion with what the villagers—so hardy,
their pantries overflowing with food to share—needed. And to produce that,
according to James, nourishing "friction with the market" that pleased and
sated the artist and his audience. Something that everyone liked and that was
what everyone expected of him, based on his geographical origin and historical situation. To be good in the most amiable sense of the word, with an
immense and baroque continental and political novel brimming with *Lonely
Planet* exoticism. With many bizarre fruits and dishes like *limón de verga* and
*chumuchuque ganso* and *budín volador* served up on flying saucers, implacable
yet patriotic brothel madams with names like *Pantaleta de Bombacha*, local
dances like *El Terremoto Florido* or *La Pingüina Acalorada*, sweet and compla-
cent cousins with nicknames like *La Renguita Coloradita Bizquita Culoncita*,
and stuff like that. All to delight the readers of a First World where none of
those hideous things, which, out of delicacy and piety, were called "magic"
though they were sordidly "realistic," ever happened.

He even had a title he considered Machiavellianly perfect, regional and
international at the same time. A title that, no doubt, IKEA would've envied:
*Minotaur Rumba.* (He'd even considered making it stronger by calling it
*Minotaur Rumbita*, since diminutives added a certain tropical flavor to the

cover: but he didn't want to complicate the lives of his hypothetical yet inevitable translators either, he thought.)

There, in *Minotaur Rumba*, the perfect fusion of the mythic and the salacious. And the barely subliminal idea—always so enticing to Europeans and Americans—that Latin America is the most winding and perhaps redeeming and adventurous of labyrinths in which to rumba. But, of course (like Henry James in his day, so many times, too many times), he'd failed. Because then, in *Minotaur Rumba*, his dictator was overcome by some irresistible urge to leave it all behind. And he gave up his bloody throne to make his real dream come true: to go to Barcelona to become a writer of the Boom and to succeed. "Is there anything better than a novel with a dictator? Of course there is: a novelist dictator!" the enlightened and delusional despot asked and answered himself. And, of course, events precipitated when he initiated a fiery relationship with a fluorescent beauty of the *gauche divine* who'd been Kurt Vonnegut's lover and John Cheever's student in Iowa. And there were also appearances by Francis Bacon and the voluntarily auto-insomniac Warren Zevon, during his stint in Spain, refusing to sleep until he died, raising his glass, and saying that thing about "We love to buy books because we believe we're buying the time to read them" back in days when people still read a lot and read slowly, and time expanded with a book in your hand instead of shrinking on a screen, because writers wrote books to give the gift of different lives and distinct deaths. And bars opened never to close serving drinks named after novelists and the color of ink. And you could hear a tribe of exiled *coya* assassins, playing protest songs with *quenas* and *charangos* in the metro. Yes, everything fit in there (though he'd forgotten to include a Nazi). Baroque rococo. And one chapter in the book would reveal, at last, the impassioned and mysterious reason why Marito punched Gabo in Mexico; it hadn't been over a woman or anything like that, but, rather, over reams of blank pages: an idea for a fucking story both considered their own but couldn't write.

*Minotaur Rumba* would include that story as a kind of appendix, written, in the end, by the ex-tyrant, disoriented by mystical visions, like a quasi-castaway on the beaches of the Costa Brava, who ends up dying in the arms of a recently arrived young Chilean or Mexican writer to whom he bequeathed the legacy of the revelations of his exegesis and whom he obliged to continue his mission. But in the next chapter it would be discovered that the entire preceding episode was nothing more than the dream of the protagonist (yes, at one time his characters had the capacity to dream, which he no longer has, and he clung to the remnants of those dreams with fingernails and eyelids, eyelids being the fingernails of the eyes), who then woke up, disenchanted, in his charming Eixample flat. And, tired of being rejected by the local *gauche divine*, he understood that his thing would always be the far right. And so he returned, resentful and furious, to his homeland. And there accepted his fate as dictator and gave everyone a new kind of boom. And his first step was to build a bonfire and burn all the manuscripts of local writers, many of them, it must be said, so bad.

And, of course, soon, almost immediately, alas, that book had already become another of his books, another book like all his previous books. A book that, nevertheless, he'd opted not to publish and to store in his file of potential posthumous materials that was turned to smoke in a possibly purifying fire (or so he'd convinced himself), the work and action of his sister. Penelope, the madwoman from the mad family, burning it all down in a gothic frenzy just before she was committed for life and who, in the end, years after that fire, burned too.

A crazy nun who'd known Penelope in another life, Maxi's sister, had followed and pursued her for years with a *Les Miserables* plan. And had caught her at last at that "wellness monastery" where Penelope had been committed. And the crazy nun, crazier than his sister, had set fire to all of it. And there, Penelope had died and been reincarnated as a literary legend. The theretofore bestselling author had ascended, living dead and beneficially malleable, to a subject of academic study, on the basis of, inevitably, "the real story behind her imagined stories." And, paradoxically and ironically, Penelope had become his benefactor, transforming him—by blood and inheritance—into her literary executor.

And so, his life was now solved and his body of work had no solution. At last, and in the most unexpected way, Penelope had become, for him, a kind of ambiguous and fraternal Medici. A strange Medici whose intentions weren't entirely about the love of art, but a Medici all the same. A patron for him, someone who—throughout his spasmodic career, in the sharing out of possible favors and assistance for his work—had previously always ended up with Borgias: freaks like ScreaMime calling on him for a demented project whose only purpose was to legitimize them as artistic personalities and who always ended up disappearing or killing each other without ever paying him his due; always knowing that nothing would come of it, that nobody would take his complaints all that seriously, because in the end he was the most unstable element of all.

So it'd gone for him: his establishment elders and his contemporaries fighting and hunting for their spot in the safari had always approached him with caution.

And so, better, just in case, to reject him, to remove him from the picture; because he always came out of focus, making noise.

The successive and ever younger litters of supposed avant-gardists respected him, yes, but always at a safe distance, on the other side of the iron bars and obeying that sign that instructed them not to feed the beast that, it warned, if you're not careful, could rip open your chest and eat your heart raw. Yes, he was, always, like an organ rejected when the time came for the transplant or like one of those cysts it's better to excise quickly for fear of metastasis. He was toxic. He had a great sense of humor. And his gifts (or *dones* in Spanish, which he sometimes referred to as his "ding-*dones*," because they had something ringing and annoying about them) turned out to be impossible to ever take full advantage of. His impact had been his influence, but it was an influence that went unacknowledged. No: he was not an influencer. And his virtues made apparent the flaws of others and his social ability was comparable to his physical clumsiness. "You're a genius, but you're not especially flexible," he'd once been told, somewhere between compliment and insult, by a powerful and superb literary agent. And, ever since, he pronounces that word "flexible" silently to himself, as if it were a singing insect, its brittle body lodged in his tone-deaf throat.

Anything he'd ever said in any important, career-related meeting had always sounded like a plummeting, free falling "Whoops!" Never like a "Click!"

Yes, no: he would've never been nicknamed LEGO.

No, yes: unlike IKEA (and, who would imagine, unlike Penelope), he hadn't been given any power. Or he'd been given rare abilities. Abilities that didn't include social networking or interweaving of webs of acquaintances or herding the names of others into his own corral like prize-winning cattle to make them his own.

IKEA collected names and liked to name them. IKEA liked dropping names. For IKEA, names of celebrities were battering rams (while for him, those same names were shields, defense mechanisms, surnames behind which to take refuge or defend himself, like that arm in the Nabokov coat of arms, saber aloft, like someone fencing with a pen, and the motto *Za hrabrost*: "with valor." What would the motto on his coat of arms be? Ah, yes: *Cut & Paste*). And so, IKEA had attained the highest pinnacle, supported by easy-to-assemble books he promoted with a sort of hypnotic speech, learned in some self-help course and whose strategy was to ceaselessly drop cosmic names and then append his own name and work to them. IKEA was a devoted influencee of influencers, producing the increasingly common misconception among the increasingly naïve and credulous that the influencer somehow ectoplasmically selects the person who claims their influence. Thus, then, IKEA stimulating the confusion by designating himself someone's disciple without granting said master the right of reply (unless by means of a successful séance session) was more or less the same as being their disciple and protégé. And this is how IKEA talked: "I blah-blah Chekhov blah-blah-blah Flaubert blah-blah Gabo (never García Márquez) blah blah blah-blah-blah Kafka blah-blah blah Borges blah Cervantes blah me." And one time at a roundtable they shared—when Penelope's success had already transcended all borders and to his complete astonishment—he even spouted off an "I blah-blah-blah the sister of this man I have sitting next to me."

Had IKEA really read all those names he ceaselessly invoked? A quick and instinctive answer would be no, impossible, absolutely not. But he wasn't so sure: it's known that exposure to the radiations of genius can traumatize or paralyze the more or less talented, but, paradoxically, have a stimulating effect on the mediocre. That's why, for every genius, there's an average of a thousand mediocre artists. In any case—there, auto-fictionalized but non-fictitious, in *Gifts Received*—what did IKEA think about, along his short walk up to harvest and give thanks for, with a stoic pride, more laurels? Easy, the same thing as before: about many more names. About many important names, about a synthetic collection of anecdotes, about cultural sketches, about summaries, easy to comment on and repeat via Google and the like, IKEA as a sort of master of ceremonies reigning over all of it. IKEA like the host and owner and decorator of a house with a library to be put together according to his instructions. Because IKEA had discovered very early on that saying "Shakespeare" repeatedly brought him closer, by association, to Shakespeare in the ears and eyes of readers, increasingly wild and anxious to feel cultured with the least possible effort. IKEA was that guy who had the courage and the nerve to publically claim "I was influenced by Shakespeare" (when anybody with an iota of intelligence knew Shakespeare had influenced nobody, yet at the same time, he'd influenced everybody, down to the illiterate man who monologues and begs for alms on his knees in the metro station) and to keep on smiling as if it were nothing. IKEA was the guy who said he was "indebted to all of them," but, far from that leaving him bankrupt, he'd gotten rich by osmosis, insinuating himself into the picture, with almost hypnotic insistence in front of judges and among critics, both increasingly open to suggestion and domestication. In the beginning, he'd been deeply outraged by the succession of crowns and medals on IKEA's head and chest. But as time went by, he'd come to take it as a kind of perverse consolation: the fact that IKEA was considered the greatest and the best did nothing but offer irrefutable evidence he inhabited an idiotic world that didn't belong to him and that, as such, didn't recognize him as anything more than a poetic mirage or a scientific disturbance. "The person who writes for fools is always sure of a large audience," postulated the energetic pessimist Schopenhauer who, of course, had a great number of repeaters of that quote (him included) who clung to the comfort of the mathematics, automatic as it was imprecise, of writing for a very limited but very intelligent few, those few for whom it was still worth the sorrow and the joy, because there weren't many specimens of that race left in the world. Or to live convinced that his kingdom was not of this world while dragging behind him the cross and the glory of an unknown masterpiece. From such certainty, it was only one step to leap into the territory of quantum physics, of multiple dimensions, of glimpsing other planes of existence where he was a sort of messiah of letters (hours ago he'd already fantasized deliriously about a global success for his latest book hoping it would make the night pass faster) while IKEA had been ripped to shreds by mobs and blogs of unpublished hyenas just arriving to the "publishing community" and living in the Age of the Professionalized Amateur.

Beyond all the foregoing, what *had* been most shocking and outrageous for him was the fact that IKEA had even figured out how to dodge the mud-slinging and condemnations of younger writers. IKEA had managed to deactivate the explosive charges of those who, supposedly, had the obligation to publically spurn him, if not like a father then at least like an unbearable older brother or a strutting and plumed cousin with too much good luck. But no. They weren't up to the task of hounding and taking him down. Rather, sometimes, just the opposite. Unlike him (who, in the early years of his career had confronted, with loving respect and humble admiration, the Saturnian titans who'd come before him, because that was his role and what he had to do, in order to, soon thereafter, be chewed up in turn by his contemporaries and successors), now the new crops only wanted to be like IKEA. The times were different. The times were times of not wasting time on generational literary squabbles like in his youth. Then, sound and fury and mockery and refounding spirit. But, so when IKEA had come up, there was no flock of flaming angels in his vicinity demanding his expulsion and fall from the heights and the demolition of his kingdom. Just the opposite. They wanted his prizes, his sales, his translations, his invitations to festivals and talks, his women, his fans. His, yes, ductility (IKEA had taken lessons in tango and kabuki theater and bungee jumping or any other activity typical of the countries to which he was always traveling for long and messy festival nights), his radio-host voice (classes in phonetics and allocution), and his look (always before one of those sessions of those photographs in which, invariably, he appeared looking out at a flaming horizon, wearing a Montgomery jacket with the collar popped), including a romantic beard and leonine mane that, it was said, was the product of periodically injecting himself with very expensive doses of the glands of baby panda bears.

IKEA's persona was to the "concept" of the young continental novelist what Derek Zoolander was to a certain type of eighties-nineties supermodel. Or, at most, in his raptures of free sincerity, one of those sympathetic amoral characters from certain Coen brothers films. Or, in his best and most courteous moments, like the social-climbing and troublemaking Eve Harrington in *All About Eve*. (And, oh, how antiquated and archaic all his pop references were now; he, who once had been distinguished and categorized for being, precisely, someone always on the avant-garde and/or beloved child of his time, was now an orphan of a time that, to top it off, didn't acknowledge and had disowned him.) IKEA like a kind of parody that transforms into what it's parodying to the point where it acquires the same respectability as the original but without being aware (and making it so *nobody* is aware of its imitation and considers it authentic) that it's a falsification. Blue Steel. Magnum. New Boom. IKEA was the diet simplification of something substantial and complex, but, even still, on sale and fat free, supposedly nutritious and rich in vitamins. IKEA was to classic literature what *Amadeus* was to W. A. Mozart. And so IKEA, on the other hand, now enjoyed the timelessness of the dead, of what's fixed forever in a time and place, and thus evoked intact, impeccable, portrayed in the colors saints are painted on cathedral ceilings. That's why, again, the young writers opted—better, just in case—to deny the omnipresent IKEA. To not even mention and much less condemn him, except in private after too much drugs; thus turning his name and brand into something deafening by omission, like someone avoiding the pronunciation of a forbidden spell for fear of reprisals, never aware of the obvious and maybe even more painful radiations of its echo. They didn't even, just in case, allude to the names or the books by IKEA's innumerable and classic "masters." The only names those up-and-coming and cool-inked kids cared about were their own and those of their closest contemporaries and, in general, friends from anthologies. The new young writers were, at that time, like creationists: for them, the history of literature began just five or at most ten years before their own appearance on the scene. And man had coexisted with simians since the dawn of time. That's why they opted to insult each other behind the scenes and among themselves and, also, in the process, murder him in the foyer. He, after all, had "discovered" IKEA and, besides, he'd become a kind of multiuse target, always ripe for reflexive mockery and automatic discredit. He was the symbol of a rotten time, they said. He was the product of the bad practices and various corruptions of the publishing world. He was someone who, in his day, in those amoral times, people read to, better, avoid seeing what was happening outside his books. He, with perspective, amounted to a distracting distraction and was accused of never having been concerned with reality and with "his time." There abounded, yes, writers who time and again declared themselves committed to society, from the comfort of newspaper columns and roundtables; and, no doubt, some of them must have dedicated hours to charity work and donated part of their royalties to charitable organizations and participated in literacy programs in low-income communities; but he'd never met any of them. Even still, he'd invented a character/personality double who responded in secret to the name Anito (simultaneously a play on Orphan Annie—because he was an orphan—and the diminutive of the Spanish word for anus) and who every now and then burst out with clichés and slogans and even sobs for his "missing in action," *desaparecidos* parents, and spontaneous performances of protest hymns/songs of the Latin American left, to the initial confusion and subsequent indignation of attendees of literary festivals and viewers of TV shows that aired at three in the morning.

And, yes, of course, his accusers had justification, all the justification not in the world but yes in their politically correct world: he—like so many others before him—had become a writer in order to read. To work with the stuff of dreams where what time it was never mattered; to get as far away as possible from his now nonexistent country of origin and city of birth, a city that now, according to footage captured by drones drifting overhead, lost in the sky, had been transformed into Venice-like wreckage, sunk to its knees in the sweaty stew of global warming. Nothing mattered less to him than reality, because, in his opinion, reality was always poorly written.

And what had become of IKEA—favorite of right-minded readers—after all of that, after his particular Swiss-quantum-accelerated episode? Shortly after publishing his prize-winning collection of stories about his prizes, IKEA had left his second wife: an actress/model, but, fundamentally, more / than actress or model. IKEA's first wife, having efficiently fulfilled—following the lineaments of the women of the Boom—her role as secretary/ mother/groupie (here the / were nothing more than that), was cast aside after acquiring a figure of the kind frequently referred to as Rubenesque, and then came a *chanteuse* who subsequently made herself a multimillionaire with impassioned torch songs dedicated to her ex, deploying a functional blend of affection and spite. Number 3 was, inevitably, a writer of bestsellers, but *risqué* bestsellers, who'd made the jump from her city of origin to American campuses and to New York vernissages with "installations" where she reproduced the crimes of Charlie Manson's girls using Barbie dolls, things like that (and, ah, from The Intruder's house, again that song and those screams and that electricity and sliding down and reaching the bottom and going back up to the top to slide down again). A perennial girl who didn't hesitate to state, with a deep voice and a sharp smile, things like "There are nights when the phosphorescent and irradiated and radioactive Amazonic ovarian tumors of Clarice (referring, of course, to Clarice Lispector) visit me in my studio . . . And they dictate to me . . . And I listen to them. . . And I take notes . . . And later I perfect and make what they told me my own" or "I also directed my own adaptation of *Equus* in which all the actors were horses, real horses" or "My stories are transgressive, but seriously trangressive: while everyone writes stories about fathers who sleep with their daughters, I write stories about grandfathers who sleep with their granddaughters."

The funny thing is that he'd known her. He knew her. Her. From back in that time that, with the passing of years, he defines as *before*, to avoid going into uncomfortable details like dates and places that many would rather forget and, if they can't, at least deny. But he couldn't deny anything; because—again, no one made him—he'd left behind incriminating written testimony and proof. On the jacket of a book. Between quotation marks that, sometimes, seem like two little hands trying to strangle that sentence you should have never thought and much less handed over, hmm, *disinterestedly*. But he'd done it, knowing perfectly well that writers never do anything disinterestedly. Writers don't work *like that*. Vocational training and occupational hazard. Writers—at least writers like him—did everything *interestedly*, because they were interested in everything, if only a little bit. And they considered even that little bit to be worthy of consideration, as if they were reading first and writing after, wondering if there was *something* there, in the lives of others, that might wind up being useful to them in their own work. Besides, she had a sublime ass. An interesting ass. Very much so. One of those asses you couldn't stop reading in order to describe later. And he'd *also* been responsible in large part for her literary breakout. Hers and her ass's. He, during his fifteen pages of fame, improvised an ingenious line for the promotion of the first book of that girl who was still just a girl and far too pretty. There she was: always slipped into short dresses that seemed to have been spray-painted on her body, in the center of one of those many centrifugal parties he was known to frequent back then, on his most famous nights (he'd always known she was very good at what she did, which wasn't the same as saying what she did was very good or that it had anything to do with literature). And years later, he'd been almost raped by her in a disturbing episode/performance in an emergency clinic. And, yes, he'd named her IKEA *too*. To complete the game, to keep playing, all alone. And he couldn't help but admire the ways reality sometimes figured out how to be so invented and inventive.

IKEA & IKEA were now IKEAS, and they were even exploring the possibility of starring in "the first highbrow reality show." He'd received a two-way call from his agent and his publisher to ask if it might not be "interesting" to "contact" IKEAS and "suggest" they included him as a "guest appearance" on the show. Perhaps for a touch of "tragicomic relief" or as an "anti-antihero": the one who was "there when they were born," now surpassed by his disciples.

He'd enjoyed lying and repeating that Zen proverb about how "if the master isn't surpassed by his pupils then he never was a master." But those two weren't his followers. No: IKEAS didn't follow anybody but themselves and they were a couple of chasers of everything, a couple of clowns clowning. And he'd felt an odd blend of indignation-disgust-uncertainty-what-if and promised his publisher and agent, to calm them down, "to give it some serious thought."

And just when he prophesized that the fusion of both monsters into one two-headed monster would give birth to the inevitable Antichrist of continental literature (Little Big Supersize Mega Maximum IKEA), IKEAS had traveled to a bend in the Amazon on the dime of some magazine, to star in a fashion production (to publicize a book they'd written together; a massive "X-rated-magical-realist" novel with immortal generals and single-breasted nymphomaniac warriors addicted to hallucinogenic piranha eggs) and they were caught in the middle of one of those sporadic uprisings where the local natives get tired of being photographed and having their souls stolen.

And all trace of IKEAS had been lost.

It was assumed they'd been devoured by cannibals and digested and transformed into a pinch of dust floating in the wind of golden and emerald jungles. But he preferred to imagine them—like at the end of that Edwardian novel—condemned to, for the rest of their days, read the complete works of Dickens to the natives. And to see if, in that way, at last, they learned something (the two of them, not the natives) and, no, better not: better to have IKEAS reading themselves to each other, but saying "Dickens has had a big influence on us."

And then—as Auden said of Yeats—IKEAS "became their admirers." And IKEAS's admirers—as admirers of phenomena unworthy of any admiration tend to be—didn't take long to head off in search of something alive and current to admire.

Whereas he, before long, realized he missed them.

So much.

Too much.

All of that was true *too*.

It was also true that he owed them something. Or that, at least, their debt to him (was there anything easier and quicker to process than a vacuum-packed literary blurb?) had been thoroughly repaid.

Besides, SHE-IKEA had shot him up to volcanic heights of a rare orgasm that night when he arrived, almost dragging himself, to the emergency room, certain his heart was breaking down inside his chest. Thinking all the while of things unthinkable in that place: possible short fictions (which he wrote down in another of his notebooks) and brief capsules of nonfiction. Example: the fact that between one beat and the next, organically and technically, the heart pauses, as if doubting its pace, to then continue on doing its thing. A true *petite mort* reminding him that, throughout this long life, everything is hanging by a taut thread or a high wire, when it comes to finding a way out of the labyrinth or across the abyss. And so, for that reason, from the day of our birth and all throughout our lives, we never stop experiencing a succession of tiny deaths. A Morse code of dots between dashes, a kind of *coming soon*; an empty parentheses between a pair of colons until the cardiac rhythm begins to slow and grow more irregular and the polarities flip and finally the pause becomes a constant and the beat a pause and a stop. Meanwhile and in the meantime, he thinks, that silence that always resides between two beats amounts to the third part of the life of the heart.

To another third part: like the slept or dreamed part.

That third part that we spend with our eyes closed and our mind more open than ever and that signifies, yes, as dreamers we all always die young: more or less before reaching an average of thirty years of shut-eyed life. The age that, in his brain and in his heart, he was and would forever remain. The age he more or less was when he published his first book, which—he discussed this at some point with several colleagues, the same thing happened to all of them—is the age writers seem to be stuck at forever. Like those silhouettes imprinted on the walls among the ruins of Hiroshima and Nagasaki by the force of the radiation of the first and unforgettable time. A debut that fixes and legitimizes you and prevents you from recalling that atomic second when you ceased to be the possibility of a mechanism to become the reality of an explosion that wants to illuminate and move the world. Something you can't and don't want to forget years later. Having made mistakes, of course, but mistakes more or less paid for whenever they don't imply homicide or suicide committed in a trance, as a way to go along crossing yourself out until you wind up, like what's set out in *Transparent Things* or in the inconclusive *Original of Laura* by Vladimir Nabokov. With a lot behind you, and yet—for a while—everything before you.

Almost three decades after his public debut as a writer—decades that amount to an eternity and not a return—he was accumulating too many small mistakes that, by accumulation, add up to one enormous error, one irreparable manufacturing defect.

It was then that (though he still went to dinners where he discovered he was the only one who'd lived through, live and direct, man's arrival to the Moon or the breakup of The Beatles) the dream began to fall apart, to kick off the blankets, to play it cool.

After turning fifty, his great crisis also reached into his nights: it was then the dream awoke. He struggled not only to fall asleep but also to stay asleep. He slept, yes; but at most a couple hours and then, all of a sudden, he would find himself lost in the darkness but lit up by too many thoughts. The childish fantasies didn't hold up to the wear and the degradation of the ill known as maturity, that stage in the life cycle of fruit that precedes rot. And he'd had the waking dream of trying, nothing more and nothing less, to destroy the planet, barricading himself inside a Swiss particle accelerator and . . .

And HE-IKEA had interceded on his behalf and paid his fine at a Swiss jail, after he'd tried to destroy the world or, better, like he said before, to rewrite it in his image and semblance and fantasizing that he would be transformed into an enlightened and all-powerful deity, after forcing his way into and pressing all the red buttons on the control boards at a hadron collider near Geneva.

A city where he'd come to deliver one of his increasingly infrequent talks about the dangers of the internet and its environs for literature in particular and human relations in general. To "denounce" for a fee how—at the mercy of those who were caught in the act—up-and-coming writers were renouncing one of the most basic aspects of their training: to paint with letters a faraway painting; to film with words a movie that's almost impossible to see again and that, when it does come back around, was a cinemateca copy, increasingly fragile or flagellated by black-and-white commercial interruptions; to hum the recording of a song on a record or cassette that played over and over until it turned to dust. And thus to change and rewrite (and repaint and refilm and rerecord) all those things in their own way and style, in order to prove that a thousand words could say something different and far more personal than any image or sound. And also to warn that readers no longer missed or wondered what their loved—and possibly unfaithful, of course—one was doing. And to remember that there was a time when the imagination flew instead of crashing into an immediate and not-all-that-creative fact checking of everything. Everyone knew where everyone was now; nobody ignored what movie Christopher Walken had debuted in (but, yes, they might not know who Christopher Walken was). And there was no longer any need to describe: because showing on the screen, pointing out with an impolite finger, was so much quicker and supposedly more precise and easy to dismiss and on to something else.

Also gone was the concept of *rarity*, of having something almost nobody else had, because, in one way or another, everything was there in the air of the internet. The exception being, yes, first editions of books: one of the few objects that continue to be tangible and palpable pieces of private property. Editions endowed with that yellowish and soulful aroma of sweaty soup in the winter that old and immortal books acquire. Therefore and on that basis, he'd "composed" a "denunciation of the state of things" (to his regret and embarrassment, as more dates on that never-ending tour keep passing, closer to the disgust of Bill Murray than the enthusiasm of Robin Williams), which once had made him "simpatico" to the tracers of sharp-cornered roundtables and the programming of "literary festivals." A kind of civil rant that combined bad jokes and serious concerns, concerns that actually concerned him less all the time. On the other hand, the threat of the electronic book hadn't amounted to much. (Suddenly, gadgets appeared in such quick succession, with no transition, annulling each other in a flash. Formats that no longer supported anything and disappeared overnight for the dawning of a new product that retired the previous one, rendering it useless; not like before, like when the VHS had coexisted for quite a while with the DVD, and the Walkman had coexisted for quite a while with the Discman, and the Homo Neanderthal with the Homo Cro-Magnon; and others have already warned that soon there wouldn't been enough electricity produced to satisfy so many plug-in-able devices and plugged-in people.) Their devotees and worshippers (the same people who had no problem paying small fortunes for unsustainable and voluminous volumes by Taschen that they only ever opened once) had lost all interest in the idea and the ease of carrying approximately two thousand pirated books they'd never read around with them. And holding sway beyond any novelty or technological temptation was the same primordial and organic fear as always, a fear that had nothing to do with the digital or the virtual or the technological: people read fewer books all the time.

Why?

Simple and even understandable: such a ceaseless procession of new and increasingly advanced models (but also more fragile and with increasingly brief lifespans of utility) had generated a complete lack of interest, when not outright hostility, toward the more solid stuff of the past.

And in the past, always and forever, were books.

All of them.

The classics and the contemporary and the immediately disposable.

Books that were written or had been written so long before to be read forever after and that demanded too much time and concentration on just one thing when it was possible to explore so many different things.

Books that sank you into the depths when all you wanted was to float on the surface of everything, without boundaries or borders.

That's why people preferred to read immediate and quick things that didn't slow you down too much in moving on to the next thing. Text messages. Twitter. Song and flight of birds, birds with the irksome ability to defecate in the air, sullying as they fly and sing. Right now. That's why people read more on phones and watches. And he still remembered times when being successful made you into someone who no longer needed to know what time it was or who was calling on the phone, someone out of reach of everything and everyone. But suddenly, phones and watches had turned into prestige objects to which everyone submitted with a dumb smile and vacant eyes and with the certainty that that was, for them, the way to be a chosen one, to belong to the *very few*. And this was confirmed every time he entered a metro or train car, or an airplane, or a bus (dreaming of any of those modes of transportation, the dream dictionaries informed him, meant "Moving up in life!!!" except when you dream they come off the rails or explode or crash, which means "Something bad is going to happen!!!"), or so many other places where nobody reads books and, as such, nobody moved forward except toward something bad happening. Or not even that: nothing happened. They read, all of them, about themselves or about real virtuous friends or false virtual friends. Or they tracked their heartbeats or the ups and downs of the atmospheric pressure. And so, it was now nearly impossible to participate in that venerable sport, around the city or high in the sky, consisting of surreptitiously and tensely contorting your neck to scan the cover and confirm the book some other passenger was reading and, much less, top off that confirmation by executing the treacherous triple-jump adolescent fantasy of, between one station and the next or over the course of several airborne hours, falling in love with that peculiar but singularly beautiful girl, reading a heavily-underlined copy of *Franny and Zooey* with exclamation points in the margins.

He felt sorry for anybody incapable of feeling what it felt like to feel things like that. Because why should he be interested in the inferior beings who, unlike him, weren't intrigued, for example, by what could be done here and now with everything the nineteenth century had to teach about the novel, without falling into pale imitations or pasty pastiches. And yet, in exchange for a few bills, they all gravitated toward the antimatter of book fairs, increasingly numerous and well attended while simultaneously selling fewer books.

The stellar moment of his odd number was when he brought his hand to his chest "where you keep your heart and your pistol" and pulled out from the inside of his jacket pocket an almost prehistoric mobile phone. A 2005 model. A mobile phone that only served to make phone calls. And then he explained to the audience in attendance that he regarded this gadget with a combination of disgust and pity. A device on which he ceaselessly received SMSs from the manufacturer requesting that he return it in exchange for a latest generation model that he would be given free of charge. Something that made him suspect—and that's how he explained it to the auditorium— that "the electronic technology of this near-fossil was probably far more efficient, it's never broken down on me, than that of its descendants; and that compromises the company's executives and techs who don't want it out there making the rounds anymore . . . There are nights when I think, before long, they'll send out a squad of ninjas to reclaim it by force." And, amid all that unfunny comedy and light humor, he'd dropped one certainty on the audience like a cluster bomb, leaving them a little shaken and not Tweeting or WhatsApping, at least for a few seconds, seconds that should be made eternal, restless, abstinent.

Then, of course, in that place, they all belonged to the first generation that grew up with mobile phones. And he could almost swear (almost) they were all squirming with discomfort when he said the following words, reading them aloud from one of his notebooks:


† Think about it a little: not that long ago none of you were going around carrying those little devices with you everywhere and you lived lives that were more or less the same as the ones you live now and you were masters of the same intelligence quotient and the same powers of internal and external observation . . . Tell me, what is it that's changed so much in your lives and the lives of your acquaintances in recent years that's made you feel the obligation or need to share everything that happens to you and everything that you happen to think of, eh? Sure, if all of you had, courtesy of some fork in

space-time, been in Dallas with your little phones that morning in 1963, we'd probably know exactly how many shooters there were and where they shot from and we'd be able to see JFK's head explode from all possible angles. But seriously, I mean it, believe me: nobody is interested in that photo of what you're eating or that sunset you're seeing or your most recent deep thought you just have to share with all of humanity unless you're interested in their reflections and their sunsets and their meals too . . . Isn't it true that not that long ago you liked many fewer things and that you took your time to think about whether something was or wasn't worthy of a *like*? Isn't it true that just a few years ago you didn't read so much and definitely didn't write so much? Isn't it true that it used to make more to sense to go to the bathroom to read than to write? Isn't it true that you used to live without wondering whether everything you did or thought was inspiring enough and worthy of being instantaneously and constantly sent out into the fullest emptiness in all of history? Isn't it true that those lives were actually more interesting and that, every so often, it was fun to sit down with a friend, live and direct and in person, and say to them: "You have no idea what happened to me last week" and then proceed to tell them with a full luxury of details, just as you had practiced in your head, with authentic tears and laughter? Isn't it true that it's more appropriate to tell people about your pregnancies or tumors in privacy and one on one and in different ways depending on the person and not to tell everyone at the same time with the same words? Isn't it true that there was a certain charm to coming home and—when it wasn't bad news—finding a handwritten note on the ground beside the door or on a desk or stuck to the refrigerator door and opening it and under that cold light reading the warmth of that message? Isn't it true that it's disturbing to think that the activity you do most throughout the day is stare at your phone? Isn't it true that it's much more pleasant not to feel that already-diagnosed-by-neurologists "phantom vibration" at the height of your pockets, as if it were the phone that we forgot and that isn't even there calling and reminding us of its existence from far away, like the reflex and memory of some unforgettable amputated body part. Isn't it true that you kind of miss that delectable torture of not being able to remember something—a name, a title, a song—and instead of finding it and terminating that torture immediately via Google, allowing that forgotten thing to live and expand and, while you try to overcome it, to awaken other memories and other songs and titles and names? Isn't it true that it used to be so gratifying to be the first to remember something in a gathering of the absentminded? Isn't it true that it was much easier to detect the early symptoms of Alzheimer's and to get ahead in its treatment without the use of instantaneous memory aids? Isn't it true that it was exciting when every time you took a photo you were also making a choice? Isn't it true that it was better to have memories that were far more precise than all those blurry photos where you can't even tell who's in them? Isn't it true that it was more exciting when every time you didn't take a photo you were also making a choice? Isn't it true that you used to film and photograph your kids less and you looked at them more and saw them better at home or at end-of-year performances or on their birthdays? Isn't it true that life was a little better when everyone who made fun of you in high school or at work could only do it from nine to five and not like now, on Facebook ("Facebook friend" was a great oxymoron, he thought) or Instagram or wherever, at all hours of the day and night, and you there promising and deceiving yourself that you won't log back on to see how they hit you and insult you and laugh in your screen-face. Isn't it true that it's better to go out into the street and meet up with friends and not to capture virtual monsters that cost you less and less money, which takes more and more work to earn? Isn't it true that it was better to go out walking in the street and randomly run into people instead of knowing where they are at all times but never seeing them in person? Isn't it true that it was so nice to go out walking and be sure that nobody could call you on the phone? Isn't it true that it was better to go out into the street when there were none of those new stoplights, on the ground, specially located to protect people who keep getting run over because they're walking, head down, looking at the screen of their phone? Isn't it true that it was nobler to immediately come to the aid of the unknown victim of an accident instead of making a video and "sharing it" first? Isn't it true that it's weird that doctors, when it comes time to let family members say goodbye to their loved ones—many of them dying because they were so concentrated on their phones they never saw what was coming at them until it was too late—have opted, I read about this the other day, to unplug the screens of the monitors that register the dying vital signs, because many people, reflexively, ignore the dying person and stare at those devices that make sounds like a video-game, and are the sounds of "game over"? Isn't it true that everything sounded better when all the phones sounded more or less the same, when their voice was more or less the same? Isn't it true that you kind of miss those days when having a good memory was something to be proud of and not something we put in the hands of that device in our hands? Isn't it true that it was exciting to memorize the phone number of a person you loved and to dial their digits one at a time, as if they were the letters of the person's name, instead of just pressing a button without ever knowing what those numbers might add to or subtract from our hearts? Isn't it true that we should be prouder of the memory of our soft brain than that of our hard disc? Isn't it true that the world seemed better ordered and fairer when it wasn't so easy to reach anybody via email, and certain levels of friendship and hierarchies of familiarity and rules of protocol were respected? Isn't it true that things worked better when someone asked the legitimate owner first before casually giving away their phone number and email address to just anybody? Isn't it true that it was a pleasure to unplug the phone or to think that you'd achieved enough success in your life that you could dispense with it, that you had someone to deal with those ring-ring-rings or with those ringtones personalized—like those car horns that used to sing "La cucaracha"—with songs from TV shows or movies or famous speeches or, even worse, the wailing of your own baby? Isn't it true that you made love more often or at least thought about making love more often or slept more and more deeply dreaming about making love and not about staring at and talking on your phone? Isn't it true that it was much more enjoyable to go to the bathroom with a book than a phone? Isn't it true that spy thrillers and love stories were much better and more exciting when their moles and kitty cats had to search for and locate a phone on the street or in a bar and weren't carrying it with them everywhere? Isn't it true that the president of the United States still looks more elegant in the oval office with an old-school telephone and not holding one of those plastic and metal wafers? Isn't it true that everything was more convenient when you didn't have to declare them at airports as if they were lethal weapons? Isn't it true that it was easier to live a calmer life in a world where phones weren't exploding and the new model of something wasn't worse than previous models?

Isn't it true that your lives were better when you were people who had a thought, and thought about it for a while before broadcasting it, and your face and name were out in the open and not the maniacal masks of avatars and aliases and anonymous and invasive body snatchers? Isn't it true that everything was much nicer when phone calls were much less frequent and lasted much less time? Isn't it true that life was more relaxed when you spent time reading absolutely nothing and maybe achieved some kind of Zen emptiness, unlike now when you read all the time, and all you read are brief inanities that, in their accumulation, end up turning you into a big inane nothing? Isn't it true that what makes you check your social media profiles every minute isn't the satisfaction of seeing yourselves there but of confronting the constant dissatisfaction of not really being seen by anyone? Isn't it true that everything was much nicer when you didn't have to take constant and interminable seminars to be able to use new applications, suspecting that soon everything would completely flip upside down and you'd have to start from a technological ground zero and take classes to learn how to hold a spoon and slurp down your soup? Isn't it true that everything seemed much grander and much more expressive when the world was much smaller and much more incommunicado? Isn't it true that everything felt much more exciting and adventurous and proximal and close when the long-distance thing existed? Isn't it true that it was easier to trust those foldable and uncomfortable and silent but oh so much more believable paper maps that, in addition to showing you where you were, pointed out where you had been and where you would be? Isn't it true that the air felt lighter and the landscape shone far brighter when the only thing you knew about writers was what was in their books or in the occasional interview and when you knew absolutely *nothing* about the life and work of readers because readers didn't write? . . .

Then he paused. And he felt them reflect, restless and even embarrassed at having succumbed to such a panacea/placebo; but the doubt and fear lasted but a sigh, no longer than it took them to type one hundred and forty characters. Then they took his picture and sent it with some little messages on their

messenger apps with texts like: "This guy is SSINF, LOL, hahaha ☺☹."
And something told him the person who sent all that could be none other
than the girl—overweight with gigabytes and inactivity, her body stuffed into
a T-shirt that, ironically and involuntarily, read WISH I WERE HERE—
whom he'd had to yell at to get up and stop blocking the entrance with her
ass and her screen. Whereas others came down on his side, but with rather
disturbing (or equally ignorant) lines of reasoning, like that the Apple logo
was the fruit of the tree of knowledge nibbled by temptation, that it was no
coincidence that the price of the first Mac had been the oh so antichristian
$666.66, and that the scriptures, in Revelations, warned about the "masses
following Satan" and . . . There they were. Some and others, people who not
only moved their lips when they read, but who, also, moved their lips when
they wrote, and barely moved their lips when they spoke, having lost all
ability to modulate their words and make them and make themselves heard
and understood. The world had been invaded and conquered by fools. No:
they weren't even fools. They were fool's fools. And yes, they detested him
and he detested them (pretty quickly he realized he had before him people
whose sole activity was to read badly and write worse, all the time, when they
never would have had to, when really they were made for other things, things
where letters and sentences were secondary or tertiary). And he thought how
much nicer the world would be if they all admitted they hated each other.
How much simpler and more comprehensible. How much easier to take. To
understand affection as an exceptional and infrequent aberration and love as
a mythological creature. And not to expect any of that to present itself or
to take place. Hating was so much more logical. Hate was a great primary
source. Hate sheltered you and provided warmth ("I write because I hate,"
William H. Gass admitted once, a writer who once also referred to the past
as that cape and hat you throw with carelessness and even disdain onto the
sofa upon entering, knowing full well that when you leave you'll have to put
them back on again). And then he tried to extract some of that thick black
bile that was filling his body up to his throat and making him gag in public.
But his was a sterile and barren hate where nothing could germinate beyond
his resigned contemplation. Just there, seeing them so busy, with the tips of
their tongues poking out between their lips and thumbs moving (thumbs

that once were one of the most important milestones of the human being's evolutionary development), ever more myopic from the work of having to stab at those ever smaller touchpads, he hated them with all the love he had.

And then he deployed his secret weapon, the last bullet in the chamber, his final solution.

And, without pulling any punches, with all the hate in his heart, as a farewell gesture, he said to them:

† I don't know if you know this, but the latest scientific studies have revealed that every time you send a text message or a tweet, you lose more or less a minute of your life. Good night and thank you for your generous attention.

And, driven from the auditorium by the wind of hate, a wave of booing that made him think, on the defensive and outside all reality, "Oh, this is how Henry James must have felt when, on opening night of his *Guy Domville*, he went out to greet the audience and—for fifteen minutes!—stood frozen under the lights amid a storm of hissing and jeering, condemned as if in a Roman circus." Then he got out of there as fast as possible and disappeared into the most sunset of horizons.

James had, of course, understood then that there was no audience worthy of his greatness in "the age of trash triumphant." And had proceeded to shut himself in and to write his masterful late novels and all those stories with writers (for him the best stories about writers ever written) always contemplating the twilight of their own careers and the dawn of those of their disciples, who never attained their giant stature, but found a way to scramble up on their shoulders all the same.

He, yes, thought and told himself the same thing. And that impulse drove him to write just one more book, one last book, belonging to the genre of last books.

Again.

That book.

A last book about a writer who refused to snuff himself out and opted to detonate an astrophysical and fulminant phenomenon far beyond all virtual-digital gadget or tech-format reader.

A last book that revealed, openly and with pride, its own concealed mechanisms and regained the pleasure of being *overwritten* and sought for its reader the same wonder of observing the moving gears of an old clock with its insides spilling out into the air, and in so doing constructing a more or less plausible idea of time that could never be precisely represented by digital devices with motionless circuits, sealed in the most inviolable of absolute voids. He'd read somewhere that the small pendularly-swinging, anchor-shaped piece (responsible for the tick-tock of the noblest clocks) was called the "escapement." And that name had cracked him up, seeing as it referred, paradoxically and ironically, to something that marked the impossibility of escaping from the passage—as martial as it was *décontracté* and as deliberate as it was rapid—of a time that was passing ever faster. Because—another ironic and paradoxical detail—there was more and more to remember. But—unlike during our childhoods when everything was novel and transcendent—we pay less attention to our present, which never ceases to be a succession of repeated situations, uninspired variations, where there lurks only the originality of other peoples' deaths and the anticipation of our own end.

And he couldn't stop thinking and feeling that all of the preceding wasn't duly recorded by the new technologies for which the hour of a night and the plot of a novel were nothing but more applications among so many, like, for example, those games where cloying-colored candies lined up in descending rows, exploding with small explosions, no doubt, calibrated to yield a kind of toxic sonic addiction, preventing you from thinking about anything else that wasn't precisely that.

When it came to this stuff, to readable electricity and the different gadgets, IKEA (who returned to his thoughts because he never left, wherever he was, alive or dead or enduring whatever terrible fate he imagined for him; because that whole thing about him disappearing in the Amazon was obviously just another of the many things he happened to think of and that didn't do him any good in any way for any reason), of course, didn't want to make any enemies. IKEA didn't allow himself the idea of losing a single customer. And so he'd declared "I like to reread my favorite nineteenth-century authors in first editions, but I like my favorite readers to reread me in electronic books."

And he listened to this with clenched teeth. And said to himself he would happily waste one of his three wishes to strip IKEA of that affected and oh so self-satisfied diction (an esperantic-babelic accent that seemed to contain skillfully balanced parts of all Spanish accents) and impose on him the little, exceedingly out-of-place voice of David Beckham: anything to make IKEA shut his mouth, to force him, at least, not to talk about anything but his books.

And everyone smiled and asked to take selfies with him.

With IKEA, in Geneva, sitting beside him, asking him through his teeth what time it was and if he'd noticed the tits on the blonde in the first row, eighth seat from the right.


So he'd shown up there ready to do his increasingly downtrodden and negative number in front of an audience wearing faces that asked *who is this guy* and not really caring about the answer that, when given, almost invariably, made them go back and ask all over again who was that guy.

And also, along the way and in the process, to write an article for an airline magazine (*Volare*, run by the person who years before had been his first boss and the editor of his early writing) about the aforementioned Large Hadron Collider. The Large Hadron Collider at CERN, searching for something definitive they called "Higgs boson" or "The God Particle." And for the exact re-creation of what happened in the seconds immediately after the beginning of all things.

Or something like that.

So he'd come to Geneva already believing in nothing and definitely not in the spiritual holiness of literature. Convinced that—as Maurice Blanchot had warned from his watchtower—"Literature is heading toward itself, toward its essence which is disappearance." There he was, heading toward himself then. Disappeared from almost every shelf in disappearing bookstores. Agnostic and atheist and excommunicated when it came to the practice of his craft. Creatively destitute and driven by the inertia of his autopilot and his reflexive writing. An outlaw lacking any rule for the practice of the most fugitive of the arts. Nothing there of mathematics or of music or the laws of perspective in portraits of landscapes or, at least, that exactitude on which to get your footing and stand up in the meter of sonnets or in the obligatory spatiotemporal coordinates of haiku. Loose, lost, disconnected from the mother ship and the name of his creative forefathers.

He'd come to Geneva clinging to a well-worn but never-waded-into-beyond-its-shores copy of *Ada, or Ardor* by Vladimir Nabokov. He'd tried in vain so many times to read it, but, mysteriously, he never managed to get past its first pages. Though *Ada* was, without a doubt, along with *Absalom, Absalom!* by William Faulkner and *Hopscotch* by Julio Cortázar, the novel he'd started the most times but never continued or finished. And in which he'd gotten, at most, past the first twenty pages, or something like that, and broken off the most times, as if blinded by a unique fever. Penned by one of his literary heroes (his relationship with Vladimir Nabokov had become more and more impassioned with the passing of the years) whom, luckily, HE-IKEA had forgotten to list in his polynomial blurbs and when he recounted his influences.

He had admiration and envy for the exemplary example of Nabokov. To him, a kind of singular specimen: someone who had always done things his way, who'd given no quarter, who'd succeeded on his own terms. Someone who'd gained access to the émigré paradise and territory of living and writing and dying in a hotel, in that no man's land where you can do anything (he'd always thought an émigré was someone who went into exile but had time, in their flight, to pack up and bring along their library, their own portable homeland, the most nomadic of rooms, made to fit anywhere; which hadn't kept him from, on more than one occasion, suffering the loss of losing books).

And for him, Nabokov was someone with whom, he felt or wanted to feel, he shared traits and gestures and flaws. Phobias and jokes, like his referential mania and his propensity for self-reference; his ease at moving far and wide in the world from an atomized and volatized family; considering himself a professional foreigner; his polyglot wordplay and polished alliterations and his distorting echoes and repeated repetitions and polyglot rants; his hatred of the roar of motorcycles and his vicarious shame, standing before the paintings of Marc Chagall; his dentition issues during his youth; his affection for the parenthetical and his lack of interest, bordering on disdain, for scripted dialogue as a narrative device in his own fiction and even in real life; his hatred of the telephone as an instrument for dialoging (in the Demonia a.k.a Antiterra of *Ada, or Ardor,* he knew this because though he hadn't read the novel he *had* read several books about the novel, there are neither telephones nor television screens); his annoyance at group activities, his disdain for any jazz (free or hot or cool or swing or acid) performance; his certainty that reality is overrated (looking down on the expression "everyday reality") and that time was something it wasn't worth believing in; that his head would never rest on a divan to recount dreams aloud; his adoration for the figure of the recurring muse; and, of course, his insomnia. (Noteworthy difference and inevitable to mention: nothing terrified him more than the proximity of nymphets and the like; and nothing mattered to him less and bored him more than the problematic movement of chess pieces.)

For him, Nabokov was the most moveable and most moving writer in every sense.

And, he thought, perhaps, the writer who sounded more joyful than anyone when he read what he'd written. Nabokov was the writer of joy (of absolute joy when it came to the act of writing), no matter the horrors and sorrows he might narrate.

That was the truth. That's why he reread Nabokov all the time. And read everything he could find about him. Vladimir Nabokov had proposed/warned that the only true biography of a writer was the history of his style. And he was right. And he'd become such an aficionado/addict of all academic studies of Nabokov that focused on his lively style. Volumes published by university presses in which the authors, invariably, wind up transformed into true Charles Kinbotes. Creatures staggered and driven crazy, haggard and burned by the carefully deployed winks of the Russian, like small but smart-delayed time bombs. Wordplay and cryptic allusions and levels of self-references that they proceeded to activate with their obsessive theories. Running the gamut from intriguing to absurd and that'd made Nabokov truly immortal, on par with Shakespeare, always *in progress* and never entirely finished being read deeply and to the end. He'd "discovered" something himself: that the phantasmagoric daughter of John Shade (who's reproached by her father for *not* haunting him) was named Hazel and that, when you break down her name into *Haze, L.* you're referred laterally and subliminally to the nymphet Lolita

Haze. And, true, strictly speaking, it should be Dolores Haze, and . . . The many and so many other books by and with and for and about Nabokov that until recently he was reading and rereading, in search of some secret key, a mysterious formula that would bring him back from the loss of his gift. Writers have—by obligation and necessity—very childish mentalities. And he thought that maybe, who knows, here's hoping, Nabokov would somehow help him, infect him with his thing.

He—who at one time, in days when plotlines never stopped occurring to him, had fantasized about the existence of a button that, when pressed, would allow him to stop being a writer for a while, to stop thinking *like that*, to unplug—now dreamed of the alms of a few lines or even just a title.

He imagined possible "solutions" that, of course, though clever, would be completely ineffective: from a deal with the Devil (he even attended a Satanist group that told him they weren't interested in "a soul of so little substance") to fasting and drinking a tall brimming glass of squid ink. Every so often—when he worked up the courage and shed unconsciousness—he reread himself with half-closed eyes, as if the written words were like those burning but moistening eye drops. And he wondered if he'd completely dried up the deposit or vein where all of that'd come from, while enumerating the five stations of the cross of Kübler-Ross-brand grief (denial, anger, bargaining, depression, acceptance) to which he added a sixth station: the parentheses in suspense of (*to be continued . . .* ). That maneuver so typical of the comics of his childhood where, when everything seemed used up and closed off, you could start over by repeating all of it, resorting to the idea of alternate dimensions or corrections to what'd already been told. Something like putting in practice an ambiguous *Aloha State of Mind*, a word that meant "goodbye" as well as "hello," the result, perhaps, of spending too much time on Hawaiian beaches, wondering if the waves were coming or going. A turning around to advance, a going back to go forward. A maneuver adopted in dark days by several of his most beloved and admired superheroes.

Another turn of the screw, indeed. Again, the Henry James strategy (to keep ascending once the zenith of your body of work is attained, by tackling a revision and rewrite and explanation of what you've already written, which is, as such, forever improvable) tempted him for a few minutes, maybe fifty-nine minutes: the attraction of functioning as a medium for his own body of work, of asking the ghost of that person he'd been and still was in his books if it was there. To demand that it knock three times and . . . But then he remembered that for Henry James, his most justified and necessary whim of a totalizing *New York Edition*, had signified for him the gravestone-memorial of a definitive publishing failure: almost nobody had been interested in subscribing or buying it. And the American died in England, deliriously raving and believing himself Napoleon Bonaparte ("Tell a dream . . .") and admired by some, who called him "The Master," but read by few. And he had to wait for the academics to bring him back to life and raise him up onto the altar of dead immortal classics. (He liked to imagine on his sleepless nights that somewhere and sometime one of those hostage exchanges from spy movies took place, on a foggy bridge outside time and space. He liked to imagine that the United States handed over Henry James to help the decadent European novel enter the twentieth century. And that, after a while, the Old World would offer up Vladimir Nabokov, who came fleeing the Bolshevik Revolution, to revolutionize the concept of the Great American Novel.) But he was so/very far from being Henry James. And he no longer had publishers at his disposal converted to his faith and who would be tempted by the idea of a beatifying *Sad Songs Edition* or, at least, consider it a viable way to launder the sinful dark money of some narco-investor with cultured pretensions. So, already from the start and with only the capital of the dead from his life, he'd neither followed his example in the end nor paid attention to James in the beginning. James, whom he'd always liked so much more than the unbearable and unreliable Hemingway when it came to advice that always corresponded to his actions. James, who postulated that thing about "To write is a solitary life . . . Because it is practiced alone and if one is a sufficiently good writer one must confront immortality or its absence every day." James, who on one occasion had referred to the art of interacting with ghosts: "If you don't believe in them, don't bother them," he'd said. And he had also recommended, when it came to structuring fictions of any kind of real sustenance, to never forget that all of life was "inclusion and confusion," while the secret of art ran through "discrimination and selection." And to leave something untold or unrevealed. To leave out the poems of Jeffrey Aspern, to not reveal the sex of the, for once, first-person narrator of *The*

*Sacred Fount*, to not specify what the extraordinary or catastrophic fact is that John Marcher intuits in "The Beast in the Jungle" or what the unexpected greatness is that Dencombe discovers in his book only at the end of his life in "The Middle Years," to not specify what "the little nameless object" is in *The Ambassadors*, and to not entirely certify the existence of the living dead in *The Turn of the Screw*.

And he'd done just the opposite.

He'd revealed everything.

He'd bothered and included and confused the ghosts (his ghosts, the ghosts to whom he belonged) only to discover, too late, that he believed in them but they didn't believe in him: that his ghosts discriminated against and didn't choose him; that they weren't even interested enough to appear and give him a slight and half-hearted fright.

IKEA had reproached him for it, shaking his head and pointing at him with an accusatory finger: "You shouldn't make fun of certain things, man. The thing with your parents, for example . . . If you turn it into a joke, the joke stops being funny after you tell it two or three times. Whereas, if you keep taking it seriously, with tears in your eyes and a trembling voice, it'll hold up forever . . . It's like an ace up your sleeve, like a hobbyhorse . . . I can't say I envy your books, but, oh, what I would've given for some *desaparecidos* parents . . . The most traumatic thing that happened to me in that sense was that, one time when I was in Mexico, a drug addict stole my rental car in Cancun. Outside a shopping mall. I wasn't even inside it, I'd left it in the parking lot; but that traumatic experience was enough for me to erect *Tremors of the Eagle*, my great, more or less autobiographical, narco-novel, soon to be adapted for the big screen, starring Sean Penn in the lead role as *moi*."

He, on the other hand, did nothing with his parents beyond one story, deemed "irreverent" by many. And they had nothing more to do with him apart from remembering his first book (while new incarnations and variations of the same thing appeared, but with a furrowed and militant brow and a stern and committed gesture) as one of the highlights of, again, "a cynical and corrupt decade that had no respect for anything." And the years and the books passed as if they were different rooms in a haunted house he couldn't get out of and now almost nobody (his dwindling readers among them) dared enter.

But after his frustrated and absurd attempt to transform himself into an avenger and Armageddonic particle ghost at a Swiss accelerator, he drew strength from somewhere. And he broke a window and made his escape.

And he found a way to write another book, the one that'd been his last book.

A book whose subject was, then, something far more revolting than the subject of his first book.

An uncomfortable and polemic subject.

A subject—the only one he had left—that'd become the most unsettling and transgressive of all.

A subject that was, yes, *delicate*.

The book was about reading and writing.

About the increasingly dreadful and depraved modalities of reading and writing.

Was there anything more perverse in a world where everyone went around plugged into something, typing brief texts, shout-singing in public, ears covered by XL headphones, scrolling through live-action photographs more than instantaneous than Polaroids and completely and absolutely unnecessary (an affront to when photographs were a big event and planned out and, before that, to those photographs where nobody smiled because being photographed was a solemn affair and, besides, it turned out to be quite difficult to hold a smile throughout the many minutes the plate had to be exposed)?

No.

The book traced the indispensable constants that determined how someone, he, would've once had and maintained the idea—the fixed idea, the unwavering and immoveable idea—of being a writer. Of how a writer was made/unmade and how a piece of writing was unmade/made.

A book that was all the books that book could possibly be.

At the same time, *all together now*: the idea of the possible book, the book while it's being written, the book finished, the book just published and read by others as something new, the book that you return to after a time to find some paragraph that might come to detonate the idea for another possible book.

How had he described and written it? Ah, yes: "A book that thinks like a writer in the act of thinking up a book, what he's thinking about when he happens to think of a book, when that book happens to him, and about what happens with that book" and "A book that would be an open book, though not consequently clear and figurative, but cloudy and abstract. A book like one of Edward Hopper's clean and well-lit rooms, but with a Jackson Pollock waiting to come out of the closet."

Something like that and of that style.

An extreme specimen with no return from what somebody had defined as *poioumenon*: a *making of* in search of that which, supposedly, could and should *be made*.

The story prior to the story that's yet to come.

A reading before writing what, in the beginning, was going to be read: the portrait of a man standing amid reefs, sharp like fangs, making desperate and titanic gestures to ships that sank without knowing they were sinking and aboard which nobody was reading on the deck anymore, because they were too busy sending crying-face emoticons while he, also in the engine room, doubling himself, wondered how nobody had come up with an emoticon whose face symbolized the end of the voyage and of the world.

The book analyzed the parameters of the literary vocation as a singular and inescapable destiny: a plan A without a plan B.

A plan X.

And its sentences were long and full of subordinate and oh so insubordinate clauses.

And it had parentheses (many).

And that exotic rarity of the semicolon.

And its paragraphs were as wide and compact as walls, offering no blank spaces where you could catch your breath.

And, let's admit it, it was varnished with a not-so-thin layer of rancor and spite and envy, qualities inherent to all writers.

And, yes, on more than one occasion, he wondered why at a certain point he hadn't stopped reading to write down certain things. Why he hadn't occupied himself with light and funny and fun matters (he remembered that his friends laughed at him a lot, at things he said, things that occurred to him in the moment, without overthinking it) far away from all that literary solemnity.

And, if he were unable to escape literature, why then had he never paused on noir fiction and on Charles Bukowski and John Fante and on Henry

Miller and Jack Kerouac. On youthful writers. On that spirit that made young people love you and sent you leaping from generation to generation, like a kind of relaxed and easygoing guru for all those who only wanted to be distracted from the fact that they didn't have a girlfriend and did have acne.

And to keep them company.

And to understand them.

And to have produced noble yet simple texts, with hard but sensitive characters, mischievous and kindly rogues, always on the road. High-speed books for uncomplicated highways. Perhaps something with walking dead or with teenagers lost in dystopic landscapes controlled by despotic adults who might or might not be their parents.

But no: he knew that, in his case, all of that would've been impossible. Because before long he would've swerved down side roads, more difficult to maneuver. And nothing is more hazardous than the vertigo produced by traveling with a genius in the passenger seat. Somebody we know to be far more expert behind the wheel, but who, nevertheless, refuses to help and only enjoys blinding oncoming drivers by flipping on his high beams. High beams like those of Barry Hannah and J. P. Donleavy and William S. Burroughs and Tom Drury. More favorites; all included in a "writing workshop" he once "taught" to an ever-diminishing number of attendees, all with the unmistakable aspect of, yes, needing urgent repairs or, better, of needing to be taken, along with their faded pages, to the closest chop shop and junkyard where he could deliver the *coup de grâce* and head off on the lam.

And no, obviously, of course: the writing workshop hadn't gone well, nothing had been fixed and no vocation kick-started. He had to admit it: his wasn't a particularly didactic mindset, apart from not being particularly flexible and exceedingly sardonic. But you couldn't fault him for it. It wasn't a crime, like selling magical cures or shares in a nonexistent company. Teaching—and attending a writing workshop—was like believing in something. And, as tends to happen in any temple, the faithful believe more than the priest. It was a comfortable rite and, possibly, the only teaching role where doing it poorly had no grave consequence (as could happen with instructors of airplane pilots or of heart surgeons, for example) and didn't even diminish anybody's chance of success. Because one could write really badly and still earn a lot of money and get really famous. A mystery far more unsettling than the multiplication of fish and bread and maneuvers (linked to sudden inspiration or the rediscovery of dead authors) like immaculate conceptions and more or less justified literary resurrections.

Even still, when he had the spirit, he'd tried to impart something, to preach fragments of the good news to his students. His thing, basically, had been to put in practice what Nabokov proposed in his famous introduction to his course at Cornell regarding "good readers and good writers," certain that none of his students would happen across the original. And so, he greeted them with a promising "My course, among other things, is a kind of detective investigation of the mystery of literary structures," then he recited from memory—as if it were his own—that "Literature was born not the day when a boy crying wolf!, wolf!, came running out of the Neanderthal valley with a big gray wolf at his heels: literature was born on the day when a boy came crying wolf!, wolf!, and there was no wolf behind him. That the poor little fellow, because he lied too often, was finally eaten up by a real beast is quite incidental. But here is what is important. Between the wolf in the tall grass and the wolf in the tall story there is a shimmering go-between. That go-between, that prism, is the art of literature.

"Literature is an invention. Fiction is fiction. To call a story a true story is an insult to both art and truth. Every great writer is a great deceiver, but so is that arch-cheat Nature. Nature always deceives. From the simple deception of propagation to the prodigiously sophisticated illusion of protective colors in butterflies or birds, there is in Nature a marvelous system of spells and wiles. The writer of fiction only follows Nature's lead. Going back for a moment to our wolf-crying, little wooly woodland fellow, we may put it this way: the magic of art was in the shadow of the wolf he deliberately invented, his dream of the wolf; then the story of his tricks made a good story. When he perished at last, the story about him acquired a good lesson in the dark around a camp fire. But he was the little magician. He was the inventor. There are three points of view from which a writer can be considered: he may be considered as a storyteller, as a teacher, and as an enchanter. A major writer combines these three—storyteller, teacher, enchanter—but it is the enchanter in him that predominates and makes him a major writer."

Then he sighed, was silent for a few seconds—looking out at that landscape of yawning mouths and half-closed eyes—and proceeded to rip apart his contemporaries to the joy of the class, always thirsty for blood and one-liners to tweet and so much happier to hear about what someone dislikes than what someone likes. His students were badly written wolves and bad readers. And when one of them would howl that classic of literary criticism/online comment in virtual bookstores ("I didn't identify with any of the characters" or "None of the main characters seems real to me"), he half-closed his eyes and responded that "They seem implausible to you, but nevertheless they are written, ergo they exist: as far as identifying with them, let's see if I can find some book about someone who goes to a writing workshop because they have nothing better to do with their life."

After all of that, his book had been, also, the occasion for his last grand promotional tour, financed by the enthusiasm of his publisher who believed in him more than he believed in himself or who, perhaps, had lost a bet with a competitor and was now paying his tremendous punishment: having to promote against the wind and tide and tsunami—oneiric terminology come to think of it—his black-sheep and *sleeper* author.

He'd been to some strange countries for the first time. In one, he'd been accused of being a narco-trafficker by two psychotic immigration officials and rescued at the last minute by the pilot of his plane who, providentially, had read one of his books, and refused to turn him over to the authorities; and that made him wonder, though he was very grateful, whether or not he felt at all calm knowing that an admirer of his was at the helm of that hunk of steel and sound; and so, ungrateful, he spent the whole trip remembering that madman who not long before had crashed with a planeful of passengers into a wall of the Alps.

He'd verified again that, everywhere, the nutritional and non-Darwinian pyramid of writers was constructed, always, with the same blueprint: many very bad writers, some very good writers, a few excellent writers, and—this had nothing to do with the survival of the most talented—too many really bad writers were considered excellent by some critic, easily seduced by schemes of connections, patronage, awards, and self-promotion.

He'd traveled across the ocean, returning to his homeland where journalists of the cultural variety asked him (always with malice, familiar with his extraterrestrial situation of uncomfortable cosmic singularity and anti-gravitational space curve in whatever critical-academic canon there was in his now nonexistent country of origin) what, did he think, was or would be the place he occupied within the literature of his generation. A question that he invariably answered by citing the exceedingly spaced-out words of Doctor Heywood R. Floyd. The man (the B-actor William Sylvester, there elevated to the highest heights, with that oh so Hugh Hefner air, so similar to many of his parents' friends) who communicates top-secret instructions to the crew of the *Discovery One* when it's already too late or too early in *2001: A Space Odyssey*. But before that—being interrogated by the Russian scientist Andrei Smyslov about the mysterious and supposedly epidemic incidents that took place and were covered up by the American government on the base at the Clavius lunar crater—Floyd responds with words he took and used whenever people came at him about his exact location within the national literary-planetary system: "I'm sorry, but, er, I'm really not at liberty to discuss this."

And no, he didn't discuss it.

And what was the name of that little childhood friend who went, so many times, with him and Penelope to see *2001: A Space Odyssey*; the one with whom they listened to that other Floyd, the Pink one.

And no, it hadn't been all bad, remembering and asking himself questions like that, revisiting those vital constants of his inconstant occupation, back for a few days in the place where he was born dead.

In hotels that for a couple days let him feel Nabokovian and monolithic. In elevators with the music of saxophones and clarinets, the typical instruments of hotel ambience. In rooms like those of the rocker Pink or the astronaut Dave. With those TVs that, when turned on, automatically tuned in that really disturbing channel devoted to that very hotel where you were staying, but that there, on the screen, looked so different, like an ideal and perfected version of that place where you were. Like a heavenly alternative to the hotel that, on this side of the screen, was more of a more or less comfortable purgatory. There, on the other side, minibars on the accounts of others and time suspended, to float, stretched out across meticulously made beds with heavy space-breathing where, sometimes, you were startled by those bright white towels twisted into the shape of a swan coming into the room. And to dive into that inviting pond of sheets to recover from the harsh savannah of airports. From those small supposedly comfortable republics that were actually tyrannical and where the worst of capitalism and communism were in communion, with absurdly high prices, overcrowding, and nobody giving you any explanation or respecting your rights, where everything could be lost or blown up and your horror is only mildly attenuated by those ghost zones, with closed shops, like secret havens where the PA system and Wi-Fi didn't reach and you could read in peace.

Outside the hotel, surrounding that safe zone, that no-place, lurked the real world of fiction. The little literary community that, for many of his colleagues, was an exciting place, but that, for him, was the closest thing to submitting yourself to drastic and invasive medical checkups of the kind that leave you impotent and trembling for days.

Various and sundry risks and discomforts.

Discovering already in the skies that you've chosen the wrong book for the flight. Encounters with once-close writers who now resemble worn-out mannequins always crammed into hideous shrunken sweaters of a grade-school sky-blue. Presentations featuring some flammable girl whose heat he got just close enough to before running away with the more-than-justified fear of getting burned. Or the unexpected—but stylistically and anecdotally appropriate—incursion into the room of his nonagenarian first grade teacher, "Señorita Margarita," who'd thrown herself on him, releasing shrieks of "I taught him to write! I taught him to write!" The woman was recently escaped from an old-folks home and was quickly subdued by a couple nurses (and all of this to the great pleasure of a number of his followers who nudged each other, so satisfied to have come and to confirm there wasn't much difference between what happened in his life and in his books). And even some readers who demonstrated they really understood his work with a presentation that was disturbing for him (readers he'd de/formed and who, in the end, frightened him a little bit, always asking super complicated questions about characters they seemed to know better than he did), who'd adopted his last monolithic and odysseic book as if it were a long-lost child, or the girlfriend they never had. And they honored it as a "living posthumous book," or something like that, and regarded him the way you regard a dead man, not knowing this dead man is also looking back at them and thinking, please, could they just stop looking at him already and let him rest in peace, right? Back from his tour, even his wilted journalistic side experienced a slight new blossoming. And he was asked—by the same massive and prestigious publications, the same ones where he'd been published in his early "flavor-of-the-week" days—for short essays about the condition of the writer in hard times. Editorial directors with the voices of children called him on the phone (they were so much younger than he was, younger in every sense) and gave him instructions and scope (set not by them but by the art directors, based on the illustrations they were planning to use) and specified due dates and length, but (he always found himself forced to ask, almost apologizing) rarely specifying how much they were going to pay him.

And he said yes to all of it. He was an easy yes. His yes was a yeah yeah yeah.

And he complied with the request to insert some or other occasional and mischievous dart/stinger for the hypersensitive and allergic communities of online writers/performers and aspirants to everything and that whole milieu into whatever he wrote.

Articles of the kind that always received a disproportionate number of quick and irascible and accusatory comments online from people who seemed to always be desperately alert and more than ready to willfully belittle anything he'd written (nobody owned what he said or wrote anymore; everything was passed from one keyboard to the next and, with each step of remove, it became degraded by successive commentators and masticators until, like with chewing gum, it got blown up until it exploded with a plop and lost all its original flavor and wound up an annoyance stuck to the soles of shoes). Everything was always analyzed vis-à-vis a display of a rather diffuse capacity for reflection, always and forever conditioned by personal issues.

Years before, those were the people who talked to themselves on the street or whose relatives opted not to invite them over for Christmas dinner or who, when flights were delayed, assumed leadership of the rest of the passengers and started in with the shouting in front of the counters, feeling themselves something like Lenin in the Finlyandsky station.

Now, on the other hand, they were sure the whole world listened to them and read them. The internet was their garden where they could go around defecating among the bushes or ripping up flowers. Not the paradisiac Garden of Earthly Delights but the purgative more than purgatory Garden of Earthly Deceits. They were, yes, strange people: people with a great capacity to hate everyone else and love themselves. Narcissuses staring into the liquid mirrors of their screens, looking out for any possible allusion to their personas or methods. And their fury at what he wrote on commission was considerable, and that reaction, for his bosses, made his piece "a complete success." Because "success" was measured by the number of comments received and they didn't have to be positive and it didn't matter if they were unintelligible or unnecessary (suddenly, relying automatically on the technological format, everyone felt technically and automatically insightful and that they had the right and obligation to say something about everything). Or to denounce errors of orthography (once, because he didn't subscribe to the specifications of Real Academia Española of the kind where "blue jeans" is turned into "bluyín," he'd committed the outrage of refusing to use "en boga" [meaning en vogue] opting instead for "en voga" and he'd been stoned online for foreignizing and Frenchifying). Or to complain that "I didn't understanded anythings" for the simple fact that what he wrote made some sense and used proper grammar. And, yes, the thing with his writing was *you had to read it.* Which is to say: you had to concentrate and devote your attention to what you were reading, something that didn't contain abbreviations or little faces or little hearts, something with sentences that sometimes exceeded three lines in length. The disturbing thing for him was, in many cases, the late-night hour when those comments were posted: didn't anybody work? didn't anybody sleep?

In any case, he had fleetingly been consecrated a kind of nemesis to all of them. With indifference and resignation and for the money. That was the dumb and lightweight enemy luck had dealt him, bad luck, oh-so-lazy luck. Devices, little devices? *Batteries Not Included*? Who was laughing at whom? Who would laugh last when there was no longer any reception? Had *that* become his subject? Why not, on the other hand, choose a rival/accomplice instead of an enemy? Take on the admirable lushness of the nineteenth-century novel not to vanquish it, but to transform it, to bring it back to the wastelands of the twenty-first century so it could germinate again, with equal power and modernized forms? (Thinking of what a challenge it would be gave him vertigo, dizziness, sighs more arrhythmic than romantic.) Or was it maybe that you got the enemy you deserved, one on your level; and he'd gotten the flatlands of screens and tablets? Was he really that worried about that whole electrified world? Was he seriously going to comment again about how the new and insensate phones had done away with the need to check the time on the faces of watches, *normal* watches, not watches bursting with functions like tracking your heartbeats and the calories you consumed at breakfast? to evoke the lost pleasure of hanging up the phone like someone delivering a slap or leaving it off the hook like someone turning their back? to laugh at that religious app that lets you confess via multiple choice thumb swipes? to compare letters on blank pages with photographs of chromosomes? to fire off a wink more silly than nervous mentioning the selfie of Dorian Gray? to lament the picture of families no longer gathered around the warm light of a fire but attached to the cool glow of their respective little screens? to call attention to the not at all random fact that they call those tools for tracking down information "search engines" and not "find engines"? and to the fact that he and those of his caste have always been surfing on waves of cerebral electricity, that there's nothing new in the idea of thinking of everything and nothing? to top it all off with something like "For the first time in history, writing is the enemy of writing"? Nah: the truth is that in the dark and stormy nights of his soul, at his three in the morning, he thought that he thought about all of that because someone still thought it was worthwhile to pay him for the fact that he thought like that, aloud, he thought.

When it came to the editors of his journalism (his other readers), he took it upon himself to include, at the beginning, some obviously out of place paragraph, like a silly little decoy, so his bosses would detect it immediately. And they could edit/cut it. And they would be content and satisfied at/for having edited, having cut, having altered something that was not and never would he his. And so, subsequently, he could do whatever he wanted and turn in a definitive version (the first one, the one he'd not sent), lying that "I have followed your instructions down to the last detail and you're right, it's much better like this."

And everybody happy.

And it surprised him—and it didn't surprise him, it pained him a little—to discover that those more or less clever texts composed in a single morning had a great impact and were taken seriously as "frenzied diatribes" or "apocalyptic preoccupations" about the plugged-in evolution of humanity. And they earned more esteem than any of his books. Or than his last book, which was about precisely *that*, about the end of reading (and, as such, also about the end of writing) as it'd been experienced up until that point.

It didn't take him long to realize that people—even people who read—no longer wanted or were able to handle the concussive shock of reading long books, book-books. And—instead and in their stead—they preferred to be moved by reading a few pages about the growing difficulty of reading deep and devotedly. And with that, their part was done. It was like going to church once a week to confess so you could go on sinning by/through omission.

He was also frequently asked to present books of others, due to his ingenuity when it came to overblown praise (the ingenuity ran through making the praise sound sharp and funny and plausible) with an immediate expiration date and implicit ban on subsequently reproducing what he said in written or visual media (he said that, when it came to the so-called "cultural life," book presentations were like Las Vegas in terms of that unquestionable dictum: "What happens in Las Vegas stays in Las Vegas").

There was also an attempt to incorporate him as a more or less stable/rotating judge on the racetrack of literary prizes where the role assumed was, in reality, far from that of judge and far too close to that of accomplice. Quickly—very quickly—he'd discovered how those things worked. You were given an amount of money in exchange for the silence of showing your face and offering justifications like "A fine and unflinching prose, perfect for capturing the iniquities of our time" and, maybe most important of all: "A novel that seems to be ripped right out of our cruel reality, something we could read in the newspapers of today and yesterday and tomorrow."

† The reading of the different sections of newspapers like an alternative form of life cycle: as children, we read the comics; as adolescents, the horoscopes (in tandem with equally imprecise political prognostications); as young adults,

the schedules in the event section and the cultural supplements; in middle age, the weather forecast as if it were some fascinating and vital thing; in old age, the curiosity and relief of not yet appearing in obituaries.

The reading of dreadful and almost violent manuscripts in their lack of talent and quality when you're a judge for a literary prize is, a little, like sadomasochistically reading the crime section: deaths, murders, absurd accidents, horrifying photographs of dismembered bodies and babies thrown out of windows by parents during a fight, and someone always explaining, with wide eyes and an empty gaze, that "I don't know why I did it." But they did do it. They wrote it. And presenting those prizes is a form of confession that seeks absolution and recognition and that—in many cases, another form of the crime and offense—is agreed on beforehand.

The system of prizes never reported in the cultural pages of newspapers—to keep you from feeling too bad and too guilty, to keep the organizers from undergoing the discomfort of directly asking/telling the jury the direction their vote should go—was that of placing the manuscript they wanted to win among a handful of monstrosities, facilitating its rapid selection.

And everybody happy.

But he—and his "out of place" comments during deliberations, discomfiting the consciences of his colleagues and irritating the organizers—had proven to be, right from the get-go, a not especially . . . flexible judge.

And soon he stopped being "summoned."

And he ceased to appear on the systematic listicles of the "Heirs of the Boom" (as far as he knew, he hadn't actually inherited anything from all of that beyond the implicit obligation to speak well of and honor all those statues; and he was so bad at admiring—or at least pretending to—marble and bronze idols) that periodically filled the pages of cultural supplements. More than an heir, he was disinherited.

And again, little by little, those offers were drying up. Those trips in exchange for a ticket and lodging and "symbolic payment" (to which he responded that he'd left his symbolic stage behind, and now, please, take into account that he was in his realist or, at least, impressionist, period);

always aboard airplanes that seemed to have something called *writer's class*: increasingly narrow seats that kept you from minimally extending your arms to half-open a book, less leg room, and apparently specially designed for the torture and execution of those people who, after all, spent a good part of the day sitting down anyway, so best not to complain, eh.

And that popular writer-photographer—famous for submitting his subjects to implausible and arbitrary poses—who called to coordinate a time and place for a shoot kept postponing over and over again. He couldn't decide—he'd told him with a voice, half hypnotist and half pediatrician, a convincing voice—whether to "photograph you naked and being chased by a pack of wild dogs or naked and chasing a flock of chickens . . . There's also the possibility of crucifying you upside down, naked, of course." And the encounter, in the end, never took place (he suspected he would've ended up with rabid Argentinian guard dogs barking at his inverted body on a cross, covered in chicken shit, or something like that).

Soon, he was only asked to offer remembrances on the successive unhappy deathiversaries of that film director/painter he referred to as The Living Dead Man (of a brief and fragile life and an invulnerable death and a wide-ranging and powerful body of work, and who was his friend toward the end, making him a kind of appendix to his legend) or to contribute words to the latest obituaries of more-or-less proximal colleagues where he always responded by (this was the not-so-secret formula for obituaries) saying something about them he would've wanted them to say about him. And sometimes—and some nights—he wondered if The Living Dead Man or IKEAS or all his other brothers in arms might not actually be creatures caught in the remnants of the original and primary ectoplasm of Pertusato, Nicolasito, pursuing him throughout all the years, one after another, calling him.

And then his phone stopped ringing all together.

And there's nothing louder and more deafening than a telephone that never rings, there, not looking at you while you look at it all the time. A telephone that doesn't ring is like a volatile loved one who no longer speaks to you (call that a "loved one" with great care, like someone handling something both delicate and covered with sharp edges) and a time bomb that never blows up (but that you think might make your head explode at any moment with the last and worst of all the bad news); but even still . . . even still . . . And he, who'd always hated the voice of telephones, now longed for it. Somewhat. A little bit. It tends to happen: you end up missing even what you hate.

And emails stopped arriving to his inbox (and he stopped getting responses to his own from the same people who were incessantly tweeting their lives every five minutes, even to share the news that he'd just written them though they didn't think to answer him; because it was so much more important to write in public than in private), with the exception of health insurance promotions and newsletters from the advertising departments of publishing houses. Promises of good care in terrible moments and announcements composed as if to relate cosmic events no observer could possibly miss. Lists of coverage for unprecedented and novel illnesses and information about the fortunes paid for post-mortem manuscripts of soon-to-touch-down-in-the-city unknown geniuses (a dead star is born) or brief and steamy and orgasmic opuscules (very SHE-IKEA) or first novels of a thousand pages (big bangs that almost always proved to be little pfffs) more like those of HE-IKEA than like his own, which were compared, always, not to nineteenth-century classics but to millennial TV series.

And then, not even that, and not even those bad books sent for his consideration (many of them by supposed "admirers," hoping for one of those magical blurbs that'd helped launch IKEAS). And that he, inconsiderate (and if Google was good for anything: whenever some brave kid asked for a shred of his old glory in the form of praise for the band or jacket of a book, all he had to do was type his own name and that of the requester and, more than once, too many times, there was the person who called himself his disciple virtually spitting on him in virtual public), traded in for other, better books, at his habitual second-hand bookstore.

And thus his name and address were vanishing from databases and electronic datebooks.

And with that, they were done with him.

And that's all folks, *adieu* and, again, where was he, where had he ended up? Of one thing he was more or less certain: light years away from what his contemporaries were doing. Not in front and not behind but far off to one side.

And ever further from the center, no doubt.

And ever closer to something extreme. But it wasn't anybody's Number Zero unless you could be your own Number Zero.

And did it make any sense to go somewhere nobody had gone and where nobody was waiting for him?

And, right, it's true that every so often it was convenient to shock your followers so they, after a while, realized they missed you and came back to you to love you more than ever. But, perhaps, he'd scared them too much.

And not only had he turned their hair white, but, also, burst their hearts with the intensity of his howling.

And others saw him and read him and compared where he was with where he'd been and, disconsolate or chuckling, didn't think "Bill Murray." No, what they thought was: "Nicolas Cage."

And what place had he occupied, in the end, in the "national tradition"? (A national tradition that was actually quite strange. A tradition whose—the only case in his language and, more than likely, in any language—canonical writers had all occupied the genre of the fantastic. And where all the great national novels were of invertebrate and tentacular and atomized structure. The short story was the reigning genre; maybe because the history of his now nonexistent country of origin had always been a succession of episodic earthquakes, where everything came to an end to start over again in increasingly brief but intensified, and more catastrophic, recurrent cycles and cyclones.) How did he confront the eternal and unsolvable problem of what one is like and how one is perceived and how does one ever manage to perceive what one is like and how one is perceived? Where did he fit on such a curved plane?

Easy: in the attic where they lock up the lunatics.

He was still there.

One of the *malditos*—a damned, accursed writer, a *poète maudit*—and, oh, but he'd never felt himself a *maldito*. He mistrusted all of them. Among the *malditos*, in general, the life was always more interesting (and of higher quality) than the work. And the *malditos* always felt and called themselves *malditos*. They set a trap, yes. He, on the other hand, would rather feel himself an outsider. An outsider couldn't declare himself an outsider. An outsider *was made* by others: the ones who pushed him to the edge or to the shore of the desert island, sometimes, without suspecting it, improving his art, suffusing it with the exquisite and penetrating scent of solitude. And in the case of outsiders, almost always, their work was more attractive than their lives. And, sometimes, an outsider even got to experience a moment of success (generally in the beginning of his career) that made him visible, memorable, and worthy of an occasional "What ever happened to that guy?" when it came to concocting listicles of ephemera. In the end, an outsider was someone convinced he did things just like everyone else in the world, but—he ran into fewer and fewer colleagues when he went out walking among its sand dunes—also more or less aware his world didn't appear to be particularly well inhabited.

An outsider was someone who, sooner or later, if there was luck or justice, found a way to return from that desert and change the world with the mirages he'd planted there to harvest later as oases. Sometimes outsiders took days to return, like Jesus Christ, in the event he actually existed. Sometimes years, like Francis Scott Fitzgerald and Bill Murray (whom he'd recognized as someone very special from the very beginning of his career, when nobody noticed him except in more or less successful comedies, and whose face, his nothing-and-everything face, a unisex and one-size-fits-all face; he'd used it over and over, like a secret mental note, to imagine the faces of the characters he'd once written, women and children and animals included). Sometimes decades, like Herman Melville. Sometimes centuries, like Cervantes. And there were strange cases, like that of William S. Burroughs, whom everyone was still waiting on and whose whereabouts were known, but, since he never showed up, successive expeditions (that never returned) had been dispatched to try to capture and apprehend him.

Among all these *rara avises*, for him, The Great Outsider had always been, once again, Vladimir Nabokov.

The universal and borderless Russian, coming and going across half the planet, and pulled out by the tides of history to later, on his own, return from exile at high sea like a triumphing king, standing atop a trumpeting pachyderm, its hoofs riding on two whales (he remembered seeing an image like that, in a medieval bestiary), shouting "Who are the outsiders now, eh?," driving so many supposedly renowned names toward the abyss.

He, conversely and to the contrary, had been and was and always would be, damn it, a small and minuscule and almost-invisible outsider.

An outsider whose whereabouts were never asked after and for whom a rescue mission was never organized until scientific motives held sway over artistic ones.

An outsider in a literary landscape where, moreover, it was easier all the time to be an outsider; because the literary establishment was smaller and less literary all the time. And there were increasingly few opportunities for an outsider to win his consolation prize: that a considerable number of insiders became interested in his outsiderness.

It was clear this hadn't been his case.

His entire tradition, now, ironically, ran through being a note (not an asterisked footnote, but a numbered footnote, one of so many exasperating footnotes) at the foot of the increasingly colossal statue of his sister and a handful of minor statuettes who people always believed in more than they believed in him.

IKEAS included.

And another irony, even more painful than the last: before that last moment of low-intensity glory, before that strange, more or less *de luxe* prestige, before the publication of what would be his last book and what, more than a discovery or a rediscovery, was for him a cover up, his own funeral; IKEAS had been there for him and had his back, at each and every funicular stop.

A funicular near his house in B (the funicular that appeared in his just-mentioned book) and (again, once more, few things make you more circularly repetitive than insomnia) one near his hotel in Montreux: the aforementioned funicular that appeared in the aforementioned *Tender Is the Night* by the aforementioned Francis Scott Fitzgerald, the favorite book by the favorite author of his parents (a funicular that also went up and down in *Transparent Things* and, transfigured and transported to Zembla, ascended from the terraces of Kronblik to the heights of the Kron glacier, in *Pale Fire*).

Yes, IKEAS were part of his book and in a way had contributed to its bitter and monologuing genesis. The book had been written *against* but also *with* them.

And now IKEAS were no longer there, or that's how he liked to feel, that he didn't feel them anymore. He projected himself, again, more or less forty years into the future. To a time when IKEAS's books were no longer talked about or recognized or sold except when mentioned as a kind of temporal aberration and passing trend immediately replaced by other trends and aberrations to be surpassed. Which for him wasn't much comfort. Because he—beyond having written that book that seemed to celebrate its own funeral rites—wouldn't be posthumous *either*. (In his imagined insomniac future, he liked to fantasize that his work still enjoyed a certain cult glow, buoyed more by his life than by the work itself, by the ever weaker yet sustained breath of the surprising survival and maintenance of his person.) On the other hand, the venerable mechanisms of righteous and poetic post-mortem consecration were already irreparably damaged. Everything was going way too fast for there to be time or patience to let a failure accumulate sediment and gain in seductive epic and anecdotal potency. Fifteen minutes of fame couldn't be reformulated as fifteen minutes of defeat and, for that reason, there was no possibility of constructing a compelling story worthy of redemption and rediscovery and success. There wasn't enough space or adequate focus for a failure to end up succeeding. Or for relationships, connections, miraculous synapses to be established that would bring the light of the masses to some obscure, unknown writer.

There no longer existed neither the slightest distance nor that clever hypothesis of those, in their day, so-oft-cited "six degrees of separation." Suddenly, in the first years of the new millennium—thanks and no thanks to social networks—everyone was inseparable. Everyone was together. It didn't matter whether they were in the same place or knew each other. What mattered was the effect of planetary communion. The connection of the link. And so, all of a sudden, everyone was a genius to him or herself and, thus, the desire for singularity was lost and, even, for one's own name, opting instead for masks and avatars and usernames and "anonymous." And, of course, everyone *knew how* to read and above all how to write (because of all the arts, writing was the one you learned earliest and the one requiring nothing additional but talent), but those who *could* read and write were ever fewer.

The product, then, wasn't what mattered. What mattered was to produce or, better yet, to constantly proclaim you *were* producing. Everything was digital and thumb and remix and disc jockeys became more important than songwriters. Everything was made immediate and, at the same time, untouchable. The culture of the autobiographical blog (whose entries specified how long it would take you to read them) emerged naturally in the self-portrait-happy selfie culture (where people died in the most ridiculous accidents, on the edges of balconies and cliffs and there was even a flourishing serial killer who stabbed his victims in the eyes with one of those sticks for holding a mobile phone and taking close-ups of yourself with the actually interesting thing as mere backdrop).

And—waking dream of the future—the dronicle (travel chronicles written from a drone, manufactured in Latin America if possible) became all the rage.

And the alka-novel (novels dissolved in water that you drank and that produced the sensation of having read them without having to read them).

And the ventrilit (where a doll sitting on your lap reads the novel of your choice in a shrill voice).

And the lettering (reading of random letters from great classics, the A and the X were the most appreciated by critics, while, in the Spanish version, the Ñ and the H and the LL, which nobody knew exactly whether or not it was still a letter, were increasingly underground and transgressive).

And on and on until what, for many, was the supreme and purest literary experience was attained: staring at books, without touching them, and from an ever greater distance ("Yesterday I looked at *Ulysses* . . . From ten meters! . . . Seriously it's really hard to look at," "I only look at entertaining bestsellers, I start off looking at them close up and, then, when I'm around the middle, I turn around and look at them in a photograph on the screen of my phone") until, at last, having them disappear from sight, or erasing all trace of them on one's mobile phone, exclaiming "oh!" and "ah!"

And that's how it all came to an end.

And that's how the end was and would be, the end that—for a few pious nights—came with the happy coda of bringing back into style, retro, the whole paper and book thing. For a few nights. A passing trend.

And so—in his late night prophesies—what began with the certainty that everything external was for everyone and everyone was someone. Nothing had owner or authorship.

And everyone would be happy like that, writing on their screens about what they were going to write, commenting the ones on the others, only stopping to follow their favorite TV shows (the once carefully considered singularity of the favorite that obliged a "one to ten" ranking had easily

pluralized into to three or four or five digits without any need to discrimi-
nate or justify the selections; quantity over quality), which, they claimed,
were better than stories and novels and, in addition, the perfect excuse: if
at one time television had been accused of being the great enemy of reading, now it went even further and erected itself as the superior substitute
to reading. Seeing was better than reading. And everybody happy, happily
complicit. And the truth is that, in watching those shows you could, every so
often, learn interesting things. Like that one—he can't remember its name,
but can remember that it was like a cross between a James Salter novel and
a John Updike novel—in which someone talks about something called "secondary drowning": the possibility that a child, rescued from the water, on
death's doorstep, could die from drowning on terra firma up to three days
after the near-mortal accident that, in the end, was just that, but drawn out,
like the slowest-rolling wave, a result of liquid that was never fully pumped
out during CPR.

He remembers that now.

And he can't forget either that he almost drowned at the mouth of a
marine river, when he was a child, before knowing how to read and write;
and that he believed he perceived then, in that living-to-tell-the-tale, the
commencement of his literary vocation, though he already felt himself a
writer in full use of his mental faculties, when he intuited that the reader
reads to escape, but, first, the writer writes to go somewhere, to depart.

The writer as an exciting/exiting being.

And he wonders if this suffocating and insomniac night might be nothing
but the secondary drowning from that first day, held in check throughout so
many years, but finally catching up to him, like a wave that fills his mouth
with water, sweet and salty at the same time.

And he remembers too that, again, James Salter (a writer who always
seemed to him underrated and overrated at the same time; a writer whose
last novel had an editor as protagonist) had written that "The death of kings
can be recited, but not of one's child."

And the blind quotation of Salter—and the certainty that the language
of personal tragedy is only spoken perfectly by one or two or three people,
six at most—leads him straight to finding Penelope and being unable to find
Penelope's son; it was never known if he died in the water or in the forest,

before vanishing from the borderland of a beach. And that unresolved mystery and that terrible pain that, he thought then, had ravaged his organism like a war. A pain that—making tumors bloom inside him like flowers—would bring him to death straight away, at most, in a matter of months. A pain he tried to put in writing as a form of cowardly suicide: Nabokov had said, "The thought, when written down, becomes less oppressive, but some thoughts are like a cancerous tumor: you express it, you excise it, and it grows back worse than before," and he readied himself for that. For being struck down. Being hit by a pain that was like a lightning bolt falling with a clap of thunder, but that, in reality, when it came, ended up spawning another kind of catastrophe, of the opposite sign but equally destructive: it made him invulnerable, unfeeling, beyond all illness.

His torment—he decided and it was decided—wouldn't be that of one killed in action before his time, but that of the eternal survivor. The bearer of an immortal agony he buffered by presenting it to second and third parties as bitterness at the state of things.

And so, now, for him, it was no trouble at all to replace that grimace of perpetual desolation (a grimace that reminded him of the petrified features of the paternal tomb robber in *Mr. Sardonicus* or *The Baron Sardonicus* and the heartbreaking smile of Bill Murray) with a permanent rictus of disgust.

And that rictus was ideal for wearing—as if it were a standard on his secret crusade—out and about. And so, best to lower the blinds and leave that house and go back to writer fairs and writer (not book) presentations, where everyone talked about shows and screens and about the complicity among those who styled themselves "internauts," to endow their activities with a touch of the grandeur of explorers without barely having to move, a touch of false camaraderie in that solitude. I'll scratch your back if you scratch mine and, together, across whatever distance separates us, we'll stab the back of that other person who, in general, succeeded in getting published in some "reactionary and elitist format" like that of a book.

And there inside, across the shining surface, everything seemed so clean, so meticulous, so composed, so . . . book. Thus, they were all successful losers or defeated winners. On the other hand, the paper manuscript had disappeared. And so there was no longer anything to illuminate in household desk drawers or editorial filing cabinets. And who knows how many *post-humifiable* masterpieces were resting somewhere, in an unshakeable trance, prisoners of hard disks gone soft, impossible to decode now with technologies that had advanced beyond them.

Maybe, to tell the truth, not too many; who knows.

But yes, but no: he was sure he wouldn't be considered vital beyond the grave, except as an important secondary figure, but a figure all the same, fulfilling the role of *sister's keeper*: the guardian of the memory of Penelope and the Drakadia books (and he had to admit: in more than one plotline in the luminous-terrorist saga of Stella D'Or, Penelope had found a way to sound much closer to Nabokov than he ever had; and when he asked her how she'd done it, she arched an eyebrow and, with a twisted smile, answered grimly, her breath gone metallic from all the medications and her voice that of a rusted robot: "Very simple. I learned it by reading *Ada, or Ardor*, from beginning to end in a couple days. It's all in there"). Penelope's oeuvre, like a second child he—though he didn't really enjoy it and understood its near hysterical and devotional commercial success even less—would never allow to get lost like her first.

And so, he was, merely, like an important part of the scene (he'd read that, again, Bill Murray had bequeathed his skull to be used in performances of *Hamlet*, in "an easy role to play, but always much-anticipated role in a very good play"); he was like a master of ceremonies who didn't remotely reach the creative stature or grace of Rod Serling, at the beginnings and ends of those episodes of *The Twilight Zone* that he'd seen for the first of many times as a child. Episodes he'd watched and learned, by osmosis, how to structure a story.

† Wishing to be Rod Serling when you're a kid and still wishing to be him when you're older though not necessarily grown up. To be Rod Serling like being a story's elegant host. Knowing perfectly how it begins and unfolds and ends. Minimal time but maximal efficiency when it comes to telling it, *to producing it*. None of the Laurence-Sternian "I progress as I digress," but, rather, a Rod-Serlingian "I progress" and that's that, period.

And new paragraph.

And on to the next one.

Episodes of *The Twilight Zone* like the dreams he remembered to perfection the next morning and discussed with his Cabrera classmates, on the playground at recess. Because they've all dreamed the same thing, they've all seen *The Twilight Zone* the night before, and after they've all gone to sleep and have dreamed those self-contained chapters/stories. Many of them related to sleeping and dreaming because—since the dawn of time—there's nothing more supernatural yet certifiable and real than the act of closing our eyes here to open them elsewhere.

Dream episodes of *The Twilight Zone*:

"Perchance to Dream": the story of a man who, distressed, goes to see a psychiatrist and tells him that he dreams in chapters. He dreams of Maya, a seductive carnival dancer wearing leopard-print tights (which were discussed at length at the school), and she lures him into a funhouse and then onto the roller coaster. And the man has a heart condition and knows that, if he goes any further, he'll die in his sleep. On the other hand, if he stays awake (and the man has been up for eighty hours without sleeping), the exhaustion would end up damaging his heart, and that would also end badly. The man realizes that the psychiatrist can't help him and, leaving his office, he discovers that the receptionist is identical to the woman from the funhouse. Terrified, he turns and runs back into the office and jumps out of the window to his death. Just then, the doctor calls to his secretary and asks her to come into his office and the man, the patient from the beginning, is there, lying on the divan. And the doctor explains to the girl that his patient came in, lay down, fell asleep, let out a scream, and died on the spot.

"I Dream of Genie": another attractive secretary in the office where the protagonist is a bookkeeper. The man goes into an antique shop and buys an antique and somewhat dented Arabian lamp for twenty dollars. But back in his office, the man discovers that a coworker of his (a very attractive and ambitious man) has given the secretary a very sexy *negligee*. The man, embarrassed, doesn't give her the lamp, he takes it home, and when he's cleaning it, polishing it, out comes a genie. The genie wears modern clothes and speaks slang and the only thing that gives him away are those absurd curving and pointed shoes. And he grants not three but just one wish. And he tells the man he's going to give him time to think it over carefully and goes back into his lamp. What follows are not sleeping dreams but waking dreams: the man fantasizing that he's married to the secretary, who has become a big movie star (and who doesn't have time for him and does have time for an affair with another movie star; so he rejects that one); that he's a magnate of such generosity it ends up complicating his life (he rejects that one too); so he settles for the Great American Dream: to be president of the United States (but the responsibility is too great and he doesn't know what to do faced with a crises caused by an alien invasion; so not that one either). But, in the end, he has an idea. In the next scene, a homeless man finds the lamp in a garbage can, rubs it, out comes the genie. And the genie is none other than that shy bookkeeper who doesn't know what to ask for.

"Where Is Everybody?": the most unsettling of all and the original pilot of *The Twilight Zone*. A man with the uniform of an Air Force service man wanders through a town where there are no people, but he has the sensation of being watched. He goes into a café, a telephone booth, a police station, a drugstore, a movie theater. "Time to wake up now! Time to wake up now . . . I'm in the middle of a nightmare I can't wake up from . . . I must be a very imaginative guy. Nobody in the world can have a dream as complete as mine, down to the last detail . . . I'd like to wake up now," the man says over and over again. His solitary desperation grows until, frantic, he ends up pressing the button at the stoplight over and over in order to cross a street where no cars pass by. Then it's revealed that that button is, actually, a "panic button" that "wakes" him up inside an isolation chamber where he's been for the last 484 hours, as part of a program for astronauts training to go to the moon. In the final scene, the (failed) astronaut in training is taken out of the hanger on a stretcher, and he looks up at the sky where the moon is shining, and he says something like "Hey! Don't go away up there! Next time it won't be a dream or a nightmare. Next time it'll be real."

"The Museum's Visitor": a man is sent by a powerful American business-man to recover an ancient family portrait that now hangs on the wall of a small provincial museum, in an unspecified European country. The envoy at first thinks the assignment is the whim of a millionaire, but it all turns out to be true: there's the painting and among the faces of the people posing in it he recognizes his employer's features. "It was rewarding, in a way, being part of a dream coming true, even if it was someone else's dream," says the traveler, who doesn't hesitate to make an offer for the painting to the museum manager who, at first, denies the existence of the painting, then admits it, but nervously slips away through a small door. When he tries to follow, the envoy gets lost in the museum's passageways and ends up falling asleep and has a dream in which he is contemplating a museum shaped like a giant wearing a hat and carrying a suitcase covered in tourist stickers, a museum of himself. The man wakes up with a start and discovers an emergency exit and goes out into a landscape that is the landscape of his childhood, in a forest, and through the trees he spies his parents and his little sister and himself, as a boy, a boy who sees him watching and smiles and lifts an index finger to his lips, signaling him to keep quiet. The episode ends with the man standing in front of the door that would take him back to the present, unsure whether to return or not; but the scene fades to black before we see if he walks through it. In the next scene, we're back inside the museum and we're treated to that oft-repeated ending: one of the paintings depicts the traveler with his back turned, outside the museum, all alone.

And, yes, he could understand it: all he'd achieved—like multiple episodes of *The Twilight Zone*, stories of lone survivors of planetary catastrophes in whose modality he now inserted himself as imaginary centenarian—was the ambiguous feat of being left alone.

Yes: he had nobody left.

And he'd achieved this (through a combination of good genes and adequate diet and priceless latest-generation medications he got access to because of his good attitude and impeccable résumé as laboratory guinea pig) without great effort.

Not even his regal solitude of solus rex on an empty chessboard, only held in check by his own shadow (which allowed him a panoramic view with the perspective of the lone survivor, of the one who laughs last, of the one who lives to tell the tale), could be understood as a success.

Solitude—which at one time had been the perfect product of the ideal sanctuary; a cheap activity in which you could come up with the most valuable ideas—had gone out of style.

It'd been eradicated.

The moments and spaces for being alone (that place where, among other things, you read and wrote and daydreamed) had been occupied by the faux company of social media. By a constant typing and staring at text, in the constant company of "friends" near or far, only interrupted by the eruption of some publishing phenomenon, fed by a mass hysteria of religious intensity, like what'd happened with Penelope's books, which, now, ironically and paradoxically, financed his solitude.

Now he wasn't lonely.

Now he was solitary.

Now he was beyond all thought of someone who might be thinking about him, wondering, "Where could he be? What could he be doing?"

And, even still, there he was, keeping himself company.

And there was a great deal of triumphal melancholy in his persistence.

And a great deal of paradoxical loss: because victory isn't victory if you don't have losing rivals to testify and bear witness to it.

And he'd understood for a long time now that the process of obtaining such comfortable and functional rivals wasn't easy. He realized then that there weren't even *that* many colleagues of his for whom it was going *that* much better and whose successes were *that* indisputably unjust. Before long, in his fantasies, with IKEAS off the map, all there would be in his vicinity were names of his same stature and talent of those who'd gotten more recognition than he had.

Why?

Because of pure chance or the skill of literary agents who'd gotten some publisher drunk during the long nights of the Frankfurt Book Fair, before it shut down forever after that Islamic-fundamentalist attack, coinciding with the visit of the cartoonist author of *Allah is Extra Large*.

Goodbye to any chance of signing a million-dollar contract there and thereby triggering a domino effect; because nobody wanted to be left out of the party when everything came to fruition and, if a small fortune were lost, well then, everybody lost; and automatic and collective amnesia; and nobody would bring it up in the coming years as a matter of protocol and good manners.

In any case, nothing even remotely close to that had ever happened to him after *National Industry*.

He'd never been "discovered" at Frankfurt.

He'd become what's known as a "writer's writer," at a time when writers had stopped reading (and, again, he still couldn't read *Ada, or Ardor*, could it be because, according to its author, its theme was "happiness," and he was so far away from that theme?) because they were too busy reading only what they were writing or, at most, what someone who might give them something they needed was writing and . . . ah . . . uh . . .

But, again, the digression is the secret language of insomnia and channel-surfing its dialect.

Insomnia's favorite song is "All Together Now."

And so, with an effort and adjustment of his pillow, he tries to return from there, to jump back a few thoughts, as if rewinding without the remotest control.

To concentrate on something.

On a fixed and unwavering point.

On, after so many years, giving shape to a more or less precise space through which to move. A handful of hours on his hands like a number of lines on a map.

And so, he opens a notebook and thinks about writing something that— he imagines he's already contemplating it from the other side, from the shore to be reached and not from the shore from which to reach—speaks and is written in the language of dreams and the dialect of insomnia.

A kind of flipside to his last book. A book that spoke in the tongue writers speak when they think, in silence, awake and not daydreaming, about what they're going to write. Now, on the other hand, to explore what a writer thinks he's thinking when he dreams, sleeping or waking.

A book that—with any luck—won't put people to sleep but will make them dream. The always difficult to ford second act preceding the third movement that would bring, with eyes half-closed, both tongues together in a single language: that form of the inventive dreaming that is making and unmaking memory.

He tries a few lines. The letters come out strange, hesitant, with sketchy profiles akin to those of his beginnings, to his first letters. He practices, short words and brief lines, at first. Nothing to do with and reading nothing like the sentences (more prayers than sentences, overflowing with dashes and commas and semicolons and colons and parentheses) he uses to think.

He, with caution, braves short distances.

Going from *here* to *there*.

To ascend downhill or descend uphill.

But, then, he picks up speed and, with it, so much to lose.

Writing, he discovers, is like riding a bicycle: it's true you never forget (and he doesn't forget that he learned to ride very late, on a bike without training wheels, his parents already gone); what you *do* forget is the desire to pedal, that maybe you could get back on that bicycle and see what doesn't happen or never get on it again and see what does.

Which doesn't mean, once you've regained equilibrium, that you won't fall again, so many times, that in the sorrow of the fall is the grace of getting back up.

And his bones (especially his skull and what resides inside his skull, with his ever tauter skin stretching across his bones, reminding him of that protective plastic, like alien saliva, wrapped around suitcases on those rotating machines in airports) are no longer what they were. The handlebars pushing back against his hands, like the horns of an animal he's landed astride of, legs spread, rodeoing through the rodeo of his life.

And, of course, he moves tentatively, first executing esses and, subsequently, the rest of the letters.


† To begin, perhaps, the way books read by the young and the not so young began back then (when children didn't only read books that were just written, new books, books freshly made and especially designed for children and only for children or for adults who let themselves be swept away by a melancholic fever). To begin the way that book that opened with "It was the best of times,

it was the worse of times, it was the age of wisdom, it was the age of foolishness, it was the epoch of belief, it was the epoch of incredulity, it was the season of Light, it was the season of Darkness, it was the spring of hope, it was the winter of despair"; and, yes, in the public schools there had been teachers who insisted that a personal and childish adaptation of a Shakespeare play was the best option for an end-of-the-year performance and . . .

And he feels a dizziness.

He loses air and strength and his eyes cloud over and, yes, he falls. Not off the bed, but almost (his legs pedaling frenetically under the sheets and blankets, searching for pedals that suddenly aren't there).

And the pen falls from his hand (Magic-Pen brand, a pen with a built-in light) and he has to execute a complicated contortion to retrieve it from the footboard of his bed and . . .

So, just in case, as a precautionary measure, he opts to drop the simile of writing like pedaling. And he chooses walking instead. Slower but safer, and so much easier to synch up with the memory of that nighttime walk.

Of that Great Nighttime Walk, when he was a boy who liked to run and for whom the act of walking was a form of reflection.

Back then, you walked to see and to feel better, you ran to get to weariness more quickly and then you could walk with your duty fulfilled.

And the night he now describes and scribbles down is the night of the Great Nighttime Walk and, remembering himself moving forward, is for him like walking backward, in reverse. Like Mr. Trip, like his perfect and functionally dysfunctional but not-broken toy. Looking up at the black sky. Counting stars in moonshot countdowns (he starts with star number ten thousand and, from there, down to star zero) to stay awake while others recount stories or count sheep in order to, then, fall back asleep. To stare up at the stars and challenge them to a let's see who blinks first and the stars lose within one second yet know themselves winners for all eternity.

But, it tends to happen, behind the stage of one definitive night is the backstage and the accumulated props and the dressing rooms and all the overlapping curtains of so many days before and so many years after.

And the days preceding that night in his life are days of austral summer. Long days with short nights when he and Penelope have, once again, been sent by their parents to Sad Songs. To the south. To what will end up being his Zembla and his Vyra; because sooner or later everyone ends up an exiled king of their own childhood, driven mad by the memory of youth in a world far wider than the world of adult life, fearing that a shadow of that past will catch up to it and sacrifice it in its name and its story.

There they go. He and Penelope. To Sad Songs. Where their other grandparents (the provincial Russian grandparents; their Russian grandparents in the capital take care of them during the school year and on weekends, with the rest of their time devoted to perfecting the simultaneously infallible and honest method of fleecing friends and friends of friends in games of blackjack) are waiting for them. Both pairs of grandparents came here, from so far, when they were children. To his now nonexistent country of origin. His grandparents had been émigrés, fleeing the clamor of red cavalries and white guards. And, oh, the irony that now, after all of that, they have to put up with a new revolution, featuring their own, grown but never-grown-up, children, dressed in T-shirts adorned with stars and sickles and hammers. And so they cling to their grandchildren as if they were sacred icons: their grandparents believe in Penelope's and his childhood as if it were a religion that worshipped the idea of better and less convulsive days. And so, the provincial grandparents receive him and Penelope during their vacations, with a combination of love and resignation. As if those restless children, kept still throughout the school year, experienced a sudden thaw in those open spaces, like an opportune and seasonal natural phenomenon. Like good stormy weather.

Between one set of grandparents and the other, a small brigade of rotating nannies (none of whom put up for long with the bipolar love-hate treatment of their parents, who never cease changing routines and menus) take him and Penelope to and from school. Those girls are, inevitably, very-more-or-less-a-little-bit-somewhat pretty. And, probably, they have approached his parents with the fantasy of being discovered as models. But, as mentioned, none of them last long. His father seduces them first and belittles them later, without ever touching a hair on their heads. His mother belittles them first and seduces them later without ever touching a hair on their heads either. Pure hysteria. Now you see them now you don't. And there goes one so another can come. And his parents have instructed them (him and Penelope; who already suspect that the girls are like mechanical dolls assembled in the basement of the house) that independent of their true names they are all to be called, always, "Rosalita." To avoid confusions and complications (with time, in his memory, they all look like just one, so similar were they, like successive models of the same brand, squirrel cheeks and high-pitched little voices and an air like distant and altiplano relatives of that creature known as Björk). And they all feed Penelope and him an exclusive diet of prefabricated hamburgers and instant mashed potatoes and big glasses of Coca-Cola and Jell-O of varying flavors ("Eating colors," he and Penelope call the only more or less variable thing on the menu until the one weekend, in their grandparent's kitchen, when they discover and enjoy the possibility of other foods and flavors and textures). Such is life, the life of their lives.

Their parents' life happens elsewhere, in a place where children have little reason to be, unless there's a camera in the vicinity to verify that they're children, always dressed in psychedelic-colored clothes, so fetching and photographable and reportable, and so different from their gray-and-blue-upholstered little friends.

And their grandparents from the capital seem a little disconcerted by this routine to which they've consented without being previously consulted and by the Rosalita of the moment dropping off their grandchildren on Friday afternoons and coming back to collect them on Sundays at nightfall, when everything seems to dissolve so it can reassume the solidity of the inevitable. The end of the weekend, like the terrible moment when everything, all of a sudden, is seen as it truly is, without makeup or poses.

Their parents, disconcerted at turning back into parents.

And their grandparents, saddened by his and Penelope's departure. Grandparents who, in their youth, were far more transgressive than their children: fleeing war-torn countries, crossing oceans in the holds of ships, vomiting up the few jewels they're carrying hidden in their intestines just to swallow them again; and they arrive to the New World with nothing and end up with everything, and, reaching these last and finally gentle curves in the race of their lives, no doubt dreamed of something that wasn't being responsible, once again, for two children. And having to prepare them exotic dishes like fish and pasta and fruits and vegetables.

But they didn't complain either: compared to having children, having grandchildren was a never-ending pleasure. And their grandchildren are so much more grown-up than their children. And the truth is he and Penelope—in city or provincial town—needed nothing but time and space.

He always remembers the city as an eternal autumn of movie theaters and TV and books.

And all summer long, in Sad Songs, time and space was in abundance.

And, also, the magic of the unknown or what, after many vacations spent in that place, is well-known but still intrigues them and is more and more fun all the time: as if from one year to the next, the script of those days was rewritten better, with added details that'd passed them by or weren't there before, but that now turn out to be inescapable and indispensable.

Sad Songs grows as they grow.

On walks down roads flanked by weeping willows that lead to a ruined palazzo (brought over stone by stone from Venice; he and Penelope look for and find Venice on an atlas) where, they're told, lives a wealthy local madwoman, famous for cohabiting with hundreds of chickens she dresses up elegantly in little doll dresses.

Along the dirt road that leads to a small airport: going to watch the airplanes landing and taking off is quite a show, in days when everything has to be seen live and direct to be believed and authentically experienced. Airplanes on TV shows and in movies are implausible and obvious and lacking any special effects, like the way the broadcast of the moon landing (the director of his ever more ruinous and crackpot school named Gervasio Vicario Cabrera, n°1, Distrito Escolar Primero, assembled them in the auditorium and they strained their eyes to make out what was happening on a small black-and-white television, coming up one by one, pausing for a few seconds in front of the screen, as if receiving a cosmic sacrament) disappointed and led everyone to question it, because it looked too *televisual*. Really: could it be true that space was so gray and indistinct and had such bad audio? Could 1969 really be so un-*2001*?

They have, yes, they'll realize eventually, the luck of being one of the last generations of children who will enjoy the pleasure and necessity of the implicit obligation to see things live and direct. And to understand the future as something futuristic, distant, sci-fi, and with XXL-size and top-secret computers that could never be in every home. For them, the future is still so far away, always in reach not of their hands but of their minds: all the time—all the present—they think about the future. Yesterday is so brief and, for them, only functions as something gone tomorrow. And today there are so many things to see. So it's not about seeing to believe but about believing in everything you see, even in the most absurd; because the present is much closer to what's passed than what's yet to come. It's a past-present with a great deal of the past present. The future, on the other hand, is constant novelty. And so, then, that imperfect moon-landing broadcast is left behind and there before them is that airplane taking off. And there they are. He and Penelope, at the small airport in Sad Songs, with handkerchiefs covering their mouths and goggles protecting their eyes and all that millennial dust suspended in the air thanks to propellers and turbines.

On excursions to a beach that'd changed little in appearance since prehistory—to that sea where a river mouth opens—and where there stands the tower of a man named Merlín Mantra. A man to whom the locals attribute strange magical properties. A man rarely seen outside that tower, towering atop a cliff that overlooks little pools the tide has carved into the stone that every night the sea fills with snails and octopuses and stones of impossible colors, which they collect thinking they're dazzling only to discover they lose all their luster when they dry out, back at home.

There, he and Penelope read classic stories in children's anthologies, altering a few words at first and then entire sections, each time they read them to each other, taking turns, until, at the end, they are something new and unrecognizable, and a little dwarf is a prince and a prince is a wolf and all Sleeping Beauty wants is to be left to sleep in peace, because she's tired of all the palace intrigue and conspiracy.

And they don't know it yet, but they are already training each other, as if shadow boxing, pounding out plotlines until their faces are unrecognizable and forcing themselves to stand up for one more final round, another turn of the screw. There they are, while the grown-ups take their afternoon siesta and they can't and don't want to sleep, because is there anything weirder than sleeping in the afternoon? anything more absurd than splitting the day in two with a false night in between?

He already knows he's a writer and doesn't suspect at all that Penelope, who suspects it even less, will *also* end up being a writer.

And they arrive and depart on the train.

They are brought to Sad Songs and taken away from Sad Songs by their volatile Uncle Hey Walrus, their mother's brother (not her real brother, but the son of some friends who're always coming around, who calls himself her brother in order not to have to admit he's crazy about her and crazy about everything else), who every so often returns to the home of his parents to recover from one of his "episodes," a euphemism used to refer to, but never detail, his successive and increasingly complex work-related catastrophes and mental problems or work-related problems and mental catastrophes (the latest of which has to do with the loss of an investment he'd made in a manufacturer of "inside-out socks" after having an epiphany that "It's far more logical and comfortable to put them on inside out, with the stitching on the outside, no?, yes?").

Retrospectively, he'll recognize that his Uncle Hey Walrus occupies— half offended but also committed to honoring his condition and never disappointing his resigned followers—the regional-classic seat of honor of "the village lunatic."

Uncle Hey Walrus is less the black sheep of the family and more the multicolor and fluorescent sheep of the town. And Uncle Hey Walrus loves the two of them so much, with that complicit love that the mentally unstable have for children who, they intuit, probably understand them more and better than anyone.

Uncle Hey Walrus brings them to and from Sad Songs aboard a train that takes more than twenty-four hours in either direction. A train where you can live more than an entire day, allowing more than enough time to read a whole novel, looking up from it every so often to take a break from reading everything and to stare out at nothing. He has loved trains ever since, considering them the greatest mode of transportation, the best possible vehicle, the unrivaled way to go places and get around. Traveling by train is like reading even though you're not reading: things happen from right to left outside while you follow them from left to right inside. Inside a train you can walk in the opposite direction of your trajectory, like how you can reread the sentence that just passed by. On a train, you travel at the speed of reading. He loved and still loves those trains of his childhood: trains that have nothing to do with the trains of today: so fast and aerodynamic, windows hermetically sealed, and authorities who communicate with passengers, saying things that, for him, are so well said, like "Ladies and gentlemen: we must inform you that smoking is strictly forbidden on this train. Especially, in the Car 6 bathroom" so that he, when he hears that, thinks: "Here we have someone who is a great writer and will probably never know that's what he is, and it won't be me who reveals it to him, because there already are or already were too many of us, though these days we are fewer all the time."

No, on the trains of his childhood—trains that now, for him, are like ghost trains—smoking is permitted in all areas and all the windows open so that, at night, amid the cricket song of the pampa (crickets the size of the beetles the Egyptians worshiped) and the lush scent of the countryside. A CinemaScope countryside that, more than landscape, is like the sweeping spine of a fragrant and immense animal, a beast that stretches on forever. Trains that stop at every station (in cities first and, as they approached Sad Songs, in ever smaller towns that, after a few hours, seem to entirely fit inside the train stations) and whose locomotive and cars seem constructed of flimsy tin and lightweight wood; as if they were pieces of a toy train enlarged by a mysterious ray. A train through which Uncle Hey Walrus cavorts and whoops and entertains the passengers (or that's what he tells him and Penelope who, as the summers pass, detect fewer and fewer smiles in those who watch the exorbitant orbits of their uncle, whom they pretend not to know) and even gets off at one station to wave to them, pretending to weep on the platform, running along under their window, frightening them with his display, only to hop back aboard at the last second, as the train pulled away. Inevitably—it was bound to happen sooner or later—on one return trip, at the Planicie Banderita station, Uncle Hey Walrus miscalculates the timing of his same-joke-as-always and fails to re-board the train. And he and Penelope travel alone all through the night, holding each other, like children in fairy or witch tales, in their compartment, watching the rest of the passengers as if they were menacing chimneysweeps, and venturing out into that rolling corridor that all trains are, until they come to the distant land of the dining car where they steal scraps of food and crusts of bread, telling each other in low voices not to scream, that they're like Oliver Twist or Little Dorrit. Discovering, for the first time, something they already know: that bad fiction can be comforting during times of bad nonfiction.

When they arrived the next morning to Confirmación, the end-of-the-line station, their parents (whom Uncle Hey Walrus had notified via telephone) were waiting for them, dying of laughter watching them disembark "like little heroic orphans from an English novel" (the same thing he and Penelope had thought to make themselves feel brave; but their parents laughed and laughed as if it were the best joke they'd ever told).

But this time it was different, and he and Penelope and Uncle Hey Walrus arrive in the capital (off schedule; it's the night of the 24th of December; their parents have ordered their return because, for once, they want to "celebrate a surprise we've prepared for them"; and their grandparents are worried, but they obey). And their parents weren't there when they arrived at the Confirmación station. There the three of them are, under arches of that Victorian station whose pieces arrived on a boat at the beginning of the century, along with the locomotives and train cars. Yes, trains that arrived on the water, and that's only one of the strange things that'd been mixed into the cauldrons of the history of his now nonexistent country of origin.

And nobody had keys to the apartment.

And their other grandparents were in Monte Carlo competing in a casino tournament.

And it wasn't day but night.

It was night.

It was that night that he remembered on this night, tonight.

That night—the next sun would rise to illuminate a world distinct from that of the sun before—when everything would be different, when, from then on, everything was going to change forever, in "the dead vast and middle of the night" when some are asleep and some stay awake, so that the world keeps on turning while dreams are made and our little life is wrapped in a dream and . . .

How to move through that night?

How to remember it and recognize it?

There's one thing that aids his memory and it's the trajectory of streets and avenues. He doesn't remember their names, but it's easy to recover them, though now, in his insomnia, they're all sleeping underwater. There are tools. There are devices. There are winged cameras the size of fat blowflies ceaselessly flying through the world's skies, recording everything, broadcasting it to the screens of a few viewers or of millions of people who, for years now, no longer care about being watched if it means appearing online and being seen and saying something and waving to their loved ones.

And so he connects to one of multiple search engines and there's that landscape of this childhood that's aged like him, but that, with the help of lenses and zooms and soaring spins, he can remember how it was then.

There he goes and there he returns now.

And there he and Penelope and Uncle Hey Walrus were, coming out of Confirmación with no explanation as to where their parents are and where to go to look for and find them.

And he combines that with this.

And, suddenly, everything has the cadence of those slides his parents projected in their living room when they returned from one of their trips. His parents with their backs turned and a sound like a masticating jaw from the slide carousel when it rotates and a colorful beam of light paints the white wall with faraway landscapes and the voices and laughs of his parents commenting on what happened, like the voices of playful and irresponsible gods, come down for a while to entertain the little mortals.

And then, all of it at the same time: those photographs of their adventures blending together, and all the periods of his life melting into one. Like in the temporal voyages and stellar transmutations of the protagonist of that movie a friend will mention to Uncle Hey Walrus in the middle of The Widest Avenue in the World, that same night, so many years ago. That movie based on that book in which there are aliens (aliens from the planet Tralfamadore that in the movie are nothing more than voices, like those of his parents; but that in the book are described as upright toilet plungers with a hand on top, a green eye in its palm). And there are extraterrestrial books that (compared to their simple but functional terrestrial equivalents, "idiosyncratic arrangements in horizontal lines, with ink on bleached and flattened wood pulp, of twenty-six phonetic symbols, ten numbers, and about eight punctuation marks") were small things "laid out in brief clumps of symbols separated by stars . . . each clump of symbols is a brief, urgent message—describing a situation, a scene. We Tralfamadorians read them all at once, not one after the other. There isn't any particular relationship between all the messages, except that the author has chosen them carefully, so that, when seen all at once, they produce an image of life that is beautiful and surprising and deep. There is no beginning, no middle, no end, no suspense, no moral, no causes, no effects," they explain. Those books inside that book and on that planet where, in the words of our former abductee-protagonist Billy Pilgrim, "when a person dies he only appears to die. He is still very much alive in the past, so it is silly for people to cry at his funeral. All moments, past, present, and future always have existed, always will exist . . . When a Tralfamadorian sees a corpse, all he thinks is that the dead person is in bad condition in that particular moment, but that the same person is just fine in plenty of other moments. Now, when I myself hear that somebody is dead, I simply shrug and say what the Tralfamadorians say about dead people, which is 'So it goes.'"

And over the years, he's going to quote those quotations so many times, as an ideal to aspire to but never attain, because, yes, it's something out of this world.

But now he's outside all things and, so, why not: why not look at himself and look back at all of that. Return to that night walking backward. Be Mr. Trip. Watch them and watch himself and there they go and there he goes.

Night falls over that fallen city. He and Uncle Hey Walrus and Penelope try first to find a functioning payphone, which is no mean feat (the payphones almost never work and their main function is to be coin-stealing slot machines) and, when at last they do, nobody picks up on the other end. And they exit the immense waiting area at Confirmación—a lobby designed somewhere far away, to be graced by kings and aristocrats—and make their way through all the Santa Clauses, sweating out the absurdity of being dressed up like that in the summer. And they begin to make their way, on foot, up The Widest Avenue in the World, which flows into the train station. And, true, they could have taken a taxi. But hailing a vacant one at that time on that day isn't easy. It's sunset on Saturday, the 24th of December (and he always wondered if sunset shouldn't take place starting just after midday, instead of during the last few imprecise minutes before nightfall begins), and the streets are bustling with people, like on a classic Hollywood movie set, and they were all extras, lugging packages around, propelled by an obligatory and collective happiness and with no lines of dialogue to distinguish them. Some are already a little drunk and well fed and are beginning to digest in their faces those twisted smiles that'll turn into menacing sneers by the time the party starts. And he and Uncle Hey Walrus and Penelope leave their suitcases at the station luggage office and walk unencumbered but weighed down by not knowing where to go. They have no keys to the apartment and so all they can do is treat the whole thing like a treasure hunt, they decide. And Uncle Hey Walrus is very good at this: at making them believe, at least for the first few blocks, that they are playing at "the definitive and three-dimensional version of hide-and-seek." "We have to find the hiding mommies and daddies," he announced. And when they hear this, he laughs a little more and Penelope laughs a little less. And there they go and he, now, in his bed, watches them set off and sighs a long and drawn-out sigh. And walking down The Widest Avenue in the World isn't easy. Walking there makes them even more tired. The perspective is exhausting: all that horizon in the distance and all that sky overhead and each footstep weighs more than it should. In the first few blocks of The Widest Avenue in the World there isn't much: bruised and bitten apples with squat family houses and neighborhood bars and people sitting on the sidewalk fanning themselves, some bare chested, the smoke of buses rolling over them as if perfuming them for the most toxic of celebrations. And, at last, they begin to approach the city center, one of the multiple centers of that decentered city. And there, that obelisk he would have liked so much to swap out for a towering and black monolith, and they turn right and head down "The Street of the Movie Theaters." One after another. Like neon giants. Signs announcing the big end-of-the-year premieres, and they find it impossible not to read all of them, wandering off and pausing every so often to check out the photographs of the movies on the doors. Movie theaters of every kind and shape. Colossal theaters with majestic names and small theaters where old movies, already too worn out and broken, with missing or misplaced scenes, wind up getting shown. Classic and artless movies that, because of their poor condition, become avant-garde. New and involuntary versions of *The Time Machine* or *Chitty Chitty Bang*

*Bang.* Movies that, when seen again in fragments, end up revealing new meaning and utility: movies about a group of kids ritually devoured by subterranean monsters and about a divorced father who invents lies to amuse his children. And they come to the end of that street and turn left down another street, where there are no cars, just people and boutiques (a pedestrian walkway, and he and Penelope regain some of their energy, because they like this urban transgression, where their feet usurp the place of tires) and maybe, who knows, their parents are around there somewhere. There's an "institute" where "performances" take place and, a little farther along, a bar where their parents took them many times: an artists' bar where, beside a stairway, there's a barrel brimming with walnuts that always reminded him of the barrel of apples where Jim hides to hear what the pirates are talking about. And, no, their parents are not there, and they head up another street and brush past a stadium where, on the weekends, a TV show of absurd yet irresistible masked wrestlers is filmed and broadcast (and where they also put on shows for everyone in the family and, no, please, can their grandparents not take them to another new version of *Holiday on Ice* this year). And there, next, is that huge abandoned factory (where, though nobody knows it yet, though everybody is talking about it, "subversive elements" are taken to be interrogated and tortured), that within a few years will be a discoteca called Coliseum and where he and Penelope will dance to Talking Heads until they bleed from the noses in their own heads, talking nonstop thanks to a powdery chemical. And they skirt the big department store that (he and Penelope look at each other and say nothing) their parents and their guerilla-chic cell were preparing to take by force in the next few minutes. And they pass by his school, looking more and more like a ruin surrounded by ruins. And they continue on past it and get back on The Widest Avenue in the World and turn up something that he'll never be sure if it's an avenue or a street. And there are all those bookstores and he already feels that thing he'll keep feeling forever: a Pavlovian salivation and addict's pupil dilation every time he passes by any accumulation of books. And the temptation to let go of Uncle Hey Walrus's hand is so great. To lose himself so he can find himself there inside, amid everything yet to be read and everything he'll never read. Someone told him once that those bookstores never close, that they stay open all night, and he has a hard time believing it; but it's also true that some of the people there inside have acquired the soft and transparent hue of creatures who haven't seen the sun in millennia; and he says to himself he wouldn't mind staying there forever, and being like them. To be able to step out of his own story (of what he knows is going to happen, something he knows will be terrible) to slip away into the stories of so many others who he knows nothing about. But Uncle Hey Walrus has been asking questions along the way, of people they run into, crossing them off one by one (before they're completely erased, not long now, by the erasers of History), and he throws up his hands. And they stop and go into one of the various pizzerias of similar names and eat a few slices, thick and suffocated in cheese, alongside other young men and old children and, yes, they're divorced fathers with their children, sampling the menu, at the time, typical of their new condition, before, within the next few years, the imported chain hamburger joints will disembark to nourish the loneliness of shared and alternating weekends. And now, they're in front of that "cultural building" with a movie theater up on the ninth floor. He and Penelope have gone up there many times (the excitement of going to the movies by way of an elevator) and have seen, sitting in uncomfortable seats on a tragic and worn-out carpet, many strange and different movies. And, among them, for the first of many times, *2001: A Space Odyssey*. They went in one way and came out different; but now there isn't even time to stop and look at the posters and see what was showing, on those programs covered in letters that he collects and that're so different from the programs of "normal" movie theaters, which contain nothing but ads and schedules and that you have to pay a few coins to obtain, because if not, the usher might take you to a little room in the back, behind the screen, and chop you up, so they say. And heading up that avenue or street or whatever it is, they come to an intersection with that other avenue and, on the corner, the stately building where they live. With many balconies and an old carriage entrance and the whisper of being haunted. And Uncle Hey Walrus and the two of them go up to their apartment door and knock and there's no answer (it's Saturday, no Rosalita there inside) but the echo of their knocking. And, out of the corner of his eye, he glances down the hall and sees a man in a top hat and frock coat who smiles at him and lifts a finger to his lips. And then the three of them continue up the avenue. And pass stalls densely laden with flowers like small jungles and newspaper and magazine stands like paper temples and kiosks selling candies like chewable cathedrals (among which the recent arrival of a foreign chocolate in prism-shaped packaging has resulted in an aesthetic-gustatory cataclysm among him and his friends, theretofore committed to a local brand that included little dolls of those masked wrestlers who they watch leap and fall on Sunday nights) and ice cream shops with a multitude of flavors and an amusement park that is closing its doors but still giving off light. And Uncle Hey Walrus points up at a tower with a spiraling slide winding around it and he says, "That attraction is called Helter Skelter." And they enter the zone of parks and statues. Generals on horseback pointing in different directions, old patriots in armchairs, a cemetery of elegant chalets with a fair of hippy folk art spreading out around it, stalls manned by kids with a romantic and Raphaelite air. More of the soon-to-die dead among them. And their parents are nowhere to be found; but a man, sitting at a table at a bar near the tombs, under the trunk-sized branches of a rubber tree, tells Uncle Hey Walrus that he'd heard something about a "Christmas celebration-happening" at the rose park in the Palermo forest, and he points in that direction, like another statue. And Uncle Hey Walrus swallows a couple more pills and there they go and there they keep going and they pass by the Botanical Garden and the Zoo (and the smell that both give off is like that smell he'll breathe in not long thereafter when he opens closets and removes the dead clothes of his father and mother) and regiments of soldiers and they cross over and under bridges. And they're tired of so many broken sidewalks and nonfunctioning stoplights and Penelope can't go on anymore and so he picks her up and puts her on his shoulders until he can't go on anymore, and Uncle Hey Walrus is speaking more strangely all the time (his vowels sounding more and more like consonants) and finally they find the site of the party. Where everyone is playing in the forest while the wolves are away. Dancing in slow motion and drinking as if in fast motion and smoking with the parsimonious speed of that green smoke that rises and rises along other streets and avenues into the map-less air. "They must be here," says Uncle Hey Walrus. And he and Penelope know they won't be. But, again, they look at each other and say nothing (a look that premieres that night, but that they'll give each other again so many times over the years) and he's the first to start crying and then Penelope cries and then Uncle Hey Walrus cries too. And, all around them, everyone is dancing in colorful dresses and the perfumed scent of the roses mixes with the scents of other plants. And there they stay, as if in the final scene of a movie that is really just beginning, with the camera pulling back and slowly but inexorably drifting away, while elsewhere, in more and more places, the TVs and radios begin to interrupt their scheduled programming to broadcast live from that department store where "an authentic battle royale is unfolding between the forces of order and a communist-terrorist cell." And a voice addresses the auditorium. The voice of a child, another child, neither he nor Penelope. A child in the performance of a play. A role for which he has been rehearsing. A voice that, almost apologizing and addressing the assembled audience, says: "If we shadows have offended, think but this, and all is mended, that you have slumber'd here while these visions did appear. And this weak and idle theme, no more yielding but a dream, gentles, do not reprehend: if you pardon we will mend."

And thus comes the end of the Age of Marvelous Moments.

*Así son las cosas.*

So it goes.


† Those who devote themselves to such matters—to telling stories—claim that one of the most oft-repeated words in the writing of William Shakespeare is "dreams."

Something gleaned from the work of someone about whose life little is known.

Dreams.

Everyone dreams there inside and on the stage.

Everyone asking all the time for night to fall so the curtain can rise.

Everyone insisting on the motif that the line—just a chalked indication on the floor of where to stand to recite the trance-like monologue—that separates the real from the fantasy, wakefulness from dream, is very thin.

Everyone dreams in Shakespeare and of Shakespeare.

There, the dream as a narrative device, but, also, as a way to make all the irrational things that're done while awake more or less comprehensible. In Shakespeare, dreams are for learning, learning more about what we call reality.

Gloucester dreams "troublous dreams" that make him sad.

Romeo and Mercutio dream that dreamers often lie, but in bed asleep while they do dream things true.

Shylock dreams of moneybags and Richard III dreams of the spilled blood of all his many victims and Macbeth dreams of the "three weird sisters" and of murdering sleep, "the innocent sleep. Sleep that knits up the raveled sleeve of care, the death of each day's life, sore labor's bath, balm of hurt minds, great nature's second course, chief nourisher in life's feast."

Julius Caesar mistrusts dreamers and Toby Belch warns of their lunacies.

Calban falls asleep weeping for his dreams and the daughter of Leontes wakes up laughing from hers and Sebastian asks not to be awoken if that which he is living is a dream.

Hamlet dreams a great deal, more than anyone; he dreams all the time, he waking-dreams dreams that make the world keep on moving while everyone else is sleeping, he dreams dreams that are "but a shadow" and of "the very substance of the ambitious" capable of making it possible for dreams to come true on the other side of death, while the angels sing so you have sweet dreams and good nights.

And Shakespeare dreams up all of them, rhyming "When most I wink, then do mine eyes see, / For all the day they view things unrespected; / But when I sleep, in dreams they look on three, / And darkly bright are bright in dark directed . . . How would, I say, mine eyes be blessed made / By looking on thee in the living day, / When in the dead night they fair imperfect shade / Through heavy sleep on sightless eyes doth stay? / All days are nights to see till I see thee, / And nights bright days when dreams do show thee me."

And he dreams of the excessively restless and creative teacher of "artistic activities" at Gervasio Vicario Cabrera, colegio n.°1 del Distrito Escolar Primero.

She came to the capital from the provinces. Full of good ideas. Too many ideas that, for a lot of people, are not wholly good. She has already been warned by the school headmaster (a man with the grumpy physiognomy of a bulldog who, paradoxically, likes to smoke the longest and finest and slenderest cigarettes, just then appearing on the market under the oh-so-feminine Virginia Slims brand name) that her "curriculum is under observation and surveillance."

A few too many parents were a little disturbed—or didn't find it at all amusing—that she taught their children a song she'd written, openly defying the bulldozers that would soon topple their school building, for the lengthening and widening of "The Widest and Soon-to-Be Longest Avenue in the World" and had them howl it at their year-end performance. "Too much protest," some of them paled; "anarcho-communist hymn," others reddened.

The next thing—the next "artistic activity" to be carried out by the students—seems less offensive or less offensive on its surface. A "loose adaptation" (this teacher can't bear the idea of leaving something unmodified, even an undisputed classic) of a play by William Shakespeare, *A Midsummer Night's Dream*, which she hasn't hesitated to rechristen *A Summer Night's Daydream*. And she presents her project with great care and passion. She explains that, over the years, one ceases to be interested in the youthful ardors of *Romeo and Juliet* and *Hamlet*, growing up with the fury of *Macbeth* and *Richard II*, and, at last, attaining the twilight wisdom of *King Lear* and *The Tempest*. But that, on the other hand, *A Midsummer Night's Dream* is an ageless enigma without expiration date: a strange artifact that fascinates all ages.

The headmaster and the representatives of the parents' association have gone to the effort of reading it.

And, at first, everything seems in and to abide by the established order.

And the other male teachers eye her top to bottom and front to back in the faculty lounge and mock her in low voices and secretly but obviously desire her and, without knowing it, turn into bumbling fools, into "rude mechanicals," like those in the play: seduced and enchanted by the magical powers of that divine girl.

There, in those pages, an ancient Merovingian legend irradiated by Greek motifs and fundamentally Shakespearized, understanding Shakespeare as the first great master of the mash-up (his only non-genius trait is his inability to come up with his own storylines) and of honest, Dylanite-Nabokovian thievery. Taking some banal borrowed material and turning it into something incandescent. A forest comedy, humans controlled by the caprices of supernatural beings, playful jealousy and spite, fleeting and indestructible romances without explicit details and popular and aristocratic weddings under the light of the moon between an Athenian duke and an Amazonian queen, magic and an ass's head and a mischievous sprite and love nectar from a magical flower and storylines within storylines and plays within the play and spatiotemporal ruptures and, ah, a magical and lost boy, an "Indian changeling," who ends up living among the gods.

There are a lot of minor roles as little fairies to be given out to students of lesser histrionic talent or ability to memorize their lines (the most sought-after role is that of Puck, "the merry wanderer of the night," and Pertusato, Nicolasito is the ideal and undisputed candidate, but . . . ).

There are, also, in that play, personality disorders and, if you look carefully, with squinted eyes, feminist and homoerotic and zoophilic winks, and even metafictional gusts where, near the end, the audience is informed that everything they have seen has been nothing more and nothing less than a dream, a collective and shared dream.

But nobody—headmaster, teachers, parents—says anything; because better Shakespeare than some "leftist writer."

And, besides, who knows how "that (other) village lunatic" (and, yes, Uncle Hey Walrus did meet her one afternoon, at the exit to the school, and something like sparks flew between them, like specimens of the same race finding each other, far from home) is going to pull off producing all of that. Though it was known she'd accomplished more complex feats: she'd already found a way—astonishing the authorities and thereby securing the position months before—to stage the patriotic flight of the soldier/general Gervasio Vicario Cabrera over the heads of the audience without breaking any of the boys' necks.

In any case, there was no way anybody could suspect the true intentions of the teacher of artistic activities.

Because what she's really interested in—what she planned to emphasize and expand upon in her version of the play—is the matrimonial conflict between Oberon and Titania, king and queen of the fairies, in perpetual discussion about the fate of a child.

What she wants to do is appropriate the timeless Shakespeare to portray a dawning era: The Age of Divorce.

The present day of the first separated parents and how it's affecting their children, picked up by the one or the other or by some relatively neutral relative, in the afternoon, at the exit to the school. She sees them every day: young people who've broken with their own parents' model and, at the same time, are breaking their connection with their own children. They're like those drivers who don't know how to park and, when they attempt to, run into the car behind them and the car in front of them. Destruction in both directions. A new and confused race that, nevertheless, descends from warriors (a good part of them emigrants/immigrants; come to this country fleeing distant continental calamities) and they'll end up creating a new crop of resistant and unbreakable children, weathered in their errors and lunacies, ready to endure whatever may come (over the years, many of their children will depart this ever-shifting land in search of more stable places).

The artistic activities teacher has planned and outlined the whole thing and her only hesitation/temptation is whether or not to accept the offer from that one couple of parents to participate in the production. A couple of parents who're not (presently) separated, though they don't seem to be exactly together either. Parents who at times resemble a body with two heads and other times two headless bodies. They're parents of that boy who's always looking at her (a look that's starting to stop being one of so-called "childish curiosity" and beginning to be a look with a different kind of eyes) and always announcing to her that he's going to be a writer, that he already is. And the truth is he doesn't bother her at all, though his writing is far worse than that of the other student who he battles over and over in "composition duels" (her idea) and who, a few months before, had been electrocuted and killed, among the ruins that surrounded the school.

The parents of the little writer who survived and who's on a mission to tell the tale are famous.

They are models.

They appear on TV and at the movies, in spots where they're always traveling. And they seem too happy to be real, a happiness that seems more a pose than something they live. And she's afraid they'll endanger her project. And yet, she tells herself, she could consider them the exception that proves the rule. And, besides, they've offered to provide wardrobe and even to film the thing. And their only request (by no means a small request for her) is to play Oberon and Titania. And that's where she is. Thinking about what to do. Wondering if it was just her—one of those shoots of her provincial upbringing she never managed to trim back entirely—or did that glowing couple get too close and touch her too much when they spoke to her at parent-teacher conferences? And the truth is they're always inviting her to come out with them some night to one of those "gatherings where there are definitely people who might interest you." But she tries not to think too much about that and, after all, she came to the city to have experiences, right? And to move with confidence and make an impression.

There are nights, alone, in the apartment where she rents a room, where she feels like a kind of Pied Piper of Hamelin. A guardian and a guide. A present observer but, also, a key figure. The one who opens the door for the children to go out and play, to get away, to reach for the future.

And she likes to imagine that one of those boys, one of her students (maybe the son of those parents, why not), will become a writer and write one of those novels where she won't be present in body but, absent, will survive and live on—better than ever, with a brighter glow and intensity, her brilliance that of a lighthouse—in the minds of everyone. One of those novels that always wear a name—hers—on the cover.

The only thing she regrets—so that the effect would be ethnically and geographically and stylistically perfect—is not having been born elsewhere, far away, and not having a Jewish surname and not being one of those tormenting and tormented Chicago girls, in one of those novels she is reading now, because she (her faith in culture as the territory of justice is unshakable) always reads the winners of the Nobel, and now she is reading one of the latest to win the prize, there, in her little bed that she barely fits in, because she feels herself expanding, bigger all the time, as if she doesn't fit anywhere, but has such great desire to fill everything up, while at the same time it's all just too much for her.

The artistic activities teacher wonders if that's happiness or anguish and tells herself that it's best, just in case, to keep on reading.


† Over the years, all the profound and torrential novels of Saul Bellow end up swimming in the same river and getting all mixed together (the same thing happens with Iris Murdoch, another exceedingly digressive novelist of ideas, of so many ideas, and also one who feeds vampirically off friends

and enemies to create her creatures). Of all of them, parts are remembered, moments, thoughts where it doesn't matter if it's Moses Herzog or Charlie Citrine thinking them. Either way, it's the same: they all end up with the same brain.

But there are a handful of pages—definitely not the most transcendent that Bellow wrote—that for him are unforgettable.

One short story—really the aborted beginning and rewrite of an early novel that never came into being or that Bellow opted not to publish—with the title "Zetland: By a Character Witness."

There, the typical Bellowian narrator/witness evokes the figure of a dead young man, Zetland, inspired like so many of that author's characters, by a real person: the brilliant and prodigious Isaac Rosenfeld, Bellow's childhood friend and accomplice and literary rival in the Chicago of his youth (studying anthropology at the University of Wisconsin, they seek each other out and recompose à deux and in Yiddish "The Love Song of J. Alfred Prufrock" by T. S. Eliot as "Der shir hashirim fun Mendl Pumshtok"), and deceased in 1956 at thirty-eight. Rosenfeld—a bit crazy as a result of a brutal Reichian therapy "seeking the full orgasm"—working and dying at his desk, alone and without anybody, in a one-room rented apartment.

"I had been thrown millions of light years by Isaac Rosenfeld's death. He died while writing something and it's something of a comfort to feel that writing something perhaps matters. Perhaps it does," Bellow wrote in a letter a few days after the funeral. "I loved him, but we were rivals," he admitted in another. "It should have been Isaac," Bellow confessed to another friend, several decades later when he received the Nobel. Rosenfeld himself—in days when another brilliant young writer, Truman Capote, was all the rage, the name on everyone's lips and the apple of everyone's eye—agreed and stated and wrote in a magazine that "No matter, someday Saul or I will win the Nobel Prize."

Which doesn't prevent that, reading the story/fragment, you can detect differences between the narrator (Bellow) and his beloved ghost that, no doubt, would have distanced them through the books and successes of one or the other.

The "witness" of Zetland is shown to be a worldly and figurative vitalist; while Zetland (the story bids him farewell in the beginning of all things,

with a splendid future, after having been blown away by reading *Moby-Dick*)
is evoked as a kind of abstract spiritual power and already not-of-this-world
even while alive. The reading of one and the other, from outside and with
perspective, confirms what he suspected: the survivor was much better than
the survived and, probably, the few phantasmal pages that the dead man
inspired were the best of his life, though minor within the body of work of
the other man who lived to tell the tale.

And Bellow—whose habitual modus operandi was that of medium-ven-
triloquist; MO/style also suffered/enjoyed by Delmore Schwartz and Alan
Bloom and numerous relatives and ex-wives, among others—lived a long
time to tell a whole lot more and many more deaths.

And he wrote almost to the very end when, already ninety, he said that,
for him, the world had turned into a cemetery. All of his historical acquaintances were underground, beneath his feet, he had strange dreams (that he
encountered Tolstoy driving a beat-up white van on the expressway, his flapping door denting Bellow's paint job; that he discovered he had the secret
remedy for curing a deadly disease inscribed on his penis and as a result he's
being pursued by agents of a pharmaceutical company; that he discovered a
library with unknown works by Henry James and Joseph Conrad). He got
himself entangled in awkward *boutades* as a conference speaker, where he
asked aloud and to the shock of the auditorium, who was the Tolstoy of the
Zulus (when, as someone said, it was more than obvious that the Tolstoy of
the Zulus was none other than Tolstoy). And in one of his last interviews,
on the BBC, with his disciple Martin Amis, Bellow explained that, "There
are moments in the day when I feel as if I'm looking back at life from the
beyond; I've reckoned with death for so long that I look at the world with the
eyes of someone who's died . . ." When Amis asked about the existence of an
afterlife, he explained: "Well, it's impossible to believe in it because there's
no rational ground. But I have a persistent intuition, and it's not so much a
hope—call it love impulses. What I think is how agreeable it would be to see
my mother and my father and my brothers again—to see again my dead. But
then again I think, 'How long would these moments last?' You still have to
think of eternity as a conscious soul. So the only thing I can think of is that
in death we might become God's apprentices and have the real secrets of the
universe revealed to us."

† Does Zetland = Pertusato, Nicolasito? No, tricky. Beyond the intensity of the relationship, they don't spend that much time together and don't come to know (like Bellow and Rosenfeld) strong emotions together, like the discovery of sex and love and the authentic intellectual battles of early adulthood. But it doesn't matter. Even still, exploring this possibility when it comes to making up an elegy and exaggerating his virtues. Almost turning Pertusato, Nicolasito into one of Salinger's genius Glass boys. Definitive revenge: to defeat someone who's been your rival by giving him the prize of looking far more talented than he was, in a prose and style not his but your own. To absorb him, yes. To think of him with apparent generosity, on the threshold of your own death, but, actually, to avail yourself of his mortal remains to undergird your own possible immortality (everyone has a plan to be immortal and, in general, it only really works until they die) while, more and more, you think you have less and less time until you'll put your last words in writing. To apply to Pertusato, Nicolasito the same treatment Sigmund Freud applies in that dream of his where his dead friends file by and he doesn't understand them, because they now inhabit a *non vixit*, a "never lived" when really (successful failure!) what Freud wanted to say was a *non vivit*, a "no longer living."

Adding a quote from one of the novels of Iris Murdoch (like Bellow, another reformulator of Shakespeare and serial fabricator of Falstaffs and Prosperos) to the mix. This one: "Death . . . How is it done? . . . It can't be difficult, anyone can do it. It could be more like a little movement, a sort of quick turning away. I shall make that movement one day. How shall I know how? When the times comes I shall know, my body will tell me, will teach me, urge me, push me at last over the edge. It is an achievement, or is it like falling asleep which happens but you don't know when? Perhaps at the very last moment it is easy, the point where all deaths are alike. But that must be true by definition too."

And—again, of course, fearing his jealousy and spite—Vladimir Nabokov (who considered Bellow "a miserable mediocrity"; his assessment of Murdoch is unknown, but there are some who, based on that silence, have found coincidences and coded mutual references that could only suggest certain complicity or sympathy).

And remembering, again, that fragment from a little while ago, from a few hours ago, from an eternity ago, from the project that, in a letter to

Edmund Wilson (with whom he would end up fighting an epistolary duel, in private and public, about a translation from Russian to English of a poem with duelists), Nabokov postulated as "a new type of autobiography—a scientific attempt to unravel and trace back all the tangled threads of one's personality—and the provisional title is *The Person in Question*." A project he ended up carrying out first as *Conclusive Evidence* (*Other Shores* in Russian, Другие берега), and then as *Speak, Memory*. And for him, it's the title that's the correct answer to that persistent and improper question posed in cultural supplements to fill their summertime pages, regarding what book you would take to a desert-but-apparently-oft-frequented island, where you'll never be able to go; because Nabokov's selective autobiography includes almost all traditions and genres and even a good number of languages.

And Nabokov's dead were always, like his own dead, in the past. There, that "Whenever in my dreams I see the dead, they always appear silent, bothered, strangely depressed, quite unlike their dear, bright selves. I am aware of them, without any astonishment, in surroundings they never visited during their earthly existence, in the house of some friend of mine they never knew. They sit apart, frowning at the floor, as if death were a dark taint, a shameful family secret. It is certainly not then—not in dreams—but when one is wide awake, at moments of robust joy and achievement, on the highest terrace of consciousness, that mortality has a chance to peer beyond its own limits, from the mast, from the past and its castle tower. And although nothing much can be seen through the mist, there is somehow the blissful feeling that one is looking in the right direction."

Yes, yes, and yes: to dream eternally of the dead (those dead who become so real again during insomnia) while you're dying, until death comes and, perhaps, you awaken on the Other Side (heaven, purgatory, hell?, limbo!) to discover that, now, there, your charge is to write about the living. That that's what ghosts are up to when they appear here: not trying to inspire fear but to find inspiration among those who're still on This Side. The other result of the Lazarus Equation that that stranger revealed to him in Montreux and that launched him into the void of that hadron collider with the accelerated and particular ambition of bringing it all back home, of standing up his fallen comrades, of rewriting his own story, elevating it to universal myth, and imposing on all mere mortals the unforgettable memory of his dead.

Dead who, once returned, would no longer be depressed but happy and out strolling through the streets.

All of that—arranged, expanded, carefully manipulated at his convenience—to end up telling how, after successfully putting on the performance of the flying founding father, following the technical instructions and diagrams of the first staging of *Peter Pan*; after composing and having the children sing a "protest" song in which they opposed the arrival of the bulldozers to demolish everything; after lovingly and passionately planning "my Shakespeare"; his beloved teacher of artistic activities was summarily fired from Gervasio Vicario Cabrera, colegio n.°1 del Distrito Escolar Primero. They accused her of something. Of having an "inappropriate relationship" with a father or a mother or both.

And—out of spite or curiosity, to get into something outside the law—the teacher of artistic activities ended up joining you-know-who's fashion cell.

And she was captured in the attack by the armed forces in that department store taken over by the chic-guerrillas on that nightmarish Christmas Eve of 1977.

And she died a week or two later, after being thrown out of an airplane flying over a river that flowed out into the sea in front of a city and, as she fell, she felt for a few seconds that she was flying over the enemy lines, like Gervasio Vicario Cabrera. Victorious but forever misunderstood. Telling herself that History—or, at least, the story that student of hers would write—would do right by her, would give her a raison d'être, a reason that now, in the air, is lost never to be found. Because there, falling, she feels as if she were dreaming that dream everyone dreams where they're falling. That dream where, eyes squeezed tightly shut, one wakes up just before crashing into the ground or into the water or into the fire or into the story.

† Notes for a story never to be written entitled "The Man Who Hated Mobile Phones" / Opening with a long diatribe against the small devices that people use for everything besides communicating. Set up as a succession of questions in an auditorium, like "Isn't it true that it was so nice to go on a walk and know that nobody could call you on the phone?" Questions that don't expect an answer from the audience (because everyone in the audience is busy

checking the screens on their devices) and that condemn the incessant hyper-kinesia and the attention deficit disorder caused by the new phones compared to the concentrated elegance and restraint of old telephones, only ringing every so often, when we needed them and not when they needed us. The flimsy plastic versus the forceful Bakelite. Smooth rectangles versus strong curves. Those old telephones that began in themselves and that were so alien to referential and polyvalent mania of the new and increasingly everywhere-at-once models. Telephones with a single mission: to transmit good or bad news, and only used to communicate something practical and urgent. You talked on the telephone when there was something to talk about, something to say, information that someone needed. Back then, he remembers, people who talked on the telephone all the time were people "with issues," because, back then, nobody liked talking on the telephone more than what was neces-sary and unavoidable. You talked on the telephone to be done talking on the telephone. You called looking for someone and often didn't find them. You dialed to distance yourself. You picked up the phone to hang it back up. You hung up and didn't go on.

With the protagonist's diatribe concluded, we discover that he's a writer who no longer writes (and who likes and hates thinking of himself as "an exwriter" who still "plays a writer"). The exwriter returns to his hotel and throws himself (collapses) into his bed and opens his copy of Vladimir Nabokov's *Collected Stories*. And he rereads his two favorites stories by the Russian author: "The Vane Sisters" first and "Signs and Symbols" after. He reads them, taking notes in the margins where there isn't much free space; because he already took notes before, on various occasions and trips and hotels, as an exwriter.

In their own way, both are ghost stories, the exwriter thinks and thinks again; stories with absent figures evoked or dreamed by others.

The first is unequivocally Nabokovian.

The second, on the other hand, is Nabokovian by opposition, by its firm resolve not to be.

The two stories function as kind of complementary opposites.

And, according to Nabokov, the exwriter remembers, both contain, in addition to an "outside," of what is read, an "inside," what is hidden. And that inside, hidden, ends up being vital to understanding it: "a second (main) story is woven into, or placed behind, the superficial and semitransparent one," Nabokov explained.

In "The Vane Sisters" Nabokov himself revealed the secret: a final paragraph where the first letter of each word delivers a message from the dead sisters, from the Beyond.

About "Signs and Symbols," however, Nabokov didn't explain anything; and its secret continues to be a subject of Nabokovian interpretations that consider it one of his most accomplished stories, many of them including it among that as-exclusive-as-it-is-hospitable genre known as "the best story in the world."

An atypical story for him, as well. Third person, minimal setting, few details (a distant but unerasable shadow of the Holocaust, the mention of a chess prodigy, labels on jelly jars), nameless characters, an oppressive air of doom, and the superficial and semitransparent anecdote of a couple of suffering parents—a couple of Russian Jews living in New York—who're going to visit their son on his birthday. A son committed to an institution for the mentally ill, afflicted by "referential mania." In one long and formidable paragraph (include it in the story in its totality?), Nabokov elaborates the diagnosis of the young man's disturbance. And he does it in such a brilliant and exquisite way that it almost makes you want to get infected and die of it. Nabokov writes: "The system of his delusions had been the subject of an elaborate paper in a scientific monthly, which the doctor at the sanitarium had given to them to read. But long before that, she and her husband had puzzled it out for themselves. 'Referential mania,' the article called it. In these very rare cases, the patient imagines that everything happening around him is a veiled reference to his personality and existence. He excludes real people from the conspiracy, because he considers himself to be so much more intelligent than other men. Phenomenal nature shadows him wherever he goes. Clouds in the staring sky transmit to each other, by means of slow signs, incredibly detailed information regarding him. His in-most thoughts are discussed at nightfall, in manual alphabet, by darkly gesticulating trees. Pebbles or stains or sun flecks form patterns representing, in some awful way, messages that he must intercept. Everything is a cipher and of everything he is the theme. All around him, there are spies. Some of them are detached observers, like glass surfaces and still pools; others, such as coats in store windows, are prejudiced witnesses, lynchers at heart; others, again (running water, storms), are hysterical to the point of insanity, have a distorted opinion of him, and grotesquely misinterpret his actions. He must be always on his guard and devote every minute and module of life to the decoding of the undulation of things. The very air he exhales is indexed and filed away. If only the interest he provokes were limited to his immediate surroundings, but, alas, it is not! With distance, the torrents of wild scandal increase in volume and volubility. The silhouettes of his blood corpuscles, magnified a million times, flit over vast plains; and still farther away, great mountains of unbearable solidity and height sum up, in terms of granite and groaning firs, the ultimate truth of his being."

The exwriter reads all of that—he reads it again, he underlines with ink where it was already previously underlined in pencil—and tells himself that he understands perfectly what it's about and what it feels like. If *that* is referential mania, then he had it and has it *too*. Though he never experienced it as an affliction but as an entertaining aspect of what he, sometimes, liked to identify as his style, as well as the fuel that fed his literary vocation. The perception of the entire universe. An everything-is-connected. A there-is-nothing-that-might-not-be-of-use-to-me. He had his first perception of the virus when he looked at, for the first of a thousand times, when he was still a boy, the cover of The Beatles' *Sgt. Pepper's Lonely Hearts Club Band*. And wondering who all those people were and what they were doing there, all together while, in the background, rose the orchestral crescendo of "A Day in the Life" after someone confessed that "Having read the book / I love to tuuuurn youuuu onnnn . . ."

The exwriter, also, knows exactly what the long-suffering parents are feeling in the Nabokov story, when they arrive to the sanitarium and are informed they won't be able to see their son, because he tried to kill himself again, and as such it's not recommended that he receive visitors. The exwriter has gone to see and visit his sister—no longer little but always his little sister—in the same situation. He knows that every one of those visits, for him, is the closest thing to committing suicide, without any of the glamour of attempting or succeeding. There, he was like a character in reserve, waiting to be called on, the night of the premiere and debut and the farewell: all

at the same time, all on one night. That's when he understands the meaning of the story: suicides are nothing but attempted suicides gone wrong,
he thinks. And every time the exwriter went to visit his committed sister,
he told himself the same thing: it won't be long before his sister fails once
and for all, forever, and dies from dying, dies from killing herself. Then, he
knew, the true actors would enter the scene. The relatives of suicide victims
(and he, as far as he knows, is Penelope's only family member) who're part of
the suicide: witnesses of the suicide. They're the starring supporting actors,
given the pieces of something that could be postponed (every suicide is a time
bomb) but sooner or later arrives. Without them there to receive it (in the
same way deaths by natural or accidental causes or illness-related deaths are
the lifetime inheritance of the survivors, as the dead only own their death for
barely a second), that suicide would be, merely, another death among many.
Suicide is a singular death. Death of an author.

And so, depressed as the dead, in Nabokov's story, the couple returns
home. There, desperate with sadness, the father decides he'll take his son out
of that institution. And then the telephone rings. Two times. They anticipate
awful news, but no: someone, a girl, has dialed a wrong number. Or the
lines have gotten crossed. Both times, the girl insists they pass the phone to
"Charlie." And the parents explain to her that she has the wrong number.
That there's no Charlie there. And they hang up. And the father begins to
read the labels on the small jelly jars that were going to be the birthday present for their son. Then the telephone rings for a third time and the story ends
there, with that sound, before the parents answer it.

The exwriter thinks something now that never occurred to him before: he
thinks that the person who is behind that third call—and this was Nabokov's
trick there—was actually the reader of the story. The reader as the supreme
and absolute referential maniac, trying to enter into the pages from the other
side, in the same way that the spectral and epigraphic sisters Cynthia and
Sybil Vane slip in from the other side.

But maybe these theories are nothing more than the result of Nabokov's
true trick: announcing a secret that doesn't exist and forcing the person who
reads it to seek out "signs and symbols" where there are none. And thereby be
infected by the referential mania of that sick man, who we're never permitted

to visit, but who all the same is watching from his cell, and laughing at us.

"Signs and Symbols" fascinated the editors of the *New Yorker* (maybe, the exwriter thinks now in his hotel bed, because in a very sibylline and sophisticated manner, it simultaneously parodies and pays homage to the models and maneuvers of classic, and admired by Nabokov, contributors to the magazine like John Cheever and J. D. Salinger and John Updike, at the same time that, anticipatorily, it foreshadows all that spacious minimalism and limpid dirty realism that'll appear in those same weekly pages decades later). But Nabokov's editor at the magazine, Katharine White, didn't deny herself the opportunity to introduce some changes. To begin with, she castled the title—the story appeared in the *New Yorker* as "Symbols and Signs" on May 15th, 1948—and, moving on, she suggested various changes in the serpentine anatomy of some sentences. Nabokov—with the amiability typical of a noble dealing with his servants—responded in a letter to her suggestions: "I shall be very grateful to you if you help me to weed out bad grammar but I do not think I would like my longish sentences clipped too close, or those drawbridges lowered which I have taken such pains to lift. [. . .] Why not have the reader reread a sentence now and then? It won't hurt him."

It doesn't hurt the exwriter to re-read it, of course.

Unless by hurt you mean reaching the certainty that he'll never write something *like that* in *that* way.

In any case, that Nabokov story resounds inside the exwriter like a fourth and definitive telephone call.

And he hears it ringing and answers.

And this is what the voice, his voice, from the other end of the line, tells him, not in the Nabokov story but in his own.

It tells him to remember, to remember himself as if he were reading himself first in order to write himself after.

And now—ellipsis, jump, going in reverse—the exwriter and his little sister are two children in their grandparents' house, in the south, and it's almost Christmas, 1977.

And he—who's not an exwriter but a nextwriter, someone who doesn't yet write, but already knows that he will, because he spends his days and nights thinking about what he isn't yet but should be writing—walks through the hallways of his grandparents' house, his provincial grandparents. All four of his grandparents are Russian émigrés, come to this country years ago, fleeing the Russian revolution.

Two of them settled in the capital and founded a meat export business whose earnings they sometimes gambled in casinos.

Two of them got off the boat and continued to the south and opened the first bookstore and newspaper distributor in a place where the winds were so strong they had no name and made turning the pages of newspapers and novels impossible in the open air. The letters moved and escaped and so you had no choice but to read indoors.

Outside, he plays in landscapes that look extraterrestrial and where the sea lions bellow on the beach and the sea dogs bark in the taverns on the port and the whales sing to the moon and to the lunatics in the asylum on the outskirts of a town where there isn't much to know, but the little that there is is worth knowing and memorizing: haunted houses and crazy locals, like the supposed wizard who lives in a tower overlooking the beach and who one night self-volatizes or something like that (and who then and there and forever fixes in the mind of the young nextwriter the fantasy of someday, in the future, dematerializing and becoming one with the air and with everything and evolving into a domineering deity of men and women, whom he would treat well or not so much, as if they were his characters, rewriting them again and again, until he likes how they look and sound). Think of a name for that town. Specify that the children those two couples of grandparents produced (those in the provinces, a daughter, those in the capital, a son) were a couple of more-than-a-little-unstable specimens quite representative of that youthful decade when everyone is young first and parents later but children forever; to the point where, more than once, being like the children of their children who watch them the way you watch a pair of tornadoes and how the landscape is left after those tornadoes pass by to come back so big they barely fit. They're a new generation of parents. They're the archetypical and paradigmatic prototypes of a soon-to-be-discontinued line. They're difficult to handle and even worse at handling themselves; they're artists of abandon, devotees of top-speed colliding stars. They're famous, but have that new kind of fame that burns brightly but briefly (allude, maybe to Andy Warhol, that his parents are like a distant version of superstars of The Factory). They're people who like to get into trouble just to see if they can get themselves out of it. And, for them, it's all a hobby, because there are too many good things to experience and so little time and so: love for the amateur and infidelity for the professional. And yet, those parents come up with a good idea and take advantage of their beauty and parade it around the world and use it to sell themselves and to be consumed. And, of course, that isn't enough to ward off boredom. And before long, political and ideological commitment become hip and those parents decide they're going to see what that's all about. And that's when the red warning lights start flashing, but it turns out to be so easy to confuse them with the flashing lights of a discoteca.

And so, that December, on vacation, the nextwriter and his little sister are in their grandparents' house. And they aren't having a bad time there. But they're angry. At their parents. Imagine what they could've done to the little sister to make her so so furious. Specify that what the nextwriter won't forgive them for is that they've abducted his favorite teacher, his teacher of artistic activities, whom he's secretly in love with (he's had, with her, his first wet dream, though he doesn't yet know that's what it's called: in the dream he's hanging, as if from a cornice of a mountain on a sloping, three-dimensional map; he hangs on until he no longer can and he lets go and falls down between the spread legs of his teacher and wakes up with his loins aflame and wet at the same time and, when the sun comes up, between frightened and ashamed, he doesn't understand what that dense liquid is that reminds him of the glue he uses to assemble his Aurora-brand monsters).

But in both cases, no doubt, same as it ever was. His voracious parents, once again, appropriating something that's his. Being seductive and spectacular. Driving his little friends crazy with their gifts and lunacies. Little friends who tell the nextwriter over and over "Oh, how I wish my parents were like yours." And he listened to them the way you listen to crazy people who have no idea what they're talking about and envied the normality of their parents.

And years later, he would fall in love with a girl (a girl with a disturbing tendency to fall into swimming pools who, fortunately, didn't want to be a writer, because she didn't need to; because she knew that she wasn't meant to write but to be written) who'll explain to him that she doesn't especially like to be brought breakfast in bed. But that, yes, "I adore listening" in bed to the sounds of someone making breakfast in the kitchen, because it reminds her of when her parents made her coffee and toast before taking her to school. "Hearing them there, like magical alchemists, preparing their secret formulas, me there, half asleep and half awake, in the darkness broken only by the light of the refrigerator and the burners," she'll say, as if in a trance, with that voice and that smile. And then he, writing her, will imagine (saying to himself why do you want to write about having all of that) all of that like the most exotic and adventurous of worlds, like visions of faraway and even extraterrestrial landscapes: parents who get up before you and make you breakfast! Stranger and more exotic still: breakfast! And then, after breakfast, they take you to school!

The only place his parents took him was to their grandparents' house. And they dropped him off there along with his little sister. Holidays and weekends and vacations.

And so, on vacation and on a weekend and on holiday, now, the nextwriter and his sister come and go through the chiaroscuro hallways of their grandparents' house (it's the hour of siesta and on the other side of the blinds, there's a wuthering heat that neither the wise nor the fool would expose themselves to); both like the characters in those comics who carry around a dark and flashing cloud over their heads.

What're they thinking about?

About ways of getting revenge.

And his little sister thinks more and better than he does, maybe because she doesn't want to be a writer (though she ends up becoming one), but has decided (the little sister is already so much smarter than her nextwriter brother) to be a reader. More than that: to be a reader of a single book, a book that, for her, is perfect—a book more hers than if she'd written it—and that she feels was imagined for her alone so she would never stop thinking about it.

The nextwriter, on the other hand, reads anything within range and fires off in so many directions at the same time to see what might hit the mark.

The nextwriter can't stop thinking about writing and books don't last him long and magazines even less, and so, while everyone sleeps during that trance-like zone that extends from after lunch until nearly the end of the afternoon, he goes down the stairs that lead to the library, to see what he can find. And he takes great care not to do so on the hour or quarter hour or half hour; because that's when, down below, the bells of a grandfather clock, pendulum like a tongue tired of marking time, toll. A clock that releases a martial sound, as if the gears inside its casement were being unstitched by needles. And, yes, he's already thinking *like that*: with those images and those *metaphors* and *similes* he applies all the time to everything.

And there below—vacillating between a comic with a voluptuous vampire and a novel with Malaysian pirates—he hears the sound the telephone makes when somebody is dialing. One of various telephones distributed throughout the house. Because, at the time, telephones are heavy as turtles and they never move and you have to go to them every time they call, calling you.

And he, curious, picks up the apparatus and hears on the other end, the high and small voice of his little sister. And the nextwriter has picked up the receiver before the call is connected—one number is still needed to complete the code on that dial where you insert your finger and push—and he hears his little sister.

And her words are terrible and not at all sweetened by the smallness of her voice, as if from an animated but motionless drawing.

And what his little sister has done—he discovers—is call that number from that television commercial where citizens are asked to denounce any subversive or suspicious activity.

And, there and then, his little sister is communicating their parents' plans, not realizing that she isn't speaking to anyone, that he's the only one listening.

And he uses his deepest voice and thanks his little sister and hears her hang up.

And hours later—during the commercial break of an episode of *The Twilight Zone*—they broadcast that "public service message" along with that other one with the man drowning and the one with the poor boy in the street.

And he writes down the number for informants and says he has to go to the bathroom, and then turns, and goes to another of the telephones, the farthest one of all, the one in the kitchen.

And he calls it.

And they answer on the other end.

And—in a voice far more believable than his little sister's—he informs on his parents, explaining and detailing what his parents have planned for that Christmas Eve. Their subversive happening and all of that.

And there are various clicks and switches of listeners and receivers and they take note and thank him and tell him that he's a true patriot, that he should feel proud of what he's done.

And the nextwriter goes back and sits down beside his little sister and says nothing to her about what he did.

And he'll never tell her she's innocent and he's guilty, but, hey, first and foremost and when all is said and done, it was her idea, and he only limited himself to revising it, right? He couldn't help but continue the story, to find out where it would end up.

And he'll never ever tell her anything; not even when—years later or right there and then—his sister loses her mind never to get it back again.

And the nextwriter tells himself he did what he did because he thought it would make a good story, though he knows he'll never put it in writing, unless he has nothing else left to tell, nothing left to write, if it just won't come anymore, and deliver us from nada; pues nada.

Days later, at sunset on December 24th, they arrive to the capital on the train and what follows is the story of a long nighttime walk through the city, in the company of a somewhat unhinged but oh-so-fun uncle.

And, there, the discovery of the night. "A Day in the Life," the summer night like a dream (lengthy temporal-geographical spiel, melting together spaces and times and streets and avenues; re-read and re-watch the nocturnal walks of *Dream of Heroes* and *La Dolce Vita*).

And searching for their parents.

And not finding them, of course. Because their parents had already been found by others.

And there, walking, the nextwriter and his little sister who, each of them, without exchanging a word, know what's going to happen, what's happening; but they don't want to know it.

And at some point during that night, the nextwriter starts to cry and his little sister does too and their uncle asks them what's wrong.

And the nextwriter asks—tears filling his eyes—how it's possible that nobody has thought to invent "mini-telephones." Small and portable telephones that don't need cords and that even allow you to precisely locate their owners and let them know that you need them, that they are in danger, to get out of there as fast as they can. Small devices, like the ones that Captain James Tiberius Kirk uses to order that they teletransport him at the last moment off of those chaotic and dangerous planets to the secure home of the *Enterprise* and the protective logic of Mr. Spock. A device that would keep children informed at every moment what their parents were up to. And would allow children to warn and save their parents from all the dangers lying in wait for them. Or—maybe, even, if they were *very* powerful inventions—vice versa. A miraculous talisman that would keep the family connected and together and allow the errors of the children and the flaws of the parents to be corrected.

But no.

Doesn't exist.

Cannot be found

All there is are the tears of the nextwriter and his little sister.

And their uncle starts to cry too, because he's a very sensitive person and because it doesn't seem right to him to be the only person not crying.

And jump forward, to the present, like someone jumping to the end of their story, like someone reaching the end of a story where a telephone is ringing (another telephone, a telephone the protagonist hears and hesitates, not knowing if he should pick up or not) and where, then, in the air of that hesitation, he hears the last sentence in the story.

And the last sentence of the story is:

"And that's why this now-immobile man has always hated mobile phones."


† After a tragedy, you turn into two people, you split in two: you are the one who keeps on living and the one who keeps on dying, who feels vitally dead. And, at the same time, the expansive wave of horror that has passed over you seems to never entirely pass and makes you feel a trembling and profound love for everything around you. The world is perfect and so interesting (because you are so absolutely aware of the absence of those who no longer form a part of it and you force yourself to feel and admire everything that they can no longer admire or feel), and everything sparkles so achingly

beautiful. With time, luckily, normality is reestablished and you become again who you always were. And you recover the gift of having almost everything and almost everyone around you.

And you smile again.

Or, maybe, you don't actually smile: you just bare your teeth, your fangs.

Either way, it's all the same: those who look at you have no reason to see you and perceive what you're really thinking, the things that occur to you, everything you look down on them for.

It's as if you'd been sleeping soundly and dreaming deeply.

And suddenly—the closest thing to a happy ending; a contented continuation—you're awake.


Awake like he is now.

And the tale ends but the story continues.

And a telephone rings.

A different telephone.

And yet, a telephone like the one in the tale.

A telephone like the ones from before.

The telephone he has beside his bed.

A telephone that's not as old as he imagined: and a bed that's not as complex and articulated as the one he'd invented.

A telephone he thought was hollow and empty and voiceless, impossible to call and make ring and yet it is ringing.

A telephone he answers with the hand not of a centenarian but of someone who is what's referred to as "a man of a certain age," that luminous or dark middle age. That age halfway between the ultracradle and the ultratomb. A comfortably troubling or troublingly comfortable place. A time when you start to think all the time about things you haven't thought about much (or didn't want to think about at all), a time when memories start to transform into something else, into what those memories have meant: the precise and decisive difference between a photograph and a portrait. The interpretation of events and the manner and style in which they'll finally and definitely be stored away and evoked.

Not what actually happened but what you tell everyone happened.

Realized reality.

That reality that's not detailed even when contemplated from near the end of life; when we want to believe that we're reading it in its totality, but we fool ourselves, inventing chapters and justifications and oversights; stranding what's happening in the slow rapids of what happened, floating in the "great shroud of the sea" and quoting that line "I only am escaped alone to tell thee."

But the voice on the telephone doesn't say that.

The voice on the telephone says, "Let me in! . . . Let me in!"

And it's a voice he recognizes beyond a shadow of a doubt, but doubts it could be true.

It's Penelope's voice.

And then he hears a tapping on the window and he gets out of bed like someone descending from the throne of a dead man, with a last breath but an inspired agility that surprises him. True, his joints do creak, but in the end, they can still bend.

And he opens the window and on the sill, standing at attention, as if awaiting the order to attack, is a little wooden soldier.

And a few meters beyond, on the path that leads to the sea and the forest, he sees another.

And, a little farther along, another.

And he goes along collecting them one by one, and it's been so long since he got out of bed and out of the house that the sound of the waves and the branches is like something he is hearing for the first time, after having heard it so many times. Like that song he hears now. He knows which one it is, but it's been a long time since he heard it. "Good Night," it's called. The Beatles on *The Beatles*. The last song on the last side of that two-disc set; and he remembers Uncle Hey Walrus telling him (when he was recalling his time at Apple and Abbey Road, Uncle Hey Walrus fell into something like a trance, with encyclopedic diction, as if he were a relatively close relative of HAL 9000) that he was there, when they recorded it. That he was a witness. That he saw and heard it all. And that it neither was nor had it been easy to be part of that, to bear witness to that collapse and that shipwreck of four people (four of the most beloved people in the world) who had loved each other so much and who suddenly couldn't see each other and much less hear each other. And who, now, recorded their tracks separately and in a self-destructive yet hyper-creative way and sent each other little messages more acidic than lysergic from one song to the next. And so it was that an ultraviolent P. played at being more J. than J. on the bestial and chaotic and screaming and primal "Helter Skelter" which, he said, he wanted to have "the sound of the fall of the Roman Empire"; and no, it's no surprise that Charles Manson had understood it as a war cry and a battle hymn and a thirst for bloodshed. And so J.—who'd distilled "the sound of the end of the world" on "A Day in the Life"—counterattacked with the orchestral and elegant and dulcet lullaby "Good Night," which he heard now, closer all the time, drifting through the tree trunks and sand dunes, R.'s voice as if giftwrapped and floating in the orchestral sweetness.

He tracks the origin of the song with some difficulty, under the light of the moon. He was never a parks and plazas kind of kid. He was never a boy scout. He never learned to dive headfirst or stand on his head. And he goes along, collecting little soldiers and putting them in the pockets of his robe and pajamas. He is good at that: at collecting what others forget or let drop or lose along the way. One after another. Nine and ten and eleven and, when he reaches solider number twelve, he looks up and discovers he's reached a clearing in the forest.

And there are The Intruders.

The fucking performance artists.

Four of them: the two parents and the two children.

And he looks at them but they don't look at him, because they're busy doing their thing. They're performing, or whatever it is you call what they do.

And then not only does he look at them, but he sees them.

He sees what they're doing.

The two adults are dressed up as his parents. They're identical. The illusion is so perfect that it's as if, looking at them, his memory of his parents were a kind of crude and rushed imitation, a hurried sketch.

And the two children are he and Penelope the way they once were.

And they all look happy.

And he's never felt the happiness they feel.

Or maybe he has, just now, all of a sudden, he's not sure.

Maybe, he thinks, Penelope has left The Intruders instructions to do this, so he remembers them and so, with that memory, he can forget them and let them rest in peace and let himself rest in peace.

And go on to whatever comes next.

Now, The Intruders—who're no longer The Intruders, but he and Penelope and their parents—announce they're going to sleep.

And all four of them, together, climb into an immense bed with all sorts of drawers and compartments built into it.

A bed like the one he imagined for himself.

A bed with parts of that time machine and that flying car from those movies they once watched, all together.

And they close their eyes.

And they dream.

Then the reflectors that illuminate them go out and a beam of light shines through the trees and lights up a screen, and on that screen he sees him, he sees him again, he was the one who filmed him: a boy with flaming red hair, smiling at him, running backward the way only certain unbroken children or certain broken toys can run. Penelope's lost son (and a son who was sort of his own) going into the forest, yelling back through his laughter and laughing through his yelling "I bet you can't come and find me!"

"Good night . . . Good night, everybody . . . Everybody, everywhere . . . Good night . . ." R. sings and says goodbye.

And suddenly he knows what he has to do.

And knowing what he has to do seems so much like knowing what he has to write and that thing that suddenly stings his face is called . . . what's it called?, oh, yes: it's called "a smile."

He already told it because, perhaps, it's the only thing worth telling: in the beginning of all things, before he learned to read and write (but already feeling himself a writer and a reader), he almost drowned.

He thinks now that slowly slipping out of a dream is something like that: to save yourself, to kick up from the depths of the dream, to reach for the light there above, on the surface of the sheets, and, at last, to find the air of consciousness and, awake and saved, not the interpretation of that dream but its performance.

Putting it into practice.

He would like to be able to write a book like that, but he no longer can. And yet, for a moment, it is as if he were seeing it and feeling it complete and finished. As if he could see it and feel it with the tips of his eyes and the concentric pupils of his fingerprints. Right away, of course, he begins to forget it. He feels that it's escaping and that he should let it escape, so it doesn't pull him under, so he doesn't sink into it. He watches it slip through his fingers and drift down toward the bottom.

He squeezes his eyes shut. Telling and convincing himself—aloud, but with that strangest of voices, like someone talking in a dream—he's sleeping. Wanting to believe it's all been a dream.

And he opens his eyes slowly, as if just waking up.

And the book—or the idea of the book, which is almost the same thing— was still there.

And the book floats now and it's like something to cling to and not let go, something that keeps him alive and breathing. He sees it through the blinds of his eyelids; uneasy because there's someone out there waiting for him or because there's nobody waiting for him; wondering what comes next, what will happen now, what's going to happen in the end.

Tell me, tell me, tell me the answer, he sings through his teeth.

Careful, because that's where he's headed, head spinning and blisters on his fingers from so much writing.

The gentle collapse that'll come when he extracts what he's been carrying around inside.

A familiar return, a state of pity ("Beauty plus pity—that is the closest we can get to a definition of art," Nabokov taught in his classes), a change in the weather, an unforgettable landscape, a loss of the center, a surge at suddenly feeling so light and swift, a waking part, a transparent thing, a speed of things. And it's been so long since he felt like that, since he felt what he feels every time he finishes a book. Like ripping out a tumor to implant a brain inside it. Discovering, upon reviewing the manuscript and the final proofs, all the new things that occurred to him to put in that book; and feeling that everything he's read written by others seemed to be in direct conversation with what he'd written: opening any novel or story or poem at random and discovering there inside little tin toys, windswept moors, dead sisters together forever, perfectly incompatible and lucky families, burning buildings, and dreams, dreams, dreams. And then, at last, closing it and closing them and going back to sleep well and deep, as if he were running like he's running now down that path at that speed.

That recovered speed accelerating down a road where there's no traveler but him, not worrying about anybody or anything, except, when the moment comes, remembering to, before departing, insert that lie that "No character herein bears any resemblance to any actual persons, living or dead, and . . . " or "Any resemblance in what is described, the people described, or the people doing the describing to reality is . . . " Like how the past once was, in the past, remember.


† The past is a book and insomnia could become a book. Insomnia that turns into a book written first and read after and reread later and then rewritten; and, at last, the writer attains his most evolved iteration: that of the rewriter, someone who can only rewrite the same thing over and over, the same night, by night.

Insomnia like the key that turns the gear that sets in motion the memory of someone who remembers in order to rewrite a book, to tell what happened and what will keep happening forever. To tell it better.

A book with all times at the same time, which, when seen all at once, produce an image of life that's beautiful and surprising and deep. There's no beginning, no middle, no end, no suspense, no moral, no cause, no effect. Nothing but marvelous moments, where invention is the control, dreams the entropy, and memory somewhere in between, somnambulant and ambulating through what's created while awake and what's thought while asleep.

A book in three movements.

Slow motion music.

The first movement, that of the dream; the second, that of the waking dream (where you don't know if it's headed toward falling asleep or waking up, toward understanding or not understanding what happened); and the third, that of eyes wide open, forcing you to see everything you wanted not to see for so long.

Dream, waking dream, dreamless.

† The past is that book that, in turn, would be a complex and rousing second act: the intermediate part between two other parts, the part that's dreamed (or the part that, insomniac, dreams of dreaming), between the part that's invented and the part that's remembered.

And so, inventing and dreaming and remembering like the three faces of memory.

Three books configuring a trilogy, not linear and advancing, but horizontal and happening simultaneously (all times at the same time, like the time of that cosmic voyager untethered from time).

Three strangers who, finding themselves together, see each other and, without looking each other in the eyes, dismayed, recognize they're all parts of a whole and, after so much spinning and circumlocutions, they say to each other: "In lak' ech" ("I am another you") and "Hala ken" ("You are another me").

"More in a moment."

"Same as it ever was."

"There is no question about it . . . I can feel it . . . I can feel it . . . I can feel it . . . "

And, once more, at last, from that moment on, feeling again that feeling of letting the bright days and the pages with bright ideas go by.

Now, again, into the blue and into the future.

Toward that place where sooner or later—deep down or high overhead, ever present—you always end up asking yourself: how did I get here?

Attempting to answer that question is why he writes.

Writing as if saying goodbye but thinking of sticking around.

Of not going anywhere, of continuing to spin around above his own body of work and his own life and . . .

At long last he's sleepy.
In the end dreams do come.


Good night . . .
Good night to everyone . . .
To everyone everywhere . . .
Good night.


Time is an asterisk.


The wind in his heart and the dust in his head.


Watch out, because here it comes.


Here comes the twister.


†*.

COUNTING SHEPHERDS:
*A Thank-You Note*


Wake up.
—David Foster Wallace
"Oblivion"


Up next, the shepherds behind *The Dreamed Part*, now headed off to slumber alongside *The Invented Part*: friends and family and readers and books and authors and movies and directors and songs and musicians and paintings and painters and scientists whose company and work and research and influence—near or far, frequently distorted, like everything you look at with your eyes shut—is felt in the waking dream of this book.

Here, with the lights turned off and my heart turned on, I count all of them, not to make myself fall asleep, but to congratulate myself for the fact that they're all there, keeping me always alert and acutely aware that, just outside, the ferocious sheep are howling.


"Dreams of Distant Lives," by Lee K. Abbott; "Canción mixteca," by José López Alavez; Carlos and Ana Alberdi; *Everyday Robots*, by Damon Albarn; Robert Altman; Martin Amis; Wes Anderson; Carmen Balcells and Balcells Agency; J. G. Ballard; John Banville; *The Brontës: Wild Genius on the Moors: The Story of a Literary Family*, by Juliet Barker; Djuna Barnes; *Flaubert's Parrot*, by Julian Barnes; *Overnight to Many Distant Cities*, by Donald Barthelme; Franco Battiato; *The Feast of Love*, by Charles Baxter; The

Beatles (all together then and now and separately); Eduardo Becerra; Saul Bellow; "Nighttime," by Big Star; Adolfo Bioy Casares; "I Never Learnt to Share," by James Blake; *Genius: A Mosaic of One Hundred Exemplary Creative Minds* and *Shakespeare: The Invention of the Human*, by Harold Bloom; *Warhol: The Biography*, by Victor Bockris; *The End of Night: Searching for Natural Darkness in the Age of Artificial Night*, by Paul Bogard; Juan Ignacio Boido (and *El ultimo joven*, by Juan Ignacio Boido); Roberto Bolaño; *22, A Million* ("29 #Strafford Apts": "Sure as any living dream / It's not all then what it seems / and the whole thing's being hauled away"), by Bon Iver; *Book of Dreams* and "Nightmare" and "A New Refutation of Time" by Jorge Luis Borges; ★, by David Bowie; *fa fa fa fa fa fa: The Adventures of Talking Heads in the 20th Century*, by David Bowman; Brian Boyd; Ronaldo Bressane (& Chico Buarque); *Wuthering Heights*, by Emily Brontë (annotated by Janet Gezari on the version in the original language for Belknap/Harvard; the translation into Spanish used is, with "interventions" and "interferences" by Penelope, by Nicole d'Amonville Alegría for Penguin Clásicos); Brontë family; *Mid Air*, by Paul Buchanan; *On Going to Bed*, by Anthony Burgess; *My Education: A Book of Dreams*, by William S. Burroughs; Kate Bush; *Nothing: A Portrait of Insomnia*, by Blake Butler; David Byrne; "Los dientes apretados," by Andrés Calamaro; *Music for a New Society/M: Fans*, by John Cale; Martín Caparrós; Jorge Carrión; *Casablanca*, by too many people, all of them; John Cheever; *El carapálida*, by Luis Chitarroni; Coen Brothers; Joshua Cohen; "Darkness" and "The Guests" ("And no one knows where the night is going . . .") and "You Want It Darker," by Leonard Cohen; Lloyd Cole; *Apocalypse Now*, by Francis Ford Coppola; Jordi Costa; Elvis Costello; *The Beatles Lyrics*, by Hunter Davies; Ray Davies & The Kinks; Robertson Davies; Iván de la Nuez; *White Noise* and *Mao II*, by Don Delillo; Sergio del Molino; Philip K. Dick; Joan Didion & John Gregory Dunne; *The Longest Cocktail Party*, by Richard DiLello; Stephen Dixon; E. L. Doctorow; Bob Dylan (for everything; but here, very especially, for "Series of Dreams"); *Sum*, by David Eagleman; Ignacio Echevarría; *At Day's Close: Night in Times Past*, by A. Roger Ekirch; Stanley Elkin; *My Life in the Bush of Ghosts*, by Brian Eno + David Byrne; Frederick Exley; Marta Fernández; Rodrigo Fernández; Francis Scott Fitzgerald; Penelope Fitzgerald; Alain-Fournier; Nelly Fresán; Adolfo García Ortega; Alfredo Garófano; Tom Gauld; *Freud: A Life for Our*

*Time*, by Peter Gay; *Time Travel*, by James Gleick; *Faithful and Virtuous Night*, by Louise Glück; The Goin' South Team: Truman Capote & William Faulkner & Barry Hannah & Carson McCullers & Flannery O'Connor; Glenn Gould; Henry Green; "Birds of the High Artic" and "The Incredible," by David Gray (& Tarjei Vesaas); *Will in the World: How Shakespeare Became Shakespeare*, by Stephen J. Greenblatt; Leila Guerriero; Isabelle Gugnon; Gloria Gutiérre; *The Glass Key*, by Dashiell Hammett; *Seduction and Betrayal: Women and Literature* and *Sleepless Nights*, by Elizabeth Hardwick; *The End of Absence*, by Michael Harris; *Something Happened*, by Joseph Heller; Felipe Hirsch & Paulo Werneck (& Mark Twain); Robyn Hitchcock; *Dreaming: A Very Short Introduction*, by J. Allan Hobson; *Ein Brief*, by Hugo von Hofmannsthal; Anna María Iglesia; *A Sound Like Someone Trying Not to Make a Sound*, John Irving; *Donnie Darko*, by Richard Kelly; *Book of Dreams*, by Jack Kerouac; Henry James; *Insomnia*, by Stephen King; Vincent Theo (KLM); *But What If We're Wrong?*, by Chuck Klosterman; Stanley Kubrick; *Train Dreams*, by Denis Johnson; Lalo Lambda (and Brandy con Caramelos); Librería La Central (Antonio & Marta & Neus & Co.); Eduardo Lago; Jonathan Lethem; Liniers; *Sleep: A Very Short Introduction*, by Steven W. Lockley & Russell G. Foster; "Clock for Night Owl," designed by Tiancheng Luo; David Lynch; María Lynch (Agencia Casanovas & Lynch); René Magritte; *I Want My MTV: The Uncensored Story of The Music Video Revolution*, by Craig Marks and Rob Tannenbaum; J. A. Masoliver Ródenas; Fran G. Matute; *Mental Floss*; Norma Elizabeth Mastrorilli; *The Family That Couldn't Sleep*, by D.T. Max; Valerie Miles; *The Brontë Myth*, by Lucasta Miller; Steven Millhauser; David Mitchell; Thelonious Monk; Rick Moody; "Early to Bed" and "The Night," by Morphine; Annie Morvan; Mrs. Trip (actually, the adorable couple of young readers of *The Invented Part* that brought her to me as a gift at a booth at the Feria del Libro de Madrid, 2014: I don't know their names, but I won't forget their faces and their affection; and it makes me happy to know that one writes for people that are exactly *like that*); *The Book and the Brotherhood*, by Iris Murdoch; Bill Murray; "On Revisiting Father's Room," by Dmitir Nabokov; Véra Nabokov and Vladimir Nabokov (the translations of fragments inserted in *La parte soñada* are by Aurora Bernárdez and Jordi Fibla and Enrique Murillo and my own; and now, yes, with *The Dreamed Part* out of my system, I solemnly swear that I will try again and this time I will get past page 10 and I will finish *Ada, or Ardor*); María José Navia; *I Hate to Leave This Beautiful Place* and *In Fond Remembrance of Me*, by Howard Norman; Miguel Ángel Oeste; Gabriel Ruiz Ortega; Pere Ortin (Altäir & Co.); Alan Pauls; Penguin Random House (Raquel Abad, Carlota del Amo, Eva Cuenca, Gabriela Ellena, Cecilia Fanti, Lourdes González, Nora Grosse, Victoria Malet, Irene Pérez, Albert Puigdueta, José Serra, Florencia Ure); Ginés "Belvedere" Pérez Navarro (for his perfect bullshots); Julio Ortega; Andrés Perruca; Ricardo Piglia (and Emilio Renzi); Pink Floyd (and Storm Thorgerson); *The Secret History of Vladimir Nabokov*, by Andrea Pitzer; *Monsters, Inc.*, by Pixar; Chad W. Post; Patricio Pron; Francine Prose; Marcel Proust; *Against the Day*, by Thomas Pynchon; *Dreamland: Adventures in the Strange Science of Sleep*, by David K. Randall; R.E.M.; *Providence*, by Alan Resnais; Mordecai Richler; *Sleep*, by Max Richter; *The Violet Hour: Great Writers at the End*, by Katie Roiphe; Federico Romani; *Nabokov in America: The Road to Lolita*, by Robert Roper; Guillermo Saccomanno; Karina Sáinz Borgo; James Salter; Julia Santibáñez; *Traumnovelle*, by Arthur Schnitzer; "In Dreams Begin Responsibilities," by Delmore Schwartz; *Umbrella* and *Shark*, by Will Self; *The Twilight Zone*, by Rod Serling & Co. (warning for obsessives in general and for my French translator in particular: the episode mentioned with the title "The Museum's Visitor" does not actually exist and its synopsis is nothing but the fusion/very-loose rewrite of the stories "La Veneziana" and "The Visit to the Museum" by Vladimir Nabokov); *A Midsummer Night's Dream* & Co., by William Shakespeare (even though it's pretty impertinent and rude and snobbish and redundant to thank Shakespeare for anything, right?); "That's Why God Made the Movies" and "Insomniac's Lullaby," by Paul Simon; *Moondust*, by Andrew Smith; "No Name # 3" and "Waltz #2 (XO)," by Elliott Smith; *The Noonday Demon; And Atlas of Depression*, by Andrew Solomon; The Spent Poets; Laurence Sterne; "A Chapter on Dreams," by Robert Louis Stevenson; Gonzalo Suárez; Louie C. K. Székely (Chapter 5, fifth season: "Untitled"); *Remain in Light* and "Love → Building on Fire" and "Burning Down the House" and "Dream Operator" and "City of Dreams," by Talking Heads; *The Affair*; "Do Not Go Gently Into That Good Night" & "In My Craft or Sullen Art," by Dylan Thomas; *The Physics of Immortality*, by Frank J. Tippler; *A Confession*, by Leo Tolstoy; "Stop Hurting

People," by Pete Townshend; John Updike (and John Freeman); Will Vanderhyden; María Rita Vidal; Enrique Vila-Matas; Villaseñor family; Kurt Vonnegut; Scott Walker; "Oblivion," by David Foster Wallace; *Lost in the Dream*, by The War on Drugs; Andy Warhol; *A Handful of Dust*, by Evelyn Waugh; Peter Westerberg; Jim White; "Night of a Thousand Furry Toys," by Rick Wright; Warren Zevon; *The Twilight Zone Companion*, by Marc Scott Zicree; Nathan Zuckerman.

Claudio López de Lamadrid.

Daniel Fresán and Ana Isabel Villaseñor.

And good night, sweet princes and sweet princesses.

And until the next part.

*Barcelona, October 13th, 2016*
"I'll let you be in my dreams if I can be in yours"

Rodrigo Fresán is the author of ten works of fiction, including *Kensington Gardens*, *Mantra*, and *The Invented Part*, winner of the 2018 Best Translated Book Award. In 2017, he received the Prix Roger Caillois, awarded by PEN Club France every year to both a French and a Latin American writer.

Will Vanderhyden has translated fiction by Carlos Labbé, Edgardo Cozarinsky, Juan Marsé, and Elvio Gandolfo. He received NEA and Lannan fellowships to translate another of Fresán's novels, *The Invented Part*, for which he won the Best Translated Book Award.

**OPEN
LETTER**

**WWW.OPENLETTERBOOKS.ORG**

**OPEN
LETTER**

**WWW.OPENLETTERBOOKS.ORG**

31192021823743